HELLBOUND

SAGA ONLINE

OLIVER MAYES

CONTENTS

Hey Stacy. It's been difficult, being without you this last year. I'm sorry our life together was trampled on. But it's okay. I'll find my way back to you and we'll build an even better one.

This is for you. X

PROLOGUE – THE FALL

It was the seventh day since Aetherius first met Damien, and he should've been resting by now. Things had not gone according to plan.

You have been killed by 'Scorepeeus63'. Your experience has been reset to the start of your current level and your body may be looted, at which point a random item of equipped gear will be forfeit.

Remember, it's only a game!

Death cooldown – 2 minutes and 26 seconds.

Thank you for playing Saga Online.

Daemien had won the competition. Adler, the CEO of Mobius Enterprises himself, had announced it just after midnight. A month-long lead over a worldwide contest thrown away by a vengeful ex-girlfriend, a brat with the luck of the devil and a nine-year-old noob-ody in the wrong place at the wrong time.

He might've lost the competition, but Aetherius was still the leader of the largest guild with the most bases and the most clout. Or at least he had been. Now he wasn't sure. Aetherius's leadership had been highly effective, but it had not made him or his guild a great many friends. With his defeat being advertised all over the internet, the many guilds he'd stepped over on his road to conquest were circling Rising Tide's twitching corpse. Daemien had removed the head. Now the rest of the Human Realm were coming to take revenge on what was left.

Godhammer, led by Hammertime himself, had attacked and retaken Rising Tide's waiting room four hours ago. Godhammer's assault left less than half the defending force guarding the waiting room alive, weakening them for the next guild that opted to reclaim a piece of Aetherius's pie. Then the next. Then the next.

Whatever Aetherius was going to do, he had to do it fast. So here Andrew lay. Waiting the last few seconds to salvage whatever was left. The timer ticked down to zero and the list of locations where he could respawn came up. He'd once had tens of locations to choose from. Now there were only three: the Downward Spiral, where he'd died. Ker-Uhel, his character's native homeland. And one last meaningful base. Aetherium. Which was highlighted in red, indicating it was under attack.

It was a shock to see how much he'd lost, but if there was one base he would've chosen to save, this was it. If it could be saved, he'd have a platform to rebuild from.

Aetherius apparated next to the Portal Stone in his seat of power, the blue sphere that shielded players as they spawned shimmering away, and took in the scene. It was chaos. The courtyard was swarming with players, their basic information blue if they were guild-mates, red if they were hostile and gray if they were dead. There were a lot of gray names. It was only when he saw two blue-named players attacking each other, both their names turning red simultaneously, that he realized what was happening.

His guild was cannibalizing itself.

Aetherius didn't hesitate. It had been a long campaign. Killing traitors was second nature at this point. He threw his arms out and fired Arcane Bolts in expanding circles around him, eliminating nearby threats first and clearing his vicinity. The first traitors were struck before they even knew what was happening, the bolts bursting on impact and throwing the less constitutionally gifted of them into the paths of those following in their wake.

The turncoats ran for cover, pushing each other out the way and even using their neighbors as human shields, if they possessed the strength and moral ambivalence necessary to do so. Aetherius had created enough of an opening to consider his next move when his Arcane Bolt barrage came to a premature end. He was out of mana. Already.

Aetherius raised his hands up in front of him and glared at them incredulously, adding his favorite spell to a rapidly growing list of traitors. This couldn't be right! He'd min-maxed his character and his spells were more expensive than average, but he had enough wisdom on his gear to compensate. He hadn't even fired half of his maxi— which is when he noticed his wrists were bare.

The bracers he'd painstakingly sourced and grinded for, stacked with wisdom and with a special ability granting mana-cost reduction for spells channeled through them, were gone. For a bare-handed caster, this was the equivalent of losing his weapon. He'd been wondering what might've been looted from his body following his death. Now was not a good time to find out it had been something crucial to his build.

He didn't have long. Some of the enemies were already starting to turn around. The bracers had been very important to him, but at least their loss meant he still had his trump card. He felt for the talisman under his robes, half doubting it would still be there. The moment his fingertips located the lump of metal hanging in the center of his chest, he folded his arms, started tapping his foot and addressed the regrouping attackers in a loud, calm voice.

"Now that I have your attention, there's no need for us to fight. I just want to talk."

He'd no sooner uttered the last word before focusing on a new one in his mind – *Decoy*. Then he sprinted toward the guild hall as fast as he could, picking his way between his enemies without them even sparing him a glance. He was invisible. Behind him stood a perfect replica of himself, copying his most recent action in a loop. Having threaded his way through the closing hostile ring as they hurled threats and insults at his decoy, Aetherius threw out a hand and willed a mana potion into it.

Nothing happened.

Of course. In addition to killing him, Damien had stolen his Bag of Holding. He had no inventory for potions, as opposed to the almost infinite supply he'd accustomed himself to over the course of the last month. Andrew had already considered that, and had tried to prepare himself for it, but old habits die hard. He twisted mid-run to avoid an assassin sprinting toward his decoy, only to have the same player unwittingly bellow right into his earhole on his way past: "He's doing the thing, the foot-tapping! Attack him quick so the re—"

There was a thrum in Aetherius's ears and he was visible again, still surrounded by skirmishes and opportunists. He'd expected a little more time. This was not a good crisis to face without a solid grasp of the situation. He was running toward the right place; there was a solid blue line of players, almost a raid party, standing in front of the guild headquarters. Many of them were players Aetherius had taken with him to the Downward Spiral. They'd extricated themselves from the skirmish and banded together to preserve Rising Tide's core.

Aetherius Blinked straight ahead, leaving the traitors behind and arriving among the blue-named players. Loyalty, perversely, is only quantifiable when times are tough. A state of affairs Aetherius had striven to avoid. It was only in the wake of his mistakes that these players could demonstrate their true worth. Aetherius was not surprised to see Judgementday among them.

"Move, boss, they're coming!"

Aetherius looked between Judgementday and the rapidly approaching mob, holding his position. It appeared his arrival had given them something dangerous: a unified direction. Aetherius had come to help and had instead made himself a target. In normal circumstances he'd have dispatched them swiftly. But without his bottomless supply of potions, or indeed any potions at all, there was nothing he could do. Not for now, at least. He pushed Judgementday's hands away and stared out at the mob. At the sea of ingrates he'd spent two months regulating and organizing, for their benefit as well as his own.

Powerlessness was not something Aetherius was used to. Grudges, on the other hand, were his specialty. He started recording and swept his gaze across the battlefield, focusing on each hostile player for a fraction of a second to bring up their name. After he'd put down this rebellion, he'd review the footage at his own convenience and cross-reference it with his Personal Kill List. Then he'd personally track down every single one. Before getting started, he needed to retreat to the vault and pick up a utility belt and a pair of bracers. These enemies wouldn't require endless potions. Five would be more than enough.

He built up his naughty list for as long as he dared. It was only when the first arrow whistled past that he submitted to Judgementday's pleading and the two of them turned tail. Once he and his best healer had passed the defensive line, Aetherius addressed the handful of followers who'd turned out to be somewhat loyal. They deserved a rallying speech. Aetherius wasn't currently of the right mindset for such a task, so he gave them the simple version.

"Hold them off. I'm replacing my lost gear in the vault. Then we'll kill them all."

He opened the guild headquarters doors from his menu and paced through them, closing them behind him without looking back. The moment the outside noise had been muffled he broke into a run. He'd need as many of those defenders alive as possible if he was going to secure this place. They were a strong party and could likely keep them at bay for a while, but it would only take one or two serious mistakes and they'd all be overwhelmed. Aetherius had to be back in combat before that happened.

He threw in the vault password as he approached. The mechanism at the center span and the doors swung open. The room beyond was lined with chests in neat rows. Each chest was assigned a different commodity. He knew where everything was. He'd organized it himself. Aetherius had spent a good third of his waking hours in this room over the last month, performing the unappreciated rituals of a good guild leader: allocating gear to people who'd earned it, checking on crafting output for sale, reimbursing successful guild quests, accepting or rejecting recruits, analyzing the trade market. The list went on and on. But his endeavors had been rewarding. Rising Tide had been an industrial powerhouse, hiding behind and feeding on glory and conquest.

The holdings he'd built up to control trade routes were gone. His player base was tearing itself apart. But the profit from over a month's worth of nearly a thousand players grinding was all contained in this room. As guild leader he'd had the option of storing it all in the King's vault, right in the middle of Camelot. The fee had been extortionate: 8% of all riches stored paid in gold as tax to Camelot per week. Aetherius had always felt very smug to have his own vault in Aetherium instead. Right up until now.

He went straight to his personal loot box, appropriating his utility belt and filling it to the brim. Bitterly, he severed the link his item chest had with the Bag of Holding. At least Damien had been disconnected before he could steal everything out of it. Once Aetherius was fully healed, he made for the far end of the vault. That's where he kept the good stuff. He'd passed his desk in the center and had the caster bracers' chest in his sights when there was a *ping* and a voice chat invitation popped up in his HUD:

Voice Chat Invitation: Magnitude, Gamer ID 000397, A/D

No. Not now. This was a different situation, Richard couldn't expect him to show up right away. He pointedly canceled the call and had no sooner reached the first chest than a black orb pulsed in front of him and expanded to a swirling disc, two meters high and one wide. The portal. Aetherius had always thought it could only be used on party members. There was a *ping* as Magnitude started calling him again. This could obviously not wait.

Even if he put down this rebellion, the team Magnitude worked with were a far worse long-term threat. Aetherius had pledged to win the competition for them and they'd given him plenty of assistance in that regard. Now their prize racehorse had fumbled the lead, begetting questions requiring answers. But did they really have to be answered *right now?* The continued ringing of the incoming call suggested that yes, they did.

Magnitude hadn't made any contact with Aetherius in a long time. Things had been especially tense the last couple of days, after Aetherius had asked him for a new Pegasus mount. To replace the one Damien had killed. Magnitude had listened to the request and abruptly hung up without a word. The Pegasus mount was in his base the very next morning, but it was clear his brother's goodwill was gone. His first duty was to his brother. Even before his own guild. He'd just have to make it fast. Andrew curled his fists and stepped through the portal.

Upon arrival he was surprised to find it dark, aside from the portal's own light. Usually they had a wisp recording meetings. He'd only ever met with his brother in here, but the rest of the group had always been watching through the wisp. Or so he was told. There hadn't been any meetings for weeks. Everyone had already decided that Aetherius's victory was inevitable. There'd only been one issue on which Aetherius and his allies had not seen eye to eye. From there, it had quickly spun out of control.

The ringing of the voice chat came to an end and Richard's voice echoed off the walls of the cave.

"I want you to tell me why you did it."

Aetherius span round toward the voice, but still couldn't see anything. One of Magnitude's racial traits was that he could see in the dark. Tentatively, Aetherius cast his own wisp and sent it to float gently forward through the air, walking with it and leaving the portal behind. Magnitude's voice came back, almost right in front of him.

"That's close enough. I said, tell me why you did it."

Aetherius stopped, his hands by his sides. This was much colder than he was used to.

"Did what? I've got a guild war to resolve, so if you could get to the poi—"

"We specifically told you to boost Damien, look after him, make a joint streaming video and give him a positive community experience. What did you do?"

"You gave me an opportunity and I—"

"—kicked him into the Downward Spiral. Right after he told you his mother was in hospital. I saw the video you were kind enough to record for us, the full, unedited recap. Setting the stupidity of it aside, what kind of psychopath does that to a fan?"

"That's the image this character has! He isn't a charity worker, he's ruthless! That's why I've got so many votes. People like him this way!"

Magnitude abruptly stomped forward out of the darkness, equipped from head to toe in full battle gear. It was quite a sight. His entire body was coated in jade, a whole suit of armor carved out of rare stone with magical healing properties. Aetherius had never seen anything like it. There were hundreds of individual articulated pieces, most of them concentrated over joints to allow full range of movement. It looked heavy. It felt heavy when the wrist piece fell across Aetherius's neck and held him up by the scruff of it. Magnitude would've pushed Aetherius off his feet, if the dwarf had been a little taller and the elf a little shorter.

"*Had*. You *had* so many votes. Because you couldn't just push Damien off any old high place, could you?"

He tightened his grip and braced a little harder, pushing Aetherius up onto his tippy-toes.

"No, that wouldn't have been insulting enough. So you brought him to the dungeon we *specifically* told you to leave alone after you'd cleared it. You might've been surprised Damien didn't die from the fall but you shouldn't have been, given the warnings we gave you. Your disobedience led directly to the end of your streaming career. I've got to tell you, when Damien won some of us were cheering. Not me. I was upset."

Magnitude span his arms around and Aetherius followed them over his head in a circle, down into the floor. Magnitude's level and class were still a mystery, both appearing above his head as a string of question marks, but he definitely had the strength and constitution to be wearing that armor. He knelt on Aetherius's chest, pinning him to the ground.

"I put my neck out for you. I vouched for you. And then I watched you throw it all away, for nothing."

Aetherius grabbed the knee that was pinning him, but there was no resisting it. He looked up at his older brother, his face dark with the wisp behind his head.

"For nothing? You made me boost the guy who took my spot against Toutatis, on the same day you had me lined up to end my relationship with Lillian, and you call that nothing?"

Magnitude raised his jade-encased hands and the dome reverberated with the slowest of slow claps.

"You threw a tantrum because you were sad about losing your girlfriend. At whose cost? I thought you were smarter than that, but she completely destabilized you. As I always knew she would."

"What's that supposed to mean?"

The knee on his chest dug in again, pressing him down tightly.

"She was never good for you, Andrew. How much more obvious can it be? She took the competition away from you the moment she couldn't use you anymore. How can you still not see that?"

Aetherius paused to contemplate his brother's words of wisdom. Briefly. He abruptly brought his hands together and they pulsed red. Magnitude tumbled backward, the Arcane Beam searing through the rock overhead and causing it to crash around them. Aetherius canceled the channel and pushed himself up, one hand preparing an Arcane Bolt while the other shielded his eyes from sudden daylight. It was streaking in through the hole he'd made in the ceiling. He hadn't realized they were only separated from the surface by such a thin layer.

Aetherius span round, his held spell lighting the ground around him, but Magnitude was nowhere to be seen. That was ominous. Whatever his secret class was, it wasn't stealth- or speed-based. So where did he go? Aetherius sent the Mana Wisp into the darkness ahead while he remained in the light beam.

"You should never have interfered in our relationship! You had no right!"

"She was using you! She could've taken Rising Tide any day she wanted! I thought I'd saved you, that so long as you pulled that off nothing else could go wrong."

Aetherius hurled a string of bolts behind him, where the voice had suddenly appeared. They didn't impact anything either. This shouldn't have been possible. Magnitude was obviously playing a strength-based class and he had the armor to match, there was no way Aetherius could imagine him moving so fast and so quietly in the enclosed space. Aetherius fired a pair of bolts around him in an expanding circle, lighting up the whole dome piece by piece. Magnitude wasn't anywhere to be seen.

"But I was mistaken."

The voice had come from right behind him. Aetherius was caught in the back with a hook, sending him hurtling to the periphery of the dome. It had been a big hit, even unarmed, and Aetherius was not built to take hits of any kind. Combined with the ground slam, he was down to a fraction of his health. Magnitude was toying with him.

"I solve one problem, you cause another. Just when I'd made you safe, you kicked Damien into the Downward Spiral, spiting him, us and yourself. After you did that, my hands were tied."

Aetherius fired an Arcane Beam back the way he'd come. No one was there. He gave up. He had no idea how his brother was appearing and disappearing. Without knowing how his abilities worked, he was outmatched. He stumbled to his feet, eyeing up the portal on the opposite side of the dome. It was still active.

Aetherius needed a gesture his artifact could convert into a natural facade. The foot-tapping had always been very effective, but was too well known. It had to match the situation.

"Forcing a breakup with my girlfriend is helping me? Really?"

Aetherius put his palm on his forehead and slowly shook his head, staring at the floor.

"I should never have come to you for help in the first place. 'Bro'."

Decoy.

He set the Mana Wisp to remain above his decoy and started walking toward the portal very carefully, popping a health potion as he went. He could barely see where he was going. His only reference points were the light of the Mana Wisp behind, the two holes he'd made in the domed ceiling and the dim glow of the portal in front. That and his brother's voice, which was coming from somewhere in between.

Aetherius was invisible, but he could still be heard and touched. The dome offered no sound to cover his footsteps. He carefully crept forward as his older brother tutted then obligingly started monologuing, his words tinged with anger.

"You're taking me for granted! I did everything in my power to make your streamer dream happen. I convinced my group to give you power most players won't ever get: a custom-made artifact, the best bag in the known game and two legendary mounts!"

Aetherius quickly checked on his decoy as he popped a mana potion. It looked pretty authentic. Halfway to expiration. The only problem was, Aetherius couldn't find his way around Magnitude's voice. Wherever he went, it seemed to follow right in front of him, always blocking his way to the portal. Maybe the acoustics were off in here? It could explain why the voice was also getting louder. He just needed to get a little closer, then his Blink would carry him straight to his escape route. But Magnitude's voice remained right in front of him.

"You were fed dungeon and boss mechanics in advance, you were told your traits and skills up to level 50, you had all the information on rival guilds we could acquire. And now you're using the artifact I built you with my own two hands to try and sneak past me?"

Magnitude had gotten as far as 'built' before the Mana Wisp was jetting away from the decoy and in front of Aetherius as fast as he could make it go. By the time it settled, the decoy was all but expired. Magnitude was standing directly in front of him. Looking almost straight at him.

"I'm not impressed."

Aetherius Blinked through his captor and ran. The portal was only ten steps away. He made it three steps before it started to drop into the ground and his feet became heavy. He looked down at it incredulously as it descended out of view, trying to figure out what was going on. It was as the air rushed over him that he realized why he felt heavier. The portal wasn't going down. He was going up. It didn't matter. At that point, there was nothing he could do.

He was slammed into the ceiling headfirst, falling over onto his face. His ascent did not slow. The ceiling crashed into his back, crushing him all the way from his ankles to the back of his head. In an instant, he went from full health to teetering on the edge of death, his body a mangled, immobile wreck. Then the pressure subsided and the crushing platform descended to the floor, the portal a mere five steps away.

Aetherius couldn't get up. He willed his last health potion into his hand and was dragging it to his lips when Magnitude snatched it away. The Mana Wisp followed close behind, giving Andrew a good view of his older brother draining his only hope at salvation. Magnitude put his foot on Aetherius's head, nudging it to look away from the portal before pressing down, and spoke to him levelly.

"You remember when I promised I'd leave the party if we didn't deliver your artifact? They didn't take too kindly to that. They didn't much like the idea I was more loyal to you than them. So they made an arrangement with me in private, to balance it out. I promised that if you screwed up, I'd handle it myself."

While he was talking, Aetherius had pointed a shaky hand

upward. His health might have been low, but his mana was full. His hand glowed red, then exploded. Magnitude's upper body was engulfed in the beam and the dome was filled with the roar of the release of pure energy. It did less damage than a double-handed cast but also cost half as much mana, resulting in eight seconds of Aetherius's go-to instant-death spell at point-blank range.

He held it until every last drop of his mana had been depleted, his hand only falling back to the ground when he was completely spent. And in its wake, found himself staring up and sidelong at Magnitude. Who had 65% of his health remaining, a slightly singed beard and a foot on Aetherius's head that hadn't budged for the entire spell-cast. Magnitude paused for effect, allowing Aetherius to see the results of his determination. To add insult to injury, Magnitude's health was regenerating. Absurdly quickly. He was back at full in ten seconds flat, without having used any skills or abilities.

Magnitude continued to talk as if nothing had happened.

"If you'd won the competition, you could've started a new life. But you dropped the ball. I can't help someone who won't help themselves, and I won't undermine my own position trying, and let you drag me down with you."

Aetherius heard everything he'd been told, even with Magnitude's foot muffling one of his ears, but his understanding was different. Maybe he and Lillian could've patched things up if he hadn't been offered a dark path at a bad time. Maybe a lot of things would be different. Now he'd never know, because he'd taken up his brother's offer and had ended up here, under his jade boot. Magnitude leaned in, his arm bracing on his knee and adding more pressure to the side of Andrew's head.

"So, here's what's going to happen: first, I'm going to kill you. Sorry. Then, you're going to forget this whole sorry mess happened. It must hurt now, and that's the last thing I wanted for you, but it's only been a few months and your life will improve. Even if it doesn't feel like it right now. But you can't come back to this game. They won't allow it. Every time you come back, they'll have me or someone else find and kill you.

Don't put me through that. Give up on this, learn from it, go live a productive life. I know how much effort you put into this, but it's over. When I'm finished, I'll be able to help you financially and make this right. But please. Please give up on this game."

Andrew drew a ragged breath and expelled it in a long sigh. He'd already made up his mind.

"Are the others listening right now?"

"No. I told them I'd deal with you, but I wouldn't be sharing it with them. They consented, though they weren't very happy about it. More trouble you've caused me, despite my better judgment."

Aetherius grimaced under the weight of the boot on his head. That wasn't half as much trouble as he felt like causing. He'd lost Lillian for good. His guild was in its death throes. All the wealth and power he'd accumulated would soon go with it. His reputation as a streamer had been shredded, his fall even more rapid and brutal than his rise. His job prospects were severely limited. His Universal Income was the lowest it could be, a prompt for him to find gainful employment. All he had to show for his whole life up to this moment were a lot of bad choices and a failed streaming career, turning him into a figure of ridicule worldwide.

But he had nothing to lose, and he knew exactly what he wanted to do with the rest of his life.

"That's a shame. You'll have to tell them on my behalf. First, I'll kill Damien. Repeatedly. Then, once the status quo has been restored, I'll upset it by killing you. Repeatedly. Then, I'll find out who your party are, and I'll kill them. All of them. However many of them there may be. Repeatedly. Over, and over, and over again, until I'm satisfied your debt has been repaid. Because for the sake of your plans, you interfered with my personal life. I'll ensure using me the way you've used me becomes your greatest regret, the biggest mistake you made in your entire life and, before that, the fear that prevents you from sleeping at night. I'm coming for you, Richard. You controlling, remorseless, feckless stain. I hope that's nice and clear."

Aetherius was smiling. It was nice, to have a life with meaning. To have a clear goal he could focus on for the rest of his existence. He was happy to know the hurt that had been inflicted on him would be translated into misery for the people who'd inflicted that hurt. He'd never been more sure of anything.

Magnitude pressed his temples between the fingers of one hand, the other keeping his knee steady as his foot pressed down on his younger brother's head. Andrew watched him struggle. Good. That meant he believed him. Magnitude raised his boot over his younger brother's head.

"I understand. I hope you reconsider."

Aetherius smiled. He wouldn't.

1

GOOD INTENTIONS

Damien sat at the foot of the steps, his head supported by an elbow on one knee, and wondered if he was making a mistake. This clearing at the base of the mountain was where players gathered and formed their parties before starting the climb to Brociliande's highest-level dungeon: the 'Lair of the Emerald Queen', the grand finale to the main questline in the region. It felt like a place with credentials worthy enough to satisfy his viewers. The only issue now was whether he could find a party crazy enough to run it with him.

It had been a good day so far. Damien had finally hit level 40. He'd got most of the way there two weeks prior, hitting level 36 before his headset was pulled off. The last four levels had taken almost as long to secure as the thirty-five that preceded them, now that he had his mother and his viewers to look after. Regardless, it was an important milestone. Now he wanted to try something new, to celebrate the momentous occasion. While his plan to join a dungeon party seemed ambitious, he felt the risk was justified by the potential rewards.

People had been complaining about a lack of livestreams on his channel, as if a stealth character who ran solo could afford to do such a thing. His only chance at not being hunted down in the process was embedding himself in a party, which would also add a more traditional experience to his streaming repertoire. It was easier said than done: as an 'Enemy of the Realm', he was automatically regarded as hostile by any 'Order'-affiliated characters. So pretty much everyone. His name on their HUDs would be highlighted in red to denote his status as an enemy, and vice versa.

However, he knew they could form parties. He'd partied up with Lillian on several occasions and they'd shared EXP as normal, although thanks to his 'Soul Harvest' trait he'd received experience from enemy players they'd killed as well.

It was very important he extend this concept to other players. His murder hobo routine was quickly becoming unsustainable; being a professional streamer was a lovely idea in theory, but in practice there were a few things he hadn't considered. For instance, how much harder it is to surprise an enemy when you've taught them where you hide. Or how difficult it is to catch large groups in an Imp-losion when your targets know the spell's range.

Fortunately, there were aspects of his class that were more flexible and less well known. Everyone focused on his abilities as an occultist, far fewer had memorized the abilities of all his minions. Which were not to be taken lightly, especially considering his 'Nine-Tenths of the Lore' trait doubled the stats of whatever he was possessing.

In fact, he was possessing a hell hound right now, using its 'Detect' skill to reveal entities hiding in his vicinity. He'd propped his own body up at the foot of the steps as bait. This allowed him to draw in and observe the potential party members hiding in the undergrowth, who in turn were obligingly observing his empty shell.

The enhanced senses his hell hound provided had illuminated his voyeurs' profiles clearly, even in the dark and through the thick foliage. He drew closer, taking care to keep his possessed unit in cover, until he was near enough for their basic stats to pop up above their heads. There were three of them, still a long way shy of the ten recommended for this dungeon. CactusLover, Akunaratana and LightLawd. All from the DeathGod guild.

It would be better to talk to them now, before anyone else got there. If he could strike up a conversation and show he meant no harm they might help convince any other players joining. Also, if he waited for more to show up before introducing himself, group think would likely prevail and they'd kill him where he lay. Well, then. No time like the present.

Damien canceled his Possession and, without moving his head, set his eyes on the foliage where he'd seen the figures hiding. Now he knew where to look, he thought he could see some of their outlines himself. Not nearly enough to form basic stat boxes, though.

He blinked hard twice, then checked to make sure his input had been received and he was streaming. The box showing his viewer count showed up underneath the red recording light. 106. Well, it was modest, but then again he hadn't announced he was livestreaming today. That would be tantamount to suicide. It was already dangerous enough without giving potential hunters advance warning.

He'd scarcely finished the thought when the number jumped. 584. Anyone following his channel had been notified that a livestream had begun. So presumably, around 106 people had been browsing his page before the livestream even commenced, and a further 500ish people browsing elsewhere had clicked their own notifications as they popped up. That was a decent start.

Damien took a deep breath, his fist still pressed under his chin so as not to trigger any reactions until he was ready. Here goes nothing. He stood up, raised his hands to either side and spun around slowly on the spot, showing he was unarmed. That might not have meant much in a game where you could materialize weapons in your hands at a moment's notice, but it was still the best gesture he could think of to show he bore no ill will. Then he hollered into the trees.

"Hey, you guys need more players? I'm DPS, obviously. I know the boss mechanics."

One of the three started to rise, only to be dragged roughly down by the remaining two. Three stat boxes popped up and were quickly snuffed out again, although Damien could still see exactly where they were. He stifled a laugh and tried again.

"Seriously, if I was looking for a fight I wouldn't be standing out in the open. Can you come out here so we—"

The same player rose up again, this time too fast for his allies to drag him back, and ran 90% of the way to him before taking a more considered approach to get within Damien's melee range. It was the level 39 ranger, CactusLover. Man, some people really don't care what they call their characters.

"Oh, wow, I-I can't believe it's you! And you're, uh, you're not killing me yet. That's great! Thank you. I've been watching you from the beginning, ever since the Touta— hey, can we get a picture?"

He abruptly put his arm around Damien's shoulder and beckoned his thoroughly compromised friends from the trees.

"Hey, guys, can one of you take a screenshot? C'mon, it's Daemien! I'll take one for you after?"

There were a few seconds before the two remaining players stepped out and clomped into the clearing. A level 38 paladin healer named LightLawd, clad in heavy armor and with a double-handed scepter that looked like it could heal almost as fast as it could bash in brains. Slightly low level for this dungeon, but as long as he knew what he was doing it wouldn't be a problem. The last of the trio quickly rounded LightLawd and strode in front of him, sword and board at the ready. Akunaratana, however you were supposed to say that, a level 42 warrior tank. He'd probably done this dungeon before. So they were only missing damage classes. Maybe another healer as well.

At least the core party roles were already filled. Now the introductions were out the way, Damien wanted to take this slow. This was the first time in a while he'd had a proper interaction with non-occultists. Damien still remembered the lesson Bartholomew had taught him when he'd first been conscripted: players were pretty much programmed to attack anything with a red name on sight. Well, anything with a red name that they thought they could beat without too much trouble.

Even if Damien's tentative allies were marginally lower level on average, they still represented a mild risk without the element of surprise. So he was a little uncomfortable with CactusLover being so chummy.

"That's...that's very flattering of you—," Damien shifted CactusLover's armpit off his shoulder and held him a little further away, "—but let's focus on the dungeon first. You're here to run it, right? Do you have room for one more?"

The corners of CactusLover's mouth turned up bit by bit. His enthusiasm was not mirrored by the party members standing fifteen paces behind him. The warrior had equipped his weapons and was standing combat-ready in front of the paladin.

"No. Cack, message HighZen, tell them to hurry up."

So they had a full party and these were just the front-runners. This was bad news. If any party ran the dungeon without Damien it wouldn't reset until the next day. He'd scouted this one and figured out when it was going to reset in advance, by shadowing the last party that ran it. There wasn't much hope of finding another dungeon that wasn't already resetting at such short notice, let alone a suitably high-level one on a Friday night.

It was peak time, it was crucial Damien record something worthwhile for his page to mark hitting level 40. CactusLover gave Damien a grimace and an apologetic shrug before obediently retreating behind his tank, where he proceeded to hammer out script on an invisible keyboard.

Akunaratana stood between Damien and his two charges. If the tank had ever dealt with Damien before, he would've known standing between him and his potential targets was a complete waste of time and space.

Damien could easily handle these three, so long as they were engaging on even terms. It helped that the ranger wasn't even looking at him, preoccupied with his own task. Well, he was looking up nervously every now and then, which was about as useful in Damien's presence as looking out the windshield of your car one second in every five. But what would killing them accomplish?

If Damien dealt with these guys before the rest of their party showed up, it would probably sink their dungeon run; losing both a healer and a tank would cripple their party, giving others time to come run the dungeon.

Another group might be open-minded, or desperate. On the other hand, killing players simply because they didn't want him in their party would not help future diplomatic endeavors. Especially right after Damien had specifically said he didn't want to fight.

Damien was already livestreaming, so odds were that the next party to arrive would be even less receptive than this one. The next group would likely come expressly to kill him, especially if he'd just showcased murdering their predecessors. Killing them would imply he'd never wanted to join a party, and had been trying to make Empire players drop their guard for easy kills. Even worse, one of the potential victims was apparently a fan. That didn't sit right at all.

Sticking around to meet and greet the rest of the group was a risk, but Damien was already invested in this exercise. There was too much to gain and too much to lose to let it go without a bit of extra effort. Akunaratana was just a scrub, perhaps this 'HighZen' would be worth talking to.

When they arrived, they came prepared for their uninvited guest. The clearing was quickly lit by torches as one player after another stepped into it. At their head was HighZen, a warrior with a difference: he was wearing all leather gear, agility-based from the looks of it, with a samurai sword as his weapon. It was a meta build, one that used speed for quick strikes and movement instead of following the traditional stat allocation for his class. Damien could relate.

The new arrivals spread out on either side of their leader in a long line, forming a wall between Damien and their point of ingress. Damien counted seven players to join the three who'd brought them there. Full party. At least their assassin wasn't cloaked, thanks in large part to the torches. Damien was better lit than him, though, courtesy of the Mana Wisp the party mage had sent to hover over his head.

Their full party had no need of him whatsoever and the light would prevent him from sneaking away as well. They were treating him as little more than a bonus target on the way to their primary objective. How rude.

His position was a great deal less secure than he'd hoped for, and the number of people watching his error of judgment in real time was increasing every second: 1,200 and counting.

Damien tilted his head and looked up to check the tree canopy, then returned his gaze back to HighZen as fast as he could self-correct. Sheesh, have a little self-control. I mean sure, there's a full party of designated enemy players with weapons drawn and spells ready, but that's no reason to give away your escape route. Quite the opposite. With all ten players amassed in front of him and no more arriving, Damien addressed the leader and made his proposal before they could make a mistake.

"I've been very nice, but I don't appreciate this reception when I've left your front-runners completely unharmed. I'm willing to compromise. I'll pay you for your services. 500 gold."

HighZen looked to his left, then his right, checking his guild-mates were ready while pantomiming to see if he'd heard correctly. Then, without responding, he gestured each way with his head for the rest of the party to go around. His group started to encircle the lone player at the clearing's center. The melee players – one assassin, one paladin tank and one dual-wielding warrior – closed the gap a little before edging sideways, making sure to keep their eyes on their target. The ranged players – a priest, a mage and a gunslinger – circled from a bit further back. The scouting party and HighZen remained in front of him, trying to occupy Damien's attention as they attempted this disrespectful, unsubtle maneuver.

"Are you really Daemien? I never had you pegged as someone who'd beg for his life."

Damien bit his tongue. Why couldn't decent people have shown up? He could've taken the "safe" option and ambushed them while they prepared for the dungeon. Yet of course they were woefully ungrateful. He replied to his adversary in kind, his voice layered with as much sarcasm as he felt he could get away with.

"*My* life? Ooooooh! I see, sorry for the confusion. I was

offering payment to join your party for the dungeon. Like a boost, except you won't be boosting me since I can pull my own weight. 500 gold covers the bounty on me in Camelot, so you get paid without the hassle and you get good PR for your guild too: I have quite a lot of followers and they'll all see you on my livestream. I made my intentions clear, didn't CactusLover pass my request along?"

CactusLover put his bow away and typed in midair as HighZen continued in the same vein as he'd started.

"He certainly did. Our resident occultist expert is the one who ensured we'd bring plenty of light to see you by. Your bounty's up, by the way. 500 won't cover it."

While HighZen babbled, buying time for his team to close the net, Damien processed. The bounty on him had gone up? Poorly timed. He was livestreaming, and this guy was trying to outsmart him in front of 2,000 viewers. As CactusLover reequipped his bow, the melee players encircling Damien abruptly took a few steps further back. They were now safely out of range were Damien to Demon Gate and combo into Implosion. His go-to initiation strategy.

Damien immediately shot CactusLover an angry look. The ranger looked pretty pleased with himself. Damien's "fan" was proving himself a problem. So much for worrying about his welfare. HighZen was enacting a self-fulfilling prophecy: he'd called Damien naive, when it was he himself who intended to punish Damien for pinning his hopes on other players.

It must be nice, being right all the time.

The leading players were just moving to the edges of his peripheral vision. A few more steps and he wouldn't be able to see them all without turning his head, which meant he'd be unable to dodge attacks in time. He unfolded his arms and flexed his fingers at his sides. Last chance.

"This isn't what I wanted," Damien started, focusing on HighZen against all instinct as the front-runners cleared him on either side, "you're making a big mistake."

His adversary showed nothing but excitement as Damien was flanked. Having got past his field of vision, they were now running to close the gap behind him as fast as possible. Time's up. Damien had tried being nice. Now they'd get the other thing. He drew his dagger with his right hand as his left shot upward, pointing at the ground directly behind HighZen. Damien raised his hooded head, sneering down his nose at the man who'd rejected his offer to cooperate.

"Imp-losion!"

HighZen and the players on either side of him immediately span round to look where Damien was pointing, their arms raised to protect themselves in advance of the pull. There was, of course, no imp there to have been Imp-loded. Had Damien sent an imp to that precise spot, the players at his flanks would've noticed and called out a warning before it got within range, or simply attacked Damien immediately. However, having diverted the attention of the players in front of him away from him, and with his face obscured by his hood from everywhere else, Damien could now make his escape without them realizing where.

Hopefully. Because the plethora of sound effects around him indicated that everyone who hadn't turned was attacking him.

Damien had already rolled his eyes to look directly upward without moving his head. Combined with his well-utilized sneer, he could just about see the only imp he was currently interested in: the one he'd nervously checked on in the tree canopy high above. With a focused glance and an expedient thought, Damien and the imp swapped places.

Damien grabbed the branch as the imp who'd taken his place was eviscerated by arrow fire and spell-casts. But not all the projectiles had connected with the much smaller target sacrificed in Damien's stead. There were some screams, prompting him to look down in puzzlement. He hadn't taken any offensive action, what was going on?

He leaned over the edge of the branch for clarification and what he saw warmed his heart. Once the imp had faded away to dust, some of the people who'd been shooting him from the flanks had hit their allies in the crossfire. His sense of schadenfreude intensified when he saw that one of those hit had been HighZen himself.

Damien had a bird's-eye view of the clearing, and his enemies were in disarray. Now he could direct his demons like a good old-fashioned real-time strategy game. This was his favorite way to play, directing his minions from the shadows without any personal risk whatsoever. Totally removed from combat. Above and beyond all consequences. Without—

There was a dull *thunk* as an arrow embedded itself in his shoulder, knocking Damien backward off his perch. It's rather difficult to play real-time strategy when you have to dodge projectiles coming out of your screen. His right arm with the dagger equipped lashed out, piercing the thick bough and preventing his fall. His momentum carried him underneath, prompting him to latch on with his remaining arm. It was just as well that agility was his second-highest stat. It had saved him from a rather embarrassing demise, at the cost of being completely exposed to everyone below.

"He's up there, everybody look up! Fire on that branch, he's vulnerable!"

The air around Damien suddenly sang with projectiles. The light from the torches didn't reach that high and there was no shortage of branches overhead, so they'd resorted to firing blindly. As long as Damien didn't let his profile show too obviously against the moonlight, he'd be safe. Or so he thought. He carefully dragged his body around the branch and was attempting to discreetly pull himself back up when a second arrow thundered into his side. It had barely struck before the priest cast a Holy Orb into the air, covering the whole clearing in bright light and illuminating Damien for all to see.

Screw it. Damien swiveled, dug his feet into the bottom of the branch and propelled himself forward and down. He twisted in midair, sinking his daggers into the tree trunk he'd aimed at. His rapid descent was jerkily halted as he hit the tree, costing him yet more health through impact damage, then he scrambled around before the next slew of missiles could catch up.

Damien shimmied down the trunk to the nearest branch in

cover, his mind furiously working. How had he been spotted? He'd taken great pains to ensure they wouldn't see where he was going with his Demon Gate, yet those arrows had come sailing straight to him, as if CactusLover knew exactly...

Oh! What a little turd! Damien had specifically told the group he was livestreaming, and CactusLover had spent a fair amount of time on his keyboard immediately after that. He was watching Damien's livestream in a window while he played, seeing everything Damien saw. If you're low profile, livestreaming barely matters. If you're both high profile and a contentious loner, you're inviting stream snipers to dump all over you. Now, for the sake of trying to appease his audience against his better judgment, he'd have to deal with this mess.

Damien's health and stamina were both suffering. He'd have to defer minion management to his second-in-command to get a handle on this situation. No way was he sticking his head around the corner to get killed by screen-watching scum. He closed his eyes, even as more projectiles hurtled around him, and focused on his thoughts. He didn't need a line of sight to his best minion to use him to his full potential.

Noigel, Bloodlust. One imp face-hugging every enemy, plus a hell hound on the priest. Send everything else to my location around the tree line.

It wasn't his preferred plan, but it was the only real option he had besides cutting and running. He certainly wouldn't end the livestream until this was resolved. He'd handle this, with Noigel's help. He patted the Bag of Holding at his waist and held his hand out to drink a health potion, just as the suppressing fire on him abated and the screaming down below began.

The Death-God party had taken such pains to keep their distance from Damien when he was at the center of the clearing. The squishiest of them were arrayed around the outside, nearest the tree line. Which is where Damien had been keeping his 30 souls' worth of minions concealed. Combined with the movement and attack-speed boosts that his succubi's 'Bloodlust' provided his summoned units, not to mention the 'Hell's Angels' trait granting his imps wings that exponentially increased their movement speed and flight, it was no surprise they were finding their marks. He'd had his tentative allies flanked long before they'd attempted to flank him.

Damien was relieved he'd survived long enough to show he wasn't as helpless as he'd endeavored to appear. He hadn't chosen this dungeon simply for the prestige, it was also an ideal staging ground if things did not go his way. Now it was Noigel's turn to capitalize on his planning.

Noigel was a fantastic unit manager. He and Damien had refined target priority, tactics and combination moves over the last couple of weeks. It was paying off.

Damien risked a glance around the tree trunk to get a grasp on the situation. Over half the players were imp-capacitated, which was Damien's shorthand for 'they were rolling around on the floor, trying to pull imps off their faces'. The priest was all but dead, an imp raking his face and a burning hell hound savaging his throat, and with no help in sight.

Face-hugging had always been effective crowd control, but only lasted a few seconds depending on the target. Using so many at once was a gamble. The more physically capable players were dealing with their imps, then assisting whoever was nearest. Removing the priest had been important, but Damien needed more value out of this.

Damien picked out the mage. Rather than leaving the dirty work to others, Noigel had taken on the secondary target personally and was clawing and biting for all he was worth. The mage had lost a quarter of his health and the rest of Damien's enemies were still mostly preoccupied.

Damien raised his arms, a dagger clasped in each hand, and Demon Gated. He'd no sooner swapped places with Noigel, his thighs straddling his unfortunate opponent's head in a purely circumstantial tea-bagging, than both his hands plunged down. Each of them pierced the top of the mage's head through to the hilt.

Casters were not generally built with high constitution, and this one was no exception. Damien rolled off the corpse and stared back at the tree. Noigel was leaning round the trunk so

Damien could see him, anticipating his return without any need for instruction.

Having activated his 'Rift Walker' trait which granted experience for killing an enemy, Damien's Demon Gate cooldown had been reset. He'd only been absent from his tree for a few seconds when he Demon Gated back into it again, safe, sound and away from battle. Noigel did not fare so well in Damien's place. An arrow sailed through his head and blew his brains out into the undergrowth behind him.

Damien liked CactusLover less and less. He'd dealt with his assigned face-hugger imp quickly and then executed Damien's best minion. Damien would almost have rather taken the hit himself. With Noigel dead, he'd have to direct his troops himself, which meant sticking his head in CactusLover's screen-watching sights.

Now they were in combat, all the torches requiring a free hand had been extinguished one by one in favor of full combat capability. The priest was dead, his Holy Orb sputtering away. The mage was dead, his Mana Wisp had fizzled out of existence. Damien was most of the way to achieving his ulterior motive of plunging the group into darkness. The last obstacle in his way was his least favorite fan, CactusLover, who was spraying the trees at the clearing's edge with one enflamed arrow after another. He was creating a ring of light around the clearing to block Damien's potential points of ingress.

Damien scowled. He should've killed this guy first. He was still processing his disgust when CactusLover, a new fire arrow notched and drawn, abruptly turned from the tree he'd been facing and loosed straight at Damien's all but imperceptible head. Damien had to pull back as the arrow whistled past his nose into the dense forest beyond. It was pretty clear by this point who Damien's next target priority was.

It's quite an advantage, seeing what your opponent sees. But at least he wouldn't be able to tell what Damien was thinking. If he was so intent on watching through Damien's eyes, that could be used to Damien's advantage. How many minions did he have left? He checked his Soul Summon Limit and found it at 17 out of 30. Sounded right, he'd lost a hell hound and ten imps, Noigel included. That left him with a succubus, a wraith, one last hell hound and four more imps. He'd have to make do.

From the safety of cover, Damien assigned his minions their orders. The hell hound and wraith would be coming with him. He'd have to keep them behind him, otherwise CactusLover would rob them of the element of surprise, but all three of them moved fast enough to make up for it. The four imps and the succubus would remain hidden until he'd provided an adequate distraction. He took a deep breath, focusing on what he wanted to happen, and started running clockwise around the outside of the densely forested circle, away from the fire arrows embedded in the trees around his location. He stayed just within the darkness the foliage provided, making sure to keep his eyes on CactusLover as much as possible.

CactusLover took the bait. He immediately abandoned his campaign for a better lit forest and started yelling orders at his superiors, his excitement getting the better of him.

"He's trying to flank us! Follow my arrows and chase him down, I'll cover you!"

Most of his allies ignored him, either because the one issuing the orders was a scrub or because they didn't feel like chasing an occultist around in the woods. Damien glanced around the clearing, looking for HighZen and wondering why he wasn't giving the orders. The raid leader was nowhere to be seen. That was a problem.

Damien had more pressing concerns. The party assassin had decided to follow CactusLover's instruction. The lack of light was a benefit for him too, and he was better suited for one-on-one combat than Damien. He threw his arms out behind himself and, following the trajectory of CactusLover's arrows, charged into the trees at Damien's back.

Damien couldn't help but groan as his new target vanished, even when he knew he needed to focus. He was aware that, in theory, holding your arms behind you made assassins run faster. Even so, he'd never submit to looking quite that much of a tryhard to do so. This guy probably had the Ninja trait and everything. For shame.

If the assassin got him it was likely game over. Since his own character was an 'assassin-lite', with most of his focus on the wisdom stat in order to have a full roster of demons, he was ideal prey. Assassins not only beat him soundly on physical stats, they also came pretty close to the heightened senses and movement speed occultists boasted in the dark.

Fortunately, courtesy of multiple experiences with assassins, Damien had developed a single-word command to address this problem.

"Fetch."

There were a few seconds where the only sounds were the snapping of twigs under his feet and the rush of arrows around him as CactusLover continued trying to guesstimate his location. Then there were a series of short, sharp pants as the hell hound closed in, the Detect skill very much in play. The silence was interrupted by half a swear word, which in turn was interrupted by a snarl, after which followed a great deal of decidedly unstealthy yelling. Without skipping a beat, the wraith delivered a stab in passing before continuing to follow in Damien's slipstream.

Damien risked a glance at CactusLover, the night vision bestowed by his 'Shadow Walker' trait becoming advantageous in the absence of light sources. The hell hound's ignition and the assassin's screaming were distracting CactusLover enough for his own screen to provide more interest than his target's. The rest of the party's attention had been drawn to the burning mass at the edge of the woods. The warrior and paladin tanks were at the front, with the rest bringing up the rear.

This wasn't exactly what Damien had planned, but it would suffice. He paused with his back to a tree and leaned out to check where the flaming arrows were. It was much easier to locate them now he'd made his way to the opposite side of the clearing. Once they were gone, this battlefield would be much more hospitable. For him, anyway. His four imps promptly flew from the trees to remove the arrows.

Damien quickly drew back behind his cover and called the wraith to his side. He turned it away from himself and thought 'Possession'. His vision jumped two feet forward and his real body slumped to the ground behind him. With any luck, even if CactusLover was watching his screen it would only register as a blip. Damien's real body hadn't finished rag-dolling behind his borrowed one before he propelled his new vehicle even further around the clearing, guiding it at extreme speed while avoiding incoming obstacles by smoothly leaning left and right.

It took three seconds of weaving through trees at breakneck pace before Damien found himself at the edge of the stairway up the mountain, where his failed attempt at diplomacy had begun. He was now precisely on the opposite side of the clearing from the hell hound he'd enflamed, exactly where he needed to be. He veered into the clearing and tore toward the center, where CactusLover had positioned himself to grant maximum reaction time.

Damien had reduced this meager advantage to nothing. His 'Nine-Tenths of the Lore' trait granted anything he possessed doubled stats, and the wraith's primary stat was agility. The imps had extinguished four of the six burning arrows simultaneously, as well as providing an unforeseen benefit: CactusLover had turned his attention to fire at them instead of looking after himself.

With his minion's agility doubled, the superior 'Shadow Beast' passive ability fully activated in the dark, the beefiest units drawn to the opposite side of the field and his target's attention diverted, Damien was in good shape to achieve his objectives.

Damien was halfway across the clearing before CactusLover's screen-watching alerted him to the danger. He turned just in time to receive an arm-blade through the neck. As Damien drove him into the floor, the object of his ire gurgled half for the benefit of his party and half in delight.

"I'm being killed by Daemien!"

Damien drew back his second arm and prepared to plunge its attached blade through the ranger's chest. The whole battle would be much easier once this guy was dead. So he was doubly perturbed when a slender curved blade protruded between his eyes, directly out of the wraith's forehead, before he could deliver the finishing blow.

Damien's vision abruptly blurred and he was back in his own body in a fraction of a second. He peered around the tree trunk from the floor. HighZen was standing over the smoldering remains of his wraith's corpse, offering his free hand to CactusLover to drag him back to his feet. CactusLover had survived with just a fraction of his health left thanks to HighZen's expedient intervention. But where had his savior come from? He'd probably Charged in from cover, with his agility-based character making it even faster. What a palaver.

"Hey—," the party leader yelled, "—we need a heal over here!"

Oh, I don't think so. This was more than worth risking his succubus for. As the party wheeled around, their brief encounter with the diverting hell hound finished, Damien's spell-casting minion started charging a Chaotic Bolt. Damien focused on the subtle purple light on the opposite side of the field of battle and possessed its wielder as quickly as possible. Possession had no cooldown, he wanted to end CactusLover by his 'own' hand, and possessing his succubus would double its intelligence to make that a reality.

He entered his new vessel just as the Chaotic Bolt pulsed, indicating it was fully charged. With very little time to tarry, Damien flung it at the middle of the field. CactusLover didn't quite have time to complete the defiant, exultant utterance he was yelling into the woods around him before it connected.

"I survived Daemien himself! Take tha—"

Then the bolt pounded into him and he exploded. Coated in his anti-occultist tactician's remains and shrouded in almost complete darkness, HighZen announced the only tactically sound decision he'd made all evening.

"Retreat!"

They'd thought themselves capable of dealing with Damien as a ten-man party, but now they'd lost their four most crucial roles and were fighting blind. Damien thought about letting them leave before deciding it wasn't appropriate. Four out of ten was not enough to compensate for his wasted planning.

He wasn't gonna catch 'em all. They were scattering, taking the nearest exit rather than leaving as a group. HighZen himself had sounded the retreat and wasn't sticking around to make sure everyone got out okay. Akunaratana and LightLawd were running to catch up with their guild leader, but HighZen was much faster than either of them and leaving them behind. These three would do.

Damien had two imps and a succubus left. The succubus was still under his Possession. He extended her wings and dropped into a dive, using the speed of the drop to boost his chase. Using the succubus's wings was much like guiding the wraith, only with an extra dimension added to where he willed it to go. It was extremely useful, being able to impart your consciousness to an expendable body. It allowed Damien to play very aggressively, not to mention granting a wide range of abilities to use in imaginative ways.

As Damien flew over the fleeing players in the dark, he pointed his vessel's clawed forefinger at the ground directly in front of HighZen and thought 'Circle of Hell'. A wide ring of black fire immediately engulfed the escape route and Damien's target blundered straight into it. HighZen had stopped nearly in the center when Damien landed in front of him, the succubus's whip already coiling forward to encircle HighZen's neck.

HighZen hadn't even decided if he was coming or going. He was not on his guard. The steel barbs pierced him around and around, then encompassed his hands when they instinctively shot upward to try and remove the obstruction. Damien took the whip in both hands and yanked it over his head, dragging HighZen onto his knees.

Damien had approximately half a second to enjoy the spectacle before his vessel burst into golden flames. His succubus had been Smitten. While his foray with her had been an immensely successful maneuver, the paladin healer and warrior tank were not far behind.

The succubus would last a few more seconds. Damien needed to get into position. He canceled the Possession and jumped to his feet, running past the tree he'd been hiding behind just in time to watch the tank run up and finish his lone demon off.

She'd already fulfilled her purpose: Damien's final two imps had caught up. The first of them was hovering above and in between HighZen and Akunaratana, right at the furthest range of the ability. Where the pull would be strongest.

The Streaming Champion pointed.

"Imp-losion."

The unstable portal cracked open over their heads and sucked everything toward it with incredible speed, pulling the two of them into the air. The rift closed a fraction of a second later, taking the imp with it, and they collided where it had first materialized.

That was only the start of their problems. The second imp had swooped in underneath them in the wake of the Imp-loding first and was ready to perform Damien's demonstration of the most stupid ability he'd seen in the game (so far). The cherry on the cake of why not partying with him had been an incredibly bad idea. Damien equipped his daggers, pointed at the second imp and, squinting his eyes, braced himself. He'd been waiting for a fitting occasion to use his newly acquired trump card, the trait he'd chosen for hitting level 40. This was as good as it would get. He pointed again.

"Ex-Imp-losion."

His new ability was the polar opposite of its paired sibling. Where the former pulled things in, this one very much repulsed them. While they both required an imp as cost, this one did not forcibly dismiss the imp and leave half a soul behind in return. It blew the imp apart from the inside out, removing it from the field in a much more direct manner. However, that was more than equitable given the ability's effect: every time Damien Imploded an imp, a charge was added to the Ex-Imp-losion icon in his HUD. For each charge, the energy and imps drawn into the rifts from Imp-losion's casting were added to Ex-Imp-losion's next cast.

Damien had charged it fully before he came. Five charges. Which meant not only was he about to receive five imps from this rift, but that they were going to be fired out of it with five times the force of an Imp-losion. Considering Imp-losion packed enough of a punch to pull tanks into the air like beach volleyballs hit by baseball bats, that constituted considerable power.

Damien was very glad to be behind his tree.

If the Imp-losion had precipitated a piercing crack, Ex-Implosion's cast was announced via a deafening roar. Two rag-dolling bodies above it hurtled high into the tree line in different directions, helpfully screaming and thus allowing Damien an acoustic approximation of their trajectories. He surmised they were going very far, very fast. LightLawd was close enough to get hit by the blast as well. He shot past Damien with a low hum of displaced air and disappeared into the woods far behind.

The trees snapped and bent over backward, creaking and shaking as the blast tore through them. Even from Damien's relatively distant cover, his head was thrown back and his hood blown off by sheer force. Imp-losion had a maximum area of effect. Ex-Imp-losion had no such discernable boundary.

One of the complications was that Damien could not control how the imps left the rift. One of them was shot directly downward at twenty-eight meters per second over less than ten meters, which translated the imp into a smudge. Another was marginally luckier, avoiding the floor but being thrown into a nearby tree before it could self-correct. What remained of it was not in flying condition.

The remaining three were fortunate enough to get thrown out in directions that did not immediately ensure crippling injury or death, and they dutifully did exactly what Damien had ordered them to do through Noigel. They used their Ex-Implosion-enhanced momentum to fly toward the nearest un-impeded enemy and latch onto them.

One was fired straight up and latched onto Akunaratana before he'd finished the ascending segment of his flight. His extended stay in the Circle of Hell had not been kind. He was still burning. Damien immediately Demon Gated onto him in midair, latched his legs around the tank's waist from behind and started frenziedly stabbing him in the back of the head.

This tactic would only work if he managed to kill his target, otherwise the cooldown on his Demon Gate wouldn't reset and he'd be committing exotic, elaborate suicide. His best chance to avoid that was by inflicting as much damage as possible before the armor reduction of Circle of Hell wore off.

Akunaratana, bless him, had absolutely no idea what was happening. Damien critically stabbed him through his armored skull three times before the armor-reducing flames wore off, at which point Damien meticulously levered the dagger that was still embedded in his helmet and rained blows on the side of his neck with his Striking Dagger instead. They'd just reached the top of their trajectory when his target expired.

Damien kicked off his body and turned his head toward the remaining screams. The raid leader was not heavily armored, so the blast had carried him a little faster and a little higher. There was no imp currently on him, but there was one flying straight in his direction. The raid leader already had low health. He'd probably die from fall damage if left to his own devices, but Damien wanted as active a role in his demise as possible.

Damien Demon Gated to the second imp and they swapped momentum. Less than half a second later Damien's dagger was embedded in the raid leader's chest. HighZen stopped screaming, his face a confused tangle of terror, as Damien brought his own face in close.

"Who's naive?"

It only took one more stab through his forehead, then gravity started bringing them both down. Time to get off. Damien looked to the edge of the forest where he'd come from and ordered the first imp he'd swapped positions with out into the center of the clearing where he could see it. There was too much at stake to play chicken with Arcadia's surface. He Demon Gated to the floor as soon as he saw the imp, in order to swap places and momentum again, leaving the plummeting imp to control its own descent.

He'd pulled it off. He had to secure the area. Some of the

enemies had been running and might, if they lacked common sense, come back. A hell hound was the priority, so he'd be alerted if that happened. Especially since a fair portion of his viewers could be running to his location at this very moment.

So long as that was taken care of, there was something else he wanted to see. In all the excitement, Damien had neglected to keep track of his most important stat. He glanced up at the viewer count on his HUD and suddenly felt extremely self-conscious. Over the last five minutes, nearly 50,000 people had tuned in to watch his first ever livestream. He'd better say something.

"Uuuuuuuh—," off to a good start, as usual, "—thanks for watching, this has been Daemien murdering a bunch of people who didn't want to do a dungeon with me. I swear it was an accident, I really did want to join up with them, but then, you see, that guy HighZen, he was really rude. Yeah. And he— you know what, you should probably watch the whole thing from the beginning and then you'll get it. Okay. I have some looting to do. Shout-out to CactusLover for being a huge pain in my— in the butt. Okay then. Bye!"

Feeling his face turning red, he blinked twice and the red recording light switched off. Well, there was at least one area of his career he could identify as requiring improvement. He was much better at preparing statements when there weren't tens of thousands of people watching him live.

He was halfway to summoning a new hell hound when a loud *ping* indicated he'd received a message. Damien opened his menu without canceling his channeled summon and focused on the message, closing the menu and bringing the message screen up in a window.

Scorpius-*beta*: Very imp-ressive! A bit gruesome for my tastes, but those people weren't very nice. Since your 'dungeon' thing hasn't worked out, dinner is in half an hour. Love you, Mom. xxx

Damien's freshly unflushed face went crimson. His mom had been watching that display. Oh dear. That would make for an awkward conversation. The hell hound had already been summoned for ten seconds, his three remaining imps were idle and Damien himself was staring off into space. He shook himself and sent them out to pillage the fruits of his labors. He had to collect all the soul energy and loot the bodies as fast as possible.

Damien knew it was completely illogical, but he had a sudden, deeply unpleasant image of Cassandra standing over his mostly unclothed body as it lay prone on the bed. Looming over him. Her arms folded and her foot tapping.

Better summon a portal first, just in case.

2

HOME IS WHERE THE HEART IS

Back in his new base, Damien squatted over the loot bags his demons had brought through and examined his haul. Aside from each player ceding him an item of equipped gear and the occasional potion, there was in fact nothing. No gold, no raw materials and certainly no choice items of interchangeable gear that had been sitting around in their inventories. Players had been so much more lax back when he'd entered the scene.

In a region where everyone had known their place and thus what to expect, players had been much more comfortable carrying the majority of their worldly possessions with them. His primary targets, the members of Rising Tide, had been incredibly comfortable in their superiority and had proven the most lax of all, to Damien's profit. Now that PvP was rampant again, everyone was much more cautious.

Of course, Damien was the root cause of that instability. Everyone had low-key hated Aetherius, but were happy to ignore what essentially amounted to a dictatorship in exchange for stability. Since Damien was not only the author of their overlord's demise but also the most prolific 'Enemy of the Realm', he made the perfect scapegoat.

This lazy sentiment was not helped by the exodus of Rising Tide players into the very guilds they'd been suppressing. These cronies-turned-fugitives had been accepted with open arms.

From there, they'd seized the narrative and infused their new allies of opportunity with their occultist hate. Damien understood. He wasn't happy about it, but it made sense. There'd been an enormous number of players in Aetherius's guild and their levels were higher than average. Turning them away out of principle would only mean more battle power for rival guilds in uncertain times.

Good thing he was a solo player, then. All he had to worry about was how many views his profile got, and today had been a good day. 50,000 viewers in a single five-minute sitting, with more to come when he put it on his page! Kevin would surely be pleased. Damien would have to give a commentary on it later to capitalize on his first legit livestream, even if it had been shorter and more 'murder-hobo-ey' than he'd planned.

First things first. Damien checked his stat page and was immediately hit with an endorphin rush. He'd secured a further two levels' worth of experience from the Death-God guild players thanks to his 'Soul Harvest' mechanic. It could've been a little more. Perhaps that's why some of them had been less than eager to engage him and were so quick to distance themselves from HighZen. More likely than not, they'd had the most experience points to lose. Too bad.

Damien went over his current stats:

Class: Occultist
Level: 42
Health: 960/960 **Stamina:** 1,010/1,010 **Mana:** 3,020/3,020
Strength: 51 **Agility:** 145 **Intelligence:** 51
Constitution: 96 **Endurance:** 101 **Wisdom:** 302
Stat points: 10
Experience: 11,896/42,000
Soul Summon Limit: 9/30 **Soul Reserve:** 5/10 (+0/1)

It was only recently that his Soul Summon Limit, undoubtedly the most important attribute for his playstyle, had hit 30. The growth of that particular class feature had been a source of constant vexation. It was obviously subject to severely diminishing returns: he'd already had a max Soul Summon Limit of 27 at just 244 wisdom points, yet it had taken a further 56 stat points to bring it to 30.

The moment his Soul Summon Limit hit 30, Damien had started investing in agility instead. Even if his Soul Summon Limit did go over 30, it wasn't worth the points to make it do so. They'd be better utilized making him move faster and inflict more damage personally. He immediately sank the new 10 stat points into agility, raising it to 155.

The fact his wisdom still rose by a point each level aggravated his OCD, since he had no need for further points in that stat yet had another 58 levels ahead before he hit the presumed level cap of 100. Fortunately he anticipated changing gear a great many times before reaching that point. He could phase out the wisdom on his equipment for other stats. Assuming he ever found any other viable equipment.

His latest haul was not comforting in that regard. Lots of nice items, almost none of which were suitable for him personally. The assassin had left behind a hood with 50 agility, which had been promising. But equipping it would interfere with his Occultist Adept Robes set bonus, so he'd be losing 15 agility, constitution, endurance and wisdom. Which meant a loss of 150 health and stamina, a minion slot and a fair chunk of the agility he'd gain, just for the sake of hitting a little harder. He threw that onto the discard pile and was left with a single item for consideration, so small that he hadn't noticed it until everything else was gone.

HighZen's Ring of Fortitude: 30 Endurance, 20 Constitution

Now this was a good find. He'd filled up the first of his ring slots long ago but had been running with the second one empty. This finally meant his character would be fully geared and he wouldn't have to remove anything in order to receive the new stats. He slid it onto the ring finger of his right hand and checked out his equipment page to appreciate the lack of empty slots. Head, chest, hands, legs, feet, amulet, two rings and two weapons in his weapon slots. Magnificent.

Satisfied, Damien sent his base minions to carry away the remaining gear for scrap. While they set to work, he paced to his Tier II Soul Well and examined it.

Soul Well II
Health: 500
Soul Capacity: 15/20

He'd saved 5 souls in his Soul Reserve for just this purpose. Today's outing had been a net loss for Damien's minion and soul counts. He'd have to get them back up eventually, but in the short term he could supplement his numbers by juggling minions between his own Soul Summon Limit when he was online and that of his Soul Well when he was offline.

He tapped the Soul Well five times to move his five internally stored souls to his Soul Well's capacity. Then he dumped Noigel, an imp and the hell hound into the Soul Well, leaving four imps attached to himself. His Soul Well currently had a hell hound, a wraith, a succubus and seven imps. It wouldn't repel a serious attack, but Damien had taken his time creating a space where he was unlikely to be bothered. He was still sore about losing out on the spoils of his fight with Aetherius, as well as the subsequent destruction of his base.

If only he hadn't been disconnected, all those riches could've been his. He'd have lost his base either way, since he'd promised Bartholomew he'd only stay in the dungeon for a week. He supposed it had been worth it, since the buzz surrounding his nemesis being killed by Scorepeeus63 had been the cherry on the cake of his victory. It had taken a lot of effort to reestablish himself, though.

The true winner of the battle, much to the surprise of everyone except Damien, had been Bartholomew. His master had respawned in a dungeon filled to the brim with soul energy and immediately restored himself and his abode to their former inglory. The conniving git had probably planned for something like this all along. On top of that, true to the far-fetched promise Damien had made in order to secure a base in his dungeon, Bartholomew had awakened to scores of level 1 players who were literally lined up waiting to be turned into fully fledged occultists.

It turned out Bartholomew was quite picky when he had plenty of players to choose from. The streams of his initiation rituals had been amusing for everyone except those subjected to them.

"Master. I know you said to leave you alone when you're thinking, but I'm starting to worry you've slipped into a coma."

Damien winced at Noigel's clumsily dumped exposition. He hadn't ever told his minion that his mother had been in a coma, mainly because he'd rather Noigel made remarks of that nature by accident instead of on purpose. His minion's loyalty had been pretty much unwavering ever since he'd been bestowed with wings, following some strict disciplinary measures at the start of their relationship. He still had quite an attitude on him, more than enough to warrant Damien picking his words carefully. Better to keep his work and home life separate.

"No, just thinking of how far we've come. How are the base upgrades coming along?"

"The Demon Forge is Tier II. We're upgrading the Gateway. Estimated construction time is eight hours."

Damien nodded. In his experience, Noigel gave himself very generous estimates. If Noigel said it would take eight hours, it would probably be complete in six. Then he'd spend the rest of the time wooing the succubus.

"Your orders are unchanged. Well done today, that mage needed to go down. Sorry you took an arrow through the head."

Noigel waved a dismissive claw at him.

"It was a good clean shot, much better than when it takes a while."

Noigel bowed before flying off into the depths of the cave. Seconds later, the predictable screaming started as he set his charges to work. There was a red glow as he ordered the succubus to cast Bloodlust and soon the whole cave was a cacophony of noise.

One of the arrangements they'd worked out between them ensured Noigel was always accompanied by a succubus when overseeing construction: Damien would bind a succubus to the base and Noigel could trigger her Bloodlust to speed up project times whenever she had the mana to do so. It was quite often, since his summons regenerated quickly outside of combat.

It was a win for Noigel too, since it all but guaranteed that the construction would be complete ahead of schedule and he'd have something to do afterwards to pass the time. There were all sorts of exploits for this class, if you had the wherewithal and the stomach to find them.

Once the Gateway had been upgraded, Damien would be able to cast portals leading to the bottom of the Downward Spiral as well as to his own base. Which was important to him right now, not simply because of the increased mobility but due to his single most pressing concern. He hadn't learned a single new ability since 'Summon Incubus' at level 30. The Gateway upgrade option had come at level 40 and would surely be useful, but his combat abilities were stagnating. The Ex-Imp-losion his level 40 trait granted had been a refreshing change, but he couldn't wait ten levels for every new development.

He had to talk to Bartholomew and seek guidance on how to progress with his build from here. If his mentor had any quests for him, that would be even better. Either option would provide him with a direction for future streams, rather than repeating what he'd been doing: dossing around attacking targets of opportunity and making ill-advised attempts to party up with plebs. He could worry about that tomorrow. For once, he was showing up to dinner on time.

"Noigel, I'm headed out. Keep up the good work."

His minion threw him a thumbs-up and set his task force back to the matter at hand. Damien opened his menu and waited the ten seconds to log out.

He woke up to the inside of his visor, the internal display asking whether he'd like to quit from Saga Online to the root menu. He threw on some light clothes and opened his door. There was Cassandra, humming as she fussed over the new food processor.

There was still a part of Damien that couldn't accept it. There'd been a time when he was all but certain he'd never see her again. That her last conscious thought would be of their stupid argument. Now she was more herself than she'd been in a very long time.

Damien pulled the door to behind him and it clicked shut, his mother's humming cutting out as she turned her head.

"Hey, you're early!"

Her face flashed in a big smile before turning back to the food processor unit, which was still complaining loudly.

Her smiles had once been thin, tight and unwavering. Hardly smiles at all. More like beleaguered battle lines, to be held at any cost. They'd been pinned down for a long time, but were now striking out to reclaim old territory: the first wave would push back her newly plump cheeks, working its way toward the interior to crinkle her nose before surging onward and upward to flank her eyes.

A real smile. Not a sick charade for the benefit of an ungrateful son.

He put on a smile of his own, making sure to push a little harder so it might reach his cheeks, and came to stand beside her. He put a hand on her shoulder. She distractedly patted it while continuing to attack the display with a pointed finger.

"Still giving you trouble? I can call Lillian, she's got the same model."

"I'll figure it out on my own, I've already got to the last stage. I'm more worried about you. Are you feeling alright? You had a difficult time at work today."

Damien stifled a snort. It was bizarre, hearing his mom refer to Saga Online as 'work'. It was even stranger, though less hilarious, to hear her describe the bread and butter of his dream job as 'a difficult time'.

"Mom, what are you talking about? It went really well. Somebody dropped a ring for me, it has some endurance and constitution. Very useful for me."

Cassandra jabbed the display a few more times and there was a positive-sounding *ping*, after which she finally straightened up and ushered Damien toward the table.

"Mmm, that's nice, dear, but it's not what I was talki—"

The two of them were barely sat down when Cassandra's guardian wristband went off. Within two seconds she'd already silenced the alarm and her hands were rummaging in her pockets, looking for medicine capsules she neither had nor needed. Force of habit. The two of them shared an awkward grimace as she turned her attention to the guardian wristband display instead.

"What does it say? Is everything alright?"

"It's fine, it's just another scheduled check. I don't know why I even bother, this thing is supposed to run ten years before it needs looking at and it was installed last week."

She tapped her chest as she talked and Damien couldn't help but grimace at the glassy *clinks* it made in reply. Cassandra glanced up in time to catch his reaction.

"Hey, cut that out. You paid a lot of credits for this thing and it's a damn sight better than the one I had before!"

Damien silently squinted at the upside-down display from the other side of the table, then at the spot where the bionic replacement's servicing panel glowed through her clothing. Granted, a working bionic heart was much better than a failing regular one. He'd still rather his mother had been given a lab-grown heart for the same price, even if they were reserved for people with lesser means and longer waiting times. They might've been a bit less durable, but they were a great deal less exotic. Or high maintenance.

As things were, they'd simply swapped one uncomfortable ritual for another. Fortunately, his mom had adapted to it pretty quickly. She seemed to be handling the lump of madness in her chest a lot better than he was. And the regular testing would only last until the end of the week, while it calibrated. Then her recovery period would be at an end and she'd be due back at work, although Damien was vying to make that unnecessary.

The food processor went off and Damien went to fetch it. He opened the top panel and immediately understood why his mom had been having so much trouble. She'd made pizza. What kind wasn't immediately obvious but it was a pretty good attempt, better than any pizza he'd personally managed so far.

By the time he got it back to the table, Cassandra was finally done with the guardian wristband display. Now she was pursing her lips and checking her fingernails. Damien assumed she was searching for well-earned praise, right up until she opened her mouth and looked at him coyly.

"How is Lillian, by the way? I'm still surprised you haven't introduced us yet."

"Well, we've both been pretty busy since you got back, but I'm sure you'll meet her eventually."

"Mmm. I've got to admit, of all the crazy things that happened to you the strangest is ending up shacked up with such a nice girl. You...you didn't get up to any, you know..."

Damien looked up at Cassandra and choked on his slice. She had crossed her eyes, opened her mouth and was pushing her eyebrows up and down with gusto. Damien held his hands out in front of him.

"It was nothing like that. Moooooom, stop it!"

"Alright, alright, I believe you. I've stopped, you can look up. After everything that happened I'd still like to thank her personally. Any chance you can bring her back here?"

Damien checked through the gaps in his fingers to make sure it was safe, then shook his head and continued devouring pizza. He needed to eat enough to sustain himself, quickly, in case his mom decided to pull another stunt. Her high spirits were having some unexpected side effects, including but not limited to a sudden redevelopment of her sense of humor at his expense.

"Well, if not tomorrow then sometime soon, hopefully. Anyway, I got distracted. I wanted to talk to you about your new job. Especially that fight you had tonight with all those other players."

Damien slowed down enough to chew his food. This sounded serious. He hadn't managed to swallow before Cassandra pressed on, her head nodding and her eyes roving the room as she thoughtfully sounded out what she had to say. It appeared as though she'd been rehearsing it for some time.

"I've caught up with all the videos you posted for the competition, and you told me what it was like getting around while I was gone. I'm sorry you went through that for me. It's all turned out very well, but I can only imagine how horrible it was. I'm pretty sure you've been downplaying it."

She fixed Damien with a sudden steely gaze and he was caught sitting there, frozen with a mouth full of pizza. Cassandra gave him a short curt nod, as if his expression were a full confession, then continued.

"That's what I thought. I know we've already agreed you can take the placement exams next year. That's all taken care of. I have no problem with you exploring a streaming career. For the time being."

Damien gulped down the last of his share of pizza and drew breath to express his gratitude. They'd been over this already, so he wasn't sure exactly why he should thank her again just for restating it. A combination of good manners and well-attuned survival instincts compelled him to do so all the same. He didn't make it.

"But!"

Oh for goodness' sake.

"You didn't seem terribly happy when you were playing tonight. If anything, you seemed more stressed than ever. Even if there are a lot of credits at stake, I don't want you doing this job if it makes you miserable."

Damien knew that getting stressed out was just a normal part of gaming. Especially in his scenario, where a few hundred thousand people swung by each day to judge all his actions. It would be more worrisome if he wasn't stressed out, that would imply something was wrong with him! Not a winning argument. He washed his last slice of pizza down with water, playing for time.

“That’s mainly because the people who showed up were morons. You know, I had a plan for tonight and things didn’t go the way I wanted. It’s okay, I’ll try again tomorrow.”

Cassandra narrowed her eyes and pursed her lips at him again.

“I’m here for you now. I’m sorry I wasn’t before, but better late than never. You can come and talk to me about anything. Whenever you like. Okay?”

Phew. It looked like he’d got out of that with minimal traumati—

“Even if you and Lillian had some hanky-panky and I need to take you to the clini—”

“Okay mom, I love you, thanks for dinner, goodbye now, bye!”

3

TEST YOUR MIGHT

Damien awoke to the dulcet tones of his H4ck0r headset blasting death metal into his skull via his left ear. It might've been the weekend, but for him that meant an early start. Saturday and Sunday would be peak time for any dedicated player, and while the majority of them would probably wake up in the afternoon he needed to hit his stride long before then. The early bird gets the worm. The late bird is worm food.

He stuck the headset on and navigated to the front page of Saga Online: The Saga Continues. The page loaded and the highlights shot into view. Damien was alert pretty quickly. His brief livestream was in pride of place, right at the top of the list.

1. **The Return of Daemien! Another Group of Heroes Fall Foul of the Streaming Champion on Their Way to Run a Dungeon.**

He didn't make it any further than that. He read it a few times, his impression growing worse with each pass. Did whoever titled this watch the stream at all? He'd worked long and hard making a video commentary detailing what happened: how he'd gone to the Lair of the Emerald Queen looking for an alliance and had instead become the subject of an unprovoked attack. Now Mobius had thoughtlessly labeled him the instigator!

He clicked the link and within ten seconds had crossed the line from indignation to outrage. The Mobius-endorsed cut of his livestream had omitted the entire conversation between him, the original scouting party and later on HighZen. The clip only began with Damien in the trees, his enemies having already inflicted friendly fire damage on themselves. The edit made it look as if it was Damien's doing. This didn't seem thoughtless. If anything, it looked intentional.

A quick check filled in the rest of the details. It had been posted at 8pm the previous night, a full two hours before Damien uploaded his own commentary on his profile page and stumbled into bed. 1.5 million people had watched the Mobius version. A million and a half! The number of viewers at the end of Damien's livestream had been eclipsed by Mobius's front page spread.

A comparison between his own video's view count and that of the highlights made him feel worse. The proliferation of Mobius's official version had not attracted attention to Damien's personal account. Quite the opposite. His thoughtful, borderline apologetic account of events had a mere 50,000 views. Why would anyone watch the same video twice? Nobody would ally with him for dungeons if this was how Mobius presented him.

Well, all the effort he'd put into yesterday was now officially wasted. He'd probably get a nice credit bump from being front page-worthy, not to mention raking in a healthy number of views. Hopefully a good chunk of them would be visitors, since their views counted for more than those of people already playing. It would be a pretty lousy first impression of him.

He'd have to talk to Kevin later and see about officially setting the record straight. Except Kevin didn't work weekends. Well, his handler had always been a pretty industrious guy, with any luck he'd show up and Damien could pick his brain.

He got up and reconvened in front of his computer with his full breakfast prepared fifteen minutes later. There was something else he needed to look at before he logged in: the increased price on his head.

Up until then, Damien's only bounty had been set by Camelot:

Wanted — Daemien the Low, dead, 500g. Recurring.

Arcadia was very much a self-contained world; you didn't submit tickets to a Game Master if you had a grievance with another player. You sorted it out yourself by learning to use the infrastructure Mobius had provided.

Damien navigated to the list of outstanding warrants and found himself at the top of the list. A second bounty had been opened on him that made the first look like pocket change. 5,000g. This was a problem. Damien didn't need a great deal of market experience to know 5,000g was a lot of currency. More than your average individual player would front, unless they were very well-to-do and you'd done them a *serious* wrong.

The list of people Damien had wronged was rather long, but he'd hardly call it griefing. He'd like to think he hadn't so inconvenienced anyone that they'd award a stranger several weeks of gold grinding to put him in the ground for twenty-four hours. Someone had. But who? Not Andrew, surely?

Rather than being added to the outstanding bounty issued in Camelot, this one had been issued separately from another location. His new bounty was registered to a settlement called Carlisle.

He looked up Carlisle. It was a neutral, humdrum border town, set in the mouth of a valley that led out of the Empire's territory. Just less than a week ago there'd been a change of governor. Some guy called Magnitude. Very foreboding. Probably a new boss, since the cultist/occultist story line and the Lair of the Emerald Queen had both been done to death. It still didn't explain why this NPC had it in for him personally.

It was 8am on Saturday, high time to get to work. Damien opened his eyes at the entrance to his base and was immediately welcomed back via intense, hair-raising, banshee-like screams. At least his structures were probably all finished with, and at least both Noigel and the succubus were still alive.

"Morning, Noigel." Damien knew by now to call for his minion before he turned around, lest he found Noigel canoodling and both their mornings were ruined. "Status report."

There was a surprised squawk and a few moments of awkward silence before Noigel appeared from behind the forge.

"All quiet, master. No disturbances since you left. All constructions have been completed."

Damien nodded and strode past to see his newly erected Gateway. Eurgh. Newly enhanced Gateway. Just don't make eye contact. His plan fell apart when Noigel's promiscuous partner appeared, leaning against the forge in what looked like an attempt at a seductive pose. It would've been less traumatizing if she hadn't bared her incredible fangs to lick her black, protruding eyeballs.

Damien briefly wondered what would happen if he threw up while he was still wearing the headset. How was he supposed to possess this succubus now? Had that tongue been anywhere he should be concerned about? He didn't want to be the one to disrupt the system while it was working; this deal made Noigel more productive and was a good way of Damien showing him respect, which the minion surely deserved given his performance. Besides, although it was *extremely* realistic, it was still only a game. He'd rather bear Noigel's discrepancies in mind and avoid possessing that particular succubus at all costs. Maybe he could leave her down here to be Noigel's permanent concubine? He'd just have to grin and bear it.

Grinning became a little easier when he set eyes on his completed Tier II Gateway. Well look at you! Aren't you a beauty? It had kept a similar theme, but had built upon it in a very stylish manner. The first ring of floating, rune-carved stones had pulsed with blue light. It was now joined by a second orbiting ring that cut through it, the runed stones of which glowed a rich purple.

"Noigel, you are to begin upgrading the...hang on."

He went into his base management settings and checked the status of all the buildings in his current base:

Soul Well II: Soul Capacity – 20/20
Gateway II: Gateway Network Destinations – 1/2
Demon Forge II: Advanced Smithing – 100%

Everything besides the Soul Well was fully upgraded. He set aside the materials needed for the Tier III Soul Well and initiated construction. He could take a more detailed inventory when he got back. For now, he was eager to test the new Gateway. It promised to be very useful; he could build a second Gateway outside of his base and Portal to it. He was limited to one Soul Well, so unfortunately he couldn't build a second base. That would've been awesome.

Even so, if he found a good place for a second Gateway he'd have instant access to whatever amenities that location had to offer. Maybe a good spot to grind souls, or nearby to the entrance to a dungeon. Until then, the second location had defaulted to 'the Downward Spiral'. Damien recognized an in-game prompt when he saw one. He hadn't visited Bartholomew in a while, but hopefully the vampire would have something of use to impart regarding his skill problem.

"Alright, I'm visiting Bartholomew. Get to work with the base team...oh, and Noigel?"

He beckoned his minion to walk with him and strolled nonchalantly out of the cave, his hands clasped behind his back. Noigel attentively followed until the two of them were alone, and Damien took on a very serious air.

"Why don't you take the opportunity to make yourself your own room? Like Bartholomew did for me in the Downward Spiral, with my own base separated from his dungeon. How does that sound?"

"Thank you, master. But if I have my own room, what will me and the succubi enjoy our "special time" on?"

"I don't understand."

"Well, it's pretty convenient on the Demon Forge, and it's great fun on the Gateway since we both have wings to mount the flying rocks. My personal favorite is right in the middle of the Soul Well. Bam!"

Noigel had pounded his fist into his open palm, so enraptured was he with his own story. Damien's lips had receded into a tight, thin, unwavering line.

"You mean to tell me you've been enjoying your "special time" with the succubus all over *my* base structures?"

"Well of course, boss, I mean, you're a smart guy. Where did you think we'd do it? On the floor?"

Noigel had gone from elegant servant to 'shameless, creepy uncle Noigel' in the span of about two utterances. Damien didn't feel like indulging that particular rabbit hole today.

"Thank you, Noigel, for registering your grievance. I take it the problem is that were you to obtain your own private space, you and the succubi would have no item of furniture upon which to perform your "special time". Have I understood this correctly, Noigel?"

"Yeah, you totally get it! That's why you're such a great master, it feels like you really understand who I—"

"I'm going to stop you there, Noigel, before I lose my mind. Your priorities have changed. While I'm gone, clean this base from top to bottom. Don't stop cleaning until I come back. Pay special attention to the three base structures you and the succubus road tested in my absence. Thanks."

Damien went into his menu and found his new Portal ability description:

Portal: Mana cost: 100, Channeling cost: 10 MpS, Casting time: 10 seconds – You open a portal to one of two locations: 'Daemien's Gateway' or the 'Downward Spiral'. Focus on which you wish to travel to as you cast the spell.

The portal remains open until you cancel the spell, you run out of mana to channel the spell or the Gateway is destroyed. You cannot use this spell while in combat or when enemies are nearby.

. . .

He could summon a portal straight back to his base after he'd finished talking with Bartholomew? Swell. Although Noigel might need more time than that to clean up. Maybe some dedicated tools. Noigel chipped in as Damien began channeling.

"Master, just checking, you want me and the succubus to perform "special time" all over your entire base?"

"No! That is not what I said!"

The spell started to glimmer and fade.

"Clean the base. All of it. And don't make it weird! I'll be back soon and we'll sort this out, but no "special time" until we do. That's an order."

The portal opened and Damien leaped through it, desperate to put the conversation on hold. He arrived on the lowest floor of the Downward Spiral. It was pitch black down there, but the night vision bestowed upon him by 'Shadow Walker' meant he could see everything without issue.

It was an interesting scene.

Three players were spread out in varying stances and states of undress. Some of them moved with caution verging on the obsessive. Others stood completely still, their ears pricked for signs of movement. They were all blindly groping around in the darkness, trying to find any advantage over their peers. There were giant rat bodies scattered across the floor, often with a dead, unlooted player nearby – examples of a rat's potent poison finishing off an already wounded player.

One of the players, clothed but unarmed, scuffed her toe on a tile. The other two twisted their heads toward the noise. She froze, but they'd already drawn a bead on her location. They held their weapons in front of them and moved cautiously toward the disturbance. With a start, Damien realized they were using very familiar tools. Rat bones.

A strong, well-manicured grip fell upon his shoulder.

"Shhhhhhh. Don't disturb them. This is the good part."

Damien sighed. Bartholomew's appearing trick never got old. Neither did Bartholomew. In fact, he looked as young as Damien had ever seen him. Long black locks of hair were parted in two places by thick, curling horns that protruded from either side of his head. He had grown and styled a small, black goatee. Of course he had.

He was quite handsome, save for the fact that his face had been trapped by a permanent sneer, a malevolent cheer, the workings of which weren't entirely clear.

It was a little clearer for Damien in that moment, standing by Bartholomew's side and seeing from his perspective. Damien couldn't say he derived much enjoyment from seeing players like this, on a personal level. Bartholomew eagerly whispered into his ear as the players drew closer to their prey.

"You missed the start of it, but I'll fill you in on the details. Heroes of the Empire arrive at the top of the Downward Spiral at all hours. They are guided into the depths by a hell hound, past the various demon hordes on the six circles above and directly through the traps on the stairs. Those who survive the traps meet me and are told the conditions for their trial, after which they hand over their meager possessions and accept me as their master."

Well, one thing about Bartholomew hadn't changed. He sure liked to hear himself talk. Damien was already well aware how Bartholomew had structured his vetting process. He was surprised Bartholomew didn't require new recruits to jump in through the top of the Downward Spiral, in order to emulate Damien's experience to the fullest possible extent. The tribute was still endearing, in Bartholomew's uniquely sadistic way.

"I queue up to forty of them at a time, the newcomers joining the veterans who have just reincarnated. I conjure up rats to fight and keep a good number of bodies around for improvised weapons. Then I throw them all into the darkness and watch them tear each other apart. Does it remind you of anything?"

"How could it not, Bartholomew? I'm touched. I do notice a slight difference between then and now, though: you had me prove my worth against rats and a skeleton. Now you have your potential students killing each other as well?"

Bartholomew's eyes remained fixed on the combatants as they closed in. His smile flashed and the iridescent runes etched into his skin and robes briefly pulsed. It started around his feet and ended in the tips of his horns.

"Oh Daemien, you grew up in a different time. You were once the only human occultist. You're not aware that we're often cannibalistic. When these new students set out, they won't just have to contend with the rest of the world as you did. They shall also have to contend against each other, and their predecessors, and those who come after. Only the strongest survive, but those that do thrive. We are not a weak species."

A yelp from the other side of the arena drew Damien's attention back to the fight. The weaponless girl had slowly drawn back, then come to a stop. The two who'd arrived to attack her had found each other instead and were fighting each other in the pitch black. It took a while, since they mostly missed each other, but eventually the occultist swinging his thighbone in broad sweeps brought down the shattered-rib stabber. Only for the previously weaponless girl to collect the shattered rib after it clattered to the floor in the dark and stab the victor in the back. She was the only player left.

Bartholomew clapped.

"Winner, winner, craven sinner!"

He began to methodically pulse purple light from his body and she relaxed. Although she still had to navigate the rats, the first of her trials was at an end. Bartholomew turned to Damien.

"I have a certain gift to bestow upon a worthy candidate. I shall return as soon as I'm done."

Bartholomew floated away, drawing in his latest victim with hypnotic pulsing purple light. Damien looked to the old location of his first and most successful base. Although the alcove indicating the entrance was long gone, Damien knew exactly where it had been. It was strange, but he kinda missed it there.

On the other side of the floor, Bartholomew was recruiting the survivor to his cause. Damien didn't bother crouching. The level gap ensured his Shadow Walker skill would be more than enough to prevent her from seeing him. He couldn't hear Bartholomew speaking from that distance, but he could easily make out the blazing lights burning demonic runes into the floor in front of his new recruit.

Damien focused. He'd heard about this, but he hadn't seen it for himself. And given what he'd heard, seeing really would be believing. The runes were all finished simultaneously, and an imp hopped out before throwing gang signs. Damien focused on it, bringing up the basic information above its head. So it was true. It was another Noigel.

As if one Noigel in the world wasn't enough.

Having "blessed" her, Bartholomew continued his speech a little longer and then floated upward, leaving her to commence rat purging. Damien could scarcely reconcile that he'd gone through the same ordeal himself. At his current level and with everything he'd learned, she seemed light years away from reaching him. Yet it had only been a few weeks.

He felt a twinge of nostalgia, accompanied by a surge of sympathy. Her first task would be learning how to deal with Noigel. Bart turned off his disco lights and floated transparently up to where Damien had awaited his return. He held up a finger.

"One more thing."

Bartholomew clapped his hands together and then spread them apart. A series of portals opened across his final floor, from which spewed a new infestation of rats. After a few seconds, and with a further twenty rats added to his dungeon's menagerie, Bartholomew lowered his hands and the portals closed.

"So all that time you were giving me quests to remove rats from your dungeon, you were the one who put them there in the first place? I'm not sure if I should be flattered or insulted."

"The former, most assuredly. The rat infestation may be manufactured by me, but the inconveniences of sharing living space with oversized rodents are extremely real. Your own experience has formed the basis of the suffering and betterment of your peers and I continue to occupy a rat feces-laden basement so they might follow in your footsteps. There is no higher honor I can bestow."

"I wouldn't mind the honor of being told the truth every now and then."

"But Damien, I already told you: I hold liars in higher regard. At least liars possess some sort of self-preservation instinct. I hope you didn't come here merely to squabble. Come, let me have a look at you."

Without waiting for consent, Bartholomew held Damien's chin and twisted his head this way and that, then skirted around to examine him from every angle. It was strange, but for all his maniacal scheming Damien trusted Bartholomew implicitly. They'd come a long way together, and everything had turned out alright.

So far.

Bartholomew finished his inspection and cooed lightly.

"I see you can contain a full demonic horde now. Excellent. Yet you still haven't achieved even a fraction of the power you're capable of. Interesting times."

"Yeah, about that. I haven't learned any new combat abilities for a while. I was wondering if you had any advice about what I should do next."

There was a long pause. Bartholomew was looking at him listlessly, a rare phenomenon. Perhaps there'd been some kind of glitch in the game? That would be even rarer. No sooner had Damien opened his mouth to pursue his inquiry than Bartholomew made his thoughts plain.

"Daemien. While you are a superb occultist, you tend toward more orthodox means of killing people rather than through the application of infernal magics. I may be capable of stabbing people to death, but I don't do it with any great finesse and it's certainly not my area of expertise. I made it very clear you were straying into unfamiliar territory from the very beginning. Did you forget?"

Damien was thrown into the all too familiar situation of feeling like everything was his fault, without having the faintest idea what his critic was referring to.

"I'm flesh and blood, Bartholomew. Not a machine, if that concept has any meaning to you. I don't have total recall and everything you've told me would be quite a lot to remember. Can you run it by me again?"

Bartholomew glazed over for a fraction of a second, then delivered a scathing review of Damien's tactics, already almost a month old, with exactly the same tone of voice he'd employed the first time round. This time he had more facial muscles and skin to convey the full extent of his snideness with. Damien wasn't a machine but Bartholomew was, whether he knew it or not. His delivery of the lines was word perfect, bringing Damien right back to his first steps with the occultist class.

"Your choice of tactics was...interesting. I'd have expected you to use Maleficium spells from afar, with imps for defense and Shadow Walker to escape from danger. Instead, you relied on imps for attack and defense and used Shadow Walker to engage your opponents in melee. You're aware that you have magic at your disposal now, yes? You don't have to use rat bones anymore."

It was eerie, but it was also spot on. Bartholomew glazed over for another fraction of a second and then he was back in the room.

"The truth, seeing as how you hold it in such high regard, is that your unique style demands you invest more in your physique than your mind. While you certainly possess an abundance of wisdom, enough to summon and control a demonic horde, you lack the intellect to employ anything beyond the most basic infernal magic."

He saw Damien narrow his eyes and rolled his own.

"You're not *stupid,* Daemien, we both know that. You're just..." Bartholomew waved his hands around in the air, searching for the words that wouldn't make this worse. "Not...cerebrally...inclined?"

"Yeah. Thanks. Low intelligence. Got it. When can I expect some abilities for more physically inclined occultists?"

Bartholomew sucked on his teeth and winced. He almost looked sympathetic. Oh holy hell. This couldn't be good.

"Daemien. Occultism is in essence a magical art. Your unique style has worked remarkably well, but since you've already mastered demon summoning, the time has come for you to return to the path I originally laid out for you."

"You're telling me occultists never get any agility-based abilities at all, aren't you?"

For once, Bartholomew was out of words. He simply held his palms up and shrugged. Damien mulled it over. He was intent on increasing his agility stat, but Bartholomew would have him put points in intelligence instead. That was not an option. He was already level 42. He'd no longer enjoy the absurdly rapid leveling he'd experienced while his class was still relatively unknown, so there'd be little immediate improvement to his combat abilities. Meanwhile, his enemies would continue putting points in attributes that granted them immediate benefit, putting him at a significant disadvantage.

Wearing gear with intelligence would increase the damage of his spells, but it wouldn't allow him to learn new ones. That was calculated by a combination of your level and natural stat points crossing over the required thresholds. If he abandoned agility in favor of intelligence, he'd still be inferior as a caster for at least twenty levels. Maybe more.

For his sacrifice, Damien would not only be forced to change the playstyle that won him the competition, he'd also lose much of the nimbleness that ensured his survival against superior numbers. Furthermore, his already selected traits worked superbly with agility as his secondary stat, but he'd passed over many others that would've been better choices were he relying on spells for damage. That alone ensured his character would be permanently gimped.

No thank you.

"Bartholomew, that won't work! I have a very specific way of doing things, and it's the reason Aetherius was defeated and you have people literally killing each other to be taught by you. I have to do this my way, but I need your help to do it. You're exceptionally wise and powerful, you must know something that can help me?"

Bartholomew crossed his arms and pouted despite Damien's overt flattery.

"I'm sorry the rare and incredible gifts I bestowed on you were only half to your liking. Let me just rifle through my Bag of

Holding and see if I have any occultist tomes on the lost art of stabbing people."

Bartholomew dramatically thrust his hand shoulder deep into the bag. A strange spectacle, since from the outside it looked only large enough to accommodate up to his wrist. Damien pursed his lips and indulged his former master as he rummaged around in a silly pantomime of actually looking for something.

Bartholomew pulled out a rabbit, which he glibly chucked over his shoulder to join the giant rats; an umbrella decorated with a green bird's head on the handle; a spidery-looking white gun with a wired-up potato inexplicably stuck on the shooty end; a silver sword with a ruby the size of an egg embedded in the handle, which Bartholomew hissed at before quickly dropping it back into the bag; and a weird wand coated in what appeared to be dwarven engineering, identifying itself in Damien's HUD as a 'Sonic Screwdriver'.

The display would've been more entertaining for Damien if Bartholomew wasn't using it to mock him. Bartholomew dropped the wand back into the bag and threw his hands up.

"How unfortunate! It appears the lost occultist art of inserting pointy things into people's bodies until they expire is, truly, lost. Perhaps because we gained the ability to blow our opponents apart from the inside out at long range? *We may never know.*"

Damien withdrew his dagger and brandished it in Bartholomew's face. He was annoyed, but not so annoyed that he'd take on his former master in a fight. Instead, having waved it around to try and provoke some sort of reaction, Damien twisted the handle so the vampire could examine it up close.

"Oh yeah? If there aren't any occultist abilities based on physical combat, where did this Sacrificial Dagger come from, then? And these Adept Robes with agility instead of intelligence?"

Bartholomew raised an eyebrow at the mentions of stats on items, but ignored the immersion break to keep a hold on his argument.

"I specifically crafted those items for you. They didn't even exist until I took you under my wing and found out you were set on ignoring my advice. I was all but forced to, when it became apparent you were headstrong and self-absorbed from day one. Let me refresh your memory."

Bartholomew blinked before launching into another sterling reenactment of an early interaction with Damien. Only this time, he was mimicking Damien. With a whiny, nasal, slightly breaking voice.

"The spells attracted too much attention. They were dangerous to me and they were dangerous to the imps as well if I missed. This way was much—"

Damien was seething. Bartholomew cut his reenactment short.

"I see you're angry. Good. How do you think it felt to have my teachings eschewed by an ungrateful little whelp who would've died without my help? Did I insist you follow my instruction? No! I encouraged you, and waited for you to come to the realization I was right by yourself. Only, as we know, that never happened. You cut a swathe through Rising Tide and eventually even brought Aetherius to his knees. Which is all the more remarkable given the strategies you employed."

Bartholomew raised himself to his full height and glowered at him. He was a full head taller than Damien, and undoubtedly more physically able thanks to his vampirism. Once upon a time, Damien would've found this extremely imposing. However, now Damien was twelve levels higher, although Bartholomew was still undoubtedly more powerful. More importantly, he knew Bartholomew cherished him. Damien was certain he would not be harmed, despite the posturing. This did not decrease the severity of his former master's tone.

"Your strategy has worked incredibly well up to this point, but has no further room for growth. The only way for you to proceed is to embrace the full extent of my gift. It might not be convenient in the short term, but it will undoubtedly reap rewards in the long term. I tell you this as a Master of the Occult, as *your* former master and as someone who has both benefited from and is still invested in your success. Tell me now, Daemien: how will you proceed?"

Damien was having another flashback, triggered by Bartholomew's carefully chosen words: 'How will you proceed?' That was the line that had followed Bartholomew's ultimatum when they first met, that if Damien didn't accept his offer of becoming an occultist he would be violently and excruciatingly murdered. He hadn't had a choice then. He did now.

He stared back into Bartholomew's face evenly.

"I refuse. Your way is great, but my way works better for me. I won't change how I operate when it has brought me success. Not even if it's your style, and not even if you compel me to. If you won't help, I'll find someone else who can. If no one will help, I'll make it work by myself. My methods define me. I won't abandon them for anyone."

He and Bartholomew stared at each other. One of the many ways Bartholomew outstripped Damien was in staring contests. Seriously, he had giant pitch-black fishbowl eyes. Damien wasn't sure he even blinked at all. But after a while, without his eyes leaving those of his charge, Bartholomew nodded slowly.

"I see. In that case, you are ready."

Bartholomew raised a white-hot finger and tapped Damien on the forehead. Given the conversation that had preceded it, Damien could hardly believe a quest notification was popping up in his HUD:

'There's Always a Bigger Fish – Find Bartholomew's master. Part 1 – Enter the Dark Tower.'

"Whoa, you have a master? You've been holding out on me, Bartholomew."

"I'm rather selective regarding who I choose to invest my time in. Though I possess far more of that particular resource than your average denizen of Arcadia, I nevertheless do not waste it. My master is considerably less tolerant and exponentially more long-lived. I would not deign to send someone in his direction unless they were worthy. This is the highest honor I can bestow on members of my flock, do not take it lightly."

"I thought your rat-infested dungeon and your kill-tastic

tribute to one of the worst hours of my life was the highest honor?"

"I lied."

Hmm. At least he'd finally provided Damien with a new quest. With this, he'd have original content to put on his channel, and with any luck a boost to his combat skills as well.

"Can your master help me advance as a close-combat occultist?"

"Oh, I should think so. One way or another. Whether he *will* help you is another matter entirely. He is not easily impressed, less easily coerced and all but impossible to deceive."

"He sounds like a laugh riot. Is that where you get it from?"

"Not at all. In fact, his main concern with me is that I'm far too kind."

Bartholomew's face split in half, his skin stretching back and his maw unhinging to reveal as many of his rapidly elongating rows of teeth as possible. It was the most sickening smile Damien had ever seen. It had been bad enough watching Bartholomew grin with feeling in his obviously monstrous, inhuman state. Seeing a vaguely human countenance encompass the same display made him seem every inch the eldritch abomination he was. It got the point across, though. Bartholomew's master was probably not a very nice man.

"I see. Well, thank you, for that. You can close your mouth now. Oh, one of your fangs appears to have snagged on your bottom li— no, you've got it. That's cool. Anyway. Where can I find this bundle of joy?"

"He is beyond. Outside the Human Realm. Past the Wastes, across the Outer Ring then through the Inner Circle. Into the most unholy site in Arcadia, the Dark Tower. And then a little further still."

"Lovely. Could you, uh, could you mark it on my map?"

4

ONE SMALL STEP FORWARD FOR A MAN

It was shaping up to be a productive morning. Damien had thanked Bartholomew profusely and left him to his endless rolling deathmatches. He was certainly a glutton for punishment, just not his own. Damien had his own grueling challenge ahead, but he wasn't fazed. He was excited. This was exactly what he needed: a long, mysterious quest, with no emphasis on player-killing and the potential to advance his character's build. He could repair the bridge between himself and the community while providing valuable information about the outside world at the same time.

For all intents and purposes, the realms of the four primary races were training areas for the real meat of the game. At least, that's how Mobius had advertised it. Damien couldn't be sure, because there was very little in the way of information about what lay outside, other than that it was considerably more dangerous. In fact, nobody knew much more than what Bart had imparted to him.

The four playable races were positioned at all four corners of the map, as far away from each other as possible. Directly outside of their fortified positions lay the Wastes: a barren stretch of rock and sand. The reward for traversing it was a whole new world of content to be explored: the Outer Ring. A land of plenty, with new resources to be plundered from rich environments, exciting new creatures to meet and kill as well as myriad settlements with the promise of lucrative trade and endless quests to perform. Which was just as well, because it served as the primary staging ground for the advancement of all four races after leaving their respective homelands.

The final area, at the core of Arcadia's map, was the Inner Circle. Bartholomew had not been forthcoming about what Damien might find there, besides his objective, but the name and location made the overall theme clear enough. Most of the late-game content would be there, and more likely than not it would be the source of the highest-level dungeons and the most dangerous mobs. So presumably all the best gear would be there, too. That's where Bartholomew was sending him.

Thanks to his Bag of Holding, Damien didn't need to worry too much about item preparation. He didn't have to think too hard about what to do with his minions, either. The wraith would stay behind for defense, since it was already light outside. Everything else would come with him. Ten imps, the hell hound, the succubus and Noigel.

Damien was interested in the new bounty issued on him through Carlisle, especially since the town had recently had a change of leadership. However, the quest from Bart had relegated the bounty to a distant second priority. Carlisle was simply an obstacle to be circumvented, which would be a much easier prospect at night and all but impossible during the day. Especially when you factored in the climate of the Human Realm's final territory. The North.

It wasn't far from Damien's base, which he'd stuck in a grinding cave near the far end of Brociliande with no known quests attached to it. As he approached the wide border, the forest started to change subtly. The trees were spaced a great deal further apart, allowing the first flakes of snowfall to drift to the frosty earth beneath their branches. Before long the middle distance was completely obscured by a veil of falling snow. In addition to moving less swiftly and having reduced vision, his and his minions' stamina points were replenishing more slowly. Words appeared in the middle of his vision, denoting both the name of the zone he'd crossed into and the sub-area it was affiliated with: The North – Frozen Forest.

Damien pressed on, and within minutes the ground lay invisible beneath a blanket of pristine white powder which was thickening by the minute. It was not long before his team was leaving a long trail behind them, advertising their location to any who might stumble across their tracks. They would be covered up again in due course by fresh snow, but each second they lingered increased his chances of being hunted. He was below average level in this area, and unfamiliar with the terrain.

Damien wasn't a complete fool. He was well aware of the environmental effects of what players had affectionately dubbed 'Frozone'. His agility directly translated into faster and more effortless movement, but if his reduced vision caused him to blunder into a dangerous situation with low stamina, the slow replenishment rate brought on by the cold meant he'd have a hard time blundering himself out of it. The name of the game here was patience. Fortunately, or unfortunately, his minions were suffering the adverse effects a great deal more than he was. With the exception of the hell hound, their stamina would deplete rapidly if he so much as jogged. At least it served as a constant reminder to keep his own stamina in check.

His winged minions took to the air, leaving only himself and his hell hound grounded to pick their way through the snowdrifts. While this greatly reduced their overall tracks and also helped their fight against the elements, it also meant he had twelve bright-red blimps hovering around him, their bodies stark against the white backdrop all around. If anything happened, they'd have to descend quickly.

The hell hound growled low in its throat and pointed its snout ahead and to their right, prompting Damien's airborne forces to land. The imps buried themselves in the abundant snow while the succubus, hell hound and Damien himself planted themselves behind the nearest trees and lay still. A bear.

Level 43 and elite to boot. Not worth the trouble of killing. It sauntered across their path at a steady gait without noticing them. Damien's party had barely set out again when the hell hound growled for a second time. This time pointing behind them, in the direction the bear had come from. They'd no sooner attempted to conceal themselves when a level 43 ranger, his attention rapidly alternating between the bear's tracks and the whiteout ahead, stumbled right into their midst.

He abruptly stopped where the tracks of the bear and those of Damien crossed. Damien sighed as the ranger's gaze slowly followed the new set of tracks, all the way up to where Damien was doing his best tree impersonation. It was not enough to satisfy the ranger. The two of them locked eyes. Well, damn.

Damien couldn't have looked all that imposing, squatting and hugging the tree for balance. He tried to dissuade the ranger anyway.

"The bear went that way. I'm not goi—"

The ranger nocked an arrow. That was enough. Noigel yelped and the snow around the ranger burst open in ten places, each of the imps adding to Noigel's cry with shrieks of their own. While the ranger's head darted left and right, Damien took his pick and Imp-loded the one in his enemy's blind spot. The ranger was hurtling backward when his legs kicked underneath him and propelled him into the air, toward the lowest branches of the nearest tree. That Double Jump trait. He hadn't even got to the tree when, still airborne, he loosed the arrow. Right into Damien's chest.

The initial damage was substantial. 200 hit points were immediately gone. The real problem was the debuff, a skull and crossbones with a red droplet hanging underneath. He was bleeding. Smart choice by the ranger in this environment, since low stamina would worsen the damage over time. He'd probably had this arrow prepared for the bear to kill it via attrition, but it would work far faster on his new quarry.

Damien cursed and rolled around the tree, the second arrow thrumming into the ground behind him. He poked his head around the other side just in time to watch the first of his imps get nailed, the ranger shooting it down with ease as it flew toward him head-on. Rangers were ideal characters for this zone, their range and low stamina weapon usage enormous advantages. This guy was not only well skilled for tundra combat, but was also clearly well versed in it.

It was as the second imp went down, only a moment after the first, that Damien commanded them to evade. The ranger missed the next shot, took his time before killing a third imp with the next, and was leading a fourth when the succubus's Chaotic Bolt smashed him back off his branch. He Double Jumped again, landing improbably on his feet. Which is when the hell hound cannoned into his chest, knocking him down and pinning him on his back. The ranger had swapped to a serrated dagger and stabbed it twice, the second stab finding purchase between the hound's armored plates, before Noigel and the last two imps sailed in to chomp down on his arms. With his limbs impeded, the hell hound ended it quickly.

Damien was gratified to have proven a more difficult kill prospect than an elite bear. He was not gratified that this ranger had completely mitigated his Imp-losion, killed three imps and inflicted severe wounds on both him and his hell hound – they were both still taking damage from the lingering bleed effects. He laboriously trudged over, being careful not to let his stamina drop too low, so that he could loot the body and absorb just 1 soul. The ranger's body disappeared at Damien's touch, leaving an empty patch of snow and a full loot bag. He threw it into his Bag of Holding without opening it and was summoning a fresh imp when the hell hound growled again.

Oh, of all the frigging—

Damien turned to run back to his tree, only to realize with mounting horror that the bleed effect had stained the ground all the way up to it. A trail of blood would follow him wherever he went till it expired in another fifteen seconds. This was not viable. He crouched down and sent his new imp out to a different tree, then Demon Gated to it, while Noigel scattered his minions to cover. The imp that had been used for Damien's

Demon Gate quickly buried itself in the snow. The hell hound, still bleeding itself, suffered the most from the rapid action required.

Damien cautiously peered around the side of the trunk. This time it was a level 45 assassin, casting her eyes around her at the signs of struggle: tracks crisscrossing in every direction, abundant blood in spatters and patches, and a deep furrow of disturbed snow where the ranger had fallen. All fresh. And not an enemy in sight. But there were also two obvious blood trails. After some deliberation, she set off after the freshest and most obvious trail: the hasty tracks and fresh blood left by the hell hound.

Damien hesitated. If she found the hound she'd know there was also an occultist nearby. So letting her get it would be doubly unhelpful, since Damien would also lose his primary defense against assassins. Yet his team was not in a fit state for a straightforward fight or a veiled one.

There was only one thing for it. He leaned the other way, spying the huddled hell hound behind a snow-capped boulder and dismissing it. Sensing the urgency in his command, the hell hound wasted no time in jumping through the portal that appeared. The assassin reached the spot, daggers drawn. Tracks and fresh blood leading to absolutely nothing. She most likely thought a player had run there and bled out, then been looted.

After a few tense moments, she retraced her steps and followed the short trail of Damien's blood, but to no avail. Her search of the area fruitless, she followed the bear tracks away. The bleed on Damien gone, he tentatively made his way to where his hell hound had departed, picking up the one and a half souls it had left behind. It's a good thing soul energy was only visible to occultists.

This zone was more dangerous than he'd anticipated. Occultists had a clear reason to kill other players, due to their experience point-stealing perk, but surely these players had better things to do than stalk targets in the woods? Weren't there quests they should be doing? He'd have to be even more careful.

He sent an imp to scout ahead and Demon Gated as far forward as his range of vision would allow. The succubus and the imps flew after him, leaving the ground between themselves and the killing crossroads pristine. Now he knew how to conceal his movements.

They'd been traveling through the forest for another ten minutes before the new strategy found them. The imp he'd sent forward to scout was dispatched via an arrow through the chest. Damien drew further back, using the blizzard to his advantage. He dismissed an imp for half a soul and summoned a new hell hound. He possessed it, then dropped down to the floor to drag himself forward on his new scaly belly, shoveling snow in front of himself to remain obscured.

A red outline appeared, perched on a tree out in front. He was moving closer to determine the player's level and class when a second outline appeared in a different tree, a short distance away. A ranger and a mage. The ranger's red outline was empty on the branch, indicating he was stealthed. How the mage had gotten up the tree Damien was sure he didn't know, but the ranger was far too close for him to believe they weren't aware of each other. Their levels were a match as well. Level 45. They were likely working together.

Damien mulled it over. It appeared players would be a more reliable source of soul energy in this zone than the mobs he'd been hoping for. So much for wanting to lay off the player-killing for a while. If he got this wrong, he'd either die or be forced to Portal home and take the souls from his Soul Well to try again, setting him back even further.

This could be done sensibly, if Damien was careful enough. He sent two imps all the way round the outside of them, paying special attention to the red outlines of each to take full advantage of their blind spots. They were not looking directly at each other. They were facing opposite directions, looking for incoming targets instead of protecting themselves. Mistake.

Damien sent the imp on the ranger in first, then directed the other to face-hug the mage. It was much easier to attack still targets than moving ones, since it allowed him to plan around them if they weren't careful. He killed the ranger quickly then Demon Gated to the mage before it could deal with the other imp. It was much easier to resolve combat quickly when he got the jump on his enemies. But these two had the right idea.

Why travel through the zone when you could have your targets come to you? Damien could set up shop here for a while to get a respectable minion count and raise his level. He could implement this strategy much better than either of the players he'd just dispatched.

"Noigel, I want you to ride the hell hound out. Make a big figure of 8 in the snow with this ranger's body in the center, way out past our field of vision on two sides. About 100 meters in each direction. Make it really wide. If the hound detects anything, come straight back."

While they were gone, Damien summoned a new hell hound. He was positioning his minions when Noigel came riding back at pace, the hound blasting hot clouds in the air as it replenished stamina. Damien instructed his imps to bury themselves around the ranger's body and was pondering what to do with the succubus and new hound as Noigel and his own trusty steed set off to complete the second loop of their circuit.

Damien wanted to lure in players who were following tracks, but a straight line only had a 50% chance of them going in the right direction. If they went the wrong way and found a dead end, they might realize what was happening. A circle with the ranger's body at the edge would work, but also seemed suspicious – why would anyone be traveling in a wide circle like that? He'd rather any potential victims had as little to question as possible. Let them think they were the ones hunting. A figure of 8 guaranteed players found the body no matter which way they followed the tracks. The two long straight sections would provide expediency and realism to the pursuit of their imaginary quarry.

With the hell hound next to him, and Noigel, the succubus and the other hell hound on the opposite side of the ranger-bait and seven imps steadfastly shivering in seven almost imp-erceptible mounds around it, Damien settled in to wait. Another advantage to this that he hadn't thought of was that his units would all be at full stamina when combat started, courtesy of their lack of movement.

The first to arrive was a warrior. Gatz. Level 44. Big claymore on his back. Not the best class to have in this weather, but the armor would still pose a problem to Damien's posse. In addition to the black plate mail, he had a bear skin wrapped around his upper body. It didn't look like a regular inventory item. Perhaps it granted him resistance to the cold? Damien could hardly ask, he'd have to look it up later. Gatz glanced around briefly, but having seen nothing out of the ordinary he ran up to the ranger's body to loot it. The promise of free stuff clearly mitigated the suspicious nature of four sets of tracks converging on one body, at least for this player.

He might've been sturdy, but he didn't have any ranged attacks. Gatz had just looted the body when both hell hounds started running toward him from opposite sides. Gatz only caught sight of the one on Damien's side and stood to face it, weapon in hand, a few seconds before it would've reached him. Damien had it halt a few feet away to keep his attention, snarling upward with paws splayed. The second hell hound barreled into the back of Gatz's neck before he'd made a decision.

Damien sent everything in. The succubus cast Circle of Hell to reduce armor and burn him, and the two hell hounds both ignited as their target went prone. Still not fast enough. This guy had a lot of HP. Damien joined the fray via a Demon Gate, taking the armor reduction and the burn for the sake of doing more damage while his foe was down.

Gatz was at less than 20% health when he started to glow red. Oh man, he had the Berserker Rage trait. No wonder he felt comfortable strolling around the tundra with an unstealthy class all by himself.

The succubus cast Bloodlust and they all set upon him with increased fervor. With three burning effects inflicted on him Gatz was still going down, but stupendously slowly. The Berserker Rage trait could only be used once every twenty-four hours, but the increased strength, damage resistance and health and stamina regen it provided constituted a full minute of game-breaking insanity.

Gatz was at 5% health when he leapt to his feet, throwing his assailants into the air. The warrior wheeled round, sighted Damien where he'd fallen and Charged. The succubus's Chaotic Bolt slammed into his face, but while it brought Gatz to the edge of his life it did not stagger him as it should have.

Damien's Demon Gate was on cooldown and he wouldn't be able to hit this guy even once in melee before he was cut in half. In desperation, he span his daggers round and hurled them at the berserker's face in rapid succession. One clanged away uselessly on the edge of his helm. The other embedded itself in his eye. 0%. Gatz paused for a moment, still standing upright, as if he had to consider whether this bizarre use of the daggers merited a kill. Then he keeled over backward and lay still.

That had not been the easy kill Damien had planned for. But if he could deal with this lunatic he could probably handle anything else wandering these woods. That was a small comfort considering how much damage Gatz had done. Damien himself had been badly burned by straddling his enemy in the middle of the succubus's Circle of Hell, since he was not a demon. The rest of them were either damaged, out of mana or disoriented. But there was no time to lose. For all Damien knew, Gatz's tracks were already being followed by another enemy.

"Reset! Noigel, the imps and the succubus cover up the tracks around our hiding places. Beat your wings over the snow until your stamina is low, then back to your positions. Quickly!"

He strode forward to remove his weapon from Gatz's eye, suppressing a laugh when it turned out that it was the Sacrificial Dagger and that it was charged with a soul for delivering the killing blow. You learn something new every day. Not that he had any intention of hurling his precious weapons at players in the future.

Gatz himself had provided him with a further 2.5 souls, which Damien regarded as a poor return for the effort invested. He left Gatz's body where it lay to act as the new bait, retrieved

Shankyou's Striking Dagger from the ground and made his way back to his tree, with all his minions already concealed again. He was wondering if he should summon any more imps when his hound started growling.

This could work.

5

ONE GIANT LEAP BACK FOR MANKIND

The next half an hour was tense. Something Damien had not taken into account was that he didn't have to kill everyone who wandered into his trap. If he didn't like the look of a target, he could simply let them pass by. The main objective was to bring his minion numbers back up, and each player only gave 2 or 3 souls at best, so he had to keep tactical losses to a minimum.

As soon as he'd replenished his minions, he'd start scouting for a place to build a solitary Gateway, to test the new Portal ability. Then it would be onward to scout out Carlisle. It would help if he got to grips with the terrain and people's tactics in this zone in the meantime.

He learned this the hard way when a party of three came through, a ranger, a priest and an assassin following in Gatz's footsteps. They came across his body and wasted no time in taking Damien's spoils for themselves. All he could do was look on as they looted, then headed out on the looping trail he'd left for them to follow. Completely unaware they'd walked into an unsprung trap.

It soon became apparent that Damien's biggest concern was not whether he could kill the players who were appearing, none of whom were anything like as sturdy as Gatz had been, but whether he could kill them fast enough to be able to reset the trap before the next player appeared. The blizzard did a good job of disguising how busy Frozone was.

Fortunately, by picking his targets correctly and matching his approach to their playstyle, success was all but guaranteed. The squishiest targets also tended to have the highest burst damage, but were dispatched fast enough with a Demon Gate in their blind spot and a quick flurry of sneak critical strikes. The heavily armored were fewer in number, so letting them pass through uninterrupted was no great loss.

He'd already dealt with three more players in this fashion before the party who'd looted Gatz returned, the figure of 8 loop leading them right back to where they'd started. Except there was what appeared to be a large, snow-covered boulder at the intersection. As they passed it, Damien directed his thoughts to the succubus hidden behind it and she cast Bloodlust. Then all his minions, save one, burst from their hiding places and charged toward the enemies. The party was quick to react, putting their backs to the snow-covered mound as they drew weapons and took aim.

Damien had often wondered how he could make the largest of his demons, the incubus, more viable. The problem was that while it was both powerful and sturdy, it was also an obscenely large target and an enormous investment of 10 souls. Not generally a sensible option to maintain a low profile or get a good return, especially on the move. This terrain had led Damien to take a risk.

The snowy boulder burst open and two massive, clawed hands shot out of it, snatching up the ranger before he could escape and the priest before he could cast. The assassin abruptly vanished, leaving his comrades to their fate, only to rejoin them as the hell hounds reconjured him out of thin air with savage bites. They wouldn't have needed the Detect skill to find him, since the thoughtless slew of swear words and hastily retreating snow prints gave him away.

Damien was quick to Demon Gate and render the fight one-sided before it reached its conclusion a few seconds later. A costly skirmish turned into a quick and painless injection of 8 souls' energy, plus another one in his Sacrificial Dagger. Only 1 soul shy of the investment in the incubus being fully returned.

With a full Soul Summon Limit of seven imps, two hell hounds, a succubus and an incubus, it was time to start filling his base. Once the succubus and the imps were finished clearing incriminating tracks, Damien opened a portal and sent the incubus and the succubus home. He immediately summoned a new succubus, so he still had a solid 20 soul-cost team to help him.

This was all well and good, but he'd killed ten players and was yet to level up. That was weird. They'd all been around his level, he'd have expected to go up at least one or two after killing so many. What was going on?

He'd finally finished resetting, paying close attention to his hell hounds the whole while, when the headset started to ring. It was Kevin. Damien checked the time. 10:48. Kevin really was a very conscientious guy, logging in on a day off to check messages. Damien answered the call.

"Hello, Kevin?"

"Damien! My man! How's it going?"

Heh. That was a far cry from how Kevin used to address him. No umming or ahhing in lieu of his name. They'd been through a lot together since then, even if they'd never met face to face. Without the opportunity to fight Toutatis that Kevin had fatefully thrown his way, his life would look very different. Whether his mom would've had the heart attack without their fight as a catalyst was anyone's guess, but they'd all come through it somehow and things had turned out well. He'd rather report to Kevin, someone he all but knew personally, than a random fill-in from the enormous Mobius Enterprises employee pool. Better the devil you know.

"I'm glad you called, I wanted to ask you about the stream Mobius edited for me yesterday, with the player raid. Did you see it?"

"I did. I wanted to talk to you about it but we've all been pretty busy here, getting the endgame in shape."

"That's good to hear! I'm headed that way myself, so I'm glad—"

"Woah there, hold up. You're still a little too early to be heading to the Outer Ring. What level are you now, 42?"

The hell hound at Damien's side started to growl. Curses. He peered out from behind the tree and lowered his voice as a new target blurred into existence at his vision's edge.

"I'm sure I'll manage. Anyway, about the stream. I—"

"Damien, I'm not sure if I should be telling you this, but now isn't a good time to go that way. There's a situation brewing that doesn't bode well for anyone under level 50."

Kevin hadn't lost his habit of cutting off Damien mid-speech, evidently. But this sounded important. The next words out of Kevin's mouth included a name that had been making the rounds recently, along with some less well-known tidbits.

"There's a player, called Magnitude, who's taken over Carlisle. He didn't do it by conquest. He bought the whole settlement. In one go."

Damien was so distracted he let the lone gunslinger who'd blundered into his trap wander past. There was a lot to unpack in that short sentence. The first, and the weirdest part, was that Magnitude was a player. Damien had assumed he was an NPC, due to the imposing name and credentials. He hadn't even been aware that players could become leaders of settlements, by conquest, trade or any other means. Kevin steadily plowed onward through Damien's already labored thought processes.

"We always planned for players to take control of settlements, but much, much later. He's removed the Carlisle quests, all of them, and put in one of his own. A player-killing quest, no less."

Damien's heart briefly jumped out of his chest before remembering the bounty set on him in Carlisle, likely by the very man they were discussing. Even if Carlisle had been Empire-affiliated before the takeover, it was no less hostile to him now.

"What's the quest?"

"Kill ten players in a row and report back, without dying. If you die, the quest resets and you have to start again."

"That doesn't sound so bad. I've managed that already."

"Damien, not everybody is an occultist. Your class is specifically designed for solo play and ambush strategies, balanced out with strong social demerits and a need for almost constant in-game presence. You, a full-time streamer playing that highly specialized class, would no doubt have an easy time of it. The fact is, Magnitude has brought all progression in the zone to a grinding halt."

Damien, who'd briefly felt pretty pleased with himself for accomplishing this goal without knowing it existed, was a bit put out to have the achievement presented as though his carefully planned success were simply a matter of course. Then the real problem burrowed its way into his head, as he realized that he'd already seen the effects of this quest. The question of why he wasn't getting any experience for his kills had been answered. If a player died, their accumulated EXP to the next level was reset to zero. So his 'Soul Harvest' trait was completely useless, and his primary source of EXP gain was gone.

It had been nice waxing philosophical, thinking he could lay off the player-killing and focus on Bartholomew's quest for his channel instead. Now the option had been taken away, he was more than a little reticent.

"That's outrageous! It's unfair! What are Mobius doing about it?"

"Nothing. Magnitude hasn't broken any rules and we're not about to start penalizing players for creative play, outstanding achievement or imaginative thinking. If that were the case you'd probably have been in trouble yourself, not too long ago."

"Come on, Kevin, that's a rubbish comparison! I fought for my victory fair and square, I didn't buy a key settlement then lord it over everyone lower level than me for funzies. I'm assuming this Magnitude is higher level, right?"

"You know I'm not allowed to give you specific details of other players. Anyway, there are at least some people progressing. A few players have already managed it, and as a reward they're being inducted into his guild and given access to more quests."

"It's a conscription exercise?"

"We're not sure what he's doing. The North is becoming more full every day as players finish the quest chains in Brociliande. Most of them died on entry, since everyone looking to complete Magnitude's new quest stayed pretty tight-lipped about it. It's started to come out this morning though. In fact, it's trending. Haven't you looked at the official Saga Online channel yet?"

Damien squeezed his temples between thumb and middle finger. He had, in fact, and had been presented with a completely different problem. One which Kevin had just unwittingly reminded him of.

"Yeah, I have, but the news wasn't there when I looked. I saw something else though, which is what I wanted to talk to you about. That stream Mobius cut for me was terrible! It didn't cover what happened properly at all! It's like they wanted to make me out as the bad guy, when all I was doing—"

"Now Damien, hang on a se—"

"—was trying to join a party, and then this—"

"—Damien, it was—"

"—moron with a samurai sword shows up and—"

"—Damien, I'm the one who cut the footage together."

The forest briefly went silent again, causing Damien to realize just how loud he'd been. Fortunately his hell hound wasn't growling, but Damien certainly felt like growling in its place.

"I'm sorry, you what?"

There was a pause, followed by the familiar swish of papers being moved around on Kevin's desk. Damien waited, his temper rising steadily, until Kevin had found his bearings. He'd obviously prepared this in advance.

"As your minder, back when you were simply testing game elements my role was to process any abnormal findings and your satisfaction level with gameplay. Now my role has switched to ensuring the success of your channel and managing your PR. I've got the numbers right here in front of me and I promise this is a good thing, even if it doesn't feel like it."

"How can you be—"

"Damien, please trust me! You should know that of all people, I have your best interests at heart. This is actually a really good situation for you."

Damien grumbled and Kevin pointedly waited to make sure there would be no more interruptions.

"The channels dedicated to mainstream pursuits, like base-building, game mechanics or guild management are very common. The channels for player-killing are far fewer, and they're all oversubscribed even though the content is sub-par. Half the time the players running these channels end up with bounties and can't make new content, since more often than not they're on death timers. But you have the class to make it work, since you're so overpowered for player-killing and you already have negative reputation with the Empire."

So Kevin wanted him to be a full-time player-killer, the exact opposite of what Damien had been striving toward.

"Kevin, what you're telling me would be fascinating if I gave a damn. I don't want to be hated by the majority of players I play this game with. I'm trying to move away from player-killing. I only did it in the first place because that's the role that was forced on me."

"You complained that your numbers were dropping even though you won the competition. This is the solution. It's a pretty good one, even if I do say so myself. With this you'll have a steady income and a secure career. This business with Magnitude even helps you, since there will be more players—"

Kevin was halfway through his pitch when Damien's hound bore its teeth and snarled out into the wilderness. He needed to end the call and concentrate on what he was doing.

"Yeah, Kevin, we'll have to finish this later. I've got work."

Damien hung up. He was just as worried about the encroaching threat as he was relieved the conversation was temporarily over. He stuck his head out to survey his surroundings, his eyes straying over the tree Noigel was hiding behind. Only Noigel was practically in plain sight, his legs sticking out from one side and his tail swishing around behind him. There were another pair of legs sticking out from behind the tree as well: red, slender and ending in a pair of hairy hooves. From what Damien could make out, which was blessedly little, Noigel was sandwiched in between them.

That lecherous little turd. Making hanky-panky when he should've been standing watch, and upsetting the hounds in so doing when they needed to be paying attention. He'd bloody well kill him.

All caution gone, Damien stepped out from behind his cover and started marching purposefully toward Noigel's impromptu love nest. The hounds were still barking, one on each side. Noigel was apparently too busy to notice. Damien was halfway there when he lost his temper.

"Shut up! I'm dealing with it! You two should be—"

Which is when, off to the left, a mage stepped out from behind a tree. He was no further from Damien than Noigel and his special interest. The canoodling couple had not been the cause of the hounds' distress, not at all. Damien knew now that they'd been barking because their master was in danger. And what spectacular danger it was.

Between the long golden hair, the pointed elven ears and the green piercing eyes punctuating Aetherius's all too familiar sneer, it was pretty clear Damien had messed up. Aetherius's presentation was a far cry from what it had once been, the coordinated style and color scheme of his equipment replaced with a hodge-podge of mismatched items, but otherwise he looked every bit as imposing as he ever had. Not least of all because his hands were glowing red.

The other imps were all still concealed beneath the snow. Damien had no choice. He'd no sooner locked eyes on his oblivious second-in-command's rump when the two of them switched places. It was hard to say which of them suffered more. Noigel transcended from oblivious self-indulgence to a screaming scattering of atoms in half a second flat. Had Damien's view of his imp not been obscured by the tree, he may simply have chosen incineration rather than salvation. As things were, the price of salvation was his tongue being matted with succubus thigh fur.

This was not the sort of momentum transferal Damien had in mind. The succubus wasn't any happier, screeching angrily as they each fought to get off the other faster. With claw marks on his face, a hairy tongue and Aetherius's sudden appearance plunging his heart into his stomach, Damien would've paid handsomely for someone to rip off his headset. The feeling mostly passed after a few moments and Damien wondered why he hadn't passed with it. He turned to look for Aetherius, expecting another spell to be coming his way. His adversary was standing in the snow, calmly drinking a mana potion.

"Everyone, get him!"

His imps had already burst from the snow while he reeled from sensory overload, their protective instincts triggered by his heightened distress. At his command, the succubus set off behind them. But something didn't feel right, and it wasn't just his tastebuds either. His hounds were running the wrong way.

Damien was redirecting them when a number of key facts popped into his clearing head. He'd ignored them moments earlier, to his cost. He'd given them a direct order, and although some of his units were more antisocial than others they never disobeyed instruction. Aetherius had been drinking that mana potion for a long time, considering most players could glug them down in mere seconds and it had once been a core focus of his playstyle. And the two hounds, who'd started from different locations, appeared to be converging on empty space. Not only that, but they were altering their paths as they ran, running in two curves. As if they were chasing something.

Damien's eyes darted from the hounds to the ground ahead of them just in time to see a tuft of snow get kicked up into the air, seemingly by the wind. Until in front of it an empty footprint appeared in the snow, the latest in a trail that ran all the way back to his potion-drinking enemy's image.

Damien started running for the nearest tree as Aetherius Blinked, becoming visible but closing the gap between them to nearly nothing. The illusion of him drinking a potion faded and the minions immediately turned back to cover their master, but Aetherius had meticulously circumvented every single one of them. Even the hounds, who'd been on the verge of catching their prey, had been left far behind. Aetherius aimed a glowing-red left hand at Damien's head, braced his feet and fired.

Damien slid forward and passed underneath the beam without stopping. Aetherius canceled it and threw his other hand up and around, curving an Arcane Bolt directly into Damien's path. Damien had to veer right to avoid it, the bolt's turning circle just too wide to keep up with him, and found himself on a collision course with his pursuer. Aetherius threw his hand back up, glowing with the light of a new beam, when the Chaotic Bolt the succubus had been charging slammed into his back. Aetherius staggered forward, caught completely unaware.

By the time Aetherius had recovered, Damien was already leaping toward him across the short distance that remained. Aetherius brought both hands around from his sides, where they'd been thrown for balance, in a desperate attempt to cast a double-handed beam at close range. Damien was faster. Each dagger met a separate outstretched palm, piercing through them as their bodies collided. Aetherius fell over backward and Damien landed squarely on top of him, his knee on his enemy's chest and the daggers pinning the spell-casting hands to the floor on either side of his head.

Aetherius struggled to free his hands, but Damien kept them held down while he waited for his minions to come finish the job. After a few moments, Aetherius relaxed. Damien was just considering trying to remove a dagger to put it through Aetherius's head when his latest victim's face contorted. Not with anger, but mirth. He started chuckling, trying to hold it in, but it quickly deteriorated into full-on laughter. It was unnerving. Damien had expected insults, or curses, or at the very least a hearty glob of spit in his face. Not this.

The hounds were closing in, using the last of their stamina to reach them as soon as possible while the winged minions lagged behind. They were on the verge of seizing Aetherius's head when Damien forced them to stop. This wasn't how it was supposed to go down. If anything, Aetherius should have been madder than ever. He was still trying to figure out what to say when the laughter stopped. While that had indeed been annoying, the bored expression Aetherius had suddenly adopted, so reminiscent of that which once accompanied his old foot-tapping habit, was worse.

"What's the holdup? Do you enjoy sitting on my chest? Just hurry up and kill me already, so I can go eat or do laundry or something."

"I was just wondering what you thought was so funny. You seemed pretty bummed out last time I killed you. And took your Bag of Holding, I might add. It's really useful by the way, but not the kind of thing you should be building a character around."

Aetherius's eyes briefly settled on the bag, narrowed, and then rose up to meet Damien's again.

"Oh yeah, that thing. Glad you're making good use of it. Means I'll be able to reclaim it at some point. Don't lose it before I kill you, 'kay?"

"Says the guy with daggers in his hands. You won't kill me, you just blew the best shot you're ever gonna get."

"You think that was a serious attempt? I just heard that you were in the neighborhood and thought I'd try my luck. And holy crap, I almost got you on my first try! This will be easier than I thought. I can't believe I gifted a pleb like you with the streaming competition. And that bag you're so proud of? You stole it. If it happened any other way they'd call it griefing, but nooooo, killing the competition leader by stealing his inventory is totally cool. At least it fits your image; you're a little kid with an edgy class and a superiority complex."

Damien was shouting now, and Aetherius's smirk just made everything even worse.

"For starters, I was about ten levels lower than you and had to fight pretty much a hundred people you threw in front of you as cannon fodder, and you're getting hung up on your whole playstyle having a single glaring weakness that I exploited? You were spouting all kinds of crap about me being a noob, when all that time you were relying on a gimmick to win? Truth is, *Andrew*, your whole strategy relied on people not knowing what you were doing. It had nothing to do with skill at all. You're just not that good a player."

Aetherius sighed and rolled his eyes. How was it that he was becoming more annoying by the second? There was a pause, and then he pulled the rug out from under Damien's feet.

"That's rich, coming from the occultist. But you're half right. I min-maxed my class and took an easy route. You know why? I was running a huge guild, looking after my players and keeping content on my channel up. Playing the class properly was secondary, so long as everything kept working."

Damien adjusted his grip and brought the minions in a little closer, so they could all jump him together if he tried anything. Aetherius seemed entirely focused on the conversation, all but oblivious to the knees on his chest and the daggers piercing his palms.

"Thanks to you, those distractions are gone. I can play on my own terms. Meanwhile, your problems are just beginning! And oh boy, it's a lot of fun watching you get yours! I saw that stream yesterday, the one where you killed all those *innocent* raiders. You enjoying being the bad guy, Damien? Being hated? Being Mobius's little lapdog?"

Damien was stunned. Aetherius had hit the nail right on the head. Effortlessly.

"Aww, lookit those wittle puppy dog eyes! You *are* sad! While the pressure on you racks up, I'll be focusing entirely on how to end the career you stole from me. If you kill me at this stage, it means nothing. But if I kill you? Man, I can only imagine how badly that'll tank your ratings. Now you're the one with everything to lose."

His grin broadened as he watched the words sink in. It took a few moments but Damien had a thought and suddenly smirked back. He knew something Aetherius didn't. Sharing is caring.

"I won't be hanging around for your second go. I'm headed for the Outer Ring. By the time you respawn, I'll be on the other side of Carlisle and you'll still be penned in here. If you've heard the news about me, you've probably heard about Magnitude taking over Carlisle. I'm pretty much built for avoidance and evasion, but I don't see you getting through. So you have fun here, with all the other trash, and maybe—"

Damien had really thought he was making headway. Aetherius had slowly been going redder and redder in the face, his eyes widening and his face contorting until it looked like it might explode. Then, he did. He screamed laughter into Damien's face. Okay. He'd completely lost it. There didn't seem to be much point in humoring him further. Damien looked up at a hound, ready to give the order, when Aetherius finally did start spitting into his face. Unfortunately, it was a secondary feature of a great deal of acerbic verbiage.

"What did I just say? A kid with an edgy class and a superiority complex! It's so gratifying to see how far you've fallen, and how quickly. It took me months, but it only took you a few weeks before you started calling other players trash! For no reason at all! And in the same breath, you're smugly talking about Magnitude penning *me* in? Oh, wow! What a disaster for you!"

He pealed off into a second laughing fit, through which he gleefully spluttered out the words Damien hadn't known he didn't want to hear.

"You're not getting past Carlisle. You're the whole reason Richard took that settlement so early! He wants to keep everyone else from getting out as well, but at least they have a small chance of serving him instead. I've fought Richard, trust me, he'll handle you without help. And thanks to your player-killing adventures here today, he'll know you're coming. No. You'll be here for a long, looong time. Your vapid supporters dwindling away as your dream fades and reality sets back in. I'll have plenty—"

In unison, the hell hounds twisted their heads back the way Aetherius had come and growled. Damien's head darted upward, following the direction they were pointing in. Aetherius filled his lungs and bellowed.

"Over here!"

Damien looked down at Aetherius just in time to catch a cheeky wink. Then his adversary vanished from underneath him, causing Damien to plop into the empty cavity that had been left in the snow. What the hell? The only skill Aetherius had that would allow him to do that was Blink, but that required facing—

A dull, slightly delayed *thud*, followed by the snapping and creaking of branches far above, attracted Damien's disbelieving gaze. Aetherius had Blinked upward, into the trees. Granted, with his low physical stats he looked like a complete tool, his legs kicking in the empty air as he struggled with the simple task of pulling himself up onto the branch. But he'd slipped out of Damien's reach, from right between his fingertips.

This guy didn't know when to quit. If he thought Damien would let him go he had another thing coming. He was totally out of his element in the tree, but Damien would be quite comfortable there. He was sending an imp up for his Demon Gate, the hounds getting louder with every passing moment, when something collided with the side of his head and his hit points plummeted. It had hit him so hard that he staggered over sideways, then toppled into the snow.

He had 120/1,160 hit points remaining. 2x damage for being unaware of the enemy, then another 2x damage on top for being struck in a critical zone. That's a lot of damage. He much preferred being on the other end of such attacks. Still lying in the snow, his hand traced its way up to the side of his head and found an arrow sticking out of it. Wonderful. And he was bleeding as well. Marvelous. Bleeding arrows sure were popular around here.

He had to hide. He looked over to where the attack had come from, hoping to catch a glimpse of his enemy, and found something much worse. Without Noigel present to guide them while he was occupied, his minions had all run with maximum aggression in the direction of the attack, following their prime directive to protect their master.

In his brief absence, they were getting mown down. There was more than one enemy. That was clear from the variety of attacks being levied against them. His hounds were the fastest, and thus the first to run into the overwhelming odds. The first was hit by an arrow, the damage of which was much mitigated by the armored plates, only to have its head blown off by a bullet. Not the typical close-range clump of buckshot Damien had seen firsthand in his own altercations with gunslingers, but a long-range, accurate, instant projectile.

That was dwarven tech! Here? The second hound was hit by an Ice Bolt, freezing its forelimbs and reducing its pace to a crawl. Without speed on its side to close the gap, the hound was practically harmless.

This group seemed dangerous to tangle with in the best of circumstances, never mind when they'd got the jump on him. Damien needed to get out of here. He commanded his imps to flee as he scrabbled behind the tree Aetherius was balancing in, bleeding profusely the whole while. It was already too late for the rest of them. The succubus had proven easy prey when acting of her own accord, flying in the open straight to her inevitable demise. She dodged an arrow and managed to release her Chaotic Bolt before an Ice Bolt hit her wing, sending her into a nosedive. She hadn't even hit the floor before a second bullet had improbably struck her through the neck. A remarkable feat given her rapid, uncontrolled descent.

Dwarven ranged weapons were some of the best in the game, but at least they had long reloading times. The next shot would likely be reserved for him. They had an ice mage as well, somewhere, who was stacking the environmental effects of the zone with his own to devastating effect. So there were at least three players. Damien had chugged a health potion while he watched and was about to draw his head back when the number increased to four.

While everyone else remained in hiding, a warrior closed in to deal with the frosted hound. It was a tank who was making use of the Behemoth trait, a tower shield that looked normal-sized on him but had the approximate dimensions of a bank-vault door and an obscene black flail, complete with a spiky ball on a long chain. It passed straight through the chilled hell hound at the end of its arc, shattering the beast into myriad fleshy shards of ice which burst and disintegrated in midair.

The rest of the party had not revealed themselves, but this

player provided enough information to confirm how much trouble Damien was in. Level 48. Off to a bad start. Damien spied his name and gleaned that the whole character was very much designed based on the principle of size mattering. He was called 'BiggusDickus'. Damien couldn't agree more. Best of all, his guild was 'Carlisle-Elite'. So these were Magnitude's boys. That went some way to explaining why they were causing so much grief. They'd already killed ten players consecutively here, they knew exactly what they were doing.

Damien could try to run, but the bleed effect on the arrow would kill him before he got very far. Assuming he didn't get shot in the back first. If he did manage to escape, they'd follow the trail of blood he'd be leaving behind for the next fifty seconds. The only way he was getting out of this would be by Demon Gating, but he'd have to get it right. Which would be difficult, because one of his three remaining imps had already been shot out of the air.

Damien thought for an instant, then flew the last two in different directions. One flew straight past him without stopping, putting itself as far away from the combat as possible. The other flew upward toward its previous target, Aetherius. The blood leading to the foot of the tree meant they'd quickly discover Damien, but he was more concerned with concealing the whereabouts of his escape imp. Since Aetherius had caused so much trouble, the least he could do was provide a distraction.

Damien looked up and waited till the imp was in range. He'd previously intended to off Aetherius himself, up in the branches where the mage's low agility would render him helpless. However, this was more important, and considerably more amusing. He Imp-loded it, enjoying the spectacle of Aetherius being torn out of the tree. There was a dull *thud* as he landed, but Damien couldn't risk watching without endangering himself. Unless...

"Possession."

Now flying his escape imp, Damien waited until Aetherius's body was starting to blur out in the snow before flying in a wide circle. His old nemesis had dropped face-first between the

Carlisle-Elite members and Damien's evacuated, bleeding body. Keeping Aetherius in his sights would give him a fair amount of warning if anyone was getting close to his position. Aetherius wasn't moving. He was lying facedown in the snow exactly where he'd fallen.

After a few seconds, BiggusDickus unceremoniously walked up to him and threw the flail through his prone form. Aetherius's body dissipated, the choice of illusion so subtle that even Damien himself hadn't clocked it. Aetherius reappeared, coming around the very tree Damien's body was propped up on, hands glowing.

This guy was relentless. Damien canceled the Possession and cast his eyes up for the imp, the thrum of Aetherius's held spell-cast ringing in his ear. He found the imp where he'd left it and Demon Gated instantly, arriving exactly as the Arcane Beam tore through the spot where he'd been lying. He hadn't even had time to land the imp, resulting in a brief fall and a splatter of blood at Damien's new location.

Time to leave. He ran directly away from the combat, spamming his Portal spell as the same repeated notification informed him the spell could not be cast while there were enemies nearby. When it was finally replaced with a notification saying that he had to stand still in order to cast, Damien darted behind the nearest cover and strained to focus on it. Far behind him a single gunshot rang out, muffled by the distance and the thick white blanket coating the environment. He didn't have the luxury of finding out if it had connected. The moment the portal appeared, he leapt through it and it quickly closed behind him.

Damien had failed in his objective of erecting a Gateway nearby. He'd acquired 17 souls' worth of minions, only to lose 16 of them. He had little to no experience gain. Yet considering what he'd come up against, he was lucky to be alive.

So much for his productive morning.

6

QUID PRO QUO

There was one thing Damien felt like doing above all others, and he still had a soul left over in his Sacrificial Dagger to do it with. He pointed it at the floor and started summoning an imp. Not just any imp, but the one that had inadvertently brought his morning's efforts to a standstill. As he resummoned Noigel, he sent the Soul Well-bound succubus to the furthest corner of the base. He'd be Noigel's sole concern, this time round.

"You ungrateful little swine! Do you know what happened, thanks to you? You knew what you were supposed to be doing, Noigel, and you decided fulfilling your disgusting urges was more important!"

Damien was jabbing his finger into Noigel's ribs, mere words not enough to express his discontent. The imp surprisingly backed away without a word of retort, cowering and remorseful. It wasn't enough to satisfy Damien, given the setback his summon had propagated.

"I told you to stand watch and you waited until I needed you most to indulge yourself? Are your disgusting urges more important than keeping your master alive? Tell me! Are they?"

Noigel had no response. He'd only just been reincarnated and had no inkling of what had transpired while he was away. He was defenseless. The same state of being he'd inflicted on Damien minutes earlier, by not doing as he was told.

"Aetherius showed up! That's who you got blasted by, and what were you doing? Bobbing up and down on a tactical asset. So not only did you not keep me safe, you were stopping the succubus from keeping me safe as well. And look where we are: back where we started, with nothing to show for it! Do I need to go back to giving you direct orders, like when we first met?"

Noigel cowered. For once, he had nothing to say. Somehow, that made Damien angrier. He'd expected snark, or defiance, or at least some of his most important imp's charisma to manifest. Which is when he realized: there were no imps besides Noigel present. Noigel didn't have the ability to speak. Not in tongues that Damien would understand, at any rate. Yet somehow, this realization made Damien angrier still. He was somehow the bad guy, verbally attacking the minion he'd relied on when it lacked the ability to speak in its own defense.

Whose fault was that? Was it Damien's fault Noigel couldn't speak? If he hadn't been so busy cavorting, they'd have dealt with Aetherius without issue and there would've been a plethora of imps in the base, in due course, to support Noigel's 'Forbidden Knowledge'. Even better, there'd be no need to berate him in the first place.

Yelling at him was only making him feel guiltier and angrier, but not in that order. Damien cast his eyes about his base, looking for a suitable course of action to further chastise his summon.

"Go sit on your hands and stare at the wall. This is your fault! I order you to stay out of my sight."

That was a pretty unreasonable order, but Noigel had behaved pretty unreasonably himself. He did as he was told and Damien looked away, then went into his menu. With Noigel as his only surviving imp and in time-out, base construction was not going to happen. Damien still needed to edit together the footage from that morning into something that implied a successful run.

He revisited the whole debacle with Aetherius and the

Carlisle-Elite, only to decide none of it was fit for consumption on his page. Which made him feel like as much of a spin doctor as Kevin.

Nevertheless, it did end up serving a purpose. He went over his conversation with Aetherius in detail, looking for one particular point he hadn't had time to digest before he lost control of the situation. Aetherius had referred to Magnitude as 'Richard'. He knew him by his actual name. They weren't allies, since the Carlisle party had attacked Aetherius without hesitation. With someone like Aetherius, it was hard to tell where the truth began and the lies ended. But what he'd said had seemed pretty sincere. Hateful, sure, but heartfelt.

After half an hour, Damien had compiled a neat ten-minute-long clip. A great deal of the time had been spent waiting, and the fights themselves had not generally lasted very long. That was the point of the strategy. He stuck the longer, more interesting fight with Gatz at the end. At least it had been pretty cool when he threw the dagger through his eye. That was a standout moment, for sure.

Right. Maybe this would look a bit better from a distance. He attached the succubus to his own Soul Summon Limit to make sure Noigel didn't get any hanky-panky in while he was away. The succubus would leave Arcadia with him and come back when he logged back in, leaving Noigel with only the incubus and a wraith for defense. And hopefully nothing else.

"Noigel, if you do anything funny with the incubus or the wraith, so help me God, I will find every imaginable way of making you pay for it. Stay there, just like that, and think about what you did."

The log-out procedure finished and Damien opened his eyes to his own room, hungrier than ever. After he'd had something to eat, it would be time to go visit Lillian. It would be the first time they'd seen each other since she'd gone with him to check up on his mom, after her operation. He'd wanted to stay away from work talk, to connect with Lillian over something other than Saga Online. Yet, if anyone could tell him who 'Richard' might be, it was her.

The ride to Lillian's house took half an hour, considerably less time than when he'd been traveling mostly on foot while pursued by the law. His reclamation of automated taxi services went a long way to making that possible. They were more expensive than the vast majority of transportation services, that went without saying, but they were also the safest by far.

It was certainly strange though, passing under the city as a simple passenger rather than as a fugitive. Spanning the gap between him and Lillian in minutes rather than days. Every now and then his eyes would alight on a tuk-tuk, or an internet cafe, or a sheltered market stall down a dark alley.

It was funny, thinking how much more secure he was now than he had been then. He never intended to go back. He had to make the most of the opportunity he'd earned for himself. He just hadn't thought it would be so complicated. A brief analysis of his profile and the myriad but underwhelming competing PvP accounts showed that Kevin was right. It had taken a little while, but the view count of Kevin's duplicitous edit had resulted in a fresh wave of subscribers to his stream channel and a marked increase in the views of all his original videos. He'd have that to look forward to when he got his first paycheck at the end of the month. What Kevin was not taking into account was the stagnation of Damien's abilities.

So while his visit to Lillian was originally intended to be a social call, there was work on his mind when he found himself outside her door. He gave it a few seconds to let the déjà vu pass, then hit the buzzer and the Mobius call-box in rapid succession. The call-box lit up.

"Hello, who's there?" inquired Lillian in her best bedside manner. A plethora of sound effects, including spell-casts, explosions and cries for help, created a backdrop of total madness. She sounded quite calm in the middle of it all.

"It's Damien."

"You're early! I thought we— hang on."

Damien's head rolled back as Lillian screamed into her microphone. A loud buzz heralded the door opening, followed by a slew of orders from Lillian. She was back to raid mode.

"Burst down the adds! You're forbidden to heal players who stand in AoE, no excuses. That means you, Judge, you soft wimp! And somebody leash— fine, I'll do it myself! Damien, get inside, shut the door and wait!"

Damien was inside and closing the door before the static emanating from the box had died away. He gave the expansive living room a sigh before settling in on the sofa, wringing his hands as he wondered what Lillian was up to. Maybe it was the Lair of the Emerald Queen? That would make sense, since she wasn't much lower level than him.

Too bad she'd end up stuck in the Human Realm, just like everyone else. At least she was enjoying the game for now. Since she was a casual gamer rather than a pro, maybe she'd be able to come back to Saga Online once Damien had sorted out Magnitude's mess.

He was still mulling over how to convey the bad news when her bedroom door opened and Lillian emerged from down the corridor, still fastening her dressing gown around her waist. She was wearing her pajamas and a massive pair of plush green slippers, modeled after goblin feet. A new addition to her line of home comforts. It didn't look like she'd been out of the house all day. Good for her.

She looked up from the bathrobe cord to shoot him a broad grin. She threw out her arms and advanced on him, still smiling from ear to ear. It appeared her raid had gone well.

"Come here, you filthy cultist! How's it going? Like my new feet?"

Damien was up on his own feet and beaming back at her just in time to get squeezed. His smile was more than a simple return of her affection. As she advanced, his eyes had involuntarily darted to her wrist to find it bare. She'd removed her guardian wristband.

She was doing so much better than when Damien had last visited. He felt a lump rising in his throat and pushed it back down while she couldn't see his face, only for his eyes to start watering as Lillian seamlessly transitioned her hug into a chokehold and an unwanted noogie.

"Oi, don't bully me! Bloody paladins, always throwing their weight around."

He was still a little bit shorter than her, and not in nearly as good shape. But Lillian relented, giving him a last embrace before dropping down on the sofa and sighing.

"Yeah, I'll admit, I've been doing a lot of that recently. So, champion! How goes professional streaming life?"

"Eh, not great, to be honest. It's not what I thought it was going to be."

Lillian nodded sagely and crossed her legs.

"Can't say I'm surprised. It was pretty exhausting supporting Andrew with it. You don't have a guild though, surely it can't be that bad?"

Damien scrunched an eye shut and looked at her.

"Funny you should mention Andrew. I ran into him today. We had a "conversation", if you can call it that. Then he signaled the Carlisle-Elite to our location and almost got me killed."

"You've been having trouble with the Carlisle-Elite as well? You didn't mention it in your stream today."

"It wasn't stream-worthy. Aetherius didn't have anything nice to say and the fight didn't go too well for me either. It was better to leave it out. He's unhinged."

"He's been unhinged for a while. I'm glad we got revenge on him, I don't think we could've handled it any better than we did. But looking back? Maybe if I'd been in a better place I'd have done things differently."

"Lillian—," Damien's hand dropped on her shoulder, "—you helped me save my mom, and you got me my dream job. I didn't mean to sound ungrateful, by the way, about the streaming gig not being what I thought it would. I enjoy it a lot, it's just more complicated than I realized."

Lillian put her hand on his and gave it a quick squeeze before moving it back down to the sofa.

"That's pretty much what happened to Andrew. He was committed, I'll give him that, but the stress turned him into a completely different person once we hit the big leagues. I couldn't let what he did slide, but...it would've been nice, you know, if things had turned out a little better. And a big part of that is on me, since I'm the one who tore it all down once he was set to win."

Damien coughed loudly and pointed at himself.

"I think you'll find *I* tore it all down. I can't have you taking the credit for my accomplishments!"

She gave him a hard whack on the shoulder. In game or out, it still hurt.

"Please! You didn't even have a proper profile page until I showed up. I could've wiped the floor with you when we first met if I felt like it, back in the Twisted Forest. Then you've got the raid on Rising Tide's waiting room I had to pretty much drag you into, which is what really got everyone's attention for the first time—"

Damien's ego was taking a bit of a battering. The big sincere smile he'd had since he got there was starting to feel strained.

"Okay, I get it—"

"—you remember? When I let you kill that Pegasus I told you about and get all the EXP?"

"Yeah, I remember."

"And how about the Rising Tide guild headquarters? Did *you* march in and destroy it top to bottom in a couple of minutes?"

"No."

"And I'm pretty sure I saved you from Andrew when he had you cornered, at the bottom of your base with the firewalls penning us in. If memory serves. And before that—"

"Alright Lillian! I get it! *We* tore it all down. You were a reliable sidekick."

Lillian looked at him in shock as Damien tried his best not to laugh, then started whaling on him without warning.

"How dare you! Take that back!"

"Alright! It was all you!"

Lillian kept on, jabbing him in all his pressure points through his outstretched hands with no effort at all.

"You're damn right it was all me! Your plan to player-kill all Rising Tide, your successful one-man raids on their dungeon runs and your one-on-one duel with Andrew had NOTHING to do with it! And don't you forget it!"

She lurched back into her seat, crossed her arms and blew a strand of hair out of her face with a huff. Even though she was grinning, Damien decided to tread a little more carefully.

"I was only joking. I know I owe you, big time. If you hadn't helped, I probably wouldn't have got anywhere."

Lillian remained quite still, but her eyes darted to the side and her lips spread in a mischievous grin.

"Oh, so you owe me? That's good to hear, since I had something in mind for you. If it's not too much trouble for the big-shot streamer?"

"Sure, whatever you want. So long as we can get some pizza after we're done?"

She eyed him sidelong for a few moments before extending a hand to shake on it with a broad grin.

"Deal. Easiest bribe ever."

"Worth it. What exactly is it you want me to do?"

"We're heading into the Inner Circle."

"Whoa, hold on a sec, why are you going there? And what do you need me for?"

"You should know why! The Carlisle-Elite has been harassing us all over Frozone, trying to kill us or push us out. They don't have the numbers yet, but they will soon enough. The other guilds aren't interested but we don't have any bases to maintain, so nothing to lose. We may as well push through and get new quests and content in the Inner Circle. We're expecting just a *tiny* bit of resistance, so it would be good to have a player-killer along. Last I checked, you're one of the best."

He could do her this favor and he'd also be helping himself out in the process. And he'd get paid in pizza. Excellent all round.

"Okay. Honestly, I'm heading for the Inner Circle as well, so this is a pretty good deal for me. Who are the other players? Is this a new group you've pulled together?"

Lillian grimaced. Damien could already tell he wasn't going to like her answer.

"It's what's left of Rising Tide. They needed somebody to take the reins after the whole thing imploded, and I thought since I was at least *partially* responsible I could reprise my old role. There aren't many who stayed, but those who did are some of the best."

"You're the guild leader of Rising Tide?"

"Come on, Damien, gimme some credit. I half ran it even when Andrew was officially in charge. I dealt with the players and he dealt with the economy. No bases or economy to worry about now."

"Don't you think that's going to be a bit of a problem? I doubt they'll want to work with me."

"Uh, Damien? I'm the boss. If I tell them we're working with you, that's what happens. Besides, they can't very well complain about you without complaining about me."

He hadn't thought of that. Lillian saw his discomfort and patted him on the back.

"Don't worry, we're all squared away in Rising Tide now. Nobody's following me who doesn't want to and I make it worth their while. Remember the dragon Andrew took down, while we were attacking the waiting room? We've been doing the dungeon every night for the last week. We have really steady runs now we've leveled up, no one even died today. Of course, if Magnitude recruits more players he'll block us from running it, so we need to get a step ahead of him."

Ah! The mention of Magnitude reminded Damien of what he'd wanted to tell her.

"There's something else I need to ask you. I think Aetherius knows Magnitude in real life. Does the name 'Richard' mean anything to you? He called him Richard a couple of times."

The smile dropped off Lillian's face.

"Magnitude is Richard? Are you sure?"

"He didn't say it, exactly, he sort of laughed it into my face. He was so busy evil-monologuing I'm not sure he realized. Who's Richard?"

Lillian gave a long sigh and delivered the bad news.

"Richard is Andrew's older brother. He was beta-testing the

game right from the start, that's how Andrew got into Saga Online in the first place. I never met him in real life, but Andrew used to talk about him a lot until...until things went south."

Lillian trailed off at the end, looking away and raising her head to the ceiling. Damien cut through the awkward silence.

"Do you still want to attack him, now you know who he is?"

"You're damn right I do. He's the one pressuring us, not the other way round. Are you up for it? I'd have thought it goes with your channel pretty well."

That was true. It would be safer to scout out Carlisle with a big party in tow, and rolling with Rising Tide of all people would show once and for all that he could cooperate with other players. He'd been planning on scouting out Carlisle before he moved past it anyway, so this played right into Damien's hands. Except he didn't have any minions. He'd be a fat lot of use without any imps to enact his strategies with.

"I'm running pretty low on minions after today, I'd like to help but I'm not sure I can. It would take me—"

"Oh! You're in bad shape? I Portal Stoned back to Camelot after we left the dungeon, but I could always come with you and help you grind some souls out, if you're in a bad way?"

She stared straight at him, eyes wide and searching. A small smile played out on her lips as she took in Damien's reaction. She knew enough about his class to know she had him. So did Damien. This offer was too good to refuse, even when he was supposed to be taking the night off.

"That would be great. It's difficult getting my minion count back up from nothing."

Lillian rose to her feet, raring to go.

"Alright! Sorry to make you work on a day off, but Saga beats a movie any day if you ask me. I've already seen all of them five times anyhow. We'll farm until six, have some pizza, I'll tell my guild to meet us at the start of Frozone at seven and then we'll head out. Sound good?"

"Better than good."

"Sweet! Just like old times."

"Not exactly. Unless your guild tries to kill me."

7

THIS IS GETTING OUT OF HAND

Damien and Lillian opted to roam the end of the Brociliande zone, looking for high-level mobs. The two of them were level 42 and level 43 respectively, which posed a problem. The lowest-level mobs Damien could expect to obtain souls from were level 37 and Brociliande mobs only went up to level 39. Also, finding a decent soul farm was difficult on a Saturday afternoon. There were a lot of players out there, it was daylight and Damien still had a large price on his head.

What should've taken less than an hour ended up taking two, with more time spent finding safe places to farm than actually farming. One of the side effects of the next zone becoming so PvP-oriented was that a lot of players were cramming into the back end of Brociliande to grind experience, often in groups for increased safety. With a lot of caution and perseverance, they netted a hard-earned 30 souls – averaging one every four minutes – before logging out to eat.

Despite Lillian assuring him everything would be fine over pizza, Damien wasn't convinced. He'd almost rather have not taken any minions with him at all, for fear of losing them all when Rising Tide turned out to have different ideas from their leader. However, he couldn't very well do that without offending Lillian, who'd helped him farm them for the better part of her afternoon.

Damien was pretty nervous when they reached the Frozen Forest and saw Rising Tide waiting for them. There were a lot of them. Once they'd stopped moving Damien was finally able to get an accurate count: thirty-six of them, all between level 38 and 44. Not as many as there had once been, but every last one of them high level.

They'd been told he was coming in advance, but that didn't stop them from staring. Damien wasn't sure where to look. He'd definitely killed at least half of these guys. He settled for staring at the back of Lillian's head as she issued orders.

"Alright you lot, just like we planned. Team Clowns to the left of me, Team Jokers to the right, the rest of you with me and Daemien in the middle. Stick to your own team's comms unless there's an emergency. Focus! This is a player-killing zone. Let's move out, it'll take a while to get there."

The walk through the forest was much less eventful with Rising Tide flushing it out in advance. The groups at their flanks, Clowns and Jokers, were especially vigilant. As he focused on each player in turn, Damien started remembering which of them he'd previously met in combat pretty quickly.

Lillian's leadership of all these different characters was an incredible feat, even before factoring in her full-time job and Rising Tide's lack of a guild headquarters. Especially since she'd personally contributed to Damien dethroning their leader. It said as much about them as it did about her.

It took the better part of an hour to traverse the whole zone, following a few altercations with players who'd drastically misread the situation. But the group eventually arrived at the far edge of the forest unscathed. Leaving his summons behind, Damien came to stand at Lillian's side and set eyes on the obstacle he'd so blithely told Aetherius he'd circumvent without difficulty.

It was not like it was in the source material on the Saga media page. Not at all. The little border settlement of Carlisle was gone. It had been replaced with a huge wall that spanned the entire valley, completely blocking off the zone's only exit. Yet while the mountains were made of stone, this thing was made of metal. That was weird, and foreboding. They had plenty of stone around they could've used instead, for much cheaper. It was almost as ridiculous, maybe even more so, than buying the settlement in the first place. Magnitude had to be rolling in gold.

It was hard to gauge the size of it, not least of all because there was nothing in front of it for comparison. The land around the base of the wall was a vast open semicircle, with no trees and no cover at all. An open field.

"Lillian, what the hell is that?"

"That's Carlisle. I did say we might hit a tiny bit of resistance."

"You call that a tiny bit of resistance? I was expecting us to go around a small settlement, not through a damn wall!"

"So was I. Over the last week, the Carlisle-Elite have been deconstructing Carlisle and turning it into this thing. I was hoping they wouldn't have finished it before we were all geared from the dungeon, but no such luck. Looks like they had a busy day today. That's not all. Look, up there."

Damien followed her pointing finger and got his first anchor to perspective. A series of thin spikes were running all the way along the top of the wall, with torches spaced out between every three spikes. The slight wavering movement of each and every spike drew Damien's attention to what they really were. Spears. Each held by a guard, their upper bodies showing through slats in the parapet. There were a lot of them, more than felt necessary and certainly more than any normal guild would have on watch duty. They were too far away for Damien to make out their basic information, but given how many of them there were, their coordinated weapons and their unerring attention to duty, it seemed they were not players.

"Are those NPCs?"

"Yup. Carlisle has a bunch of them. They aren't as strong as your average player, but they're much better at being guards. We've counted fifty, and they change shifts four times a day, so they have anywhere between a hundred and two hundred NPCs. Maybe more. If you could run interference while we smash our way through the front gate, that'd be grand."

Lillian put her hand up to her ear and started talking, prompting everyone to turn their heads to face her regardless of whether they were within range of her voice.

"Remember, we aren't looking for a prolonged engagement here. Play defensively, I want as many of you alive after this as possible. There's a good chance they're waiting for us. Not much we can do about that, but we can at least be prepared for it. I'll be taking point on this one. If I'm in combat, I expect all of you to be with me. If you see me retreating, you'd best run. Get your potions in order, maintain your gear, refresh your food buffs and be ready to go in five minutes."

As Rising Tide set up a quick camp, Lillian turned her attention back to Damien.

"I know you're more a solo operative, so while we hit the gate I'll leave you to it. You've got this, right?"

"Don't know about that, but I'll give it my best shot. I'm moving away from you lot to hide myself and find a better vantage point."

"Alright, see you on the other side."

She gave him a gentle shove and a nod. Then she turned back to her team, her features hardening before her face was even out of sight. Damien took a deep breath and left them behind. At least he'd avoided being killed by Rising Tide. He ran around the edge of the clearing, distancing himself from them as much as possible in the short time he'd been given. His minions eagerly came to join him, relieved of his confusing instructions not to attack the humans any longer.

Damien ran for four minutes before coming to a halt. His route had taken him most of the way round, though still not quite to the edge of the terrain. The wall was easily larger than any of the human settlements, with the exception of Camelot.

Damien took stock of his minions and tried to decide what to do. His first plan was to fly Noigel to the top of the wall and Demon Gate to him directly, but getting past the guards would require more than just an imp nonchalantly flapping its way across the gap. Even at night, the white snow on such open terrain would make moving targets pretty obvious against them.

Fortunately, the wraith's stealth mitigated that problem. He'd start with the wraith, then move the minions in while the guards were distracted by Rising Tide.

He placed the wraith at the threshold of the forest. Then he cast his eyes out to the right, waiting for his cue.

Thirty seconds later, a steady stream of players started filing out from the wood. Damien squinted and could just about make out Lillian at the front. They'd barely left the tree line when a bell rang out, echoing down into the valley below. As Rising Tide broke into a run, a second and then a third alarm pierced the night.

Go time.

"Possession."

He'd no sooner taken on his wraith's form than he leaned as far forward as he could go, the ground disappearing underneath him as he tore across it. The lack of obstacles may have prevented him from moving in cover, but the wraith had superior stealth and blinding speed in the dark. 'Shadow Beast' was one of the best unique skills in his minion roster, putting even his own 'Shadow Walker' to shame. Despite starting out after Lillian's party, Damien reached the wall long before. He did not stop, hitting it and immediately gliding up it without losing speed.

It was strange, looking at the wall from this angle. Usually an ascent in this form would take no longer than three seconds. This wall was massive. Damien was still marveling at the size of it when the harsh shriek of metal heralded a series of slats opening above. Flaming arrows poked out of the gaps, all of them facing toward Lillian's encroaching party.

The arrows themselves were not too much of a problem for Damien personally, but the fires were a mild threat. If they cast enough light, the wraith could lose its grip on the wall. Damien slowed to a stop and waited for the arrows to be loosed, but it appeared none of the guards were close enough to Lillian to fire. They were just holding their arrows there, lighting up the wall in a long line and blocking his path. Only further down the wall were they loosing their arrows.

The first light of priest-conjured Sanctuary spells encompassed Lillian's party, a radiant impenetrable dome under which the outnumbered party grouped as they ran forward. The domes could not be pierced by projectiles, but it cost mana to keep them deployed and each projectile would drain the caster's mana directly. The light projected by the spell as an unavoidable secondary effect ensured there were a lot of projectiles coming their way.

Damien turned and sped along the wall toward the middle, underneath the firing archers, then went straight through before they could prepare another volley. Their coordination might have been imposing and impressive, but it left gaps ripe for exploitation.

As he neared the top of the wall a volley of spears shot over the side, whistling past him on their way down. Lillian's party was nearing the gates, and they were now in range. The spears weren't just for show: they could be hurled at enemies from above, and Damien could only imagine how fast they'd be going by the time they reached ground level. Sure enough, the first wave of spears was immediately followed by a sound not dissimilar to shattering glass as the first of the Sanctuary spells shattered to pieces.

Everyone was definitely focused on the gate now. Damien ordered Noigel to move all the flying minions in, instructing them to head for the edge of the wall, where it met with the mountain. Until they arrived, he'd have to do what he could with the wraith.

Damien drew level with the top of the wall at the same time as a guard leaned over it, hurling a spear toward the clustered mass at the gates. Damien had a perfect shot at his exposed chest. He drove his arm through it without a second thought, then pulled him over the edge for good measure.

They were leaning over the ramparts to throw straight down. How convenient. Damien zipped between the holes in the wall, waiting for the NPCs to predictably lean over each time. He killed a third the same way as the first two, allowing gravity to do the bulk of his work for him, then decided it was still too slow. He'd have to do something a bit more drastic to pull any meaningful amount of aggro off Lillian and onto himself.

Alrighty. He could use this wall to his advantage. He zipped over the edge, stabbed a guard through the side, then another one, then ran back over the other side. It was risky and unrewarding. The guards were level 50, he hadn't killed either of the two he'd stabbed and there was an abundance of torchlight all across the ramparts. He'd certainly draw more attention this way, even if it was less effective.

A chorus of cries rang out behind him as he disappeared over the edge, but Damien was already gone. He moved further down the wall, to a place that hadn't been alerted to his presence, and did the same thing again.

It was when Damien came up for the third time that he saw the results of his hard work. Most of the guards had drawn back from the edge of the wall and were on the defensive. Progress. Too much progress. He was spotted almost immediately as he came up and all the guards in his vicinity were on their guard, waiting to repel him.

Damien went straight over the other side of the wall without touching anyone. No damage, but he'd definitely bought Lillian some ti—

A series of bright blue orbs below caught his attention. There was a Portal Stone placed a distance behind the gate, and players were arriving at it. Besides the Portal Stone, there was nothing behind the wall whatsoever.

He'd thought the rest of Carlisle would've been relocated to stand behind the wall, but there was nothing. As perplexing as it was, Damien had other priorities. The blue orbs had stopped coming, for now, and they'd heralded the arrival of only a handful of players. Damien saw no more than fifteen, each of them presumably an elite player-killing success story. He caught sight of BiggusDickus pretty effortlessly, although it was harder to make out the less physically gifted of them from so far above.

One did draw his attention, though. A player had appeared right below him on the ground, seemingly out of nowhere. The new arrival pressed a hand against the wall and almost immediately twisted his head up to stare exactly at where Damien was. Which was odd, because between the wraith's Shadow Beast and the pitch black it shouldn't have been possible to see him, even with night vision.

A door had opened up next to this player and a battalion of NPC heavy infantry was filing out of it in two ranks, forming up in front of the gate. They had spears, like their comrades above, but they were also far bulkier, equipped with heavy armor and huge rectangular shields. They were locking into each other as they arrived in position.

So the town guard were all stationed inside the wall itself. And this guy was calling them out. There was only one person this could be. Now he was looking up, Damien could see his face and the name had appeared above his head. Magnitude. No class name. No level indication. All question marks.

A secret class at least ten levels higher than Damien. The main event. The leader of the opposition was directly below him. If Damien killed him fast enough, neither his class nor his level would matter very much. It was probably a coincidence he was looking up. He was just looking at the guardsmen throwing spears over the wall at Damien's retreating form. Yeah. That made sense. Damien had gotten lucky. He could kill this guy, here and now.

Damien changed course to position himself directly above Magnitude and dropped straight downward. Magnitude's gaze followed him all the way to his new location. Hmm. That's not good. But he still wasn't moving.

Damien's arms were all the way back and ready to scythe through his adversary's head when, without looking away, Magnitude slammed both fists against the wall and his health dropped by a third. Damien was laser-focused on his adversary, trying to figure out why his health was dropping. Magnitude couldn't have done that much damage to himself just by hitting the wall, surely?

It was the wrong question to be asking himself. Damien

didn't notice the two blocks of metal forming left and right, rising out of the wall's pristine surface ahead of him. He was already in between them when the walls literally closed in on him. The cubes smashed into each other, with Damien's wraith perfectly caught in the middle.

Damien Blinked and opened his eyes. So much for ending this quickly. The hell hound was standing at the base of the tree, growling back into the forest. There may have been enemies nearby, but Damien's primary concern was with Lillian's group at the gates. Damien rang Lillian immediately but she didn't pick up before he realized a different problem. Noigel's group had arrived at the far end of the ramparts. He stared at the conflict and concentrated his thoughts into a single order.

Noigel, I need to Gate in! Give me an option!

He turned back to the gate and could just about catch the cluster of Rising Tide players outside it, a new Sanctuary spell apparently holding. The archers at the mid-level were all focused on bringing it down and sparks were flying off the top of it. Damien's attention was drawn back to the end of the ramparts by a small, burning figure. It was an imp. Noigel had sent it into a torch to set it on fire so Damien could find it across the vast distance. The evil little genius.

Damien braced himself, then Demon Gated. His senses were overwhelmed as he went from peace and quiet to utter chaos. His party of imps and succubi were outnumbered and outmatched. Guards were moving back to them from the middle, where they'd reconvened to pelt spears at Lillian's group, to deal with the new threat.

Right then. He sent an imp flying over them, then dropped it down and Imp-loded it as best he could. The succubi cast Circle of Hell directly over the seething mass, burning the guards and threatening to burn anyone else who wanted to reach them. He'd been too slow; one of the guards had rushed past the Implosion's radius and was en route to run him through.

It was at this moment Lillian chose to answer Damien's call.

"Busy! What do you want?"

"Fall back! We're not gonna make it!"

He sent another imp to whap into the guard's face, but the guard kept on running at him. Damien barely avoided impalement only to be pushed to the ground as the rest of the guardsman crashed into him.

"We're going through the gate, end of story!"

At such close proximity and with the guard's sight still blocked, Damien's daggers were a far better choice. Which would've been fine if his dead enemy was not wedged in on top of him and there weren't more guards on the way.

He wanted to give Lillian all the information he had to convince her to turn back, but his circumstances were making it difficult. More guards were coming in the Imp-losion's wake, and Damien was still indisposed. They'd have a much easier time stabbing him now he couldn't dodge. Damien flew an imp into them, keeping it low, and yelled out the only spell that might help him survive.

"Ex-Imp-losion!"

The arriving guards were thrown up and back the way they'd come, if they were lucky, and over the wall if they weren't. Damien only had three charges on the spell, but that had been enough to disrupt the offensive, temporarily. The imp had been just above the floor and two of them had been fired out of the rift unfavorably, hitting the floor or the balustrade at high speeds. Ex-Imp-losions created a lot of ex-imps. The third had been launched at speed into the air at an angle.

Damien himself had been closer to the Ex-Imp-losion's cast than he'd have liked. At least he had a cushion to absorb the impact with. The blast sent Damien and his dead adversary tumbling backward to hit the mountain at the wall's furthest end. Damien extricated himself from his foe's remains before leaping to his feet and giving his full report.

"Lillian, they're prepared for you behind the gate and Magnitude is with them. He's some kind of crazy metal mage thing. We aren't going to make it, we should retreat!"

Given how concise and informative Damien had been, he'd

expected Lillian to finally consent. So her blend of barely contained anger and sickly sweet sarcasm came as something of a surprise. Especially since it was punctuated by successive shattering hits on the gate, so forceful he could hear the strikes echoing from below.

"Why thank you, Damien. Tell me, have you seen what's behind us?"

Damien obligingly turned over the parapet and grimaced. Players were pouring out of the forest in droves, running toward the clumped mass of Lillian's party at the gate. Rising Tide had turned to fight them, but it may as well have been a zombie horde. They were even attacking each other en route to the party, with isolated skirmishes breaking out all across the area. Damien could see why his raid buddy was frustrated.

If she wasn't retreating, he had to at least do his best to give her a fighting chance. He also needed to make a break for the Inner Circle himself. Damien sent his remaining four imps and the succubi over the edge of the wall, on the enemy side. A few moments later, he followed after them.

He was now in freefall. He ordered three of the imps to push toward the ground as fast as possible. If he got there before they did, he was screwed. The last flew off to the middle of the wall, toward the group of NPC heavies.

With that done, he resumed his long-running altercation with gravity. He needed the imp to slow down before it hit the floor as well, otherwise he'd be speeding up his death rather than preventing it. Crap. Well...it would be nice if he could keep the imp, but in a situation like this he had to put himself first. Sorry dude. Damien ordered the imp to hit the ground as fast as possible. It weighed less than him and had wings, so it would both survive an impact better and be able to slow itself down faster...hopefully. The imp was only a second from impact when Damien ordered it to stop. It threw out its wings immediately in a futile attempt to slow down, but still hit the snow with a sad *plomph*.

Damien didn't bother checking the damage before Demon

Gating, finding himself flat on his face with all the imp's kinetic energy already very much dispersed into the tiny crater he was lying on top of. His own kinetic energy had been transferred into the imp, which hit the ground for the second and final time about half a second later, this time with a cut-off yelp and a hearty squelch. Not his most compassionate tactical choice, but notably better than the alternative. The bodies of the guards thrown over the edge by the Ex-Imp-losion reinforced that viewpoint. They'd adopted the traditional, time-honored strategy of all human bodies fighting against gravity: unceremoniously dying.

A final loud *clang* drew his attention back to the gate, which was now a way off to his right. The gate had indeed been breached, although not in a particularly impressive fashion. While its durability bar was still at approximately 90%, Lillian had focused her efforts where it was weakest and she could reach: the bottom point where the steel plates of each massive door met. They were crumpled and folded, leaving barely enough room for her troops to start ducking through in single file. They were then greeted by a wall of shields and spears, which advanced on the group as a single block.

Damien pointed at the imp sailing in above their heads and eyed the cooldown meter for Imp-losion. Still five seconds to go. Curses. And Lillian's troops were already running in, only to stop as they saw what was waiting to greet them. They started running forward again when Lillian hurtled past them, their own rather less bloodthirsty battle cries joining her own. The aura of her Divine Might suffused her entire body and her war hammer arced over her head as she prepared to swing. Then she saw what she was facing and slowed down. Damien thought she was reconsidering the engagement, and that his warnings had finally come to bear. Nope. She was just recalibrating. The hammer disappeared out of her grasp and was replaced with her sword and shield before she lunged forward.

She took a running start and hopped, the power behind her stride carrying her to her enemies with a single pump of her legs. All the guards simultaneously dug their shields into the dirt and pointed their spears to use the power of her charge against her.

With the Imp-losion on cooldown and Lillian too close to avoid Circle of Hell herself, Damien could do nothing but watch. They were higher level than her, but despite being a tank Lillian had invested heavily in strength. Which was doubled by her Divine Might, putting her far above them in terms of raw power. With her shield squarely in front of her, she was not altogether unlike one of the cubes of metal that had crushed Damien's wraith. The spears attempting to strike her bent on the shield she was holding close to her body, then snapped and splintered. Lillian crashed into the ranks holding them with the approximate force and subtlety of a cannon ball.

A Lillian-shaped hole appeared in the front line, while the Rising Tide members running through the gap took advantage of the broken formation to lay into them with arrows, spells and brute force. Having found her point of entry, Lillian was creating space by running up to enemies and punting them back with her shield, knocking them into their allies and completely obliterating any sense of order their lines still had. Whenever she came across an immobilized enemy sprawled on the ground, she'd execute with a strike through the neck and then return to shield-bashing.

The Carlisle-Elite players were now running in. Ah, a chance for Daemien, Champion of Arcadia, to show his quality. He maneuvered his imp over their path and—

A hairy block of green rock popped out of the ground in front of him, blocking his line of sight. Damien leapt backward as a pickaxe swung through the area his head had just been occupying. The back of his head hit the floor, his legs following his movement to put him back on his feet as Magnitude pressed forward, trying to prevent him from escaping.

Damien kept the distance between them. It was quite easy. Magnitude was a dwarf. Which meant his legs were moving almost twice as fast in order to match half Damien's running speed. It should've been funny, but when he was running at you with murderous intent it was actually quite scary. At least he clearly wasn't agility-based, so Damien would have no trouble staying ahead of him.

Damien caught sight of something much scarier than Magnitude's pumping legs. Magnitude's health had been at 80%, but over the course of a few seconds it had risen back to 100%. When it hit max, he hopped up in the air with his arms over his head. It was a modest hop, but his feet didn't touch the ground again. The ground simply swallowed him up, as if he'd pencil-jumped into a swimming pool.

This was how Magnitude had gotten the first hit in, appearing right in front of Damien out of nowhere. Well, there was a simple solution: if that's where he currently was, it wasn't where he was going. Damien dug his toes into the ground and leapt forward, turning around to see if he'd been right. Magnitude popped out of the ground, already swinging the pickax in advance of his arrival. He was back down to 80% health.

Every time Magnitude used this skill, he took damage. This would've been a lot more comforting if not for his obscene health regeneration. Damien could only get a percentile reading, since he couldn't see Magnitude's stats, but aside from Berserking warriors he'd never seen anything with HP regen so high. Magnitude was back to running after him again. As he backpedaled, Damien willed a health potion into his hand and started glugging. Magnitude immediately stopped and slammed both his hands against the floor. The same thing he'd done against the wraith.

Damien came to an immediate stop and there was a rush of air behind him as two cubes of tightly packed earth slammed into each other. Magnitude was now at 64% health. He stopped advancing, waiting for his health to rise back up, as Damien drained the potion.

Damien took the time to condense all the information into a single package. Slight delay on spellcasting, so spells are cast predictively. Changing direction is a good preventative measure. Fast movement from underground "tunneling" is tempered by a 20% health cost. The trash compactor move appeared to be the same, 20%. He'd thought Magnitude was a metal mage, but it was broader than that. More like an earth mage.

Damien had enough information to start guessing.

"That's a neat class. What's it called?"

Magnitude stared at him angrily, his health still rising at about 4% per second. That wouldn't do. Damien hadn't had the focus to order his minions when he was getting to grips with this secret class, but he did now. A Circle of Hell formed directly around his enemy. Magnitude ran out of it as fast as he could, which was gratifyingly slowly, only to turn and find he was being chased by imps. Even more gratifying was that the moment the black flames took hold, his health regeneration completely stopped.

Suddenly, Damien had the upper hand. Magnitude ran a hand through the ground, manipulating the burning earth as if it were no more than butter, and propelled a sphere of condensed rock and dirt at the nearest of the imps. It was obliterated, the ball passing straight through it and smashing into the wall behind them. Damien looked at Magnitude's health. It cost him around 10% health for the nasty long-range earth ball.

"You're an earth mage? Nah, too predictable. Geomancer maybe?"

The question marks above Magnitude's name in lieu of his class persisted, but he was getting agitated. The rock he pelted at Damien was evidence enough of that, but Damien already knew how his class worked by this point. Hands above head, ground diving. Hands hit the earth, nasty crushing blocks of death. Single hand through the ground, mud ball. The burning from the Circle of Hell stopped as Magnitude reached the outside of it and his health regeneration kicked back in. More information. So long as he was taking persistent damage, he wasn't regenerating health.

While it was a known mechanic that passive regeneration stopped in the presence of damage over time, it had never really mattered before; passive health regeneration was only 1% of full health every ten seconds, whereas Magnitude was sitting pretty regenerating around 40% over the same period.

"An alchemist? Sorry, that was a long shot...deep mage? Earth-bender?"

The imp caught up with Magnitude and whapped into his face, but it turned out this particular strategy did not work very well on this target. Magnitude grabbed it with both hands and squeezed it like a toothpaste tube. The imp behaved much the same way you'd expect a toothpaste tube to, albeit louder. The poor thing's eyeballs were the last extremities to vacate its now lifeless body. *Pop, pop.*

Magnitude ran a hand over his face to remove the fluids, then started running away. It was good to know his skills, but Damien was yet to figure out a way to finish him off. Most of his damage was from backstabbing, and this guy did not seem like a fun character to get within range of. There was one thing he could try. Damien flicked his wrist at Magnitude's retreating back and cast a spell he hadn't found use for in a long time.

"Corruption."

Damien might not have focused on his intelligence stat much, but this situation didn't require high intelligence. He just needed a persistent damaging effect. At the very least it would stop Magnitude from casting at random, which would relieve pressure.

All this time, Lillian and her team had been fighting and he'd been preoccupied with Magnitude. Damien turned, fearing the worst. Rising Tide was pincered in between the Carlisle-Elite and the gate, through which the influx of reinforcements was long over and a steady stream of injured enemies was filing through instead.

Lillian was still standing, although she'd brought herself a lot of attention with her stunt. BiggusDickus had gone straight for her and she was on the defensive. Her Divine Might had burned out and her stamina was more likely than not low from dealing with the NPCs that had been placed to absorb the brunt of the player attack. The imp he'd wanted to disrupt the enemy formation with was long gone.

Damien looked back to Magnitude, who was smiling and still at 65% health. His health regeneration wasn't working, but

Damien's Corruption was doing almost no damage. Time was up. Damien abandoned tact and ran straight toward him. If Lillian was going to lose, the least he could do was finish this guy off. Magnitude had other ideas. The dwarf grabbed his own wrist, opened his palm and placed it on the floor.

The floor in front of Damien rose up and started to curve inward. Damien ran up it and saw that it wasn't just in front of him. Magnitude was creating a dome of earth and rock, with himself at the center. Damien was no slouch and could move pretty fast, especially in the dark, but he was only barely catching up with the growth of the dome. This spell had a longer cast time than the others, and Damien noticed something new. Rather than all Magnitude's health disappearing in one go and the dome immediately appearing, this was being cast over a long duration. A channeled, free-form spell, with health instead of mana as the resource.

In practical terms, what this meant was that when Magnitude was finished casting he'd have very low health. If Damien could get in there with him, he'd be able to finish him off reasonably easily. With the Rising Tide forces all but overwhelmed it would be a Pyrrhic victory at best, but it could open the floodgates to further consequences. With Magnitude and many NPCs dead, their gate damaged and their strategies exposed, their defenses would be strained and more guilds could come to finish what Lillian had started. But killing Magnitude would be by far the most important factor. Damien had to take this chance.

The dome was always developing just slightly ahead of him, as if it were teasing him. He could see Magnitude just over the lip of it, eyeing him warily as his health continued to drop. This was shaping up to be by far the most costly spell he'd employed. He'd started the cast at about 64% health, was already down to 30% and was still afflicted by the Corruption spell.

The dome was almost done and the hole in the top was rapidly closing. If it closed over him, Damien would have no way of getting inside and Magnitude would be able to regenerate freely. Damien might have a shot at making a break for the Inner Circle, but that paled in comparison to removing this player from the game for twenty-four hours. He owed Lillian that much.

Besides, it would look really good on his profile page.

Magnitude was at 18% health and the opening was still staying just out of reach. Damien braced his feet and dived forward, half expecting to get caught by the dome and severed in two. Instead, it slowed at the last second and he plunged into the darkness headfirst. He'd no sooner rolled than the dome sealed and the dim twilight became total darkness, which his eyes adjusted to quickly. Magnitude was at 14% health. Too low to tunnel out, by Damien's calculations. He had him right where he wanted him.

Except as Damien ran forward, daggers raised, Magnitude uttered a single word.

"Renewal."

A burst of green light emanated from him, lighting up the dome completely. Damien shielded his eyes, blinded out of nowhere, and hopped back. When he could open them again, Magnitude was at full health. The Corruption was gone, too, ahead of time. It was hard to tell through his beard, but Magnitude looked pretty jovial all of a sudden. Damien couldn't blame him. He was now trapped in close proximity with his enemy and all his minions were still outside. This instant healing ability meant that Magnitude had been completely safe the whole time. Damien had been played.

Magnitude threw his hands above his head and hopped while addressing Damien for the first time.

"Don't go anywhere."

Then he vanished into the earth and was gone. Damn. That had not gone well. Damien ran up to the wall and stabbed at it in a futile effort to escape. He knew it was hopeless before he even started: the walls of the dome were at least a couple of feet thick. He was trapped in there, while Magnitude dealt with Rising Tide and Noigel's ragtag party at his own leisure. He had to get out, fast. He was already past the wall, if he could figure out how to break through the dome he could make a run for it.

He tried to Portal, but was informed he couldn't cast the

spell if there were enemies nearby. Par for the course. He'd picked up some souls from the very high-level NPCs, but only six. Not enough to summon an incubus. Which was the only summon that might've got him out of here. He was still pondering his options when something grabbed him by the back of the head.

"You're a pain."

Damien was flipped over by the back of his head, his face hitting the floor hard. He struggled, but it was pointless. Magnitude had overwhelmingly high strength.

Damien had moved to the wall yet Magnitude had arrived right behind him. How was this possible? Damien mulled it over while he ate dirt. He'd already seen this, back when he lacked context to make sense of it. When Magnitude had touched the wall, he'd immediately found Damien's wraith. Even when Damien had been in stealth mode and a long way above, where Magnitude had had no business anticipating an enemy. It fit the profile of his other abilities. Magnitude could sense where enemies were standing if they were touching the ground. (Or whatever else they were touching, judging by the failed wraith attack.)

Well, even if the situation was bad, it was a plus to understand how he'd got there. This situation seemed somehow extremely familiar. Magnitude was employing the Bartholomew methodology of negotiation. But unlike the last time Damien found himself in these circumstances, his mom was waiting for him at home. This wasn't a big deal. He took a leaf out of Aetherius's book.

"Just get on with it."

Magnitude pressed his head into the ground a bit harder and muttered under his breath. The ground suddenly glowed with faint blue light.

"Believe me, I'd love to. But you're lucky. We have an offer for you."

Wow, the situation was becoming more familiar by the second. Damien uncomfortably twisted under Magnitude's grip to find his captor's face contorting, as if even looking at Damien were a painful prospect. Which was all the more annoying coming from a guy making him eat dirt.

"Could you maybe offer to take your hand off my head? Or does sadism run in the family?"

Magnitude released him surprisingly quickly, allowing Damien to his feet. There was a new entity inside the dome: a Mana Wisp, the same as the ones Aetherius used for recording purposes.

"You can insult me as much as you want, but if you talk about Andrew again I'll put my fist through your face."

Damien opened his mouth to reply, only for Magnitude to stare up at the wisp and shout at it out of nowhere.

"No! It's bad enough you want him alive. You can watch, but I'm handling it."

Magnitude turned his attention back to Damien, looking extremely cross. The dwarf's features naturally lent themselves to that particular emotion. Damien's eyes darted from the Mana Wisp back to Magnitude. Someone else was watching. These must be the people Aetherius had been talking about. Damien chose not to acknowledge them. If he could get Magnitude mad enough, maybe he could speed this up by catalyzing his own death to get the killer in trouble with his teammates.

"Wow, two sadists and two anger management cases lined up in a neat little row. What a happy little family. I'm surprised you don't get along better. Oh, wait. No I'm not."

Threat of physical harm doesn't mean much to someone actively trying to hasten their demise. Damien was hoping Magnitude could assist him in that regard, if he pushed the right buttons. The dwarf flared momentarily, his hands raising to pummel the earth. Unfortunately, whoever was talking to him must have said something severe, halting Magnitude in his tracks before he could achieve Damien's goal. He crossed his arms in front of himself tightly, likely to prevent himself from killing Damien on a whim. Then he started passively intoning an offer as if he were reading it out from a script. More likely than not, it was coming directly from the mystery third party and Magnitude was just a mouthpiece.

"Here's the deal. You're not going to the Inner Circle any time soon. But, if today is the last time we see you here, we'll instruct the Carlisle-Elite not to attack you. They can even help you, if you call for assistance. We can set that up. We're increasing our patrols into the forest shortly. After that, it will become extremely difficult for you to exist. If you accept the terms, you'll be able to keep making your streams in—"

Damien shot a hand into the air. When Magnitude stopped talking he immediately filled the gap.

"So your offer is that I help you repress the players in the forest, who have no EXP for me because of the player-killing format you've introduced to the zone. In exchange, the Carlisle-Elite, the only players who might be worthwhile targets, help *me* to help *you* achieve your goals. So once they're all high level they can kill me anyway, like they did Andrew? No thanks."

Magnitude tightened his arms across his midriff.

"It's a good offer, Damien. You should take it. If it were up to me I'd make your life impossible. It wouldn't be difficult. Fortunately for you, for reasons I don't pretend to understand, my peers are genuinely concerned for your well-being."

Damien had a good laugh at that.

"Yeah. I can really feel your concern. About as much concern as it turned out Aetherius had for me, when he managed to get me into this position."

Magnitude sighed and stared down at the floor, then came back on a different tack.

"Do you know why Rising Tide was attacked by all the player-killers in the zone? I put on a special offer on the official Saga Online channel. Rising Tide players are currently worth five kills each toward my quest. I made the kills on them redeemable even after death, so killing two guarantees instant Carlisle-Elite membership and, with it, passage beyond the wall."

Ah. So that's why the players had attacked with such wild abandon, when before they'd been more concerned with their safety. That was undeniably a good reason to risk your life, especially if your current kill count toward the quest was low. Even if a player died in the process of killing a single Rising Tide player, it would cut the number of player kills required to join Magnitude's guild in half.

"All I have to do is announce a deal and the whole forest comes running to protect the wall that's fencing them in. They don't want the wall to be destroyed. They want to be a part of it. That opportunity does not extend to you, due to your competition victory and your class. With a single message, I could put out an offer on you. Kill Daemien once, instant membership. I did the same for Andrew already, he's having a rough time of it. Three deaths and counting. You'd hardly be able to play the game again. But I will refrain from posting such a message and allow you to go about your streaming in relative peace, if you stop making a nuisance of yourself. Otherwise, I'll take great pleasure in stamping you out of existence."

Now Damien had something to think about. If Magnitude were true to his word, this would offer him a relatively stable position in the forest to improve on his streaming activity. His foray into the forest earlier that day had been mostly successful until it was interrupted by Aetherius and the Carlisle-Elite. This deal would remove that problem. He'd be free to hunt the lower-level players as he saw fit, improve on his already successful strategies in the Frozen Forest and carve out a small, comfortable niche in the game from which to build his channel. Maybe, in time, someone else would resolve the Magnitude problem for him.

But that wasn't what he really wanted. Even without Magnitude's offer Damien could've decided to camp in the Frozen Forest of his own accord, but he hadn't. He wanted to explore the new content and give his viewers something really interesting. He wanted to move away from player-killing, not to get forced back into it. He wanted a significant increase in power, the kind that only the world beyond the wall in general and Bartholomew's quest in particular could offer.

Any offer Magnitude made him was specifically tailored to deny him that. It was also turning him into unpaid labor, helping him keep the number of players succeeding in the quest low, and thus the value of joining the Carlisle-Elite high, without reward.

Magnitude was quite the spokesperson, to present such unfavorable terms as if they were both fair and benevolent while simultaneously showering him in condescension and threats.

That would not do.

"I pass. Thanks for your generous offer to acquiesce to your control and be grateful for it. I'm starting to see how Andrew turned out the way he did, if you fed him that warped logic long enough."

Damien crouched down, his hands on his knees so that he could stare his captor in the face.

"Now. I'm pretty much sick of listening to your deluded, self-aggrandizing garbage, although I'm very happy to have all this recorded footage of you, revealing how you play everyone against each other for your own benefit. I need to upload it, so if you'd be so kind as to kill me I can go reveal what a conceited troll you are. Or I can just kill myself. It would be better than listening to you go on. Or you could let me go, in which case maybe I'll keep the footage to myself. No promises, though, because you're a massive jerk-off."

Magnitude, shaking slightly as he stared Damien dead in the eye, opened his mouth to address the Mana Wisp.

"Did you get all that?...You saw it! I tried, and I'm not trying any harder than...really?"

And then, much as his younger brother had done earlier that day, Magnitude smiled big and broad.

"He doesn't listen to me though, so you'll have to tell him...sure. I'll do it now."

Magnitude's eyes stopped staring through Damien and stared into him instead, his smile broadening still further till his beard was rising up his face on both sides. What was this miserable git suddenly so happy about? Magnitude spoke directly to Damien this time, and things got a whole lot weirder.

"Alright. Let's remove this dome, shall we?"

Magnitude clapped his hands together and the dome crumbled into dust all around them, the flakes sinking into the ground as they made contact until all evidence of Damien's subterranean prison was absorbed back into the landscape.

Damien was nonplussed. He'd been hoping for a quick death and was not sure what to do with himself having been released.

"So I can go now, right?"

"Yeah! Yeah. You can go."

Magnitude put his hand out and a purple tinged parchment appeared within it. He seemed completely carefree as he unraveled it, chatting amicably the whole while.

"Or you can stay. It doesn't really matter. You're no longer my responsibility."

"I thought you were going to stamp me out of existence?"

"So did I, but this is much more satisfying. This guy might be the only person who hates you more than I do. I almost feel sorry for you. Almost. Have fun."

And with that, he started to read. As he uttered a stream of unintelligible, guttural words, the scroll seemed to absorb the scarce light around it. It wasn't long until the area surrounding Damien and Magnitude was as dark as if they still stood within the confines of the earthen dome. Darker than that. Darker than Damien could see through with his night vision. A set of glowing runes, much like those that appeared when Damien summoned his demonic minions, was slowly etching itself into the floor at Magnitude's feet.

Someone was coming, and Damien had a choice to make. He could try to take on Magnitude and interrupt the summoning. The prospect of that working was pretty bleak, even without taking the rest of the Carlisle-Elite guild into account. Or, already on the other side of the wall with no enemies in sight, he could make a run for it.

Damien pegged it. His strategy was simple: first, he needed to get outside of Magnitude's sensory range. Which was pretty large, if his earlier experiences were anything to go by. If he could just manage that, his innate stealth in the darkness should manage the rest.

He didn't look back to see how Magnitude's summoning was going. The snow behind the gate was in patches, and the environmental effect that had hampered stamina regeneration in the

Frozen Forest was gone. That was a relief. Every second here would count.

Damien was forced to control himself when his stamina got to 25%, slowing to a jog. It was frustrating, but not as frustrating as stopping altogether would be. He was pretty fast, especially in darkness. He'd been running as fast as he could for a full minute when the valley walls at his peripheral vision fell away and he found himself, officially, in the Wastes. The area was even less vibrant than he'd expected. Nothing but arid plains and rocks as far as the eye could see, which wasn't too far at this hour.

Damien had a lot of experience in choosing hiding places by this point. The best analogy he'd come up with was that picking a place to hide was a lot like picking a toilet cubicle. You don't want to go for the nearest one, where everyone in the most desperate need goes, or else you'll have a bad time. You also don't want to pick the least convenient one, because that's where everyone who's avoiding the nearest one goes. You also don't want to go with the second nearest or second least convenient options, for the same reason. Damien skirted past all the obvious bad choices and all the less obvious bad choices until he found an area that barely registered on his radar. He ducked in.

He was doing well, but he had an option now that would cement his achievement. He had to build a new Gateway. Then, as soon as it was done, he had to leave. Maybe he'd escape the pursuer Magnitude had put on his tail. Maybe not. But if he had a Gateway already set up, so long as it wasn't found he'd be able to Portal back past the wall at his leisure.

He set Noigel to the task and started summoning more imps to assist him, increasing the construction speed every ten seconds. Noigel, in a rare display of restraint, kept his mutterings low but urgent as he directed new arrivals to their tasks. His charges echoed the sentiment, carving out rocks from the surrounding walls as quietly as they could with their razor-sharp claws. They were sacrificing haste for hush, and given the circumstances Damien could not fault them.

By the time he'd used up all seven of the souls he'd obtained from combat, including the one in his Sacrificial Dagger, the construction was only 10% complete. Even with Noigel urging them on, the constraint on their noise levels meant they were working only a little faster than normal speed. Damien joined them, lugging the blocks into the formation illustrated by the shaded area in the middle of the outcrop. He specifically ordered Noigel to have the imps focus on cutting rocks out rather than wasting energy on heavy lifting. The estimated construction time dropped. That might be enough.

Damien had gone out of his way to pick a far-flung, inconspicuous hiding place. There were only two possibilities he could see for his pursuer. Either they would run onward, not realizing their quarry was hiding rather than fleeing, or else they'd have no recourse except to check every single nook and cranny. He could've run in any direction, which meant the number of hiding places they'd have to check would be far greater than only those Damien had seen. Whichever of these options they chose, they were highly unlikely to find both Damien and his new Gateway. Once its construction was complete, the advantage would be decidedly his.

He started to relax a little bit. Magnitude had underestimated him. He was going to get away with it. Only twelve more blocks, or three and a half minutes, and his victory would be all but guaranteed.

"*Miiiit-Suuuu-Keeee-Taaaa.*"

Damien froze, the block he was hauling falling from his limp fingers, and slowly turned his head toward the sound. He hesitated to call it a voice. It didn't sound humanoid enough. But no, the thing blocking the entrance was definitely humanoid. It had arms, legs, hands, feet and a face. That was where the resemblance to anything human ended. It was hideous. Its eyes were a pair of enormous black orbs, set above a slit nose and a gaping underbite full of oversized teeth. The jaw was framed on either side by fangs protruding from above and huge tusks from below.

As terrible as that visage was, it was the second mouth that gave Damien pause. Embedded in the creature's distended torso, aligned over where the belly button would've been, was a perfectly circular wormhole that occupied the entirety of its stomach. It was lined with hundreds of serrated teeth, extending back into the creature's guts. A long slimy tongue lolled out from the depths, the tip drawing itself around the 'lips' as it moistened them.

As Damien watched, the tongue withdrew back inside and the mouth gnashed, the circle closing before the teeth ground across each other. First from above, then from the sides, then from every other angle in an appalling hypnotic pattern. It was speaking. The syllables were long, lazy and languid, matching the movement of the elongated slug-like tongue that flicked around within its confines. The tone was gravelly, grating and deep, the rumblings of an endlessly hungering stomach.

"My eyes are up here, Daemien-chan."

Jesus wept. Damien declined the invitation to make eye contact and made what limited assessment he could. The thing was mainly body, but the arms and legs were bulky enough to support it. It had no gear. It looked more like a dungeon boss than a player. However, it was speaking very much like he'd expect a player to speak.

Damien looked up at the head for a name. It was called 'Archimonde'. A second name next to it in cursive script indicated a Saga Online-designated nickname: '*Batara-Kala*'. It was a player. With question marks in lieu of a level, indicating it was at least ten levels higher. Damien looked at the class name, expecting more question marks, and found something far worse. Archimonde was an occultist.

It appeared Magnitude had not been kidding when he had said he almost felt sorry for his worst enemy. Damien was starting to wish he'd read into Magnitude's sudden carefree attitude a little more deeply.

Archimonde was blocking the only entrance. Damien might not be able to escape, but his imps could squeeze through the gaps and he could Demon Gate to them afterwards. If he could get by, perhaps he could run. It did not look like Archimonde could move especially fast. Damien sent the message and his imps swept into the air, each of them aiming for the gaps. From behind Archimonde, creatures emerged to fill those gaps.

Two of them were dog-like and on fire, casting light over their surroundings. Damien had never seen hell hounds that weren't his own before. That explained how he'd been found. Three more were small and more like monkeys, shambling forward on their knuckles to meet Damien's host of imps. The two sets of imps were identical, except Archimonde's did not have wings. The moment Damien saw his enemy's minion composition, he knew he was doomed.

Archimonde compounded his dismay in two utterances, this time coming from the fanged mouth in its face. The voice was gruff and throaty, though nothing like as deep as the one that came directly from its intestines. It was only as it uttered the words that Damien realized Archimonde was an orc. Or at least it had been, once. Archimonde's finger flicked between first one of Damien's imps, then one of its own.

"Corruption. Imp-losion."

One of Damien's imps was ignited in black flames. Archimonde's own imps barreled into the cave until one of them was picked and a portal opened, sucking Damien's escape stratagem toward it. As the imps were pulled into each other, the black flames spread from the afflicted to encompass them all. Their screams barely lasted a moment until each and every one of them was ash.

Noigel had been further back and had avoided the carnage. He stayed high up, avoiding the gnashing teeth of the hounds as he flew for one of the meager gaps left by Archimonde's considerable form. Another Corruption would've sufficed, but Noigel was not so fortunate. As he neared freedom, Archimonde's tongue lashed out. It wrapped around Noigel before elastically drawing him into the teeth like a bungee cord. Noigel's screams were the worst, more pathetic and desperate with each slow, measured bite. Damien was entirely alone.

"*You don't know your place, Daemien-chan. I'll show you.* Circle of Hell."

Damien hadn't seen it coming. He braced to leap backward

just a fraction of a second too late and found himself stuck. The flames were lashing around his legs, holding him in place as he burned. Archimonde lurched forward into the circle to join its prey. The flames lashed around Archimonde as well, but they neither burned nor held it in place.

"You told the whole world of the existence of occultists. That did not belong to you, Daemien-chan."

Archimonde's tongue encircled Damien's waist and pulled him out of the flames as the root ended, drawing him toward the growling stomach. Slowly, this time. Damien equipped his daggers and screamed as he plunged them into the tongue. The damage was paltry, barely registering on his enemy's health bar, but the flames rushed up Archimonde's body toward the puncture wounds and...restored them. Archimonde was regenerating in the flames.

Archimonde's burly red arms grabbed an arm, then a leg, and twisted Damien sideways, holding him across his midriff before the tongue slowly fed him into the meat grinder, talking around him the whole while.

"If you post your chat with Magnitude, I'll be posting this. Let's not fight, Daemien-chan. Let's be friends."

He was already within the mouth. It was stretching and contorting itself to fit him across the middle. Damien had a free hand, and he was stabbing at the arm holding him there to no avail, yelling himself hoarse all the while. Then the mouth crunched down on his torso and grated across him, like the teeth of a chainsaw. It encompassed him from his armpits to his waist, the teeth dragging through leather and then flesh. Even with pain settings reduced, being eaten alive was awful. His health was already low and Damien had seen what the teeth had done to Noigel. One bite should've been enough, but Archimonde was dragging it out. Savoring him. The tongue now unoccupied, the mouth paused to speak around him.

"Yuuuummy! Gooo-Chiiii-Soooo-Saaa-Maaa-Deeeee-Shiiiiiii-Taaaaaa!"

Another careful, deliberately prolonged bite. Then another. And finally, mercifully, a fade to black.

You have been killed by 'Archimonde'. Your experience has been reset to the start of your current level and your body may be looted, at which point a random item of equipped gear will be forfeit.

Remember, it's only a game!

Death cooldown – 23 hours, 59 minutes and 56 seconds.

Thank you for playing Saga Online.

8

THE WORLD IS A VAMPIRE

Damien jolted upright and cried out, his arms flailing around his body. The gradual easing out of the simulation had not been enough for him to disengage from the game, this time. What Archimonde had inflicted on him was more visceral than any nightmare he'd ever had. In a state of numb shock, he lay back down and stared at the timer for a while. After a minute had passed and he still hadn't come to terms with his death, he went to confirm the nature of what he'd just come face to face with.

Damien's trait choices were listed, including those he hadn't taken. Some of the answers were there, but not all. It was a start. Archimonde had taken the 'Contagion' trait at level 10, allowing Corruption to spread by touch. That's why all Damien's imps, and Archimonde's too, had gone up in flames after they'd been pulled in by the Imp-losion. At level 20 Archimonde had taken 'Purgatory', which gave Circle of Hell a rooting effect for five seconds and increased damage the longer someone stood within it. Archimonde had finished it off by improving Circle of Hell a second time at level 30, taking the 'Unhallowed Ground' trait that healed demonic minions within its area of effect. Which had worked on Archimonde as well, apparently. So Archimonde was officially classified as a demonic minion.

As to which of the level 40 traits Archimonde had taken,

there was no knowing. None of the abilities those traits pertained to had been used. Archimonde hadn't needed them. There was certainly nothing there to explain the manifestation of its grotesque form, otherwise Damien would've seized it with both hands himself instead of taking the Ex-Imp-losion ability.

There was also at least one more trait, the known unknown, that Archimonde received at level 50. Archimonde was at least level 53, given that Damien was level 42 and his killer's level appeared as question marks. Maybe it was the level 50 trait that allowed for the insane transformation? That seemed to make sense, given that halfway to max level was such a big milestone. Even if Damien could be certain that was the source, it was not helpful. He had no way of surpassing this foe the way he was now, no matter how cleverly he played.

Even without taking Archimonde's physical stature into account, one thing was perfectly clear. Damien had built his character wrong: he was an oddity, a weird alternate build that had avoided using the occultists' primary stat in favor of taking the long way round. Archimonde's player had built the character the way it was designed for and the benefits were clear. Damien had put all his points into having a large horde of demons, yet in the face of the character-centric build Archimonde had employed they were all but worthless. Damien and his minions were weak and vulnerable, whereas his enemy was both sturdy and effortlessly powerful.

Damien was cycling through the recording to take another look at his enemy, free from immediate danger, when he was startled by a loud crash from outside. He pulled off his H4ckz0r headset as Lillian stomped from her room into the kitchen, muttering angrily the whole while. Then the footsteps stopped and there were more crashes as she went about her business with considerably more force than necessary.

Damien tentatively opened the door. Lillian was roaming around the kitchen in a whirlwind, slamming down processor paste canisters on the counter top and attacking her food processor unit with them. Damien edged his way in and stood in front of the door, waiting to be seen. When that didn't happen, he closed the door behind him, gently, to announce his presence. Lillian's eyes flashed up at him, full of rage. She turned away and went back to taking out her emotions on her kitchen appliances, slightly more softly than before.

"What happened?"

She banged down a canister so hard that paste flew out the top of it. Then curled up her fingers and set them on the counter, staring down at the floor. After a few deep breaths, she looked up at Damien.

"I called everyone into our forum for discussion, but some of them didn't show up. Then I found out why. Some of the players who arrived had some enlightening screenshots to share. Their death screens. Who do you think they were killed by?"

Damien was already aware of Magnitude's big power play. He'd seen the effect of it with his own eyes, even before Magnitude had explained his subjugation of players who weren't even in his guild.

"Yeah, it's a problem. But now you know what to expect, we can devise countermeasures. The players in the forest won't be much of a problem; if they're going to be aggressive we can cull their numbers first, then—"

Damien had fallen prey to the classic blunder. He'd assumed he could calm Lillian down by fixing her problems. Which presupposed not only that he knew the extent of her problems, but that she was asking for help. She was not. She was trying desperately to vent, and him talking instead of listening only fanned the flames.

Lillian's voice cut across him, low but forceful.

"No, Damien. You think you get it, but you don't. Most of them weren't killed by random solo players. They were killed by MY people. A bunch of them decided it was easier to join the Carlisle-Elite. Six players, nineteen of us dead between them. One of them, a lowbie warrior called TwinBlade, killed five of us. FIVE! Three of them were priests, so that's where our healing and support magic went."

Damien stood very still as his peripheral vision gradually

expanded, the room becoming improbably large and detailed as if everything in front of him were a display on a screen.

"He was part of the rearguard, assigned to protect the casters while our vanguard went through the gap I'd made. They waited for the strongest players to go through the gate, then butchered our casters before they could follow. I stood up for TwinBlade, way back in the day, when he was still worthless. Even Andrew was fair to him. And he asked for...no, he DEMANDED the loot after we did the dragon today. And I *gave* it to him, because I thought he *deserved* it, and he *took* it, and he said '*Thank you, boss*', and then—"

Lillian had failed to vent. Without warning, she swept her arms across the tabletop, through the canisters and the plates, throwing everything to the floor. The tools were all synthesized and none of the cutlery broke, but there was plenty of mess. Having done the deed, Lillian stuck her fist under her chin and regarded the sloppy mixture decorating her kitchen thoughtfully. Damien pursed his lips and looked at it with her, as if they were enjoying a piece of post-post-post-post-modern art together.

What a waste. Damien could only imagine what his mother would have to say if he'd been subject to such an outburst. Then he realized he'd done something pretty similar during his time hopping between pod hotels, if only with a flask of nutrient juice. At least Lillian was making a mess of her own things, rather than the charitable gifts of other people.

It took a while but eventually, as the pastes started to blur into a bubbling murky brown where they overlapped, Damien snapped out of his malaise. Now was not the time for such judgment, of Lillian or himself. Nor would it achieve anything. Now would be a good time to offer his support, such as it was.

"I'm sorry, it sounds like you put a lot of energy and goodwill into your role as guild leader. You deserve better than the way they repaid you for your hard work. Come on, let's get this sorted out."

He was walking toward her when she threw out a hand for him to stop, then pointed him at the sofa.

"Don't take another step. I made this mess myself and I'll

clean it up myself, you'll have no part of it. I've already involved you in one mess today, and it didn't help either of us. I'm assuming Richard finished you off eventually? Wait, you came back much later than I did, what happened?"

Damien rolled his eyes into the top corner of the room and ran his tongue over his teeth. There was a brief moment of revulsion as he drew the unnecessary parallel between his own mouth and the one he'd been eaten by, which he steadfastly powered through in order to construct a brief summary of his evening.

"Magnitude, his superiors and I had a long talk about all the terrible things that would happen if I didn't fall in line, which are now pretty much set in stone. He surprisingly let me go when I refused to make a deal with him, and then bad things happened. Namely I was eaten alive by his extremely powerful, occultist, demonic, fat weaboo associate named Archimonde."

Lillian absorbed this information slowly while Damien folded his arms and gently nodded, assisting her in ticking off the key points.

"Ah. His superiors? There are more of them?"

"Yeah."

"Oh. Terrible things such as putting you on the kill list, same as he did with us?"

"Among other things, yeah."

"I see. I assume when you say you were 'eaten alive' by his associate, you mean this Archimonde beat you really badly?"

"Well yes, but also no. *It* beat me really badly *and* it also literally ate me alive."

"Ah."

"Yeah. Via the giant bobbit mouth in its torso."

"What's a bobbit?"

"Don't look it up if you don't know what it is, it's not very nice."

"That sounds messed up."

"It did it while talking in Japanese, out of the stomach mouth, as if it were a cute girl."

"That...that's much worse."

"Immeasurably. I'm going home."

"I feel bad though, this is the first time I've seen you since your mom got out of hospital and it's been a complete disaster. Are you sure you don't want to stay over? I've got tomorrow off, so it wouldn't be—"

"Nope, no way. Sorry, I've got to be back with my mom before morning. Still a bit worried about her, you know? And I have to come up with something to put on my stream. Which will be tricky since I'm dead."

"I hadn't thought of that. I'm sorry, I...I thought this would go well."

What had happened? They'd always gotten along and now out of nowhere everything was awkward and weird. Was one bad beat all it took? Standing around here wouldn't make it any better.

"Don't worry about it, Lillian. I reckon this will look better in the morning. Let's call it a night, and maybe I'll see you tomorrow evening."

"Yeah, okay. Sorry about this. I'll try and sort something out. Keep an eye on your messages. Could you send me the footage of your talk with Magnitude, and maybe the encounter with Archimonde as well?"

Damien didn't feel like sharing the sour fruits of his evening's labors with anybody, but he didn't want to make this any more painful than it already was.

"Sure. I'll review it and send you something when I wake up tomorrow."

Lillian nodded sadly and came around from behind the counter to give him a hug, then led him back to his room to collect his things.

"Alright, thanks. It'll be good to know what we're up against."

Damien grimaced. No it wouldn't.

He woke up late the next day, not having set an alarm since there was no point, and things did not look better. His online persona, the one everyone actually cared about, was still very dead. He still had nothing worthwhile to put on his stream.

Everything had gone more or less okay until Magnitude showed up. He couldn't simply show everything up to that moment. That would invite Magnitude and his cohorts to complete the picture. The final brush-strokes of that particular portrait would have very grim consequences for Damien indeed.

Damien would've been perfectly happy to end up on the Carlisle-Elite recruitment kill list in exchange for exposing Magnitude's underhanded tactics and his dim view of the player base. Players would come after Damien hard, but it wasn't as if he were Mr. Popular. Instead, Magnitude's associates had played a card that showed him exactly how much trouble he was in. A big part of the interest in Damien's channel was due not only to being the competition winner, but also thanks to being the highest-level occultist. If he started making waves now, they could easily post his humiliating death at the hands, and teeth, of an occultist far above his level and ability. His entire channel and his fledgling streaming career would suffer an enormous blow.

There was no question Archimonde had gone out of its way to make the encounter as terrifying as possible, not only to intimidate, but to make the footage hanging over Damien's head as damaging as possible. Introducing Archimonde was a far worse threat than the talk with Magnitude had been. They'd already had him right where they wanted him, yet had only shown their full hand when he turned down the safe option.

Damien checked out the Carlisle-Elite page. Despite the low number of members, there were nearly a thousand people following the page and thus receiving notifications. Lo and behold, a large banner across the top announced yesterday's big offer. Members of Rising Tide were now permanently worth five kills toward the recruitment quest. There were several videos showing different viewpoints of Rising Tide's inglorious defeat, including a few from the perspectives of former Rising Tide members who had turned traitor.

There was also one acknowledging the 'brave heroes' who'd helped to defeat the enemy from within, honoring them by formally inducting them into Magnitude's elite standing army.

Damien could hardly believe people would swallow this

without question, but the likes and comments sections told a different story. Either they knew better and had bought into the illusion on the basis it would serve them one day, or they'd sincerely fallen for Magnitude's warped rhetoric.

It was, of course, not immediately obvious which was which. The players spreading his rhetoric out of the arrogant notion that they'd be the human sewage that rose to the top of the septic tank had remarkably similar online footprints to the players who simply didn't know any better. They looked exactly alike. For all intents and purposes, they were actually the same people.

The important thing was that there was nothing whatsoever on the page about Damien. That pretty much confirmed his theory, and meant he wouldn't be posting anything about the raid from his own perspective. He felt a wave of relief. Closely followed by shame. Then anger. He'd been left in no position to disillusion anyone. He was caught more deeply in Magnitude's web than any of them, and the personal cost to him was too high. Besides which, if speaking out resulted in his destruction it would be worth absolutely nothing.

He drummed his fingers on his desk. What was he supposed to do with the rest of his day, while the aspect of him that mattered to anyone was still dead? Which is when Cassandra knocked on the door. Damien composed himself.

"Come in!"

The door swung open, and in walked his mother with a tray of food and a wan smile.

"Good morning, sleepyhead! How is everything going?"

He smiled back at her. He hadn't thought it possible, but following sixteen hours without food he was very hungry. Late breakfast consisted of bacon and eggs, his favorite thing and Cassandra's failsafe option for him. He lied without even pausing to think about it.

"Everything's fine. Good, even. I'm just doing some research into current affairs."

"Oh, you mean the thing going on with Magnitude? Yeah, I

saw Lillian took a beating yesterday, bringing the fight to him. She's very brave, standing up to a bully like that."

Cassandra was really following everything. Damien pulled his lips good and tight. He even managed to make them turn up a little.

"Yeah, she's very brave. No doubt about that. I'm sorry, mom, what I'm doing is really important and I have to get back to it. This breakfast is exactly what I needed. Thank you."

Cassandra placed his food in front of him as he spoke, at once completely ignoring the implication of what he'd said and barely batting an eye.

"I'm sorry, it's a bit cold. I heard you get in late yesterday and I made it a bit later, but since you didn't wake up when I knocked I thought you could use the rest more than the sustenance."

"Thanks, mom, I'm starving."

She paused with her hands on the tray to nosily inspect his screen. Then she gave him a look.

"How did Lillian take it? I guess you were still with her after it happened, since you got back so late. I'm glad you were with her when she was having a tough time."

Damien tensed his cheek muscles a little more, holding everything in place.

"Yeah, it was good to see her again. I've got to get back to it. Thank you so much for bringing me breakfast, I'm surprised you don't want me to have it in the kitchen!"

"I know how busy you must be, and how hard you're working. Keep at it. I'll bring you lunch as well, in a while. Fancy a curry?"

"I'll eat whatever you make me. Love you."

"Love you too."

She turned and had her hand on the doorknob before spontaneously turning and delivering what had actually been on her mind.

"I'm going back to the daycare tomorrow. I'm fit for work, the heart's running perfectly, I've never been a stay-at-home person and I miss my kids. They miss me too, I hope. But I need to get started on my prep. I've got a favor to ask, if you have time?"

Damien groaned before he could stop himself, then swiveled in his chair, back toward his computer, so that his misgivings might be less obvious. He wasn't happy Cassandra was returning to work so soon after her operation, but he knew better than to argue. If she'd made up her mind, debating it with her was a one-way street to an unnecessarily long talking to, followed by her doing what she'd said she would anyway. Besides which, she was obviously doing much better. There wasn't much for him to complain about.

"What do you need?"

"I'd like for you to pick up groceries from the market street. Veggies mainly, some fruit as well, so we can get some actual nutrition for once. Before lunch would be ideal, so I can serve them up. Can you get them after you finish breakfast?"

"Sure, I'll manage."

"Thanks, honey. I'll leave the list on the table."

Damien grunted and Cassandra kissed him on the head before seeing herself out. The moment she'd closed the door behind her, Damien slumped down in his chair. There wasn't much he could do here beyond moping, but that didn't mean he felt like going outside. He sat up and started eating the food, slowly at first, but increasingly quickly as the joy of eating vanquished his distaste at having been eaten. Hunger was a powerful force, even more powerful than disgust. He went to have a look at his own channel while he ate, so he could do a quick review before heading out.

There was a private incoming message, from someone he actually knew as a friend in game. He desperately hoped it wasn't Kevin. He was already under enough pressure without Kevin riding him for going against his advice. He squinted one eye shut as he opened the message window, then breathed out gratefully. It was from Lillian.

Lillian: Send me your footage from yesterday, please. I'm hustling and I need it.

Damien squinted at her politely framed, unreasonable

demand. What did she need it for? He hadn't edited it yet, he didn't feel too good about sending it raw. Not even to Lillian. But he had other stuff to do today. Like eating and wallowing in self-loathing. He mashed out a reply into the box.

Daemien: What do you need it for? I might need it for my own stream, so don't give it to anyone else."

He'd barely gone back to looking through his channel comments when the chat box pinged.

Lillian: Not sharing it. Just need to see with my own eyes. Ammunition. We need help and I need to know what our enemies look like. If you want me to fix this, you'll give it to me. QUICKLY."

Jeez. Ever the negotiator, our Lillian. It couldn't be helped. There was almost half an hour of footage there, he didn't have time to review it before he went to pick up groceries. Pursing his lips, he picked up the video file and dumped the whole thing in the chat box, along with a flat statement of his own interests.

"Don't put this anywhere near the Saga Online official channel. I'm doing this for a living now, and this whole thing you got me into yesterday is jeopardizing it. Hope you understand where I'm coming from."

He clicked 'Send' and several gigabytes immediately moved out of his own personal control into the purview of a second person. What he'd said seemed a little mean, but he needed her to understand that this footage was very private.

Her reply was quick and by all rights should've had a 'TM' symbol next to it.

"Piss off Damien, I won't send it to anyone. You must be pretty stressed out to insinuate that. Thanks for passing it to me despite your overwhelming paranoia. You'll be eating your words before this evening, if I get this right."

Well, that was pretty final. She sounded almost as stressed out as he was. Guess it was justified, but at least she unequivocally knew where he stood on distribution rights. Now he could move into his comments section and have his late breakfast while he read people's hateful comments in peace.

There was a lot of the usual rubbish, with a higher proportion of people complaining about the lack of content than usual. He considered sending a message and decided against it. Things were bad enough already without inflicting his almost nonexistent charisma on an unsuspecting public. He'd been scrolling through his page for about fifty comments when something interesting, and altogether a little disturbing, showed up. A comment from a vaguely recognizable name, sent that morning, complete with a link invitation.

Scorepeeus63: Praise Be, Dark Lord! We would be honored if you could take some time to fill out our **survey**.

Hmm. That made an interesting change from the usual negative feedback. This guy was a Scorpius clone! Man, that sure brought back memories. Technically, they were the ones who'd killed Aetherius, when they'd guided a nine-year-old boy into combat as a joke, only for him...wait a minute...

Damien gave the messenger's name another look and his mouth fell open. Scorepeeus. 63. The nine-year-old. It was this guy! This was the guy who'd killed Aetherius! He hadn't heard anything from this lot since he'd returned to the game after his mom settled. He'd always thought they'd hit their peak as a group and disbanded, not least because the character they'd named themselves after, 'Scorpius' from his beta-testing days, had faded out after his big occultist reveal. He'd been a little surprised and more than a little put out at their disappearance. They'd proven themselves a very committed sect of mega-fans, bordering on extreme, right up until they'd vanished.

Why on earth were they inviting him to do a survey? That was a bit incongruous with calling him 'Dark Lord': 'Good afternoon, Dark Lord. On a scale of 1–10, how would you rate your pain?' He wouldn't have even seen this message if he hadn't been killed yesterday. Not much of a silver lining, but it was something. Better than backlash from people he'd killed, at any rate. He clicked on the link, not entirely sure what to expect, and was presented with bold white words on a black background, with absolutely no further information:

'Type the name of your sponsor: _____, and wait until your membership is processed.'

Well, Scorepeeus63 was the one who'd sent him the link, right? He input his name and the screen went blank, save for a loading icon in the middle. Didn't surveys need to be easily accessible, so people wouldn't bugger off and do something else? Requiring not only verification but 'membership' on top seemed a little counterintuitive. If it weren't for the weird form of address and the person who'd sent the link, he'd have closed the window. It seemed a little too strange to write it off completely, though. He decided to leave the page open while he went to do the groceries that had been requested of him. With any luck, by the time he was back it would be ready and he could see what this was all about. He single-mindedly chomped down the last bites of his breakfast and got dressed. It was time to take a trip down memory lane.

He turned out of the compound, giving the security camera outside the gate a glance, a wave and a grin, before heading into the alleyway. It was an improvement, not having to worry about his face being seen as he left his own home. The summer was nearing its end and the temperature had become 'sweltering' rather than 'actively hostile', but the greatest improvement to his comfort by far was not wearing a headset. It hadn't bought him as much time as he'd hoped for, but at least it had been enough to sort himself out.

The worst mistake he'd made by far was waiting for the Central Union agents to show up at the internet cafe before he'd started frantically withdrawing credits from his mom's card. He'd played the 'what might've been' game a fair few times in his head since that day, a deeply unhelpful hobby that lent itself to him naturally as a chronic overthinker, and generally found himself grateful. Had the idiots assigned to him blocked his mother's card before they invaded his unsafe haven, he'd have been left with no credits at all. He'd have known they were coming, too, but without credits he'd have been dead in the water.

Even at his most self-deprecating, he found it hard to fault himself for the lapse of judgment. Maybe what he'd learned about the permissions of CU Child Services would be useful, next time he was traumatized from giving his mom a life-saving shot directly into her heart before she was kept in a medically induced coma as he attempted to win a streaming competition from scratch to save her life while simultaneously evading the aforementioned authorities. *Ya never know.*

Well, he was pretty sure it wouldn't happen again. Fingers crossed. The important thing was not to demean himself for a simple mistake made under extreme duress. Not his forte. He was just glad this information wasn't available to the general public; they were a pretty judgmental bunch, and he was plenty judgmental of himself already.

He came out of the alleyway and emerged into the bustling market street. The stalls were all different, as they were every day, but somehow it all seemed the same. With a couple of notable exceptions. He hoped the fish vendor had stayed home on this particular outing. The veggies could be anywhere, but he expected to find at least a few of the ones with less nutritional value staring at screens in the internet cafe. So when he looked into it on his way past, he had a bit of a shock.

There were red signs in the window, marked with 'closing down' in bold white text with red borders. He'd seen a lot of these signs in shop windows before, from shops that seemed to be in a permanent state of foreclosure with cut-price items that were not all that cheap. There were a couple of shops on that street that had been holding 'closing down' sales for years. People being what they were, they were generally full of would-be opportunists. Damien had a shorthand for them: gullibles.

Damien peered through the gaps in the internet cafe window as he passed it by on the opposite side of the street. It did not appear to be employing this as a tactic. It appeared to be very much closing down. The entire place was empty, as it had been when Damien had last visited it himself. 'Closing down' signs didn't work as well for people who sold fast internet and judgment-free spaces as it did for retail, apparently. The door was wide open in a feeble attempt to invite people in. Damien peered through that as well, all the way to the back wall, and what he saw made his heart sink. The VR pods at the back had been wrapped around with red tape, as if each one were the centerpiece of a crime scene.

Damien quickly turned his head away and down to the floor as he walked past, as if taking his eyes off it would prevent it from existing. Even he'd clocked the pod distribution as being unsafe when he had last entered. At the time he'd viewed it as a positive. It meant that CU didn't have eyes on that place. He hadn't conceived that Tweedledum and Tweedledee would trawl through the footage manually, or that he'd inadvertently draw them to find the violation of an internet cafe which he'd considered to be off-grid.

He'd not given it much thought since he had left it – there'd been a lot on his mind – but his impact on the small business had clearly not been beneficial. While he'd somehow managed to come out of the ordeal relatively unscathed, he'd led CU on a red-tape path of destruction in his wake. That old man obsessed with his phone game was one of the few people who'd been kind to him, and this is what he'd got in return. If Damien hadn't found a place so quickly, there was little doubt all his efforts would've been for naught.

The same went for the other place...what was it...Freja's Freakshow Palace? No, that name was a bit off. The sentiment was right, though. She'd let him in as well, although she'd been a lot more reluctant to do it, given his age and the venue's orientation. Damien hadn't been to see the aftermath of that visit, but he had chucked nutrient juice all over the walls in a rage fit and fled. Not his finest hour.

He'd all but forgotten about them in the wake of his victory, but he doubted they'd forgotten about him. Not in a good way. The rush of traffic prompted him to look up. He'd gotten all the way to the end of the road while staring at his feet. He huffed and checked his pockets before turning on his heel, pretending for the benefit of exactly zero onlookers that he'd realized he'd left something at home. It wouldn't do for the strangers around him to think he'd suffered some sort of mental lapse. He confirmed to himself that he'd suffered exactly that when he found the grocery stall right next to the internet cafe. He kept his eyes down as he picked out the choices his mom had made, half expecting a kind old man to run out and start heckling him in the street, before heading back home at double pace.

The groceries dumped in the fridge and his past behind him, Damien slumped into his chair and focused on the screen. To find utter pandemonium. His 'membership' had been approved. The 'survey' was most definitely not a survey. A large pentagram occupied the vast majority of the background as he scrolled through a block of very supportive, deeply disturbing communications:

Scorepeeus63: Behold, the prophet is come! My lamentations have summoned him from the abyss. Praise Be.

Scorpenis: Praise Be! My mother is also happy!

Daemiaemiaemien: What if Daemien, was, one of us? (dododoDOdo) Just a pagan, like, one of us? (dododoDOdo) Just a danger in the dusk, tryna harvest some soooooouls?

Scorpious666: He is risen. The slumbering one has awakened. I was there at the dawn of his creation: I stared into the void and the void said 'No, that's ok, you go ahead.' The first words of our abyssal master! I failed to recognize their worth, and lo, I shall crawl across the earth on my belly for all time. Praise Be.

BabySharkolomew: Oooooh, it's what you'll do to meeeeeeeyooooooh, and all humanityeeeee. Oooooooh, you raise demon armiiiieeeeeeeesoooooooh, to kill everyone slowly, and then I'll say Praise Be.

Vargus: Be me. Eat a bag of dicks for breakfast. Go home for lunch and eat another bag of dicks. Finish work and start preparing my bag of dicks for dinner while I warm up 'The Saga Continues'. No Aetherius. Me sad. Chew dicks pensively. Some guy called Scorpius fighting instead. Level 28. Total noobcake. ROFL, wut a tryhard. Noobcake kicks demi-god in my three meals a day and cusses him out in livestream, with broken arms and legs. Dicks spilling from my gobsmacked open mouth (soooooo many dicks). I inhale too hard and my dinner gets lodged in my throat. Stars in my vision, blacking out. Try to call my mom for help, but multiple phalli are blocking my respiratory organs. Tumble out of my chair sideways and hit the ground, hands around my throat to dislodge all the penises I've been chowing down on. There's no hope, there are too many. Everything goes dark.

Wake up, my vision is blurry and my throat is blissfully unburdened by inadvertent deep throating. I'm being transported somewhere. Am I on my way to heaven? How will I explain my eating habits to Saint Peter? Big blurry white words are floating into perspective in the center of my vision. I try to focus on them, my brain still struggling to replenish oxygen. The words clear, and it is obvious that my diet has not gone unnoticed. I am in hell. 'The Elder Scrolls V'. Oh no, oh god no, anything but that! 'SKYRIM'. Please, St. Peter, I can change, please don't forsake me, PLEA- "Hey you, you're finally awake". Thanks Todd.

10/10, would eat dicks and watch Daemien kick a demi-god in the schlong again.

Praise Be.

Daermiern: Finally we will be together, Dark Lawd! Finally we will be together! I feel your embrace, Dark Lawd! I love you so much! AHAHAHAHAHAHAHA! Praise Be.

Scawpeous69: I was blind, but now I see! I am Daemien, and Daemien is me! Praise Be.

ScawPious: Bid my bloodlust ru - CAN'T WAKE UP - cancel possesio - SAAAAVE MAAAAAAAIII - Save me from the Noigel I've become. Praise Be!

Daemiaemiaemien: Oh, and Praise Be.

What in the name of all that was tasteful was this? Damien's eyes roved around the rest of the page, searching desperately for some sort of anchor to reality that he could cling to in this sea of depravity. There was not much to be found. The page had a member list, going at more than sixty strong, with not very many online. That made sense, given that these reprobates came across as creatures of the night.

He scrolled back up and found a banner at the top of the page, designating this far-flung corner of society as 'The Nine-Year-Old Army'. What a bunch of nine-year-olds were doing flinging profanity around for his benefit in a dark corner of the internet, Damien was sure he had no idea. His instincts said 'flee', but his ego said 'let's see what happens if I type a message into the comments box'.

Damien typed a message into the comments box.

Daemien: Good afternoon. (1:1)

Just when he thought it couldn't get any weirder, it did.

ScawPious: It speaks! Shun the nonbelievers! Shuuuuuuuu-uuuun! Praise Be.

Scorepeeus63: The first words of the prophet! Bow before his Dark majesty! Praise Be.

TheWhater: Praise Be!

TheWherer: Praiiiise Be!

TheWhener: Praise Be.

TheWitcher: I hate you guys. Praise Be.

Okay. So this was definitely a cult. A very silly cult, but a cult nevertheless. He was pinged with a private message which popped up on his screen.

Vargus: Hi, thought I'd help you out a bit. I'm the page developer. Thank you for coming, we're all really excited! Praise Be.

Daemien: Uh, thanks. What is this, exactly?

Vargus: This is a private group for Occultists. It started with the original Scorpius fans, as you can see from some of the names, but a few of us are new. We made this community for support in game and conversation – it's quite lonely in game as an Occultist, so we got together to form a big family. Didn't think you'd be joining us! Praise Be.

Daemien: Thanks. Why does everyone say 'Praise Be' after everything?

Vargus: It's a rule. We make up new rules all the time, but that's one of the core precepts. You're the prophet though, so none of it applies to you. Pretty sure you can do whatever you want. If you want to talk about things normally there's a discussion board on the side, along with a members list, ranking system and a rules list for newcomers. None of that applies to you either, but you can have a look to see how it works. Please check it all out and let me know if you need any help. Praise Be.

Daemien: Thank you, I'll have a look around. Nice job with the page, it's very unique.

Vargus: Ty! PB.

Not only was his hardcore fanbase alive and kicking, they'd all become occultists and were working together. After what Bartholomew had told him regarding occultists being cannibalistic, he didn't think such a thing was possible. If anyone was going to manage it, though, it was always going to be this lot. Damien smiled. Now this was a welcome surprise. He eyed up the tabs on the side and clicked the 'Members' tab first.

Scorpius clones were the most numerous by far, making up almost 60% of membership. It also showed their levels. They were doing quite well! There were a few lowbies, maybe 10% of the group total, who had yet to reach level 10. Then there was a huge jump, with the next largest group of 30% of the membership occupying the 20s. After that, the vast majority of the group were absurdly high level, given the time since Damien had announced how to become an occultist. More than thirty members out of sixty-six were pushing level 30 and a select few had reached level 30 already. The highest-level player was Scorepeeus63 himself, the Aetherius killer, at level 38.

Wow! The kid who'd been afraid of the dark had grown up real fast. What a turnaround. The rest of them weren't far behind. How were they so successful? Maybe the rules list would provide answers. He clicked it and the sidebar got pushed down to make way for a set of clearly explained rules, some more predictable than others.

1. Praise Be.
2. All comments on the main page must show proper respect for the hierarchy, which is available on the rankings page. See rule 1. This rule is not applied to discussion groups, but civility remains a high priority.
3. The highest rank in this community is Low Priest. The

Low Priest guides group activities for the day, following approval from the Council of 9 (year olds).

4. The sole aim of the community is to raise the level of our Low Priest as fast as possible. To qualify, a prospective Low Priest must log on every day for no less than two hours each day for seven days, and must integrate with the hub. The lowest level eligible player will be selected. If application for Low Priestage is approved, the new Low Priest will be leveled as much as possible over the course of a day and all affairs will revolve around them.
5. Tuesday through Sunday are days of sacrifice. At the end of a '*successful boost*' (minimum 5 levels total), the current Low Priest acquires at least 1.5 x EXP levels of the next nominated Low Priest. Boost time is 24 hours, or however long it takes to complete the Low Priest boost (not including sacrificial EXP gain), whichever is shorter. The new Low Priest then kills the old Low Priest and the cycle begins anew.
6. Monday is poker night. All participants welcome.
7. Failure to follow the rules will result in a day ban, then a week ban, then a permanent ban. For the duration of your ban, you will be removed from the channel and shunned by the group in game. Shuuuuuuuun! All Council decisions are final. Please follow the rules and ask questions if you're not sure what you should be doing.
8. We are blessed by the arrival of Daemien, our Dark Lord! You stand in the presence of greatness. Conduct yourselves accordingly.

Alrighty then. Damien checked the rankings system and found it extremely simple. The current Low Priest was one of the level 20s, a non-Scorpius clone called 'Nightman'. Directly below him were the Council of Nine, which included Scorepeeus63, Vargus and a few of the other people who'd posted upon Damien's arrival. Members below them were simply designated as 'Normies'. Damien's name was in a separate box from the rest of the group. He was designated as 'Dark Lord'. He probably had Vargus to thank for that.

He was receiving a lot of messages from other members as well. They were mostly brief and quite a lot less disturbing than what they'd greeted him with on the main page, but they were all followed by some variation of 'PB'. Damien thanked each of them in turn as he clicked his way through the discussion pages.

There were a variety of silly posts, where members were honing their skills in adulterating song lyrics and language in general. But tucked away at the bottom, as if as an afterthought, were a collection of occultist class FAQs: discussions of stat distribution (Int–Wis ratios were most popular, but a fair few factored in other stats as well); level and stat requirements to unlock different spells/buildings; spell order in combat; survival strategies; what role you fit with your specific skills in occultist raid parties; minion deployment and compositions...it went on and on. Damien was speechless. This was a huge trove of information!

From the various discussion boards, an obvious trend emerged: the majority of players had pumped intelligence as their primary stat. That suited Damien fine. He could use their input to get a glimpse of Archimonde's skills. The next most common group were people emulating him, with higher wisdom and an emphasis on minions. A very small number of them were emulating him too much by putting most of their stat points in agility. Oops. So this was what being a bad role model felt like. It was more their fault than his, as far as he was concerned, but still.

There was one discussion board with more traffic than any other. Every single member of the group had visited it at least once: 'How do you make Noigel stop acting like a gee golly?' It was by far the question Damien was most interested in for his own purposes at that exact moment. He clicked it in a hurry.

The answers were not very useful. Damien wasn't sure whether to be pleased none of them had been as successful as him, or annoyed they had nothing to offer regarding his most recent problem. Many were derivative of his own work in the earliest stages, which was readily available online. Beyond that, most of the answers tended toward one focus. Suppression. It seemed none of them had brought Noigel to his full potential. The highest-voted recommendation in the group was to account for an extra half soul when summoning and dismiss Noigel after summoning the last imp.

While Damien completely understood the sentiment, it was a far cry from the best way. He tentatively typed out a message, barely believing that what appeared on the screen had originated from his own fingertips.

Daemien: I cannot overstate how annoying it was to get Noigel onside. I also can't overstate how crucial Noigel's input was to my success. He requires a lot of attention and very, *very* careful instruction. Even then, sometimes he still goes his own way. Despite all that, he's worth it. He's a superior UI for minions in combat scenarios and massively increases construction speed in base when 'Forbidden Knowledge' is active. I'm having trouble with him, even now. He's still the most valuable minion in my lineup, every time, by far. Try to endure him.

Damien hit 'Send' and immediately wondered what he'd been thinking. It would've been easier and more acceptable to just agree with everyone, but he'd gone against their opinion on this issue on his very first day. Well, hopefully what he'd said would help those in the early stages. If this group got a little more invested in Noigel's mechanics, maybe they'd progress things and Damien could reap the rewards. They'd probably quite enjoy watching Noigel fornicate his way through their demon rosters, judging from their collective sense of humor.

Perhaps they'd create an event to see which Noigel was the least tolerable. They could run it consecutively with their poker night. Perhaps a table of Noigels playing poker, and the Noigel who won could have "special time" with all the other players' succubi. Although a whole cult's worth of Noigels with Forbidden Knowledge right next to each other was a very dangerous prospect.

Damien turned back to the discussion boards and had been

absorbing information for almost another hour when he received a voice call from Lillian. He squinted a little bit, half expecting to get shouted at, and answered the call.

"Yeah?"

"I'm in the middle of a big meeting. I need you here with me."

"Can you give me more information?"

The moment he relaxed was when the shouting started.

"Just get in! It's a very important chat group, we're talking about dealing with Magnitude and the wall! What part of 'I need you' don't you understand? Does that seem like a request I'd casually throw out? You think I—"

"Fine! Send me an invite if it's so important. If you're making that big a fuss it better be a big deal, I don't need you—"

You have been invited to join Round Table Council Meeting.

"—shouting every...time...oh, shit."

"Click 'accept'! They're grilling me Damien, I need you here!"

Damien accepted and a chat box with exactly twenty-six names in it popped up immediately afterwards. Twenty-four names belonged to the guild leaders of the twenty-four guilds who held the highest reputation with the Empire. One of them belonged to King Bedivere, the NPC Ruler of the Empire. And then there was 'Daemien'. He was slightly out of his element.

The first comment came almost immediately, and the source was King Bedivere himself.

King Bedivere: We bid you faint welcome to this meeting, Daemien the Low. I would not ordinarily consort with your kind, but Lillian the Immortal beseeches me you know much of our enemy and insists we would be remiss to neglect your council. Speak.

Daemien the Low? He knew that was his Empire-sanctioned nickname, but it hit differently when someone was calling him it directly. It was just as well he was outside of Empire influence and their designated nicknames weren't applied to him, because if they were he'd have to abandon his plan to go to the Inner

Circle and start a murder campaign until they gave him a more fitting moniker. Lillian interrupted his teen-rated murder fantasy.

"Make sure you start or end every message with 'O Mighty King', capital M and K, and tell him what happened with Magnitude and his guild. You've got two minutes before he gets impatient and starts rushing the conversation."

Oh good, a timed challenge. We wouldn't want to accidentally offend old kingy-wingy by typing too slowly, would we? Damien wrote the first three words and then tried to match the way he was being addressed, so he could prove the hostility unwarranted by being polite. Which was tricky when he was doing it through anger and didn't have any time to edit.

Daemien: O Mighty King, I and my previous enemies turned sudden allies from Rising Tide assaulted the tyrant Magnitude's fortress yesterday and were met with staunch resistance. There is a large wall barring entry, manned by at least two hundred men, all of whom are trained in spear, javelin and bow. I assailed the ramparts while Lillian led her forces in breaching the wall, but we were met with former heroes of the Empire who betrayed their cause and were slain. I fought with Magnitu—

"Thirty seconds left, finish the sentence and send quickly!"

Most of his time had been wasted on thinking rather than typing. Writing in old-timey language was difficult, but he wanted to make a good first impression.

—de personally, and he is a very dangerous adversary, as are all who have fallen under his power.

Send. Damien hadn't even finished sighing in relief before King Bedivere had sent a fully composed response. Perks of being an AI, Damien supposed. Although however this one was tooled up, it clearly wasn't designed to cut Damien any slack.

King Bedivere: You mock me, at my own council? Lillian is a new leader of Rising Tide and as yet has not regained any physical holdings in our lands. The reputation of her guild has plummeted in recent times, along with the number of men at her disposal following her ill-advised offensive yesterday. I found her claim that your presence here was warranted dubious, yet I entertained it to honor her guild's past. Despite having arrived at her behest, your first action is to mock my speech. You provide no information besides that which she has already offered, and given your standing I find your word wanting. I invite the rest of the war conference to pass judgment.

Damien stared at the screen openmouthed as Lillian laid into him.

"What were you thinking? You think we all talk like that when we communicate with him? It would take hours! Now he – oh come on!"

Rising Tide's name was dropping down the list as the various verdicts of the arrayed guild leaders rolled in. They were a bunch of yes men, all of them hopping on board their king's comments and giving their AI leader a verbal tonguing. Their comments conjured up a powerful image in Damien's mind of the leaders of the strongest guilds in the Empire, all lined up with their Mighty King bent over in front so they could take it in turns to stick their faces between his cheeks and give him an enthusiastic cleaning. The first responder's name gave Damien a pretty clear indication of how this would go down.

HighZen: O Mighty King, well said. Daemien has no place here and we don't need his input. Kick him out, and cut Lillian's reputation for the waste of time and the insult.

TheRickestRick: Wow, that's embarrassing. Talk about someone trying too hard. Kick this guy so the grown-ups can get back to talking about our next step, O Mighty King.

Hammertime: I'd like to hear more. This is his first statement in an unfamiliar setting, I don't believe he meant to cause offense. Quite the opposite, he was obviously trying to be polite. He may possess valuable information and we are letting our prejudices get in the way of acquiring that information. We should give him the benefit of the doubt. I withhold judgment, O Mighty King.

BlackNwah: O Mighty King. You're right. Kick him.

And so it continued for another twenty comments. Each of them was also getting upvoted or downvoted by everyone else as they rolled in. Hammertime's comment was largely left alone, but the rest of them were upvoted almost immediately as they were posted, before any human could've had enough time to read them all the way through.

Damien couldn't help but draw a parallel with his own recently discovered hole in the internet, but where those guys were just having fun and supporting each other this lot were vindictively toeing the monarchical line. Damien was not allowed to judge his own piece, which was no surprise, nor was he allowed to 'like' or 'dislike' any of the comments judging it. Although he'd been invited into their conference, he was still 'less than them'.

Lillian posted toward the end.

Lillian: O Mighty King. I wouldn't have invited Daemien here unless it was important. He's confirmed everything I said. If you're patient and willing to work with an open mind, he might even be convinced to show you some parts of the video so you can see it for yourselves. Your dislike for Daemien is less important than the future of your guilds, the players under your care and the Empire itself. King Bedivere, it seems your court has already decided, so I put this to you. Please do what's best for your people.

Damien was barely halfway through the first sentence when Lillian switched from typing to babbling at him through the speaker.

"Damien, if you share the video, even just the part where Magnitude talks about his plans, they'd have to eat their words. Our reputation with the Empire is all Rising Tide has going for it at the moment. We have no headquarters and nobody in the Empire likes us, even though Andrew is no longer the leader. I'm trying to get these morons together so we can attack the wall with a proper force, before the Carlisle-Elite get any stronger. Can you do me a solid and share it with them? Even just a small piece? Please?"

"I'm thinking."

He didn't have long. Thirty seconds after the last comment had rolled in, King Bedivere sent his next message. It completely undercut Lillian's claim that sending the footage would endear him to them, because he was demanding it by force.

King Bedivere: Judgment: 23 votes negative, 1 vote abstaining, 1 vote positive. You have made a poor first impression, Daemien, and it shall cost Rising Tide dearly. I shall allow you one chance to redeem yourself and your ally. Share the vision of your failed incursion that Lillian claims you have in your possession, in its entirety.

They really wanted that footage, didn't they? But they were trying to strong-arm him into giving it when it was obviously a valuable asset. Bad move. Even if Bedivere had demanded just a segment as opposed to the whole thing, he wouldn't have sent it on these terms. Damien got to typing. It was a lot easier now he wasn't unnecessarily standing on ceremony. It was much easier to convey how he actually felt in two minutes than when he'd been unnecessarily filtering himself.

Daemien: As Hammertime stated, I was trying to be polite. The knowledge I have is valuable and you'll need it to prepare a successful attack. I came here to share that knowledge with people who hunt me down on a daily basis, but you decided to bully me, holding my friend's reputation hostage when you could've just asked nicely.

You're right, 'o mIgHtY kInG'. This is a crap welcome for someone you're asking for help. And since this is how I've been received, you'll get no help from me until Rising Tide's reputation is restored, you have something to offer me in return other than threats, and you gain control over the suck-ups fawning over you for their own reputation instead of doing what's best for the Empire. You're not fit to rule and they're not fit to serve. Have fun fellating yourselves while Magnitude poaches your players and the Empire is destroyed.

He sent the message and, neither knowing nor caring what King Bedivere would have to say in response, closed the window. They were enemies before, and they were enemies now. He was more concerned with how Lillian would take it. The message had only just been sent. Lillian was still reading, and quiet. Damien pressed his lips together and cranked down the volume in advance. He didn't want his windows getting blown out by the shockwave that was surely coming.

There was a long intake of breath. Damien braced himself for the shouting, but it didn't come. She just breathed back out again, long and slow. Then back in. It took a few moments to realize what she was doing, but when he did it hit him hard. Lillian was trying to prevent herself from having a panic attack. She'd talked about it with him before, when Andrew had pranked her so cruelly at the hospital and when she'd "lost her temper" after being killed by him prior to Aetherius's defeat at the hands of Scorepeeus63, but he'd never actually seen her have one. Or heard it, as it were. It ran so contrary to everything else he knew about her that he'd not given it much thought. He'd certainly never thought he'd end up giving her one directly. Especially since she was no longer using the guardian wristband.

He thought about speaking, then decided against it. He'd stay on the line and she could talk to him when she was ready. Not before. Lillian kept it up for a good minute before she got it under control, and even then there was only silence. Shouting would've been a considerable improvement. At last, she spoke.

"You have no idea what you've done. Do you?"

"I stood up for you, and for myself. You can see that they're a bunch of tools, right? They'd have ta—"

"Those 'tools' are the highest-tier players in the Empire! And you've just insulted them all, when I was the one who'd invited you there. So everything you say is on me, and none of the—no! Nooo!"

The long slow breaths came back as Lillian mashed away on her keyboard. It wasn't long before the key-clacking died down. Then there was a smash.

"They've kicked Rising Tide out of the Round Table! So we have absolutely nothing going for us now, and I have you to thank! Thank you, Damien! Thank you for taking my trust and screwing me over with it!"

So this was his fault now? All he'd done was stand up for them and *he* was the bad guy, not this collective of douchebags Lillian had expected him to pander to? He thought not.

"You know what? You're welcome! And thanks for promising something I'd already made it clear I didn't want to give, inviting me to a group to get insulted by a bunch of strangers on your behalf and then yelling at me for not doing what you wanted! How is it my fault they're jerks and I told them where to get off? If you'd at least briefed me before the meeting, I might have known what to expe—"

The call was cut. Great. So Lillian was probably in a full-blown, anger-induced panic attack by now, and Damien was the cause. Perfect. Well, at least he didn't have to worry about being invited back to the council. Which was just as well, since he had much ruder things to say to them. By the time he was done, Rising Tide would've been declared Harbingers of Chaos.

He'd always hated the Empire forces, mainly by conditioning, but now he'd interacted with them it went much deeper than that. They'd attacked him, he'd defended himself, yet somehow he was to blame. He tabbed back to the Council of Nine resource page and ran over the words without taking them in while he brooded. He'd done this for all of five minutes before he got a new invitation. It wasn't from Lillian. It was from one of the guild leaders with a seat at the Round Table. If it had been anyone else, Damien would've immediately rejected it. But this was the only one who'd shown any sense, and was also one of the only ones he'd encountered in the game.

Group Chat Invitation: Hammertime, Gamer ID 006226, A/D

Hmm. If they'd sent this guy as an envoy, maybe they had more sense than he'd thought. He could see about getting Lillian put back in. At her original standing or higher, of course. And one or two concessions for him specifically as well, at the very least. On the other hand, if they were making more threats and nasty demands using Hammertime as a mouthpiece, it was roast time. Win-win.

Damien accepted and a new box opened. He knew it wouldn't take him directly to the council meeting, since it was just a regular group chat invitation. He'd assumed it would be a few select members of the Round Table, come to ply him with nice words before they got back into negotiations with a bit less bite and marginally more compromise. He was surprised to find that there were only three players there. Himself. Hammertime. And Lillian. They weren't wasting any time, bringing them both in together. An apology from Hammertime wouldn't mean much, though, since he was the only member of that group who didn't owe them one.

The conversation didn't go the way Damien expected.

Hammertime: I'm sorry for the way you two were treated. But I have some questions for the both of you. Lillian, could you tell me why you decided to attack the wall without requesting help from the other guilds first? Daemien, what was your stake in this?

Daemien: Lillian doesn't need to tell you anything until Rising Tide is back in the Round Table and they've apologized for what they said. It's nice you saying sorry and all, but that doesn't mean we'll happily tell you everything we know so you can run back to them and get your brownie points.

Lillian: I had to attack the wall to show we're team players now, since no one else was stepping up. I thought some footage of the problem might encourage the rest of them to act, but so much for that. Daemien had his own plans.

Hammertime: Daemien, the two of you have been permanently banned from the group and Rising Tide has been formally removed. They won't reverse that decision. They don't know we're talking and I'd like to keep it that way. I'm here for my own reasons, which might overlap with yours.

Daemien: Nice, Lillian. It's not my fault the favor you asked for was suicidal, and that you demanded another one you knew I wasn't prepared to give. Stop playing the victim when you're the instigator.

Hammertime: Sorry Lillian, but I don't believe you. I think there's more to it than that, and would appreciate if you could be candid. I could've easily joined everyone in ousting you from the Round Table. Instead I urged restraint and was your only ally. Please be open with me.

Lillian: If I hadn't helped you, you wouldn't have that job.

Period. Boo-hoo, you lost a day. As if you didn't have your own reasons for being there. Learn to take the blame for your own bad choices. I should've just showed them the video myself instead of relying on you. Now I've lost the last of Rising Tide so you don't have a couple of days of bad publicity. After everything I've done for you, I never thought you'd be so selfish.

Hammertime: Enough. If you feel like arguing with each other, do it in a private chat. I'm here to talk about something else. You're going for the Lady of the Lake quest, aren't you?

Lillian: That's conjecture, and unhelpful. I didn't sacrifice my standing with Camelot and the loyalty of half my guild-mates so you could throw conspiracy theories at me. Sorry to disappoint.

Hammertime: You underestimated the defenses and ended up dying, and then you came to us because you realized you couldn't do it by yourself. If I'm wrong, say so again and I'll be on my way. But if I'm right, I'm here to help. And given you could take screenshots of this and get me thrown out of the Round Table with you, that is not a statement I make lightly.

Daemien: So sorry, the occultist social reject would like some filling in. Who's the Lady of the Lake?

Hammertime: There's a quest we all got when we first signed up to the Empire, called 'The Lady of the Lake'. It was question-marked and grayed out, so most people just removed it from their quest chains. At level 40, the question marks disappear. It's probably a level 50 quest. If you ask around in the right places in Camelot and have the necessary reputation and resources, you get a quest destination in the Outer Ring. Research suggests there's an old myth tying the Lady of the Lake and Camelot to a sword called Excalibur. The unbreakable sword of a king. A potential legendary weapon, the first of its kind. Ringing any bells, Lillian?

Lillian: What do you want?

Hammertime: I want in.

Lillian: Why?

Hammertime: Bedivere should be rallying everyone to attack Magnitude before he gets too powerful, but he's trying to play it to his advantage. Preventing anyone from completing the quest and usurping him. At this rate, it won't be long before the game becomes unplayable for us without joining the Carlisle-Elite. I'm a streamer as well, not as prolific as Daemien by any means, but Magnitude is not good news for me. Magnitude set up that wall to prevent people from pursuing this quest, since humans level up faster than other races. Which means pursuing it is likely the best option available to us if we can't procure the forces to destroy the wall outright.

Daemien: Did this not seem worth sharing, Lillian? I could've been a lot more helpful if I knew what you actually wanted. And after all that talk about me being selfish. I'm pretty pissed.

Lillian: So you want to muscle in on the quest and steal my plan for yourself, and you want to use my manpower to help you achieve it? Good one.

Hammertime: If you can do it by yourself, more power to you. Go right ahead. You wouldn't have come to the Round Table if that was the case. Not to brag, but I myself am extremely specialized and my presence alone would make breaking through exponentially easier. You don't have the luxury of choice.

Lillian: Not only can I not trust you, I can't trust the guild members under you. I thought my own people were trustworthy and some of them turned against us halfway through the raid. If we're not doing this with Camelot's backing, we need to make it a small, reliable force. They need to be willing and able to enact the plan tonight. How many high-level, serious players in your guild are readily available that you can trust? I mean REALLY trust.

Hammertime: Three.

Lillian: That's low enough to believe you're taking this seriously. I also have three. If we're both attacking the wall we might get through it faster. It took me sixty-five seconds just to make a breach big enough for individual players to duck through. From watching Daemien's replay it looks like they're using the guild alert system, so their response time is quick, even offline. We need to hit them in the early morning, around 3 or 4am. With work and school starting tomorrow, that will give us the largest window. We'll also need to shave off as much time from the gate destruction as possible, and source methods of reaching it unnoticed.

Daemien: Glad the video footage I sent you was some use after all. I can help destroy the gate. Don't know how a possessed incubus stacks up against you two but it should be decent. Speaking of, if we include all three of Hammertime's trusted allies that gives us nine people total. What classes are they?

Hammertime: Nice to have you on board, Daemien. I've got a pistoleer gunslinger, a paladin healer and an arcane support mage. Very devoted players, all very good at what they do. My mage may even have a solution to reaching the gate unseen. I'll check with her. Can you fill the gaps Lillian?

Lillian: Not really. Between the betrayal yesterday and losing our seat just now, I don't have a huge pool of players left to pick from. The one I trust the most is another paladin healer, then a support priest and a scout ranger. We have two support casters, two healers, two ranged damage, Daemien in a support/damage role and us two as tanks. It's not terrible, but we lack magic damage. Do you have any damage mages you can trust?

Hammertime: Afraid not. Is it that important?

Lillian: Do you remember how Rising Tide broke through your headquarters gate last time? It's important. If you don't have anyone to nominate, I have a suggestion.

Hammertime: You're insane. No. I thought you said they needed to be trustworthy? He's the worst choice available, outright.

Lillian: If breaking down the gate in a hurry is a crucial factor and we currently lack magic damage, he's the best fit by far. He's a known enemy of Magnitude's. He'll jump at this chance. If we know what he wants, and what he wants aligns with what we want, he's trustworthy...insofar as we can trust him to do what he wants.

Daemien: Please tell me we're not talking about Aetherius.

Lillian: Aetherius's biggest problem at the moment is Magnitude, not us. The combo we developed for breaches would massively cut down the time it takes to get through the gate, which is crucial for the plan to work. We need to destroy that Portal Stone before the reinforcements arrive, every second is crucial. I don't have anyone else who can work that strategy. We need him and he needs us.

Daemien: Someone will have to talk to him.

Lillian: It has to be me. I'll get in touch with him through one of his old friends in Rising Tide and lay it out.

Daemien: Last time I saw him, he alerted the Carlisle-Elite to our location to try and get me killed. What if you tell him the plan and he leaks it?

Hammertime: That's a good point. Does the potential reward outweigh the risk?

Lillian: I'll be sparing on the details. Worst-case scenario, we all die. At Magnitude's current recruitment rate this will be the last good opportunity we have and it needs to count. Aetherius is many things, but he's not stupid. Helping Magnitude win guarantees he'll lose. He'll take the opportunity to strike a blow at Magnitude, who represents the greater threat, and he'll ally with us.

Daemien: I'm against this. But if it's enough reason for you to talk to him, you must be pretty sure it's the right option. We've taken a toll on each other today. I'm not happy with how things have gone, but I don't think you deserve to deal with him for a second. Especially if you're not feeling 100%. Are you sure?

Lillian: I'll manage. Hammertime, get your three players together as fast as possible and brief them. I leave how much you want to tell them to your discretion, but let me know how much that is so we don't cross our lines. Stay in touch and let me know your progress. We'll hash out the details between us.

Hammertime: Time for a crusade.

9

BREACH

Damien opened his eyes and found himself in a deserted cafe. All the noise associated with the setting was absent. The low hubbub of conversation, the clatter of cutlery, even the hum of traffic in the distance. In its place, there was only void. His own breathing was the only disturbance, disrespectfully loud in this sea of disquieting tranquility. That, and the faint ticking of an old-school analogue clock from behind the service counter. Cassandra had taught him how to read these things when he was little, not that it had come in handy much outside their one-on-one sessions. He looked around and winced as the squeak of his sneakers echoed off the walls.

"There you are."

The voice was so sudden and so close that he jumped, turning to find Lillian in the cubicle right behind him. Given how badly they'd fallen out earlier that day, Damien had been surprised when Lillian invited him to talk face to face (or at least the Mobius Enterprises-enabled next best thing).

He breathed through his nose and smirked to alleviate his embarrassment, but Lillian did not share his mirth. She'd opted for all the defaults, wearing the same gray jogging outfit that Saga Online opted for during calibration and avatar creation. Damien had been excited to test the software of Mobius's 'Second Life' system, running through the free options available that day to find some branded choices he felt complemented his sense of style: baggy jeans crisscrossed with decals, a pair of ultraviolet boot/sneaker hybrids and a massive denim hoodie that felt much too big, even though the app had made it clear this was the correct size for him.

It had been beyond cool when he was reviewing himself. It did not seem quite so cool now. He sheepishly sat down across from her, every movement making more noises that heightened his embarrassment. With no background noise and no hustle and bustle to mask his own impact on the surroundings, his every action felt ill conceived, poorly executed and uninspiring. It would probably not have been so awkward were he not being closely observed. Lillian had her hands clasped under her chin, as though in prayer, while staring at Damien over the top of them. Waiting for his chair to stop creaking as he shifted his weight, each minor movement and accompanying sound effect more awkward than the last.

At last, after he'd held himself uncomfortably still for what seemed like an eternity, she started to speak. Her words offered no comfort. If anything, they made the whole experience stranger still.

"I am recording this conversation for the purpose of sharing select parts of it with other relevant parties. I will not use it publicly. If this video or any parts of it reach the public domain without my consent, I will take action against those responsible, including but not limited to the application of the law."

That was a very formal opening line. Not promising. Damien was recording as well, mainly because he'd never used Second Life before and had been considering posting it to his profile as a 'slice of life' update in the absence of any in-game footage. Lillian's intro did not do much to promote that as a viable option. She'd only paused for a couple of seconds before she continued talking, only slightly less tersely than she'd begun.

"I spoke to Andrew."

"How did that go? I hope he wasn't rude."

"No, actually, he was surprisingly polite. He was a bit smug when he figured out I was asking for cooperation, but did his best to keep it to himself."

"How much did you tell him? The last thing I need in the middle of all this is to get killed by him before we even start the plan."

Lillian didn't immediately reply. She just stared at him, the noise of the clock becoming more prominent with each tick.

"Andrew is very interested in helping us. But he doesn't trust you any more than you trust him and he's not a huge fan of Hammertime's, either. It was difficult to convince him this wasn't a trick, given our history, but I showed him some footage to bring him around. My footage of our failed attempt. As well as some of yours, actually."

She wasn't apologizing for it. She wasn't rushing to explain herself. She was just sat there, letting him absorb the information. Was she trying to upset him? Why was she baiting him like this? The clock ticked onward and Damien sat there, holding himself back. Until he could no longer.

"I thought we were friends. Why are you trying to make me angry on purpose?"

"Okay, so we're friends. What's my second name?"

Tick, tick, tick, tick...

"What's my ambition? What do I want to achieve in life?"

Tick, tick, tick, tick...

"Tell me everything you know about my past; how many siblings I have. When I decided to be a medical student, and why. How long I was with Andrew, before everything went wrong. What I enjoy besides playing Saga Online. Tell me anything you know about me at all."

Damien leaned forward, struggling to keep his voice level.

"I don't know anything about you besides what you've told me."

"That's exactly right. And I've told you nothing. But you seem to have built an image of me in your head. One where I give, and you take. That was fine when you needed help, but the crisis with your mom is over. She is safe, and you have a stable future."

Her voice had been very calm throughout, but now it was starting to build. And unlike his own choices, her every move and word was well thought out, crystal clear and full of weight. All the weightier in this room without distractions.

"You're still completely focused on what you need. And your needs will never end. They just come one after the other, all in a neat little row, lined up to infinity, that which you've just fulfilled immediately replaced by whatever it is you need next. I saw Andrew do this when the competition consumed him. Now the same is happening to you directly, at my expense. Your needs are more important than my needs, even when I'm helping you fulfill yours. Do you know what that makes us?"

Tick, tick, tick, tick...

"Allies. As long as we want the same thing, no problem. But if it doesn't benefit you directly, or it has even a slightly negative impact on you, you immediately become hostile. You're still doing it, right now: you didn't even bother asking which part of the footage I showed Andrew. You rushed to confront me, and I'd rather not respond in kind. It clouds my judgment and makes me less than what I am. So we're going to slow this, *all* the way down, and proceed as allies. Not friends."

Damien had never been broken up with before. He'd never had a girlfriend before to afford the possibility. He imagined this is what it felt like. It was not pleasant. Lillian took him in, watching his face carefully for a few seconds, before proceeding in the same vein as though nothing had been said.

"I showed Andrew the part where Magnitude was talking to you about making a deal. Once he got through the first bit, you know, the part where you lumped him in with Magnitude and insulted both of them, he was surprised. He thought you'd take the deal. He's a pretty easy read for me, I may have even detected some respect."

"I don't much care about the respect of someone I don't respect myself. I'm assuming there's a point to this, besides telling me we're not friends anymore, and I'd like you to get to it quickly."

"He wants something in return for his assistance. The bag he insists you stole from him."

Oh. So that's what this was. Lillian's grand scheme to bring Aetherius into the lineup would cost him the best item he had. Which he got fair and square, by the way.

"And had you already decided we were allies, rather than friends, before you agreed to that deal?"

"The deal started with him saying he wanted to kill you in a widely publicized duel and for you to post some unflattering messages afterwards on your own wall, as well as returning the bag, but I haggled him down to something I thought you might agree to. On my terms, he only gets the bag if the operation is a success and we get past the wall and out of immediate danger. I haven't told him when and where we're meeting yet, so his ability to interfere with our operation in the event of him not joining us is limited. If you don't want to give him the bag, I will relay that to him and continue negotiations."

"Why would you need to meet with him after this if I say no? In fact, what if I don't want him on the team at all? We can manage this just fine by ourselves and as far as I'm concerned he's a dangerous, unwanted presence. Why should I be the one who sacrifices the most valuable thing I have for something I don't even regard as a benefit?"

Lillian shifted in her seat and glanced away from him, the first time she'd moved since they started talking. She scrunched her eyes shut and refocused on the floor, then stared at him even more piercingly.

"Frankly, Damien, his abilities make him more valuable to our objective than you. I'd rather have both of you on side, but if that becomes impossible I will strive to make sure he is on board so we have the highest possible chance of success, even at your expense. If it's a straight choice between you and him, I'll choose him. If you're not prepared to part with the bag, I will try to find some other way of coercing him to join us. If that includes you not being invited, which I imagine it will, that's what will happen."

"You're not serious? After everything he's done to us, you're prioritizing him over me?"

"I'm not debating this with you. You have a straight choice between agreeing to hand over the bag, in return for which you are guaranteed a spot on the team, or refusing and dealing with whatever the consequences of that decision may be. I didn't have to tell you what those would probably look like, but I did. Mainly because I'm hoping against hope you have some common sense you've been keeping hidden. Decide."

There was no way out of it. He needed to get through the gate, and he couldn't do it by himself. The bag was extremely useful to him, but not nearly as important as getting on with his quest. The main problem he had with this exercise was making a concession to Aetherius. He consoled himself with the knowledge that if they didn't manage to break through he wouldn't have to.

"Yes. If we get to the Outer Ring, I'll give the bag to Aetherius."

"No. You'll give him the bag if we get past the wall and out of immediate danger. Look at me and say it clearly."

"I will give Aetherius the bag if we get past the wall and out of immediate danger."

"Thank you for your time, and your cooperation. Go away."

It was past 3am. Damien was on his way to the rendezvous point, bleary-eyed and not in the best of moods. The preparations were all complete. He was meeting with Lillian and her group at the entrance to the zone so they could travel together. They'd link up with Hammertime and his group near the border to Magnitude's wall. Aetherius would be the last to arrive, since Lillian had diverted him to a separate location as a bare minimum countermeasure. It probably wasn't necessary, due to what had been promised. Which, in addition to the lack of sleep, was why Damien wasn't feeling particularly chirpy.

Things were not looking too hot. It had taken six hours to get his minion count and Soul Reserve back up by himself. What made it worse was knowing it could've been avoided. Potentially. Only Damien would likely never know. When he'd first logged back in, he'd been given an option he hadn't considered: he could respawn in his base, in Camelot (certain death) or where he'd died. He could go straight back to the location he'd made it to, beyond the wall.

Except, he knew it was a false option. If Archimonde was camping that location, he'd be dead on arrival. Besides which, by that point he'd already pledged his support to Lillian and Hammertime's offensive. Even if Archimonde and Magnitude had overlooked this, which he sincerely doubted, he'd be leaving Lillian and her party to fend for themselves. She'd take that pretty poorly, given the talk they'd had prior to his login.

The biggest insult by some margin was that his body had not been looted. There probably hadn't been enough of it left to loot by the time Archimonde was finished with it. Regardless of why, his enemies had forsaken the chance to break his Adept Robes gear set. That's how *nice* they were being. They may as well have patted him on the head.

It was with a heavy heart that Damien arrived at the rendezvous point with two hell hounds, a succubus and seven imps in tow. His base was completely defenseless, his minions either integrated into his own Soul Summon Limit or dismissed for soul energy. He'd filled his Soul Reserve to 10/10 and left his Soul Summon Limit 10 points clear in anticipation of summoning an incubus, although he'd resorted to dismissing the incubus in his base to acquire the last few souls. He wouldn't be the one to get them spotted early and ruin the whole plan by trying to walk that hulking thing across the zone unnoticed. Although he didn't have much hope for the plan to begin with.

One of his hounds snarled and Damien followed the direction it was looking in as Legolias, one of Lillian's party, stepped out of the trees and beckoned him to follow. Damien stepped in and found all four stood at a fire: Legolias, the scout-spec ranger. Judgementday, the paladin healer. MrHealyFunTimeYeah, the support priest. And Lillian, who required no introduction. She decided Damien didn't need any introduction either, inviting him to join the group through an in-game message and setting off without a word. Legolias neatly leapt between the trees, placing himself in the highest branches and matching his leader's pace from fifty feet above the ground. The other two ran a bit to catch up while Damien consigned himself to the rear guard. He assumed that if Lillian 'expected' anything of him, she'd make it known.

They had to stop a few times and wait for Legolias to find a path around when he reported ambushes in the trees ahead. It went some way toward highlighting just how desperate players were to join the Carlisle-Elite, that they would wait for passersby at nearly 4am. Fortunately, Legolias seemed very good at fulfilling his role. He had to be. With five players in their group, bulldozing through and expecting people to move was not an option. Especially since there was a hefty reward for killing all of them now. Occasionally, they even ran into some mobs that had found the time and space to respawn in the early hours of the morning. They were circumvented as well. Lillian only had one thing on her mind, and it wasn't petty grinding.

It took a while, but the faster speed from having a smaller group made up for the rerouting issues until Lillian brought them to a halt with a single closed fist. She typed a few messages and soon they were joined by Hammertime's team. Aetherius was already with them. It was hard to tell who in the group looked more upset by this development. Damien was pretty unhappy himself, but personally he'd have put his credits on Lillian, even though he couldn't see her face. He could certainly hear her hissing at Hammertime.

"Why is he here? He was supposed to be the last to join us."

"He found us of his own volition. It didn't seem practical to send him away to have him return later, although I assure you that was my inclination. Especially since he's already fallen out with my gunslinger."

Damien drew level with the rest of Rising Tide, leaving his demons behind, and took the second party in: Hammertime, the berserking behemoth. Trinytea, a dual-pistol gunslinger. Sabrina, the support mage. OhHolyLight, the Godhammer paladin healer. And, of course, Aetherius. The trickster. He was looking a lot less smug and a lot more uncomfortable than Damien had thought he would. That was good. He caught sight of Lillian's face, wondering if she'd keep her cool now she was face to face with Aetherius in game. Her ire, much to Damien's surprise, was directed not at Aetherius but the gunslinger.

Lillian paced toward her, her fists balled up and her shoulders hunched. Trinytea backed away and Hammertime came to stand between them. Lillian turned on him instead. Everyone's hands shifted to their weapons.

"What—," she enunciated with utter contempt, "—is she doing here?"

"She's one of my best, and has remained faithful and hard-working ever since she left Rising Tide. If we're entertaining both Daemien and Aetherius, I'm sure you can manage her."

"She didn't leave Rising Tide. I threw her out. She knows she isn't welcome in my company, or Legolias's, or even Aetherius's for that matter. You don't strike me as incompetent, Hammertime. This wasn't a simple mistake."

"No, it wasn't. We're shorthanded and the choices below her were untrustworthy, unfitting or both. Your reaction justifies my choice to withhold her identity, but only if you don't push this any further. Times have changed. Your vendetta against Trinytea counts for nothing against the challenge that lies ahead."

Lillian stared at him, her chest rising and falling as the rest of them held their breath. Lillian returned Hammertime's chiseled, disdainful gaze.

"It wasn't a vendetta. It was a promise, which you've maneuvered me into breaking. You say you brought her because she's trustworthy, but you've proven yourself untrustworthy in so doing. Not a good start to this alliance."

"Wow, and I thought I was unpopular. Everyone here hates each other so much we better divvy up who fights who before we get started. Dibs on Damien."

Everyone turned and stared at Aetherius. Who threw his hands up and shrugged.

"Don't look at me, I'm not the one who assembled this 'team'."

Legolias dropped down from the trees right next to him, short-swords drawn, and scissored them over his throat. Nobody rushed to defend the mage.

"If this doesn't work out, we'll all be in line to kill you first."

"Cool, very confidence-inspiring. I'd like to get through the wall before the next streaming competition, though, so I promise to shut up if you lot promise to pull up your pants and stop acting like children. Everybody wins."

He looked at Lillian imploringly, motioning to the blades against his neck. She rolled her eyes, but motioned for Legolias to leave him be.

"Those are favorable terms. Everyone gather round and we'll go over the plan."

After everyone had figured out where to sit without being next to a mortal enemy, the briefing began. It took about ten minutes, much of it repetition as players took it in turns to stifle their yawns, but by the time they were done the plan looked good. Better than good, actually. While it wasn't an ideal group of ten, the players were all highly specialized and there were a wide variety of abilities and utilities to bring to bear. Some of which Damien hadn't even heard of.

As the rest of them trudged toward the gate, still eyeing each other warily and choosing their walking partners with care, Damien pointed at the floor and summoned his incubus. Then he dug into his bag and grasped the weapon he'd commissioned Noigel to equip the incubus with and tipped the bag upside down, allowing the weapon to fall to the snow with a *thud*. It was a double-handed quauhololli. While the name was exotic, the weapon itself was crude and brutal, like the incubus itself: a huge orb of dense iron, strapped to the end of a long wooden shaft.

The armor choice was not armor at all. It was a simple leather harness, providing almost no protection. A niche item for transporting resources, the leather straps supported a large basket on the back where materials such as lumber, rocks, ore and loot could be collected and transported en masse. It had never been very useful to Damien, since he'd always relied on the Bag of Holding. He'd found a combat application for it instead.

If Damien was possessing the incubus, and the incubus was wielding a massive two-handed weapon, that meant Damien needed to sort out travel arrangements. This was the best he could come up with at short notice. The incubus had equipped the harness, but try as it might, with its stamina rapidly depleting, it could not comfortably hold the weapon Noigel had crafted for it. It was simply too heavy.

Damien possessed the incubus and his 'Nine-Tenths of the Lore' trait doubled all its stats. He grabbed his vacant body with his new gargantuan hands and dropped it into the open top of his gathering bag first, then strained to pick up the weapon before resting it over his shoulder with one hand. The beast's stamina stabilized, then rose back to 100%. Sorted.

Damien trudged his way to the rest of the group, Noigel corralling his minions to gather around him on either side. The players looked at Damien in alarm and made way as he took his place at the front of the line, next to Hammertime. The guild leader gave him a quick once over, looking up at a player taller than him for the first time in a good long while, and nodded in satisfaction before bringing his attention back to the gate.

There were three major components to the plan, all with strict time frames. The first phase was actually reaching the gate through the no-man's land, which spanned an area slightly longer than two football fields. The wall was manned by archers in the walls and 'spear-chuckers', as Lillian affectionately dubbed them, on the ramparts.

The second phase was getting through the gate. Breaking it down was fairly implausible, since it occupied the approximate dimensions of a four-story house and according to Lillian's footage was made of wooden beams arrayed four meters thick, reinforced with steel. Once they started hitting the gate, their presence would be noticed without a doubt and the timer would begin. If things went well.

The final phase would be destroying the Portal Stone to prevent reinforcements from arriving, which would only work if the second phase were to be completed within about thirty seconds. That would allow any Carlisle-Elites who were already online and ready to go time to join, but at 4am on a Monday morning they were counting on those players being in short supply. After a minute, they could count on offline, serious players arriving, having been informed by the guild alert system.

This data set presented an immediate concern. While breaking down the gate was the most challenging individual component, it was not the most problematic. Simply getting to the gate already took nearly half a minute for those who were not athletically inclined, and it had already been demonstrated that even in the dark, encroaching players would be spotted against the snow long before they reached the gate. That meant the plan was doomed to fail right from the start. Unless they could reach the gate undetected.

So it was a good thing Hammertime had brought his support mage. While they were generally shunned in favor of arcane or elemental-based damage dealers, a large number of unique skills were available to them. Most were combat-based, such as the Anti-Magic Shield Sabrina had deployed on Hammertime when Damien had first encountered him in the Twisted Forest. Some did other things, generally disregarded in PvE and only forming a small portion of the meta for PvP. This was a good time to be thinking outside the box.

"You ready, boss?"

Hammertime nodded, his eyes fixed on where he needed to be. Sabrina counted him down.

"Three, two, one, Phase Shift."

Hammertime had hardly begun charging when he blurred around the edges and vanished. Well, not quite, but close enough. There was a shimmer in the space he occupied, which was a considerable amount of space. Damien could see the profile of his legs as they pumped relentlessly forward, the profile of his shoulders and even the outline of the war hammer strapped to his back, if he squinted. Everything within those confines was a distorted version of the terrain in front of him, as though he'd been turned into a hastily frosted window. So long as he didn't take or deal damage, the effect would last for thirty seconds.

It wasn't true invisibility and wouldn't work for a frontal assault: anyone looking directly at it in daylight would know something was up. However, at that range, in the dark, they thought it would be enough. It had to be enough. The other problem was that Phase Shift could only be used on one target at a time, and had a thirty-second cooldown. So they had to send the party over this way individually.

Everyone waited. It was an excruciatingly long thirty seconds. At last, they heard Hammertime murmuring over their comms, his voice a deep baritone even when lowered.

"I'm here. Next."

Sabrina hesitantly tapped Damien on the arm.

"Ready?"

He grunted, the steam of his hot breath pooling out between his jagged teeth, and reached for Noigel.

"Three—"

Noigel, Bloodlust.

"—two, one, Phase Shift."

The effects of the two spells arrived simultaneously and Damien kicked forward. Then he Charged. The incubus he was currently possessing was a powerhouse in terms of stats, but it only had two abilities: Enrage, and Charge. Enrage would only take effect once he was at less than 50% health, doubling his strength and endurance. Charge was his mobility move, a break-neck run with 50% increased movement speed for ten seconds or until he hit a target, expending no stamina and with a mere thirty-second cooldown. It was designed to put him in combat quickly and effectively. In this instance, he was using it to prevent combat from happening.

He'd made it halfway when the bonus from Charge gave out. It was frustrating moving so slowly when he was used to his occultist body, but at least the snow meant there wasn't much noise. He trudged the rest of the way across to find Hammertime huddled at one side of the gate, and then he ran for the other side. The incubus wasn't built for hiding. Hammertime could just about stand in the narrow alcove on his side of the gate, but Damien's tail prevented him from sticking his back against the wall. He stuck his face against it instead, standing straight and still with his tail glued to the floor. The guards would likely not be looking at the gate directly, since they were looking out and scanning the forest for signs of activity. Though that didn't make Damien feel any more comfortable.

Next on the priority list were Lillian and Aetherius. Aetherius had made it clear in the briefing he didn't need any help to complete the maneuver, at which point Lillian had said the two would cross simultaneously. A sensible decision, keeping the dubious ally surrounded by those who were best equipped to survive him and wouldn't hesitate to punish him for any deviation from the plan. There was a low *whoomf* as Aetherius arrived out of his Blink, followed almost immediately by a clatter of Lillian's armor which made Damien wince. He supposed so far as noise went there wasn't much to worry about, since the guards up above were too far awa—

"There it is again! Did you hear it this time?"

The voice had come from the other side of the gate. Barely audible, but extremely concerning. Damien twisted his head and found the other three members of his quartet frozen like statues. There were at least two characters, right on the other side of the gate. Only a few feet of timber separated them, the conversation humming through the grain.

"I think the lack of sleep is getting to you. We're due to be relieved in twenty minutes, just hold on."

"No, no, I definitely heard something."

"Shall I gather some men to have a look outsi—"

"No! Fool! What, there might be someone outside so you want to open the gate and let them in?"

"The guards haven't seen anythi—"

Then the voices faded as the two of them moved away.

Dammit. Even with this huge wall and NPCs on night watch, Magnitude had found actual players to stand on guard. Lillian was on the comms immediately, whispering directly into the whole party's ears.

"We've been detected and they're checking. We're starting now. The rest of you run across the gap on my command."

Hammertime had already left his corner and taken his hammer in both hands to stand over the center point. Lillian took her position on the other side, with Damien looming over her. Aetherius leaned back on the alcove where Hammertime had been and folded his arms as he tapped his foot. Even knowing his input would come later, it was still annoying for Damien to see him being himself.

They were all in position. Lillian double-checked around her, her hammer resting on the floor, and whispered into the comms.

"Me, Hammertime, Damien. Three rounds, then Beam. Go, go, go!"

She lit up with Divine Might and lifted the hammer, then plowed it into the gate. The quiet was ruptured with a low boom and a louder crunch. The wood caved and splintered, but the gate barely moved. As soon as her weapon was withdrawn, Hammertime's came in to take its place directly over it. With just two hits the outer layer was crumbling, but there were cries of alarm from beyond.

Hammertime's weapon was withdrawn. Damien's turn. He swung over Lillian's head and the metal orb struck, but missed the target zone. He'd hit a little over them, the orb cratering an aesthetically but not technically pleasing divot about two feet above the target. The gate rocked back fractionally, but the larger weapon penetrated less deeply than those of the two guild leaders. A rallying cry from above was swiftly followed by the shunting of metal slats as the archers mobilized. Even now, the mechanisms to alert offline players would be firing up.

The second time Damien hit the target, although he nearly took Lillian's head off doing it. She ducked it without so much as a backward glance then took her last strike, this one with everything she had. The center of the gate had been turned to mulch, but they were only penetrating halfway deep. She jumped backward, the glow of her Divine Might fading away as her sword and shield appeared in her grasp.

Hammertime struck still deeper, then Damien placed his final strike directly in the middle, the orb sinking deep into the gate with the impediment of Lillian's well-being removed from the equation. He was shocked the gate was still largely intact, let alone still standing, given how much brute force the three of them had buried in it. He'd only just landed the hit when Lillian cried out.

"Clear!"

From behind Hammertime, Aetherius put his hands together and they pulsed red. He was pointing not at the gate, but straight at Lillian herself. She gave him an appraising look, then smashed the base of her shield into the ground. Aetherius narrowed his eyes and yelled a single word of warning.

"Breach!"

He fired. Lillian's shield lit up with the light of her Repent a fraction of a second before the beam hit her. The shot connected with her shield then reflected back toward the gate, twice as wide and twice as powerful. Damien barely dragged his weapon free before following it backward into the snow, narrowly avoiding vaporization. Aetherius's Arcane Beams had always been disproportionately powerful, but this one's power was doubled by Lillian's trait ability.

Damien knew about the theory-crafting and had seen a couple of the videos. Being there, having an actual presence in the wake of this ability combination, was nothing like watching it on a screen. It was truly awesome, in the traditional sense of the word. He was within inches of something that would completely destroy him were it turned against him. And it went on for a few seconds, all the while feeling like it would continue endlessly.

It did not. In the last second of the cast, it withdrew and became narrower and narrower till it winked out of existence, burning the core of their combined efforts a little longer before it was completely expended. It had created a wide hole where the structure was weakened in advance of the pummeling, but everything around it was only half cooked through. As impressive as the beam had been, it had not penetrated all the way through the gate.

This had not been the plan. Damien swiveled his head to the remaining six party members and his demon retinue, who were traveling across the gap in a tight group. Scores of not only arrows, but musket balls as well, were ricocheting off the Sanctuary spell enveloping them.

There were gunners in the defense on the wall now, as well as the archers that had already caused Rising Tide so much trouble on their first attempt. Magnitude had upgraded his men. The rest of the party weren't even close yet, and once they'd arrived not only would Mr. Healy's mana be drained, but all the projectiles would be focused on their stationary tight cluster rather than the moving targets running across no-man's land.

Hammertime turned his head from the gate to the imminent arrivals, then glowed red. He'd activated his Berserker Rage to try and finish off what was left of the gate. He knew that if the group arrived and the gate hadn't yet been breached, they were done for. It seemed they all understood that much.

Aetherius was drinking a mana potion, his smug and distant propping up of the alcove a thing of the past. They were supposed to be through already, and everyone had slammed into full improvisational panic mode. Hammertime was knocking chunks out of the area surrounding the breach, but even with the structural damage and his strongest ability in effect he couldn't reach the depth of Aetherius and Lillian's combined Arcane Beam with his weapon. Lillian had just retaken her place on the opposite side to join him, hammer in hand, when the first of the new party members announced her arrival.

"Get out of the way!"

It was Trinytea, who'd effortlessly sprinted ahead of the rest of her group in half the time. Hammertime, despite the good work he was doing and the short time his ability would be active to do it in, immediately withdrew. Lillian ignored her, but stopped in mid-swing when she saw what Trinytea was doing.

The gunslinger removed her entire inventory and jammed it deep into the hole left by the beam. She gave it a last wistful look before fleeing back into the no-man's land, back toward the group where the light of Mr. Healy's Sanctuary was shimmering in protest. The mana potion he was drinking did little to allay Damien's fears. They were under extremely heavy fire. Lillian and Damien looked at each other, then fled backward as well. Hammertime took over on the party comms.

"Someone hit the bag with fire! Do it! Do it now!"

Damien watched as Aetherius stopped running after him and Lillian, planted his feet and put his hands together facing the gate. He fired his second beam straight at the bag. The cast had only gone for a split second when the explosion shook the earth. Gunslingers carry gunpowder to reload between shots, and Trinytea had packed for a long trip. In their haste, unfortunately everyone had neglected to plug the opening of the gate with anything to prevent the explosion being thrown back in their faces. Aetherius's Arcane Beam was prestigious, but did not compare to the instantly unleashed, pure concussive force of an entire backpack's worth of gunpowder. The narrow opening in the gate funneled much of the explosion back the way it had come, interrupting Aetherius's casting and throwing him through the air.

Before Damien had time to think, his arm stretched into the air and caught the mage at the top of his arc, taking all the momentum out of his flight and saving Aetherius from a crushing death by then revolving at the shoulder as if Aetherius were a misshapen, morally repugnant baseball. Damien checked the palm of his hand to make sure Aetherius was unharmed and found his archnemesis looking up at him in surprise.

"Nice catch, tha—"

Damien couldn't express himself as he'd like, but the incubus's lack of speech didn't prevent him from getting his feelings across.

"Euuuurrrrrgghh!"

He held his palm flat and roughly shook it over the floor behind him. Aetherius plopped into the snow and Damien turned back to the gate, just in time to start absorbing shots into his inadequately armored torso. He and Hammertime were both large targets, and they were now out in the open. Hammertime was drawing fire, the projectiles ricocheting off him. Damien was unarmored. Two arrows embedded themselves in his chest and a bullet tore through his abdomen. He had to keep his front to the enemies, or else they might hit his real body concealed in the bag.

There was no point in standing around here. Damien Charged what was left of the gate. His health was quite a bit less than 50%, so Enrage was already active.

Bloodlust!

Noigel had his drawbacks, but his reaction time was not one of them. Both hands on his weapon, the Bloodlust reached Damien as he drew the quauhololli back and put everything he had into a single strike. Double stats from Possession, strength and stamina doubled again by Enrage; attack speed and movement speed buffed by Bloodlust; and extra momentum from the Charge on top meant Damien was a living siege engine.

The majority of the gate was intact, but the center of it was a charred, broken mess. The party had accidentally created a fantasy-based blasting charge, complete with a magic-powered drill. There was a wide hole centered around the blast zone, but everything in the immediate vicinity looked to be hanging on by only a thread. The hole was not wide enough for Damien to pass through, not by a long shot, but it was wide enough for Damien to hear one of the Carlisle-Elites extolling the other players before he made contact.

"You are the Carlisle-Elite. No matter what comes through that gate, you will stand your ground!"

Damien planted his weapon directly into the weakest-looking section. This time there was no resistance. His weapon passed straight through the charred remnants, pieces of the gate projecting forward left and right. The rest of him crashed through in its wake. Then he was standing on the other side, with ten Carlisle-Elites all pointing their weapons at him.

BiggusDickus was at the front, advancing with his flail held above his head and his shield close. The leader, no doubt. TwinBlade, the dual-wielding warrior who'd received his membership and an instant promotion for killing five Rising Tide members the day prior, was standing beside him, ever so slightly further back. He looked very nervous. It was clear that the incubus's possessed form was not what Magnitude's night watch had been expecting.

Damien's ability to express himself was still limited, but once again words were of secondary importance. He tensed every muscle in the incubus's considerable frame and roared into them. Those still advancing stopped in their tracks, those standing their ground stepped back. The channels in the casters' hands were interrupted as they flinched, and one even fled back toward the Portal Stone, screaming and crying. Someone was up past their bedtime. They all were, to be fair.

Behind them, blue orbs started popping up around the Portal Stone in rapid succession.

Hammertime blitzed through glowing red on Damien's left and Lillian was glowing white on his right, each wielding Hammertime's hammers past and present. Lillian locked onto TwinBlade almost immediately. TwinBlade had resolutely stood his ground as Damien roared into him at close range. When he saw Lillian, his weapons dematerialized and he fled. He was not as fast as Lillian.

Trinytea slid through on the ground, then leapt into the air and sailed over the front line as the guild leaders crashed into them. She planted both her remaining shots into the top of BiggusDickus's helmet, dropping him to his knees as he was passed on either side by the two guild leaders. Legolias, lacking another vantage point, arrived on Damien's shoulder and began loosing arrows into the vulnerable casters who'd remained at the back. Aetherius Blinked through and emptied Arcane Bolts into BiggusDickus's body as he lay prone, finishing him. The hell hounds and imps had also been Bloodlust-buffed, and they arrived to savage anyone still standing as the party laid into each of them in turn.

They had to destroy the Portal Stone. If any of the players

arriving were Magnitude, which seemed likely, the whole ordeal would become far more difficult. Damien had no Charge and couldn't make it, but Hammertime and Lillian both knew the score. The Anti-Magic Shield appeared on Hammertime from Sabrina, a Sanctification buff appeared on Lillian from Judgementday, and both of them ran straight toward the Portal Stone without any loss of momentum. The players standing in their path may as well have been made of smoke. They reached it simultaneously and their hammers connected with it in the center at once, turning it into rubble and dust. The blue orbs winked out and were gone. The wall was obviously their guild's rally point, but it was not a hot spot that people purposefully logged out at. Finally some good news.

All objectives complete. Now they just had to leave. Damien received a full Soul Reserve from passing through their enemies' remains, but that wasn't his primary concern. Mr. Healy had drunk his second mana potion in advance of their escape and was running for the far side, but too slowly. Even Damien's incubus was faster than he was. Damien discarded the quauhololli in order to further increase his speed, then reduced it again a fraction by running up behind Mr. Healy and snatching him up as the spell kept running.

Now he had a portable magic shield. Cool. The rest of the party crowded around him as Mr. Healy complained bitterly, but Damien needed this. There weren't any arrows or musket fire coming for them, because Magnitude had neglected to put any slats in the back of the wall for people to fire out of. There were still the spear-chuckers on the ramparts to worry about though, and his unarmored, unprotected body was positioned exactly where any NPC with any sense would be aiming. He was in far more actual danger running away from ranged enemies than he was attacking them.

It wasn't long before Mr. Healy's Sanctuary spell gave out, but by that point they were nearly clear. A few steps more and the javelins were falling only behind them. They were out of range. They'd made it.

Damien's health regenerated quickly now he was out of

combat. Perks of possessing a demonic minion. His stamina had held out pretty well thanks to his Enrage skill – better than that of most of the players who'd been forced to keep his pace. Lillian bodily dragged them to their feet and pushed them onward.

"Not done yet, up. Up! We're not safe until we're out of the valley. Walk it off! Let's go."

Aetherius popped up out of nowhere in front of them. He'd avoided crowding under the shield by using his special ability. Sneaky. He stuck his hand out.

"We're past the wall. I'll have my bag back now."

Damien groaned and was about to cancel his Possession, but Lillian gave him a warning glance and a quick shake of her head.

"We agreed you'd get the bag when we were out of immediate danger. We aren't. Bag after we're out of the valley, not before. Shift!"

Aetherius's face turned even more sour, but he lightly jogged away without further complaint. When he was out of earshot, Lillian whacked Damien in the arm.

"Nice job with the gate."

He grunted. Not really much in the way of alternatives.

She checked the rest had moved further ahead, then lowered her voice.

"The rest of them don't know about Archimonde, except for Hammertime. We didn't want them worrying before we'd even got through the gate. Us three are the only ones who have any idea about it. Him. Whatever it is."

Damien grunted again. There was plenty he wanted to convey, such as how if they were getting along better they could've gone over this in greater depth beforehand. For now he could only grunt.

"Hopefully Archimonde won't show," Lillian continued unabated, "because it's 4am, but since you're here...well, they'd probably call it in even if it was just us, but it's pretty much a given since you're here as well. Don't worry, I factored that in before I decided to bring you along. Those healers might not have been very useful earlier, but they'll make for a strong party if Archimonde does show up."

Damien grunted, this time not bothering to hide his exasperation.

"You know what? I like talking to you more when you're an incubus. Not sure why. Can't put my finger on it. What do you think?"

Damien very slowly turned his head and stared at her, silently, as they trudged through the snow. She was suddenly in a good mood. It probably had something to do with TwinBlade's timely appearance, which had been swiftly followed by his untimely demise. It was nice to see her happy again, though, and even nicer that she was talking to him. Even if it was mainly to taunt him because he couldn't talk back.

He raised his hands and the customary keyboard appeared, resized for his gargantuan form.

Daemien: Haha.

Lillian couldn't stop herself from smirking, breaking the silence with another sudden punch that did make him grunt.

"Well, we're nearly there now. If we're lucky, Archimonde won't show and that wall will be—"

"Lillian! There's something up ahead, it looks different."

The sparkle went out of her eyes and she immediately returned to business mode.

"Of course not. Let's go."

They ran up ahead, the snow fading away as the pass leading to freedom came within sight. Archimonde was standing directly in the middle of it, its huge body easily visible in the center of the gully. It had been hard to gauge exactly how large Archimonde was in the depths of panic. Gauging it now only inspired a second round of anxiety. The thing was easily larger than Hammertime. It was roughly the same size as the incubus Damien was inhabiting, maybe a little bigger.

On either side of Archimonde, there were summons. More than it'd had on the first encounter. Damien counted six hell hounds and twelve imps, all stretched out evenly and blocking the path. Archimonde was fielding a Soul Summon Limit of 30. That meant it had at least 300 wisdom. There was no knowing how much higher Archimonde's wisdom was than that. It probably didn't lack stat points elsewhere. Especially in intelligence, since it was a caster.

Each of the minions would be stronger than Damien's own, since their stats were determined by level. How much stronger would also be unknown, until they made those question marks disappear. At least they didn't have to worry about wraiths, since the entirety of Archimonde's maximum Soul Summon Limit was accounted for.

While Damien tried to size up their opponent, his party were whispering among themselves. Aetherius had summoned a Mana Wisp and was guiding it toward the obstacle while the rest quarreled. Trinytea was reacquainting herself with her former guildmates, starting with Legolias.

"You think we're stupid? That's not a player," she said to him.

"It is. It's an occultist. I didn't take the Night Strider trait just to avoid doing damage, Trinytea. You see all the little dots next to it, with the bigger ones every two spaces? Imps and hell hounds. Just like our friend here. Daemien, you know anything about this?"

Why did everyone suddenly feel like speaking to him when he couldn't speak? Lillian interjected for him.

"Damien can't speak when he's possessing a minion. Even if he could, that's obviously not a friendly. So it's simple. We kill it and move on. We might be past the wall, but they'll reorganize and catch us if we take too long. The only way is through. Everyone, get combat-ready, prioritize—"

Which was when a window popped up on Damien's screen, showing Archimonde up close in all its glory. The feed was live from Aetherius's Mana Wisp, and he'd shared its viewpoint with the whole party. The same disgust Damien had succumbed to when he had first met Archimonde face to face spread through the players surrounding him in small doses.

"Aetherius, turn that off!"

"I'm sharing intel, doesn't that seem pru—"

Which was when Archimonde began to laboriously churn out speech from its stomach. Even Lillian stopped marching toward the broadcaster, her lips parting. Everyone stopped processing their disgust with chatter, and did so the only way such a spectacle warranted: in fascinated, horrified silence.

"Bring me Daemien-chan. I want only him. When he is mine, the rest of you may pass. You have three minutes."

Archimonde flicked its wrist toward the wisp, as if dismissing it. It burst into black flames and was gone in an instant. The group was silent. Aetherius was the first to speak, and what he had to say did not improve matters.

"That's one of Magnitude's associates, isn't it?"

He was looking at Damien, who remained silent and unmoving. He hardly needed to reply. It had been more statement than question, and the lack of response from Damien's ineloquent incubus was interpreted as confirmation enough. Aetherius's query was followed in short order by everyone talking at once. Lillian and Hammertime were trying to calm them down, but the quandary Archimonde had thrown their way had completely split the party. Trinytea raised her voice above the hubbub, saying what was surely on many of their minds.

"This isn't what I signed up for. It wants Daemien, right? Let's just give it what it wants and get going."

Lillian wheeled round and glared at her as the rest of the voices died down.

"We wouldn't have got through the wall without him, don't you have any shame?"

"I'll tell you what I don't have. An inventory. You wouldn't have got through the wall without me, either, but I don't see you showering me with praise. Now you're asking me to fight that thing with no ammunition? I wouldn't fight it *with* ammunition. It's Daemien's problem, not ours, I was asked for help getting through the wall and I did my job, this wasn't the deal! Give it Daemien!"

"Trinytea."

Trinytea's gaze snapped toward Hammertime, who had his arms stretched forward and was stepping toward her slowly.

"If everybody just calms down, we can come up with a plan. That player is trying to divide us and it's succeeding. There's no guarantee that if we give it Daemien it'll actually let us through. Then we'll have lost the only player in our party who's faced it before and knows it best, and it'll deal with the rest of u—"

"Nobody said Daemien had seen it before. Did you know about this? Who else knew about this whole deal? I'm guessing Lillian, seeing how she was so cavalier about fighting it. Anyone else? Who else knew about this?"

The party members all turned and faced the guild leaders. Hammertime fell silent. Lillian shot Hammertime a furious glance, but her cheeks were burning. Trinytea scoffed in her face.

"I wanted to show you I'd changed, and I threw all my best gear into your project to show goodwill. This is what I get as thanks. What a waste of time. GG, everyone, I'm going to bed."

The ground around Trinytea lit up and she started to log out. Everyone started yelling at once. Lillian and Hammertime both approached her at once entreating her to stay, the former more threateningly than the latter. The party members in turn all gathered around, ranting and raving into their leaders' ears as they tried to deal with the more pressing issue of Trinytea's imminent desertion.

Aetherius remained exactly where he was, staring at the enemy which was catalyzing his party's collapse. Trinytea was about four seconds into her departure when he threw a hand out and fired a single Arcane Bolt across the gap, watching intently for Archimonde's reaction. Everyone immediately stopped bickering and stared at Aetherius openmouthed.

Archimonde remained where it was, its jaws stretching wide open. The bolt splashed open across the gaping maw before it ever connected, the light turning from blue to golden. It disappeared into Archimonde's belly in a stream of glowing trails, the cavernous mouth munching down on them as though they were strands of ethereal spaghetti. Go-Chi-So-Sa-Ma.

Aetherius squinted at the teeth, now well illuminated, until all the light had been consumed. The attack had done no damage, but it did have at least one positive effect. The party was officially in combat. Trinytea's logout had been automatically canceled.

"Did...did it just eat my Arcane Bolt?"

Trinytea was the first to react, moving over to spit fury into his face.

"What did you do that for? Now I'm stuck here! Nobody said you should fire at it!"

Aetherius's eyelids flickered at the rush of hot air, but he didn't look at her. He was tapping his foot, arms folded, as he examined the opening that led to freedom from one side to the other.

"No, they didn't. And I did it anyway."

He threw his hands out and started firing Arcane Bolts in rapid succession, all going in the same direction. Straight toward Archimonde. He'd got off six before Trinytea roughly shoved him, interrupting his casts.

"Don't do it again! You'll make it—"

This time Aetherius did look at her, his hands glowing red. Trinytea abruptly shut up. Aetherius looked back just as Archimonde's belly was expanding to consume the latest offering. At the last second, he stuck his hands out with the middle and index fingers extended before dragging them violently to the right. The Arcane Bolts curled round in unison, away from the maw. Directly into the units on Archimonde's right flank. The first landed short of an imp, but the light it offered helped Aetherius connect with the next five bolts as he deftly altered their path. One hit the imp. Another hit the one next to it. Then three bolts collided one after another with the hell hound which was behind them, leaving all three dead.

Archimonde started summoning a new unit. Probably a hell hound. Archimonde was very well lit in the light of the runes forming on the ground by its side. Aetherius turned to the rest of the party.

"If we handle the minions first, especially imps, an occultist loses a lot of their utility. Kill the minions, then focus on the big ugly. Sound okay to you, Damien?"

Damien was surprised to have been asked his own opinion, especially from this source. He nodded enthusiastically. In truth, any option other than being fed to Archimonde in order to get the rest of them a hypothetical free ticket looked pretty good from where he was standing. Aetherius turned to Lillian.

"Lillian, do you—"

He hadn't completed the sentence before he was engulfed in black flames. Archimonde was methodically plodding forward, casting its gaze between party members and flicking its wrist. The Corruption hit Lillian next, then Hammertime. Mr. Healy, the only party priest, Dispelled each of them in the order the Corruptions had landed as the two paladins fired up their heals. There was only one way to solve this now.

10

FACING YOUR DEMONS

Even before the flames had left Lillian, she was yelling out orders to the rest of the group.

"Mr. Healy, when you're done Dispelling I want light! Legolias and Aetherius, you're on imps. Kill them before they get near our party. Hammertime, you're on point with me. Keep hounds and anything that gets past the ranged damage away from our squishies. Judge, you're primary healer. OhHolyLight, stop healing, you're off-healer. Unless someone's in crisis, Smite demons in range. Sabrina, I don't know your spells aside from Anti-Magic Shield and Phase Shift, stick to support rather than damage. Trinytea...you'll be first to go around, testing their responses. Might want to talk to Sabrina about that. Play evasive, keep yourself safe."

She looked at each of them in turn, making sure they were going about their assigned roles, before sidling up to Damien to talk to him privately.

"It wants you dead more than the rest of us. That's obvious, or else it wouldn't have made the offer. I'd quite like for you to live through this."

Damien clumsily typed out a six-fingered, two-thumbed reply before hitting 'Enter'.

Daemien: Thanks, me too.

"Get your imps overhead and past Archimonde, so you can

Demon Gate out of danger. The way I see it, you should have the easiest time getting past thanks to your abilities. Don't engage it in direct combat, you don't have a weapon and I regard you dying as an automatic fail. Just look mean and handle any minions trying to get through to our casters. Can you do that?"

The way Damien saw it, Archimonde wanting him dead the most and him getting past Archimonde easily didn't line up. But he didn't have a better plan and was glad Lillian had opted for him not to engage. His last death had left a scar and he was more than happy to give it time to heal. There were nine of them besides him, eight if you didn't count Trinytea. Whatever else Archimonde was, it was a lone player. As an occultist, it had already freely thrown away its greatest asset. Surprise. They might be able to handle it. If not, Damien had his own minions to throw into the mix.

Daemien: Got it.

She nodded and they got into position, Damien moving front and center with Lillian flanking him far off to the left side and Hammertime already in place on the other. The Corruptions had stopped. Archimonde must have seen them being Dispelled and realized it was a waste. Free from Dispel spamming, Mr. Healy sent a Holy Orb into the air, lighting up the battlefield with the intensity of a miniature sun. For the next thirty seconds, everyone had light.

Aetherius and Legolias opened fire, aiming for the imps as instructed. They were grounded, and quite a bit easier to hit than Damien's flying variant. After another three went down, the survivors ran to Archimonde for cover and clambered onto its back. The hell hounds remained well spread out, waiting to intercept runners Archimonde was moving, slowly and purposefully, straight toward Damien's incubus. It was somehow more menacing than if it were running. It was out in the open, walking straight toward a ten-strong party, its minions dying on either side. Yet it didn't seem at all fazed.

Damien relayed his commands to Noigel, and three of his seven imps all took to the sky as his succubus's Bloodlust set in. The order had barely been given before Archimonde stopped, looked over its head and flicked its wrist. Damien turned around just in time to see his airborne minions burst into flame, one after the other. It wasn't using Corruption on any of the players, but hadn't hesitated to use it on the imps. They died so quickly that the effect could not be Dispelled before they perished. It seemed like a waste of mana, but Corruption couldn't be dodged and almost half of Damien's escape plan was gone. Archimonde was preserving resources to kill Damien himself.

"Damien, watch out!"

Damien turned back and was hit with the full extent of his blunder. He'd only turned for a few seconds, thinking Archimonde would continue its steady pace forward. Lillian's warning came just in time for the Chaotic Bolt to plow into the incubus's shoulder. The damage from a single Chaotic Bolt was excessive. Constitution was the highest stat the incubus had. Doubled, Damien had 2,400 hit points. The one bolt had taken out 800 of them.

That wasn't the only reason to panic. In turning, Damien had inadvertently shown Archimonde the innocuous bag strapped to the incubus's back. Had he not turned in time to face his enemy, that's where the bolt would've struck. Too late, the reason why Archimonde was advancing so slowly, with so many hounds spaced out, became clear. It had been searching for Damien, taking its time to make sure he didn't slip through the net.

"Naaaaan-de? What's in the bag, Daemien-chan?"

Archimonde started lumbering toward him faster and the hounds pulled in. Trinytea seized her moment, sprinting down the side as close to the wall as she could get. Archimonde didn't even bat an eye. Even its minions didn't change course to intercept her, moving in to crowd around their master. While Trinytea was probably delighted to be ignored, Lillian and Hammertime were used to more attention.

They both ran in on either side without hesitation to meet Archimonde, weapons at the ready. Aetherius had finished drinking a mana potion and was firing Arcane Bolts straight into the air. OhHolyLight raised a hand and clenched his fist, burning

Archimonde with Smite. It was no surprise that Archimonde was classified as a demon, rather than an orc.

Archimonde stopped as the Smite took hold, its hit points dropping slowly but steadily. The Arcane Bolts were spiraling back down from above, on course to land all around it. Lillian and Hammertime were both on their backswings as the demon pointed at the ground at its feet.

"Circle of Hell."

The two guild leaders were rooted at opposite edges of the ability. The demons in Archimonde's thrall swarmed forward to attack the immobilized tanks, with three hell hounds taking point on each of them. With no means of dodging or blocking, their armor cut in half and their health burning away, the two strongest on the team were quickly overrun. Mr. Healy barely managed to Dispel Lillian before they arrived on her, removing the root but not the damage over time. Even with Legolias pouring piercing arrows into them as fast as he could, she was still in deep trouble; Archimonde's minions were also healing within the circle's confines.

Hammertime had it much worse; unable to move his feet and unsupported, he nonetheless still took out a hell hound with a single swing before the next two barreled into him. A few moments later Sabrina's Anti-Magic Shield turned the tide in his favor, removing the burning damage. Her mana would drop the more damage he took, but that would at least buy him time.

Aetherius's Arcane Bolts plummeted down from above, avoiding Archimonde's problematic stomach. Archimonde was eclipsed in bright light as they landed one after the other, hitting it in the head and its recently vacated back. The mass of flesh and sinew barely even budged as they impacted. After the last of them had connected, Archimonde still had 80% of its health remaining.

OhHolyLight's Smite was still upon the demon, but with the damage of the circle increasing over time and the trait to heal demonic minions within it stacking on top of each other, Archimonde was healing faster than Smite did damage. Considerably faster. That spell had been the bane of Damien's existence when he was in the early stages of the game, cutting through his minions with little effort in no time at all. Yet Archimonde was regenerating through it.

Archimonde was definitely a demon, but its facial features indicated it was also still an orc. What perks demons had, Damien was sure he didn't know, but orcs had Magic Blood: a 25% increase to health, stamina and mana regeneration. Regular regeneration was next to useless, but the orcish perk extended to extra healing, mana replenishment and stamina replenishment from abilities over time, which Archimonde was abusing to the fullest. Between Magnitude and now this thing, there was a growing and intensely undesirable trend in the tank/caster hybrid department.

"I'm hungry. I want a tasty snack. Yummy yummy yummy."

Archimonde twisted and its terrifying barbed tongue lashed out around Hammertime's chest. Then it started to drag him across the floor. Hammertime unequipped his weapon, took the tongue in both hands and dug his heels in, but Archimonde braced back and the tongue stretched taut before reeling him in faster. Hammertime had bashed in the brains of an imp and a hound under extreme duress, but it wasn't enough. The three remaining imps retreated to the relative safety of Archimonde's back while two more hounds confounded Hammertime's efforts to stave off a deeply unpleasant end. Archimonde took strides forward while reeling the tongue back in, its arms braced against its sides and a thick stream of drool pouring from its open mouth in anticipation.

Thirty seconds had passed. Mr. Healy's Holy Orb expired, leaving them all in darkness. Archimonde was preoccupied. Damien was one of only two people in his party who could see. He had to do something. He threw all his remaining minions, save for Noigel and the succubus, into the fray at once. The succubus would have little mana left after, but Bloodlust was required and there was no better use for her in this fight. Damien set the hounds alight and directed them to head straight to Archimonde, trying to prevent Hammertime from suffering the same fate he had. If the rest of the party watched Hammertime get eaten, it would not do much for party morale.

Archimonde looked away from Hammertime and stared the first of the hounds down. It stopped in its tracks. Damien could see no reason why. It wasn't in the circle yet, so it shouldn't have been rooted. He'd made his order very clear. It was only as he reiterated the order in his head that he noticed the hound had undergone a change. It now had a red name. By the time he realized, the other had taken a red name as well. Both of them ran toward Hammertime and sank their teeth in, joining the two he'd already been struggling with.

Archimonde had taken control of his minions? Just by looking at them? How could this be possible? Wasn't Archimonde strong enough already? Damien had already known he couldn't face this opponent alone, but this made it go from futile to insulting. If he couldn't even use minions against this player without them being taken away from him, there was no hope. There was absolutely nothing he could do.

Noigel took command while Damien floundered. The imps came flying in at Archimonde from above, claws extended and pointed forward on hands and feet, all of them going for the face. Archimonde reached behind its back, cupped an imp of its own, and hurled it into them. A clever solution to mitigate their lack of wings. A flick of Archimonde's wrist to cast Corruption and an Imp-losion put an abrupt end to Damien's meager assault. At least these minions hadn't been turned against them.

Even though the hounds had been appropriated, they'd served a purpose: they'd bought Lillian time. The battlefield was illuminated once more as she activated her Divine Might, unequipped the shield that had been reduced to scrap in her defense, then ran over the corpses of Archimonde's dispatched minions toward her enemy. She was still burning, though the timely Dispel of her root had allowed her to deal with her allotment of minions in short order. Archimonde's eyes were still cast up to where it had just triggered the Imp-losion. She took her sword in both hands, leapt forward with both feet, and dragged her blade downward. Through the monster's glistening, taut tongue.

Archimonde's anchor snapped and it staggered backward, the wretched maw shrieking and what was left of its disgusting appendage snapping back into its depths. Hammertime broke through his loosened bonds and took up his hammer to fight the hell hounds, caving one of them in instantly. Lillian landed, turned on her heel and ran straight back in.

All Smiting and Dispelling had ceased. The three players with healing capabilities were doing everything in their power to keep Lillian alive. Then Sabrina's Anti-Magic Aura sputtered out and Hammertime was once again engulfed in flames. She'd run through all three of her mana potions in less than twenty seconds, but when the flames returned to Hammertime the increasing damage over time had reset back to zero.

While Hammertime had been protected, Lillian's sustained damage from the black fire was increasing as she remained within the circle. The two paladins and the priest were intermittently chugging mana potions as well. Keeping up with Archimonde's damage was taking its toll.

Lillian wasn't paying much attention to her health. She knew when she had the upper hand in a fight and she intended to keep it. Archimonde's health had dropped notably. The exact number of hit points it had left was unknowable, but the red bar showed it was below 60% of them, in spite of the circle's healing. It appeared the tongue it was so keen on throwing around was a critical hit point. But Archimonde was still in its circle, and without a suppressing Smite and with the circle's effect increased, it was regenerating absurdly quickly.

Archimonde stopped staggering and saw Lillian running toward it. It had used its root. It had no tongue. It could not stop her. Lillian was almost on it when Archimonde pointed at her and shrieked. That it was clearly afraid was gratifying. The ability it produced when cornered was not.

"Shedim!"

Damien paused, horrorstruck. That was one of the level 40

traits he'd forgone in favor of Ex-Imp-losion. The description had been memorably awful:

Adapts Possession to be used on players and NPCs as an offensive ability. The target is blinded and afflicted with nightmares as their health, stamina and mana are channeled into you.

Damien had been glad his playstyle did not warrant choosing this ability. It seemed unnecessarily cruel. As horrible as the description was, Damien knew Archimonde had chosen its target poorly. Lillian wasn't afraid of anything and the spell wouldn't stop her from moving. All she had to do was keep running forward with her sword in front of her and she'd cancel the ability by herself. Lillian kept running, lifted her sword above her head...and stopped dead, only five strides short of her target.

Her Divine Might was canceled and the battlefield plunged back into darkness. Her arms dropped to her sides, her sword clattering in the dirt. She fell to her knees. Clutched her face in her hands. And wailed. A piercing, broken, grief-stricken cry. As though she were an infant. The second-strongest woman Damien knew, reduced to a gibbering wreck.

Archimonde was frozen in its pointing stance. Its hit points were regenerating even faster, and Lillian's were disappearing faster as well. Damien could see her health points diminishing in the party sidebar. 500 per second, give or take. It was hard to tell, with the burning effect on her and the heals barely sustaining her against it. The circle was nearly expired, and Lillian had been within it for the entire duration as the damage increased. With this on top, the healers could no longer keep up. They could only see her by the faint light of each heal landing in close succession. She would die if this was not stopped. That didn't matter. This was only a game. But her suffering was very real.

Damien had thought he knew what rage felt like. He'd led a very short life, all of it against a backdrop of simmering anger. The kind of surly, slowly accumulated misgiving that stacks up when you are wronged, or powerless, or when you're made to feel as though you're not good enough. His youth made the occasions his anger had festered within him all the more potent, because he had less to balance it against. He'd been angry with CU for a long time, since he was old enough to understand his family was forsaken. He'd been angry with Aetherius for a shorter time, but more intensely. Most of all, he'd been angry with himself. For as long as he could remember.

As his guardian angel smashed her head into the ground, the dull *thud* of it punctuating her party's stunned silence while her long scream continued unabated, Damien realized something important. Though he'd felt the sting of injustice many times, he'd never known real hatred.

His feet were moving before he'd made a conscious decision. He was Charging before Mr. Healy's ill-fated Dispel on Lillian landed. His hands were curled into fists before Noigel realized his intent and directed himself and the succubus to come to his aid. But he was still a long way out when Aetherius Blinked into the black flames, calculating it perfectly to arrive by Lillian's side. Even in complete darkness.

His archnemesis's feet were immediately snared and he was engulfed. Aetherius summoned a Mana Wisp instantly upon arrival, providing light for the casters to see Lillian by so they could measure out their heals more carefully. Damien Charged on, hellbent on their mutual enemy's destruction.

Aetherius clumsily grabbed Lillian by the shoulders, then lay over her. Embracing her, and simultaneously trying to pull her up. He lacked the strength to do so. She cried out in terror and pushed him away, hard enough for Aetherius to land fully on his back, his arms extended straight in front of him. Now he was much more effectively rooted.

Damien was approaching the edge of the circle, dull instinct prompting him to reach the nearest point of ingress, when Aetherius pointed his open palms at the abomination towering over him and Lillian. He'd somehow possessed the wherewithal to keep his hands off the ground when he fell so they'd be free to channel the purest display of wrath Damien had ever seen.

They glowed red, white and blue.

"Prismatic Storm."

A flurry of Fire, Lightning and Frozen Bolts tore out of

Aetherius's hands, aimed at close range into Archimonde's prone form. Miniaturized fireballs, followed by jagged streaks of lightning, followed by shattering orbs of frost. Five bolts of three damage types a second, each imbued with extra abilities from his traits, alternating between each hand.

Despite being cast second, a Lightning Bolt struck first. The Fire Bolts struck twice and the Lightning Bolts three further times before the first Frozen Bolt touched base. Each landed strike after a Fire Bolt did more damage than the one preceding it, and it was as the second Frozen Bolt landed that Archimonde's Possession was interrupted by the rapidly stacking damage.

Still they continued, and Aetherius had been channeling long enough now to find his rhythm. From his position on the ground, coated in black flames, his arms remained braced as his open palms twisted back and forth. Directing each bolt where it needed to go in a ceaseless blur of malicious focus and unerring accuracy.

Aetherius managed an astounding spread, avoiding the cavernous stomach and hitting all around it. Archimonde had been reduced from full to half health, even through the healing. The fire and lightning had mostly landed across its upper body and face, the ice had completely encased its legs. Nothing had missed. A feat bordering on savant, given that the twenty-five elemental bolts had cycled through each of Aetherius's hands.

The Possession had been negated and Lillian's sobbing had stopped, but Damien could still hear it. Ringing in his ears. The circle dissipated and he immediately changed to a direct path. Archimonde saw him coming and strained against the ice rooting it to the floor. It heaved twice and one foot came clear, the shell of ice cracking as it tore itself free. It was halfway to unrooting the second when Damien, as though he'd been pursuing this goal for a lifetime, planted his incubus's Charge-imbued fist squarely in Archimonde's face.

There was a wet *thud* as Archimonde's facial features caved inward. Its foot broke free of the ice and flew into the air as the back of its head was propelled into the floor. Damien stepped over it and expended the entirety of his stamina to keep Archimonde in place, one fist descending after the other into the wounds left by Aetherius's onslaught. He hadn't known the incubus's hands could move this fast without weapons. He'd never tried. He wasn't thinking about it now. It was not as effective as he'd have liked, but he'd keep doing it as long as he could.

Hammertime's voice blared out over the comms.

"Now's our chance, everyone get clear before it gets up again. Quickly! Daemien, wait until we're clear, then disengage!"

No. He needed to kill it. It was only a game, and it wouldn't be enough, but it would have to do. His blows didn't do much damage, but consequently his stamina wasn't much affected either. He felt like doing this all day.

"Daemien, we're clear. Disengage!"

The players were passing him on either side and he was being left behind, but it didn't matter. Archimonde had raised its arms to defend itself from the onslaught, but Damien's possessed incubus was stronger. Or so he thought. At the exact moment Damien started to slow, his stamina finally waning and the Bloodlust expired, Archimonde swept its arm out and redirected Damien's punch. Straight into the yawning meat grinder. It immediately clenched, rows of teeth digging in all the way from Damien's closed fist to above his elbow.

Damien roared in outrage and tried to pull free, but it was an extremely nasty trap. He punched Archimonde again, but it grabbed his remaining free arm with both hands and held it steady. Archimonde was obviously not strength-based, but still had enough to redirect one of Damien's punches and restrain another with two hands. It's much harder to catch a punch than it is to throw one. How high were this thing's stats?

Weaponless, Damien had only achieved a fraction of the damage Aetherius had managed, bringing Archimonde's health down to 24%. The mouth chewed his arm delicately. Individual rows of teeth bit in while others held fast, rippling up and down Damien's arm with excruciating care, and that number became

34%. Damien barely had 50% health left when Archimonde stopped eating.

"Daemien, we're all clear, we're just waiting for you now. Disengage!"

Easier said than done. Archimonde was eyeing him up rather than continuing with its meal. Very uncharacteristic. Damien's head was clearing, now his uncontrolled rampage had been brought to a toothy end, and he suddenly realized Archimonde's dilemma: if it kept eating, Damien would Enrage. His strength would double and Archimonde wouldn't be able to hold him still, inviting dangerous damage, or more likely an escape attempt.

If Archimonde removed a hand to channel a Chaotic Bolt, Damien would interrupt that by punching it in the face, or redirect the bolt by forcing the arm away. If the damage didn't kill him outright, Damien would have a good chance of Charging out of there after the five-second root was finished. Corruption, which required less than half a second and a flick of the wrist, would spread and burn Archimonde as well. They were in physical contact. Very close physical contact, since Damien's arm was embedded in its guts.

Damien had his own set of dilemmas, but there was one he could deal with quickly. He looked at Noigel and the succubus, who'd been hanging back, waiting for the onslaught to finish.

You're dismissed.

They leapt into their respective rifts and were gone. At least now they couldn't be used against him. The very last thing he needed was for Archimonde to take control of either of them, as it had with the two hounds. The situation was precarious enough already without offering a decisive advantage on a plate.

The other dilemmas were not so easily reconciled. If he canceled his Possession and tried to climb out the bag to make a run for it, Archimonde's strength would easily be greater than that of his incubus. If he stayed here, doing nothing, Archimonde's mana and cooldowns would continue to replenish. But then, so would those of Damien's party. The situation was actually advantageous for him if it was drawn out. The stalemate would end if the party came back after they'd realized the tables had turned.

Damien was still fighting to free his hand from Archimonde's grasp when the creature looked up into the air behind him and grinned. Damien followed its gaze and saw an imp. It was a Noigel, though it had nothing in common with Damien's own. Archimonde had clearly gone with the mainstream occultist-touted strategy of suppressing his imp rather than trying to appease it. The Noigel flew back toward Magnitude's wall, away from the spent players who'd already evacuated and might have killed it.

"Let's end this with a bang and a whimper, Daemien-chan."

Archimonde let go with one hand and pointed. Not at Damien, but up into the night sky. The spell-cast was over in two words.

"Dark Omen."

Damien's fist descended into Archimonde's face immediately afterward, which was as marginally satisfying as ever but inflicted minimal damage. He only got the one hit in before Archimonde's hands returned to Damien's and renewed their grip. Archimonde had only pointed into the sky for a second. There'd been no channel. There was nothing to indicate a spell had been cast. Was it a bluff?

There was not much light to begin with, but there is a distinct difference between meager light and no light at all. Through Damien's night vision, he saw a perfectly round shadow visibly form on the ground around him as it started to grow. The absolute pitch black was so dark he had to blink for his vision to recalibrate. He sincerely doubted that was a coincidence. Archimonde lay back, sniggering to itself.

Two seconds later, Hammertime came back on the comms.

"Daemien, is the black sphere growing above you an ability of yours? If not, you might want to...disengage!"

Damien turned his head and looked up. The moon was being eclipsed. There was a black mass hanging high overhead, just above the top of the valley, and it was getting bigger. It had covered the center of the moon and was working its way outward to cover the entire surface. Dark Omen was a fitting name.

"We need to get clear! You need to come now!"

Right. So much for waiting this out. Damien needed to Enrage. If Archimonde wasn't going to oblige, he'd just have to do it himself. Damien braced his bitten arm and violently twisted it within Archimonde's stomach. The teeth shredded his limb and Damien's vision blurred a little, but he'd accomplished his objective. He had less than 50% health. Enrage was activated. Right. What's next?

He used his newfound strength to wrench his punching arm out of Archimonde's hands and grabbed the other before pulling as hard as he could. It was both painful and ineffective. The teeth were lodged in deep, and even with quadrupled incubus strength he couldn't lift Archimonde's bulk. Archimonde was not eating it, opting instead to keep a strong grip.

Right. Okay. What are we doing here? Oh, of course! That's why Archimonde had been so happy to find its Noigel, and why it had sent it somewhere safe. Archimonde had an imp to Demon Gate out of its own spell's area of effect. How could Damien do the same without any imps?

Time had passed, and Archimonde's most reliable and heavily trait-invested ability was off cooldown. It twisted its head to the floor and pointed directly in front of its own snout.

"Circle of Hell."

Oh good. Damien's health was dropping, and Archimonde's was regenerating. Great. He'd probably die from the fire before he had to concern himself with the Dark Omen looming above. Although the low hum emanating from above implied it would be a close-run thing. The incubus might die from the flames, but then his real body in the bag would die from whatever was coming. And the Circle of Hell positioned directly over them was preventing him from canceling his Possession and leaving without being rooted.

Archimonde had chucked an imp off its back at Damien's imps earlier. That idea had merit. But he needed to prevent Archimonde from casting spells at his vacant body, not to mention whatever the effects of the spell looming over them would be. Damien could only effectively restrain Archimonde if the incubus's stats were quadrupled by Possession AND Enrage together. If he chucked his vacant body out of the way but couldn't cancel the Possession, his corpse could die on the cold ground instead. He assumed something with as long a charge time as this would do considerable damage. Still, he'd thought his way to a measurable improvement of dying a few meters away! But what if...well then. Now he had a different problem. Trying to convince Hammertime to run toward the danger zone as expediently as possible.

He brought up his menu with his free hand and mashed in a nostalgic message to Hammertime with his inferior three-fingered-incubus typing skills, making up for it with his superior inflammatory verbiage. There was no time to think about what he was sending, and certainly no time to spell-check. Either Hammertime would get it or he wouldn't.

Daemien: cm gt sum if u thnk ur hrd enuf pls.

"Saying goodbye to your loved ones, Daemien-chan?"

Not exactly. The root was over. Damien delicately and deliberately placed a foot on the side of Archimonde's face, then less delicately and even more deliberately pressed it over so it faced away from his allies. Corruption required a directed glance in addition to a flick of the wrist. No Corruption for you. In the distance, he could see Hammertime running toward him with Aetherius's Mana Wisp hovering in front to see by.

What an incredibly fast response from both parties. Still got some residual anger from when I lured you to your death with a variation on that message?

Gooood. Use your aggressive nature, boy.

It was either that, or Hammertime had a much better sense of humor than Damien gave him credit for. Or he was just plain legendary. Maybe a mishmash of all three. Damien churned a second, shorter message into the chat box.

Daemien: go long

He reached into the bag with his hand, being careful to keep his weight on the foot pressed into Archimonde's face. How to throw his own body: by the leg? Nah, the bloody thing will just fall off. No time to overthink it. If the first option is terrible, the second will have to do. He squashed his vacant body into a ball, then chucked it as hard as he could at Hammertime's approaching figure outside the new Circle of Hell's area of effect.

Considering the impending danger, Hammertime was running very resolutely. Damien would have to thank him, if either of them survived. Damien's body unfolded a quarter of the way into its arc and spiraled in the air. His limp corpse had lousy aerodynamic properties. It was only as Damien released himself into the air that he realized the one variable he hadn't accounted for. Hammertime couldn't see in the dark. He roared, the only way to warn him in time, but the hum of the Dark Omen above drowned it out and Hammertime didn't stop. At least it had been a good throw.

Damien's lifeless vessel rag-dolled out of the air and into the light of Aetherius's Mana Wisp, giving Hammertime exactly 0.12 seconds of warning before wrapping itself around his head. Hammertime leapt back to his feet, looked at the body, understood instantly, picked it up and started running back to the party as fast as he could.

Nice. Twenty-four seconds and an insane ally had cracked the puzzle. It was a bit hectic for a moment there. Damien removed his foot from Archimonde's face and smirked at his foe as efficiently as his own disgusting face would allow. Archimonde smirked sidelong back at him without turning its head. The hum of their impending death was consuming everything, and it was growing nearer. Dark Omen had begun its descent and would surely be upon them in seconds.

Archimonde's eyes turned back to its Noigel, which was standing a fair distance away. Hammertime was just about to pass that point on the opposite side. A good omen. The incubus's health was already low and Archimonde's was now comfortably high. Why would it not be smirking? As far as Archimonde was concerned, everything was well in hand. And hand was well in stomach.

Damien tried to lever the thing's head off the ground to face it away from its only hope of salvation, but both his archnemesis's hands immediately arrived to fight Damien away and Archimonde even began biting his hand with his regular, facially based mouth. Damien couldn't simultaneously fight three extremities with one. As he fought it, he realized something unsettling. There was no sound. The scuffle of them clawing and fighting each other was making no noise. The hum wasn't loud enough to drown it out. The sound just wasn't there.

The damage of the Circle of Hell was stacking too quickly anyway. The incubus would be dead in a couple of seconds. Might as well show Archimonde its efforts had been for naught. Too late for it to remedy the situation, now. He wanted it to suffer as much as possible, and while he'd been unable to inflict that physically he'd proven more than equipped to do it intellectually.

Damien bent over forward a little and opened the flap in the top of the bag, pointing it directly into Archimonde's face. He stood up straight and returned Archimonde's appalled sidelong expression, the massive googly eyes that once inspired terror now reduced to the epitome of indignant comical fury, with the most insincere thumbs-up Damien had ever had the pleasure of delivering. It would be the last action he took during this extremely successful Possession. The long-suffering incubus finally burned out the last of its hit points and died in flames. Had Archimonde tried a little harder, Damien would be dead. Its complacency, its failure to predict the variables Damien had painstakingly sought out, had invited Damien's success.

Damien was back in his own body, just in time to appreciate what he'd escaped. The Dark Omen had dropped halfway into the valley. Damien was hung over Hammertime's shoulder like a piece of meat as the guild leader fled in a justifiably undignified fashion, his arms and legs pumping furiously as he Charged toward the exit. It should've been loud, but it was utterly silent. There was no sound of any kind left, other than the hum.

The black mass Archimonde had conjured was no easier to conceptualize from Damien's new vantage point. It looked two-dimensional from every angle, as if part of a painting the artist had decided could only be improved by slapping a black circle in the middle. The only way of discerning its 3D dimensions was to assume that it extended as far forward and back as it did horizontally. By which standard, it was much closer than it appeared. A perfect sphere of black energy, boasting a circumference of about thirty meters. There was nothing about it that suggested coming into physical contact would be survivable.

As relief washed over him, he looked down to where he'd spent the last odd minute of his life. His nemesis's bulky body had already been replaced with the most unfortunate Noigel of all time. It moved to flee but was instead pulled upward, sucked into what Damien now recognized as a miniature rendition of a black hole. Archimonde's Noigel had been relocated to the very epicenter of the spell with only a second to impact. It had no chance. While the Dark Omen had taken a long time to completely manifest, it was not lollygagging now. It took on a visible third dimension as it sank into the ground to commence 'integrating' with it.

There was no explosion. There was no collision to propagate an explosion. It just buried itself in the landscape with no resistance, like a scalding-hot ball bearing dropped into a stick of butter. It was half immersed in the blink of an eye, persisted for another three seconds, over which duration there was a tangible pull toward it that Hammertime had avoided with his expedient movement, then shrank and winked out. It had formed a perfectly smooth bowl in the center of the valley.

Hammertime ran Damien the rest of the way to the opening, then unceremoniously put him down on his own two feet. Damien turned to examine the party that had navigated two far more extraordinary feats in a row. They were battered and drained, but alive. His elation was tempered when he saw Aetherius supporting Lillian. Her health was full, but she wasn't even motivated enough to carry herself. Her eyes were cast down, locked in a thousand-yard stare, not really seeing anything. Damien looked away, unwilling to inflict her pain on himself any longer. They'd escaped the carnage. But his victory over Archimonde, satisfying though it had been, was insufficient.

Despite their accomplishment, murder was back on his mind.

After twenty minutes of running through rough terrain (following Hammertime's quest directive in the absence of Lillian's leadership), they found the lights of a town. Damien realized this was where they would part ways. He was pretty sure his Enemy of the Realm 'perk' would ensure he was unwelcome in any civilized establishment. They'd be logging off at an inn for safety, but that option was not available to him. He was exhausted. All of them were. It was 4:56am. He'd sleep well that day. Then he looked at Lillian, who had one hand slung over Aetherius's shoulder as she dragged her feet, and realized he wouldn't. There was something important he needed to do first.

He drew to a halt at the back of the party as they dragged onward. Steeled himself. And called out.

"Aetherius. I need to talk to you. Alone. Please."

They all stopped. Aetherius looked between him and the rest of them, considered, then gently lowered Lillian. She didn't even lower herself. She collapsed, allowing Aetherius to guide her down, and curled up on the ground. The only proof she was alive was her chest expanding in short bursts. Seeing her like this broke Damien's heart. She was supposed to go to work in a few hours. She'd put this team together and had ended up suffering more than any of them. Because she'd decided to bring Damien, knowing it all but guaranteed a confrontation with the horror she'd seen in his petulantly shared footage. Then she had confronted his trauma herself, to try and spare him it.

Aetherius looked between the two of them, his gaze lingering on Lillian. Then he motioned for Damien to come to him instead. He was unwilling to leave her side. The rest of the party uneasily shambled onward, allowing them the space to have the private conversation Damien had requested.

Damien stepped up to his former nemesis and they briefly eyed each other up. Aetherius had his arms folded. Aside from holding them above his head, there was no more he could do to show lack of hostility. Or defensiveness. Damien followed suit. He looked back at the ground between Aetherius's feet. Andrew's feet. He reached into his Bag of Holding and withdrew the rat-skin bag Bartholomew had crafted for him, long ago. It was prepacked, in advance of the unlikely event their combined efforts tonight would succeed. He took a deep breath. Then removed the Bag of Holding from his belt.

"This is yours. Thank you for your help today. We couldn't have done it without you."

His eyes were still fixed on the floor, but he felt Andrew gently grasp the bag. He let go. Then, still looking at the floor in a desperate attempt not to show his face, he started walking away. He'd made it less than ten steps when Andrew replied.

"Goddammit...wait."

Damien kept his eyes on the floor. Took another shaky breath. And turned around. Still looking at the floor.

"You...you haven't disconnected this item from your inventory. I can access everything you have."

Oh. Damien paused. He walked very slowly back, thinking about it. Then slowly raised a hand before cramming it back against his body.

"It's fine. Take whatever you need. For you, and everybody else. I'm sorry there isn't more in there."

"Thank you. That will be useful."

Damien's eyes strayed past Andrew's feet, back to Lillian. It was awful, watching her embrace helplessness like that. The wrong kind of nostalgic. Aetherius still had to carry her into town and get her into a state where it would be okay for her to log off. The moment she did, she'd be alone. A difficult burden, to put it lightly, given the state of their relationship. But of all the people there, Andrew was still the one who knew her best. That much had been made clear. Damien struggled but managed to raise his head, only to find Andrew staring at the ground as well.

"Andrew?"

Andrew's head jerked upward at his name, and Damien saw someone who felt exactly the same way he did. They'd succeeded, and yet he looked completely defeated. More hopeless than when Damien had cornered him, by stealing the bag he'd now returned with all its new contents attached. It was hard, looking into the eyes of someone unhappier than he was. His own pain was worth less, knowing that Andrew had suffered more and would suffer further still before sleep took him. But Damien didn't look away. He owed him that much, after what he'd done. If Andrew hadn't been there to end this when he had, Lillian's condition would be worse. She'd have been left alone, immediately after having been killed by the ability that had put her in this state.

Andrew was staring back. Also refusing to look away. Damien's face contorted, staving off embarrassment and tears, as he made his last request of the man who surely needed no more burdens.

"Please look after Lillian. She needs you."

Andrew still stared. He was much better at hiding how he felt than Damien. He was still not good enough to completely conceal his misery. Damien had seen him work, and knew this: Andrew possessed an unnerving intellect. Damien was glad of it. He was glad that this man, who he'd once hated, was the one who would protect Lillian now. And in the journey to come, where Damien would not follow.

Out of the blue, Andrew smiled at him. It was broken, but it was a smile nonetheless. Damien immediately averted his gaze back to the floor. How could he even pretend? How could he pretend he was happy? The sheer gall, the audacity—

Andrew's hand fell on his shoulder and squeezed it.

"Of course I will. Go to bed, you've earned it. Make sure you talk to her tomorrow, she'll be happy to hear from you."

Another squeeze. Then he turned, ushered Lillian to her feet, and led her away. Damien remained where he stood until their uneven footsteps had faded into the dark. He waited longer still, as long as he could. When he finally thought himself alone he dropped to his knees and held his head in his hands, unprovoked by nightmares or poorly conceived abilities. His worst enemy had become someone he was relying on in one night. After Damien had destroyed everything he'd worked for to claim it for himself, Andrew had shown him kindness.

It was the greatest humiliation he'd ever suffered.

11

THE INNER CIRCLE

Damien did not wake up early. He did not even manage to wake up in the morning. He pulled off the bedcovers and was upright just before 1pm. The rigorous schedule he'd set for himself with the H4ckz0r alarms had gone down the toilet, following first his death at Archimonde's hands and now this early-morning breakout exercise. But he was officially past the wall. He hadn't come all this way to mope about. He had to follow through.

He had some other matters to attend to first. Food was a high priority. He made his way to the kitchen and found a hand-written note on the table:

Gone to work, wish me luck! Love you, should be back around 6pm. Mom (obviously) x

She'd really done it. Damien hoped she'd be alright. He couldn't imagine rushing back to his studies if his heart had been replaced with a piece of machinery. He'd have scrounged every second of medical leave available. She had to really like her job. Damien was starting not to enjoy his own job as much as he had previously. The gameplay was fine and he was good at it, so far as he could tell. No, the main problem Damien had with his job was much the same as that experienced by practitioners of every other vocation: the irritation of people he was forced to endure while doing it.

Then again, he wasn't doing an outstanding job of being a streamer at the moment. The whole weekend had passed him by and the only footage he'd posted was his foray in the Frozen Forest on Saturday afternoon. Even that had been interrupted when Aetherius had rocked up. Andrew.

Man, it was weird trying to reconcile how he'd felt about Andrew before and now. It was conceptually easier to divide him into Aetherius and Andrew, like a pair of good and evil twins. The whole pushing-Damien-naked-into-a-deep-dark-pit thing was definitely a mark against him. Might not have been quite such an Aetherius move, if Damien hadn't told him of Cassandra's dire situation about a minute before the 'boost'. And let's not forget the hospital prank Andrew/Aetherius pulled on Lillian. You know, the tasteful one? Where he'd shown up at her hospital pretending to be dead? Classic Aetherius, even offline. That had resulted in her being strapped into a guardian wristband for a couple of weeks. After what happened yesterday, Damien could see why.

Andrew had clearly seen her go through this before, considering how he'd jumped in without a second thought to comfort and protect her. In that order. It had been more terrifying than Damien could possibly have imagined. Lillian seemed so strong. He'd always thought the worst her symptoms could get were the bursts of anger, which he'd experienced personally on several occasions. Or panic attacks, one of which he'd admittedly...inflicted on her himself. Classic Aetherius. Ouch. That was a bit too close for comfort.

Funny, how Lillian had become the cause they united behind. Seeing as they both could have treated her better. Although if Lillian had been the pull factor, Archimonde was definitely the push factor. Damien definitely needed to contact Lillian today and find out how she was holding up. He wondered if she'd made it to work. He hoped not, for the same reasons as he was skeptical about his mom wading back into the fray. The last thing Lillian needed was a long day at work. There was someone else he needed to talk to as well. Damien might not have been a beta-tester anymore but there was a game element that desperately needed tweaking.

Damien gathered up his late breakfast and moved into his bedroom to browse while he ate. At least that was one habit he was keeping up with. It was generally stacked with a slightly worse habit: miring himself in a crushing sense of disappointment with the human race. Conveniently localized on his profile page. The complaints about his lack of content had peaked at 9pm yesterday, when he was in the middle of preparations to breach the wall which was keeping the equally disappointing human race of Saga Online locked out of mid-game content.

He considered interacting with them. Nah. Not today. He turned instead to the Council of Nine page, hoping for a more welcome reception. Only to find that they, too, were concerned with the content he was not providing. They were nicer about it, but they were all still asking, begging, demanding or, worst of all, predicting content. There wasn't much he could do for them in that regard right now. The situation had definitely changed in his favor, but despite having got past the wall he was not in a great position to be throwing out livestreams. Archimonde hunting him down was far worse than any price on his head.

As for the footage of them breaking through the gate, that had been marred by Lillian's experience with Archimonde. Damien wouldn't dream of showing that to anyone. Maybe he could cut it. He'd talk to Lillian first and make sure his cut was okay with her. In his own case, he'd made it clear he didn't want the footage involving both Magnitude and Archimonde beating him shared, yet she'd gone ahead and shared portions of it with other people anyway. It had turned out well, in the end. Now their roles were more or less reversed. This was not the time to pressure her about that.

So no, the cultists...occultists...predicting content would go wanting. But there was something else he could share, just for them, that would get them excited: the list of level 40 traits. Pop it into one of the discussion groups and help them plan out their build. He pulled it all off the headset, including the trait neither he nor Archimonde had taken, and planted it into his own discussion board. Entitled:

DarkLord Daemien's Tasty Tidbits

There. That should fit the profile of this target audience, judging by what he'd seen. He'd done a thing. A little thing, but it was positive at least. Food finished, Damien went into his recorded footage and found the worst part of it, saving it as a separate five-second clip. He needed to share it with Kevin. They were going to have a serious chat. He needed to get into the game and pursue Bartholomew's quest in earnest. He could see if Lillian or Kevin were online already and have a chat with each of them, or leave them messages for later.

He was back in Arcadia. In the Outer Ring. In the end, there was only one way he could conceive of making himself completely safe from Archimonde. He'd resummoned Noigel and flown him to an otherwise inaccessible ledge. Demon Gated. Then logged off standing on it. Better than Archimonde finding where he'd logged out and eating him immediately upon login. At least this way, Damien had guaranteed himself a little advance warning before horrible things started happening.

After logging back in, he peered over the edge and looked around. Nothing out of the ordinary, besides the geography. Noigel did a surveillance lap while Damien took in the scenery of the new world. He hadn't seen it in the daytime before. It was different. He'd never experienced anything like it. He'd made it past the rocky crust and had reached the lush interior. It was a virgin, untouched land.

Har. Har har. Heharhar. Har.

But, seriously, it had almost never ever been played on. All the creatures were there. No one had done any of the quests for the first time yet. Damien was in unchartered territory. He was waaaay ahead of the curve on this one. This was exciting.

Noigel gave him the all clear and Damien stopped scanning the horizon in order to check his location. The quest marker led all the way out of the zone he was in, trailing into the unknown depths of the Inner Circle. He'd have to get closer before he had a sense of the distance. Whatever it was, Damien would have to make it work to his advantage.

But first, a word with our sponsor. He scrolled through his friends list and found Kevin's name. He was online, Lillian was not. While the call went through, he went into his library and got the footage ready. It took Kevin a little while to answer. When he did, it took Damien off guard.

"Hello there, Damien. Long time no speak! How's everything?"

That was a surprise. He'd thought Kevin would be laying into him, after the lack of content over the weekend. Instead, he seemed very cheerful.

"Not good, Kevin. There's a game issue I wanted to bring up with you, something quite serious."

"Don't worry about it Damien, I'm well aware. It's alright! Difficult times for everyone at the moment. As long as you keep your head down now while the big players are moving, you'll come out pretty well on top. That player-killing niche I found will serve you well until things get moving again."

Oh dear. Damien reconsidered showing Kevin the footage for a moment, but decided it was more important to get this issue seen to than it was to avoid falling out with his PR guy. What had happened to Lillian was unacceptable.

"Sending you a brief clip, there's an ability used here which gives a player a very bad reaction. I'd like you to get it reviewed as soon as possible."

"Still beta-testing for us, even after you've moved well beyond! That's very noble of you, Damien. Honestly though, other people will be on the lookout for that stuff and the game's already in good shape, I'd rather you were...concentrating..."

He'd started watching the footage. Damien had cut it as short as he could, a brief clip of Archimonde using his enhanced Possession on Lillian. It started when he said the words and ended just over four seconds later, when Lillian had driven her avatar's head into the ground for the first time. Her wail started near the end, at just the moment her sword had stopped clattering on the ground. It was enough, Damien felt, to convey the depth of his concern.

Kevin was silent. He was probably watching it over a few times, absorbing all the information. Damien piped up.

"We ran into that yesterday, an ability used by a thing called Archimonde. It's not very nice all round, but I'm mainly concerned with the ability. It's an advanced Possession I had access to at level 40 with a trait. I'm sure what it—"

"Have I understood this correctly? Was this footage taken from your viewpoint? If so, what are you doing consorting with Lillian while she tries to get past the wall? I thought we talked about this, Damien, I thought I made you understand that this isn't the best thing you can be doing right now!"

"I'm not here to talk to you about viewer counts, subscription niches and channel mechanics, Kevin. I'm here to tell you about this very specific ability, which has obviously been implemented completely wrong. Look at Lillian again, please. Is that what the good people in Mobius Enterprises were aiming for when they configured this ability? I doubt it. Focus on that."

Kevin was getting flustered. The more flustered he became, the angrier Damien got.

"Why, Damien, why oh why, are you involving yourself in the attacks on the wall? Magnitude has already been putting out rewards on players attacking his wall, all of Rising Tide has gone under because of it! That's not something for you to be—"

"Kevin, listen to the *soothing* sound of my voice. Really listen to it. This conversation isn't about my streaming career, it's about what happened to Lillian. It's about this ability, which seems like it needs *serious* tweaking before it can be inflicted on living, breathing human beings. If this happened when I was a beta-tester, I'd be slamming the emergency buttons. I'd be leaving you nonstop messages demanding your immediate attention. It looks about as bad as having the headset ripped off while you're still playing. I'm not here to discuss my gameplay choices, I'm here to make sure this gets fixed."

Kevin was scoffing at him over the chat. Had Damien stuttered? Was the focus of his message somehow unclear? It was hard to say. But Kevin was utterly fixated on the overall ramifications of Damien's footage, rather than the specific case his attention was being drawn to.

"Damien, I've done everything I can to dissuade you from this course of action. I'd be remiss not to question your logic in pushing these barriers. So far as content goes, late-game issues like this are exactly what I'm trying to prevent you from running into while we deal with concerns that manifest at a higher level than our beta program covered. It's very complicated, and there's—"

"Kevin—"

"—no guarantee that we'll be able—"

"Keeeevin?"

"—to prevent all players who push ahead from experiencing—"

"KEVIN! I don't care! Fix it! Or talk to whoever needs to fix it. The rest is irrelevant. I don't care about everything else that's going on, I just need you to tell me someone will deal with what happened to my good friend yesterday so it doesn't happen to anyone else. That's all."

"I'll talk with the developers and have them patch it. Can we please discuss your streaming channel as well? I developed a good plan for you, keeping you out of danger while playing to your strengths, and it's still not too late for you to go back to that plan. Could you please return to building your channel from a place of stability, rather than trying to plow ahead?"

"No can do. We broke through the wall yesterday. As we speak, I stand at the edge of the Inner Circle."

Damien was more than a little proud of his achievement. Kevin stayed silent for a while. He sounded a little more enthusiastic when he began speaking again, about ten seconds later.

"You broke through the wall?"

"Yup."

"Wow, I didn't think that could be done! Great job. How many of you?"

"Like ten of us, altogether."

"With such a small group. Extraordinary. Well, congratulations, I guess you proved me wrong. What's your agenda now? If you got past the wall I'm assuming you have some sort of goal in mind?"

"Yeah, I'm continuing with the occultist questline. Bartholomew gave me a map point, I'm heading for it now. Should be good for ratings, if I can be the first to show everyone what the late-game occultists look like. Sorry for not sharing my plan, I don't think it would've gone down with you very well before I managed to get past the wall."

"Excellent! No, no need to apologize, I completely understand. You should definitely go and do that. I've got to get back to work now, but thanks for sharing your progress. Stay in touch!"

He hung up. Okay. That had turned around oddly quickly. Kevin's praise, coupled with his acceptance of Damien's plan, only enforced that getting past the wall had been a remarkable achievement. One that Damien was now completely free to capitalize on.

He Demon Gated to the floor and summoned two hell hounds and three more imps. Then started his journey to the center of Arcadia, following the marker Bartholomew had put on his map.

The scenery here was more eclectic than that in the vanilla Human Realm. This particular area was dotted with stone pillars, just like the one Damien had taken refuge on before he logged out. They were towering formations that narrowed at their center and expanded again, forming a ceiling with gaps that were bursting with vines and growths. It was a nice place to be an occultist. While there was not an abundance of players to spot him, Damien was nevertheless much happier out of direct sunlight. He attacked targets of opportunity on the way, such as wild animals that had strayed too far from their herds, and replenished his Soul Summon Limit as he went.

The most abundant enemy in this instance were weird white goats, called 'Poznan'. They were higher level than him, spanning anywhere from level 45 to 50, but proved easy targets when isolated. They started off hyperaggressive, but immediately fled when their health dropped to less than 50%. Damien had one on the run and thought it cornered, his minions encircling it and pinning it against a stone column. To his amazement it ascended the column as if it were flat ground, running around it in circles as it continued to climb. Fortunately, he was equipped to deal with this evasive maneuver. He sent the imps up to intercept it, where they latched onto its horns and dragged it over the edge. The impact damage was severe, the hounds were quick to capitalize and Damien obtained a nearly effortless 2 souls. Along with a decent chunk of experience on top! Very nice.

Damien hadn't killed any players directly during the attack on the wall, but his minions had gotten involved and granted him some assists. He was more than three-quarters of the way to level 43. He could've stuck around to get to the next level, but decided instead to continue hitting targets of opportunity and raising his Soul Summon Limit on his way to the objective.

He reached the end of the stone pillar plateaus and grudgingly stepped out into the light, his minion entourage moving beside him at full pace. He checked his map. An on-screen message informed him he'd left the 'Hourglass Plateau' and was now entering the 'Inner Circle'. The larger section of which was called the 'Olympian Plains'.

Creatures here were even higher level and very strange indeed, though some were familiar. He watched a flock of ivory-white birds gliding over the mountains, getting bigger as they came closer, until Damien realized it was not a flock, but a pack. Pegasai. Pegasuses. Pegases? In Damien's limited experience, there'd never been enough of them together to warrant knowing the plural form. It was certainly a sight to behold.

He watched as they circled round, maintaining their 'V' formation, before using a flat grassy ridge on a mountaintop as their landing runway. Maybe this was where Magnitude had sourced Aetherius's ill-fated flying mount before Damien beheaded it, back in the competition days. A theory that made Damien acutely aware how little he actually knew.

Damien could've used a Pegasus himself. He'd already gone two and a half hours on foot with his mind working nonstop, striving to avoid any unfamiliar mobs which came between himself and his priority quest. The further he went, the less comfortable he became. The Inner Circle did not follow established gaming patterns. Until now it had proceeded much like every other: each new territory you came to brought new monsters, and their levels increased according to how far along you were in the game. Not so here.

Mud-crabs coated in slurry, waiting to attack nearby trespassers on the river-shore. Dropbears holding completely still, waiting to strike unwary passersby from the trees. Transparent Jellybirds floating almost imperceptibly above the plains, waiting for someone to move within their translucent tentacles so they could go for the kill. They were all dangerous, but most of them were within Damien's level-detection range and his hounds at least let him know there was danger nearby, even if it took triggering the enemies' attacks in order to understand their nature.

Those were ambush predators, though. Enemies who struck from the shadows and used surprise to their advantage. Damien understood this strategy, and only suffered one encounter with each before he knew their methods. Other creatures were more flamboyant. A little easier to avoid, but many times more deadly if they decided to focus on you. Sharpies: birds of prey acting in tandem clouds that swarmed and shredded prey in seconds, leaving nothing but bones behind. Rhinoceroses: solitary, grumpy, armored herbivores with foul tempers and worse eyesight. Damien came a little too close while discerning their ocular range and discovered they were also extremely territorial.

Worst of all was the uncompromising, undisputed apex predator of that region. This one was a unique elite enemy, which offered some comfort. One of these existing was already too many. It was called Scolopendra-Millicornu. A flying segmented bug the length of a jumbo glider, hovering high in the glare of the sun to keep prey blind to its presence while it swooped in. Damien only escaped because he noticed the shadow approaching his position on the ground and Demon Gated.

Like Archimonde, its level was unknown. In relative terms it seemed more dangerous than Archimonde, which was quite a shock. Fortunately, this ugly thing was a lot less focused on Damien's destruction than the ugly thing he'd tangled with yesterday. It went after him for a little while, abandoning the sky to skitter after him as Damien fled at full pace, then settled for the less nimble and much more fulsome meal Damien led it to: a rhinoceros that had failed to foresee Damien using it as bait. Damien watched it flying away, carrying its meal as though it were no heavier than a kitten, and gulped. This place had been intriguing for a while, but that thing was bang out of order.

It was just as well he hadn't stayed behind to level up on the goats. There were plenty of high-level targets that wanted him dead all along his route. Bit by bit, he scraped his way through lower-level mobs and past high-level mobs until he reached level 43. Picking his engagements carefully was crucial. One wrong move would invite death. He'd rather take it slow and get where he was going alive than have to respawn where he'd died twenty-four hours later without any minions to his name.

He'd traveled for hours before he started to get close to his objective. The quest marker indicated the Dark Tower should already be in sight. He looked up and saw a huge construction, piercing the clouds. Still a long way out. The Inner Circle was massive. Damien crested a final ridge and took it in. This had to be it. The arrow was pointing straight toward it, and it definitely looked the part.

Sticking out of the ground, set into a circular basin full of red flowers, was the tower. It was the only structure Damien had seen during his travels, and it was a doozy. A huge cylinder with no gaps, as if the whole structure had been chiseled out of a single piece of rock. Damien observed the height of it and decided that was exactly the aesthetic it was intended to have, if the rock had been the size of a mountain.

That wasn't the only reason it was strange. There were no windows. It looked completely alien. More like a monolith than something made by men. Flocks of Sharpies flitted around it, black clouds that split across the tower and merged again on the other side. The only evidence it was a building rather than a bizarre topographical feature was a narrow doorway facing exactly south. Damien turned his eyes back to the earth and immediately spotted Archimonde. It was hard to miss. Its base structures were arrayed around the tower, all far more grandiose than Damien's own.

There was a Tier III Demon Forge adorned with the demonic equivalent of bells and whistles: spikes and skulls. The Demon Forge's opening, into which resources and fuel were fed, had become a demonic mouth, and the fire within made the eyes set above it smoke and glow. There was a Tier III Gateway, too, which had been stylized with a river of blood that oozed from the floating rings of stone spheres, then flowed down the steps to pool into the earth. There was one structure that was easy to recognize, since it was no different from Damien's own: the Soul Well. It might not have been the most imposing, but it did pose the biggest problem. The Dark Tower was encircled by demons divided between the Soul Well and its master.

Most of them were the usual: succubi, imps, hounds, a much more easily distinguishable incubus. They were mainly concentrated around the doorway, but were looking out in every direction. The wraith was absent, a poor choice in daylight, but there was something else in its place that Damien did not recognize.

It was a huge, rotund, blob-like creature. About the same size as the incubus. It was working the Demon Forge with its back turned to Damien, so it was hard to see more from that range, but given the company it was keeping it had to be another of Archimonde's minions. Those that were not on guard were hard at work, constructing trenches and walls around the Dark Tower in increasingly wide circles.

Damn. It was only to be expected. Archimonde had probably completed the orcish equivalent of this quest already, given its higher level. Now Archimonde was doing its best to ensure Damien could not do the same. With Archimonde there, his odds of making it through the door were nearly zero.

The Sharpies alone made descending into the basin a dangerous prospect, but they paled in comparison to the threat Archimonde represented. Unfortunately, the Sharpies were leaving Archimonde well alone. The latter's Corruption trait paired with Imp-losion probably made dealing with them all but effortless. Another reminder of how Damien's character-build choices were not working out.

Archimonde would have to log off at some point. Damien had made it this far, he wasn't turning back now. It was time to build his first Gateway away from home. He'd have to find somewhere safe for it. He struck out west, away from the path he'd taken, and tuned into his "clean toilet cubicle" radar. It was fifteen minutes before he got a *ping*, but it was a good *ping*. His imps hollowed the cave out a bit further to procure the resources required for building. With fourteen imps, including the Forbidden Knowledge-buffed Noigel, and a succubus to spur them on, it was refreshingly quick work. As it was completed, he received a notification:

'Downward Spiral' will be replaced with 'Fields of Eternity'. Confirm. (Y/N)

At least if he died now, he could come back close to his objective. He covered up the only entrance with brush, then Damien distanced himself from it as much as possible. Staying too close would defeat the whole purpose of having it. He traveled around the ridge to a point with cover, overlooking the door. Possessed an imp. Flew it to the top of the ridge to keep watch. And settled in for a long wait.

At 17:25, Lillian dragged herself across the threshold of her home, shut the door behind her and fell back onto it, closing her eyes. That had not been a pleasant day. She'd barely slept. She was glad she hadn't missed work, but the looks of concern and disappointment her colleagues shared when they thought she wasn't aware hurt almost as much. How embarrassing.

She'd thought that was all behind her. Yet here she was again. The endless circle, coming back for another loop. Kicking her when she was down, and when she least expected it.

The day wasn't even finished yet. The most stressful part was still to come. Her memory of last night was hazy, after...after that ability she'd been subjected to. But she knew Andrew had stayed with her until she was ready to log off. The last person she wanted to rely on. If it had come to that, it went without saying she'd made a spectacle of herself.

Now she had to go back into a group who'd seen her at her lowest. A group that was already unstable before she'd debased herself in front of them. To lead them. She'd spent the whole day doing a lackluster job being directed in her work team, now she could round things off by doing an appalling job of directing her game team. Assuming they'd even consent to following her, after the dis—

This isn't helping. You're thinking yourself into a hole. Focus.

She pushed herself off the door, leaving her satchel where she'd dropped it, and lurched into the kitchen. Food processor was prepped. She needed fuel, something fast and simple. Carbs. Pasta? Pasta.

She limped over to the bathroom, ignoring the ding of the food processor as she washed and did laundry. Once finished, she grabbed a fork and ate straight out of the processor as she turned her attention to what still needed to be done that day. They were in a town. There might be members of the Carlisle-Elite there. She hoped everyone who'd been playing that day while others were at work had remained on guard.

No point wasting time. Lillian headed to her room, got out of her work clothes and logged into the game.

She opened her eyes on the timber ceiling of the town's inn and immediately sat up. She was not alone. Andrew was sitting at a table in the center, arranging items into piles. He heard the *chink* of her armored boots hitting the floor and turned, his face lighting up for an instant and then relaxing again.

"Welcome back. How are you holding up?"

Lillian ignored him and moved to stand over him, analyzing the items on the table. There were nine separate piles, arranged in a circle around Damien's Bag of Holding. So, the two of them had managed to make good on the deal she'd authored without adult supervision. The age of miracles is upon us. Then she thought about it a little harder and realized Andrew couldn't have attached the Bag of Holding to his own inventory yet. Which could only mean one thing.

"I'm glad to see Damien handed over the bag without trouble. Why are you ransacking his inventory?"

"It's not like that. He told me to take whatever we needed, so I've been organizing it all day. I crafted gunpowder for Trinytea, divvied out potions for everyone and he even had some gear that might help our party. As party leader, how it's distributed is up to you, but I've done my best."

So Andrew was lying. He must have thought she was completely fried, to believe he could get away with such an outrageous fib. Lillian could only imagine how upset Damien would be when he found out Andrew had emptied his inventory. He'd probably blame her for this, even though it was solely on the two of them. Damien for being a cretin, Andrew for being himself. She couldn't handle this right now.

"I'm checking in on everyone. I've taken a screenshot of everything on the table. I'll ask Damien if we can use it. Don't take anything else out of that bag."

"He really di—"

"Don't. Take. Anything. Else. Out of that bag."

"Okay."

Satisfied, she went into her menu page and checked her messages. There were quite a few. One from Aetherius, just after she'd logged off. One from Damien less than an hour ago. Then several from the party chat at varying intervals. She checked them in alphabetical order.

Aetherius: If you need to talk to someone, please call me. I hope you get to work tomorrow. I'll be waiting in the inn when you come back online.

Urrgh. What, Andrew thought he could be a little nice after everything that had happened between them and she'd fall back into his arms? Probably because she'd shown signs of vulnerability. Creep.

Daemien: I've made it to my objective, but Archimonde is standing in front of it. I'm waiting for it to leave. I gave Andrew the Bag of Holding and told him to take anything your party needs. You were right, we really needed him yesterday. Thank you for making sure he came with us. I hope you're ok. Please ring me up if you want to talk.

Urrrrrrrrrrgh. One bad episode. Just one bad episode was all it took for these unmanageable, self-centered, juvenile delinquents to shower her with false sympathy. If having a breakdown was what it took for them to play at being kind, she'd rather they remained as they were. At least they were also pretending to be kind to each other. That was one less thing she had to worry about fixing today.

She turned her attention to the party chat and found that all the messages within were from Hammertime. They were much less emotional and far more productive than those from the other two. Just the way she liked it.

Hammertime: The town is called Glastonbury. The quest trail ended when we arrived. I'm setting out with my guildmates to explore the area and find the source of the quest. Check it in your HUD when you can. Lillian, yesterday was nasty, and you came off worse than any of us. I understand if you can't make it today.

Hammertime: Glastonbury has its own militia. It's not Empire, but it basically runs on Empire rules. The faction is called Knights Templar. The Carlisle-Elite have an embedded base here and there are lots of them around. We're guessing this is where they quest from, with Magnitude's wall as their Portal Stone rally point. They can't engage us in town without being destroyed in retaliation by the peacekeepers, but we're being watched.

Hammertime: I think we found it. There's a lake covered in mist to the north. We asked the guards about it and got directions to a shrine, in an abandoned church. Took a screenshot of the message etched into the stone.

Hammertime:
Over the misty sea lies Avalon, wheryn
The ladies live who knowe al the magic yn the world,

To unravel their mystery and bryng back the age of kyngs,
A set of knightly challenges must be upheld.

The first, the easiest, lies yn playn sight,
Goon water's edge as day turns slowe to nyght,
Ther ye shal fynd passage o'er the byam,
'Till fall of dark fades lofty quest to dream.

Hammertime: So we need to be next to the water before sunset. We're meeting back at the inn at 6pm. Sunset is at 8pm. Travel to the edge of the water should take half an hour from here.

At least Hammertime had proven himself reliable. Lillian decided Damien merited a message, despite the toll getting him this far had exacted on her.

Lillian: Just got back from work. All fine. Thank you for letting us use your supplies, Andrew is dividing them among the party. I'll keep track of what we use. If you were recording yesterday, please don't post anything online. We don't need to draw any more attention to ourselves than we already have.

The answer came almost immediately.

Daemien: I won't send anything from yesterday. Would you like me to send you the footage though, so you can see what you missed? If you see the footage externally, you might be better prepared for next time. The modified Possession Archimonde used on you wasn't even the worst ability it had. It has something like an ultimate, called Dark Omen. Big black hole thing.

What she missed? That was one way of putting it. His offer of sharing the footage was even less tactful than his euphemistic interpretation of her mental state. Besides which, whatever Dark Omen was, Damien was wrong. Archimonde's modified Possession was definitely the worst ability it had. Besides which, she'd already seen the footage, not that she wanted a long conversation about it.

Lillian: No, I do not wish to see myself bawling on the ground. Good luck with your quest, hope you find your way around Archimonde.

At least Damien was on his way. It was Andrew's turn to follow suit. Lillian reapproached the table and put on her best matter-of-fact voice.

"Thanks for the items. They're not necessary, but they'll be helpful. The rest of the party will be here shortly. You need to be gone by then."

"Did Damien confirm we can use his inventory? We have a difficult task ahead of us, we'll need all the help we can get."

Lillian stared at him, waiting for his nerve to break and for him to look at her. Instead, after a long silence, his hand went back into the bag.

"I'll take that as a yes."

"The inventory? Sure. You coming with us? No chance. We got you past the wall, as agreed. You got your bag back, as agreed. This is the part where you leave."

"Is it because you don't want me to know what you're up to? It's not complicated. You're on the Excalibur quest."

He turned his head just in time to catch her surprise. Then nodded before returning his attention to the bag.

"I was a level 40 guild leader in the Round Table Council long before you and Hammertime. You wouldn't ally with him for funzies. If you needed me to get past the wall, you'll definitely need my help on a legendary quest."

Lillian drew her sword.

"I'm sorry, you seem to have mistaken me for someone else. Get out of my room."

Andrew didn't even look up.

"After what happened yesterday? I think not. With Hammertime in your party, Carlisle-Elite all around us and Archimonde who knows where, you need someone to watch your back."

Lillian set the edge of her blade against the back of Andrew's neck. That did make him sit up.

"I could've done with that when you pulled the "prank" on me in the hospital. You know what I saw yesterday, and you knew what you were doing. We're long past the point where I'd rely on you to watch my back. If you don't leave, I'll send you."

Andrew bowed his head, exposing the back of his head

further, and sighed. He interlocked his fingers in his lap and turned to face her. Finally. He kept his neck tilted open and gave her his undivided attention.

"You'll have to kill me then. Honestly, I don't have much to lose: I've already set my Portal Stone to this inn. At least this way we'll both know I tried my best. If things go badly, I'll make sure I'm available if you need my help later. I wasn't there for you then, but I am now. You might as well make the most of me."

Lillian took her sword in both hands and drew it back behind her head. Andrew didn't move an inch, save for his eyes, which he closed. Lillian held her position. This didn't feel right. This didn't feel right at all. It was only when Andrew opened one eye, saw he was still about to die, then closed it again, that Lillian knew the moment had passed.

As Andrew himself had just said, she may as well make the most of him. She twisted the blade and slapped the flat of it against his open neck. The high-pitched yelp he made went some way to making her feel better, which was sorely needed.

"One wrong move. If you put a single toe out of line, it's over."

Andrew's lips strained, trying and failing not to make him look too cheerful.

"I'll be on my best behavior."

Lillian grabbed a chair from under the table and carried it to the farthest corner of the room, then sat down to wait for everyone else to arrive. The first of them started logging in some ten minutes later. Lillian got a few searching looks, reminiscent of those she'd received in hospital earlier that day. She stared them down until they averted their gazes. Their gazes mostly averted to Andrew, who kept his eyes cast down but responded by pushing their care packages across the table to them. When Trinytea arrived, her eyes nearly fell out of her head at the sight of him. She looked to Lillian to complain, thought better of it and redirected her anger back at Andrew, who was quick to respond: her care package was the largest of all of them.

It included three health potions, a full sack of gunpowder, a leather satchel (which judging from the default name, Andrew had personally crafted out of Damien's materials) and a Swift Hood with 50 agility. Andrew had displayed utter submission to the rest of them, but Trinytea's items were paired with his very best meaningful stare.

Lillian was not in the mood for stirring up any more old conflicts, but this she did approve of. Trinytea had fallen out with the two of them while still in Rising Tide, way back when, following an ill-fated attempt to ninja-loot a bow she couldn't effectively use from the recently deceased Legolias. She'd followed up this absurd demand with a load of guff about Aetherius surreptitiously taking the potions for himself, when he'd allocated them to guild storage. Lillian had taken charge of the situation by giving Trinytea a sound beating and kicking her out of the guild. Aetherius had taken offense, since he was both party and guild leader at the time, declaring that Lillian had undermined him.

The argument Trinytea precipitated between them had heralded the beginning of the end of their relationship. Half the people here had been present when Trinytea's career with Rising Tide was cut short. The rest of them knew about it second hand. All of them were staring at her. It was almost worth having Trinytea here, to watch Aetherius make her squirm.

Trinytea took the hood in both hands, but didn't equip it.

"I don't deserve this. I did nearly nothing yesterday, after we got through the gate. The gunpowder and potions are more than enough. Legolias, is this any good for you?"

Legolias looked to Lillian, who remained completely impassive. She was staying well clear of this one. He gave Trinytea a single curt nod and she handed it over. Hammertime had arrived while this exchange was going on. He elbowed Lillian in the shoulder, gently, then lowered his head to her ear as Aetherius kept giving out supplies.

"I had to work on that for a long time. She was a handful, but not completely irredeemable."

"Too little, too late. I'm not big on second chances."

"Is that so? Why might I have trouble believing that?"

Lillian's gaze tracked back to Aetherius, looking away as soon as he glanced in her direction. Hammertime lowered his voice even further.

"He shouldn't be here. I didn't even like him coming with us to get through the wall. That might have gone well enough, but coming with us on the Excalibur quest? He's a liability."

"I know that better than anyone. I can handle him. In case you don't remember, I'm the one who dealt with him when he got out of hand last time."

"Yet now he's back again, like a tumor. There isn't a single good reason for him to be here. You're the party leader, it's your responsibility to get rid of him. His presence puts the entire party at ri—"

Lillian smiled sweetly. Before Hammertime could finish, she'd grabbed him by the scruff of his breastplate and led him outside. She turned to close the door and caught Andrew looking after them, his face a perfect blend of concern, amusement and nostalgic reminiscence. Half a second later his face was carefully blank, and he'd gone back to distributing items. Lillian closed the door and turned on her ally, who'd forcefully reminded her that they were also long-term rivals.

"Look. I'm glad you came with us. There's no way we'd have got here without you and you did a great job today, sourcing out the information for the quest. But I'm not here for your advice. If you keep on this way, thinking you can criticize how I run things in front of my team, I'll knock your block off."

Hammertime, as if he hadn't heard a word Lillian just said, went into his menu. A few clicks later his helmet faded away, making his block available for inspection. She'd toggled off her helmet visibility and left it that way for a long time, but Hammertime had never entertained that option, so far as she knew. Lillian had never seen him without a helmet before. He was ruggedly handsome. Square-chinned, deep brown eyes paired with dark brown hair, a single lock of which hung preposterously down one side of his face. He was positively dreamy.

Definitely a full-on editing job. But Hammertime hadn't removed his helmet to show off his avatar.

"I made those comments about the manner of your leadership as an aside, not for anyone else's ears as you've implied, and I did so in a cordial, discreet fashion. Your escalation and distortion of events is unnecessary and unwarranted. And for the record, this is our team. It's your project, which I've joined, but half of these players are my charges."

He paused to see if Lillian had any complaints she felt like voicing so far. She was angrier than when she'd started this conversation and had plenty of complaints, but none she could voice at that precise moment without shouting. Hammertime had saved his most pointed criticism for last.

"I gave you the benefit of the doubt yesterday, when you threatened Trinytea and almost finished this excursion before it started. Tensions were high enough already. But know this. If you treat *my* people like that again – the same way you're treating me now, trying to stamp your authority over me by force – we'll fall out. That won't help anyone except Magnitude."

Hammertime was annoyingly calm. That was why he'd toggled off the helmet. So Lillian could see every inch of how calm he was. He was waiting, patiently, for her reply. Lillian narrowed her eyes and tried, unsuccessfully, to match his temperament.

"If anyone causes any problems, like Trinytea did yesterday when she almost collapsed the party, I won't come to you for a second opinion. I'll deal with the problem first and you can complain about it afterwards. I'll treat your players exactly the same as I treat my own."

"Acceptable. I'm much happier to retain a backseat role, but if you demonstrate weakness or poor judgment it will be my duty to take over from you for the benefit of everyone here. Especially you. However, I don't count Aetherius as one of our players. Our players come first. If you don't deal with him when the time comes – when, not if – I will."

He ducked through the door ahead of her, his helmet appearing back on his head with a few practiced clicks. Aetherius was waiting with his allotment of resources. Lillian pulled the door to behind Hammertime, remaining in the relative privacy of the corridor as she inhaled deeply through her nose.

To think that just a short while ago she'd been raving internally about Andrew and Damien's juvenile conduct. Hammertime was insufferably mature.

12

PIGGY IN THE MIDDLE

Damien was bored. Not just bored, but angry bored. Archimonde had remained parked in front of his objective for almost two hours, without so much as a bathroom break. It appeared to be watching videos, judging by the hand movements it made every few minutes. Chilling out and preventing Damien from progressing simultaneously.

He'd had lots of time to think about what Archimonde was doing, and why. If Archimonde had wanted to prevent him from completing the Dark Tower, it would've made more sense to wait inside and gank him. At the very least, it wouldn't have required building the entire base outside, directly on top of Damien's objective. This seemed designed to stop Damien from entering altogether.

Damien had only got through yesterday morning, but all Archimonde's structures were already Tier III. The construction happening was all with a view to fortifying the position. There hadn't been enough time to upgrade the structures from scratch since yesterday, so the base had already been here before they'd broken through Magnitude's wall.

If Damien's theory was correct, this meant the Dark Tower was instanced: one of the special dungeons that split reality when you entered, preventing anyone not in your party from following after you. If that wasn't the case, Archimonde could set its base up *inside* the Dark Tower rather than outside of it. So all Damien had to do was get into the tower and he'd be clear. He just couldn't figure out any way of doing it.

He'd be dodging Chaotic Bolts for almost the entirety of his descent to the tower. He wouldn't have the option of dodging Corruption. He could sneak some of the way, but that would mean leaving his minions behind, and eventually Archimonde's hell hounds would detect him. If they got him without minion support and Archimonde started attacking him at the same time, he'd be dead.

If he tried to drink one of his three health potions to counteract the damage of Corruption, his attention on the incoming bolts would be reduced. Paired with the Corruption that brought on the drinking of the potion in the first place, he'd be dead. If he got snared by the Circle of Hell, he'd be hit by a Chaotic Bolt in the five seconds following and he'd be dead. If he managed to avoid the Circle of Hell by jumping into the air, Archimonde could hit him with a Chaotic Bolt while he was in midair and he'd be dead.

If he didn't drink a potion and focused simply on dodging the bolts, assuming the first Corruption didn't kill him outright (a fairly forlorn hope), the second Corruption would follow it up and finish the job. He'd be dead. If he got too close to Archimonde, which was blocking the door with its bulk, the tongue would come into play. The tongue was a critical hit point, but Damien had already discovered in his first encounter that his damage was too low to matter. He'd be dead.

If Archimonde took control of Damien's minions during combat, the odds would turn against him even further on top of all the aforementioned points and he'd be very, very dead. Of course, that hardly mattered, because Archimonde also had 60 souls' worth of minions gathered around him. 30 attached to Archimonde's Soul Well, 30 attached to Archimonde itself. The same strategy Damien had used against Rising Tide when his base was in the Downward Spiral. Dead, dead, dead.

Damien had now been watching long enough from his imp's eyes to discover the new demon's utility role. It took up 8 souls of Archimonde's Soul Summon Limit. The other 52 were all accounted for. Imps and an incubus would bring it raw materials at fifteen-minute intervals. Exotic ores from underground. When they left, the demon turned to the pile of ore and began eating it with the big mouth embedded in its stomach. Even across the distance, the mouth was easy enough to make out. Ewww, make out. Not the best turn of phrase when regarding this creature. When it was finished, it would spit the ore directly into the Demon Forge. So it had a construction function of some kind.

There was no mistaking it. Archimonde had taken this new demon's form. Was it possible to learn this power? How? Was it the level 50 trait? That meant the 'Dark Omen' ability would be unaccounted for, and that seemed too powerful to warrant being learned just from leveling up. But so was this. Was it a level 60 trait? Hopefully Archimonde wasn't level 60 yet. That would be a lot of catching up to do.

Damien could reverse engineer Archimonde to figure out the combat options. The mouth was the first combat choice, clearly. The tongue was probably a given, too. It was likely slow, but was otherwise well rounded. Literally and figuratively.

So it was a tank. Maybe even more so than the incubus. Archimonde had showcased at least one other ability it might have yesterday, when it ate Andrew's Arcane Bolt. So the new minion was well defended against frontal magic attacks. Definitely tankier than the incubus.

He'd learned a lot, but it made him aware of how much more was left unknown. So long as Archimonde stood in front of that doorway, that was how it would remain. What could he do to make Archimonde leave? He could Portal back to his old base and start a livestream, killing players in the area until Archimonde came for him. If Archimonde was intent on shutting him down, following Damien's streaming channel would be a no-brainer.

There were two problems with this plan. The first was that the moment Damien shut down the stream and used his Portal spell to get to his new Gateway, Archimonde would likely do exactly the same. Leaving them exactly where they were now, except Archimonde would be aware Damien had built an out-of-base Gateway nearby to the objective. He would also know Damien was trying to trick him into leaving, as well as potentially figuring out the location of Damien's second Gateway. Not a good move.

The second problem was that the only way he could be certain Archimonde had left was by seeing it appear elsewhere. He didn't rate his chances of survival, if Archimonde could both plan its attack and see through his eyes on the livestream.

But what if they weren't his eyes?

Damien thought about it for a while. He had nothing but time. He analyzed everything at his disposal. He considered what he knew about streaming. Then he went into his menu, the imp's fingers marginally more nimble than the incubus's, and accessed the external browser. Making his way to the Council of Nine page. His level 40 traits reveal had resulted in the front page turning into a churning sea of irreverent discussion. Damien declined to scroll through. He was on a mission. The board was quickly drowned in 'Praise Be's following his arrival while he typed out his request.

Daemien: I need someone here to pretend to be me. I'm on a top secret mission and there is an obstacle, which I need someone to lure away by acting as bait. It will result in your death, for my advancement. If you're interested, I'm opening a discussion group. I would be very grateful for your help. (2:1)

He went straight into the discussion forum and opened a new page, entitled **False God**. Almost everyone who was online, just less than thirty occultists, piled in immediately.

Daemien: Thank you for coming. Who here is working with a build similar to mine, with wisdom as their main stat and agility as their secondary stat, and has the same playstyle as me? (2:2)

TheWitcher: I am!

Scorpious666: I'm wisdom and agility, but flipped. Does that help?

Scorepeeus63: I can do it.

Oh! Scorepeeus63 was following in his footsteps. He was the highest level of all of them. That seemed like the best match.

Daemien: The more similar you look to me, the better. Your demons should also look the same, so ideally you'll need the 'Hell's Angels' trait for imps with wings. Higher-level players preferred. Who can do this for me? (2:3)

Scorepeeus63: I can.

That was fast. He was committed. It was hard to believe this was the little boy whose absurdly frightened Aetherius kill-steal had made waves around the world. Damien remembered it and was a little worried.

Daemien: Are you sure? I'll make it as easy as possible, but even if you do a good job something ridiculously dangerous and frightening will be coming for you. (2:4)

Scorepeeus63: I'm not scared. I'm a real Scorpius. I'm low level, but I can help.

The exact words he'd used in his viral video, when his comrades had goaded him down the stairs of the Downward Spiral to cement Damien's competition victory. The previously silent onlookers erupted with 'Praise Be's and an inordinate number of exclamation marks. Damien could hardly refuse him now.

Daemien: We have a winner. Come private chat with me. Thank you everyone, and Praise Be. (2:5)

Scorepeeus63 invited Damien into a private chat first, so eager was he to get started, and then it was just the two of them.

Daemien: I'm sending you the location of my base. I want you to sit in it and send out a broadcast, where I'll be talking to my subscribers. All you have to do is follow my instructions. I need to trick someone into thinking that's where I am, so I can get around them.

Scorepeeus63: Easy! Sure you don't want me to go kill players to make it legit?

Daemien: It's too high level for you. You're level 38, some of the players in the Frozen Forest are almost ten levels higher than you. It's not ideal, but I don't expect you to go to the Frozen Forest for me.

Scorepeeus63: Frozen Forest! I can do it. Don't treat me like a kid!

Damien smacked his imp head. It had nothing to do with him being a kid, although that wasn't perfect either.

Daemien: I'm sure you can do it, but that won't be necessary. I just need you as bait, no killing required. But you will possibly die. Are you sure it's ok?

Scorepeeus63: I get to be Daemien for a few minutes? Hell yeah! Praise Be!

Daemien: Here's my base location **Rotten Vale**. How long for you to get there?

Scorepeeus63: I'm on my way! Twenty mins!

Daemien: Thanks for your help. We'll sort out the streaming settings after you get there. Let me know your progress.

A few minutes passed.

Daemien: How are you holding up?

A few more minutes passed. No response.

Daemien: Scorepeeus, please respond.

Scorepeeus63: Sorry, I was just killing some people.

At least he was enthusiastic. It was a bit disturbing, seeing those words coming from a nine-year-old. Quite funny though, in a perverse way. Maybe slightly too nonchalant? He was probably a decent player then. Either that or playing it cool.

It took Damien a fair bit of fiddling around with the streaming settings before he found there were some problems. All the details from Scorepeeus63's HUD had to be toggled off so his lower hit point, stamina and mana bars wouldn't be on display. Damien was level 43, Scorepeeus63 was five levels lower. For the purposes of Damien's plan, it would be easiest to turn off all of his assistant's HUD displays entirely. Which would be wise to implement as soon as Scorepeeus63 arrived in the area, in case he felt compelled to kill any more people before he got to Damien's base.

While he moved into position, Damien made his own preparations: he withdrew his watch over Archimonde and returned to his base in advance of Scorepeeus63's arrival. About five minutes later, Scorepeeus63 arrived. He was oddly adult-looking for a nine-year-old, but then again it would've been far stranger if the game had allowed him to play with his real-life physical settings. Even realism has limits. Damien assumed his assistant had acclimatized himself to the different dimensions of his game-rendered adult body through trial and error. He had a full entourage of demons in tow as well. Top-level enthusiasm. Damien made his presence known and came out to shake his assistant's hand. By the time the nine-year-old was done shaking it, Damien felt like it might fall off.

"Dude, this is such hax! I get to be Daemien for a day, Praise Be! Who's blocking you? Is it Aetherius? Why don't we team up and get him instead? I'm way better now than—"

"Score, dude, I need you to focus. If you talk while I'm broadcasting they'll know you're not me. You've got to be calm. I need you to stay quiet while we do this. Can you do that?"

"Yeah, totes! I can be calm and quiet! It's great to meet you! Praise Be! Where's your base?"

Damien scrutinized his follower, mulling over whether or not this would work, then started channeling his Portal. His base was right over their heads, through a hole he'd excavated in the ceiling, but most of their minions would not be able to physically pass through it. The only way he'd been able to keep his headquarters hidden for all this time was by creating his own dungeon infrastructure. His winged imps had helped with that, although they'd had to do it in shifts.

Once there was enough space, Damien had built a Soul Well then deconstructed it and moved it back as his minions continued excavating. By degrees, his own private kingdom had become almost as large as that which Bartholomew had granted him in the Downward Spiral. It had taken an entire morning, but that was a small price to pay for privacy.

Damien ushered Scorepeeus63 and all his minions through the portal, then his own, before passing through it last.

"I formally transfer ownership of my Demon Forge and Soul Well to Scorepeeus63."

He still needed his Gateway in order to open a portal back to the Inner Circle. He'd just have to make sure his accomplice didn't look in that direction while he enacted the plan. Scorepeeus63 clicked in the affirmative on the notification that appeared in his HUD. The structures immediately went from blue to green, indicating they were now in possession of an ally rather than being personal properties. It was no longer Damien's base. Damien invited his newly ordained host to take a seat on his own Soul Well and gave him the pep talk and technical guidance required, entering his settings to talk him through the necessary changes.

"When I start the broadcast, all you have to do is watch without moving too much. I'll be playing some video files from my own menu, it'll look suspicious if you're running around all over the place or looking around you while you're supposed to be focusing on the video yourself. Can you do that?"

"Yeah, totally! When are we getting started?"

"Sit here. In about twenty minutes, after I'm in position, we'll begin. Keep your head still! The more you look around the less likely this will work. Understand?"

"Yup, got it, just look straight ahead and wait for your cue to show my location."

Damien nodded. He remained on call with Scorepeeus63 as he Portaled to his new Gateway in the Inner Circle and led his full force back to his original lookout point. He'd be doing the same as Score, keeping his head still and looking forward. Fortunately, Noigel finally had enough imps for his Forbidden Knowledge to take effect. Noigel would watch over Archimonde while he enacted his plan, informing him of Archimonde's movements. The rest of his minions – thirteen more imps, two hell hounds, a succubus and a wraith – lay in wait on the other side of the ledge. The sun was setting. Damien wagered by the time he got a reaction the wraith would be very useful. He had at least one very specific purpose for it in mind. Everything was in place.

"Score, are you ready?"

"Yeah, I'm yours to command!"

"Okay. Remember to stay calm. Just look straight ahead and you'll have done me an enormous service."

"All good!"

"Send me a livestream."

It came, and Damien expanded it till Score's vision filled his entire HUD. He moved his head around a little to see how much leeway he had. Not much. If he turned too sharply, his own surroundings became visible outside of the window he'd maximized showing Score's vision. Damien would have to keep his head relatively still as well, moving only his eyes to choose settings.

Damien activated his own livestream, sending all Scorepeeus63's vision out to his viewers as if he were seeing his own base through his own eyes. All Score's own settings had been turned off, so Damien's settings overlaid them. There was nothing to indicate this was not coming directly from Damien.

"Good evening, and welcome to my latest livestream! I'm recording from within my own base today, because I want to have a discussion with all of you instead of the usual killing. We have a common enemy that requires our immediate attention."

The numbers had already started to climb. Damien kept his head completely still. Score had done an admirable job of doing the same for the last few seconds. He could hear what Damien was saying but would only be able to see the whole stream on repeat later, despite being the closest to what was happening. Damien could only hope his resolve persisted.

"I know I haven't been streaming very much lately. I do apologize. Today, I want to show you why."

He opened the first of the videos he'd lined up. An excerpt of his conversation with Magnitude:

"All I have to do is announce a deal and the whole forest comes running to protect the wall that's fencing them in. They don't want the wall to be destroyed. They want to be a part of it. That opportunity does not extend to you, due to your competition victory and your class."

"That's Magnitude. The guy who bought out Carlisle and turned the Human Realm into a prison. He's some kind of earth-manipulating dwarf thing. He's keeping us all penned in, by making us work against each other."

He reached out to Noigel. They couldn't talk plainly, because anything shared between them would be transmitted in the livestream. But the viewers couldn't read Damien's thoughts. Noigel could, if he made his intent clear enough.

Squeeze twice if Archimonde is responding.

Noigel squeezed Damien's arm twice. Good. Very good. He'd got Archimonde's attention. All was proceeding according to plan. Time to move this along.

"I pushed through despite the threat, and was presented with this thing. It's an occultist, working with Magnitude. It's higher level than me, with abilities I don't completely understand. It's pretty horrible. Viewer discretion advised."

Damien clicked on the second video, showing his first 'altercation' with Archimonde. It was painful, showing everyone just how inferior he was to someone that shared his class. But it was necessary. He had to give as much credence as possible to this ploy. Everything about it had to ring true, save for the fact he was not broadcasting from his own location. His bait of falsehood would be obscured with liberal application of the truth.

Magnitude's group had attempted to use the humiliation Archimonde heaped upon him to their advantage, to keep him silent. He could shout no louder than by spreading it around the internet in a livestream. Archimonde's deep, throaty voice echoed out into the ears of almost a million viewers:

"*You told the whole world of the existence of occultists. That did not belong to you, Daemien-chan.*"

Damien cut the footage. No need to show himself being eaten. He was sure everyone watching had the gist of how their confrontation went. Time for the next phase.

"As you can see, all the players in the Human Realm have been penned in by this alliance and are being held here first by coercion, then force if they resist. I'm arming all of you against this as best as I can: by revealing everything I know about how Magnitude and Archimonde's abilities work. My base location is here. I'm opening my map to reveal my base's location."

Scorepeeus63 was still looking steadfastly ahead. Damien coughed, then made it as plain as possible.

"I'm *opening my map to show my current location*, so Magnitude and Archimonde can see *where I currently am*."

There was a pause, and then Scorepeeus63 tabbed straight to his map. There was the indicator, showing where he was. The trap was set.

"I will continue broadcasting Magnitude and Archimonde's known abilities and potential weaknesses until one of them comes to kill me. After I'm dead, they will open negotiations with me in private so I can advance without further revealing their capabilities and motivations. If they don't contact me, I will continue this tomorrow after I respawn until I get an audience. I don't recommend anyone else search for me here unless you want to die. Horribly. Archimonde and Magnitude, your time starts now."

Damien took a deep breath. This was the fun part.

"Magnitude is a magic-user who manipulates the earth in order to do damage, move rapidly underground and create defensive barriers. He can detect incoming enemies around himself in a wide radius, so long as they are in physical contact with surfaces around them. I don't know his class name. It's hidden, just like mine was. However, his abilities require health instead of mana, which means forcing him to cast in rapid succession—"

Noigel was squeezing his arm nonstop. Damien had no way of knowing how Archimonde was responding, but something was definitely happening.

"—will result in him being unable to continue casting without killing himself. He is very tanky, with jade armor, high health and ridiculous health regeneration. Using damage-over-time effects on him completely cancels his natural regeneration, rendering him unable to cast abilities. He has another ability, called 'Renewal', which brings his health back to full and removes all debuffs in a blinding flash of light. I assume this has a cooldown, so the best way to kill him would be to force him to use Renewal, then apply pressure. He looks much stronger than he actually is."

Damien stopped talking and Noigel stopped squeezing soon after. Archimonde had stopped as well. Damien had them right where he wanted them. But he knew from what Magnitude had said that Archimonde and Magnitude, even if they were allies, did not get along. He'd reviewed his footage, while he'd been waiting fruitlessly for Archimonde to get out of his way.

It had become obvious that Magnitude had been talking about Archimonde, not Damien himself, when he said: "He doesn't listen to me though, so you'll have to tell him." Archimonde was more interested in itself. It had taken offense to Damien revealing the existence of the occultist class. It had complained to him about it directly, just before it ate him. Damien had initially revealed his class and the location of his base to lure Aetherius into the Downward Spiral. Now he was recycling the trick, with new elements in play, to obtain a new goal.

Archimonde had asserted that the occultist class didn't belong to him. How much more offended would Archimonde be when Damien started revealing what he knew of his adversary's build specifically? Let's find out.

"Archimonde is more complicated, but it also shares my class, so I can provide much more in-depth information on how it works."

Noigel began squeezing again, twice as hard.

"Archimonde is at least level 53—"

The intermittent squeezing stopped and Noigel just grabbed his arm as hard as he could, with both hands. There were shouts and orders echoing from over the ridge which was keeping Damien out of sight. He continued speaking over them, the sound of his own voice drowning out the frenetic activity in the crucible below.

"—with a primary focus on the Circle of Hell ability, which it has imbued with at least two traits at level 20 and 30 respectively and upgraded to the maximum to increase the damage and area of effect. It also has some sort of ultimate ability called 'Dark Omen', which—"

Noigel's claws were digging into Damien's skin, through the fabric of his occultist robes.

"—summons a large black hole over the caster. It collides

with the earth after approximately thirty seconds. It pulls in anything not nailed down within a wide radius, much like the pull effect of 'Imp-losion', and probably does incomprehensible damage. Archimonde is an orc, benefiting from the orcish trait 'Magic Blood' in combination with its occultist traits. It also appears to have spell-vamp on top of that; I've reviewed the footage and its health noticeably recovers when it inflicts magic damage. It has obscenely high health, but is weaker when Circle of Hell is on cooldown. This is because—"

Noigel tapped his arm twice. Archimonde was gone. Damien kept it going a little longer, mainly out of spite but also to continue the illusion for his own benefit. If Archimonde was concerned enough to have left its post to hunt him down, this was a much desired opportunity to make it suffer. Score had already indicated he was willing to die on Damien's behalf. This was a very worthy use of his life.

"—the upgrades Archimonde invested in make the Circle of Hell last longer, thirty seconds instead of fifteen. However, the cooldown has also gone up. Avoid the Circle of Hell and attack Archimonde with high-burst damage while it has no ability to help it regenerate. Archimonde's demonic form has made its stats incredibly high and has granted it some additional abilities revolving around the mouth in its stomach."

Damien looked at the viewer count. 15,000 people were watching this. That would do. He checked the time. It was just past 8pm. He couldn't see around him while viewing through Scorepeeus63's eyes, but it would be dark by now. He just needed to sign off and let Scorepeeus63 get out of harm's way if at all possible.

Damien had always been very nervous about talking with so many people watching. However, now that it had this purpose behind it, Damien found himself extremely calm. They were all part of his plan. He was in control of them, not the other way around. While offering them content, he'd used them as an elaborate disguise for his own personal agenda. They'd inadvertently bolstered his illusion just by showing up. It was a lot of people to mislead for the sake of his own advancement. Damien couldn't say everything he wanted to, but he could say enough. He worked it out in his head as he delivered his last lines.

"Knowledge is power. I'm off to go get some. Wish me luck."

He sent the signal to Noigel. He and his minions immediately crested the hill and descended into the rose-filled crucible below. Damien closed his menu the moment he started running, removing the illusion and giving everyone a glimpse of reality. The Dark Tower loomed in front of him. The answers he sought lay within. The greatest obstacle had been removed via his deception, but this was the part that really counted.

They were nearing the Dark Tower when Archimonde's Soul Well-bound minions realized there was a threat. He was almost all the way there before the Gateway started to glow, indicating that Archimonde was returning to base.

The demons were indeed dangerous, but without an adequate Noigel to guide them and their master absent they were easily dealt with. Most of them were still working to build the uncompleted defenses and their cohesion was nonexistent. Damien's own minions moved from one to the next, pulling each apart in groups before moving to the next as Damien himself ran onward.

The sole exception was the big one. Archimonde's doppelganger had left the forge when the alarm was sounded to stand directly in front of the doorway. Damien summoned the wraith to his side. The creature's tongue had no sooner latched around Damien's torso than the wraith broke stealth to cut straight through it. All Damien's minions converged on the monstrosity and took it down in a flurry of stabs, bites and strikes while it was still recovering from the critical hit. Then Damien left them behind to run down the passageway, using those of his minions that were not yet fallen to block his path and ease his passage.

Archimonde announced its return, and the return of the 30 souls' worth of minions following it, with a scream of fury that echoed after Damien into the tunnel. It would not be long before all his own minions were either dead or in Archimonde's thrall.

Damien didn't know where to go from here. He hadn't been completely convinced he'd get this far. All he could do now was continue down the passageway, hoping there was a way through. The tunnel was improbably long. Longer than the tower was wide from the outside. He'd been running for half a minute when he saw a light in the distance. It was a portal. There was nothing else, just this at the very end of the narrow space. There was no choice. He leapt through, into the unknown.

13

SERVING THE 'BYAM'

Lillian had divided her party to head for the quest. She knew if they all left together it would attract more attention. She also had to ensure any single group would be able to deal with what was thrown at it. Of course, any single group would have a hard time dealing with the entirety of the Carlisle-Elite. However, their smaller group was better coordinated, which meant splitting up would buy them time compared to being a single clump of nine players.

It was quite the puzzle. Lillian needed to ensure as best as she could that all the players arrived at their destination. She had no way of knowing how many enemies would leave in pursuit of each group. Maybe they'd all go after the first group? Maybe they'd wait for the guild leaders to show themselves? Not only did she have to give everyone the best chance of success, she also had to consider interpersonal relationships so that group members wouldn't jeopardize the plan by falling out with each other, or have bad ability synergy.

Aetherius, Legolias and Trinytea left first, but not together. That would be an automatic fail. Lillian was tired, but she wasn't stupid. Each departed from a different gate. They were all competent solo players, with either great evasion or superior movement speed in addition to their combat skills. Grouping them with other players would only slow them down and wasn't the best way to utilize them in this scenario. Lillian could only imagine the bounty on each of their heads within Magnitude's guild. They'd appear vulnerable, and by using them separately they'd siphon off as many of the enemy waiting for her party to move outside the city walls as possible. Meanwhile, the rest of the party waited within the sanctuary of their room at the inn, hidden from prying eyes.

It worked. The trio had been outside the city walls for two minutes when they started reporting pursuers. Aetherius had the most, which was probably for the best. If anyone was capable of giving them the slip, it would be him. She'd sent him through the East Gate, closest to the dim light and abundant cover of the Hourglass Plateau, with the express purpose that he could use it most effectively to escape. He'd need more help than the other two, since he'd be relying on his undisclosed stealth ability and his Blink rather than pure agility to give his enemies the slip. Legolias had a forest out in front of him to the west, which provided him with his ideal working environment. Trinytea took the South Gate, the gate through which they'd initially entered Glastonbury, and would be relying on her absurd movement speed to shake her enemies and return to the party.

After ten minutes, the remaining members of Lillian's party headed through the North Gate, the only one unused and the one closest to their objective. Lillian had decided she'd bite the bullet, insofar as interpersonal relationships went, by traveling with Hammertime. So long as he kept his unwanted opinions to himself, she wouldn't clobber him. He'd already had his say in private, hopefully he wouldn't have anything further to add among company. Lillian was still lining up her response to his chastisement in her head, although she was a little busy to give it her full attention.

With extravagant support magic at their disposal, the two guild leaders together would be able to look after all the slow casters if there were any Carlisle-Elites left who hadn't pursued her diversions. They made their way across the rolling hills and scattered woodlands until they reached the shores of Avalon.

It was technically a lake, although it was pushing for status as an inland sea. The visible portion of it was vast. While the cerulean water was shrouded in a thick layer of fog, the shoreline stretched out far on either side, with tiny waves lapping against a modest beach of pebbles before it gave away again to the viridian grass at their feet.

There was no sign of a 'byam', or anything else of interest for that matter. The whole area was devoid of life. Aside from the gentle wash of the waves, it was eerily quiet. The sun was setting far off to the west, still a ways off from touching the top of the hills in the distance. They were running out of time and had no leads. Yet there were no obvious options available.

They all pored over the riddle, without success. The dodgy spelling, the cryptic nature and unnecessary rhyming scheme were all points of consternation to the party, especially Lillian. She preferred her problems out in the open, where they could be measured, confronted and beaten down. Riddles were not her idea of a good time. Much less when the stakes were high and three members of her party were putting themselves at risk while it was being solved.

Sabrina was the first to think outside the box.

"The quest will be out there in the water, right? Why don't we just swim?"

Hammertime grunted and shook his head.

"It's probably not a good idea. If there's a quest for this, there'll be something preventing you from doing that. As your guild leader, I forbid it."

Lillian was already bitter, and this assertion of Hammertime's authority over a member of her party, who'd approached the problem from another angle and immediately been chided for it, set her off.

"Nice of you to bring the problems with Sabrina's idea to our attention and shut that whole train of thought down. Do you have anything useful you'd like to share?"

"Actually, yes, I do. I've done some searches and the rhyme appears to be in a dead language called 'Middle English'."

"And?"

"The second stanza is the important one, so I've been

focusing on that. The third and fourth lines are where we're at now. We need to find the 'byam', which is actually a 'beam', as the rhyming scheme suggested. The fourth line is about the time frame. So we need to figure out what the beam is."

Lillian grumpily sat down. Served her right, she supposed. She was well aware of her own temper at the best of times, let alone when confronted with exhaustion, high-handed criticism and Ye Olde Englishe cryptic messages. Mr. Healy sprung to cover up the awkward silence.

"So what kind of beam? Like a wooden beam, yeah? Maybe we should chop down some trees and float on them into the water?"

When Hammertime did not grace this suggestion with a response, OhHolyLight chimed in.

"If it was that easy, we could simply build a boat and sail it into the water. The time of day wouldn't matter."

"It might! Maybe the quest is only accessible during this time, but we need to build a boat and sail out to find it."

Lillian appreciated the gesture, but was starting to see this Hammertime's way. This conjecture was silly and taking them further from the solution, not closer. It was already approaching 19:30. Whatever the answer was, it probably didn't involve a boat.

"Mr. Healy, that's not a bad idea, logically, but Hammertime's right. There's nothing logical about this. There'll be some stupid play on words, or some hidden meaning that whoever authored it thought made them really witty when they're actually a pretentious twat."

Blessed, uncomfortable silence. But not productive. If nothing else was being done, she'd better check the status of the three diversionary units. She turned to the party chat.

Lillian: Status report on diversionary units.

Aetherius: Shook them, omw. ETA 15 minutes.

Legolias: Lost them in the trees. On my way. ETA 10 minutes.

No reply from Trinytea. Either she was in trouble or Godhammer guild's discipline was lacking with regards to communications. As much as Lillian wanted a reason to rag on Hammertime, she doubted his basic communication training was lacking. Although Trinytea was extremely agile, besides her speed she had little in the way of abilities to shake enemies. She'd been the best choice for that path by a long margin, but was probably the weak link of the three.

"Hammertime, Trinytea might be in trouble. She's not replying in the party chat. Please contact her privately if you can."

While Hammertime moved away to talk to his errant guild-mate, Lillian continued messaging in the party chat to ask her own absent team members if they had any input. It was mainly Andrew's wisdom she sought, but messaging through the party chat avoided asking for his help directly.

Lillian: Do either of you have any ideas about the quest?

Legolias: Aren't you there already?

Lillian: We're here, no joy. Looking for the 'byam', or beam.

Aetherius: When I get there I can make one for us, don't think we'll find passage along it to anything except death timers though.

Lillian: Serious, HELPFUL replies only p—

She stopped typing and frowned. She looked up at the sun which was continuing to descend, indifferent to their plight. The whole quest was tied to it. Once it set, the passage would be gone. The answer was in plain sight. It wasn't a wooden beam. It was much closer to what Aetherius had flippantly offered.

It was a light beam. Lillian tracked the sun to the nearest edge of the water. They were in the wrong place.

"Everybody up! We're moving to the west shore of the lake. Now!"

She set off at a run with the keyboard still in front of her as she typed into the party chat.

Lillian: Change course to the west shore. Marking it on the map now.

Aetherius: Omw, ETA 20 minutes.

Legolias: Omw, ETA 5 minutes.

While she'd been typing, Hammertime had caught up with her.

"Why are we running to the west shore?"

"Because that's where the passage will be."

"Are you sure?"

What kind of question was that? Of course she wasn't sure. She ignored it in favor of the more pressing issue.

"Where's Trinytea?"

"She's on her way, but she didn't shake the party following her. She's having trouble."

"Where?"

"About twenty minutes away, to the south. Following your plan."

That meant the enemies she was pulling with her would wind up in Aetherius's way, since he was out to the east.

"Tell her to track west first, through the forest Legolias was in. Get her to shake the enemies, then head north."

"Why?"

"Because I said so. End of discussion."

They ran onward, the slower casters setting the pace for the rest of the group as they followed the waterline. Legolias was already waiting for them at the most westerly point of the lake when they got there fifteen minutes later. Only ten minutes until complete sunset.

"What now, Lillian?"

She ignored Hammertime and looked out over the water. There was a clear reflection of the sun's light on its surface, which disappeared out into the mist at the lake's center. She strode up to it purposefully and stuck her armor-plated foot on top of it. Her foot immediately dropped through the water and sank into the mud. Lillian's tolerance for riddles was already low without feeling as though she'd answered one correctly without reward.

"It should be right here! I figured we needed to travel on the light beam, and this is where it should be!"

She kicked the surface of the water, scattering the light that flickered tauntingly over its surface and achieving exactly nothing. Even Hammertime was sympathetic as he gently wrested control from her, which irritated Lillian even more.

"That was a good theory. It's a shame it didn't work out, but it was better than doing nothing. We can regroup, find an area outside of town to make camp at so we don't have to dodge players tomorrow, and try—"

As he spoke, the edge of the sun had dipped just below the edge of the horizon. The light on the water was glowing noticeably brighter. Lillian placed her foot over it again. It tapped down and rested above the waves. The surface of the water was solid.

She went immediately from elation to panic. Aetherius and Trinytea weren't there yet. There was no time for text messages, the rest of the group would just have to deal with it. She threw her hand up to one ear to activate the party comms.

"Andr—Aetherius, the passageway is here! Where are you?"

"I'm closing in, should be there in five minutes."

"Not good enough! Use your Blink whenever it's off cooldown, we need you here right now!"

"I'd do that, but there's a large group out in front of me. I think they're following Trinytea. Didn't she tell you?"

Lillian's blood ran ice cold. She wheeled around to face Hammertime.

"You didn't relay my instruction to Trinytea, did you? She just kept on following our path. Now she's here, with all her pursuers in tow."

Hammertime folded his arms and shrugged.

"And it's a good thing I didn't, because otherwise she wouldn't have made it in time."

"No, it's *not* a good thing. She brought all the people following her, Aetherius is stuck behind them! I gave you a simple order—"

"We needed Aetherius to get through the wall but from here on he's a liability, like I said. You think I didn't understand why you wanted Trinytea to circle around? Not only have I removed her from danger, I've also saved us the trouble of bringing Aetherius on the quest, and I've done so in such a way that you don't need to take the blame. You're welcome."

He shook his head at her, then attempted to walk past her. He bounced off when Lillian activated her Divine Might and pushed back. Then staggered and crashed to the floor when she punched him clean in the side of his head. She stood over him and raised him up by the breastplate, her other hand raised up threateningly.

"Not your decision to make. If you'd done as you were told, everyone would be safe."

Another punch, keeping Hammertime pliant as the micro-stun persisted.

"I don't punish players for following my orders, regardless of who they are. That goes just as much for Trinytea as it does for Aetherius."

She deactivated Divine Might and let Hammertime drop, then strode back along the riverside, her sword and the new shield Andrew had procured for her from Damien's inventory settling into her grip. Her hand rose to her ear.

"Aetherius, we'll hold them off but you have to Blink and stealth through. Can you do that?"

"I'll do my best."

She turned to the rest of the players at her back and spoke without using party comms, so Trinytea and Aetherius wouldn't have to worry about the group falling apart while they were already under stress.

"Rising Tide players, with me. We're saving Aetherius, or dying. Or both. Godhammer is formally relieved of duty. Remove yourselves from my party. It's clear you won't do as I tell you and I won't rely on anyone who has their own plans, but I won't abandon anyone following me."

The members of Rising Tide immediately, unquestioningly, moved to stand with Lillian. She gave Hammertime a last stare, with all the disgust she could muster, then lined up her guild-mates behind her. Trinytea was running around the lakeside. Not at full speed, but comfortably ahead of the players pursuing her. She was still a long way out when she staggered forward, almost falling, then turned and began to run backward. Achingly slowly. Lillian focused and saw. An arrow was sticking out of the back of her leg, and more were landing all around her as she hopped left and right to avoid them.

She was leaving a trail of blood in her wake. She'd been pipped with a bleeding arrow in the final stretch, and couldn't go faster without losing incrementally more health. Her armaments were not long range and there was no way she could retaliate without moving into close proximity. That would be suicide, as there were more than ten players following her. A score of Carlisle-Elites hunting a single target. Cowards.

Lillian watched as Trinytea raised a health potion to her lips, trying to offset the damage inflicted by the bleed while she kept dodging. The party pursuing her drew closer and she diverted to full evasive maneuvers, reducing her straight-line speed even more.

She wasn't going to make it.

Unacceptable.

Lillian ran forward at full speed. Her guild-mates following behind. When that wasn't fast enough, she activated Divine Might and ran faster still, draining both mana and stamina to leave everyone in the dust. Her investment in the 'Swift Justice' trait at level 10, which increased her agility by 50% of her strength, was the best she'd ever made. It still wouldn't be enough for all of them to make it out alive.

What she'd do when she got there, she had no idea. Her resources would be mostly drained, and even with full mana she wasn't sure she could take on ten players who had advance warning of her arrival. That was besides the point. She'd always intended for everyone to make it. The only way to prove that now was by making sure that if anyone died, she was the first to go. She preferred it that way.

It was fine. They'd solved the riddle, Lillian would respawn in the inn tomorrow and go again. Alone, ideally, if everyone else made it. At least it would be less complicated.

Lillian was as close to Trinytea on one side as her pursuers were on the other when the thundering of feet caught up to her. There was a slight blur and a rush of air as Hammertime Charged past. He'd been Phase Shifted by Sabrina, turning him into a translucent bullet train. Trinytea peeled off to the right, away from the water, drawing the attention of her pursuers from the veiled incoming danger. They were still focused on finishing her off before Lillian got there when Hammertime appeared in their midst, his Charge-imbued hammer already embedded in a front-runner's ribcage.

They were woefully unprepared. The best defense against a behemoth is distance. The second-best defenses are roots and movement-speed-reducing abilities, preferably from a distance. The third-best defense is raw damage, applied over as short a time frame as possible. The Carlisle-Elite players who'd participated in Trinytea's marathon were all short on stamina already. None of these options were available to them. Hammertime lay waste. Lillian joined him shortly afterwards, mopping up the would-be escapees.

Lillian looked up at the sun. It was already halfway below the horizon. Aetherius was visible, but a long way out. She raised her hand to her ear.

"Everyone back and over the pathway, now! Andrew, the way is clear, Blink and use all your stamina to get to me."

Hammertime finished off the last of the players. He left them where they lay, slung his hammer over his back and ran past Lillian.

"You can thank me later."

How kind of him, to expect gratitude for saving one of her most hated players of all time. Lillian kept her hand to her ear.

"Hammertime has done his best to fix his mistake, but party members are still in jeopardy. If Aetherius or I don't make it, he is solely responsible."

Andrew had Blinked and was running as fast as he could, which was not very fast. It was only when he Blinked for the second time that he arrived at Lillian's feet, short of breath and on his knees.

How had she wound up putting herself in this position? For goodness' sake.

She activated Divine Might, picked him up in both arms and ran him back, his weight barely slowing her down. They'd not yet reached the pathway when the Divine Might faded and she slowed. She was out of mana. The sun was nearly completely descended. They had less than a minute. No sooner had the Divine Might faded when Andrew raised a mana potion to her lips.

"Drink."

She hated it, but he was right. She took the first gulp and reactivated Divine Might as she opened her throat to let the rest of the liquid pour down. Her speed once again increased as Andrew's burden became less. She was literally carrying him. Talk about a blast from the past. God, how she hated her life.

She turned onto the path of light as it started to wane, the rest of the group far out of sight through the fog ahead of her. Andrew provided intel on the sun's movements as Lillian focused on her feet. He was trying to be helpful, although Lillian was all too aware what the sun was doing.

"We've got maybe fifteen seconds."

The glow of the pathway was dimming. They were already completely enveloped by mist but the light somehow persisted, if only barely. Lillian ran forward, only able to see a few feet ahead. The pathway ended at nothing. She'd not come all this way not to give it her all. She planted both feet onto the end of the pathway and jumped forward as it faded completely. The two of them crashed into the water and were pulled down into the depths.

14

THE DARK TOWER

Damien fled through the portal, and Archimonde did not follow. He span round to confirm he was safe. The portal was gone. The dungeon was instanced, just as he'd calculated. As if in confirmation, the words he'd been hoping for appeared in the center of his vision.

The Dark Tower

He checked his surroundings and found no immediate danger there either: just a long, empty corridor leading to a doorway. Damien lay down on the ground, spreadeagled, and pumped his fists into the air. He'd done it! As he let his success wash over him, he noticed the notifications in his HUD. He was up to level 44! He also had a quest notification:

'There's Always a Bigger Fish – Find Bartholomew's master. Part 2 – Pursue your chosen path and clear the first trial.'

The first portion of the quest alone had given him enough EXP to take him through nearly an entire level! He was in that sweet spot: the EXP from the quests was increased due to his low level, yet the quests were still achievable. Then again, entering the dungeon in the first place was probably the easiest part. Getting there had taken all day. He'd have to pull his finger out.

First things first, he needed to resummon Noigel. Not only for the utility, but to give his minion some much deserved praise. The plan had turned out well, and his second-in-command had played a crucial role in bringing it about. He finished the summoning and beckoned Noigel closer.

"Noigel, you outdid yourself today. As soon as it's convenient, you'll get all the succubi you can handle."

Noigel began to cheer, only for Damien to clap his hand over his minion's mouth. The summoning had gone without a hitch, but he didn't want to draw unwanted attention to himself until he had a better understanding of this place. Which was when Damien realized he was still livestreaming. He'd promised Noigel his own private harem in front of 20,000 people. Oh dear.

"Well, looks like we made it." He took in his surroundings a little more slowly, allowing everyone watching on the livestream time to take it in. Not that there was much to take in. "Sorry about earlier. Archimonde was blocking my way, I had to make it leave. This is where Bartholomew told me to go to progress. I guess Archimonde doesn't much like the idea of having competition, so it was fortifying the entrance. I'm assuming you're still watching, Archimonde. Thank you for your time, and your cooperation."

He could see why Lillian enjoyed that turn of phrase. It was as satisfying to deliver it as it had been belittling to receive. More satisfying than punching Archimonde in the face, by far. It would've been even more satisfying if he wasn't murmuring it under his breath. His adrenaline was still running and it was hard to keep his voice low, but needs must.

At least he wasn't having problems livestreaming, for once. He'd always found it easier to record privately first and upload with commentary later. Knowing his every action was being watched and his every word heard, with no opportunity to edit out mistakes, had always made him less sure of himself. Now it felt more as if he were talking to himself, giving his inner thoughts voice for his own benefit. He'd do whatever he saw fit, the people tuning in were just along for the ride. If they didn't like it, there were plenty of other channels they could watch.

"I have no idea what this place is, what the layout looks like, what kinds of enemies there are, whether there are any enemies in here at all, or even – and this is pretty crucial – whether Archimonde can follow me in and kill me. Let's find out together."

The corridor was as preposterously long as the one that had led Damien there, but when it finally came to an end it was not back at the doorway by which they'd entered. There was a chamber with three portals set into alcoves, each with a different glowing silhouette etched into a stone plaque above it. The silhouettes showed three different occultists, all clad in varying armor and wielding different weapons.

From left to right, the etchings were blue, purple and red. They were characterized by fiercely glowing dots, as if each were a constellation of stars, with the fainter swirls of galaxies filling in the details. The first, in blue, bore a weighted scepter in one hand and a Sacrificial Dagger in the other. The figure was pointing the scepter and a Chaotic Bolt was perpetually forming at the tip. The robes it wore were the most familiar of the three, a little longer and more flowing than Damien's own tailored fit but undeniably more ornate.

The second, in purple, almost looked as though it were another class. The hood and cloak were still present, but it wore leather armor rather than robes. The weapon was bizarre, two weighted barbed spikes on each end of a long chain. It was in the process of being flung, the chain arcing back and forth as the rest of the image remained suspended. Where the last figure had been static, this one was frozen mid-leap.

The third, in red, was furthest from the concept of any occultist Damien had ever imagined. It looked more like a paladin gone wrong. This figure was clad in spiked plate mail with a skull emblazoned on the chest. It was swinging an oversized two-handed scythe, trailing a red swirl that looked like a fountain of blood.

Damien spoke his thoughts aloud.

"We appear to have three choices here. First one looks to be for intelligence builds, which is what I'd expected from this. Y' know, since all the occultist skills are based on either wisdom or intelligence. But it seems they've got options for occultists building around agility, like me, and even for strength! To each their own, I guess. Not sure how you'd build a strength occultist to be honest, but I'm sure that armor and scythe would help."

He pondered it a little longer, privately. He supposed that if an occultist ran with wisdom first, as he had, they'd be free to change course later, maintaining their wisdom stat and selecting a new primary trait to go in a new direction. If the gear was as good as it looked, it would go a long way to making most builds viable. He could choose any path he wished. This would be his last chance to decide how to build his character.

All three were tempting. The strength gear in particular looked all kinds of gnarly. He'd have a much easier time engaging in melee tactics wearing that armor and wielding that weapon. But his strategies had always relied on evasion, not taking hits. He'd been intent on building up his agility, even before it had seemed like a viable option. Now there was a path specifically for what he'd chosen, which most suited his playstyle, how could he refuse?

"I'll be running with this middle path, with the chain weapon. Let's see what this looks like."

Noigel clung to his shoulder and they entered the portal together. He'd no sooner set foot in the chamber when the portal once again disappeared behind him and the message popped up indicating where they were:

The Dark Tower: Path of Deceit

How very edgy. They couldn't have just called it the 'Path of Agility', could they? From here on there'd likely be trouble. Best to leave Noigel behind while he made sure the coast was clear. Damien crouched and headed inside. This chamber was much larger, with a solitary chest in the middle. Behind it there was a door, barred with iron slats horizontally and vertically. So there was something he had to do in here. Better start with the chest. He made his way to it while looking all around.

His night vision allowed him to see into every dark corner, but there were no signs of danger. The coast was clear. Sweet, free stuff! He flipped the latch, stood up straight and threw the lid open. From each topmost corner of the chamber echoed the tiniest, most insignificant *plink*. The four missiles struck him simultaneously, turning Damien into a pincushion. He had black spikes sticking out and through him: two through his chest and two through his shoulder blades.

Panicking, he looked up and found the source of the problem: the top four corners of the room were now adorned with health bars, hovering over four black spiny masses that were settled into the nooks. He wasn't the only one in that room that could mask its presence. It was called a 'Cave Urchin'. Level 50.

Plink.

Damien threw himself backward and the second round of spikes stuck into the floor and chest, barely missing him. The first round had taken him below half health. If he got hit again, he'd be dead. Nope. He turned back toward the chamber and sprinted.

Plink.

He'd thought his quick movement would result in his safety. It was a costly assumption. Apparently the Cave Urchins could aim predictively. The third round of spikes also struck him through. Damien watched in numb shock as his screen faded to black and his least favorite word combination of all time occupied his vision. It was even worse than usual, because apparently the Dark Tower had another unique feature: crushingly annoying death text additions.

You have been PERFORATED by 'Cave Urchin'. Fatality. Your experience has been reset to the start of your current level and your body may be looted, at which point a random item of equipped gear will be forfeit.

Remember, it's only a game!

Death cooldown – 23 hours, 59 minutes and 59 seconds.

Thank you for playing Saga Online.

His stream was still active. Everyone who'd watched him succeed in getting past Archimonde had now watched him fail. At the very first room. He was taking it all in silently for fifteen seconds, watching the streamer count fall and the timer tick ever so slowly down, before he managed to find words. When he did, he talked as if he were thinking aloud rather than to his rapidly dispersing viewers. He did modify his internal monologue for them slightly though, by removing all the expletives from it.

"That...that did not go well. It's okay. I got past Archimonde. I'll be able to respawn in here tomorrow and try again. What time is it...okay. I'll be here again at eight fifteen sharp to give it another go, and I'll send out another livestream. I'm very disappointed, but I won't give up. See you all tomorrow."

He logged out and opened his eyes, then started doing his damage report in earnest. All his souls were gone. All his experience toward level 45 was gone. His body would probably not be looted, so that was something. The stream had been short, but he'd accomplished his main goal that evening already by circumventing Archimonde, and had run his most viewed livestream since the days following his competition victory. The day was actually a success. He just hadn't thought the Dark Tower would be so punishing.

He'd been so intent on getting past the first obstacle, he hadn't ever considered whether he was ready to take on the challenge behind it. It was too late, now. If he bailed, he'd have to get past Archimonde all over again. A very unlikely prospect. He was locked in. He'd have to see this through to the end.

He suddenly felt an intense longing for the Bag of Holding he'd given up. There were any number of tricks he could've pulled with those resources at his disposal. It was a shame he couldn't both do the right thing and put himself in the best position to deal with his own challenges. At least those resources were helping Lillian's party instead. Damien hoped she was having an easier time than he was.

Lillian had never died by drowning before. She had no idea what Saga's version of it was like and no intention of finding out. There wasn't much she could do about it at that point, though. It was her intentions that had led her here, with Andrew along for the ride.

Right. There was something she could do. Lillian grabbed Andrew's Bag of Holding, went into her menu and deposited the entirety of her gear into it. She'd just made herself about 100kg lighter. Game mechanics for the win. Except not in this case. Despite the decrease in weight, their descent through the water was not slowing. Andrew was wearing robes and she was wearing basically nothing, there was no way they should still be sinking.

She reactivated Divine Might and started kicking toward the surface. Their descent still did not slow. That settled it. They were going to die. Great. She'd never paid much attention to water mechanics in this game. She'd never spent any time there swimming. Saga Online had always been a fairly accurate depiction of reality, the insane creatures and thoroughly augmented players still adhering to the laws of physics. She'd never thought there would be such a lame automatic drowning feature. How anticlimactic.

The two of them broke the water's surface and instinctively gasped for air, then looked down wide-eyed. They'd exited the lake not upward, but downward. The water was still all around them, but it was held back. They were in a giant bubble. Below them was a grassy plain, in front of a castle. That meant there was a castle at the bottom of the lake! They should've been plummeting at that point but were still descending at the same speed as they had within the water.

The two of them touched down lightly in the middle of a grassy knoll, surrounded by their allies. They were all looking at her, wide-eyed. Hammertime stifled a laugh. Oh. Lillian dumped Andrew on his feet, grabbed his bag again and reequipped her gear. Then she turned on the party, furious that her quick thinking had resulted in embarrassment, and even more furious that no one had thought to offer her an apology.

"You were all here long before us. I thought you were all already dead. If I'd known we were supposed to get dragged down, maybe I wouldn't have tried to lighten myself in the water. Why did no one give us any warning?"

She knew as she said it. They'd been too preoccupied with drowning, then taking in their insane surroundings. That was on her. How Hammertime replied was on him.

"The rest of us managed to get down here without issue, and without resorting to taking our clothes off. If you wanted assistance, party leader, there was nothing preventing you from asking."

Lillian's filter was very much expired. She wouldn't be getting a new one until she'd had a good night's sleep. Given what Hammertime had just done, he'd have to make do without.

"So you can't think for yourself? I have to tell you what to do? That's funny; you were perfectly capable of thinking for yourself earlier, when you didn't pass on my order to Trinytea."

She turned to the rest of the group while Hammertime's face was still souring.

"Well done, everyone. I'm glad we're *all* here. I invited Godhammer to leave earlier, but since we're all here, let's take a vote. If you're not satisfied with my leadership, don't waste our time. You can try the quest separately, after our group has logged off. If you stay, I expect cooperation. *And honesty.* Raise your hand if you want to leave."

Nobody looked comfortable. Nobody raised their hand. Not even Hammertime.

"Great. Let's find out what the next step looks like."

Lillian trudged off in the direction of the castle, her mood worse than ever. The constant need to keep Hammertime in check was depriving her, and the less subversive members of her party, of what little enjoyment this adventure might have had to offer. Their negotiation of the riddle should've been a time for congratulations, praise and a well-earned breather; especially since it had apparently come with a big chunk of EXP. A full one and a half levels, the very maximum that could be awarded for a single instance of experience gain.

They should've been celebrating. Now Lillian wanted to push for another victory instead, so they could distance themselves from the farcical nonsense Hammertime had inflicted on them.

She strode up to the castle gate, which was wide open. Then she laid eyes on the plinth next to it, the same kind as the one Hammertime had screenshotted and posted in the group chat earlier that day, and groaned. Another riddle. Please, no, she just wanted to fight something. Instead, she found herself stumbling through another passage. At least they'd significantly cut down on the rubbish Olde Englishe; the riddle itself was bad enough.

The second quest is tied to decency,
A ruler must be pure of heart and mind,
If you've erred and don't unwrite your history,
Your palms will fill with hair as you're struck blind.

What kind of weird threat was that? The doors to the courtyard were wide open. Lillian could even see across the pristine lawn to the doors of the castle keep proper, where another plinth lay in wait. Goody goody gumdrops. She managed to restrain herself from marching in. Neither of those consequences sounded good, and the last riddle had become functional with a bit of work. They could handle this if they just applied themselves.

"Gate's open, come on in!"

Lillian looked up from the plinth to find Mr. Healy applying himself. He was standing out in the courtyard. She hadn't explicitly told him *not to*, but still had to prevent herself from yelling at him. At least he'd spared everyone else having to test the consequences. Which appeared to be nonexistent. Mr. Healy was perfectly fine.

For about three seconds. Then the confused yelling started. The rest of the party watched in alarm.

"Guys, I can't see! What's going on? Guys?"

He had his hands stuck out in front of him to feel by, creating quite the spectacle: the plinth had not been kidding. Hair was pooling out of the bottom of his gloves, the same color as that on his head but far longer. After a few seconds, it was long enough to drag on the floor. He tripped over it with a pained yelp, which prompted some in the party to greater alarm and more to peals of laughter. It was absurd. Off to the side, Hammertime was still glancing between Lillian's hairy-handed healer and the plinth that had foretold his condition. Judgementday was among the more concerned of the party.

"Come this way! Over here, just follow my voice!"

His assistance was hardly necessary given the amount of noise the party was making in response to Mr. Healy's plight, but the priest eventually managed to make his way back across the threshold of the door, his new luscious locks dragging behind. Almost as soon as he'd crossed, the hair began to recede back into his body. It was only as it was all gone that he blinked and looked around himself in relief.

"What was that? What does that mean?"

"It means—," Lillian started, "—that you should read the instructions. It also means, apparently, you're not pure of heart and mind. Are you completely fine? Can you see again?"

"Yeah, all good. That was super freaky! I'm gonna do it again!"

"No, please don't do it again. I'd like to get through this as fast as possible."

She turned to Hammertime, who was still reading the plinth. Andrew was standing to the other side of him, his brow furrowed in thought. These two were more likely to provide useful input than the rest of the party, even if they were also the two Lillian felt the least like communicating with.

"Hammertime, you did all the groundwork finding the last riddle and your research was crucial to the solve. Aetherius, it was your comment to me about the beam that got us the rest of the way to the answer. You're actually taking the time to think about this rather than blundering in or laughing. Any thoughts from either of you?"

Hammertime didn't even look up from the plinth. To be expected, but not promising. Andrew was frowning.

"So long as there are no long lasting consequences...scientific method?"

Lillian nodded. That was a good idea.

"Alright everyone, line up. We're trying this one by one to see if it's the same result for all of us."

She thought about it a little more. It was Andrew's idea, he could handle it. There was something more important to be done.

"Andrew, if you could please watch the rest of them and tell me how it goes? I'd like to talk to Hammertime. Alone."

Andrew swiftly left to overlook the proceedings, just as OhHolyLight started yelling as he pressed his hairy hands to his eyes. Hammertime was still staring at the plinth. He was still sulking.

"You said if I became unfit to lead, you'd take over. How was I supposed to react? What choice did you give me? How would you have dealt with me, if I'd done what you just did?"

Hammertime still didn't look at her. He just waved a hand at her dismissively, then went back to irritably tapping a finger against his lips. That wouldn't do. Lillian needed an answer.

"This quest could take all night, or even longer. Neither of us is going to get through it by not talking. I need you to communicate with me."

The finger stopped tapping. Hammertime went into his menu and started clicking and typing away, but he began talking to her. A measurable improvement, Lillian felt. Until he'd gotten enough words out for the meaning to kick in, along with the tone. The longer he spoke, the more obvious his anger became. Much as Lillian's own did.

"I did talk to you. I told you exactly what you needed to do. You had to choose between *Andrew*, as you keep calling him, and the rest of the party. I can't believe, after all this time, you chose him. You sent him toward the best cover and sent Trinytea through dangerous open territory, when you could've easily removed him from play by swapping them round. I gave you the benefit of the doubt. Then, you gave an order that put her at direct risk for the sake of his safety. If she'd followed it, she'd have run out of steam and been killed long before she got within our reach. Finally, when I took the initiative and gave you what was best for the party on a silver platter, you put yourself and all your own followers at risk on his account."

He stopped typing and closed his menu, then turned to face her directly. Looking down on her.

"I wouldn't have believed it until I saw it: the mighty Lillian, putting her abusive ex-boyfriend ahead of her own party. There's a good reason I didn't want him getting this far. Don't you see? He's using you. It's obvious to everyone else. It's embarrassing. If you get Excalibur, it may as well be in his hands. I won't allow *Andrew* to run Camelot the way he ran Rising Tide, least of all with you as his obedient little puppet. Fortunately I'm not stupid, Lillian. So that's not going to happen."

That was a lot to process. She knew where Hammertime was coming from. From his own perspective, that must have all seemed very reasonable. He was so hopelessly wrong, on so many counts, in such a short span of time, that it was hard to know where to start untangling the thread he'd so meticulously knotted in his own head. Especially when he'd made her so very, very angry. She'd thought they had something resembling mutual respect. In his eyes, she'd only ever been Andrew's lapdog.

It would be easier to kill him. His Berserker Rage was on cooldown and that was the best tool he had; killing him while he didn't have access to it would be child's play. Kill him. He thinks he knows what he's talking about when he has no idea. He's beyond reasoning. He's too dangerous to be kept alive. Kill him. For the good of the party. If you don't kill him now, you'll regret it later. He's told you in plain terms that he doesn't want you to complete this quest. *Kill hi—*

"Lillian, everyone's run through the threshold and I have the results. Trinytea and Judgementday are completely unaffected! We might have enough data to figure out how the riddle works."

Lillian ignored Andrew completely and kept staring at Hammertime, her hands clenched into fists. Her killing instinct was so strong that she had to actively concentrate on preventing her Divine Might from activating. Hammertime took the initiative away from her.

"Not everyone has gone over the threshold. Lillian and myself are also members of this party. Ladies first?"

Lillian stared at him numbly. If she killed him, the party would dissolve. Many of the other party members, Rising Tide and Godhammer alike, were squishies with high damage. Many would die during the infighting before she finished Hammertime off and could turn her attention to restoring order. She'd be at the epicenter of her party's fracture. Hammertime wanted her to fight him, even if he died. This was his goal.

She wouldn't give him the satisfaction. She stalked over the threshold of the gate to stand with Judgementday and Trinytea and folded her arms, bracing herself. Everyone was watching her. Again. Waiting to see whether or not she'd fail. Whether or not she was pure of heart and mind.

Ten seconds passed. Nothing happened. She was clear.

"Hammertime, it's your turn. Get—"

Her vision started to blur. Her palms were itching. Dammit. Why was this happening? Which was when she saw the outline of Hammertime purposefully walking toward her, over the threshold, his hammer materializing in his grasp. She tried to do the same, focusing on equipping her sword and shield. They materialized in her hands, then fell to the floor. She couldn't hold them. The hair in her hands was blocking her grip. She'd been rendered completely helpless by this stupid curse. The last of her vision faded away and she was left in the dark.

Hammertime brought his head down to her ear.

"Let the record show, if I wanted to kill you it would be easy. You've played right into my hands, just as you're playing into Aetherius's hands. Sort yourself out."

Andrew bellowed out to them from behind the threshold.

"Did you solve the riddle? Share it with the rest of your party and put your weapon away. Now."

Five seconds went by in complete silence. Lillian needed to see what was happening. She started feeling her way forward, back to where Andrew's voice had come from, when she was pulled back by the scruff of her breastplate. Hammertime was holding her there.

"I'll need you to stay for a little longer, Lillian."

"Let her go."

"Don't play hero, *Andrew*, it doesn't suit you. Lillian will be fine. I won't do anything to her. Unlike what you've done."

There were footsteps all around her. Lillian tried to fight off Hammertime's grip, only to have the hair growing out of her palms yanked and then held. It was humiliating, painful and disgusting. She cried out, her voice cracking despite her best efforts.

"Andrew, what's happening?"

"Hammertime and Godhammer are splitting the party is what's happening, but you knew that already."

Hammertime was pulling Lillian backward, one hand on the back of her breastplate, the other occasionally yanking the hair on her hands when she failed to comply.

"If you were in my place, you'd have killed her outright. Then bragged about it."

"You're holding the party leader hostage, taking advantage of her, but you want to spin this on me?"

"We'll be on our way in just a few seconds and she'll be all yours again, unless she learns better. Everyone, any side effects? Blindness? No? Good."

Hammertime dragged Lillian back to talk in her ear.

"I'm sorry it has to be this way. We're moving ahead. You're hereby relieved of command."

He roughly shoved her forward, leaving her to stumble shamefully back to safety. Andrew grabbed the backs of her hands and held her steady.

"Are you hurt?"

Yes. She was. She felt like crying, but that would only make her look even more pathetic. Light started reentering Lillian's vision, and the hair on her palms started to recede. Judgementday tentatively walked across the threshold to retrieve her sword and shield, which had been left in the courtyard. Where she could not go. Hammertime and all of his own guild-mates were at the far end, gathered around the plinth. He'd figured out the riddle on his own and shared the answer with his guild-mates in private chat, leaving the rest of them behind. At the same time as he'd been putting Lillian down.

Andrew was the first to break the long silence.

"Lillian, we need to solve this riddle as soon as possible. We can't fight them unless we figure out how to stop the ailments from happening. Judgementday is immune, so it's not impossible. OhHolyLight and Sabrina were both affected when they crossed the first time, but not the second. Whatever the solution is, it can be implemented almost instantly. If we act now—"

Lillian shook her head. She was in no state to do anything. She should've quit while she was ahead. Today was her failure. She needed to sleep.

"I'm logging off. I recommend you all do the same. If I'm not here, Hammertime's group can come back and finish off the four of you pretty easily. Sorry I let you down."

She went into her menu and logged off without another word. The four people still following her remained completely silent, right up until she arrived back in her own room. She was hungry and tired, but at that exact moment, more than either of those things, Lillian just didn't want to be awake. She removed the headset, rolled over and struggled with her hatred until she finally fell asleep from complete exhaustion almost an hour later.

She woke up in the pitch black, immediately wide awake. Her headset was wailing at her from her bedside table. It wasn't her morning alarm. It was the one she'd used back in the competition days, before they had everything under control. She hadn't heard it in a long time, but her reaction to it was still the same.

It was only as she stuck the headset on and hit the 'Quick Log-In' button dominating the screen that she started thinking about it. This was Andrew's private alarm. She'd forgotten she even had it. She'd never thought to disable it. What time was it? 6am. She was supposed to be up in two hours. Why was he summoning her now? Why was he online at all, for that matter?

She'd find out soon enough. She prepared herself for combat, the timer to release from the blue protective sphere counting down. She'd need to be completely ready the moment she arrived. Three. Two. One.

Lillian's sword and shield were equipped before her eyes were open. They were raised up defensively before she'd blinked. It proved unnecessary. The only person there was Andrew. He was looking nervous, despite not appearing to be in any immediate danger. Or because of it.

Lillian put away her gear and took his trademark for her own, crossing her arms and tapping her foot.

"There'd better be a good reason for this. It's six in the morning, I've—"

"I solved the riddle."

That was a good reason.

"You must be very proud of yourself, to wake me up with a siren at the crack of dawn to show off about it. Is there also a good reason you couldn't just send me a message?"

"I'm...blocked. On all your social media."

She really needed to fully wake up before she started throwing rhetorical questions around.

"So you are. I wonder why? This could've waited until evening."

Andrew threw his hands out.

"Could it? Could it really? Hammertime got through the third riddle at 1am. I lost sight of him. I'm pretty sure if you found out I had the answer all day, then didn't share it with you, you'd be pretty—"

"Fine! You win! Can you tell me the answer, so I can go back to sleep?"

Andrew had gotten pretty animated for a moment there, looking her in the eyes and actually answering back. It was like watching a worm spontaneously grow a spine. Now he was back to being nervous again.

"You won't like it."

"There's a lot of that going around lately."

"Yeah, there is, but I'm not trying to add to it...anymore. Do you want the version where you don't know how the riddle works, so you don't have to be embarrassed for us? Or do you want the version where you know how it works, so you hate yourself and everyone around you?"

"You're the only person 'around' me."

"Yes."

"I don't hate myself, but I hate you plenty already."

"That's why I threw an 'and' in there."

Lillian rolled her eyes to look at the lake above them and exhaled through her nose. Same old Andrew: meticulous, snobbish and obsessed with never being wrong. Even when he was putting himself down. She looked at him sidelong as she considered his offer properly. He was insinuating he could guide her in passing the riddle without her understanding how he'd done it.

Challenge accepted.

"Game on. If you can get me across that threshold without me knowing why, you win."

"Nonono, that's not how you're supposed to play the game! This is a team exercise, the whole point is you don't think about it and we win cooperatively."

"You'd rather I didn't figure out how it works."

"Yes, that is exactly my preference."

"How long have we known each other, exactly?"

Andrew smiled. He knew what was coming, it was written all over his smug face. It was hard not to smile back, but she managed.

"Just over four years. Not long after we started med school."

"And over the course of those four years, do you recall a time when someone said 'Lillian, don't push yourself, it's too much', and I said 'You're right, I'll take it easy'?"

While Andrew still smiled, it was starting to wear thin and he was staring just over her shoulder. Resignation.

"Not off the top of my head."

"You can't stop me from being who I am."

"No. I can't."

"Take your best shot at stopping me from being myself."

Andrew tilted his head, shrugged, just a little, then started giving his instructions in a flat monotone.

"Open your menu."

"Menu."

"Go to 'Settings'."

"Settings."

"Go to 'Multimedia Options'."

"Multimedia Options."

"Go to 'Browsers'."

"Browsers."

"Click 'Restore Factory Settings'."

"What?"

"Do you want to catch up with Hammertime or not?"

"Done."

She closed the menu to find Andrew sweeping his hands toward the open gate of the castle, bowing insipidly as if ushering her down a red carpet. She walked up to the threshold, her palms already feeling itchy, and forced herself over the edge. Andrew sauntered over to join her, his hands clasped behind his back. Lillian was counting the seconds.

"It's okay, if you did what I said nothing bad will happen."

Lillian waited a full half minute anyway. Nothing happened. That was it? That was all they had to do? Why? What did that have to do with anything? She stalked back over the threshold to have another look at the plinth. Andrew strode along behind her, a faint tremor to his voice ruining an otherwise brilliant performance in the role of someone who couldn't care less.

"Yay, we can push on, fantastic. It would be even more fantastic if our direct competitor wasn't at least one step ahead of us, so we'd better not spend too much time...retracing...our own."

Lillian was boggling at the text. While Andrew had gone out of his way to make his solution as discreet as possible, it's still much easier to solve a problem when you're attacking it from two angles. She rechecked the plinth.

If you've erred and don't unwrite your history—

She checked the fine print of the reset button she'd just selected.

'Warning – selecting this option will erase all browser data from your Mobius Enterprises headset. This includes, but is not limited to: passwords, cookies, bookmarks, preferences and history.'

Her history. It had sounded so grandiose, buried in text that spoke of decency, rulers and purity. But all along, she only needed to clear her browser history.

She turned back to Andrew, who had one eye scrunched shut. She felt quite relaxed. She had no idea why he'd made such a fuss about it.

"Neat trick. Erase your browser history, unwrite your history, very clever. Still don't know why you were so uptight about telling me, though."

Andrew, far from relaxing, clenched his other eye closed. Then he turned away from her and stuck his fingers in his ears. Lillian was about to shove him when the penny dropped. Purity. Erring. What did her browser history have to do with...oh. Oh God. OH GOD.

"You've got to be kidding me!"

Andrew didn't turn, but he raised his head into the air and jammed his fingers a little deeper into his ears.

"There it is. Knew you'd get there in the end. Despite my best—"

"I don't do that! I've never used the headset for anything like that! That's a lie!"

Andrew's fingers obviously weren't working. He pulled them out and turned around.

"You sure? Never? Because I have a very specific memory—"

"Shut up."

"Oooookay then."

Lillian folded her arms and glared at the plinth. Well, Andrew had promised, then she'd promised, then they'd both delivered. If anyone was to blame in this situation, it was her. Just the way she liked it. Though not so much as usual under these circumstances. Andrew, now the bubble had already burst and he'd been proven right, as usual, was regaling her with his methodology. Accompanied by his usual, refined, 'I told you so' aura.

"I mean, logically, we knew we were on a crusade. The very least we should've done was delete our browser histories. If it makes you feel any better, the only two players who passed the test were underage. Everyone who could use the headset to look at adult material, did. Hammertime figured it out before he crossed over. He's probably whacking one off right now, while he admires his own avatar in the third person."

"Says the guy who spent half a day making his own avatar. It took Hammertime about two minutes to find the solution to the riddle. How long did it take you, again?"

Now that did make Andrew's face pucker. A small consolation prize for Lillian's own lost face.

"That's a low blow. You said I needed to make my avatar look good, so I'd be a contender. And I never said how long it took me to solve the riddle, but it was around six hours. In fairness, it was pretty hard to concentrate when Godhammer could come back at any moment and murder me."

"So you hung around here watching them? I thought I told you to log off?"

"You 'recommended' we all log off. The rest of them did, wisely. I "stupidly" stayed behind so I could test the second riddle and watch them solving the third. I could only do it in thirty-second shifts but it was enough to get the gist."

Lillian felt her hard facade waver, just a little. Andrew had stayed there until 1am. At least. Then he'd woken up at 6am and incited her wrath, just to give her all this information, privately. Considering the state of their relationship, he was pretty brave to summon her here and convey the nature of his discovery. Which led to another question.

"How will we tell the rest of our party to deal with the last riddle?"

"Same way I told you, but more nonchalantly so we get less friction. For all our sakes. I doubt they'll overthink it like we did. Hammertime was in a heck of a rush, though. If he just sent a message saying 'delete your browser history', I'm pretty confident his whole party is aware they're surrounded by perverts."

Lillian brayed laughter before she could stop herself. That observation took some of the sting out of her ordeal. She got it under control as quickly as possible, only to find Andrew wistfully smiling ahead. Another point to him. Curses. She hadn't thought she'd find any joy over the course of this encounter. Now she had, she needed to allocate more energy to concealing it. She coughed in her throat, then went back into business mode.

"We'll have a look at the next riddle together, then I'm off to get breakfast and coffee. I'll be back on tonight."

"Sounds good. If you unblock me, somewhere, I'll update you on our progress. But once you're offline I'm going to bed. Need to catch up on sleep, it was a long day."

"Thank you. I'll have a much better day myself, now I know this is in good hands."

Andrew's smile grew, until he realized it might be a little too big. He coughed to cover his face while he regained his composure. Lillian let it slide. He'd earned it.

15

MEMORY LANE

Damien kept his head down as he passed the internet cafe for the third time in ten minutes. Each time he committed to entering, he found a convincing alibi to change direction at the last second; he wasn't going inside! He'd just been crossing the street, he'd mistaken the internet cafe for another shop further down the road or he'd left his wallet at home. While none of these scenarios were true, they were all perfectly feasible alternate realities that precluded confronting the one he resided in.

He'd been out shopping for groceries, making himself useful while 'Daemien' was dead in yet another alternate reality. He could only stay at home reading the comments on his profile page for so long before the walls started creeping in. His stunt yesterday had certainly attracted a lot of attention. A lot of it was good, but not all of it.

The complaints in this case were wide ranging. Anger at being misled, dissatisfaction with the short length of the stream (which seemed particularly selfish to Damien), too much emphasis on in-game politics rather than gameplay, and – get this – 'shoddy camera work' while in combat. If Damien started slowing down so his viewers could get a clearer look at whatever was killing him, his streams would be *a lot* shorter.

Had those same people been watching this grocery run through his eyes, they'd have crucified him. Not the ones admonishing stream length and camera work, though. They'd be complaining in other directions by now. Damien had bought his groceries between the second and third runs to ensure, one way or another, that he would soon return home. He passed the door for the third time. Then stopped in the street, turned around and marched inside.

The gloominess had been desirable when Damien had first passed through, but it made a very different impression now he wasn't looking for somewhere to hide. A few seconds after he'd stepped off the street, his unaugmented eyes still acclimatizing to the dingy interior, all the lights were thrown on. Damien squinted at the man responsible and he squinted back, a vapid smile plastered to his face as though his retinas weren't flash-frying in their sockets. It was not the old man Damien had feared seeing. He relaxed, then became more concerned in a new direction. Where was Gian? Who was this guy? He was much younger, maybe in his early twenties. Or late twenties. Early thirties? He wasn't very good at eyeballing that yet.

The new proprietor made it a little easier with his opening statement.

"Hey! I mean, hello. Please, have a seat, you've got the whole place to yourself. Not the pods, they're unavailable until...until later. If you like, I can...oh, but first you have to pay at the desk...sorry. Haven't been here long. How can I help you today?"

However old he was, early thirties was way out. This guy was too polite, too bad at talking to people, and most important of all, he obviously cared too much. Damien knew it was an unfair pigeonhole, but his brief experience told him that the older people got, the less they cared about stuff. Either that, or they learned to stop showing it. He himself was still waiting to find out which. The shop had been completely empty when Gian was behind the desk, and the old man couldn't have cared less. This guy was falling over himself just to say hello.

Damien gave his first hidey hole a once over while his host

stumbled through the introduction. The old, manky curtain concealing the bathroom stalls. The computer desks, still gathering dust as the age of screen games settled into its long-lowering coffin. And the haphazardly stacked pods, now laid to rest before their time. Mummified, as it were, with extravagant amounts of red tape. How wrapping them up made their presence any safer was a mystery, but the CU officials who'd performed the embalming had obviously considered their work done before moving on to spread their tidings of bureaucracy to the next struggling establishment. They hadn't caught the shop down the road that had feigned closing down for the last decade. Of course not. That might've been useful.

There was no sign of Gian anywhere. This was a problem. Damien had assumed he'd be identified the moment he walked in. With this stranger in his place, he'd have to take the additional step of identifying himself as the harbinger of their misfortune. It would be easier to come back when Gian was working and let the misery commence organically.

"Sorry, I was looking for Gian; older person, on his antique phone a lot. When will he be back?"

"Oh, I'm sorry, it's just me and dad running this place for the next few weeks, until we shut do— until business picks up. Gian won't be coming back. I can pass hi—"

"Why won't he be coming back? Did he get fired?"

The words tumbled out of Damien's mouth before he realized how incriminating they were. Fortunately, the new manager was still focused on customer service rather than putting two and two together.

"I've taken over for him, and Antonio still runs the night shift. I'll see Gian when I get home, so I can bring him a message if you like. What would you like to tell him, and who should I say was looking for him?"

"That's okay. Thanks for your help. I hope the pods get sorted out soon."

Damien turned and was out the door before the new host could even reply. They were a family business. Damien wished he'd minded his own. Things were not going well for them. It sounded as though Gian had been permanently removed from duty, thanks to his interference. It would've been easier if he'd just moved on. An apology wouldn't fix the mess he'd made. He headed back home, wishing all the while that he'd left the past where it belonged.

"You're early."

Lillian gave Andrew a cursory nod, walked straight up to the plinth and read it again. It had been a nice change of pace, talking to him again yesterday, but she'd rather not get too chummy. They still had work to do. She'd spent every available second thinking about it all through the day, without any means of testing her theories. All she had was conjecture, which had taken her no further than she'd gotten with Andrew in the early hours of that morning. Reading the riddle face to face was no more helpful than reciting it at work.

The third quest houses key that's hidden near,
But looking for it makes it hard to find,
Don't focus on the path and it shall clear,
Or focus and be trapped by your own mind.

It was gibberish. The whole riddle was self-contradictory and unhelpful. Since when did looking for something make it difficult to find? They had to unlock the door, clearly, it was right there. What was this garbage about being trapped by your mind? More unwanted melodramatic flair. Lillian walked up to the gate and double-checked it, just to make sure she hadn't been seeing things when she and Andrew first looked it over that morning.

There was a prominent keyhole set into the middle of the gate, large enough to suggest the key was about the size of a short-sword. 'Near' had to mean within the courtyard. She and Andrew had searched for an hour that morning without success, but they knew they were on the right track as Andrew had watched Hammertime's group go through the same process.

According to Andrew, the four players had combed the courtyard for nearly five hours before they finally found the key. He hadn't seen who got it, but it was the only logical explanation. They'd taken a ten-minute break sitting together in a huddle, presumably to congratulate themselves, and passed through the open gate a short while later. It started closing immediately after they'd left.

They'd considered whether or not Hammertime's group would be able to take the key with them and had decided against it. Even if they did, it probably respawned somewhere when the doors closed, as with any other dungeon that had notable on-site requirements, although this 'dungeon' was unlike any Lillian had ever been subjected to. The alternative, that only the first group could pass through, didn't bear thinking about.

Lillian checked her friends list and found Mr. Healy, Judgementday and Legolias conspicuously absent. They needed the additional bodies to help reduce the length of the search. She thought Andrew had said he'd get that covered.

"Why isn't everyone else here yet?"

"They're all logging on after dinner. I got them into the courtyard individually over the course of the day, don't think any of them figured out the implications. I sent you a message saying so. Thanks for unblocking me, by the way, but I guess you didn't check before you logged on."

Lillian nodded and went back to what she was doing. She couldn't focus on the path, but had to find the key. Their current theory was that the key was invisible and hidden somewhere in the massive courtyard. If that was the case, it would be the least absurd of the three riddles they'd encountered so far. It was the only theory they'd come up with where the last line and Hammertime's actions tied together to make any sort of sense. You couldn't find the key by looking for it, so you had to open your mind to other possibilities. Such as the possibility that the key was invisible.

No wonder Hammertime's group had wanted a ten-minute

sit-down by the time they were finished. If she and Andrew got lucky and did a good enough job of searching, maybe they could all start the next riddle once the rest of the team got back. She turned to Andrew, who was standing and watching her. Waiting for orders. They could pick up where they left off that morning.

"I'll start on that side, up against the wall. You start on the other side. Make sure you sweep it thoroughly. If we meet in the middle and haven't found anything I'll have to assume you missed it, then I'll have to check your side as well."

"And likewise, I'll have to assume you missed it on your side. So if it comes to that, we'll check each other's sides."

Lillian grunted. If he moved into her half and found the key somewhere she'd missed it, she'd be mortified. She gave him a nod, then headed to her position.

She'd already decided the most efficient means to check for the key. She could push her sword in front of her over the ground, sideways, and listen out for any noises. That would require her to be on her hands and knees, so it would take longer. Alternately, she could drag her hammer behind her, although that would drain her mana through Divine Might quickly, and would be less sensitive. She'd test them both, then—

"Actually, Lillian, before we get started I'd like to talk to you. If that's alright?"

She groaned and shambled back around, setting her sights on Andrew. Who hadn't moved from his spot. She just wanted to get on with the quest. Hammertime could be ten riddles ahead by now. They needed to catch up and didn't have as much time to do it in as the professional-streamer-turned-amateur-betrayer did. Every second counted.

There was also a good chance that the Carlisle-Elite would figure out the first riddle for themselves and follow them inside. They could already know the location and the time, having followed Trinytea there yesterday. There wasn't much more to the riddle than that. At least they'd still be kept at a distance by the second riddle. The courtyard that had fractured Lillian's authority would now provide a barrier against the vast majority of encroaching enemy forces. Solving the third riddle would be a lot more difficult with enemies breathing down their necks, though. Better they figure it out as soon as possible. She reasoned with Andrew as gently as she could bring herself to.

"Is it important? More important than this? Can't it wait?"

"It can, but this is of long-term importance rather than short term. While you had a whole party to deal with I didn't want to get into it, but now it's just us. I'd like to use this time before the rest of our players get here to have a conversation. Ten minutes, before we start doing the quest."

She hadn't come here to have a sit-down and an awkward chat. She'd come here to get her party through that door.

"No. Definitely not. And Andrew, sorry, but they're my players now. Just because Hammertime threw away his role as 'co-leader' doesn't mean I'm considering someone else for the position. We'll talk after we're through the quest. Maybe. Not before. We don't know how many more riddles there are, Hammertime could already be on the last one. Go do your side, we'll meet in the middle."

She turned and made her way to the furthest edge of the courtyard, then dug her shield into the corner and wiggled it around, looking for a telltale sound. A *clink*, most likely, if it made contact with this infernal hypothetical key. The corner clear, she put the edge of the shield about a millimeter away from the wall and started lightly dragging it backward across the ground. She was completely focused on what she was doing. So Andrew's voice from just a few feet behind her came as a bit of a shock.

"Lillian, if we—"

"What are you doing here? Go check your side! I'd like to get through this riddle before I eat, so we're all fresh and rested for the next part. Is that too much to ask?"

Andrew scratched his head, but didn't move. It *was* too much to ask.

"I know you want to get on with this. So do I. But I think it's *very* important we sit down and talk things through first. I did spend the whole day getting everyone organized, solving the hairy hands riddle and applying myself to this one while you were at work. I just need ten minutes. Please?"

Lillian stared at him. Andrew might've said please, but he wasn't pleading. If anything she could detect just a hint of frustration bubbling under the surface. It was obviously important to him that they have their long-awaited talk. The circumstances of their breakup were messy, to say the least, and Lillian could also do with a chance to vent her feelings. Just not right now, when there were other things at stake.

She had to admit, he'd gone above and beyond on her behalf the last two days. If it was anyone other than him asking for this, after doing so much, Lillian would've immediately accepted. It was only because of their history that she didn't want to talk to him.

She couldn't afford for them to fall out, now that he was one of the only people she could rely on. That was one issue. The other was the crushing paranoia that Hammertime could complete the quest chain at any second. If they couldn't spare ten minutes, it was likely already too late. Ten minutes. If it got out of control, she'd call it off and get back to the matter at hand.

"If we have this talk, you have to promise there won't be any more distractions. Even if you don't like how it turns out. We'll both focus on the quest for the rest of our partnership. Deal?"

Andrew's hand shot out to shake on it. This all seemed very formal. Well, that was preferable. If he'd tried to play their history off casually she'd have been furious. Lillian grabbed his hand and they shook, then he turned and motioned for her to follow.

"Come sit with me. We'll have a good vantage point if anyone comes for us from either side."

Lillian shrugged. Fair enough. She followed him and he sat down cross-legged, right in the middle of the courtyard, before beckoning her to sit opposite. She was looking back toward the gate by which they'd entered, with her back to the gate they needed to pass through next. They shouldn't have to worry about anyone coming from her side until sunset, but better safe than sorry.

Andrew let her get comfortable, spared himself one last glance at the keep gate separating them from the continuation of their quest, then focused entirely on Lillian. He didn't waste any time.

"So the way you screwed me over with Damien was pretty cold-hearted, huh?"

"That's how you want to start this? You're not serious?"

"I'm very serious. We put all that work into making my life viable again and you tore it out of my hands at the last second."

"Okay. First up, it's your fault your life fell apart. You were in your final year, exams coming up, all you had to do was study your way through them and you'd have been done. You'd have been placed in an apprenticeship, like me, and your future would've been on rails. Then you got into the Saga Online Alpha."

"I told you all about it, you agreed it was a good idea. Saga had been in the pipeline for years, nobody knew when it was coming out. Then my brother invited me to join the alpha test. Only a thousand people invited and he gave me his only plus one! You said so yourself, it would be a good way to blow off steam when I wasn't studying."

"Oh, you blew off steam alright! You didn't study at all! How many times did I wake up to find you still on the headset? You slept through the day and played all night. You barely ate. Worse than that, you lied to me. You told me you were studying while I was asleep. Then the exams rocked up. Lo and behold, you failed. Not just marginally, they wouldn't even let you retake the test. All those years, wasted."

"It's Richard's fault. He should never have invited me to the alpha when he knew I had exams. It was the worst time to have any distractions, and Saga—"

"It's got nothing to do with Richard. That was entirely your fault. You're not a child. If someone offers you something, it's up to you whether you accept it. You're responsible for your own actions. Magnitude isn't my favorite person but you don't get to blame him for this, any more than you get to blame me. Own your mistake."

Andrew had been speaking levelly for the duration of their 'chat'. This was the first time Lillian had given him pause. She could read him so easily. They'd been together for a long time, and she'd seen him at his worst and his best. Right now, he was some terrible place in between.

"You're right. You're completely right. I let my emotions get the better of me and ruined everything. I lied to you, because I knew what I was doing was wrong and you'd stop me if I told the truth. I was just so fed up of studying, and I wanted to forget all the pressure and the stress. That part was definitely my fault."

"But it gets better, Andrew. You didn't just ruin your own life, you took your best shot at ruining mine. I gave up my holiday to get you established in the same game that put you in that position. It was the only viable option you had left and I didn't want to support a deadbeat. You're too clever to live off my back, it would've destroyed you. But I could still support you. I did so the best way I knew how, by coming to stand by your side when you needed me. You showed me the ropes, you gave me all the information you got in the alpha about paladin skills and traits. I studied how to play Saga as hard as I ever studied to gain my apprenticeship. I kept your people in line and destroyed everyone who got in your way. How did you respond? By putting my career at risk."

"We'd always—"

"After two months of co-running Rising Tide with you – leveling, budgeting, researching, planning, fighting, editing, conquering, all of it – after all that you 'pranked' me, by showing up at my hospital on a gurney pretending to be dead! Aside from the humiliation of investing in you as a human being, I also had to deal with the shame of not seeing through your trick. My peers couldn't believe I'd fallen for it. I was off work for *two weeks* recovering from your stunt. As if you hadn't already—"

She hadn't realized she was ranting. Everything she'd wanted to tell him was pouring out of her. This was why she hadn't wanted to talk about it until they were done with the quest. No good could come of this. But they were here now, at his request, and he was going to listen. So she found it hard to grind to a halt when Andrew threw up his hand, asking her to stop. She did, but just barely.

"Lillian, it's no secret that you're angry with me. You've made that abundantly clear. But please, let me speak. I can't explain myself if you're trying to do it for me."

"Why start now? I did everything else for you! What more could I have possibly done? How did you think—"

"Lillian! Please! I've needed to talk to you about this for so long, and you're taking it from me. I know how badly I screwed up, but I've had time and distance to process it and it's time you heard my side. When I'm done, you can keep—"

"It's always about what you need, isn't it? You need to talk to me for ten minutes. You need to tell me your side. You need to unwind from exam prep. You need help managing Rising Tide. You need this, you need that, when will your needs end? If you're really sorry, you should consider what I need: I need you to shut up and listen!"

Andrew shut up. Andrew listened.

"I ran into Damien after he killed all the players in that Twisted Forest raid. I went there to do it myself, but he got there first. He even brought Godhammer into it and got all of them killed as well. He was in the middle of announcing his victory, and rather than stopping him I let it run. I was happy he'd shown up to give you grief in the last days of the competition, when I knew it would hurt you most. I wasn't planning on taking it from you. I just wanted to show you your actions had consequences. I needed to let you know you hadn't beaten me, after you turned me into a social outcast of the guild we built together and ended our relationship in the worst way imaginable. I was stuck on forced leave at home, nothing better to do. I couldn't just let it slide, even though I knew how stressed you were and how much you needed to win."

Andrew had stopped trying to interject. He wasn't complaining, or interrupting her. A pleasant change from usual.

"Then I saw Damien getting attention. I could hurt you even more by supporting him. Good! He wouldn't win, but he'd make a stir and you'd suffer for it. Good. I invited him to my house, so I could help with his campaign. The same way I'd helped you. What do I find? His mother was dying. He came to you for help. And you kicked him down a hole. I had to leave him alone and cry when I finally realized what a *monster* you are. That's when I decided to destroy everything. I would've liked to turn the other cheek and let you be on your way, even after you took everything from me. I wasn't strong enough. I'm sorry I made myself the final nail in your coffin. But you had it coming! You deserve all the misery that's come your way! It's no one's fault but your own. Learn to accept the blame for your own mistakes."

Lillian was done. The quest ahead of her was completely out of sight and out of mind. Andrew had eclipsed it by pushing her into this discussion, and she'd given him both barrels. Lillian was relieved to have finally unburdened herself on him, having carried the weight of her revenge for weeks. The only question now was how he'd react. It was hardly a question, given how well she knew him. But he still had the right of reply. He was staring at the floor for some time before he answered.

"The competition ended up being more stressful than the exams, but I had nothing left if it failed. Richard was messaging me the whole time, trying to convince me to cut you out of Rising Tide and end our relationship. He wanted his party to support me, but they'd only do so if you were out of the picture. I got the whole 'This guild ain't big enough for the two of you' speech. He also said you were unstable. Not good for me, in general."

"You never told me about that. So the whole time I was helping you, you were keeping that from me. As if I didn't have enough—"

"He made that offer at the end of the summer, when you'd almost *left*. Look, I let you speak without interrupting, even though there was plenty I wanted to say. Will you let me finish?"

Lillian folded her arms. Fine. She'd just have to save her grievances for the end. This would probably take longer than ten minutes, but they were invested now. If it took too long, she'd hold that against him as well. In the midst of her own indignation, Andrew's 'air quotes'-accompanied intonation of the word *left* did not ring the alarm bells it would have otherwise. Andrew glanced at the closed gate behind her, muttered under his breath, then picked up where he left off.

"As well as the two-leader problem, he said you were stealing my limelight and you'd take votes from me just by staying in the guild. After everything I'd seen, I knew he was right. You were getting way more attention than I was, even though you were trying to redirect it to me. But I refused to throw you out. I owed you too much to do that to you. So I told him no. Then, right after we took Godhammer's base and turned it into our highest-level outpost, you told me you were leaving. Later the same day, we had that argument when you kicked Trinytea out of the guild. I was handling it my own way, but you took over without asking me. You were leaving, but you wouldn't hand over control. That argument was the last time we spoke. I left your apartment the next day, while you were on your first day at work. I messaged you that evening, but you didn't reply. I kept messaging you. Nothing. You ghosted me. For the whole final month of the competition."

This was taking a turn for the worse. Andrew had nailed it. He'd been watching and analyzing her every bit as intently as she'd been watching him. And he was circling the truth of it, which she'd worked so hard to keep from him.

"I told Richard you were out and he rewarded me with high-tier items, including this bag. Thanks to that, I was able to deal with your frontline duties as well as my own administrative duties. I had to. With no one else I could trust, managing the game's largest guild alone, I had to be online eighteen hours a day. I spent most of the time coordinating from in base, just trying to hold onto what I had. My leadership sucked compared to yours, so I compensated with severe consequences. I didn't have anything else. I kept messaging you, asking for advice, begging you to get back in touch. You never replied. So when Richard said I needed to prove we'd severed ties with a stunt, I agreed. At least I'd get your attention. Then he told me what the stunt was. I refused, point blank. He threatened me to go through with it, or else lose his support. I was terrified, but I couldn't do what he asked. I was alone, scared and tired. That night, unable to sleep, I logged into the game at 5am. I thought since I couldn't sleep I might as well get some organization done. I think you know what I saw."

Lillian had really, really hoped he hadn't noticed. But now he was presenting it like this, everything was starting to make sense. And he was building up, exactly the same way she did when she was so sure she was in the right.

"I saw *you*. On the Rising Tide player list. Leveling up your character in secret, in the early hours of the morning. You'd blocked me to make sure I couldn't see when you were online, as I found out not long after, but as guild leader I could still see you on the list of Rising Tide members. Which you well knew. You logged out about thirty seconds after I logged in, just in time for me to pull up the list of online players and watch your name fade to gray. You were level 36. Eight levels higher than when you had announced your "retirement". None of my night watch had told me you were still playing. They respected you more than me and were veiling your actions from me, right under my nose. Do you know what that looked like? No contact with me, leveling up in secret, bringing in guild members to keep it secret with you? You were organizing a coup. Richard must have known about it, which explains why he was pressuring me to do something so horrible to you."

Lillian had completely forgotten about getting through the gate. This was awful. She really thought she'd gotten away with it. Instead, it was her own actions that had triggered the whole series of events leading to Andrew's defeat.

"That was the last straw. I consented to the prank on you and pulled it off later that morning. I hated my entire guild for the rest of the week, because they'd all lied to me on your say so. I couldn't punish them all, but I punished the ones who'd been on night watch when I saw you log out without bothering to tell them why. It was better left unsaid. And then, for good measure, I kicked Damien down a hole. I was already planning on it, just to upset my brother. First he'd gotten his own way by making me consent to that horrible prank, and wouldn't stop going on about how he'd been right all along. Then, the very next day, he wanted me to chaperone some kid who'd taken my spot on 'The Saga Continues'. You know, that guy you made competition leader in my place? Damien made it much easier when he fed me that tear-jerking story about his mom being in hospital. I mean, what a cliche, right? I dealt with ten scammers a day at my peak, all coming to me with sob stories like that. The story wasn't even particularly creative! I expect at least a little effort from people scamming me. Except it turned out his mom really *was* in the hospital, and that I'm a psycho for not accepting his ridiculous story at face value. What a *horrible* person I am. Even Richard's party agreed I was a psychopath. But let's all *praise* Lillian and Damien, for taking down the big, nasty bully. Damien got his mom out of hospital by taking me down. Good for him! And you were by his side, using inside information to kill the mount Richard sent me, destroy the waiting room you'd once helped me capture and set the stage for my downfall after your own takeover bid failed. *Good for you.*"

Lillian hadn't been looking at Andrew for the last portion of his rant. She couldn't. She was holding her hands over her face, trying not to scream into them. All this drama because she'd been trying to hide her intentions from him. How had such a simple plan gone so horribly wrong?

She was still playing the events over in her head when Andrew coughed, pointedly. She drew down her hands to look over her fingertips. He looked exhausted, and smug. He had a unique smugness to fit every occasion. This must be his trademark vindication smugness. He pointed over her shoulder and she followed it to find his smugness was even more justified than she'd thought. What she saw did not quite outweigh Andrew's storytelling showmanship, but it came pretty close.

The gate leading forward was wide open.

"What the—how did—"

"No time. Let's go before it changes its mind. I'm still not 100% sure how this thing functions, technically."

He Blinked forward and stood at the gate as Lillian struggled to shift gear, gathering herself and running to meet him. He turned inside as she arrived and the two of them passed through together. Her EXP bar shot up another level and a half, bringing her to level 46 in the blink of an eye. She'd never been less interested in her character's progress. As they crossed, the gates swung closed behind them. Lillian was still reeling as Andrew went into his menu and started typing. Her internal workings were in complete disarray. There was only one thing that was clear, so she started from there.

"You tricked me through the riddle. Why did you do that? Why couldn't you just tell me how it works? Was it all an excuse to take out your anger on me?"

Andrew didn't look up from his task. His movements indicated he was sending several messages. To whom, Lillian had no idea. She was still waiting on the answer to her first question, while processing everything Andrew had laid on her. He stopped typing, closed his menu and set his sights back on her.

"No. Of course not. I did it because I had to. We misread the riddle this morning, and we misread how Hammertime and his group solved it. We assumed they'd done it by searching the courtyard. They actually solved it in the last ten minutes, while they were all sitting down doing nothing. The way to pass through the gate is by not thinking about passing through the gate. The headset measures our brainwaves to see if we're problem-solving, while the game tracks our movement to see if we're searching for things. Simultaneously. I know, because I had three test subjects to get through it over the course of the day."

He folded his arms and started tapping his foot. Old habits die hard. Lillian was about to speak again when the first bubble appeared, then the second and third in rapid succession. They contained Judgementday, Legolias and Mr. Healy, who were all looking very relieved to see both Lillian and Aetherius. He'd got them all through the riddle without letting Lillian know. But how had Andrew gotten hold of them so quickly if they were all offline? Andrew was all smiles.

"Well done guys, it worked. You can unblock Lillian, now."

One by one, they all went into their menus to do as Andrew had requested. He turned to Lillian and came very close, but she was the first to speak. Her anger lacked its usual weight, but there was still enough of it to push her words.

"You didn't need to have them block me. You could've just told me how it worked and then we'd have distracted each other normally. Or you could've found a different way of distracting me."

Andrew turned back to the three players, who were awaiting his orders. Notifications saying they'd come online had popped up in Lillian's HUD, one by one.

"Alright guys, I want to discuss our next step with the party leader. We might need to eat before we get started properly, but I wanted to show her the three of you had made it here already. I know it made you feel bad, but it was only temporary and I can assure you it was *very* necessary. If you could give us some privacy, I'd appreciate it."

The three of them turned away, all looking psyched to get started. None of them had any idea what Lillian had just been put through. Andrew turned back to her, keeping a careful, cheerful smile on his face. The words he told her could not have been more at odds with his presentation.

"Wrong. You're wrong on all counts. We both know how your mind works. If you knew the objective was not to think about getting through the gate, you'd have thought about it every five seconds. If I tried to distract you with funny videos, like I managed with the rest of this lot, you'd have insisted we get on with the quest. Mr. Healy went blind and grew hair out of his hands halfway through our first attempt, I had enough on my plate without keeping all of you preoccupied at once. 'Hey, Lillian, I've got a really *funny* video of a monkey riding on a pig, let's watch that for a few minutes instead of catching up with Hammertime.' I think not. That room was the worst possible challenge for you, because you don't know how to switch off. I had to trick you through it without you knowing what I was doing. Which it turns out I *can* do, by the way."

He called out to the rest of the party, his voice suddenly cheery and light.

"I'll head off first. I've been online all day and need to eat something. I leave you in our party leader's capable hands!"

He turned to Lillian as the blue light enveloped him, still smiling.

"It turns out I lack the strength to keep my misgivings contained, as well. But at least I'm here when you need me, rather than ghosting you and stabbing you in the back."

The bubble vanished and Andrew was gone from within it. Lillian stared into the empty space he'd vacated, trying to unknot everything she'd just heard. She'd rather do it in private. She turned to her three guild members, who were still all looking happy as clams and eager to get on with the quest. She'd have to disappoint them.

"Sorry, guys, Andrew just got me through that last riddle and I haven't eaten yet. Let's meet up here at...eight thirty. Make sure you're all rested and ready to play for as long as possible, I want to get through whatever the next riddle is before the end of the night."

She gave them a wave and they all waved back, none the wiser, then all four of them logged off simultaneously. Lillian immediately sent Andrew a message directly into his inbox.

"I completely understand why you're so angry. You have every right to feel the way you feel. I had no idea you'd caught me out, I'd really hoped you hadn't, but there's a good explanation. I'd be grateful if you could come and meet with me privately at 20:15. You worked most of it out yourself already, but you're missing some vital information that might change your mind. I hope to see you then."

She clicked 'Send' and pulled off the headset. That had been an enlightening exchange. And painful. What an idiot she'd been. Good intentions don't count for much when they carry consequences this dire. Good deeds, even less so.

After she'd finished eating, she'd have to pull together all the proof she could and show Andrew what he was missing. That would be easy. The hard part would be doing it with all the kindness she could muster.

After what the two of them had put him through, she'd have to come clean. Even though it would hurt him more than what he already believed.

16

SQUARE ONE

Damien logged in. He'd been presented with the Dark Tower as a place to respawn, as is standard, and had ended up back in the opening room of the Path of Deceit. He'd wondered if he'd be placed in the initial chamber, where all three paths would be available to him. It would've been nice to have the option of trying one of the other paths, but since he'd started by choosing the one that was most suitable for him it was no great loss.

He'd promised he'd livestream again at the end of his last broadcast. While he could do without the scrutiny, he could definitely do with the views. This was the unchartered territory he'd been pining to share with his hungry audience. He just hadn't factored in that the unchartered territory would be a dingy murder tunnel and that everyone would be tuning in to watch him die.

Hopefully he was wrong, on that score. He'd probably do better this time, although that was a pretty low bar given he'd been skewered in the very first room. He walked up to the wall, unsheathed his daggers and attempted to chip at one of the stone blocks hemming him in. Each dagger lost a whole point of durability and the stone was completely unaffected. Yeah. This dungeon hadn't seemed like it would give him such an easy option, but at least he'd tried.

Either way, it was 20:19. Go time. He started livestreaming and the viewers piled in. He quickly minimized the chat box, leaving only the viewer count in the very top right-hand corner of his peripheral vision. This challenge would be no easy feat, he needed as little in the way of distraction as possible. But first he'd have to acknowledge his viewers and let them know what was in store.

"Welcome back, everyone. I'm glad you've all tuned in for the Dark Tower, the Path of Deceit, take two. Yesterday wasn't what I was hoping for, so I'll be taking it a little more seriously this time round. For one, I won't be providing much commentary unless I'm sure I'm completely safe. A lot of people complained yesterday that they didn't get a good look at what killed me, but I'm afraid that goes with the territory. It was a super-dark chamber with four stealthy spiky death balls in the corners, and we now know they can kill me in two volleys. We also know they predict movement. Full disclosure: I'll be moving my head around and changing direction a lot. If you didn't like the blurry camera angles yesterday, avert your gaze."

He equipped his daggers and twisted them in his hands experimentally. He had no opportunity for a warm-up before he started and needed to be at the top of his game the moment he entered the room. It was a daunting prospect. A single misstep could result in another twenty-four hours before he could try again. But that was still less daunting than the logistical difficulties of the enemies he was facing. The least he could do was outline the exact nature of the problem these enemies posed, to clue in his viewers as to why he was very likely about to die. At least explaining it would buy him a little more stream time.

"So the enemies yesterday were called 'Cave Urchins'. It may have been a little unclear given they killed me in about six seconds, but they appear to be immobile long-ranged masses set into the top four corners of the chamber. If you watch the replay of the livestream I posted yesterday and pause it at seventeen minutes and nineteen seconds, you'll get a good look at one. I've thought about how to deal with them for the last twenty-four hours and would like to share my thoughts with you: I have absolutely no idea how to deal with them. The core body is completely protected by the spines, so there's no way I can stick my hand in there to stab them without getting murdered myself. But that won't be an issue, because they're too high up for me to reach and I have no ranged weapons."

He was still spinning his daggers around in his hands and had started hopping back and forth on the spot, the paces getting a little wider each time to stretch out his comfort zone while still maintaining the same speed. About three steps a second. He was a long way from draining his stamina yet. It was hovering around 95%.

"If I still had Noigel, I could Demon Gate up there and stab one. Theoretically. In fact, I'm pretty sure he'd be killed before he got anywhere close and I'd also probably be stabbed dozens of times in the process. Then I'd probably be finished off by the remaining three, while I was still in the air. They predict movement, remember? I imagine that includes falling. I'm not willing to test that theory anyway."

His paces were getting wider and his legs were starting to pump. He was maintaining the time between each step as the distance increased, so even adjusting the distance a little required significantly more stamina. His hops were now two meters apart and his stamina was sitting pretty at 75%.

"In other words, even if Demon Gating was an option I don't have the means to kill these things. Which means there are three possibilities. The first is that I'm not supposed to kill them. I'm supposed to avoid being killed by them. But the door ahead was barred, so I clearly need to do something in that room in order to move forward."

His feet were now far apart enough between each step to qualify as jumps. His stamina was no longer holding steady. It was draining, down about 10% with each leap. He reduced the distance a little and the stamina reduction became about 5% per hop. Okay. He reverted to his original hops and it stabilized.

"It could be that I need to open the chest, take whatever's inside and move through undetected. Except, I isolated a still image of the stream at sixteen minutes twenty-one seconds that shows the door was still barred after I'd already opened the chest. Maybe there's a delay before the door opens, but that seems unlikely."

He stretched out his steps as far as he could while still maintaining the same speed. They were good, long strides, definitely enough to move him out of position at short notice. His stamina was already too low to support it for long. He'd only managed three and a half when he stumbled as his movement was tempered by the cost. He tried to revert back to short hops immediately afterwards and nearly fell over. Okay. He paced on the spot to let his stamina replenish as he continued talking, his eyes flitting toward his viewer count: 20,000. He'd retained all his viewers from yesterday. Wow. Shouldn't have looked. Damien didn't let it interrupt his flow. He kept doing exactly what he'd been doing before he knew he was under such heavy observation.

"The second option is that there's something in the chest that will help me deal with the Cave Urchins. I never got to check it yesterday, so I have no idea. But I know this is the agility path for occultists and long-range options are much more accessible for the traditional intelligence route, using spells. Although I think an intelligence occultist would be killed before they got anywhere close to killing these things."

His stamina was at 63%. High agility allowed for increased movement speed for less cost, but abusing it would still drain his stamina quickly. He hadn't invested in his endurance stat whatsoever, besides what he was receiving from gear. He'd never paid much attention to it in the past, since his strategies had never overly relied on it. If it was low, he Demon Gated and hid until it was restored. If it was high he acted on it, then Demon Gated and hid until it was restored. His daggers didn't require much stamina to wave around, all he had to do to attack was essentially move his hands up and down over his target. The only thing he'd ever really needed stamina for was running away. His tests indicated that repeated, rapid changes of direction required a lot more stamina than running in straight lines.

Which was a shame, because that was the only kind of movement that would keep him alive in this scenario.

"I guess a tanky occultist might last a little longer, depending on what they had equipped. But since the spikes are being shot from all four corners at the same time, even a shield wouldn't completely protect them. And a tanky occultist wouldn't be very well equipped to kill the Cave Urchins, either. This is the agility path, so I'm assuming the solution lies in using agility to deal with it. Which means there should be something in that chest to help me."

His stamina was full. Damien zigzagged around the room in a series of short leaps, his upper body pivoting at the waist to push his momentum in the direction he wanted to go. The issue here was control. His feet had to be near the floor at all times, so they'd be ready to kick him in a new direction at any given moment. If his movements were unnecessarily large he'd lose balance, drain stamina compensating and end up a stationary target. If they were too small, he'd run the more immediate risk of being dead.

He'd only ever done this once, when he was up against Magnitude, and his technique could obviously use improvement. Moving in a random direction was much more difficult than between two spots, since he had to ensure his body lined up in mid-leap to prepare for where he was going next. In actual combat, random directions wouldn't do. With such conservative movements, he'd have to choose where he moved next carefully. If he dodged in a straight line directly away or toward one of the Cave Urchins, the spine it fired may well still hit him. He managed twelve jumps, some better than others, before he stumbled and ground to a halt. It would have to do. He couldn't stretch out the stream by practicing this all night.

There was one other possibility he'd left for last. The worst-case scenario. He'd tried to think his way around it, to no avail. He had no raw materials in his inventory with which to build a Gateway, having given up Andrew's Bag of Holding. He had a hunch he wouldn't be able to create structures in this space anyway, but since it would've made things much easier he had to try. He'd failed to harvest the necessary resources from the wall before he started his stream. He couldn't even use Ex-Imp-losion to get imps and refund them for their soul energy, since triggering that ability required him to have an imp in the first place. Besides which, employing that strategy in such close quarters would achieve nothing except decorating the walls with their pancake remains. Probably his own, as well. Better to make his viewers aware now to dull their potential disappointment. Or foreshadow their glee.

"The last possibility is that I'm not ready for this yet, there's nothing particularly helpful in the chest and this exercise is doomed to fail. I'm much lower level than the mobs in this dungeon. I'm mainly invested in wisdom, not agility, but I have no minions with me to take advantage of that. If I was supposed to come in here with a full Soul Summon Limit of demons and maintain it in order to progress, it's already too late. I won't get past Archimonde a second time. Let's hope there's something in that chest. The weapon that was foreshadowed at the entrance to this path, for example."

That was a bit of a stretch and he knew it. He found it highly unlikely Mobius would present him with the signature piece of gear for that path in the very first room. It had to be something vaguely helpful, though. He hoped. He crouched down, activating his Shadow Walker-augmented stealth, and lowered his voice to a hush.

"I won't find out by staying here. We'll figure out what's in the chest and go from there. I've got you all on silent so I don't get...distracted..."

His eyes had strayed to the viewer count in the top right-hand corner. 30,000. Right. He was a thing now. He closed that as well. Out of sight did not equal out of mind, but he could do without glancing at it while he was supposed to be focusing on what he was doing. 30,000 was considerable stakes. Now the only indicator that he was being monitored was his oldest Saga Online friend, the little red glowing dot. He focused on the task ahead of him again, saying his last words for his own benefit:

"Open the chest, don't get stabbed, take what's inside, don't get stabbed, exit the room, don't get stabbed, three, two, one."

Showtime.

Damien crouched his way through the alcove into the room and stopped, waiting for the telltale *plink*. It remained deathly silent. They hadn't shot him when he came into the room yesterday. He had no reason to believe they'd shoot him until he gave away his position. The only reason he was hesitating now was because he was aware. He'd happily made his way straight to the chest when he'd had no idea the Cave Urchins existed. He looked up into the nearest corner and saw straight into it without obstruction. In Saga, full stealth meant you were functionally invisible rather than hard to spot. The urchins would be visible again once they attacked. No reason to force it. Opening the chest would accomplish that all by itself.

Damien walked in front of the chest and carefully opened the latch. Still crouched, he walked behind it and levered it open from either side.

Plink.

The four projectiles either pinged off the floor or shlunked into the lid of the chest. Had he opened it from in front, he'd have ended up in exactly the same situation as yesterday. By opening it from the back, the lid had acted as a shield for the two spines that had been shot into his shoulder blades on his first try. Hooray for not getting stabbed. Yet.

He turned and looked up into one of the corners behind him, his body tensing. The Cave Urchins were visible and he was able to get a long look at one. There wasn't much to see. It was a spiky black mass. Damien wasn't interested in performing a scientific analysis, he just wanted to make sure it wasn't about to do something undesirable. Like firing around the chest at random, for instance. He waited, his legs still tensed and ready to pump for the door. After five seconds, the Cave Urchin faded away into the corner of the room, becoming completely invisible again.

He crept his way back in front of the chest and peered inside.

At the bottom of the chest lay a bundle of knives, attached to a studded leather cord. He picked it up and inspected his loot.

Throwing Knife Sling
Durability: 20/20
Description: A leather strap that can be attached to your body, allowing quick and easy access to mid-range throwing knives.

Bingpot. Jacko. Who cared? He was saved!

"Yesss!"

Plink.

Damien didn't have time to jump. He was still in his menu. He started throwing himself flat on the ground, but even the slight delay in thought was too much. He got hit in both shoulders and on either side of his back. His health was at 400/1,180. This seemed familiar. He'd been hit and was no longer in stealth. He hastily closed his menu and scrabbled to his feet.

'Pli—'

Damien leapt backward, a little further than he'd planned, and the spines shattered into the floor in front of him. He immediately span round and ran for the chamber he'd entered by. The way ahead was still barred and he wouldn't last long in here. It was his only viable option. Three steps later—

'Plin—'

In the heat of the moment, Damien had forgotten everything he'd practiced. His steps had been too wide while he was running. He planted both feet on the floor mid-run and leapt right, but leaping further did not make an entirely suitable substitute for leaping on time. Three of the spikes missed, but the one fired from the corner ahead of him struck him straight through the opposite shoulder. 205/1,180. Not good.

Damien stopped moving completely. His stamina was at 45% from overdoing his movements. At this rate he'd run out before he got to the exit, at which point he'd definitely be dead. He'd performed his evasive maneuvers just fine when he was practicing, all he had to do was set aside the mistakes he'd just made and do everything perfectly from this moment onward. No pressure. It was a reaction speed test. All he had to do was wait for the—

'Pli—'

Damien leaped forward and all four missiles missed. He was down to 35% stamina. He walked slowly toward the doors that led to safety. Stamina was actually replenished while he was walking at a slow pace. Not as much as he was losing, but this way he remained completely balanced and would be able to react in time when the—

'Pl—'

He jumped forward. Harder this time, because the angle was becoming less forgiving the closer he came to the opening to safety. If he jumped forward from this point on, the two far behind would still hit him. If he jumped sideways from this close to the door, he'd be hit by at least one of the two ahead of him. So much for jumping randomly. He was five jumps from the exit. He stepped forward, trying to keep his feet as close to the ground as p—

'Pli—'

He jumped sideways, hard. The projectiles had all missed, but he had 19% stamina remaining. His jumps had taken him off to one side. He couldn't head for the door directly. If he was walking toward the door, he had to pick a different direction to jump in. That was no good. Which was when he realized he could use the predictive nature of these enemies to his advantage. He'd been focusing on making sure he wasn't predictable, but the urchins were far more predictable than him. He'd been using the jumps to avoid projectiles while he ran toward his objective. He should've been doing it the other way round.

He turned on the spot and ran parallel to the doorway. He had to run, but he couldn't forget to keep his feet close to the floor. The doorway leading to safety was passing him by on the right-hand side. If they didn't shoot again soon, he'd have used up his stamina running, he'd have passed his target and his ef—

"Plin—"

Damien leapt sideways through the doorway, as fast and as far as his remaining stamina allowed. The Cave Urchins on the far side of the room had been aiming at where his run would've taken him half a second later, since they were further away. The Cave Urchins above and on either side of him were shooting almost directly downward, and it was his sideways movement that saved him. He sailed through and tumbled to the floor in the next room, his stamina not even high enough to recover from the fall. He took minor damage when he hit the ground, bringing him embarrassingly close to death. But he was alive.

He was lying prone. If one of the Cave Urchins on the far side could see him through the doorway, this was it. He flipped himself over and crawled on his hands and knees to the wall, then placed his back to it. They hadn't been able to follow his movement into the first chamber, after all. If they had, he'd definitely be dead. He started laughing, uncontrollably, as the pressure was finally released. He'd done it. It wasn't nearly as smooth as he'd hoped, and he'd almost ended up dead from hissing his relief at finding out what was in the box, but he hadn't. He was alive.

His laugh gave way to panting breaths. His stamina wasn't high enough for that yet. While he waited, he reopened the viewer count in his menu. 40,000 viewers. It was a good thing he'd kept it closed before he'd started. Any distraction at all would've spelled the end of him. His viewers had gone for a while without him saying anything, other than the poorly judged "Yesss!" he'd hissed through his teeth. This was a cause for celebration. He raised the Throwing Knife Sling, holding it up for all to see, and said the first thing that came to mind.

"I got it! We're still in the game! Suck it, Archimonde!"

Lillian checked her menu for the third time. It was 20:23. Andrew was late. While he wasn't perfect by any means, punctuality was not one of his flaws. Not that she was in any position to make a checklist. She brought up his message box and inquired after him.

Lillian: Hello. I'm ready when you are. I'd rather do this privately, and I'd also rather do it face to face, but if you're not up to it today we can do it tomorrow. Let me know when you can.

Aetherius: I'll be there in a minute.

Alright. Finally. If he said he'd be there in a minute, he would be. That gave her a full minute to apply conscious thought to her new surroundings for the first time. Best to front-load the bad part: the dreaded plinth that hinted at how they'd be wasting their evening.

To err is human, this riddle is divine;
Can you do right when others do you wrong?
The line betwixt a cuck and saint is fine,
A king is neither. Thread it, or begone!

Of the four riddles that had been thrown at Lillian, this was by far the most annoying. She'd never been so sure they held the sole purpose of mocking her. The previous three had all been annoying in their own unique ways, and Andrew himself had commented that the last of them was specifically designed to prevent people with her Type A personality traits from clearing it.

She hadn't thought the one directly after could be any worse, but it had hit her at a personal level exactly when she needed it least. She was literally about to try and do right by Andrew, after he'd done her wrong. Well, she'd done him wrong too, but not intentionally. Not until after he'd done her wrong, anyway. Then she'd turned it on him and done him wrong back again. That didn't seem much better.

A thought occurred to her, but she couldn't decide if it was funny or troublesome. A few moments were all it took for her to extend it to its illogical conclusion and she entered a full-blown panic. What if the course of action she was now committed to turned out to be the solution to the riddle? Andrew had tricked her through the last riddle by using their past to keep their minds off the task at hand. What if she was about to accidentally get them through this one the same way? Doing right when others did her wrong? Would the headset read their brainwaves for this too?

If the way forward opened as a direct result of this, Andrew would think she did it on purpose, to one-up him. That was the opposite of what she wanted to achieve! What she wanted to share with him was sensitive enough already, if doing so accidentally removed their next obstacle...if it solved the riddle...it would be nice to get through this stage, sure...but...

Oh no. She cared more about making things right with Andrew than she did about progressing through the quests. *She cared about him.* No! Why was this happening? The competition was over. Her involvement with Andrew was over. Damien's victory had drawn a line through the past so she could focus on the future. She'd moved on. She was happy, fulfilled and focusing on herself now. Even as she thought it out, she knew she was lying to herself.

If everything had improved after she got her own back on Andrew, why had she gone straight back to Rising Tide? She could've joined any guild she liked, or stopped playing altogether. Instead she'd worked herself to the bone, trying to restore their combined project to its former glory. Why? She'd even led them on the biggest quest she could think of. Only to find that the player standing in her way, Magnitude, had been Richard all along. She hadn't left anything behind. She was still in the endless circle, and it had come back for yet another loop.

Lillian wasn't happy. She'd been trying, but she hadn't been happy for a long time. She hadn't been able to pick Andrew up and set things right, so instead she'd torn it all down in the hopes of finding closure. It had seemed like the right thing to do at the time. It hadn't felt right afterwards, though. Having revisited the picture she'd buried deep in her subconscious and heard what Andrew had to say, she knew it never had been.

"Lillian?"

She span round, shocked and appalled. Andrew was standing right there. How had she not noticed him come in? He'd arrived in a glowing, humming blue ball of light! Oh. She'd zoned out. She really was regressing quickly. The only person more surprised than her, judging by the concerned look she'd received all too often from far too many people over the last two months, was Andrew.

"Sorry I'm late, I was watching—"

She had to tell him now, before he said something to change her mind.

"It doesn't matter. I need to show you something. Open your chat."

She went into her own menu, picked out the screenshot and put it into the box. She hovered over it. What if it all went wrong? There was still time to take it back. She could pretend she was sending him something else. Anything else. She only hesitated for a few moments longer before she sent it. Andrew stared at it, nonplussed.

"That's the Godhammer headquarters."

"Yes."

"They appear to be having a party of some kind."

"No, it was preparation for a party."

"Right. That's why there are no people. I'm guessing this was to celebrate taking our waiting room back...they removed the stables I see...and the date is wrong."

"The date is right. This picture was taken during the competition. Before the stables were built. While it was still occupied by Rising Tide."

"That makes sense...it also says it was taken at five thirty in the morning? Oooh. I see. You're behind this. Did...did you use Rising Tide funds for this? Wait, I recognize that banner! They sell them in Camelot for 1,000 gold!"

"Yeah. It was huge. It had to be, to go from one side of the courtyard to the other. I actually bought three of them, because our players kept telling me the wrong sizes."

"You bought three of them?! They're a complete waste of money! They serve absolutely no function except for decorative purposes! How did you hide that from me?"

"Don't worry, I sold the two we didn't use back. The last one was sold back too, in the end."

"You'd only get half the gold refunded! That's 1,500 gold,

gone! More if they were customized. I guess they had to be customized, if they were that big, and you bought them all for nothing! What about the stage? What was that for?"

Lillian was doing her absolute best to stay calm. She didn't want to hurl this in Andrew's face. It would already hurt without throwing it at him. He'd realize it himself, soon enough, if she just kept answering his questions.

"That's where everyone was going to dance, have duels for betting on the outcome with guild-issued prizes for the winners, then gather for the group photo at the end of the night. I had it all figured out."

"Yeah, I can see that. And you managed all this behind my back! You took prizes out of guild storage for this, without telling me? I knew I should've turned off your vault permissions sooner, but I never thought you'd screw me like this! How much was the stage? I didn't even know that was available for purchase."

"It cost nothing but time and energy. I can't take the credit for it. I had some of our artisans construct the pieces, then one night they put it all together and took the screenshot so I could see. It was deconstructed before morning. I didn't want you to know about it."

"This is how you were garnering support while I was offline? Organizing guild parties in the early hours of the morning? No wonder everyone was so eager to do night duty!"

Oh, come on. He was still angry. If he was thinking straight, he'd have figured it out by now. She had to be patient. He deserved it, even if it didn't feel like it just at that moment.

"I didn't take anything out of the vault. It was all from me, and the players. I organized all of it and threw down all the money I had, but I could barely cover a fifth of the costs myself. I accepted donations from our guild members for the rest."

"So while I slept, you and the rest of Rising Tide were having group-funded dance parties and dueling events? No wonder they liked you more than me!"

"No. Andrew. I was planning for just one party that never happened."

Andrew's eyes widened in understanding.

"I see. Finally, it all makes sense."

Lillian breathed a sigh of relief, glad she'd managed against all odds to let Andrew down gently. It was only as he kept talking that she realized her relief had been premature. Andrew's tunnel vision had taken him as far from the truth as he could possibly get.

"This was the celebration party for after you took over Rising Tide. Now I know why Richard made the prank so severe; he stopped it from happening at the last possible moment. Why are you rubbing it in my—"

This was as far as Lillian could go. She blurted out the reality, before Andrew could dig any deeper.

"The party was to celebrate you winning the competition."

She'd done her best. As usual, it hadn't been good enough. She watched the realization settle in over his face. She watched his anger twist and writhe, fighting to remain present in its death throes. He was halfway done when she started to speak, her words forced and low so her voice did not break.

"I told you I was going back to work, and I did. But I changed my schedule. I woke up every day at 3am. Waited for you to go to sleep. Logged in. Found out about current affairs in the guild from the night watch. Organized the night watch schedule, so anyone who needed a severe talking to could explain themselves to me in person. Vetted new players. Kicked out players who were giving you trouble. Went questing, to keep my level as close to yours as I could and earn gold to pay for your celebration party. Double-checked your accounting, which never took very long: you've always been better at it than me. Instructed our highest-ranking players to take pressure off you wherever I judged it was most needed. Provided advice for them to feed you over the course of the day. Focusing on the cultist questline was my idea, to improve Rising Tide's standing with the Empire, solidify your position and keep you in the public eye with minimal risk. At 8am, I logged off and got ready for work. I worked all day. Then I went home and slept at 8pm, so I could do it all again the next morning. I did this for the whole final month of the competition. Right up until you enacted Richard's 'prank' in my hospital."

Andrew wasn't looking at her anymore, but Lillian forced herself to look at him. This was her fault. She thought she'd been so clever. She thought she could do all this without him noticing, to let him think he was entirely responsible for his own success. The celebration party would've been more difficult to sell as a spontaneous event, with all the planning it had required. Given the stress he'd been under, it was the very least he'd deserved. He'd still deserved it after she'd decided to turn against him. She just hadn't seen it.

"This is my fault. I didn't want you to know I was still there. I wanted you to think you'd done it all by yourself, so you'd regain your confidence and go back to the way you were before we started playing. I couldn't tell you that you weren't good enough, because it wasn't fair. You are good enough. But no one can run a guild that big by themselves. I thought I could do this behind your back, to boost you up. I didn't know there was more going on under the surface. Please, forgive me. I'm so sorry."

So much for her voice not cracking. Andrew had turned away from her. Lillian was grateful. She didn't want him to see her like this, either. They stood there, in silence, for about a minute. Then, without a word, the blue Logout Sphere appeared around him for ten seconds more. Lillian stood there in silence until he was gone. He hadn't shouted at her. Was that good? She didn't even know. He'd come back when he was ready, and then she'd know for sure. She hoped he would come back. She was loath to admit it, but she needed his help.

Lillian went into her menu to check the time. 20:31. The rest of them would be coming online any second now. She had to make herself look presentable. She took a deep breath and set her attention on the challenge ahead. Nothing had happened in the room after her and Andrew's conversation. So it hadn't affected the quest, after all. Lillian was both relieved and annoyed. She felt she deserved some token of appreciation for doing the right thing, but at least her testimony hadn't been cheapened by providing her with measurable gain.

It was now 20:33. None of the players were here. What was going on with everyone today? First Andrew, now the rest of them as well? She went into the party chat and did what she did best: motivated them.

Lillian: Some of you aren't here yet. We don't have much time tonight. If you're not coming, I'd like to know why.

Then she quickly opened Andrew's chat box and typed him his own message.

Lillian: The message I just sent in the party chat doesn't apply to you. Take as long as you need.

She hadn't finished typing out the message to him when the first of the blue orbs appeared. It was Judgementday. Looking flustered. Her guild might have fallen apart but she hadn't lost her signature charm. The other two orbs appeared behind him in quick succession as he garbled out perfunctory excuse number one.

"Sorry I'm late, I completely lost track of time."

"That's alright. You're here now. Thanks for coming."

Legolias was next, quickly followed by Mr. Healy. Legolias was more forthright about the reason for his tardiness.

"Sorry I'm late. I didn't realize it was already eight thirty. I was watching Daemien's stream."

"Me too! I laughed my head off when he nearly died! He was doing so well, right up until he said 'Yesss'!"

The three of them burst out laughing and turned to face each other. They'd all forgotten she was there. Judgementday was quick to pick up where Mr. Healy had left off.

"I know, right? Those jumps, though. I can hardly see what's going on!"

"Meh. I could do better. I'd have that room done in about fifteen seconds. He doesn't have nearly enough stamina or agility to support what he's doing, and until he got the throwing knives he wasn't even able to hit them back."

"That's why it's so much fun to watch! I mean, come on, Legolias, you're a ranger. I could cast Sanctuary and completely negate all the projectiles at the same time, but that wouldn't make for good viewing now, would it?"

"I could Smite them, probably. They look plenty demonic to me. Don't know if I could heal myself through the attacks, though. Daemien was completely right about what was in the chest, now he has a chance!"

Lillian had stopped paying attention to the conversation halfway through. The final blue orb had appeared. Andrew materialized into their space while the rest of them were still in full swing. They hardly even registered his arrival. It was just as well. He did not seem particularly happy.

Lillian had specifically told him to take as long as he needed. He didn't look much better than he had when he'd left, five minutes ago. Yet he'd shown up anyway. Hadn't he said he was watching something, before she'd cut him off to send him the picture? He was probably watching the same thing as the rest of them. Lillian had unsubscribed to Damien's channel prior to starting the quest. She hadn't wanted any distractions. Had he posted any of their fight against Archimonde, she'd rather not know about it until she'd finished her own business. Their argument had helped her decision. But her decision had left her out of the loop.

Judgementday was the first to acknowledge Aetherius's presence, by bringing him into the conversation.

"Boss—," he looked over at Lillian, terror in his eyes, "—I mean, Aetherius. Sorry. Aetherius, you're watching Daemien's stream too, right? What do you think? Legolias isn't very impressed, me and Healy think he's doing alright. What's your take?"

"He's doing well."

"There! See? If Aetherius says he's doing well, there's no denying it!"

Lillian cleared her throat and the conversation died.

"Everyone, I'm glad you're all enjoying yourselves, but there's something we should be doing right now."

She let her words hang in the air, making sure no one felt like contradicting her. When she was left unchallenged, she started issuing her orders.

"Open your menus. Open the Saga Online media page. Navigate to Damien's profile page. Then we'll all watch his livestream, together. We can take it in turns to guard everyone who's not looking. I'll go first."

She'd watched the smiles slowly growing on their faces as she delivered her instructions completely deadpan. By the time she got to the end, Judgementday, Mr. Healy and Legolias were ecstatic.

"Thanks, boss! We'll give you a running commentary!"

Lillian gave Judgementday a cursory nod, then turned her attention to Andrew. The rest of them were already in their menus, scrambling to return to the stream that had made them forget their own quest. Andrew was not buried in his menu. He checked to make sure the other three were all occupied, then spoke levelly to Lillian.

"You didn't need to do that for me. I know you only did it because I'm still distracted."

"That's not entirely true. They deserve a break and they're all distracted as well, just by Damien instead of me. I wanted to give them a reward and do something besides pursuing this quest with them, but after what happened with Hammertime...I've been pushing pretty hard. It's time I...what did you call it? Switched off. We'll watch how Damien does, together, then get back to it when he's finished. We're ahead of schedule, thanks to your hard work today. But I still need you in good shape for whatever comes next. You're my co-leader, after all."

Andrew's face shot to the floor. She'd gone too far. He turned around, sat on the ground and opened his menu. Welp, at least she'd tried. No regrets. She hadn't made it to her lookout position before one of her chat boxes pinged.

Aetherius: Thank you.

Lillian took a deep breath. And smiled. Finally. She'd achieved something of actual worth. She made sure the rest of them weren't looking. Opened her menu. Navigated to Damien's stream. Set the window in the corner of her HUD, so she could keep a lookout and watch simultaneously. Then, for the first time in a long time, she half switched off.

17

WHAT WE DO IN THE SHADOWS

Damien threw another knife. It sank satisfyingly into the center of his emptied rat-skin bag on the other side of the modest entry chamber. He'd increased the distance by degrees, trying various throwing techniques to see which one had the best success rate. His preferred technique had turned out to be palming the knives directly from his newly acquired sling, then throwing them in a straight line, point first. He'd been quite lucky to kill Gatz, the berserking warrior he'd inadvisably taken on in the Frozen Forest. Damien had thrown Shankyou's Striking Dagger, which was much heavier and not at all designed for throwing, directly at his target's face without any practice. He'd thrown that one from the handle. Oof. Hindsight remains 20/20.

He was considerably better at it with his right hand than his left, but it hadn't taken long to make his left-handed throws passable. The knives did not survive being thrown into walls at high velocity. The durability had turned out to be related to the number of knives on the belt, and he was down to sixteen of them. Four of his left-handed throws at varying distances had not proven ideal. He was clearly better at it now, although he had no idea how much damage they'd inflict. Now he could at least hit his enemies and his health had finally fully regenerated, it was time to go test on live targets. Or whatever it was the Cave Urchins qualified as.

He'd left the viewer count up in the corner as he practiced, comfortable with adding a little pressure since he wasn't at immediate risk. It had been hovering at around 42,000, but over the last five minutes it had steadily decreased. Time to get a move on.

"I guess that'll do. Thanks for your patience and sorry for making you wait, but I'd like to get this right first time. These knives are much lighter than the daggers I'm used to. I still keep the stats from my holstered daggers while I'm using them, so that's nice. It's definitely a better option than throwing my equipped weaponry—"

His chat box pinged.

"Uh, I'm getting a message. Let's see what's up."

It was from Lillian. Why was she messaging him now? He read the message out in his head quickly, tutted under his breath, then read it out for the benefit of his audience.

"Lillian writes: 'Legolias has some "constructive feedback"'" – Damien did the air quotes, sticking his hands in front of him so everyone could appreciate the gesture – "'regarding your movement. He'd like you to add him so he can write to you directly.' Okay. Thanks, Lillian. You know what? Legolias is a ranger in Rising Tide I've met a couple of times. He clearly knows what he's doing. I'm willing to see what he has to say. I'll just pop his name into my friends list over here and wait for him—"

Legolias accepted his friend request the moment it was sent, and the text came up in the box two seconds later. He'd obviously copied and pasted it and hit 'Send'. Good of him not to waste any time. Less good of him to use his precise word choices while Damien was livestreaming. Well, there was nothing inappropriate in there. Damien had already established how he'd respond to fan mail when he read out Lillian's message. If Damien didn't read this one out, he'd look petty.

"Legolias writes: 'Duck and roll. You'll use less stamina, you'll be a smaller target, you'll move more quickly over short distances and you'll reenter stealth after not attacking for five seconds. It's the basic evasive move for assassins and rangers! What's wrong with you, man?' Thank you for your valuable input, Legolias. I'm not an assassin or a ranger and have received exactly zero instruction on how to move efficiently in combat, since my class trainer is focused on spell-casting. I've had to pick it up as— Legolias writes: 'Sorry, I didn't know you'd read all these out loud.' The more you know, Legolias, the more you know."

It was a handy suggestion. Damien would try it, if the opportunity arose. It was time to get ready. He retrieved his bag and started replacing the items he'd strewn a safe distance from his makeshift target range. It was a modest assortment of equipment compared to having easy access to everything in his chest. He'd manage. His gear was not yet in total disrepair, not even the bag he'd just used for target practice.

For now, he'd focus on putting the new skill he'd just acquired to the test. He palmed two throwing knives off his sling and held them at the ready, the tips of the knives edging out past his fingertips and the flats of the blades secured under his thumbs.

"Here we go again. Hopefully we'll see a new room for the first time in twenty-four hours. Three, two, one."

Damien crouched and entered the room, sneaking to the very center of it to stand out in front of the chest. That would give him the maximum amount of time and distance to dodge the incoming projectiles. It also made the angle each projectile would be fired from as predictable as possible, the same angle from all four corners.

Throwing knives were a welcome addition to Damien's tactical options, but he had no direct reference point for the technicalities of their use. The nearest comparison he could think of were stealth rangers. They always became visible shortly after firing, so he could only assume the same would be true for him. His ability to remain in stealth was directly proportionate to the ability of enemies to detect him.

If the Cave Urchins could locate him with a single carelessly uttered word, it was difficult to imagine he could throw knives at them without being fired on. The worst part about these enemies was the limited delay between each shot. Once he was detected, he'd have no time to reenter stealth before they fired again. Unless what Legolias had imparted to him became applicable.

Using the throwing knives did not take a huge amount of stamina either, but that would be on top of his dodging. Once he engaged, it wouldn't be over until either he or the Cave Urchins were dead. At least he had time to get the first throw right. He knew where his targets were despite their stealth.

Still crouching, Damien drew back his arm and snapped it forward, his fingertips pointing into the corner. He let go exactly as his arm was fully extended, the knife skimming the palm of his hand and shooting toward his invisible target in a straight line. There was a wet *thud* and an unexpected shriek as the knife sank in and the Cave Urchin it had sunk into appeared. 28% health remaining, from what Damien's HUD indicated was a sneak critical attack.

Damien could understand it being a sneak attack: he'd left stealth only a fraction of a second before it connected. It was the attack's designation as a critical hit that surprised him. The Cave Urchin was a spiky blob with no obviously defined hit zones, and Damien hadn't been targeting any specific part of it. He'd literally thrown it in the thing's general direction. That implied the entire body behind the spines was a big critical area.

Next came the important part.

'Plin-'

Damien dropped and rolled forward, his right hand moving to his sling while still in motion. The spines passed harmlessly overhead as the core of his body dropped to the floor. He transferred the momentum from the roll as he rose back up, through his extended arm and into the second knife. Very nice. No amount of practice on an empty bag could've taught him that. The Cave Urchin screeched and disconnected from the wall, its hit points at zero. Damien ran to the next target.

'Pli-'

He rolled again. All the projectiles passed harmlessly overhead. This would never work more than once against players predicting movement, but it was superb against these mobs. This allowed Damien to focus entirely on his newly acquired knife-throwing technique. Which is how he hit the second urchin with two knives simultaneously, with both arms outstretched toward his target and his left hand mirroring the movement of his right.

He was hardly losing stamina. He'd hit with all five knives so far, which he quickly made six as he finished the urchin off. This was easy! With only two urchins left the rolling technique was even more effective. As he rolled across the room, remaining crouched in between, he reentered Shadow Walker. Even easier!

Damien finished off the last two with no trouble. All enemies defeated. Zero damage sustained. This room had been reduced to a plaything. The iron slats covering the back of the room lifted, their removal highlighted with a plinky, optimistic tune reinforcing his success. The tune was nice, but the level-up notification he received with it simultaneously was nicer.

He was level 45! He was sure his celebration would result in some complaints about camera angles, since it involved a fair amount of spinning on the spot, but he was also sure he didn't care.

"Done. They're all dead, I'm alive, the next room is open and I didn't take a single hit. And I get full EXP just for completing part of the quest chain! That's more like it!"

He pumped his hands a few more times before he got that under control as well. There were things he was supposed to be doing, such as checking how many knives could be salvaged from the bodies of his enemies and how many souls he'd obtained. He'd have minions again! Things were looking up.

"Bear with me while I loot and prepare myself for the next room. Shout out to Legolias for the rolling strat. Thank you!"

He walked upright to each corner in turn, checking where the bodies had fallen. Upon their deaths the black spines had disintegrated, leaving only spherical white husks behind. They'd seemed much larger when they were covered in spines. He commended himself for how accurate he'd been with his knives without knowing how small his targets were. The soul energy they'd left pooled toward him as he placed his hands on their creepy skeletal remains to loot.

The materials they had to offer to mark Damien's achievement were urchin meat (mmmMMMmmm) and the throwing knives he'd embedded in them. They offered exactly 2.5 souls each, bringing his Soul Reserve up to its full 10 souls. Save for the one knife that had shattered on the wall, all the knives he'd thrown were also recovered. That brought him back to 15 out of 20 durability on his sling. He'd lost more knives during testing than he had in actual combat. This is why you test. He put his unattributed 5 stat points into agility and considered his windfall.

He could summon minions again. It didn't seem wise when he didn't know what lay ahead. He'd scout out the next room first, then determine what was required in order to deal with it...no, there was a better option available. He pointed at the floor and summoned a wraith. It had better stealth than him and was more expendable. Sorry, wraith. He escorted it to the newly opened pathway as he spoke to his audience, which was holding steady now he was back in action.

"I'm sending the wraith in to look around. After we're done investigating, I'll have it come out of stealth to check if there are any hidden enemies. Then I'll head in myself."

He sat down with his back to the wall, possessed the wraith and floated inside. There were two chests in this room! One in the near corner on the left, one in the far corner on the right. The rest of the room lay completely bare, identical to the one Damien was currently sitting in. The way forward was not blocked this time. It appeared he could walk straight through from one side to the other without any issues. Suspicious, given how the first room had appeared equally benign at first glance. There were almost certainly more Cave Urchins in here. At least Damien had his wraith to scout it out for him. The wraith's movement was extremely fast, he'd be able to dodge after opening the chest without too much difficulty.

He tipped himself forward and accelerated toward the nearest of the two chests. He'd made it only a few feet when he found himself impaled on the spines of a Cave Urchin. This one was on the floor. Just by floating into it the wraith had sustained serious damage. Even a single point of damage was enough to remove stealth. Damien had no time to react, but he knew what was coming next. What he hadn't been prepared for was the scale of it.

'plinkplinkplinkplinkpli-'

The first spine, projected rather than blundered into, was enough to end Damien's Possession. He could still hear them ricocheting not only around the space where the wraith had been but all across the walls, even from the next room over. One of the spines flew through the doorway, whistling past Damien's head, to shatter on the far wall. It was brief, yet exceptionally noisy. There were a lot of Cave Urchins in there. He could live with that. All he had to do to prevent them from firing was remain in stealth. What he could not live with was that they had now found their way to the floor. Where he could stumble into them at any given moment, ending his stealth and his stream immediately.

There was at least one Cave Urchin on the floor, almost right next to the door. He had to find out how many more there were, and where. The rest of his minions did not have stealth as their ally, so they'd be destroyed upon entry. There had to be another way of revealing the location of those on the floor, so he could avoid them on his way to the chests. He'd have to figure out a way of opening the chests without ending up on the receiving end of a fatality as well, but the first step was identifying where his enemies were. He'd require assistance to do that without dying. Sorry, Noigel.

He pointed at the ground and summoned the imp. Noigel arrived, but Damien was making his apologies before the imp had even finished his customary salute.

"Sorry, Noigel, you're going to die now."

At least he'd been honest. Noigel, understandably, did not appreciate Damien's forthrightness. He started back-chatting in his usual tongues, but Damien saved them both time by talking over him.

"I wouldn't normally ask you to do this, but there's an obstacle here I can't get past without possessing an imp. I'm short on soul energy and summoning another imp would just result in you dying later, because I can't take—"

Noigel folded his arms and sat with his back to Damien. Great. He supposed it was fair. He needed time to offer an explanation for why he was reneging on their usual deal.

"You don't know what I'm dealing with yet. Let me show you what the problem looks like so you know I'm not being lazy."

Noigel swiveled back toward him, still looking unimpressed. Except Damien wasn't sure how he could...wait, yes he did. He might not have any rat spleens at his disposal to lob around, but he had other resources that could act in its place. He went into his inventory and placed one of his five stone blocks on the floor. He didn't need them for construction just at that moment. He removed his dagger and chipped at the corner, creating a stone and a slightly damaged building block. He thought about it, then created a few more. He ended up with five stone chips and a building block that was so damaged it shifted in his inventory to occupy a new slot there. It could no longer be used in construction and would no longer stack with the pristine building blocks.

He kept chipping away. Eventually, by the time the block was completely worn down, he had a stack of twenty-six stone chips. His dagger had only taken a few points of durability damage, because he'd been careful about it. It was nothing like as taxing as when he'd tried to do the same thing to the walls of the Dark Tower, which had proven completely impenetrable.

Damien gathered up his fascinating rock collection. With both him and Noigel out of line of sight, he tossed one of the chips around the corner, into the Cave Urchin-occupied room. About a second after he'd thrown it in, before it had even hit the ground, the noise of tens of spines striking all around the room echoed into their hiding spot. Damien had no doubt whatsoever that many of them had hit the tiny stone chip while it was in midair.

"There are Cave Urchins in here that shoot projectiles when they sense sound or movement. They're stealthed and very accurate, but immobile. I died because of them yesterday, remember? When I left you behind to investigate the room by myself? You must've been automatically dismissed when I died, now you know why. I need to get a clear idea of where all the Cave Urchins are so I can avoid them. Which means you'll have to go into the room after I've made them visible so I can see where they all are."

Noigel blew a raspberry and turned his back again. He clearly wasn't keen on dying. Damien sighed. He'd become aware that he was livestreaming again, in the wake of Noigel's insubordination. He needed Noigel's help, but he couldn't waste time here. There was a way of doing this.

"Alright. I'll cut a deal with you. You want to have your "special time" with a succubus, right?"

Noigel span round very slowly to face him again, arms still folded. He was listening.

"If you do this...I'll summon a succubus after I've got through the room. The two of you can have your "special time". I'll just turn my back and let you get on with it. How does that sound?"

Noigel stroked his chin, as if he were considering the proposal. Damien knew very well how attractive it must be. He was counting on the draw being too great to resist and was not disappointed. Noigel stuck his hand out and they shook on it, in front of all Damien's viewers. They might not have known exactly what "special time" entailed, although many of them could probably guess. Damien felt like a pimp. He suppressed a shudder, but the deal was done.

"I'll throw another stone in, then immediately cast Possession on you. The Cave Urchins will fire at the stone and there will be a three-second delay before they fire again. I'll have three seconds to put you way up in the top of the room so I can see where all the Cave Urchins are while they're still visible."

Noigel stuck his thumb and forefinger together. Sorted. While Damien could simply summon a second imp to perform this task, there was more at stake here. He still wanted to reward Noigel, and making him work for it would further reestablish the pecking order between them that had been disregarded of late.

"Ready?"

Noigel nodded and braced himself with his hands and feet on the floor, ready to push off. Damien threw the stone and a half second later he'd possessed Noigel. He kicked forward just as the splintering of spines around the room began. As he passed through the doorway, Damien got his first glimpse of the latest obstacle. It was bad. There were a lot of Cave Urchins in there, all of them on the floor. As if they hadn't been bad enough consigned to the corners of the ceiling. Damien flew straight up as he passed through the doorway, all the way to the ceiling. The imp's field of vision was greater than Damien's own, courtesy of his enormous fishbowl eyes. Each bottom corner of the room had just come into his range of vision when the Cave Urchins arrayed below all fired at once. Damien tried to dodge, but there were too many projectiles coming from too many different angles. He had no chance. The Possession ended.

At least Damien had been honest regarding the outcome. Noigel had sacrificed himself on his behalf, now it was up to him to make good on his promise. That would not only require staying alive, it would also require killing at least one Cave Urchin. He only had 6 souls left in his Soul Reserve, having summoned the wraith and Noigel. He needed at least one more for a succubus. How he'd achieve that he had no idea, but the first room had seemed unbeatable when he started it as well.

He brought up his own livestream in his menu and stifled a snort. With any loss of focus in the Dark Tower inviting death, he'd do well not to make a habit of laughing to himself. It was difficult, though, since he was looking at the infinity window he'd inadvertently created. Damien was watching himself watching himself watching himself watching himself watching himself. After that the window became too small to see any further.

He scrolled the livestream back a few seconds and watched

himself fly Noigel into the room. Then he paused it on a frame where he had a good view of the whole floor layout. There were a lot of Cave Urchins. They were forming the walls of a pathway, although one particular placement was obviously more tactical. The chest in the far corner was completely encircled by a cluster of them.

The near chest did not pose the same difficulty. While there were plenty of Cave Urchins preventing him from traveling to it directly, it was not blocked in the same manner as the further one. He could start from there. He examined the still image he'd taken from his own stream and plotted out a route to it. He'd have to start by walking straight in about halfway through the room, then take a sharp left, then another sharp left before he got to the wall, then there was a gap he'd have to thread to reach the chest.

He wouldn't be able to make a single sound once he entered the room. It was time to address his viewers as his player character in what could well turn out to be the last time in twenty-four hours. He whispered, even though he was still safe.

"I want to see what's in the first chest before I get through the room. Let's hope it's not more knives. I'll do my best, but this could all be over very quickly if I get it wrong. Wish me luck!"

He crouched down and tiptoed into the room, his picture of the Cave Urchin-riddled layout pulled into the corner of his HUD for reference. The first part was easy. All he had to do was walk forward. He got about halfway there, checking the picture constantly, before the nerves kicked in and he stopped moving. He hadn't taken the stress of what he was doing into account.

While there was clearly plenty of room to move, the spines of the Cave Urchins were very long and extremely pointy. A single pinprick would be enough to remove stealth. Worse still, he had no frame of reference for the distances. The floor was a single slab of impenetrable rock and the Cave Urchins were all invisible. It was very difficult to judge where he stood in relation to the picture he'd chosen to rely on so heavily.

He took another step forward. Not dead yet. Great. He took

another half step forward. Looked up at where Noigel had died as he examined the picture. Looked at the walls on either side, availing him nothing. Took another half step forward. And froze. He had no idea whether or not he was supposed to turn left yet. He examined the picture intently, hoping there would be some answer. There was not. He had to make a decision: turn left or keep going straight. He inched another step forward. Still not dead. Then he turned exactly 90 degrees and took a deep breath. It felt like he was in the right place. He checked the picture again. Looked at his own position. And raised a foot into the air.

His chat box pinged. In the dead silence, Damien almost jumped out of his skin. His lungs felt like they might explode from the pressure. His nostrils were whistling, ever so slightly, as the air he was trying to suppress was forced from them. He tightened his lips into the tiniest of openings, forcing himself to breathe exceptionally quietly. It seemed so very loud, and the enemies he was encircled by could register it at any moment. He was frozen like that for about half a minute, until he trusted himself enough to replenish the air in his lungs by degrees.

All this for a bunch of Cave Urchins that he thought he'd already made himself the master of. Twinned with the exceptionally poorly timed message. Who'd thought it would be a good idea to ping him at that precise moment? He opened his menu and found out.

Lillian: Aetherius hasn't stopped ranting for two minutes. He thinks you're about to die. It sounds accurate. You've blocked him, he can't message you. Please unblock him.

So Andrew had almost killed him again. This marked the fourth time Damien had nearly been killed by Andrew, but only the first time it had happened indirectly. Scowling twice as hard to make up for the noise he couldn't make, Damien slowly turned around on the spot, went straight back through the doorway and set himself down with his back to the wall, where he'd be safe. As annoyed as he was that he'd been messaged while he was concentrating, his relief not to be in that room was greater. So much for his plan.

He was about to go through with Lillian's request when he

remembered his viewers, and the implications. Was he really about to take advice from Andrew, aka Aetherius, on a livestream? That would be odd, to say the least. His career had been built around Andrew's destruction. How would his followers react to this twist? What would it do to his ratings?

He wasn't sure what his followers would think, but it could only push his ratings in one direction. Up. He found a new reason to complain. He wanted to solve this by himself. Accepting Andrew's help not only seemed wrong, it seemed...he wasn't sure how to put it...counterintuitive? He'd come to Andrew for help before and it hadn't exactly worked out in his favor, in the short term at least.

Damien started typing out a message to Lillian, asking if she could just tell him herself without having to unblock Aetherius, but he promptly deleted all of it. That seemed worse. He couldn't just pretend Andrew didn't exist, after what he'd seen him do against Archimonde when Lillian needed him. It would've been easy enough to just let her die, to run around Archimonde while it was clearly focused on killing everyone else. But he hadn't. He'd put himself at risk on their behalf.

Damien would probably have immediately unblocked Aetherius and taken his advice if he wasn't being watched by so many strangers, worrying more about what they'd think than what he himself believed. Which was when he realized that all the text he'd been typing out to Lillian had been on display in his livestream. Including to Andrew himself, who was watching. Obviously. Deleting the message hadn't prevented it from being seen, it had just given everyone a clear view of his reservations while leaving them open to interpretation. Andrew would probably not interpret it well.

Now he had to unblock Andrew, didn't he? Super. The joys of livestreaming. Damien went into his meager friends list, noting Kevin's absence only briefly, and highlighted the name. Then he unblocked his erstwhile nemesis. Almost immediately as it was unblocked he received a response. Not a message, but a voice call. While it rang, he decided to enlighten his viewers as to what was happening. At least he could set the record straight before Andrew stuck his oar in.

"So...here's the thing. I got past Magnitude's wall in a party with a few other players. Aetherius was one of them. He was really good, he didn't stab me in the back or push me down a hole or anything! Anyway, he turned out to be really helpful. I gave him back his Bag of Holding...didn't need it, it's a trash item anyway...and it was a good deal to have him on our side. Let's see what he has to say about this next room."

Damien answered the call and was met with complete silence. For about three seconds.

"A trash item?"

"Alright fine, it's really useful and I didn't want to give it to you. Happy?"

"Livestreaming isn't easy, is it? I saw you typing—"

"Yes, Andrew, I know you saw me typing. I'm under quite a lot of stress right now. There are a lot of people waiting for me to get on with this, so I'd appreciate you sharing your insight sooner rather than later."

"Your picture idea was good. Really good. But that room doesn't have any frame of reference to work with. It's probably designed that way, to stop you from doing exactly what you're trying. Ironically, the Cave Urchins are the only thing you can use as a frame of reference in there, but if you could see them there wouldn't be an issue. I couldn't work out where you were standing just from looking at the picture, so I doubt you could manage it...with all that stress you're under."

"Nice save, Andrew."

"Thanks."

"Well now you've outlined the problem, do you have any good ideas?"

"Of course I do."

Yeah, of course he does. Damien waited to be clued in. Andrew didn't care to elaborate.

"Could you share it with me?"

"I could."

"You're really enjoying this, aren't you?"

"Yup. I'm having a great time."

"I'm glad one of us is. If you're not going to hel—"

"Your first option is to level up and come back when you're ready for this. It'll be easier to detect enemies in stealth if you're comparable in level. This dungeon doesn't look like it was designed for players before about level 48 or 49. You're making life pretty difficult. I'm surprised the Cave Urchins haven't detected you yet, since you're wandering around so close to them. You're lucky they don't work with conventional mechanics, or else you'd be dead already."

"Can't leave until I'm done with this place. It's now or never. Do you have a suggestion that doesn't involve giving up?"

"I do, but you'll find it even less attractive than the first one. Earlier you were throwing rocks into the room. Do that again, inside the room."

"Oh, brilliant! Wish I'd thought of that. Except doing it will break stealth and I'll get murdered before it hits the ground."

"That depends on how you throw them."

"Go on?"

"The headset first registers whether an attack is made based on intent. Not on whether or not the attack is successful. That's why making an attack removes stealth, regardless of whether or not you hit your intended target. With me so far?"

"I think so? Hit me up with the second half, please."

"If you're not making an attack, you won't go out of stealth. Chucking a stone won't count as an attack. Well, unless you hit something with it, then it'll be an accidental attack. That would unstealth you. If I've understood correctly, the Cave Urchins only follow movement and sound. So long as you're in stealth they can't detect you at all. The stone will become visible about a half second after it leaves your grip, the same point at which you'd become visible if you threw it with malicious intent. So throw the stone, but not anywhere it will hit an enemy before it becomes visible. Your picture should be good enough to find somewhere safe to throw a stone."

"You're a mage. Why do you know so much about stealth mechanics?"

"Stealth enemies are particularly dangerous to me, a mage, so I make it my business to know as much about their mechanics as possible."

"Come to think of it, you also have an ability that uses stealth."

"That's also a factor, but it's a different mechanic. It's much more flexible and less delicate than remaining in stealth, otherwise I wouldn't get much use out of it at all with low agility."

"What do you suppose I should do if I try your rock-throwing strategy and I get torn to pieces?"

"It's up to you whether you want to try it, but I'm telling you this in good faith. If it doesn't work, sue me."

"I think I'll try it. Thanks. Is that everything?"

"Yeah, I think that covers it. I'll send you a message if I have any further thoughts."

"Please don't do that while I'm in the room. When Lillian sent me that message I nearly died."

"You're tempting me, Damien."

Damien knew Andrew was playing this up for his audience, but that was a bit close to the bone.

"Do I need to block you again? This is important to me, but I prefer not having your name permanently grayed out on my friends list."

There was a pause. The first time Andrew had paused during their whole exchange.

"Alright, I'll be good. I also prefer not being grayed out on your friends list."

Their conversation was cut across by a loud cry. Damien hadn't heard the voice's source speak often, but the irreverent tone of voice coupled with the silly sense of humor allowed him to discern the point of origin as Mr. Healy, who'd been unable to contain himself.

"Now kiss!"

Damien and Andrew groaned in unison. Damien hurried to conclude as the laughter of Lillian's party came over the call from afar.

"Okay. Thanks for your help. I'll try it out."

"Good luck in there. We're all rooting for you. Hashtag if-you-die-it's-totally-not-my-fault, Aetherius out."

Andrew hung up before Damien could reply. Could've been much worse. The real test would be to see whether or not his advice worked. Damien palmed a stone in his hand and crouched back into the room. Just as before, he was fast enough at first but each step made him less eager to take the next. The reference picture was still inadequate, even following his break. He thought about what Andrew had told him, carefully, then tossed the stone in a lazy arc forward toward the next room, high overhead.

The stone was shredded to atoms before any of the Cave Urchins had even become visible. They all appeared simultaneously at once, the majority of his field of vision becoming black with spikes. Damien remained exactly where he was and made sure he didn't move. He'd put the rock somewhere where none of the ground-launched missiles would hit him by mistake. This was the moment of truth. If throwing the rock had taken him out of stealth, he'd be looking at the death screen in about two seconds' time.

His HUD said Shadow Walker was still active. But Shadow Walker had still been active when he got shot for saying "Yesss" in the last room. He held his breath. Five seconds later, all the Cave Urchins simultaneously disappeared. They weren't firing on him. He wouldn't have to sue Andrew after all.

Now he knew he could get away with this behavior, Damien decided he'd do what he did with all mechanics that worked out in his favor in games. He'd abuse it. He wasted no time in chucking the next stone into the air, and started moving the moment the urchins became visible. Five seconds of safe movement per stone, twenty-two stones left, just under two minutes of movement. Plus whatever Damien felt he could get away with. That was more than enough to get to the first chest.

The next part he'd done before, only not with so many enemies. The angle they were at would make it easier, the volume harder. Not so much 'harder', as more intense. He flipped the latch on the front of the chest. Gently. Moved around the back of it. Carefully. Then lifted it from either side. Gingerly.

The number of spines launched into the lid was so great, it was thrown open without Damien's continued input. Which would've been fine, if he wasn't standing underneath it. It tipped over and smacked him on the head, knocking him onto his back. He only took a few points of damage. It was a few points too many. Damien was out of stealth. He had three seconds.

3

Damien crouched to hide behind the chest, then gave up. There were two Cave Urchins, one on either side of it, that had clear firing lines from each direction. Only they would fire, because he was only in their line of sight. He could survive two spines, but not two spines every three seconds.

2

Damien made a run for the door back to the chamber he'd already cleared, preparing to leap over the urchins on his way to safety. He'd reached the side of the chest when the hopelessness of that plan hit home. There was no time. He'd still be in midair when the next volley came, with absolutely zero chance of changing direction. There was only one place left to go.

1

Damien turned, ducked and rolled, straight into the open chest. It was not designed for a person, but the chest was not conservative. It was large. Everybody loves large chests. Right then and there, Damien loved them much more than anyone else. He flopped into it, landing on his back, and tucked his legs in as the number of spines sticking out of the inside of the concave lid doubled. All of them had passed through the space where his knees had been, the last parts of his body he'd withdrawn in time. Damien counted to three. The chamber was completely silent once more. It had worked. He was out of line of sight and wasn't making any noise.

This raised some interesting questions. If he had a Bag of Holding attached to a chest and climbed into it, would he be in his own inventory? He'd never been compelled to climb into a chest before. It was a shame he didn't still have Andrew's bag, or else he could've tried it then and there. He doubted the result would've removed him from this predicament. Unless of course it opened a rift in space and time, which might be the only end more violent than poking his head out of the box and turning his face into an instant reverse Cave Urchin. The inside of the lid was not looking pretty after absorbing two volleys.

First things first. He'd managed to get into the chest, first figuratively, then literally. He could feel the item it contained digging into his back. If he made sure to take it before trying anything more ambitious, at least he wouldn't have to go through this again. If it was more knives, he'd be very disappointed. Damien awkwardly reached underneath himself and transferred the item into his inventory for inspection.

Darkstriders
Description: A pair of demon-hide boots once worn by the Sunset Emperor: Bartholomew, Scourge of the World. They carried him far and wide, all the way to his ignominious end.
Level Requirement: 50
Stat Requirement: 200 Agility
Stats: +30 Agility, +30 Endurance
Special Abilities: Soul-bound
Set Bonus: Sunset Emperor – +30 Agility, +30 Constitution, +30 Endurance, +30 Wisdom (1/5 pieces): Shadow Walker functions in broad daylight

"WHAT THE F—"

'plinkplinkplinkplinkpli-'

Another round of spines smashed into the lid of the chest serving as Damien's temporary lodgings. The implications of what he'd read were so unexpected he hardly cared. The boots constituted an exceptional piece of equipment which was soul-bound so he'd never run the risk of losing it along with a truly wonderful set piece bonus if he could attain all five pieces. That was less than half of what prompted his outburst.

Bartholomew had once been the 'Sunset Emperor', an agility-based occultist, just as he was. Bartholomew had mocked him for pursuing this route, had urged him to play with intelligence as his primary stat, yet he'd been the perfect candidate to provide him with tutelage all along. Instead of mentoring Damien, Bartholomew had withheld his knowledge and mocked him for insisting on following what was now, canonically, a potential chosen path.

They'd have words, assuming Damien ever got out of the Dark Tower. Well, getting out of the Dark Tower would be easy enough if Damien chose to turn back. They'd definitely have words sooner or later. For the moment, Damien was not pleased. He was dedicated to finishing what he'd started, so he'd have to put a pin in the argument that was already building inside him. After that, his vampiric mentor was gonna get it. 'Let me just rifle through my Bag of Holding and see if I have any occultist tomes on the lost art of stabbing people.' From Mr. Stab the World, himself. What a duplicitous scumbag.

Damien contained himself, his breath coming in short bursts through his nostrils. He couldn't yet equip the new boots since he was still five levels away from the level requirement for doing so, but he was glad to have them. He could now focus on how to get out of this box without dying.

If he could kill the two Cave Urchins with line of sight to the back of the chest, he'd be able to get there, reenter Shadow Walker and leave. Now he had a goal, he could start working toward it.

He equipped a rock and threw it out of the chest. At the exact point it started to hover, the spines struck. Three seconds. Damien rose on his knees and threw three knives in rapid succession. The first urchin he needed to kill was near, and he didn't miss. Damien was down again before it had finished screeching. One more flick, closely followed by one more Damien-in-the-box performance and both urchins were dead.

Now would be the worst time to mess this up. It was also the part he was most likely to mess up. With only one second left before the next volley, Damien threw the final rock high overhead, toward the opposite corner of the room. Then he crouched down, making sure the projectile was the only visible target.

His timing was adequate. The noise suggested all the urchins had fired, not just those in his vicinity. He was free! He clambered out of the chest as fast as he could and scurried behind it, accidentally scraping himself on some of the spines that had penetrated the lid of the chest in the process. But he was out of line of sight of all remaining urchins. He waited for five seconds, just to be certain he was back in Shadow Walker.

He started by collecting the knives, urchin meat and soul energy from the two urchins he'd painstakingly slain. In the cleared room, when he'd killed them at level 44, they'd dropped 2.5 souls each. That was now down to 2 souls each. It was just as well his Soul Reserve couldn't contain any more than that. Everything had to be done in complete silence. His rocks were running low. He made his way back to the already cleared urchin chamber, slowly and carefully, then set his back to the wall.

"So, that sucked."

Damien produced a new building block and reduced it to twenty-six brand-new chips of rubble as he kept talking.

"Sorry that took so long, and sorry I spent so much of it with my head buried in the bottom of that chest. It wasn't my first choice, believe me. I'd like to get this room out of the way now, so after I've finished making more stones I'll get on with it."

He finished off the block, granting him a grand total of twenty-nine stones to keep him alive, before checking his messages. He'd received three, one each from Lillian, Legolias and Aetherius:

Lillian: You're an idiot. A clever idiot, but definitely an idiot. I have no idea how you get yourself into these messes, let alone get yourself out of them.

Legolias: Okay. I can't do that.

Aetherius: Nice job.

He read each of them out in turn, heavily intoning Aetherius's reply. That was high praise, coming from him.

"Alright, all that's left is to get through the room. I promise I'll make it as boring as possible."

He did. It took twelve stones to weave his way through the death maze, but Damien got all the way to the end without incident. It was only as he reached the far doorway that he stopped and examined the second chest, placed in the opposite corner from the one he'd been stuck in for so long. It was completely surrounded by Cave Urchins. There was no way he could remove them without being attacked, the chest was simply unreachable. Was it there as bait, to tempt players into walking straight into the urchins guarding it? If that was the case, why was it on the far side of the room? Anyone approaching it would be well aware of the danger posed by the urchins before then.

There was another strange feature, clearly intentional but completely inscrutable: a wooden beam, set diagonally into the corner of the room high above the chest, with a black 'X' over the middle. Was he supposed to throw a knife at it? What would that accomplish, besides possibly getting him killed for making an attack with intent? It seemed like a cruel trick, to prompt the greedy or careless into triggering their own demise.

He'd spent far too much time in that room already and had promised his viewers he'd make it as boring as possible. He could come back to it later. He gave it a last wistful look before exiting the room.

There was a longer corridor here, granting a degree of separation from the room that had come before. No sooner had Damien crossed the threshold than he leveled up again. The EXP for clearing the second stage of the quest carried him into level 46, and halfway to level 47. There was the gratification he'd been searching for. As far as Damien was concerned he deserved level 50 for the trouble.

The new room was small. Barely larger than Damien's own bedroom. There was no point in taking any chances. Damien threw a stone up into the air, but it landed without anything happening. There were no urchins in here. He could do with a chance to relax after the endless tension of the room before.

The way to the next chamber hinted at why he was being granted a temporary reprieve. There was a large cast-iron door, with a silver demon skull split across the opening. A mini-boss door. Not all dungeons had them, but those that did ensured any who entered would not leave until either they or the boss was defeated. They existed not so much to keep adventurers out as to keep whatever the boss was in.

A side table, carved of the same impenetrable stone as the rest of the dungeon, had a single health potion and a brand-new sling of knives on top of it. Games only ever gave away good stuff so liberally when something bad was about to happen.

Before that, Damien had made a promise. He'd told Noigel he'd summon him and a succubus back as soon as he made it through the room, in exchange for his sacrifice in providing Damien with the room's layout. It wasn't Noigel's fault his efforts had proven insufficient. Nor would Damien have made that promise if he'd known there was a boss chamber up next. But he'd given his word. It was time to uphold his end of the bargain.

Damien summoned Noigel, then immediately summoned a succubus. This brought him back down to just 2 souls. Needs must. Hopefully the succubus would prove herself useful in the fight ahead, since the cost of summoning her was so dear. It was what came next that Damien really dreaded.

"Alright, Noigel. As promised. "Special time". Make it snappy, boss room in five minutes."

Noigel did not complain about the time constraint. He could work under pressure. He saluted smartly then leapt through the air toward the succubus, who had her arms outstretched and a toothy smile spreading over her monstrous face. Damien quickly turned on his heel and examined the wall, then went into his menu. He wouldn't have made this arrangement if he'd known how small the space they'd be stuck in would turn out to be. This deal was getting worse all the time.

No matter. He'd made good progress already. His sensibilities would suffer a little but at least he wasn't in mortal peril. Just moral peril. He went into his menu and spoke to his followers, trying to explain his minion's behavior away in hushed tones.

"Noigel is...smarter than you think, even without his 'Forbidden Knowledge' active. He's fiercely loyal, although that took a lot of work to get out of him. And...he's a bit of a horn dog. He's been acting up recently, following his urges out in the field and getting us in trouble, so I took his "special time" privileges with the succubus away. It's best to think of him as...a devious pet. If you establish clear boundaries and good rewards, he'll be responsive. This seems to be the most effective reward, unfortunately, so we're just gonna have to deal with it for a few minutes while I take stock."

Whatever Noigel and the succubus were doing, they were being quiet about it. Thankfully. Damien may have been forced to cut the sound if it had gotten too raunchy. He went into his stat page and examined it intently.

Class: Occultist
Level: 46
Health: 1,200/1,200**Stamina:** 1,350/1,350 **Mana:** 3,060/3,060
Strength: 55**Agility:** 174 **Intelligence:** 55
Constitution: 120 **Endurance:** 135 **Wisdom:** 306
Stat points: 5
Experience: 28,940/46,000
Soul Summon Limit: 8/30 **Soul Reserve:** 2/10 (+0/1)

Good progress. He put the 5 stat points he'd attained for his last two levels into agility, bringing it up to 179. He'd have over 200 agility by the time he was level 50, factoring in the single point granted to each stat with each level. That would be enough to equip Bart's gear, assuming he found the rest of it. That was pretty much a given. Damien would tear this place apart before he left without acquiring every last scrap. Good gear for occultists was hard to come by, let alone a gear set with a passive bonus that applied to one of his best skills.

He nodded in satisfaction and turned around, ready to move onward. Noigel and the succubus had been so quiet that he'd forgotten they were there. Or what they were doing. They'd appropriated the stone carved table for their "special time", moving the health potion and the Throwing Knife Sling off to one side while they lay over the rest of the table. Noigel was on top.

It wasn't what Damien had expected. They weren't doing

anything untoward. Damien had never lingered over what they did in private, since he'd only imagined one scenario that did not bear lingering on. Noigel was...cleaning her. He was using his tongue, granted, but if anything he resembled an affectionate cat rather than a miniature adult movie star. Noigel was busily lapping away at the succubus's hoof hair while she stroked his head. Now he was facing toward them, Damien could just about make out a low purr.

All this time, Damien had assumed they were doing something dirty. In fairness the way Noigel described it, coupled with the screams whenever Damien had logged on, suggested a more sordid kind of relaxation. Then again, Noigel generally described just about everything in those terms. Unbelievable. Oh! That's why Noigel had asked if Damien wanted him to perform "special time" all over his base, after Damien ordered him to clean it. It was Damien's fault for coining the term 'special time'. The little git knew what Damien had been thinking all along and teased him with it instead of explaining himself. He'd improved immensely, but was still the same Noigel he'd always been.

The succubus noticed Damien looking and hissed. Noigel turned, saw his master's eyes on him and started angrily garbling at him in tongues. Damien did not look away, because he'd noticed something very strange: Noigel's horns had grown. Damien had no sooner noticed them than they began shrinking back into Noigel's head. In a matter of seconds it was as though nothing had happened.

This was new. The perks of inadvertent voyeurism. Maybe this was why Noigel was so keen on pursuing this activity. Maybe it was why he usually went for howling loudly whenever Damien returned; Damien had assumed the noises were a by-product of "special time". Now they seemed more like a deterrent. Regardless, he couldn't sit there and experiment. His viewers were probably already making fun of him, he didn't need to push it any further. That would be better done once he was out of here. Of course, Noigel would still have to work for it.

The shoe was on the other foot now: Noigel had revealed it was in fact he who objected to being seen pursuing this activity, whereas Damien was perfectly comfortable using it to his advantage. The spectacle was no more offensive than a cute cat video on the internet, although it was being acted out by considerably more horrific beings.

"Sorry, Noigel, time's up. We've got a boss to kill. There'll be plenty more opportunity for "special time" in the future, if your performance merits it."

He grabbed the Throwing Knife Sling off the table and equipped it, only for the one he'd already been wearing to appear on the table in its place. He tried to put it in his inventory but it would not comply. So he could carry a maximum of twenty knives, only in the sling, and none in his inventory. Not very realistic, but if he went down that route he'd also have to explain how his tiny rucksack could contain blocks of stone and metal without encumbering him in the slightest. Better to take the good with the bad than complain about every tiny detail that didn't please him. Twenty knives should be enough. The health potion next to it was equally useless, since he was still at max capacity on potions. Also ungrateful, now he stopped to think about it, but three potions should also be more than enough.

He could've done with a full complement of minions, but he'd have to make do with what he had. He summoned two more imps, the only thing he could summon with his last 2 souls. He wasn't prepared to dismiss the succubus for a mere 3.5-soul refund. She could be every bit as cost effective as a hell hound or a wraith. There was only one way to find out. Damien took a deep breath and put his hand on the door.

You are about to begin boss fight: 'Mordred'. Are you prepared? (Y/N)

Damien nodded. The doors swung open. Damien strode inside, his minions around him. The moment they were clear, the doors swung shut and clicked behind them. Let the fun begin. This chamber was unlike the others. They'd all been open space, with no visible obstacles. This one was riddled with rings of boulders, spaced wide apart but blocking vision to the center. Damien took note. The scenery would probably be a staple of this boss fight. The chamber was much larger, customary in epic battles, and cylindrical. It reminded him of Bartholomew's final floor.

His analysis was interrupted by a sound that did not belong: the cries of an infant. He paced forward, moving past the first ring of rocks to find a second, then a third. After that, the boulders ended and the floor opened up into clear space. He put his back to the boulder that was blocking his line of sight and stared out into the middle of the dungeon floor. It was exactly what it sounded like. A newborn babe, wrapped in cloth, howling into the dark.

Damien didn't trust it. Not even for half a second. It was either the boss or bait. Even so, he couldn't very well throw a knife at it. That wouldn't curry any favor in his viewers' eyes (or his own, for that matter). He wouldn't have even done it if he wasn't being watched, as suspicious as these circumstances were. But he sure as hell wasn't going out there to get it. That's what imps are for.

Damien directed the imps and the succubus to move in and find their own cover, very slowly. They didn't have any stealth abilities, but provided they were careful they wouldn't be seen. The chamber was dark and the boss fight had not yet been triggered. They took about half a minute to get into position. After that, there was only one course of action Damien could contemplate. He ordered one of his two marginally more expendable imps to walk into the center of the room and examine the baby.

The imp strode out as Damien observed. It got all the way to the middle of the room without incident and without any inkling of how much danger its master was putting it in. So far so good. What was he supposed to do with this baby? He didn't want it anywhere near him, that much was for sure. Assuming he didn't get murdered by the thing, its cries would draw unwanted attention to his location. Better to get it out of the way. If nothing happened, he could search the room for signs of how to proceed. He ordered the imp to pick it up and walk it away from him.

The imp picked up the baby. It immediately stopped crying. Aww. That's nice. At least now it wasn't howling it would pose less of a tactical threat. The imp made it three steps before it stopped. Damien reiterated his order. It still didn't move. It was just staring down into the baby's face, completely rigid. Damien made the order more forcefully as the bundle the baby was wrapped in ripped, pierced by a long, spindly leg. Then another. A predictable six legs later, the bundle was reduced to rags as the baby developed into a 'not baby'.

The not baby quickly became far too big for the imp to carry. The not baby was perfectly capable of carrying itself. Of the two faces Mordred possessed, the traditional spider face that was staring the imp in the eyes was actually the less horrifying. The face of the baby had enlarged and become a perfect circle, changing location during the transformation. It was embedded in the top of Mordred's abdomen.

Damien was starting to wish he'd thrown knives at this thing from the beginning, although it would be folly to believe the fight could be ended so effortlessly. The good people of Mobius Enterprises had clearly put a lot of time and energy into rendering this nightmarish masterpiece. Damien doubted they'd reward those who tended toward infanticide with circumventing the primal dread inspired by Mordred's design.

Mordred raised a single limb and stroked the imp's face. Tenderly. The only movement the imp made in response was a slight trembling from head to foot. Mordred brought its face closer, still stroking that of the imp. Its jaws flashed and a chunk of the imp disappeared. Usually when imps died, they turned to ash. This room was not so merciful. The health bar had already disappeared, yet the imp was still there. This was an extended execution. The imp was being eaten alive.

Mordred entered a feeding frenzy. It started with the limbs, working its way from the outside toward the juicy, crunchy center. While it ate, its abdomen was raised up. The baby face was in plain view. The eating would not last long, there wasn't much meat on an imp and Mordred was already halfway done. Damien stepped out from behind the rock and threw first one knife, then—

Froze. The eyes embedded in Mordred's abdomen had opened wide, and they were staring straight at him. It was not the realization that he'd been seen that caused Damien's hesitancy. He couldn't move. Even his left arm had stopped halfway through throwing the second knife, holding it in place. The first knife fared no better. One of Mordred's legs lashed out and struck it out of the air, absurdly fast. The less creepy of Mordred's two faces turned away from the snack and eyed up the main course. Which was when Damien heard it speaking to him. In his head.

Come over here, where I can see you better.

Damien obligingly walked forward. He had no control over his own body. His steps were not fluid, but they were more than sufficient to carry out Mordred's instruction with minimal resistance. This must be how his minions felt, when he gave them orders. They had no choice but to obey, regardless of how they felt. He still had three of them. They had to do something.

Damien didn't grasp the irony as he threw them all in to save himself. Noigel was the first to go. He'd directed himself toward the weak point on Mordred's back, but what worked for the knife worked just as well for a soft, squishy imp. He was pierced as another leg lashed out, striking him straight through the chest. The succubus did marginally better. She at least survived her feeble attempt at slowing the creature down. She threw out a Chaotic Bolt, which Mordred did not bother to intercept. It splashed over its hide to no effect.

So much for that. The last imp was swooping in. It wouldn't turn the tide of this fight. Damien could see it out of his peripheral vision, even though his eyes were locked onto the compound eyes of the creature he was approaching. He could not speak but Demon Gate did not require an audio cue. He Demon Gated, which was less than helpful since the imp was flying through the air toward Mordred. It was even less helpful when the eyes of the supposed weak point locked onto his. His hand had not even made it to his sling when the command came.

Go limp.

Damien tumbled off Mordred's back, onto the floor. There was a Circle of Hell there, set by the succubus. It burned Damien but had no apparent effect on Mordred. Mordred positioned itself over him, staring into his eyes, then plucked him up and put him outside the circle as the root ended.

Drink a health potion. I expect a full meal.

Damien's hands moved on their own, withdrawing a potion and drinking it down, much of it splashing over his cheeks and chin as he struggled to disobey. Mordred observed him. Its legs were shuffling back and forth, as if struggling to contain itself. Another Chaotic Bolt splashed off its back while it waited. Mordred was not paying the succubus the slightest bit of attention. It was locked onto Damien, staring at him from very close, so Damien's whole field of vision was spider mandibles and a plethora of individually winking eyes. The health potion was finished.

On your knees.

Damien dropped to his knees, his hands in his lap, as Mordred continued toying with him. He'd never felt so completely powerless. Not even against Archimonde. At least with Archimonde, he'd still been able to resist before he was consumed. There was no illusion of hope to be found here. He was less than a fly. Flies do not obey instruction.

Pop out your tongue.

Repulsive. Demeaning. Inevitable. Damien felt himself stick out his tongue, and hated himself for it. Mordred raised a limb and gently stroked his face. A single tear rolled down Damien's face, the only form of self-expression he'd made since Mordred locked eyes on him. Damien's screen abruptly went completely black. He gasped. The game had ejected him, immediately. So much for being slowly eased back into reality. He could feel his own hot breath bouncing off the screen in front of him, the nodes of the headset pressing into his scalp. He was so relieved they were no longer transmitting.

Which was when the sound of his own screams, coming not from his mouth but generated by the game itself, began. The customary message appeared, with all the insincerity of the one that had come before it about twenty-three hours prior:

You have been DEVOURED by 'Mordred'. Fatality. Your

experience has been reset to the start of your current level and your body may be looted, at which point a random item of equipped gear will be forfeit.

Remember, it's only a game!

Death cooldown – 23 hours, 59 minutes and 59 seconds.

Thank you for playing Saga Online.

His stream was still active, he just wasn't delivering it while logged in anymore. He could see the viewer count in the top right-hand corner: 60,000. 60,000 people had watched that happen to him. He wanted out, but his mind was in tatters. He started trying to talk over his artistically rendered screams in the background — tongueless, if his critical faculties were not so suppressed as to deceive him — continued for a full five seconds.

"I...that wasn't...I need to go. Bye."

He pulled off the headset and it shut down. He was in his own room. He pulled his arms around his shoulders, rocking gently back and forth on his bed. Then quickly went to turn on the light before adopting the position again. This would take more processing time than he was accustomed to.

18

WALK THE LINE

Lillian tried calling again, but this time it was automatically declined. Damien had turned his headset off. She couldn't blame him for seeking solitude, following that showstopper.

First Archimonde, now Mordred. Damien really knew how to pick 'em. Which of the two was worse? The Possession-based ability Archimonde had used on her was centered around pure fear. There was no denying it, given what she'd seen when it was used on her. Mordred's abilities seemed little or no better. She'd heard the spider's voice resonating in Damien's head and had watched as he obeyed, powerlessly. It was a toss-up, but she reckoned his most recent death had been just about the worst she'd ever witnessed, by a hair. Well. No. That wasn't technically true. The worst in Saga Online, maybe.

Arcadia was very realistic, but it was not real. The least real thing about it were the lack of consequences following death. There were a lot of factors surrounding death it could emulate passingly well: fear, anger, pain. Regret. The reality is far worse. People who die don't get to feel anything afterwards. In reality, those feelings are only carried by those who are still living on behalf of the dead.

Lillian had seen death. She knew the real thing, the consequences it held, intimately. She wasn't afraid of it. She was afraid of what she might feel right before it happened. All the things she could've done differently flashing in front of her, until the endless loop came to an abrupt halt, for her at least, on her final thought. A lot of people playing Saga prioritized staying alive rather than giving it their all. Lillian knew this was no way to live, or die, in game or out of it.

Not dying came second to living well. The two were closely tied. If you're dying for something, it had better be more meaningful than what you'd achieve by continuing to live. In Saga there was a vast gulf between the two rather than a fractional overlap. Playing well was easily more important to her than suffering a laughably lenient twenty-four-hour "death".

She'd died a lot, to Andrew's dismay, when they started playing. He'd mistaken her overenthusiasm for continually misreading the odds. This lasted for about a week, until she calibrated her character with the requisite skills, stats and traits that allowed her to survive odds no one else would even consider facing.

Gradually, she died less and less without changing the way she operated. By the time Lillian hit level 20, she didn't die at all. Constantly testing her limits to breaking point, then calibrating her character so her limits were broken rather than her, had resulted in the ability to cheat death by repeating the split-second decisions that led to it.

Funny, how her nickname was 'The Immortal', given how often she'd died acquiring the expertise to earn it.

Damien did not work like her. Not even remotely. He prioritized staying alive, meticulously planning out as much as he could to remove as much risk as possible. That's why she was so quick to accept his death. Had she been in his place against Mordred, she'd have fared no better.

Lillian called him yet again as Legolias and Mr. Healy echoed the conversations happening all over Saga Online media.

"That was bad. He should've waited until it wasn't on alert before it attacked."

"Oh give over, Legolias! It was eating one of his imps, that was the best window he was gonna get."

"Sure, Healy boy, sure. Except he didn't attack it from

stealth! The whole dungeon is built around stealth, he's needed it at every stage. How did he decide not to remain in stealth when he was attacking the most dangerous enemy he's come across so far?"

Andrew's voice cut through their dispute, loud yet singsong in its lilt and sway. Lillian knew that voice. He used it to mask his anger.

"How many bosses have you come across that needed to be killed from permanent stealth, Legolias?"

Legolias stuck his chin out.

"None. Because I've never been in the Dark Tower, on the Path of Deceit. He should've seen it coming."

Andrew closed his menu and looked straight at Legolias, who stared back. The rest of them watched. All the singsong dissipated from Andrew's voice, replaced with pure derision.

"Yet I don't believe anyone saw it coming, not even from behind the safety and separation offered by a screen. Are you seriously telling me you knew, categorically, that if Damien locked eyes with the boss he would become bound to its commands and it would inevitably eat his face?"

"I knew leaving stealth wasn't a good idea."

"He had to start somewhere. What seems safer to you, a ranger, than a ranged attack from long distance? You're surely aware that would require Damien to stand upright so he could achieve—"

"You're not our leader anymore, Aetherius. Just because you got us through the last couple of riddles—"

Lillian stepped in, marking the end of their recreational activity. While it was a shame it hadn't ended on a more positive note, it did not bear the hallmarks of becoming more positive if she let this discussion continue further.

"Aetherius *did* get us through those riddles. You included, Legolias. Which is why he's now co-leader, effective immediately. The two of you can argue in your own time. Does anyone want to take a guess at what this plinth means?"

Andrew walked over to the plinth first, with Legolias staring sullenly at his back. Lillian gave him a warning glance and they huddled around the next problem. The five of them mulled it over in silence.

To err is human, this riddle is divine;
Can you do right when others do you wrong?
The line betwixt a cuck and saint is fine,
A king is neither. Thread it, or begone!

Judgementday was the first to voice something of value.

"I think the first line is about forgiveness. 'To err is human, but to forgive is divine.' The second line makes it seem that way too, doing right when others do you wrong."

"No wonder Aetherius can't get us through this one, forgiveness isn't his—"

"Legolias? Focus."

"Sorry, Lillian."

Mr. Healy squinted around the plinth into the next room, which appeared to be the Great Hall. Despite the grand scale of this particular castle, the layout so far was identical to the standard Empire guild headquarters design: Outer Keep, Inner Keep, Great Hall, War Room and Seat of Power. Rising Tide had previously presided over many headquarters, all of which had a Seat of Power, the most private of rooms reserved for whoever was in charge. Considering the nature of the quest they were on, the Seat of Power here would probably be named the same way as in Camelot: the Throne Room. Where this quest would surely end.

There were no signs of life in the Great Hall. Not even Hammertime and his lot, which was a bad sign. If they didn't catch him soon it might not happen at all. Either that or they'd logged out for the night and this would put Lillian's party ahead.

While Lillian's mind flailed with the possibilities, Legolias squinted back at the plinth, then through the alcove again, before making his own observation.

"Who are we supposed to forgive? There's no one in there."

Lillian looked into the Great Hall. He was right. Except for the chandeliers and the staircase at the far end, the Great Hall was empty. Lillian already knew forgiving one of her peers wouldn't work, since she and Andrew had done that fairly convincingly without any result. Her eyes strayed to the same place they always strayed when she broached a suspicious room in a new dungeon. The top of the doorway, just in case. What she saw there made her smile.

"I wouldn't be so sure."

They looked where she was pointing. There was a small skull carved into the top of it. It was subtle, barely larger than a thumbprint and not in the same gaudy gold or silver as would indicate a boss or a mini-boss. But it was a skull, all the same. She could smell combat.

It was about damn time.

"Alright, you all know your roles. Except you, Judgementday, you'll be off-tank. Sorry, I know it's not your favorite thing. You brought your shield with you, right?"

"You know I did. I heal if Healy goes OOM, right?"

"If he runs out of mana we're in trouble, but yes. Don't do anything brave, just protect Mr. Healy. Aetherius as well, so long as he's standing in range. I'll try to keep the biggest threat off you. Legolias, retreat back to Judgementday if you're in trouble, otherwise you're running evasion for defense and targeting the boss from the flanks. Aetherius can—"

Andrew raised a hand.

"Lillian, if I may?"

"Yes, what is it?"

"We need to answer the riddle, first and foremost. Killing may not be the answer here. It says we need to thread the line between a cuck and a saint."

Lillian held her tongue, but Legolias was quick enough to say what she was thinking.

"So you're saying we need to fight the boss, but not kill it?"

"Maybe. I have no idea. You have all the same information I do."

Lillian put her sword away and pinched the bridge of her nose. As much as she didn't like it, he was right. Answering the riddles had always been the way forward. That complicated things.

"Alright. Let's take it slow. Everyone else, speak up if you notice anything that seems important."

They all nodded. Good. Lillian was itching for combat. She hadn't used any of her combat skills since the fight with Archimonde, which had gone poorly. It was time to let loose...but not too loose, since they needed to solve the riddle. Freaking riddles. They ruined everything, even boss fights. Urrrrgh.

"Everyone, stay close behind."

She strode into the Great Hall, her party following in her wake. Despite the abundance of light sources, this room was shrouded in shadow. The flickering candlelight from the chandeliers illuminated many different knightly crests hanging from the walls. Some of these shields were clean and fair, some were foul and stained with blood, some were smooth and unbroken and some were cleft as though by battle of knight with knight.

Lillian raised a closed fist as they drew to the center of the Great Hall. There hung a huge banner, much like those that Lillian had ordered for Rising Tide's victory party that never came, at least in size. It was far less gaudy, the words were much smaller and the message conveyed was far more somber. Andrew muttered to them under his breath.

"We should read this. It might be relevant to the room."

Lillian nodded. She was glad to have a good reason to focus on it longer. The riddles had all been annoying, this was straightforward. It was a decent creed. She didn't appreciate all of it, but she was a big fan of most of it.

The Code of Chivalry: To live one's life so it is worthy of respect and honor by:

Fair Play: Never attack an unarmed foe. Never charge an unhorsed opponent. Never attack from behind. Avoid cheating. Avoid torture.

Nobility: Exhibit self-discipline. Show respect to authority. Obey the Law. Administer Justice. Protect the innocent. Respect women.

Valor: Exhibit courage in word and deed. Avenge the wronged. Defend the weak and innocent. Fight with honor. Never abandon a friend, ally or noble cause.

Honor: Always keep one's word. Always maintain one's principles. Never betray a confidence or comrade. Avoid deception. Respect life.

Courtesy: Exhibit manners. Be polite and attentive. Be respectful of host, authority and women.

Loyalty: To God, Sovereign, Country and the Code of Chivalry.

Lillian wasn't much for God or Country. She blamed that more on the world she lived in than herself. Aside from that, the basic tenets of the Code of Chivalry were good. Surprisingly so. Which made those rules she had not followed all the more hurtful. '*Never abandon a friend, ally or noble cause*'. That hurt the most. '*Avoid deception*'. Harder than it sounded.

She was still reading when Mr. Healy piped up in a whisper.

"Can we go yet? I'm done, is everyone else done?"

Lillian groaned. He couldn't have read it properly in such a short span of time. She was only halfway through her third reading.

"This could be crucial. There's likely a boss and this is a pretty big clue. Take it seriously."

She finished her third reading, then took a screenshot of the banner for good measure. They made their way to the end of the hall in silence, each of them waiting for an enemy to lurch out of the dark. At the far end of the Great Hall stood a single flight of ornate stairs, at the top of which stood not an ordinary door but a portcullis: an immense grate of iron that would've been more at place on a capital city's gate. Lillian span the hilt of her sword in her hand. Strong boss vibes all round.

They made it most of the way across before finding their guard had been up preemptively. At the base of the steps hung a huge black shield and a brazen mall to strike it with, as though the shield were a gong. No one felt the need to point out the challenge written in shades of red beneath the shield:

Whoso smiteth this shield

Doeth so at his peril.

Cool. Lillian was familiar with peril. This was pretty conclusive evidence there'd be a boss fight. Everyone knew what to do. She seized the mall in both hands and struck the shield so violent a blow that the sound echoed back from the walls of the Great Hall, and from the rafters in the rooftop on high, and from the antechamber behind them and the walls of the hallway beyond the portcullis, as though twelve other shields had been struck in those places.

In answer to that sound, the portcullis was drawn and they heard steps, heavy and armored, coming closer. A knight came to stand atop the stairs, clad all in black, as the portcullis dropped and the way through was once again barred. He was as big as Hammertime, but did not give off the same cute 'n' cuddly vibes. Not that the man who'd betrayed Lillian in front of her party was especially adorable.

His main weapon was a regular blade for him that would be too large to serve as a claymore for anyone with a normal character model. Good. Lillian was familiar with their use and power. That wouldn't pose a problem. She focused on the space above his head. 'The Black Knight'. Level 50. She'd fought plenty of bosses higher level than she was before, albeit with adequate preparation. His voice boomed into them from the top of the stairs, his sights set squarely on Lillian.

"Why didst thou, having read those words yonder inscribed, smite upon my shield? Now I do tell thee that, for thy discourtesy, I shall presently take thy shield away from thee, and shall hang it up upon yonder wall where thou beholdest all those other shields to be hanging. Wherefore, either deliver thou thy shield unto me without more ado or else prepare for to defend it with thy—"

This was the aggro stage, and boy was it long. Lillian had thought being the one to strike the shield would suffice to make her the primary target. However, as the boss prattled on she decided to spare herself and her team the monotony.

"Look man, it's really late. Can you skip to the good part?"

"That I will so."

An icon appeared over his head as she uttered the last syllable of her counterchallenge. It was two swords, crossed over each other. She focused on it and a description popped up in her HUD:

Knightly Duel: the actions of those not participating in the Knightly Duel shall have no effect on anyone in the room and vice versa.

Lillian frowned. She didn't have that effect on her. She

checked behind her. Nobody else had it either. The Black Knight clanked his way down the stairs and walked up to the shield Lillian had struck, then removed it and strapped it to his arm. He glowered down at Lillian, who was standing next to him with her weapons drawn.

"Three shall be the number of duels from your party, no more, no less. Three shall be the number of the duelists, and the number of the duelists shall be three. Who shall be the first?"

A one-on-one fight? That...that made sense on a quest like this. Almost all dungeons had a hard cap on the number of players who could run them as a group. If other allied parties significantly contributed to completing the dungeon, the boss would have no experience or loot to offer and everyone's efforts would be wasted.

In this dungeon, the EXP and loot were not the primary concern. The Black Knight was an obstacle to be circumvented on the way to the true objective. This mechanic ensured he couldn't be cheesed by bringing hundreds of players to the room and fighting him all at once. Not that they had that option, even if it had been allowed.

This was probably not good news. It seemed pretty likely Hammertime and his group had gotten through this, now she knew the nature of the challenge. His Berserker Rage would be ideal for it. He was easily the best suited of his party for a solo deathmatch. If he could do it, even if it was by leveraging his Berserker Rage, Lillian could do it. If he couldn't do it, she could do it anyway. She clanged her sword against her shield, drawing the Black Knight's gaze, and took up her defensive stance.

"I'll be—"

Lillian turned around to find Andrew walking toward them, shouting and waving his hands across each other.

"Time-out! Black Knight, we're going to confer."

He led her back to the group, though Lillian kept her eyes on the Black Knight the whole time. They'd scarcely got there when Lillian threw off his hands.

"Why are we still here? Who's fighting him if not me?"

"We only get three chances at this. If we mess it up there

might be a reset before we can try again, which lets Hammertime get even further ahead. Assuming we get to try again at all. You should be the last player we send out, that way you'll get two chances to see his move set and adapt."

Lillian couldn't argue with that. There was one small problem.

"Alright. Raise your hand if you want to try soloing the level 50 named NPC with the Behemoth trait. Anyone?"

Andrew immediately raised his hand, the only one to do so. She should've seen this coming. Lillian couldn't decide if she was more annoyed with herself or Andrew.

"You're a mage. There's no denying your damage, but this is a boss in close quarters. You won't survive long enough to give him a proper test."

"I'm just following your instruction. If no one else is up for it, I'll go first."

Judgementday tentatively raised his hand.

"I guess I'm the best option. I'm not much use as a tank and I won't win, but I might survive longer than Aetherius. You'll get a better view of the attack patterns that way."

Lillian looked between the two of them. They'd both stepped up but she had to make a choice between one or the other sacrificing themselves for the benefit of the team. Exactly the kind of decision she'd trained herself to avoid making at all costs. She looked them up and down.

"I'd still rather go first myself. I'm the one who's designed for this type of fight, why would we send anyone else? That's committing to failure."

The two applicants looked at each other. Whatever Andrew saw on Judge's face, it was enough for him to turn on Lillian and speak as frankly as he had in a long time.

"Don't be selfish. We're not here to be your cheerleaders, this is a chance for us to be useful. If you aren't willing to put us at risk, even when we're aware of the danger and decide to face it ourselves, why are we here?"

Lillian hadn't figured out a valid response before Judgementday picked up where his former boss left off.

"I've done nearly nothing over the last few days. I'm better suited to survive and Aetherius has done plenty already. Let me do this."

Great. Now Lillian was expected to throw her players away like cannon fodder. If she didn't, her concern for their safety would somehow reflect badly on her as a leader. Wasn't the entire point of her role as a paladin tank and the party leader to keep those under her from falling in harm's way? That became a lot more difficult when they insisted on it.

"Judge, you sure?"

"Yup. Just make sure you're watching how he kills me closely."

"Think positive, stay focused. You're first up, Aetherius comes after. Good luck."

Judgementday nodded and walked forward, drawing his weapons. He bashed his weapon against his shield rather less enthusiastically than Lillian had.

"I'll be your opponent."

The Black Knight looked Judgementday up and down. He peered at the rest of the party, as if expecting them to reconsider. When no one did, he set his sights back on Judgementday and the 'Knightly Duel' icon flashed over his head. The fight was on.

It was Judgementday who went on the offensive, to Lillian's surprise. The Black Knight raised his shield in front of himself, the first movement he'd made, as Judgementday ran up to him and bludgeoned it with his sceptre. He bounced right off, the only possible outcome.

Lillian winced. Knowing Judgementday was a healer didn't make this easier to watch. Never mind his character being all wrong, he simply had no aptitude for combat. The only reason to attack someone's shield is if you're planning on breaking it. As she made this connection herself, Saga Online agreed with her: a line was slashed through Judgementday's 'Knightly Duel' icon from top left to bottom right.

This was new and probably not good. That was confirmed when Judgementday's much bigger adversary tapped the shield into his front. It was wide open following his failed strike. As

Judgementday toppled over backward in his heavy armor, his footwork converting a mild shove into a complete collapse, a second slash appeared through his 'Knightly Duel' icon. Paired with its twin, it formed a cross from each corner of the icon through the middle.

Lillian was glad Judgementday hadn't been required to off-tank. He wasn't much more useful in this capacity, although at least he'd revealed this fight had conditions. By Lillian's reckoning, Judgementday could only make one more mistake. He made it almost immediately after she'd finished her analysis.

Judgementday tortoise-rolled to his feet, turning his back on his enemy in the process, and ran away. He only noticed he'd received his third strike after he'd turned at a safe distance. Lillian saw his eyes glance up and to the left, where the buffs and debuffs were defaulted to display in his HUD, then watched the tension leave his body. The Black Knight beckoned for the next challenger.

Lillian turned to talk with Andrew and found he'd vacated his place. He was standing back in front of the Code of Chivalry. She had a screenshot of it. She brought it up and put it on display, reading it through against Andrew. There were too many rules involved to keep the screenshot in the corner of her HUD while she fought. She wouldn't have time to reread the rules while she was fighting this guy, and making the image big enough to do so would block out all her vital statistics.

She still had unattributed stat points requiring allocation. That would give Andrew a head start. She was party leader, he wouldn't dare start fighting without consulting her first. Except he might. Better decide quickly. She was bringing up her stat page when Judgementday's heavy footfalls carried him in front of her. She'd managed to tune out the noise, right up until he started talking.

"Sorry, boss. I didn't know I could lose on technicalities."

"It's fine, you did well. Read the banner with Aetherius. We're working on it."

Judgementday cleared Lillian's field of vision and Lillian

focused on her stat page, leaving the Black Knight firmly in the background of her menu.

Class: Paladin
Level: 46
Health: 1,650/1,650**Stamina:** 1,600/1,600 **Mana:** 1,100/1,100
Strength: 290 **Agility:** 55 **Intelligence:** 55
Constitution: 165 **Endurance:** 160 **Wisdom:** 110
Stat points: 15
Experience: 24,625/46,000

Lillian put all her points in strength. She could micromanage constitution, endurance and wisdom later. She was punching above her weight here, and a significant strength boost would make the most of her 'Swift Justice' trait. That was her overwhelming priority.

With the extra 15 points invested, 'Swift Justice' raised her functional agility to 208. She couldn't get any use out of agility skills or weapons, but coupled with her high strength she was fast. Not as fast as rangers or assassins, but faster than any strength-based tank.

With Divine Might activated, her strength would hit 610 and her functional agility would rise to 360. 360 was a lot of attack and movement speed, especially with 610 strength behind it. She was level 46, so Divine Might would cost 46 mana per second. That gave her about twenty-four seconds of use.

Her opponent was a level 50, behemoth-grade warrior. As well as his huge reach he'd likely have a ton of health, since the Behemoth trait granted 30% of natural strength as constitution. Lillian's level 40 trait would kick that pillar of support out from under him. She just needed to apply it without breaking the rules.

She returned to the Code of Chivalry and reread it. By the time she'd finished, Andrew was waiting for her to initiate talks.

"Aetherius, I'm guessing you've understood all this?"

"Yup. There's a rule framew—"

"Yeah, I know. Don't see any reason for anyone else to go in before me. Pay attention to the banner and don't speak on voice chat unless it's important."

Lillian strode forward, sword and shield in hand, ignoring the calls of her teammates behind her. She had no interest in sending Andrew in next. It was unlikely he'd win, but nothing would annoy Lillian more. Aside from him dying, maybe. Throwing away his life to advance her cause, with their history? She'd never live it down.

Lillian had been waiting to reassert herself ever since the incident with Archimonde. After all those irritating riddles, this place finally had some combat to offer and she was ready for it. It would make for a good warm-up before she caught Hammertime. Lillian took up her stance not a few feet away, but directly underneath her adversary. She stared into his visor.

"Let's go."

The Black Knight drew his sword and raised it high above her head, the tip pointing down toward the top of her skull. He'd only have to drop it as soon as the fight started. Lillian held her place, inviting him to go ahead. There was a reason she'd walked up so close. She could draw an aggressive, highly telegraphed attack, at which point all she'd have to do was move faster.

The 'Knightly Duel' icon lit up in her HUD and she activated Divine Might in the same instant, sweeping her shield above her head. The sword was rediverted and her combatant's arm was stretched out over her.

All the chinks in his armor on the right-hand side were as exposed as they could be. Without moving her feet, Lillian stretched her sword arm forward and plunged it into his abdomen. As expected, the Black Knight had a lot of health. This level 50 mob was a signpost for what a great duelist should look like. Lillian needed to establish dominance immediately. She had a trait for that.

The level 40 paladin traits were comprised of three holy seals costing no mana, each tailored to a specific subset of paladin. 'Psalm:30' could be applied to a target at range and increased all healing on them by 50% for thirty seconds, with a fifteen-minute-long cooldown. This skill had saved Lillian against Archimonde and was great for healerdins, but healing wasn't Lillian's area.

'Psalm:23' was applied to yourself and offered significant raw increases to all stats, based on character level, for the duration. The holy seal lasted two minutes and had a cooldown of ten minutes. Lillian had decided the downtime was too much to rely on, besides which the increases to her stats were overall less useful than her Swift Justice/Divine Might combo. She could not afford to be at maximum efficiency only one-fifth of the time. It worked for Hammertime, but to her the concept was absurd.

Which is why Lillian had chosen the last holy seal, which could only be applied on hit but was available whenever it was not currently in use.

"Numbers:14."

Lillian's sword glowed and the light bled into the Black Knight's wound. A crack appeared in his character model, not his armor, over his shoulder. Light spilled out of it. 'Numbers:14' was set.

This was the tanking trait, although it didn't look like it. Its value was hidden in its complications – Numbers: 14 lasted for forty seconds, over which duration the target would have their total constitution reduced by 1% per second for forty seconds. In the fortieth second, the reduced constitution would be inflicted directly to the enemy's hit points as 40% true damage. The only way to remove this debuff was either through a high-grade cleansing spell or by killing the caster, which would immediately restore all the constitution lost and prevent any damage from happening.

It was complicated. Lillian had been forced to do some research and had eventually decided to invest in Numbers:14 after coming across a thorough, comprehensive, coma-inducingly detailed breakdown of how the skill worked by a helpful commenter in a forum.

ItsUpToYou88: Let's imagine our target has 100 Constitution Stat, 1,000/1,000 hit points and is afflicted with Numbers:14. This is unlikely since you can only apply Numbers:14 with weapon damage, but imagine it anyway. Numbers:14 reduces their Con Stat by 1% per second, reducing their Max Health. After one second, the target has 99 Con and 990/990 hit points. After forty seconds, the target has 60 Con and 600/600 hit points. One second later, the ability is finished and the 40 Con is returned to the target, but the missing 400 hit points are not. The target is reduced to 600/1,000 hit points.

That's the easy part. The hard part is that Numbers:14 takes from current health and missing health evenly. For example: our target has 100 Con Stat but only 500/1,000 hit points and is afflicted with Numbers:14. After one second the target has 99 Con and 495/990 HP. After forty seconds, the target has 60 Con and 300/600 HP. One second later, the ability is finished and the target is reduced to 300/1,000 HP. Numbers:14 has done 200 true damage rather than 400, because there was 50% less current health to take. In other words, the more damage the target takes over the forty seconds, the less damage Numbers:14 will do when it resets.

Did anybody understand anything I just said at all?

Lillian got the gist. In theory, this meant she could inflict 40% true damage over 40 seconds. In practice that would never happen. Using it on any entity that understood what it did ensured she'd get their full attention. Bosses and raid groups alike had access to high-grade cleansing spells, but those have cast times and cooldowns. She could tether high-priority targets with this ability, freeing up her team to enact their own strategies.

Lillian withdrew her sword from the Black Knight's ribcage and thrust her shield upward in one swift motion. The shield's rim smashed into his armored jaw. He reeled out of melee range, marking the end of the exchange. All of which had gone in Lillian's favor.

She checked his health bar: the damage she'd dealt had been carved out of his hit points – 1,220 for the sword strike she'd slotted through his armor, another 610 inflicted as blunt trauma by the shield-enabled micro-stun to the head. He still had 63% of his HP. That put him at about 5,000 max HP. Ridiculous.

A white mark was creeping across the right side of his health bar, the true damage component of Numbers:14 stacking up. More cracks of white light had appeared on the Black Knight's character model, a persistent visual reminder to both combatants that one of them was on the clock.

Lillian deactivated her Divine Might. No need to waste her mana while she had the upper hand. The Black Knight took stock of his situation and stomped back into melee range, swinging his sword in a broad sweep.

This was the true value of Lillian's latest ability. It made her opponents commit to killing her quickly, prompting them to use up all their stamina early. All she had to do was stay out of range, let them tire themselves out and then finish them off when they overextended. Assuming she didn't just bulldoze through them in the first place.

She ducked to one side as his ebony sword cleaved the air above her and a new exchange was opened. Lillian had dealt with plenty of shield-bearing enemies before, player and non-player alike. Not to mention that she was a shield main herself. There was an appreciable gap in a shield-bearer's defense whenever their sword arm was extended, and this gap was all the more telling on a behemoth-sized body.

Lillian's hit-and-run strategy came to an abrupt end when the Black Knight's knee arrived in her midriff, followed by an armored elbow in the back, putting her on the floor. He'd baited her to his weak spot and had an attack specifically designed to punish her for it.

Lillian span onto her back and pulled her shield across her body as the Black Knight reversed his grip. She reactivated Divine Might and swept her shield across the blade as he drove it downward, leaving it to grate against the cold stone floor.

The longer she stayed within the Black Knight's attack range, the easier she'd find it to remain there. Here, for instance, was a point in time when her opponent had already presumed everything was under control. This was when players left themselves most vulnerable. AIs, too. Lillian lunged straight upward, stabbing through his visor.

Lillian had achieved an armed Divine Might critical hit. 305 strength, doubled by Divine Might to 610, inflicted by a Holy Sword that did 2 x strength damage with no base damage for 1,220, doubled again by hitting a critical zone for 2,440 damage.

The Black Knight reeled backward, reduced to 15% of his max health after ten seconds of combat. Lillian had taken two unarmed attacks, and they'd hurt. She'd felt it. She deactivated Divine Might to check her hit points and found them at 1,250/1,650.

That was a lot of damage for unarmed attacks through armor. This guy could one-shot her, definitely. She could one-shot him by now as well, but she'd have to be careful about it. Which was why Lillian was so annoyed when the Black Knight dropped his massive shield directly in front of himself and entrenched his position.

"'Tis but a scratch!"

Yeah, says the guy with 20% health and fifteen seconds of Numbers:14 under his belt. He was baiting her. It wasn't as though she had anything better to do.

Lillian approached, activating Divine Might before darting to the flank. She was looking for an opening, minding her opponent's sword arm, when the shield swung in from behind her. She'd assumed it would be a stationary obstacle, but it was moving almost as fast as her top speed.

Lillian jumped back and the shield screeched across the ground in front of her. This was new. The Black Knight hadn't been that strong when they'd started this fight. Now he could move the slab of metal attached to his arm as if it were a paperweight. His strength stat had increased and he was running a new defensive strategy, utilizing a zoning technique to keep danger away and pressure on.

Lillian had come across this playstyle often. Players designed to operate at peak performance under specific conditions. She always made sure to destroy these enemies as quickly as possible, before they had time to get comfortable. It appeared the Black Knight's strength had increased as his health decreased. By how much Lillian couldn't say, but it fit the bill. That would be a pretty excellent trait for a behemoth-class warrior.

Lillian had wanted to finesse this, but she wasn't opposed to using brute force if he was deploying this method. He was hiding behind the shield, so she'd have to destroy it and destroy his win condition in so doing. Lillian had long searched for a way to convert her stats into raw power. Her search had ended with Hammertime's behemoth-grade war hammer. It converted 2.5 x her strength stat into crushing damage and unlike her Holy Sword came with considerable base damage of its own. It had a very respectable strength stat bonus on top, which was also doubled by the Divine Might she had to activate in order to wield it effectively.

Only behemoth-class heroes were supposed to use their own grade of weaponry. Their character models were the only ones big enough and the strength requirement was doubled for normal-sized players. Yet so long as Lillian had Divine Might activated, she could wield the war hammer without issue. She was aware how it must look. Her small frame was holding a weapon easily larger and obviously heavier than she was without difficulty. Intimidation was a bonus perk.

Divine Might and this hammer were an ideal combination for blowing through defenses most players would regard as "impervious". She simply attacked their weaponry directly and ground it, then them, into dust.

She ran forward, aiming her strike right at the center of the shield as it swung out toward her. The two of them struck, the unstoppable force versus the immovable object. Only one could be true.

Lillian's hammer connected at full swing. It was a valiant attempt at handmade nuclear fission. The shockwave was enough to push back her players and rattle the shields hanging on the walls. Not that Lillian could hear it over the sonic boom she'd created at arm's length.

In the split second their behemoth-grade armaments made

contact she thought she'd been successful. The resounding *clang* had been followed by a give, which Lillian sensed through her weapon's handle. Then her arms were thrown back as the shield barreled into her, striking her across the front of her body.

Lillian felt her nose flatten and break, the rest of her face squeezing in behind it. Her strike had been mighty and had taken most of the power out of the Black Knight's swing, but the shield was immense. He was beating her at her own game.

Lillian hit the foot of the stairs far behind and lay there in a crumpled heap, just for a second. She tried to stand up, still clinging to her hammer as the stun persisted. Without Divine Might, she couldn't pick it up.

The Black Knight was running toward her, much faster now he could carry his armaments so effortlessly. Her head was still reeling but she had to move. She released her grip on the hammer and staggered to her feet, preparing to dodge. The moment she stood up, the Black Knight stopped. In the same instant, a mark appeared through her 'Knightly Duel' icon. Mr. Healy's voice came through the party chat a half second later.

"Never attack someone who's unarmed! That works against you if he can't attack you either. Equip something!"

Andrew cut in halfway through with his own information.

"His shield is wrecked, hit it again."

Her team had provided her with all the information she needed. The stun finished, Lillian reset her nose, burst back into white light, took up her hammer in both hands and ran back toward the enemy that had just sent her flying.

Numbers:14 would be over in ten seconds. Lillian wanted to wrap this up before then. She had enough mana left to keep Divine Might activated for that long, all she had to do was use it. Andrew was right: the shield hadn't done much better from the attack than she had. So it was no surprise when the Black Knight juked her, pulling the shield back against his body and bringing his claymore scything down in one swift motion.

Lillian's hammer was cocked and ready to strike. While it wasn't a defensive weapon, she'd done stranger things in combat. She swung into the flat of the blade on its way down, turning the sword away. She followed through and the Black Knight staggered sideways as she rotated on the spot. His shield was coming into view and he wasn't braced behind it.

Lillian span a whole loop and brought the hammer crashing into the very center. The huge *clang* was replaced with a loud *screech* as the metal gave. It was rent straight across the middle, leaving both pieces hanging uselessly from the straps on the Black Knight's forearm and pushing him even further off balance. He was toppling over. His defense was down and he was vulnerable.

Lillian swapped between her weapons and prepared herself for the final strike. Which was when Mr. Healy blurted out two words into the party comms.

"Respect life!"

Mr. Healy had the most important attributes of any great healer: awareness and timing. Lillian planted her sword in the crook of her target's sword arm, where there was a nice chink in the armor to allow for movement. That would give her thinking time. He drew back his shield-free arm to strike her, resulting in Lillian delivering a prompt shield bash to his face. He tumbled to the floor and Lillian stood over her downed opponent.

The Black Knight's health was very low. Andrew was concerned.

"Lillian, the riddle. Don't kill him!"

"He's resisting."

"Ask him to surrender! Politely!"

Lillian raised her shield over his head, keeping his sword arm pinned with her sword buried in the crook of his elbow, and was the very politest she could bring herself to be.

"Surrender or death?"

"Spare my life and I will yield myself unto thee."

"...I accept."

The portcullis standing above the stairs was raised, immediately followed by a cacophony of *dings*. Everyone in the party had leveled up simultaneously. Lillian had leveled up twice, to 48. It was definitely over. It felt satisfying, though not as satisfying as if she'd killed him.

She grudgingly stepped off her opponent's breastplate and regarded him, arms folded. Then she extended her hand to him, reactivated Divine Might and pulled him to his feet. The Black Knight was a pain and a very difficult challenge but at least he wasn't a sore loser. He took a knee in front of her, still holding her hand.

"Madam knight, I know not who thou art, but I do pledge my knightly word that thou art the most potent knight that I have met in all my life."

A blessing arrived on her from Mr. Healy, quickly followed by a larger one from Judgementday. Her face filled itself in, her nose reset and her body was as new. The entity which had broken her face in the first place was now simping on her. Once again, Lillian was as polite as she could bring herself to be. She patted the back of his hand sympathetically.

"It was a good try. You did your best."

She finished her sentence and he faded away. Ah. That old chestnut. If only all simps were so easily deterred. In the center of the room, a fat golden chest faded in as the Black Knight faded out. A welcome trade. The chest was for Lillian. It literally had her name hovering above it in her HUD. She gathered her party up next to it for the after-fight talk.

"Nice shout-outs there, Aetherius, Healy. Judge, thanks for taking the test run for me, that really helped. It says this chest is for me, let's see what it is first."

Lillian opened the chest and could scarcely believe her eyes. It was a full set of crusader armor: head, chest, arms, legs and feet. There was no set bonus, but the gear was resoundingly better than hers for at least one good reason. It was all level 50. Even for level 50 gear, it was far beyond Lillian's expectations.

She had to be fair. She put it to her party.

"Should we split it five ways and I pay you for the pieces? Or does anyone want to roll against me for this gear?"

Legolias and Mr. Healy were already shaking their heads when Andrew spoke up.

"It's pretty clearly for you, the one who completed the duel. You deserve it and it'll be a nice souvenir of your victory."

Judgementday had been a little slow to shake his head. Lillian couldn't say she blamed him. He knew it wasn't for him, but it was good gear and he'd helped. She acknowledged his sacrifice.

"Thanks, Judge. This will help me a lot once I can wear it. If you're up for it, we can find you some tank gear and I'll take you through the basics when you have time?"

"You're offering private tuition on tanking?"

"Absolutely. I can't be surrounded by people willing to die for me when I need them alive."

19

BREAK THE ENDLESS LOOP

Lillian rearranged all the items in her inventory to make room for her haul, and was still forced to ditch her maintenance items to accommodate all of it. By the time she'd finished organizing her possessions, the rest of her party had started chatting to pass the time. The real prize still lay ahead. Lillian appraised her party.

"We all set to go?"

At once, their smiles became strained. Lillian checked herself. She folded her arms and waited for the complaints to start. Judgementday nervously stepped forward.

"I'm really sorry, but I can't be on much longer. I didn't get much sleep yesterday and I've got a full schedule tomorrow. Class starts at 8am for me on Wednesdays."

Right. She knew that. She was still figuring out what to say when Legolias chipped in.

"It's been a lot of late nights in a row, I'm falling behind on my assignments. I need to catch up before I go to bed. Not sure how long I'll be able to come online tomorrow, either."

Lillian scrunched her eyes shut and opened them again. It didn't help. Her grand vision of saving Camelot was being waylaid by homework.

"This was the Great Hall. Only two rooms left, the War Room and the Throne Room Two rooms and we're finished."

Judgementday wasn't having it.

"It's taken us two days to get through the last four riddles, and that's leaving out Sunday when we had to get through the gate and fight Archimonde immediately afterwards! All of them school nights."

"Come on, Lil—"

And now Mr. Healy had joined them.

"—that was a good fight, but it was a bit intense. Let's call this one a win and come back fresh tomorrow, I'd like to end on a positive note for once."

"Do you have anything important to do tomorrow, Healy?"

"I'd like to sleep before midnight, if it's all the same to you?"

Lillian kept her cool, although she didn't feel like it. On the same day she'd given them a break, letting them watch Damien's stream when they could've been pressing on, everyone had started complaining about the grind.

There was no sense in bringing up that she'd let them watch Damien's stream. They'd earned the break and following it had performed to the best of their ability. They all deserved better than her ire. Her problem was that none of them seemed to be acknowledging the stakes. She laid them out to them as simply as she could.

"If this were just about us and there weren't any mitigating circumstances, I'd understand. But Hammertime is still ahead of us. Godhammer could be in the very next room, about to get through the riddle unless we stop them. Even better, they could be in the last room *right now*. Aetherius, back me up here."

Everyone turned to Andrew. Andrew looked between them. He gave Lillian a long, hard stare. Then, to their combined amusement, he started typing. Lillian was less amused than the rest of them.

"Whatever you want to say, can you just say it? If you're typing it to them because you don't think I can take your honest opinion, that's kinda offensive. And if you're typing it to me—"

Her chat box pinged. She was glad he'd typed it to her instead of saying it out loud.

Aetherius: Do you remember complaining, earlier today, that

I had no self-control because I played Saga Online instead of focusing on my studies?

That was completely valid. But completely different! It was different because the stakes here were higher. Besides, she had a higher goal here, even if...the rest of them...didn't. Crap. Either they had the same goal, which they had every right to compete with her for, or they didn't and she was really insisting that helping her with the game was more important than focusing on their studies. What she was doing was wrong either way.

She blew out a long breath between her pursed lips. This was a lost cause. However, she could convince them to do one last thing before they all logged off.

"Can we at least move into the next room before we log off? I don't know if the gate will still be open by the time we come back and I don't much feel like fighting the Black Knight again. We're lucky we got through the first time round."

There was a bit of grumbling, but Lillian drove the point home.

"If Hammertime and his group are in the next room we'll have to fight them to log off safely. Which means we'll know the earliest they can respawn and we'll take control of the quest chain. If Godhammer are in the next room we'll deal with them before we log out. No riddles. Does that sound fair?"

Andrew nodded his approval.

"Fair. Works for me."

One by one, the whole party agreed. If Godhammer weren't there it would be very bad news. But if they were, Lillian would sleep much easier that night. Unless the fight didn't go their way.

They gathered at the foot of the stairs. With Lillian leading the way, they ascended and cautiously made their way through the open gate. The moment all five of them were across it, the portcullis dropped shut with a *clang*. If Hammertime's party was in the room ahead, they'd know they had company. Then again, the battle had been loud enough. Godhammer would've had time to prepare for their arrival. Not a comforting thought.

"I'm going in. Channel your heals in advance. Look for space. Prioritize their damage dealers."

She set her shield ahead of her and ran into the room, scanning for health bars. No sign. Godhammer had to be concealed behind the huge round table, the only point of interest in this otherwise bare room, waiting for a single player to wander into their attack range so they could even the odds before the real fight began. Lillian jumped onto the table and circled the entire perimeter, her sword pointed over the rim, as Legolias cautiously checked underneath it.

Nothing. They were alone. There was no obvious way forward. The room was stone on all sides. It was over. Mr. Healy's Logout Sphere enveloped him.

"I guess that's it. Post a time in the party chat tomorrow, I'll be there if you need me."

Legolias gave Lillian a nod before following in Mr. Healy's footsteps.

"Sorry they're not here, Lillian. I'll be online tomorrow evening, or call me if there's an emergency."

The Logout Spheres blipped their players out of Arcadia and back into the real world not long after. Only Judgementday and Andrew lingered. Judgementday walked up to Lillian, who was keeping her face turned away.

"I really thought they'd be here."

"Me too, Judge. It's alright. See you tomorrow."

"Are you sure? I can stay if—"

Lillian closed her eyes and gathered herself before she set them on Judgementday. She opened them and saw what she'd expected. Pity. She wouldn't fault one of her most loyal players for saying what was on his mind, nor would she allow him to feel sorry for her.

"Judge, I can't have you playing when you have things to do. I've been pushing hard recently. Sorry I got carried away. Go study."

"No, it's okay, I can—"

She slapped him hard on the back.

"Get out of here! Study hard and I'll see you tomorrow, okay?

We'll figure out your tanking lessons as well."

She held her hand on his arm and gave him a quick nod, beckoning him to return it. When he did, Lillian patted him on the shoulder before sitting on the table to see him off.

The moment he was gone, she slumped over and held her head in her hands. She heard Andrew pacing in front of her but didn't look up. Maybe if she didn't pay him any attention he'd leave her alone. She heard him clamber onto the table beside her and pace to the middle. Curiosity got the better of her. She couldn't help but draw her hands down her face to see what he was doing. He was scrutinizing the table intently.

"It's over, Andrew. Either they're in the next room or they've finished the whole quest already. We should leave."

"If they'd taken Excalibur, all Saga Online would know. Hammertime wouldn't be quiet if he'd succeeded. We need to figure out this riddle as soon as possible."

He'd found it. She'd completely ignored the middle of the table over the course of her search for hiding players. The whole table served as the last plinth. She climbed up as Andrew finished reading, turning away to scan the rest of the room. Lillian took his place and read the inscription:

The fifth quest is a pair, with two ways through;
The path to greatness parts at no small price,
A tribute worthy of a king is due,
By you or made by one in sacrifice.

These virtues are the parents of their kin,
Aligned in disregard to personal wealth,
It is said a man's gift opens doors for him,
And brings him before great men, such as himself.

Two ways through, it said. Lillian looked up and saw none. The War Room was a dead end. She chided herself. Psychological barrier. If they could find out the requirements, the way forward would open to them. The requirements were named: price, tribute, sacrifice, personal wealth. The question was how to make the offering in the first place. Whatever it was, it was not apparent.

"Andrew, any idea how we—"

Andrew stood upright and began pacing around the table again, shaking his head. They wouldn't get anywhere like this. She got off the table, intercepted him and put her hands on his shoulders.

"You need to sleep. You slept late yesterday and not for long enough. You were online all day getting everyone through two of the riddles. Three if we include—"

"Don't patronize me. I'm not leaving until this is done."

That sounded more like the old Andrew. What was Lillian supposed to do with that? Leave him here alone? Try to convince him to log off again, presumably making it worse? Or just cut to the chase and argue with him, like the good old days? None of these options were appealing. She wasn't having the best day herself, she'd rather avoid slipping back into old habits and making it worse for either of them.

She decided to watch. She was no more capable of focusing on the riddle than Andrew was, not when he was acting like this. She sat down on the table edge to wait him out. It wouldn't take long, given her experience and his current temperament. Andrew made it a quarter of the way around the table before he looked back to find her staring at him.

"Oh, I see, you're letting me do this by myself? I got us most of the way here, I thought you might—"

"I've been meaning to ask you about that. Why are you here?"

"What?"

Lillian drummed her fingers on the tabletop. She just couldn't help herself, could she? Even after everything they'd shared, even seeing how tired and frustrated he was, she couldn't sit there and let him speak to her that way without pushing back. There was no audience for them to keep up appearances in front of. She'd reopened the box. Or perhaps it was a joint effort. There was no closing it now.

"I thought once you were clear of the wall, we'd go our separate ways as agreed. You insisted on sticking around. To watch my back, you said. But we didn't have our talk until a few hours ago and up 'til then, you thought I'd stayed hidden to steal Rising Tide and the competition from you. Now I'm watching you lose it, because Hammertime is out of our reach. Or should I say your reach? Were you ever here to help me? Or were you always going for Excalibur, right from the start?"

The two of them stared at each other for a long time. Andrew walked back over, his eyes still not leaving Lillian's, and stopped dead in front of her. When he spoke again, he wasn't ranting like before. His voice was low and tight.

"Is that how little you think of me?"

"No, Andrew, that's how much I think of you. If you want to try and take Excalibur, you have every right. You've done more work to get here than I have, that's for sure. But if that's what this is, I'd like it out in the open. There's no Rising Tide, not anymore. No competition to worry about. Probably no Excalibur, either. We may as well be honest with one another, for a change."

He looked at her for a couple of seconds, saying nothing, then returned to circling the table. Lillian took a deep breath and let it out. At least Andrew had stopped ranting at her. He hadn't made it another quarter of the way round the table before he drew to a stop, staring at the ceiling. Then came back to her again.

"You know what? I wanted to make up for what I did. I wanted to show you I'm not what you think I am. I wanted to help you when you needed it most, even though you gave up on helping me. Then you told me you'd never left, that you'd never really left, and I knew nothing I could do would ever be enough. All I had left was getting you through this quest. Now Hammertime's taken it away from me, and you don't believe me. You helped me for years; I wasn't even good enough to help you through a few days."

The longer he spoke, the more his face contorted and the further his eyes drifted away from hers. It was hard to watch. But Lillian did. He showed no signs of stopping.

"I thought that if I just worked hard, I could make up for not being good enough before. But I've failed, again. It's all I ever do. I had everything I needed, and I threw it—"

Lillian grabbed his hands. It was too much. She couldn't take it in one sitting. She had to do what she could to close the box again. One particular sentence came to mind:

"Stop blaming yourself. You always take responsibility for everything, even when it's beyond your control. You're not perfect, and you never will be. But you are amazing."

Andrew choked out a laugh and squeezed her hands back.

"Don't throw my words back at me. They were for you, and you deserve them. I don't."

"You do. You really do. What I want right now is for you to get some sleep. We'll have a lot to think about tomorrow if Hammertime gets his hands on Excalibur. I know it's not what you wanted, but can you do that? For me? It would make me happy."

He was a mess, but he managed to nod.

"Okay. I'll be online tomorrow morning. I'll fix this."

"You already have. Go ahead. We'll try again tomorrow."

Andrew's shoulders dropped. He was ready to leave. He toggled into his menu and lit up to log out. A few seconds later, Lillian did the same. The moment he disappeared, Lillian canceled her logout.

She might've been a big fan of the Code of Chivalry but if she had to pick between being honest or protecting people, she'd deceive them every time. Even if it hurt. Andrew was in no state to handle this. He'd done more than enough. She'd finish this alone. Not only to get Excalibur, but to catch Hammertime and give him an earful. It had always mattered, but now it was important. She'd tear down the goddamn walls if she had to.

She took out her hammer to do exactly that. The door was supposed to be here. She was more than capable of making her own if one wasn't provided. She drew the hammer back...then set it down on the table as her Divine Might faded. This was not a question of strength, or even of will. She had to abide by the rules. The riddles had always been the way through this. She couldn't afford to lose her temper, the consequences could be far worse than cleaning up a mess in her kitchen.

She let go of the hammer, raised her pain settings and had positioned herself to do squats – less effective in game, but still a viable distraction – when the notification came up in her HUD:

Current offering – Hammertime's Behemoth-Grade Iron-Crusher – Level 35. Accept? (Y/N)

She froze, staring at the hammer. Why had that happened? Tentatively, she took out her sword and shield, placing them reverentially on the table.

Current offering – Hammertime's Behemoth-Grade Iron-Crusher – Level 35, Holy Sword – Level 40, Brawndo's Tower Shield of Mutilation – Level 36. Accept? (Y/N)

It was as simple as that. Offerings on the table. Right. She could get through this! Okay. If she got into the next room, she'd have to deal with Godhammer.

Should she call everyone back online? No...no, she couldn't do it. They'd made it clear they'd had their fill and she'd let them go. Even if she'd already opened the way forward, it would still be breaking her word. Always pushing for just a little more out of her people. Besides, she didn't even know how this worked yet.

She'd give it everything she didn't need. If she ended up fighting Godhammer in the next room, she'd need her weapons. They went back into her weapon slots and her inventory. She had a very high-end bag, enchanted for reduced weight and size so it was easier on the eyes and the thighs, although it couldn't hold a candle to Andrew's Bag of Holding. With the recent addition of the armor set from the Black Knight, it was full to bursting. Hmm. She was halfway to level 49. If she got through the challenge, she'd probably level up twice again and be able to wear the new gear.

She mulled it over. No. It was too risky. She was nearing level 50. If the location and the boss's level were any indication, these were level 50 quests. If she threw away the armor she could definitely wear, only to end up fractionally short of the level requirement for the armor that would replace it, she'd have completely screwed herself. The Black Knight's drops had been good, but they'd have to go.

Of course, that would make everything even harder. The Godhammer player who'd got through the quest might be wearing that armor if it hadn't constituted part of their offering. Which would put her at a serious disadvantage in both quantity and quality of enemies. Only some of her current armor was over level 40, most of it was in the high 30s. She'd likely be outnumbered, and whoever was wearing the level 50 gear, assuming they'd reached level 50, would be seriously dangerous. It was probably Hammertime. She was screwed either way.

What was she supposed to do with this? The best she could, that's what. She had to commit. All the level 50 gear she'd been so happy to receive went on the table. Something about it felt right. Hadn't that been a lot of gear to receive from a single encounter? Yeah. At the time she'd been happy, but now she saw it for what it was. A trick. The key to the next riddle, subtly laid down before it had even begun, camouflaged by greed. That was it. This was the way through. She could always replace the level 50 armor later, but the opportunity to go after Excalibur was irreplaceable.

Her odds had significantly improved. None of Godhammer who'd got through would have the level 50 gear either. Even better, if that was the price and the only thing left to gain was Excalibur itself, there probably weren't many of them competing for it. Especially if Hammertime had gone through first. Lillian wouldn't like to be the member of his party who showed up in the last room immediately after him. She couldn't say, for certain, if he'd be as fair-minded as she was. The requirement was quite a lot to throw away, in pursuit of a reward Hammertime had demonstrated he was willing to adapt his moral boundaries for.

This was all in her favor. Just a little thought and she'd cracked it. While it certainly wasn't her favorite aspect of these quests, she'd just needed a little more motivation to do it properly. Andrew would be very pleased when he woke up tomorrow and found she'd got Excalibur after all. The fight with Hammertime wouldn't be easy, but if she could handle the Black Knight she could handle him.

With all this in mind, she reviewed the window dominating her HUD:

Current offering – Crusader's Helmet, Chestplate, Gauntlets, Greaves, Boots – Level 50. Accept? (Y/N)

She was ready. Well, not completely. She equipped her sword and shield. Now she was ready. She set her feet, focused on the notification and nodded. The items began to fade out, exactly the same way as if they were being unequipped. It was working. She was on her way. She had to be ready. The moment the way forward revealed itself, she—

Offering rejected.

She stared at the message. Then she stared at the table, waiting for her rejected offering to reappear. It did not. She kept staring. Nothing. She'd been so certain it would get her through, making the loss worthwhile, but now it was all gone for no gain. *Now* she missed it.

She stared at the table for a long time. To her credit, she only took her hammer to it once, to curb the desire to destroy anything in her house upon returning to reality. It was as ineffective as she'd assumed it would be, although had she somehow managed to break the table she'd have been torn between satisfaction and regret. Then she did what she should've done five minutes earlier and followed after Andrew.

20

GIVE AND RECEIVE

Damien was out on a walk, which was unusual. Not least because it was raining. Whether his stroll would turn into something else was as yet undecided. He'd have to figure it out pretty soon, though, because the internet cafe was coming up on his right.

The market street was as busy as ever, despite the weather. Damien's first pass made it abundantly clear the internet cafe was not. As ever. If it had been, perhaps he could've walked home and granted himself an early night. If only life were so easy. He'd suffered a big loss that day. He needed a win. It only took a single pass to decide he was not simply taking a walk after all.

He pushed his way into the internet cafe and walked up to the counter. The man standing behind it was somehow familiar, even though he'd never seen him before. When he looked up from his screen to smile at the new customer it clicked: this was Gian's son. The father of the obsequious man who'd greeted Damien that morning. The missing link in the evolutionary chain. Antonio, if Damien remembered correctly.

As Damien came closer, his face was illuminated by the light over the service desk. Antonio's smile faltered and then went completely flat. Damien pulled back the hood of his coat, then jammed his hands in his pockets.

"You must be Antonio. I met your son earlier today, but I was looking for Gian."

"It's Mr. Vasquez. And you must be Damien. Haven't you caused enough trouble already?"

At least the social barrier of explaining who he was had been unceremoniously removed.

"How do you know who I am?"

"You're pretty well known in this industry. Not the first time you've been in, though. You brought CU with you last time, and they demanded to review our footage. They caught my old man letting you in without your ID card. He can't work here anymore. Only figured out who you were when I checked them again today, after my son said he was harassed by someone he didn't recognize. What makes you think you're welcome?"

Well, not that reinterpretation of the facts, for a start. Damien didn't appreciate being accused of 'harassing' someone. Damien had come here to apologize and see about helping, but this attitude was not working for him.

"Nothing. But I still wanted to thank Gian for being kind and letting me in without ID. Because of that, I was able to get my mom out of hospital. Without him, I'd be in foster care and she'd be dead. I didn't mean for anything bad to happen to him. So please tell him I'm sorry, and let him know his actions saved someone's life."

"That won't pay my bills. Or the fine on the pods in the back, which I hadn't even fully paid off before they got impounded, thanks to you. Or the fine my dad got for trusting you, which prevents him from coming back to work until it's paid. My son had to take leave from his actual job to help us while we shut down, so you've disrupted his life as well. Gian's kindness killed our business, because he was kind to the wrong person. Get out of my shop."

Damien pulled his hands out of his pockets and scratched his chin. He made no move for the door. While he'd been focused on his own culpability rather than that of the other parties involved, apologizing had come easily. He'd come here to accept his portion of the blame. Not to soak up everyone else's.

Antonio might have been aggressive and imposing, but he was not a gigantic blob demon with a mouth where his stomach should be, nor was he a were-spider-baby with mind powers. Of course, Damien was not an occultist. But he could deal with this as himself.

"That's an interesting take. Because as kind as Gian was to let me in, and glad as I am that he did, I didn't *force* him to. He's a grown-up, and he made a choice."

"I'm asking you to leave, but I'll remove you by force if necessary."

"Come to think of it, I don't remember stacking the pods in the back of your internet cafe so dangerously, either. I'm assuming you're the one who put them there, seeing as you run the place. I'm just a teenager, I've certainly never run a business, but even I could see it was poorly done. That's part of why I thought I'd be safe here, actually."

"Do you want me to contact CU?"

"Great idea! Go ahead. Ring up the people who punished Gian for being kind, when they weren't too busy chasing me down for breaking exactly zero laws. That'll improve things! You've already got the 'closing down' signs, I'm sure a second CU visit will bring the customers surging back in."

Antonio turned the screen toward Damien so he could see, opened the phone line and started punching in numbers.

"Doesn't make any difference. The first time you brought CU was enough to stop people coming. Calling them again—"

"You know what, Antonio? I'm trying to talk to you honestly. I really did come here to apologize, and the other reason I came here is to help, if you'll let me. I won't do it if you keep lying: I was here for two days and I never saw a single customer, not even once. That was before CU came. I'm sorry things were going badly before I even showed up. That doesn't mean I'll let you pin the whole blame on me where it's not due."

Antonio had been holding his finger over the dial button throughout. Damien waited for him to push it, so he could leave without regret. However, Antonio slowly drew his hand back to the desk before folding his arms on it.

"How do you want to help, besides late apologies and empty words?"

"Give me a device."

Antonio looked over the desk and selected a touch pad, before pushing it across the counter to him. Damien briskly typed in his information before placing it back on the counter.

"This is my e-mail. Send the files related to Gian's fine and I'll see about paying it. I don't think a person should be punished for kindness, even if in a purely legal context the responsibility falls squarely on him. There's more I wanted to discuss, but given the way you've spoken to me I won't be discussing it with you. Let me know when your son's gone and your father's back to work, so I can talk to a mature adult. Copacetic?"

"Copacetic?"

"Satisfactory?"

"No. Anything—"

"Well that's too bad, because those are my terms. I'll be waiting for your e-mail."

Damien walked out of the shop without looking back and went straight home. Antonio's e-mail got there before he did. Antonio really was desperate. At least he hadn't let his pride get in the way of his family's comfort and security. Damien got ready for bed as he recounted the conversation in his head, wondering if he'd done the right thing.

Cassandra was very quiet as he relayed the exchange to her over breakfast the next day. She asked what time he'd headed out on this errand, knowing it had to be late. Once she'd extracted that information, she listened in silence to the end.

"Run that last part by me again."

"I said those were the only terms I'd give him the credits on, then I walked out."

"No, honey, the part just before that."

Damien eyed his mother over his bacon and eggs, trying and failing not to cow his head.

"I said I would only discuss it with a mature adult, like Gian."

"And why did you say that?"

"Because he was talking and not listening, which made me angry."

"So you spoke out of anger."

"Yeah, I did."

"Did it make you feel good?"

"You know what? It did. It felt good to stand up for myself when someone was putting me down, using me as a scapegoat for all his own problems."

"Antonio sounds like he has a lot of problems, doesn't he?"

"Don't do that."

"Do what? I'm just saying, it sounds like he's having a really tough time. His business is going down, the pods he's still making payments on have been impounded, his father is—"

"Yes, mom, I get it."

"What do you get?"

"That he was talking out of anger as well."

"Now you've figured that out, I'll leave you to it."

Cassandra finished her OJ and stood up. Damien forgot to keep chewing as she wandered back to her room, apparently with no intention of continuing the discussion. He leaned around the table, still caught by surprise.

"Is that it? You don't have anything else to say?"

Damien leaned back in before she reappeared in the doorway, sunglasses on and her satchel over her shoulder. She put her hand on the back of his chair.

"No, I don't think so. I'm glad you stood up for yourself, I'm proud you're paying Gian's fine...how much is that again, out of interest?"

"Five thousand credits."

"It's your money, you have the right to do whatever you want with it. I'd like it if you talked with me before you make any more big purchases though, okay? Just in case."

"Yeah, mom, we already agreed that. That's a big part of why we're talking about it now."

"Fair enough. What I'm proudest of, though, is you could've

made yourself look better and Antonio look worse, or not even told me about this at all, but you told me the whole truth instead. Thank you, that means a lot to me."

She kissed him on the head and made for the door.

"See you tonight. Let me know how things with the internet cafe turn out."

"How do you know I told you the whole truth?"

Cassandra turned in the doorway and dropped her sunglasses to the end of her nose.

"I just know."

She drew down her sunglasses and pointed first at her own eyes then at Damien's, closing the door without breaking eye contact. Damien huffed and collected their dishes to take to the bio-washer. That had gone better than he'd expected. Now, aside from his self-inflicted errand, he had the whole day to himself. Better get to work on his profile. As much as he didn't want to see it, the footage he'd got during his livestream yesterday wouldn't edit itself.

Most of it didn't take very long. The acquisition of the Throwing Knife Sling followed by the fight with the four Cave Urchins was short but sweet. The second room was largely edited in double time to compensate for how slowly he'd been moving, with a couple of pauses to analyze his prolonged stay in the chest and explain what he was doing, and why. It seemed a lot less obvious, looking back on it. He hadn't been able to explain it while he was doing it at the time, because making much more noise than he already had might have got him killed. Now he could explain at his convenience.

He edited out the part with Noigel and the succubus. It was odd, but it felt wrong to broadcast it on his channel. Noigel was an NPC, but he was also Damien's closest working partner. He'd been pretty vocal regarding his displeasure at Damien's inadvertent voyeurism, so he probably wouldn't be too happy to know his intimacy had been intentionally circulated to a wider audience. Either that or he'd embrace the role and become the latest cat video/meme template. Noigel had shown plenty of awareness regarding Saga Online media, at least when his Forbidden Knowledge was active. Better not take the risk.

The real problem was Mordred. Damien skipped through the early preparations, up to the point where his imp had picked up the baby. Then he watched through, slowly. From the moment the imp had looked down, its gaze had never strayed away from the boss. Right up until it was eaten. Eye contact. He watched himself throw the first knife, prompting Mordred to turn his way before he froze halfway through throwing the second. Eye contact. Then he fast-forwarded to his Demon Gate, during which he had a good half second of flailing his arms around to achieve balance before the eyes of the baby body were focused exclusively on him. Eye contact.

Mordred's ability to control the movement of enemies was based entirely on eye contact. That was useful information. He just had to learn to throw knives at relatively tiny critical hit points without looking, or else he'd be eaten alive for the third time in less than a week. Superb.

He rewound to the start of the encounter and began editing sincerely. It didn't take long. His fight with Mordred had been even shorter than his fight with the Cave Urchins in the first room, although it had proven quite dense with information. Damien opted not to regale his subscribers with the strategies he was still incubating. Better to play his hand close to his chest, rather than vocalizing his plans to thousands of people before finding they were not so brilliant as they seemed. Better to be quietly confident than brazenly optimistic.

"And now, if you listen closely, you will hear the soothing, simulated sounds of a sixteen-year-old being eaten alive."

Right on cue, the death screen came up and his avatar began screaming. Those were just about the funniest words Damien could think of to belittle what had happened to him, although they still didn't seem sufficient to offset the brutality of his most recent death. He could only hope they'd be funnier to those who hadn't suffered it personally. Somehow, it was worse that the exact circumstances of his death had not been shown. It left more to the imagination. Damien had run through countless variations of what might cause him to make those exact noises, were his pain settings higher and his self-consciousness lower. He'd do his utmost to ensure that it didn't happen again.

"I'll take another crack at it today, see if I can find any weak points or exploits. Tune in tonight, Thursday the 8th of August around 9pm, to see if I kill Mordred or if I feed it again. Peace out."

All done. What to do with himself now? Coffee and networking. Maybe a closer look at assassin and ranger playstyles, so he could find more efficient ways of moving. A search on throwing knives to see if anyone had any better methods for using them, though Damien had never heard of them prior to getting his hands on the sling. Lots to do. Starting with coffee.

He settled back into his chair and started from the Saga Online front page. He sipped his coffee as he read through what admins deemed to be the biggest Saga events of the last twenty-four hours. Magnitude was up in the top five, as he had been for the last week. At exactly midnight, the Carlisle-Elite had lowered the requirement for recruitment by half.

Weird. Wasn't the whole point of the wall and the kill count to limit progression and maintain quality control? Getting five kills in a row without dying would be more than twice as easy as ten. Why were they upping recruitment so quickly? He found part of the answer a few stories further down, squeezing in at number five. It was him. He'd made the front page.

#5: Daemien Breaches New Solo Dungeon: The Dark Tower.

How about that? He'd been on the front page a few times after becoming competition leader. There'd been a story about his mom being in hospital, detailing how he'd paid for her surgery with his prize money while leaving all the unsavory bits out. There was another one when he returned to the game, after Cassandra had recovered. After that, the spotlight had drifted away. There were only so many times you could spring an ambush and stab a lot of people in the back to hold the attention of an audience. It's not like he was a bad player. It's just his actions lacked...significance.

It was a shame, then, that the people compiling these stories hadn't made the connection between him breaching the Dark Tower and the Carlisle-Elite speeding up their recruitment strategy. They weren't quite so close to the story as he was. Of course, that wouldn't be the only reason the Carlisle-Elite were speeding up: Lillian would be out there too, doing her thing. He wondered how she was getting along. She hadn't made the front page, which suggested she hadn't got Excalibur yet.

He scanned the rest of the stories, but none of the others were relevant to him:

1. Orcish civil war over! Orc Clan Chief Gilgamesh renames orc capital Waaarrghkanda.

2. Carlisle-Elite ramp up Recruitment, Camelot receives no reply to angry letter.

3. Kryton takes us through a cooking tutorial for his latest discovery: the Deep-Fried Haggis.

4. Tensions rise as Elvish emissary shot outside Ragnar-Rock. Score 25 – 23 to the Dwarves.

5. Daemien breaches new solo dungeon: The Dark Tower.

There was more than enough happening in the Human Realm to be worried about the rest of them just at the moment, thank you very much. He was honestly surprised he wasn't higher up the list. It was better than not being on the list at all, though. Damien redirected to his inbox and sent Lillian a message. She'd called him a few times yesterday and he hadn't responded. It would be good to show it hadn't been anything personal.

Daemien: Hey, sorry for not staying in touch like I should. Things have been difficult over here. It was great having you guys watching me and chipping in, thanks for connecting me and Andrew. His advice was really useful. I hope you're having a better time than I am, and you get Excalibur soon. Our small corner of the game would be a lot better off if it were in your hands. Send me a message if you're free to chat sometime.

He considered it. Then he decided he'd better send Andrew a message as well.

Daemien: Thanks for helping me out yesterday. Not many people can pull off altruistic trolling. Are things going well with Lillian? Hope the stuff in my bag is helping.

That was enough for now. He'd been sat at the computer for an hour and a half, it would be a good time to get his chores done. He drained the dregs of the cold coffee and had just stood up when his chat box pinged. Andrew had already written him back.

Aetherius: You're welcome. I'm not sure about that second statement but I'll take it as a compliment. Things are going okay, we've hit a snag but I'm working on it. I have bad news: the Bag of Holding hasn't been connected to an inventory since your livestream on Monday evening. I see what you did there. Nice move. But your inventory is gone. Your base is likely gone, as well. Sorry.

At least he had confirmation. Damien settled back into his chair and keyed out a reply.

Daemien: I'm the one who's sorry. Should've told you first, so you could take anything you needed before I did it. That's my fault. What's the snag?

Aetherius: Hammertime split the party and took Godhammer ahead. Long story. We're stuck behind this riddle:

The fifth quest is a pair, with two ways through;
The path to greatness parts at no small price,
A tribute worthy of a king is due,
By you or made by one in sacrifice.

These virtues are the parents of their kin,
Aligned in disregard to personal wealth,
It is said a man's gift opens doors for him,
And brings him before great men, such as himself.

Ideas welcome.

Hammertime had split the party? Just when Damien was starting to like him. People are invariably disappointing. There was one line in there which sounded familiar. He focused on it: *These virtues are the parents of their kin.* That sounded a lot like something he'd been forced to read in his literature classes. Or was it history? Where had he heard that before? He drummed his fingers on the table. Virtues. Oh! He hadn't heard it in a class at all! It came from a conversation Cassandra had foisted on him one night, when he was complaining about his lot.

Daemien: "Gratitude is not only the greatest of virtues, but the parent of all others." One of the two virtues it's talking about is gratitude. I'm guessing the other is charity, because of the '*disregard to personal wealth*' bit. So charity and gratitude are your '*two ways through*', whatever that means.

Aetherius: How do you know so much about virtues? Was it part of your occultist training?

Daemien: Harhar. My mom works in a virtues-based kindergarten. Virtues are very much her thing. Speaking of which, I have to go, I have errands to run. That's called diligence, by the way, although you've never had trouble with that one.

Aetherius: Do you know all the virtues?

Daemien: Diligence, Chastity, Forbearance, Forgiveness, Charity, Gratitude and Humility. There are different specific names for them and there are a lot more besides, but those are the seven primary virtues.

There was a long pause. Andrew had stopped responding. Damien gave him a minute, then raised his hands to start typing when the answer came through.

Aetherius: You're a genius! Thank you again! Gtg.

So Damien was a genius now. He had it in writing from Andrew, and with two exclamation marks, no less. Damien wasn't sure knowing the seven primary virtues qualified him as a genius, since his mom had been drumming them into his skull for as long as he could remember. The important thing was he'd obviously been helpful, to prompt such an outburst.

He put himself together, shower and all, before starting on

his chores. It wasn't enough just to know the virtues. He had to try and demonstrate them from time to time. Patience wasn't a primary virtue, but it was the one most useful to him then and there. He'd get back into the game soon enough. He just had to be patient.

21

IN THE PRESENCE OF GREATNESS

It was 1pm when Lillian got home. Having taken an automated taxi against her principles she was on edge, but it was the fastest way home and her misgivings came second to necessity. She'd found a colleague to cover for her, although arranging it at such short notice had come at a price. She'd be covering half their Saturday night shift. The worse half, from 8pm through to 1am, although the second half on that particular day of the week was not much better.

None of this mattered. Andrew hadn't stopped messaging her since 11:30. He said he'd solved the riddle.

Lillian had the headset on and was logged in thirty seconds after she'd closed her front door. Andrew was waiting for her.

"I didn't think you'd actually come."

"Never mind that, you said you've solved the riddle?"

"Couldn't do it without you here. I have to put my gear on this table in exchange for your passage. Lillian? What's wrong? You seem upset."

Lillian drew her hand the rest of the way down her face. She thought he'd discovered something new. He was at the same place she'd reached yesterday, just before the disappointment starts. Time to fess up.

"I stayed online after you logged off and did exactly what

you're trying now. I gave my whole level 50 set as tribute and it didn't open the way forward, but I still lost all of it. Sorry I pretended I was logging out. You needed to sleep and I didn't want you thinking about it."

"Yeah. I knew all of that already."

He didn't seem surprised in the slightest.

"How did you know already?"

"Uh, let's see. I knew before I logged off that you were more worried about me than the riddle. I realized you weren't coming when I checked and found you were still logged in. I knew why you'd done it and stuck around to see what happened. Five minutes later you logged off. You gave up. You weren't on a death timer but you'd given up quickly, so something bad had happened. Once I figured out what this table did, I knew exactly what had happened."

Lillian was annoyed, although she knew she had no right to be. It wasn't very useful to do the wrong thing for the right reasons when you got caught five seconds in.

"You did sleep though, right?"

"Yeah, I did. Eventually. I got over it. Never mind that, are you ready?"

"Hold on, didn't you hear me? I tried this yesterday and lost all the gear, it'll be no different for you."

"Damien said the two virtues this riddle's referencing are charity and gratitude. The last four riddles were based on four of the seven primary virtues: diligence, chastity, forbearance and forgiveness. This room is charity and gratitude together. It's not charity if you're doing it for your own gain. The riddle states the person trying to pass through can give tribute for themselves, but it's a better fit if one person does it on behalf of another."

"That's a good point. When did you become so wise in the ways of charity?"

"After two hours' research on the subject."

She knew he was joking, but the delivery was so dry and so quick it was completely believable. He kept going in the same, somber tone.

"That alone is a good enough reason to try, but I also have better gear to offer than you do."

Andrew had better gear than the level 50 crusader set she'd thrown at this yesterday? That seemed unlikely. She'd believe it when she saw it, but there was an even more obvious issue that came first.

"What about you? How will you get through?"

"If I'm the charitable one, you have to be the grateful one. Hopefully, if you feel grateful enough, you'll trigger passage for me as well."

"I don't know about this, Andrew."

"Why?"

Lillian shifted her feet, trying to find the words. What if she didn't feel 'grateful' enough for Andrew to come as well? What would that look like? Not good, to put it lightly. She'd have to get him through by any means necessary. She still had all her equipped gear to throw at this. But she'd need it if Hammertime was waiting for them.

What if Hammertime had already finished and was waiting until they'd already made similar sacrifices, just to rub his victory in? Would he do that? She couldn't rule it out, not after—

"Lillian, you're worrying."

"No, I'm not."

"Yes, you are, I can see it."

"What if it doesn't work?"

"We've come too far not to commit now."

"What if I get through...but you don't?"

"Then I don't get through. Which will mean all the conclusions I made were wrong, because I know you want me to come with you."

All that stress for nothing. He was looking at her straight on, letting her see him completely. None of his tells were there. He wasn't lying. He had no reservations at all.

"Do you really mean that?"

"Of course I do! You'll need me for backup to deal with Hammertime."

He was still holding that straight face. Lillian groaned. She was far too stressed out for all this humor.

"You're not as funny as you think you are, Andrew."

"Maybe, maybe not. I am about to get you through this. Ready?"

Lillian reluctantly consented. Andrew seemed pretty confident his bid would succeed, which only worried her more. She'd been certain her plan would succeed as well. At least he'd been warned. They didn't have any better options.

Lillian remained unconvinced until Andrew took a deep breath, held out his hand and took hold of the item he intended to offer as tribute for her passage. His palm literally glowed with the worth of his offering. Lillian knew what it was immediately, despite having never seen one in person before. She did a double take, not trusting her own senses. It was an artifact. A permanent one. The real thing.

Only two other artifacts had ever been announced by players. Their existence had been widely reported on Saga Online media, evidence that the ceiling for what was possible in game was far higher than anyone had conceived. The two players who'd advertised their good fortune had experienced vastly different fortunes afterwards. The first had their artifact forcefully taken in an ambush less than two days after they'd announced their windfall. The second had recently become leader of the orc capital, Waaarrghkanda. It made sense that Andrew had kept his acquisition to himself.

The design was elegant. Two silver serpents wrapped around each other, their forms interlocking to hold the structure steady. There was a square opening at the center, holding the component people had learned to stay quiet about. A vibrant green gem, emitting its own light. The name of the item and its description appeared in gold above it as Lillian stared in disbelief.

Loki's Lesson in Trickery: You summon a decoy that performs a predetermined action for 30 seconds. You obtain true invisibility for the duration of the effect. The effect is canceled when you or the decoy take damage, when you cast an ability or when you inflict a new source of damage. Cooldown: 30 seconds.

Lillian finished reading and the world made a little more sense. The questions rolled off her tongue as she caught up with reality. Andrew answered them as quickly as she could throw them out, without either of them taking their eyes off his most valuable possession.

"That's an artifact."

"Yes."

"How did you get it?"

"Magnitude made it for me."

"When?"

"Right after you left me. Right after I *thought* you left me. I found the artifact material the same day, after we had the fight about Trinytea in the Malignant Crypt."

"So this is why you started folding your arms and tapping your foot."

"Yes."

"This is how you've been using the Bag of Holding to drink mana potions."

"Yes."

"He gave you those two items and fixed all your character's weaknesses in one go."

"Yes."

"And now you're offering it as tribute, for me?"

"...Yes."

"Why? Why the artifact? Why not save the artifact and give it everything else you have?"

Andrew lowered his hand and tilted it sideways over the tabletop. The amulet chimed as it bounced off the stone, then fell flat and lay silent. The rarest item Lillian had ever seen. It seemed so insubstantial for something so overpowered. Andrew stared at it a few moments longer. Then looked at Lillian.

"This is the only item I have that I can't afford to lose."

He nodded at her, then the table. The artifact began to disappear. Neither Andrew nor Lillian looked around the room waiting for the way forward to reveal itself. They were both focused on the fading artifact. That's how special it was. After a few moments, it was gone.

Lillian couldn't believe Andrew had owned something so incredible. Let alone that he'd give it up for her sake, for something that might not even appear. It took a while before she realized that no rejection message had come. She looked up, to the other side of the table. There it was.

"Andrew. You did it."

She caught his eye and the two of them looked at the back wall together. Lillian could see the corridor leading to the Throne Room, through the alcove that had appeared while they weren't looking. She readied her weapons.

"Let's go. We might still be in time."

She was reviewing Hammertime's character information in her head. If she was going to make him listen, first she'd have to put him out of commission. A more difficult prospect than simply killing him, as the Black Knight had shown. It would take at least thirty seconds, or up to a minute and a half if Berserker Rage was available to him. That was just Hammertime. There could be other players as well. At least Andrew would be there for support, but she'd rather ensure his safety and let him hang back. It hadn't even occurred to her that she might not have another choice until Andrew called out after her, his voice trembling.

"Are you mocking me?"

Lillian stopped. She turned. Andrew had not moved from his spot. She looked between the way forward and him.

"What are you—"

"I thought I'd really done it. I was terrified I'd just given up my artifact for nothing, then you said I'd opened the way forward and I believed you. Why? Why would you hurt me like that?"

Lillian's eyes widened. Her worst fear had come true.

"You can't see it, can you?"

"It really worked?"

"Not if you can't see it. Come here."

Andrew, still looking skeptical, walked over to Lillian. She grabbed his hand and dragged him through the alcove. Or she would've, if she could've. She crossed the threshold without any problem and a notification popped up as she hit level 49, just shy of level 50. She hadn't even processed her level when her arm was yanked back: Andrew's fingers had hit an invisible wall, which to him remained very visible. He pulled out of Lillian's grip and nursed the hand she'd made him punch the wall with, smiling all the while.

"Lillian? Are you still there?"

He couldn't see her at all. Lillian stepped back into the room and he locked eyes with her immediately. To Andrew, the room was still sealed. It had been a long time since she'd seen him look so happy.

"I did it."

"Why can't you go through?"

"I don't know. I guess I was wrong. Worked for you, though."

His eyes widened.

"What are you doing standing around here? You might still be in time!"

"That's what I said!"

"Go! Go get Excalibur! I'll be waiting for you here, just message me for help with the last riddle after you've dealt with Hammertime."

"I'm not leaving you here."

Andrew wrung his hands at her.

"I gave up my artifact for this! We don't have time to figure out how to get me through as well, just go!"

Lillian looked over her shoulder. Andrew was right. It would be far more terrible if his generosity came to nothing because she was being hardheaded. But she had something to say first. The riddle had made her seem ungrateful. Andrew might've been putting a brave face on for her, but she wouldn't leave until she'd had her say. She took his hands in her own.

"Andrew. Thank you. I'm so lucky—"

"Lillian, stop talki—"

He was trying to shake his hands out of her grip. He was still intent on rushing her along. This was more important to her, even if Andrew didn't share her sentiment. She grabbed his hands a bit harder.

"Shut up, this is important. I'm so lucky you came with me and we got the chance to fix things between us. That's more important to me than the quest. No matter what happens with Magnitude, Hammertime and Excalibur, let's—"

Andrew had been trying to contain himself, but it had proven impossible. Justifiably so.

"That's lovely! I agree with you! But you said 'Thank you', I can see the way through now, stop talking and move!"

The moment her grip loosened he grabbed her by the shoulders, roughly turned her around on the spot and started pushing her into the corridor. His hands were still on her back after a few steps, then Lillian started running herself. That was it? She'd been delivering a big heartfelt speech when all she had to do was say 'Thank you'? She could not wait to be done with this place. One way or another, that was about to become possible.

"Lillian, weapons!"

Her sword and shield appeared in her hands and she broke into a run. Andrew couldn't keep up. After a few seconds she arrived in the Throne Room. It was larger than any of the other rooms in the castle, including the courtyard. Stained-glass windows stretching from head height all the way to the ceiling shone prismatic light into every corner. The walls and floor and all else were hewn of white marble, the ceiling a vast mural composed of great and valorous deeds, with a shining sword at the center of it all. Excalibur.

Lillian was standing on a red and gold carpet which led all the way to the steps at the far end. Atop them stood the throne. It was empty.

Lillian eyed it up as Andrew came in and began his own evaluations. It could not be so simple as to sit on it. There was a riddle. There was always a freaking riddle. Her primary concern was making sure the area was secure.

Her eyes tracked backward into the corner behind her. The darkest part of the room, but not nearly dark enough to conceal Hammertime's bulk. He was curled into a ball, peering out at her over the crook of his arm. He was wearing nothing. He had no armor, no weapon, no apparent inventory item. Just the loincloth, less than the rags players entered the game with. Andrew followed where she was looking. Then they all stared at each other.

Andrew was the first to break the silence, albeit by murmuring into Lillian's ear.

"I'm glad I didn't know he'd be like this."

"Why?"

"I'd have gladly given up my artifact to see this. Which means it wouldn't have qualified as a charitable act."

Hammertime rose to his feet. He was bigger than them, but that hardly mattered. With all the stats from his gear absent and no armor, he posed no threat at all. Even Berserker Rage wouldn't help him. Which was just as well, because he'd activated it and was running toward them. Whatever he lacked, it wasn't courage. Lillian braced herself behind her shield and called out her warning.

"Don't do this, I want to t—"

His bare shoulder dropped into her at full tilt. He managed to push her back, to her surprise. It was still not enough for her to lose her footing. Andrew had run to the side of them and his hands were glowing red.

"Andrew, no killing! That's an order!"

She activated her Divine Might and shoved Hammertime back on the second push. If she could contain the Black Knight without killing him, this would be child's play. Except that Hammertime had now set his sights on Andrew.

"Hammertime, if you attack Andrew I won't—"

Off Hammertime went, his hands extended forward to wrap themselves around Andrew's throat. Andrew twisted sideways and Blinked to the far side of the room, appearing in front of the wall. This was ridiculous. Hammertime had to know he couldn't beat either of them like this, let alone both of them. Lillian was tired of him embarrassing himself.

Hammertime turned toward Andrew, ignoring Lillian in favor of the unarmored mage with Blink on cooldown, and Charged at him. Lillian knew her enemy was in a desperate situation, but how could he possibly imagine he could get past her? Sure, killing Aetherius was a much more realistic prospect than killing her. It still lay beyond the realm of fantasy. She couldn't reasonably expect Andrew not to kill Hammertime if she didn't stop him first.

She deactivated Divine Might and jumped sideways. It wasn't quite enough to block Hammertime's path, although she could've if she had wanted to. Hammertime curved, trying to pass her. Lillian's feet hardly touched the ground as she jumped again, right into his side, swinging her shield directly into his torso.

Hammertime doubled over around it and his hit points dropped. Good thing she'd deactivated Divine Might. He still didn't fall, although he'd been brought to a complete halt, and his health was replenishing quickly. Berserker Rage was unreal. He turned on her and drew back his fist, teeth clenched and eyes wild. Lillian promptly reactivated Divine Might, drew back her unhelmeted head and snapped it forward to meet his closed fist. Hammertime took more damage than she did, although his health pool was restoring faster than hers. Brawn meets brains, except Lillian's brain had plenty of brawn behind it. Hammertime hadn't even dredged up enough damage for a stun.

Lillian unequipped her sword. She didn't want to kill him by accident. She caught the second punch, plain and simple: her 'Swift Justice' trait, coupled with Divine Might, made it relatively simple against someone with less than half her pure strength. She twisted her wrist and rotated her arm in a wide circle, which Hammertime followed all the way to the floor. His health was very low now, which was okay as he'd heal in a few seconds anyway. Then she unceremoniously dragged him across the floor by his wrist, back toward the War Room.

"Andrew. Stay here, discover what you can. I won't be long."

Hammertime kicked and struggled the whole way there. Getting him through the doorway required a little more oomph, but after that there was nowhere for him to find purchase. Lillian dragged him down the corridor by his wrist until they were back in the War Room. She deposited him on the floor and stood in the doorway, keeping herself between him and Andrew. She didn't want to have this conversation in front of him without knowing how it would play out.

"I'd like to talk. I'd rather not kill an unarmed opponent but if you keep attacking me I'll have to. Would you like to talk?"

Hammertime sat there in surly silence until his Berserker Rage was finished. He knew it was over. The red aura surrounding him dissipated, marking the end of any threat he posed. Where once he'd been all but equal to her in the party, now he was at her mercy. She wanted to show it, if he'd allow her to.

"What happened to your gear? I'm guessing it had something to do with this room?"

"Just kill me. Don't gloat about it. You beat me. Congratulations."

"I wanted us to do this together. You're the one who turned it into a competition. A competition with no winners, only losers."

Hammertime pulled himself up to sit cross-legged, his hands braced on his knees.

"Aetherius is the winner. He's used you, again, to get what he wanted. While we're sitting here talking, he's getting Excalibur. You didn't listen to a single word I said. I was right to try and do this without you, since you insisted on putting 'Andrew' first. You're just a silly little girl, being emotionally manipulated by an evil, selfish man."

Lillian looked him over. He was so confident he was right. She was equally confident he was wrong, with good reason. She laid her cards on the table.

"A few minutes ago, Andrew gave his artifact as tribute so I could get to the last room. Yes, he had an artifact. That's how he was pulling his tricks. It's only a lucky accident he's in the Throne Room at all. He did most of the work getting us through the riddles after you split the party. He never left anyone behind. Everything he's done, he did for me, as a way of apologizing for his past behavior."

She thought this would be enough, but Hammertime was more set in his thinking than she'd imagined.

"Yet now Andrew is in that room, alone, and you're here talking to me. You think he's helping you when he's been using you all along! That's how he's always played this game. He worked to mend your trust so you wouldn't suspect him, waiting for the opportunity to stab you in the back. His patience has paid off! You've given it to him!"

Lillian considered it. Hammertime's position was logical, were Aetherius the person he'd presented himself as publicly. Hammertime did not know the finer points of Lillian's relationship with Andrew, or his personal life, or the conversations they'd shared on the way to this moment. He was completely disregarding everything she'd told him, with less than half the information.

Setting that aside, what Hammertime was saying was not completely impossible. Andrew might, given the circumstances, have a crack at taking Excalibur for himself. That didn't bother Lillian. She'd already told him he had every right to try. It would be less than perfect, but given his circumstances she could accept it.

"It's not too late," Hammertime said. "If we stop talking now you can kill him before he gets Excalibur. To be honest, I don't think you have what it takes to be a great leader. You won't handle the stress and you'll be manipulated by the first person who offers you a few kind words. Better you get it than it ends up in the hands of that manipulative trash!"

This was pointless. Hammertime had already made up his mind. He was stuck like this, forever. She should've just killed him at the start, when he'd told her frankly how little he thought of her, and nipped this whole fiasco in the bud.

Since she was already here and hadn't needed to kill him outright, she could at least give it her best shot. Not for Hammertime: she didn't owe him anything. She owed it to herself, so she could look back on this and know there was nothing else she could've done. He wouldn't be receptive in this state unless he had something to gain, so she gave it to him.

"I'll tell you how things look from where I'm standing, then you can come through and try for Excalibur with us. You don't need to say a word. You can, if you want to, but you don't have to. If you stay quiet and actually listen for a minute, two minutes tops, we'll be done here. There's no hurry; Andrew has no interest in finishing the quest himself. I can't convince you of that, since I'm a 'silly little girl', but it's true. I don't mind if you interrupt or don't pay attention, but we'll stay here until I'm satisfied we've hashed this out properly. All I ask is that you listen."

"I don't believe you."

"Yeah, I've gathered that. But I know you're recording. It won't look great if I go back on my word, will it? I promise if you hear me out, you can try for Excalibur with us."

She stuck out her hand and looked to it, waiting for Hammertime to accept. It wasn't as though he had any other option. He took it and they shook. Now came the hard part. She stared at him, her mouth tightly closed but working in every direction, her eyes narrowing and widening. It must've looked like she was having a seizure. It was only as Hammertime drew breath to speak, which could only make her task harder, that she finally managed to force out the words.

"I'm sorry! Sorry. Sorry I've been a mess. I was in decent shape to lead the group when we set off, but things went downhill right from the start. That's not something I wanted any of you to see, and it's definitely not anything you should have to worry about. I did my best, but I wasn't in a good way even before we fell out over the first quest. I could've conducted myself better. Sorry."

"Apology accepted."

Lillian suppressed the urge to grumble. She'd apologized, and meant it. She'd been far too aggressive with Hammertime at the inn. He'd behaved himself better than she had, for the most part. The problem wasn't that her apology was unwarranted; she knew she wasn't perfect and didn't mind admitting fault. The problem was that Hammertime had far more to answer for. She couldn't expect him to meet her at the middle ground if she didn't take the first step. He showed no intention of joining her there. She coaxed him along.

"Is there anything you'd like to apologize for?"

Hammertime was still looking at the floor. Lillian wouldn't let this one go. He'd acknowledge what he'd done. She waited. It was his time.

"I took you hostage and split the party."

"Close enough. Let's give you credit where credit's due: you looked at the riddle. You figured out what it wanted in under a minute. You're very intelligent. I wish you were stupid, that would've made this so much easier. Then you used what you'd learned for your own gain, to enact what you thought was the right course of action. The right course of action, as you saw it, was to manipulate me into a position of vulnerability and use me as a tool in your plans. Did you ever stop to think that's no different from what you hate Andrew for?"

Hammertime didn't look up from the ground. He could no longer meet her eye. He was decent after all, and he was embarrassed by his despicable behavior. Good. There's nothing wrong with making mistakes, so long as you learn from them. She'd made her point. It was about time to wind this down.

"Now we've both had our say. Unless you have something important to add, I'm ready to move on. Would you like to move on?"

Hammertime's head didn't move from the spot of ground between their feet. Lillian got to her feet and held out a hand.

"Let's draw a line under this and see if Andrew doesn't try to kill you."

He took her hand and allowed her to hoist him up. Pretty

quickly, all things considered. She led him back through the corridor, into the prismatic light offered by the stained-glass windows on all sides. Andrew was there, arms folded and tapping his foot. Lillian put it down to habit.

Whatever he was doing, he hadn't tried to do the quest by himself. The death knell of Hammertime's argument, the rock-solid foundation of everything Lillian had told him. Not only did she know herself better than Hammertime did, she knew Andrew better as well. Obviously. If he didn't comprehend the scale of his blunder now, he never would.

Hammertime approached Andrew with Lillian walking by his side. This would be the very last time she extended the benefit of the doubt to Hammertime, unless he acted appropriately. His body language was positive in that regard: his arms were stuck rigidly by his sides, his fingers flat against his thighs. Andrew's hands, in contrast, were already glowing red. Hammertime stopped about ten feet away from him, rigid as a board.

"Sorry."

He turned to Lillian.

"Sorry."

He straightened and marched into the corner of the room, where he'd been waiting to ambush them earlier. The Logout Sphere consumed him. Lillian and Andrew watched until his presence was gone from that world. Andrew stared into the corner for a few seconds after it had been vacated, then looked at Lillian, raising an eyebrow.

"Damn. What did you do to him?"

"I'll show you the recording later. Did you find out anything while I was gone?"

"Nope. Sorry. Didn't want to trigger anything."

"Alright. Last stretch. Let's get on with it."

Lillian drew her weapons and walked the red carpet, Andrew a few paces behind. They were halfway there when a figure emerged from behind the throne and began floating toward them slowly, her hands held in front of her at the midriff. She was dressed neither in robes nor armor but a dress of pure white samite. Her arms were encircled with several bracelets of wrought gold.

She was small and not threatening at first glance, but there was something off about her. More than just the fact she was floating above the ground, which was a pretty pedestrian sight in Saga Online. She drew to a stop ahead of them and her hair flowed above her head and about her face. It was a glamor, like the one Aetherius had used back when his presentation had mattered. Aetherius's had been an air enchantment, letting him float off the ground until he entered combat and giving him a windswept appearance. This had to be water. Her bracelets only briefly touched upon her arms, her garments flowing out around her. Her eyes were pitch black, yet bright and glistening. Her skin was completely pale, save for the red lips which bore the faintest of smiles. She was undeniably, eerily beautiful. And more than a bit intimidating, if you knew where to look.

This could be the boss, which would explain why Hammer-time hadn't got anywhere with no gear. That would fit the usual layout for a dungeon: dodgy stuff, dodgy stuff, mini-boss, dodgy stuff, boss. This was not a normal dungeon, though. Not to mention, bosses tended to be a bit more talkative. Lillian kept edging closer and suddenly what she'd been waiting for appeared above the mysterious stranger's head. She breathed a sigh of relief. It was in green writing. Whatever this thing was, it wasn't hostile.

'The Lady of the Lake'

Lillian briefly recalled Mordred, the baby that had turned into a giant spider and eaten Damien. He'd been right to be suspicious of the baby. That had been very obviously something that did not belong. While the Lady also seemed out of place, she was far too suspicious to warrant her placement as an ambush attack. Mobius would've made her less weird. Lillian put her weapons away and introduced herself.

"Hi. I'm Lillian. This is Aetherius. We're here for Excalibur."

The Lady looked at each of them in turn. Then she began to speak.

"Those who fain would wield yonder sword..."

Oh no. That's why there was no visible riddle in here: this watery tart was feeding it to them verbally. Lillian cleared her mind to absorb the Lady's words as she finished the first sentence.

"...Must be beyond all fear and all reproach,
But claiming these traits falsely is abhorred,
So clad yourself in truth, lest you encroach."

It seemed simple enough. Don't be scared. Don't be...reproachable. Tell the truth. This riddle was playing Lillian's jam. Her bread and butter, too. The Lady of the Lake stepped aside and Lillian gave her a nod as she strolled past.

"Well at least that was easy. It's the next part I'm worried about. Andrew?"

She looked back to find Andrew behaving in a very peculiar fashion. He'd stopped a few steps past the Lady and appeared to have adopted the same water-based glamor, except he was also floating up off the floor, thrashing his arms around in slow motion. He was drowning in thin air. He swiveled round and waded forward a short way before falling to the floor on his hands and knees, dry as a bone. He got up and ranted at their host, but despite the short distance between them there was no sound. Lillian raised her voice.

"I can't hear you! Can you hear me?"

She'd spoken to him over party chat, yet he still hadn't heard anything. Andrew held up a finger for her to wait and started typing. There was no sign of any barrier, but it was clearly there. It made sense. You couldn't have two people going for Excalibur at once. She opened her menu to see what Andrew had just sent.

Aetherius: The riddles have all been based on the primary virtues. The only one we haven't seen so far is humility. Try to be humble. Look behind you.

Lillian did as she was told and found the throne occupied. By whom, she could not fathom. He did not look like a king. Nor did he look like a boss. He didn't look like anything Lillian had ever seen. He was beautiful, but undeniably alien. It was hard to say whether he or the Lady of the Lake was the stranger of the pair. He was old, judging from his neatly coiffured silver hair, but his face bore none of the signs of old age. Not so much as a single blemish. His features were sharp, from his pointed nose and chin to his piercing blue eyes.

Stranger than his appearance was the way he sat on the throne. He didn't look like he belonged there. He was poised on the very edge of the seat bolt upright, his limbs tightly pressed against his body. He was composed entirely of straight lines. His clothes were not unfitting for the seat he occupied: a silver quilted robe, held across the waist by a metallic golden sash beset with jewels of several sorts that gleamed in the light from the stained-glass windows. The robe ended just below the knees, beneath which there were garments of a very different nature. Tight black leather pants, ending in gold plate boots.

Who was this character? Lillian looked above his head and decided he was stranger than the Lady of the Lake, if only by a hair. At least she was named. This individual was not.

'?????????'

As Lillian reached the bottom of the steps an icon appeared in the top right of her screen. She recognized it immediately: it was a heart rate monitor. Her heart rate was currently sitting at 75bpm. That was higher than usual for her. Was that in game, out of game or simulated? She had no idea. What she did know was that she'd been told to be beyond fear. The situation was tense, the NPCs were unnerving and the stakes were pretty damn high. Lillian could still do better. She took a deep breath and let it out, slowly. Her heart rate obligingly dropped to 65bpm, and was going lower before the man in front of her spoke.

"Tell me about yourself."

"My name is Lillian. I'm nineteen years old. I graduated—"

She'd been told to clad herself in truth. This did not appear to be the truth the stranger in front of her was searching for. A single commanding syllable put an end to Lillian's first attempt at an introduction.

"No."

Then softer, but authoritative.

"Tell me about yourself."

Okay. Saga Online-based truth then.

"I co-led a prominent Empire guild, Rising Tide, for over two months. During that time we were the most active guild in the Empire's service, with a combined—"

"No. Tell me about yourself."

Her bpm was starting to steadily rise. What did he want?

"I'm trying. Can you phrase your question more clearly?"

He stared at her and Lillian stared back, keeping her breathing slow and steady. When he spoke again, her heart rate jumped to 85bpm.

"Why do you want to wield Excalibur?"

Did she answer the last question correctly? Seemed unlikely. She wasn't dead yet, so she wasn't out of it yet either. Stick to the truth.

"Because it's a legendary weapon. Anyone would—"

"No. Why do you want to wield Excalibur?"

"I want to rule Camelot."

"Why?"

A new pattern. Was she going the right way? Better to answer quickly than hit whatever the threshold was that would cause her to crash out by default.

"Because I think I'd be pretty good at it."

The man's eyes flared. He looked over her shoulder at the Lady of the Lake, then swept a hand over his knee, as if he were clearing away some dirt.

"My associate will show you out."

Lillian didn't even have time to ask what he meant before she found out. There was no warning when the hit came. It struck her in the chest, picked her up and smashed her into the ground. Every time she hit the red carpet, she was picked back up and smashed into it again from a great height. An invisible wave, without the wet. The wave itself did not hurt too much. The repeated contact with the ground did. She'd been thoroughly pulverized by the time she found herself approaching Andrew from a great height.

The Lady of the Lake stepped neatly to one side and Andrew had to Blink out of the way as Lillian crashed to the ground. She lay there for a few moments, her hit points teetering on the brink. At least she wasn't dead, although a quick check of her HUD somewhat diminished the relevance of her survival. At some point during her transition from interviewee to flotsam, the bpm monitor had been replaced with a new message:

Time to next audience: 12 hours

"Lillian, what happened?"

Lillian gingerly pushed herself to her feet and several of the armored plates covering her clattered to the floor. Her gear had held up against Archimonde and the Black Knight, but this was the last straw. She and Andrew picked up the pieces and started putting them into her inventory.

"Well I didn't get Excalibur, in case you were wondering. Now it's making me wait twelve hours before I can go again. I don't think he liked me very much."

She gestured at the throne, only then noticing that the strange man sitting in it was nowhere to be seen. At least she'd have twelve hours to prepare for her next go, unless Andrew got it first.

"Fancy a crack at it? I can tell you the questions, so you'd be better prepared than I was."

"Pass. Why take a beating for something I don't want? I don't get the impression I'd be able to just give it to you afterwards. I can still help you with it, though, if you like? I couldn't hear anything you were saying in there, did you do the humble thing?"

"No, I did not. I'll have another go at it next time. If failing the riddle always ends like that, I won't survive the next one. I've already lost most of my constitution and armor from my equipment. Any gear Hammertime didn't lose in the room before this one, he probably lost to this. He should be back to take his turn in a while, if he doesn't succeed we'll give it another shot."

"Are you feeling okay?"

"Uh, yeah, besides getting beaten up by the floor. Why do you ask?"

"Why do you suddenly not care if Hammertime gets Excalibur?"

"I already told him what he needed to hear, although he didn't make it easy. Magnitude is a bigger threat. Every day, the Carlisle-Elite recruits more players who can take quests in Glastonbury, access the Inner Circle, level up past 50 and get new gear and traits. It won't be long before the power gap is huge. Regardless of who does it, someone needs to sort this mess out in a hurry. I can live with Hammertime having Excalibur if it means Magnitude is dealt with."

"That's *very* noble, Lillian. Can't say I agree. I didn't come all this way to watch you gracefully step aside for a bully. Rather than rooting for the flavor of sewage we hate less, how about you get your head back in the game?"

"Andrew, it's been nothing but drama since I logged in. For once I'm about ready to take a break. Besides, twelve-hour timer, remember? Unless you want to try it there's nothing for us to do but wait."

"If you're free...maybe you could show me the talk with Hammertime and we can talk about the riddle. Together? Over lunch."

"Over lunch?"

"If there's no point in us being here for the next twelve hours, we may as well do something useful. You said we should let Hammertime attempt Excalibur and I've made it clear I disagree. That means keeping me logged out should be your top priority for the next twelve hours. Or am I mistaken?"

"Is that so? What if I gave you a direct order not to kill Hammertime?"

"I'm not saying I'd disobey your order, I'm just subtly implying it's possible unless you come have lunch with me. Besides, it's lunchtime, the time at which regular humans eat lunch. You still eat, right?"

"Occasionally. You know what? Lunch is on me. Can we maybe figure out the details after we log out? We've got a bit of a third-wheel situation here."

The two of them slowly turned their heads to look at the

Lady of the Lake, who was just doing her thing: staring at them while looking all floaty and mysterious. Andrew gave her a grin and a wave. No response. Creepy. He kept his eyes on her while talking to Lillian out of the corner of his mouth.

"Agreed. I'll be waiting, so you better actually log out this time."

"Stop rubbing it in! I'll see you on the other side."

The two of them followed each other out of logout, leaving Saga behind them.

22

HIDE AND SEEK

Damien was back in the first chamber. Now he knew what he had to deal with, he wanted to be in as good a shape as possible beforehand. He turned on the livestream as he accustomed himself to his enhanced movements, waiting for the numbers to increase. He reached for a throwing knife, only to find it wasn't there. The sling was gone. Great, so now he'd have to do that all over again. At least he knew what he was doing this time round.

As the viewer count picked up, he prepared new stones from his inventory and addressed his audience for the first and last time.

"Hi everyone. Today is all business. I'll be saving commentary for the review video. Enjoy the ride."

He turned the viewer count off. No distractions today. He was all set. He knew what he needed to do. They could just enjoy the show, or find something else worth watching. It's not like he was the only creator of content. If they didn't like his footage, rather than whining about it they could always find something they enjoyed.

Damien crouched down and headed back into the danger zone. He opened the chest in the first room and found a brand-new knife sling. Good, the chests reset when he died. He wouldn't have got very far if they didn't. He took a knife in each hand and made his final checks:

Knives out, *knives out*, elbows in, *elbows in*, knees apart, *knees apart*.

A-do-be-da-be-do-be-da-be-do-be-da-da.

In Damien went, the two knives leaving his hands and the next two entering them halfway through his first evasive roll. He already had the system down for this room. After his second well-timed roll, Shadow Walker bolstered his stealth and he was once again able to position himself for the next easy double throw. It was essentially a warm-up, with the additional benefits of easy experience and soul energy.

Those benefits were diminishing as he got closer to level 50. He finished the room and recovered the throwing knives and souls, only to find the urchins had again dropped 2 souls each rather than 2.5. They were down half a soul from yesterday. At least the number of souls per urchin was stable, unlike outside of the Dark Tower. He'd just have to kill more urchins than he originally planned.

He made his way through the room, throwing rocks aplenty. His higher level allowed him to see the urchins without throwing rocks if he came a little too close to them for comfort. He was still a little too low level to be attempting what he was doing, but it was an improvement. With 8 out of 10 souls, his first port of call was to kill the urchins behind the chest. One would suffice for filling his Soul Reserve, but he'd have to kill both of them to get out safely afterwards. There were plenty of other urchins in range too, which he'd start with after he'd drained his Soul Reserve.

It was much easier to repeat the process when he was doing it on purpose rather than by accident. Much faster, too. Damien opened the chest without allowing himself to be struck by the lid and found it empty. Shame. While another pair of Darkstriders would've been more than welcome, he only needed the safe space it provided in the middle of this hostile environment, where a single misplaced word would be enough to draw unwanted attention.

His vantage point in the chest occupied, secured and finally vacated, he followed the urchin road into Mordred's antechamber and summoned ten imps. For the first time since they'd entered, Noigel's Forbidden Knowledge was active and he could speak properly, which was not to be confused with appropriately. The moment the tenth imp dropped to the floor, Noigel reminded Damien of everything he'd been missing.

"Why no succubus? Come on, master, I was murdered by a giant spider yesterday! And the time with the succubus wasn't even five minu—"

"The succubus isn't useful for what we're doing. If we fail this run, that's another twenty-four hours without a succubus for you. Hold all the imps in this room. I'm going farming."

Damien was heading back out, checking for more stones to throw, when Noigel landed on his shoulder.

"What if we succeed?"

"Why are you still talking to me? I gave you an order: hold the imps in this room!"

"Yeah, I'm following the order. Look: see how all the imps are still here, in the room? I'm just that good. No succubus for another twenty-four hours if we fail. What if we succeed? Another not five minutes with you watching? Come on, give me something to work with here!"

Oh no. Noigel was becoming pushier by the day. He'd been much more compliant when they'd been focused on base-building, allowing Damien to leave him to his own vices and devices at length. That still hadn't stopped Noigel from pushing his luck in the field, though. And now here, trying to bargain with Damien instead of focusing on the task at hand.

The stakes were high for Damien. If he wanted maximum performance, he'd have to make them high for Noigel as well. He could do that, in both directions.

"As you wish. I can fit four succubi into a Soul Well, plus you...and a spectator imp, to look on and see how privileged you are, if that's something you'd be into. If you act out in this dungeon, like you did with Aetherius, you'll be watching imp number two."

It was like flipping a switch. Noigel gave a sharp salute and glided back to his team. They all gathered around the table as Noigel organized them into pairs and they began what appeared to be a rock/paper/scissors tournament. Good enough.

Damien retook his position in the chest. He was sure this wasn't what Mobius had in mind. This room had all the hallmarks of a stealth test, not a farming opportunity. After much rock throwing, knife slinging, repositioning and somehow a complete lack of cursing, Damien killed another five urchins, filling his SouL Reserve. His throws became less accurate as his targets got further away, his knives shattering when they hit stone instead of flesh. He still had a full knife sling waiting for him in Mordred's antechamber, so no big deal.

The imps were so focused on Noigel's latest game that they barely noticed Damien's return. Noigel had tired of rock/paper/scissors and had used the available resources to come up with something a bit more engaging. The resources were the knives from Damien's as yet unclaimed knife sling and the table they'd been placed on. The game was 'Five-Finger Fillet', more colloquially known as the 'Don't Stab Yourself in the Finger' game. The imp variant was, of course, 'Four-Finger Fillet', a category also open to humans who'd hard failed at Five-Finger Fillet.

The rhythmic *tink* of metal on stone was halted with a meaty thunk. Noigel slapped his hand over the imp's mouth before it could scream and the rest of them fell about, snorting with laughter as quietly as they could. Damien rose up out of his crouch without announcing his presence. And waited. As the imps stopped laughing one after the other, Damien understood for the first time why Bartholomew enjoyed sneaking up on him so much. The looks on their faces were priceless, Noigel's most of all. Damien figured that might have something to do with the knife shards that had been pushed to the edge of the table.

"Noigel. How many knives have you broken?"

"Three?"

Damien strode over to the knife sling to inspect it, the imps moving out of his way. Sixteen left of twenty. Damien was about to comment when Noigel pulled the knife out of the imp's finger, prompting another muffled scream, flipped it over and handed it to Damien handle first. All while smiling sweetly and fluttering his nonexistent eyelashes. Good enough. At least Noigel hadn't killed any imps while he was gone.

He gathered twenty knives into a single sling. No harm done. Then he pointed at the floor and summoned three wraiths and another imp. His Soul Summon Limit was at 20 out of 30, a big improvement on yesterday. He couldn't gather any more souls without using the knives he'd kept reserved for Mordred. This was as good as it was going to get. This was it.

Damien reviewed everything he needed to do, then placed his hand on the door:

You are about to begin boss fight: 'Mordred'. Are you prepared? (Y/N)

As prepared as he reasonably could be. Damien nodded and the doors opened. Before setting foot inside, he stared at Noigel for a solid five seconds, conveying his plan. It was as simple as Damien could manage. He couldn't hope to overwhelm Mordred with numbers, it would just murder them all. He couldn't move eleven imps and three wraiths into the killing zone, either: they'd just die one after the other as Mordred found them. They'd all sit around the outside as he attempted to deal with it by himself. Less complicated. He'd call on them for help when it was needed.

Noigel was very serious now. After all, Damien wasn't the only one to have died yesterday and there was a succubi harem on the line. The imps and the wraiths all spread themselves around the outside of the chamber evenly, the wraiths forming the points of a triangle. Damien couldn't see them, but he wouldn't have to. Hopefully.

The door closed behind him as he moved in last. He'd moved past the outermost ring of boulders and up to the second when the baby's wailing began anew.

How to trigger the encounter had been a source of some contention between Damien's morals and pragmatism. Since it was a known enemy he'd be more than justified to plant a knife between its eyes. It still didn't sit right with him. Not least of all because he didn't know what would happen. It might make things even worse. On the other hand, sacrificing one of his imps to be eaten was wasteful. He compromised, chucking a rock at the bawling bundle of joy, and it began to shift.

He pulled back, readying a throwing knife in one hand and a rock in the other. He could hear the ripping and tearing of cloth. Some of the legs were emerging. Damien might've been stealthed, but he had no idea how far Mordred could detect him from. There was only one way to discern that information, and it made about as much sense as carrying an open flame toward a leaking gas station to see when it would blow up.

As the noise finished, Damien cautiously peered around his cover, hoping for a glimpse of a leg, or the bulky back of the abdomen. Anything that wasn't eyes would work for him.

Mordred was gone.

Moving seemed like a bad idea. Not moving seemed like a worse idea. He had to do *something*. His odds would not improve by waiting for his enemy to make the first move. Damien took his rock and pelted it at the opposite side of the circle, without even looking where he was aiming. So long as it wasn't nearby.

There was a *clunk* as it hit something. Damien peered around his cover again, full of dread. He watched the rock fall to the floor from where it had struck a boulder on the far side. No further sound followed. So much for that. At least it hadn't cost him anything. He'd have to use live bait. He was contacting Noigel to send an imp in when he caught movement. The briefest flash of black as Mordred skittered between rocks. It stopped running when it reached the boulder Damien's rock had struck, then the first of the slender, hairy black legs hooked over the top of it.

The good news was that Mordred wasn't stealthed. The bad news was that Mordred was very quiet, very nimble and had excellent hearing. All the attributes of stealth save for the game-imbued effect of invisibility.

Damien watched it scuttle silently up the boulder and perch on top of it, peering at the rock on the floor. It turned on the spot, shifting first left then right. It couldn't turn its head. It had to turn its whole body to make eye contact. That was a very useful piece of information that would make this encounter much easier, Damien thought to himself. Until Mordred raised its abdomen into the air, twisting the baby-faced body to allow its crimson eyes to scan the area.

Firstly, ewww. Secondly, ahhh. The baby face was definitely a primary critical hit point. It was also, unlike most faces, not possible to attack it from behind. Attacking now was high risk, high reward. This was so obviously the most dangerous moment. It was also, clearly, the moment of opportunity. The two were not always paired, but it was not uncommon. Mordred was as close as Damien could contemplate it getting to him. Maybe a little closer than that. This was as good a shot as he could ask for.

Damien edged back before the abdomen faced him directly, palming a knife and trying to convince himself to engage. He hoped he hadn't misjudged the speed of the 'Baby Monitor' sweep. He leaned around the boulder, flung a knife as hard as he could, then turned and fled.

He was using the mechanic Aetherius had taught him. The knife, and he, would become visible a half second after he released it. Not only did he have to be in cover by then to maintain stealth, he also had to be close enough for the knife to reach Mordred in less than half a second. Otherwise the attack would be deflected, just like yesterday.

His stealth wouldn't be very useful if Mordred came to investigate. Which is why Damien was moving away as fast as he could while mantaining stealth, which was nerve-rackingly slowly. He'd been close enough for the knife to hit; Mordred was dual shrieking, half that of the monster below and half that of the one on top. Damien's shoulders hunched up in a futile attempt to cover his ears. The scream ended and was followed by a deceptively quiet *pitter-patter* of feet drawing closer, not unlike a set of fingers drumming on a wet cloth.

Damien rolled behind the first boulder he came across, all too close to the cover he'd just left. There was total silence, then another piercing scream, issuing from where Damien had been hiding three seconds ago. He played his fight and flight instincts off against each other and held his ground. Moving now was exactly what not to do. The scream coupled with the speed was designed to make him panic and give away his position.

To avoid being controlled, Damien simply had to avoid eye contact. The problem with Mordred was that not keeping an eye on the creature was every bit as dangerous as looking directly at it. Every second he left Mordred alone, it would be hunting him instead of the other way around. Even if Mordred didn't find him, it might find and eat his contingency plans. He had to lead the creature, both to keep it from roaming and so he knew where it would be. He couldn't afford to let up on the pressure or else—

A long, black, hairy foreleg extended over the top of the boulder he was hiding behind. Damien was about to be examined at close range. Whether he was looking at Mordred or not would hardly matter by then, since his peripheral vision would be full of fangs.

Noigel! Help!

Ten imps swept their wings and jumped into the air, appearing around the outermost circle in perfect synchrony. Damien picked out one far off to the side and Demon Gated. The imp he'd traded fortunes with screeched, drawing Mordred's attention from right underneath it. The imp would last less than two seconds, if that, but it didn't have to last that long. Damien pointed as he fell back down to the ground.

"Imp-losion."

Mordred's grip was strong. Imp-losion could not drag it off the rock it was perched on. Too bad. There were two other benefits though. The first was that Mordred would be left hungry. The second was that this most tried and tested of Damien's combinations wasn't merely covering Damien's escape, it was also covering the approach of his first wraith.

Damien's feet buckled under him as he hit the cold hard floor. He pushed himself up and ran back in. This was when he most needed to be present. A fresh shriek before he'd rounded the first boulder told him his wraith had arrived. With any luck it had attacked from stealth, maybe even with a critical strike on top. Regardless, it had at the very least covered for the tail end of Damien's absence. It would likely last no longer than an imp, but it was only supposed to inflict one good hit. Keeping his target busy while Damien reset.

Damien spied the back of Mordred's abdomen, perched over the boulder the creature had clung to, as Mordred lashed out against the wraith that had wounded it. A health bar appeared above Mordred: 86% health. 14% more damage than Damien had inflicted on it yesterday.

This thing was not so strong as it appeared. It could definitely die. He had the tools to make it happen.

Damien stood completely upright, palmed a knife in each hand and flung them at the back of Mordred's raised torso together, diving behind cover as it screamed. The attacks had no modifiers for being critical hits or from stealth, but throwing two of them while stood upright from a safer distance was a good compromise. Mordred's shrieks intensified and the *pitter-patter* of feet came again. Damien moved around his cover, keeping the faint sound between himself and his target. Mordred was running up to where Damien had been when he'd thrown the knives, not where he'd dived and rolled for cover afterwards.

Damien was an ambush player. While most enemies required an 'all in' to get the most out of such a strategy, this fight had to be more measured. So he'd constructed a string of ambushes, each ensuring the success of the next, allowing Mordred nothing while maximizing the utility of each minion in a single use.

All he had to do now was keep Mordred contained in this space, away from where his minions were concealed, until he could start the cycle again. Damien already knew how to do that. He moved forward in Shadow Walker to new, further cover, then threw another rock to the other side of the arena. Mordred went pitter-pattering after it. That's when Damien knew for certain he was in business. It became even better when Mordred faced directly away from him as it scanned for his presence.

Bartholomew would never have fallen for such a trick. Even some players wouldn't fall for it twice. When Mordred had had eyes on Damien and he could hear it in his head, it had come across as calculating, mocking and cruel. It had taken extra time to torture him rather than ending the fight quickly. Not so when Damien avoided falling under its influence. Without him in its thrall, it was reduced to little more than a desperate, frenzied, instinctive animal. Damien had a procedural four-step plan, and it looked like it might be good. He kept Mordred in his sights as he palmed a knife in each hand.

And so it went for two more rounds. Rocks, knife-throw critical strikes, full ability combo with wraith support and finally another double throw to reset on the way back in. On Damien's final cycle he even managed a double throw in the first step, aimed into the more unsettling of Mordred's two faces. The knives sticking from the glistening, lightly furred hide gave it the appearance of weeping tears of blood. It was a good thing Damien had his routine to focus on, a framework through which he could rationalize his proximity to pure nightmare fuel.

But as Damien willingly entered Mordred's domain for the fourth time, his wraiths were spent. Without those precious seconds of distraction while he was falling loudly to the floor, Mordred would hear or see him as he Demon Gated and run straight to his location, bringing him back to square one. He had nine knives, eight imps and a handful of stones left. Mordred's health was not nearly as low as he'd hoped for, but it was now down to 28%.

Damien's method was sound, so far as he was concerned, but his damage was too low. Bad gear, low level, not enough soul energy available to employ his strategy to the fullest. His next attack had to be decisive. He'd hoped it wouldn't come to this. He'd rather get it over with than have to go through it all over again.

This wouldn't require Noigel's guidance. The order was simple enough for Damien to deliver it himself. He waited the last few seconds until his cooldowns had reset, keeping tabs on Mordred's location. He could continue trying to throw knives and dodge around, but he was more likely to get caught out before he could finish. Without wraiths for support, his strategy had a hole in it. There was no benefit for Damien in drawing this out. Time for the 'all in'. He sent the imps up and over, directing them to attack the face. Specifically, the eyes.

They reared up and swooped toward their target from all angles. Mordred stared two of them down, taking control of their bodies in rapid succession and allowing them to plummet to the floor. It turned and struck a third, then a fourth out of the air with the pointed tips of its feet. Damien Demon Gated to the fifth as it blitzed in past its fallen brothers, then screwed his eyes shut as he scythed his daggers down.

They plunged into the softer, more giving hide proffered by Mordred's weak point. The screeching reached an even higher multi-tonal pitch, with Damien's legs spinning behind him as the baby-gorgon-spider whirled round and round to throw him off. Mordred's legs could not articulate to attack him if he was directly on its back, but this was of little comfort. If he lost his grip, this would be over in a heartbeat. Or better yet, it would be an excruciating rerun of yesterday.

He alternated between stabbing with one dagger and anchoring with the other, eyes still tightly shut. They were not good hits, but they had to be doing something. He lost count of how many times he'd stabbed, but kept going anyway.

It was a while before he realized the shrieking and spinning had stopped. It was completely silent, save for his continued blows to a probable corpse and his panicked breathing. Damien paused, briefly, to confirm the kill. Then withdrew his daggers, slid off the creature and onto the ground. All still with his eyes closed. He turned his back and walked a distance away. Happy thoughts. When he finally convinced himself to open his eyes, the game gave him something to smile about.

He was up from level 46 to level 48 and then some. He had no business dealing with this dungeon when he was too low level for it, but at least that meant his experience gains were disproportionately high. Yay. Not that he'd recommend anyone following in his footsteps. Maybe he'd acquired some new skills? No? Too much to ask? He'd better get some loot from this horrible thing he'd just put behind him.

"Noigel? Are you there?"

There was a squawk of acknowledgment. Noigel had survived. They wouldn't be having any debates with only three other imps for him to draw intelligence from.

"Gimme a minute."

Damien opened his menu. Somehow it felt like he could still stay a step away from what he'd just put himself through by not acknowledging it. His stat bar would provide a welcome distraction.

Class: Occultist
Level: 48
Health: 1,220/1,220**Stamina:** 1,370/1,370 **Mana:** 3,080/3,080
Strength: 57 **Agility:** 181 **Intelligence:** 57
Constitution: 122 **Endurance:** 137 **Wisdom:** 308
Stat points: 10
Experience: 29,360/48,000
Soul Summon Limit: 4/30 **Soul Reserve:** 10/10 (+1/1)

More good news. He'd absorbed 10 souls and had another one from his Sacrificial Dagger. Yay. How fortunate. Right. That had been horrible, but it was over. He'd pick up the gear, summon new minions and move on. It was definitely time to move on. He put all his new stat points into agility and moved on.

Mordred had been converted into a loot chest. A big fancy one. He hadn't even needed to tell Noigel what he wanted before it was done. This, in addition to his sterling service in combat, meant his imp had a new assignment. Damien pointed at the floor with his Sacrificial Dagger and began summoning.

"Well done, Noigel. You were awesome. Here's one succubus for now. Our first deal still stands but you're on track. Go find a rock somewhere private. Come back when I call."

Noigel saluted and ran off with the succubus in tow. Alright. Another immediate source of drama temporarily rediverted. He got to looting and felt a little better still.

Heartbinder

Description: A demon-hide chestpiece once worn by the Sunset Emperor: Bartholomew, Scourge of the World. They kept his heart and soul protected, an empty shell protecting an empty shell.
Level Requirement: 50
Stat Requirement: 200 Agility
Stats: +30 Wisdom, +30 Constitution
Set Bonus: Sunset Emperor – +30 Agility, +30 Stamina, +30 Endurance, +30 Wisdom (1/5 pieces): Shadow Walker functions in broad daylight

It almost made the fight worthwhile. So far as Damien could tell, he'd gotten through most of the immediate shock. Did Mobius have dedicated therapists? It should. Big company. He could ask Kevin if they had any therapists they could refer him to for this sort of thing. For now, he needed to take a breather for a few minutes. Perhaps Cassandra still had some leftover heart medicine he could borrow? Maybe two therapists. Yeah. He was fine.

23

KA IS A WHEEL

In the absence of any therapists, Damien made do with what he had available: online blooper reels, courtesy of the external browser. A band aid was better than nothing. At least Noigel wouldn't have any complaints about how much time he was getting with the succubus. Well, any valid complaints.

"Noigel, come here, please."

It took thirty seconds, but he didn't need to call a second time. Noigel landed in front of him, his horns already completely receded.

"Find the way forward."

While Noigel and the minions panned out, Damien took stock. He had four imps and a succubus. He still had 4 souls left but was in no rush to use them until he knew what he'd need. He waited for Noigel to scout the way forward. After a minute, Noigel flew back to him, shaking his head and shrugging his shoulders.

Damien stood on top of a boulder and looked around. There was no doorway besides that which he'd entered by, which was now open. He looked up and around. He circled the entire chamber. There was nothing there. The only way was back. Confused, Damien made his way through the doors and they closed behind him, then locked. He placed a hand on them, just to be certain. They were inert and would no longer open for him.

What was going on? It was only as he stepped away that a new chest shimmered into view in the center of the antechamber. This one was far more ornate than usual: gold trim, carvings, varnished finish. If it was a trap, it was the meanest one Damien had ever seen.

He had the imps open it, just to be sure. When nothing terrible happened to them, Damien peered inside. He recognized the weapon immediately. The two blades looked a lot heftier than they had in the light show preceding the Path of Deceit. He inspected it.

Shirai-Ryu Chain Kunai x 2
Description: A pair of melee/throwing weapons granted to Bartholomew as a customized gift from a like-minded specter of the Netherrealm. They brought him closer to his goals and his goals closer to him, one corpse at a time.
Special Ability: When thrown, the chains linking these weapons extends. Pulling on the chain draws you to the target, the target to you or both, depending on the forces acting on both parties. Twisting the chain disengages the weapon.
Demon-Spear: Mana:1,000. When a target is pierced at range with both kunai simultaneously, flipping the chains pushes a wave of black fire along them. If both flames reach the target they are ignited, reducing armor by 50% and inflicting half your agility as direct damage per second for 5 seconds. Cooldown: 2 minutes.
Level Requirement: 45
Durability: 100/100
Damage: 300 + (Agility x 1)
Stats: +100 Agility

This was an incredible piece. It was a two-handed weapon, of sorts, with one blade for each hand. The damage and stats more than justified taking up both of his weapon slots. 100 agility! A 1:1 ratio on damage, with 300 damage for the base calculation! He knew his old gear was severely outdated, but this was insane.

Then there were the special abilities. The first was a way of getting into range quickly without relying on his imps for Demon Gates. The second granted Circle of Hell's damage over time and armor reduction without the need for a succubus, although it cost a whole lot of mana and would only be applied to a single target.

He considered the level requirement. Why was this gear only level 45 when the rest of the gear in this dungeon was level 50? Whatever the reason, it meant Damien wouldn't have to wait. He put his daggers away and equipped the kunai. The chains wrapped around his forearms, passing behind his back to connect to each other and through his hands to the blades, which dangled below his wrists. He pulled on the chains and they slickly ran backward through his grip, the blades snapping into his waiting palms.

He could get used to this. It was worlds beyond any weapon he'd ever seen in this game. Why had it been given it to him here, rather than presenting it to him in Mordred's boss chamber as a reward? He remembered the unopened chest in the corner of the previous room, the block of wood above it with the distinctive 'X' carved into the center, and formed a hypothesis.

He took a throwing knife in each hand and passed them to Noigel.

"That's your quota of knives. Maintain order here while I scout. Same as before, keep everyone quiet."

Noigel tipped a knife to Damien in a modified salute and motioned at the table with the other. The imps immediately piled in, shushing each other as they jostled for space. Noigel had made staying quiet part of his game. Smart imp. The succubus stood to the side with her arms folded, looking bored by the whole affair. All as it should be.

Damien crouched down and returned to the silent room. He tossed a rock overhead and assessed how many urchins were left. Many on the far side had already been culled but this side was still rife with them. The urchins reentered stealth and the chest he'd previously left behind became visible, taunting him.

He looked from the chest to the wooden beam above it with the 'X' in the middle. Here we go. He double-checked the description of his newly acquired weapon's special skill. Right. Seemed a bit insane, in a logical way. As logical as anything else he'd done in this room. The wooden beam was about two meters long and one wide, tucked right into the corner. The chest was very slightly in front of it with a small gap behind. That's where he would drop down, if he went through with this.

Would throwing a weapon at a block of wood qualify as an attack made with intent? Would he become visible and get perforated? Why risk it? Damien reequipped his new weapon, drawing one blade into his hand and taking a rock with the other. He flicked the rock into the air and the moment all the urchins fired, flung the kunai at the beam as hard as he could. The kunai had a great deal more heft in it than the throwing knives and took a fair bit more stamina to throw. It didn't seem likely, but he hoped he wouldn't break the beam by mistake. More importantly, if his Shadow Walker was deactivated, he'd have to make a very hasty exit.

While the weapon looked very different, it worked exactly the same way as the throwing knives. The chain unraveled from his arm seamlessly and soundlessly, without requiring any additional effort. The kunai sank into the wood with a satisfying *thunk*. It had been loud, yet he was still in Shadow Walker. Attacks on inanimate objects with no health bars didn't break stealth. Probably. He'd have to try it without throwing a rock first to be sure but didn't feel like doing so in his present company.

Damien pulled on the chain. He was drawn through the air, over the urchins, until his hand was back around the weapon. He was still in Shadow Walker. A twist of the wrist and the kunai disengaged. He dropped to the floor, behind the chest. Okay. He was now trapped behind a chest with urchins on the other side. This was familiar. He'd rather secure his way out before he started rooting around in the chest.

Damien positioned himself so only one urchin had line of sight to him and flung a kunai at it. The kunai struck the urchin in the middle and it was immediately destroyed. His damage was much higher now. He pulled on the chain, intending to bring the kunai back, only to find it was still embedded in the urchin corpse.

He'd been certain twisting to release wouldn't be necessary if he'd killed the target. So certain it hadn't even occurred to him to do so. Damien had been attacked by plenty of corpses, never an unanimated one. He twisted his wrist and the kunai disengaged, snapping back into his hand empty. That didn't do anything to slow down the upward trajectory of what it had been attached to. He was lucky urchins immediately dried up on death, shedding their spikes and most of their weight, although when it hit him in the head his first thought was not how lucky he was.

He set his back to the chest, grumbling and rubbing his forehead. The weapon was great, but the mechanics behind it provided endless opportunities for stupid deaths if he wasn't careful. He'd have to practice more. He took his time with the remaining four urchins, killing each of them with a stealth critical strike over the next minute. They were only providing one soul each. At least it was a good chance to get accustomed to his weapon mechanics. Throw, twist, pull.

With them gone, Damien was comfortable enough to open the chest. He braced his arms as the lid was struck with spikes from further afield, then sidled round to withdraw the item before retreating behind the chest to examine it.

The Last Grasp
Description: A pair of demon-hide bracers once worn by the Sunset Emperor: Bartholomew, Scourge of the World. The more holdings he seized, the more of himself he lost. At the exact moment he held the entire world in his grasp, he lost everything.
Level Requirement: 50
Stat Requirement: 200 Agility
Stats: +30 Agility, +30 Wisdom
Set Bonus: Sunset Emperor – +30 Agility, +30 Constitution, +30 Endurance, +30 Wisdom (1/5 pieces): Shadow Walker functions in broad daylight

Three set pieces down, two to go. The only question was where to head next. If it wasn't through Mordred's room it had to be somewhere around here. Giving him the weapon after he'd returned here was signposting. It was because using it would open new ways forward, as it had done already with these bracers. If the way forward was only accessible with this new weapon, it likely lay overhead. He examined the ceiling and found only one thing out of place: there was a square hole right in the middle of it. He pulled up the screenshot Noigel had taken of the floor and found a matching gap in the center of the room, void of urchins. He'd have to go there to see upward clearly.

There were now a lot less urchins in the room than when he'd started. His level was also high enough to see them from a reasonable distance. Reasonable not to walk headfirst into them anyway. He made it to the middle without throwing any rocks and looked directly up. There it was. Another wooden beam above the opening, this one without an 'X' through the middle of it. The gap was just wide enough for a person. The problem was Damien also had his minions to consider.

There was no way his imps and succubus were getting through that room and into the opening before becoming pincushions. It required a great deal of self-control for Damien not to groan, which would've killed him in his present company. More busywork, more waste. He returned to the antechamber and dismissed all his minions, picking up 2 souls and leaving the rest behind.

Throwing the kunai at the block of wood hadn't disrupted his Shadow Walker before, although it had definitely made a noise when it connected. So long as he had a rock in his inventory, or even an item he regarded as less valuable than his own life, there was no way he'd take that for granted. He tossed the rock, threw the kunai up and was pulled through the gap before there was any chance of a second volley coming.

He had a quick look around. No sign of any enemies or anything else of interest, save for the wooden beam stretching over the narrow passageway he'd passed through. A rock hurled into the air confirmed he was safe. Then he looked up and took in the latest obstacle.

This room was bigger than all the rest of them put together, only upward. If Damien wasn't mistaken, it represented the interior of the tower he'd seen from the outside. It was mostly empty, save for a multitude of wooden beams crisscrossing the room all the way to the top. They always cut directly across the room, all of them overlapping in the middle, yet looking up Damien could not see the exit from any point at his own level. There were hundreds of them, extending far into the distance.

Damien summoned ten imps as he sized up the weird environment above him. He could send an imp up as high as he could see and Demon Gate to it, but with the cooldown that would still take a long time. It clearly wasn't what this room was asking for: it wanted him to practice with his new weapon. Damien was game. He'd keep the imps on standby and have Demon Gate for insurance. He threw a kunai at the first beam and pulled the chain, drawing himself underneath it. Then he awkwardly clambered around and pulled himself over the edge.

This didn't seem right. Doing it this way would barely be faster than Demon Gating and took a lot more effort. Damien eyed up the next beam and took his experiment a step further. He threw a kunai, then swung out on the chain into the air. It was cool for a moment, but then he reached the end of the arc and began to swing back. Whatever he was supposed to be doing, this wasn't it. He pulled on the chain to reset so he could try again.

That was when the problems started. He'd assumed pulling the chain would take him in a straight line to his destination. It did not. His swing was amplified as the chain grew shorter, dragging him over the top of it. If he didn't disengage he'd be smashed into the beam at high speed. He twisted the chain and the kunai was immediately withdrawn. Without a tether, Damien flew upward and backward. He hurtled past one beam, then another, until his ascent was brought to a halt upon colliding with a third.

He'd lost most of his momentum before he hit it anyway, so

he didn't take too much damage. Now he was falling, which was a lot more consistent in the damage department. He threw a kunai in midair at a beam as he passed it, then the chain went taut as he dropped below it. He flew around it in a spiral, the chain shortening as it wrapped around the beam continually. Each rotation brought him one step closer to bashing his brains out. He twisted the chain again on the upswing, and so the cycle continued.

He could build bigger swings now. Dandy. What he needed to know was how to make it stop, please. As he started to slow, he aimed for a beam above him rather than below. As soon as the blade landed, while he was hovering perfectly between rising and falling, he tugged on the chain and was brought to it in a straight line. The moment the blade entered the palm of his hand, all his momentum was canceled out. He hung out there for a while, unwilling to move, until the imps caught up with him. The one sniggering had to be Noigel.

This would work, he just had to control it. He'd been working with just one chain, he hadn't tried with two yet. It might give him twice as much control or it might take twice as much control to master. Probably somewhere in between. Or both. He jumped out and threw a kunai, pulling to fly upward. It was much better this time, since he knew what was coming and was facing the direction he was moving in. As he passed that beam, he threw at the next one with his free hand and released the former. The chain went taut and he circled upward again. This was manageable, provided he didn't miss. He soon found that even missing was okay. He just circled the beam he was on and took another shot on the next rotation.

All he needed now was practice. He'd have plenty of that, seeing as how this tower went on forever. He swung out again, his eyes acclimatizing to seeking out the next target earlier and earlier. He'd passed ten beams before he realized he had it down. It was all natural now: he was looking four beams ahead to plan his movements in advance without even thinking about it. Everything had become real smooth. Right up until he heard a familiar noise.

'Plin-'

Damien went into full panic mode, his hand twisting. It changed his direction in time to avoid the needle, although recalibrating at such short notice was tricky. He had to find the urchin. If he left it, at least one of his minions would be killed when they flew through. Damien swung around again, passing through the same space to provoke another response. It came and Damien disconnected on the loop.

As the needle flew over his shoulder, he followed the trajectory back to the source. Now he had to figure out his next anchor point and fire on the urchin at the same time. Anchoring was the priority. He could take a few urchin needles, but he wouldn't survive a bad fall. He anchored and hit the urchin with his second throw, making sure to twist as soon as it landed so he wouldn't fly into it or pull it into himself. It took a few rotations and there were a couple of misses while he worked the angles but the urchin died on the second hit. He was clear.

He kept working his way up, the number of urchins increasing steadily but surely. He'd been at it for half an hour when a mass of five urchins spanning two beams appeared. In other circumstances he'd have considered passing them by, even if he lost his minions for it. However, these circumstances included a chest, placed at the very center of the beam. He took a few hits while he was swinging around, and even had to retreat downward to drink a potion at one point, before he picked the wrong route to come in and didn't release fast enough.

It was a steep learning curve with a lot of literal steep curves. After he'd dealt with one, the whole thing became much easier. Each urchin he dispatched after that made it easier still. He finished them off and landed right next to the chest, utterly full of himself. He was even more pleased when he retrieved the fourth of five pieces of Bartholomew's set.

Kusazuri of Imminent Misery

Description: A demon-hide protective skirt once worn by the Sunset Emperor: Bartholomew, Scourge of the World. Bartholomew always assumed the imminent misery referenced

those who acted against his interests. He was right. What he failed to recognize was his place as first among them.
Level Requirement: 50
Stat Requirement: 200 Agility
Stats: +30 Constitution, +30 Endurance
Set Bonus: Sunset Emperor – +30 Agility, +30 Stamina, +30 Endurance, +30 Wisdom (1/5 pieces): Shadow Walker functions in broad daylight

Four down, one to go. He could see the faintest glimmer of light filtering down from above, although he could only guess how much further he had to go. Maybe this was the halfway point, if he was lucky. He hadn't realized this would be a marathon.

The urchins he'd killed on the way were starting to accumulate. His experience bar was filling up and he'd accustomed himself to the bizarre environment. The further he went, the more comfortable he became. What had once required conscious effort was now second nature, both in and out of combat.

It was something of a surprise when the number of urchins began to ramp up. Soon there were at least three urchins for every ten beams. Damien adapted to the pattern after the first two rounds, changing his movement to deal with what he knew would be coming. He calculated his trajectory from below, timed his releases when he was above and removed himself from combat immediately after his attacks by retreating to the lower levels he'd already cleared.

He'd been accumulating new minions the whole while, leaving them in Noigel's care to keep them from harm as he dealt with the threats himself. It was tricky, since the souls would drift down and he had to try and catch them before they fell too far. He had a full group worth 30 souls again. He was limited to picking minions who could handle the 'terrain': imps, succubi and wraiths. None of which would be very useful for this. He'd settled on sixteen imps and two succubi. That was a long time ago.

He didn't realize just how many urchins he'd killed until he heard a telltale sound, different from the *plink* of the urchin spines, the *schlunk* of a kunai embedding itself in the beams or the unworldly screeches of his quarry. A happy noise.

Ding.

He'd hit level 49. Killing Mordred and ending that section of the quest had only brought him halfway there. How many urchins had he killed? An ungodly number, for sure. He hadn't been counting, but he could check the time to get a vague answer. Forty-five minutes. He'd been at this for forty-five minutes already. Did it ever end? The fourth piece of Bartholomew's set had definitely not been the halfway point. Maybe it just went on forever like this. There was no final piece of the set. There was no end to the long climb. He was supposed to fail.

Damien kept going all the same. He hadn't logged out in the Dark Tower before – or in any dungeon, actually. Nothing would be worse than logging back in, only to be dumped back at the beginning. If this really did go on forever, that would be an incredible joke. Terrible for him, but undeniably brilliant and very much in keeping with his experience so far. At the very least, he'd get as far as he could before he had to sleep. Then he could try logging out on one of the beams and cross his fingers that he kept his place until the next day. There was no reason why it shouldn't work. Then again, there was no reason why this shouldn't have been over already.

He scrunched his eyes shut and focused. This place was making him paranoid. He had to keep himself together and make sure he didn't get killed by an urchin, or worse, by falling. He had to keep climbing. Anything else was a distraction. There was no thinking himself out of this. He just had to endure. Maintain his flow. Give the very best performance he could, so if it did go wrong he'd know he'd done his best. He invested his stat points into agility and kept going.

He'd been at it for over an hour by the time he saw light. It was a long, long way away. But it was a change. Something different, something to look forward to. He was going to make it. A short while later, the urchin numbers noticeably dropped.

There were less of them, and those that did appear were all gathered underneath the beams, where the light couldn't reach them. Some thirty beams later, they were gone altogether. He was on the verge of finishing.

Now he'd had so much practice and there were no urchins in the way, Damien could really let it rip. He was ready to see the back of this place. He threw himself upward as high and as fast as he could, picking his spots and tearing toward the sunlight. He was nearly at the exit when he heard a faint screech from below. Then a whole chorus of them. His minions were yelling up at him for some reason.

Maybe he was moving too far out of range? He'd left them far behind and undefended. What if he'd passed some urchins without them detecting him? He knew imps wouldn't be able to do anything about urchins, and he had no idea if the succubi's attacks would be any more effective than they had been on Mordred.

Damien twisted in midair and swung near the outside wall, where the density of the beams was reduced. He positioned himself above one and threw both kunai into it, let gravity take him and pulled on both chains together.

He'd done this a few times upward already, but never down. It turned out doing it downward was faster. Much faster. Too fast. Much too fast. He'd badly miscalculated this. He could see a swarm of red bodies flying up to meet him. As soon as he was close enough to make out an imp at the front, he Demon Gated to swap places and momentum.

He was out in midair, but that was fine by him. A quick look around and a kunai throw returned him to stability. The bulk of his problems had already been handed off to the imp that screamed its way past him faster than terminal velocity, which was ended with a loud *splat* and an abrupt silence somewhere below them.

The two succubi stared at him, jaws agape. The imps, all fifteen of them so far as Damien could tell, let out a gasp simultaneously. He yanked on the chain and pulled himself onto the beam. Why wasn't Noigel making himself known?

"Noigel, where are you? What was the screaming for?"

There was a brief pause, then all his minions dropped out of the sky, shrieking and choking. He leaned over his perch to watch as they landed on the beam below him and leaned over each other helplessly, wheezing for breath. What was wrong with them?

"Noigel! Status report!"

His minions started to howl. Only then did Damien realize they weren't in danger. They were laughing at him. He double-checked the information above each of the imps' heads in turn, just to be sure. Noigel wasn't there. Oh dear.

He turned on the beam and gingerly began summoning a new imp to replace the one he'd obliterated in his stead. His minions clammed up as Noigel dropped out of the portal.

"Noigel, I promise that wasn't on purpose. I heard you screaming—"

"—and decided to murder me."

"No! I came as fast as I could and Demon Gated to the first imp I saw. I didn't know it was you!"

"You can't tell me apart from the other imps?"

"You were a long way away and the first imp I saw."

"And you rewarded me for being the fastest to reach you by murdering me?"

"It was an accident!"

"Oh! I didn't realize it was an accidental murder! My mistake, *master*. No harm done."

Oh no. Noigel had acquired enhanced sarcasm. It was probably a symptom of his repressed anger, which he was not repressing very effectively: his shaking was now so pronounced it looked as though he might spontaneously Imp-lode.

"It wasn't a murder. You sacrificed yourself for me when I needed you, and I'm grateful."

"You sacrificed *me* for yourself because you acted carelessly, and I'm not grateful."

"You don't mind when I do it with the other imps."

"You don't mind when I kill other humans."

"Because they're usually trying to kill me!"

"They're usually trying to kill me as well."

Damien couldn't argue with any of that. Even worse, he'd realized halfway through that he was the guilty party; he'd changed the argument repeatedly instead of conceding any of Noigel's points, he hadn't apologized directly for what he'd done yet and was all round not doing a very good job of keeping Noigel on side.

Damien grabbed the knife sling from around his waist and unequipped it, then held it out to his minion. Noigel had shown he had uses for the knives already, if only in playing games.

"Can you equip it?"

He tentatively held his hand out and Damien placed it in his open palm. Noigel wrapped it over his shoulder like a bandolier and it tightened. He looked like a little demonic pirate, equal parts cute and dangerous. Most importantly, he looked extremely pleased. He must've realized how happy he looked, because having examined himself for a few moments he abruptly scowled and folded his arms. Damien held out a closed fist to him.

"Now I'll definitely be able to tell you apart from the other imps without any delay. I don't know how good you'll be at throwing the knives, but you can use them to increase your damage and assert your authority over the rest of our team. I'm sorry I got you killed for no reason. We good?"

Noigel pouted, then submitted. He gave Damien a surly fist bump. Damien was nodding in satisfaction when Noigel crouched, took a knife by the edge of the blade and sent it spinning toward the beam below. It was a different technique from the one Damien used, but the pained squawk of an imp below indicated it was effective.

Noigel's first knife attack had been a sneak critical. Damien's Soul Summon Limit dropped to 29 out of 30. Noigel could no longer conceal his glee. He clapped his hands together and cackled manically as Damien held a hand over his own forehead. Maybe this had been a fresh mistake. He pointed at the ground to summon a new imp as he tried to remain reasonable.

"Please don't use it like that or I'll have to take it off you."

"They were laughing at me! I'm using the knives to assert my authority, like you told me to. If I don't keep them in check they won't follow my orders as effectively."

"I'm pretty sure they were laughing at me, Noigel, not you. Ask me for permission before you attack our own team, okay?"

"But master, If I'd asked permission you'd have said no."

"Your logic is infallible. I'd have definitely said no. Don't do it again. Now, what were you screaming about?"

Noigel had withdrawn another knife, prompting the minions below to take to the air. They needn't have worried: he was only using it to pick his teeth. Noigel was making full use of his new accessory. He spoke through his closed jaw as he continued to pry at his gums with the blade.

"Oh, we saw a loot chest a bit further down which you went straight past. I thought you might want to open it. Master."

"Noigel?"

"Yes, master?"

"Would you have told me about that chest if I hadn't given you my knife sling just now?"

Noigel put on his best display of shock and hurt, his vocal cords grating against Damien's inner ear. Damien wasn't sure if it qualified as sarcasm, which meant if it was sarcasm it was extremely high grade. Deeply troubling.

"Of course, master! How can you doubt me, master? Haven't I always—"

"Would you have told me before or after we left the dungeon?"

"I suppose we'll never know. Master."

"I'm glad you're feeling better. Keep serving me well and I'll keep rewarding you. Lead me to the chest."

Damien followed Noigel down, more carefully this time. It was a little harder going down than it was up. He had less practice at it and gravity was now speeding him up instead of slowing him down, which conversely meant he had to take it slower. The effort was worth it, since he knew what he was moving toward. There was a hole in the wall, at the back of which sat the last chest. Noigel puffed his chest out and pointed at himself with his thumbs, signaling for a Demon Gate.

Damien chose to show he could do it unassisted. He opted for the more difficult route, swinging around three times to get the trajectory right before landing perfectly in the gap. Noigel shrugged and squeezed past Damien, attempting to juggle knives as his master retrieved the final piece of Bartholomew's set.

Hooded Cloak of Self-fulfilling Prophecy
Description: A Nether-weave garment once worn by the Sunset Emperor: Bartholomew, Scourge of the World. To satiate his endless gluttony, Bartholomew aligned with forces he could not comprehend. He thought he was carving out his own destiny. Only when the cost came due did he realize he was a puppet, manipulated by the one who claimed to be his benefactor.
Level Requirement: 50
Stat Requirement: 200 Agility
Stats: +15 Agility, +15 Wisdom, +15 Endurance, +15 Constitution
Set Bonus: Sunset Emperor – +30 Agility, +30 Endurance, +30 Constitution, +30 Wisdom (1/5 pieces): Shadow Walker functions in broad daylight

Damien read the description of each piece of new gear in turn. There was a pretty clear message: someone had used Bartholomew the same way Bartholomew had used him. His master, presumably. Was Damien ready to upgrade his tier of manipulative master?

He'd already achieved most of his goals. He was level 49 and halfway to level 50. He'd acquired a whole gear set that would give him the ability to Shadow Walk at any time of day as well as providing an enormous boost to his stats. He had this magnificent weapon, along with all the utility and damage it provided. He could just leave, right now. He could make a portal and head to Bartholomew to demand an explanation, or go back to the Inner Circle where he'd left his concealed Gateway (assuming it hadn't been discovered and destroyed in the meantime).

Yeah, right. He'd breached the Dark Tower and now he'd climb it, all the way to the top. His enemy was Archimonde, who'd almost certainly finished the whole dungeon already. Not to mention Magnitude. Damien would need all the help he could get. He'd come too far not to see what was at the end of all this. This was the path of progression the game had to offer him. He'd see it through.

"Alright, Noigel, let's get this done."

Damien resumed climbing, the light getting brighter and brighter. After five minutes of continuous upswings he found the source. There was a hole in the middle of the ceiling. Now he thought about it, he wasn't sure how it could be so bright. It was already past midnight. He swung to the opening and the sun baked down on him, blinding him. Apparently this dungeon had no regard for such paltry concerns as the movements of celestial bodies.

He grabbed the sides of the hole and pulled himself through, his entire field of vision turning white as he tried to squint through it. He set foot on the platform above and a faint noise ran through his head. One of Damien's all-time favorites.

Ding.

He was level 50. Glorious. Even better, three additional notifications arrived with it:

Level Up!

Summon Consumer Unlocked!

A new trait is available for selection. Choose wisely.

Building Upgrades Unlocked!

First things first. He'd been waiting a long time for this, and had worked hard for it. Damien put his last free stat points into agility, threw on all five pieces of Bartholomew's gear set one after the other and admired his character page.

Class: Occultist
Level: 50
Health: 1,990/1,990**Stamina:** 2,140/2,140 **Mana:** 3,850/3,850
Strength: 59 **Agility:** 333 **Intelligence:** 59
Constitution: 199 **Endurance:** 214 **Wisdom:** 385
Stat points: 0
Experience: 19,850/50,000

Soul Summon Limit: 30/30 **Soul Reserve:** 8/10

Clothes really do make the man. The second notification was pretty much self-explanatory. Running his own private victory parade, Damien clicked it and was taken straight to the relevant section of his skill list.

Summon Consumer: Mana: 1,500, Souls: 8 – You point at the ground, searing it with runes to open a portal to the demon world. After channeling for 10 seconds, the portal is opened and a consumer arrives on the mortal plane. The consumer will serve you until it dies or is dismissed. Consumer stats improve every five levels.

One step closer to Archimonde. He still had the level 50 trait to assign! He went into the menu and read through his options.

Dark Omen: A black hole forms overhead then drops onto the location it was initially cast, inflicting catastrophic damage that ignores all armor and resistances.

Entropy: Spell damage reduces the damage resistance of enemies by 1% once per second, stacking infinitely. All stacks are lost after 5 seconds of spell damage not being applied.

Legion: Your maximum Soul Summon Limit is increased to 50.

The most important factoid was that wherever Archimonde had received his transformation, it had not come from this trait. Damien was further behind than he'd hoped. He sized them up one by one.

Having experienced 'Dark Omen' firsthand he knew it was highly situational: difficult to land, but conclusive if it did. He'd love to know the details, but not enough to take it as his trait. 'Entropy' was interesting. It was also no use to him at all. Damien relied on shock tactics and quick combat resolutions, not attrition. He wasn't disappointed though, because 'Legion' was freakin' sweet.

Five incubi. Seven succubi. Sixteen wraiths or hell hounds. Fifty imps. Fifty. Imps. The possibilities were mind-boggling. So long as he kept Noigel on his good side, he'd be able to manage a horde like that to devastating effect.

Damien selected 'Legion', nodded through the notification asking if he was sure and watched as the other two options grayed out. It was decided. He went back to his stat page, expecting his Soul Summon Limit to have increased to 50. It was a rude shock when he saw it stood at 30 out of 44. Hmm. Crap. His Soul Summon Limit had increased, but so had the wisdom required to reach the cap. Looks like wisdom's back on the menu, boys.

It didn't really matter. He'd have taken 'Legion' regardless. It was mildly annoying, that's all. He'd just hit level 50 for crying out loud! Where was his instant gratification? Ah, whatever. A Soul Summon Limit of 44 was nearly 50% more minions than he could field ten seconds ago. What did he have to complain about? His wisdom was approaching 400. That was already incomprehensible.

Last, but not necessarily least, he had building upgrades to look forward to. A quick check indicated his Demon Forge could now be upgraded to Tier IV. If he had one. Ditto on his Gateway. That would require a bit more effort on top, after this was all done with. At least he'd extended the glass ceiling. More of the game was available to him, entirely due to his hard work.

While he'd been mulling over his new stats, abilities and trait, his minions had caught up and his vision had cleared. He closed the menu and saw something even more ridiculous than his stat page. Arcadia. All of it. He hadn't realized just how high he'd climbed. If he jumped, he was at risk of exiting the stratosphere and leaving the planet. Assuming Arcadia was a 'planet'. The curvature he could see from here implied as much.

He turned and found spectacle in every direction. He could see the homelands of all four races from here. The gleaming spires of Camelot, surrounded by the luscious plains of Tintagel.

The sprawling metropolis of Orgri— no, wait, it's Waaarrghkanda now: the sprawling metropolis of Waaarrghkanda, where resident clans fight for adjacency to the vast Sukhavati Oasis. The floating fortress of Ker-Uhel and her arrayed islands, held in orbit by magic and spite. And the site of V-Au-lt01, hidden at the heart of the largest natural landmark in all Arcadia: the supervolcano, Ragnar-Rock.

Humans, orcs, elves and dwarves, arrayed across the four corners of the world. All visible from a single place, through the clouds and under the baking sun at just past midnight. What a trip. Damien was so enthralled he didn't realize the hole he'd come through had disappeared. He was not so enthralled that he failed to notice the enormous doorway that appeared in the middle of the platform. It was adorned with the biggest golden skull he'd ever seen, along with a message in gold cursive script across the top of the frame:

Go then, there are other worlds than these.

Damien stepped forward and noticed for the first time the practical application of his agility, which had all but doubled since he started playing a few hours ago: his body felt weightless. That wasn't the only factor in his increased speed; he was excited. What better way to test run this absurd new gear than against an unknown boss? He put his hand on the door and, upon reading the text informing him of the boss's name and asking if he was prepared, found his imagination had been wanting.

Damien tilted his head to the stratosphere and howled with laughter. He braced his hands on his knees and laughed at his feet. When that proved insufficient, he kneeled on the floor and held his sides, still laughing his heart out. For once it was Noigel who was disturbed by Damien's behavior.

"Perhaps you should return to your own world and rest before we attempt this, master?"

Damien grabbed Noigel by the arms and dragged him into a headlock, giving him a noogie as his captive choked out an indignant screech. Damien kissed his bald head, spat when he realized what he'd done and went back to laughing twice as hard. It was only when Noigel got the knives out and brandished them threateningly that Damien relented, letting him go and wiping the tears from his eyes.

"No way. We're doing this right now!"

He summoned two hell hounds and two imps, draining his Soul Reserve and bringing his Soul Summon Limit to 38/44. Then he put a hand to the door, nodding furiously as the text reappeared.

"Everyone inside!"

The doors swung open, revealing not Arcadia's skyline that lay behind it but a completely new room that lay through it. Well, not completely new. Damien had seen it once before, about a month ago. The underground arena had much more in common with the lower levels of the Dark Tower Damien had just left behind. He had an inkling that once the boss appeared, that would no longer be the case.

The minions filed in and the door closed behind them. Damien had Noigel disperse them around the outer walls. Then he reconsidered and gave Noigel new orders, having him place them behind each of the four vast stone columns that stretched to the ceiling.

"Master—," Noigel started irritably, "—could you make up your mind?"

Not even a grumpy Noigel could spoil this moment. Damien grinned at him and raised a hand in acknowledgment.

"Sorry, I forgot how the start of this goes."

"You forgot how the start of this goes?"

"That's what I said. Don't move from there."

Damien strolled out toward the middle of the arena, densely packed golden sand crunching under his feet. He was waiting for the sign that combat was about to begin. He was nearly at the center when the low rumble started under his feet. Damien immediately turned tail and ran back to the column Noigel was hiding behind, his arms and legs pumping up and down in a pantomime of sneaking as he giggled under his breath. He looked every inch a naughty child who'd lit a firecracker under an abandoned junkyard TV.

Damien could move very fast now. He'd already reached safety by the time the low rumble had become a deafening roar and the entire arena had begun to shake, as if in the throes of an earthquake. Damien stuck his fingers in his ears, still snorting while Noigel stared at him incredulously. The rumbling stopped. In that moment of silence, Noigel gave voice to what he'd been trying to process:

"Master? What do you mean by—'"

Before Noigel could finish his question, the ceiling exploded. Damien and his minions were quite safe behind the columns as the walls were bombarded with rubble. One and a half seconds later there was a second, heavier impact, followed by an immense shockwave. Damien waited until it passed and then, unable to contain his glee any longer, jumped out from behind his cover. The gear was great, the trait was great, the weapon was great. It all paled in comparison to a second chance against the enemy that had set him on this path in the very beginning.

In the middle of a smoldering crater, surrounded by shards of glass where the sand had been superheated, lay Damien's true prize for reaching the end of the Dark Tower. Resting on one knee, with an obscenely large serrated blade thrust into the ground in front of him, was Toutatis: The Mad Tyrant.

Damien equipped his kunai and held them out to either side. Toutatis rose to his full height, dragging his sword out of the ground with one hand before setting his sights on Damien. A red icon in the shape of a menacing eye appeared in Damien's battle HUD: In the Sight of the Gods – All stats reduced by 40%. They'd doubled the debuff. Damien didn't care. If this was what was waiting for him, he'd climb the Dark Tower a thousand times. So long as he never gave up, his victory was assured.

Damien gripped his new weapons tightly and yelled into the god's face.

"Where's my backpack, you filthy animal?"

24

THE VIEW FROM HALFWAY DOWN

When Damien had first fought Toutatis, he'd been playing a beta version of Saga with notably different mechanics layered over the vanilla game. Limbs could be broken or severed, his stats were reduced if his headset detected fear and there was more exposure to explicit content (not in a good way), to name a few. Saga Online had been just that little bit more unpleasant for Damien than it had been for paying customers.

He'd chosen to play a warrior, which had offset much of the unpleasantness tremendously. Heavy armor allowed him to avoid dismemberment, for the most part. A relatively high constitution stat served as a buffer against fear, at least until his hit points dropped anywhere below half. Armor and hit points didn't do anything to protect his innocence, so it was just as well he wasn't overburdened with that in the first place.

Having occultism thrust upon him in the regular version of Saga Online had been difficult in different ways, even before taking his circumstances into account. Nowhere was safe. He was forced to travel everywhere on foot, through hostile territory. His only realistic means of leveling had been player-killing, a risky business in any game, and more so if you've been playing your character for less than a day. He'd spent much of the following week alone, playing the class with only Bartholomew and Noigel to guide him. A very loose definition of 'guide' indeed.

Yet despite all the difficulties he'd overcome, the majority of commentators offhandedly diminished his accomplishments by saying occultists were overpowered. As if his success had nothing to do with him at all. As if killing well over a hundred player characters in a week had been handed to him on a plate. What did they know? He doubted any of them could've got as much out of the class as he had. His gear was always lacking, he was squishy, his minions had lower health than him, he dealt very little damage at great personal risk, and while other players could fail willy-nilly and bounce back after twenty-four hours, a death for him was a huge setback.

Until now. Now he had a high-tier, level-appropriate gear set to complement his chosen playstyle. *Now* he was OP. Now he could give Toutatis a proper fight. Once the formalities were out of the way.

Toutatis roared, as Damien knew he would. He braced himself on all fours, leaning into the wind. Even with 40% reduced stats, his agility was higher than when he'd entered the dungeon. His feet dragged backward through the sand, but he remained standing at the roar's end.

The preliminaries were finished. The stage was set. On with the show. Damien ran forward, hurling a kunai at Toutatis's bare midriff. Toutatis took the hit and the kunai sank in. That was a surprise. Damien had expected him to deflect it, as Mordred had done. It was only when Toutatis grabbed the chain before Damien could twist and release that he realized this was not a good thing.

Noigel was quick to react, the minions all screeching to announce their presence as they rounded the columns. Those in range of the succubi were Bloodlusted and heading his way fast. Damien didn't rate their chances in melee against Toutatis, although a distraction would certainly be useful right about now. The only thing more useful than that was an exit. He thought *Stop* as clearly as he could and all the minions immediately halted where they were. Not a moment too soon.

Damien had not been foolish enough to pull the chain himself, so Toutatis obliged him: the eight-foot deity jumped backward, yanking Damien off his feet, then pulled on the chain with all his might. As Damien hurtled toward him, Toutatis raised his ten-foot sword above his head with a single hand.

Damien set his eyes on an imp on the far side of the room and Demon Gated. He turned as the helpful imp was sliced in two in his stead, ran behind the column as Noigel reasserted his command over the minions, then crouched.

In the wake of his near death, the excitement was starting to wear off and logic was kicking in. This was a boss fight. Just as it had been with Mordred, there would be a specific way of handling this. He would've rather fought Toutatis with all his experience combined with his newfound raw power, but the fight was not set up that way. This was the Path of Deceit, not the Path of Honorable Combat. Even if he was willing to do so, he'd rather not have to climb all the way up here again.

In the Sight of the Gods reducing his stats meant he was supposed to attack without being seen, just like Mordred but with a different flavor. He'd acquired a gear set that would allow him to do just that, even with the sunlight streaming in through the ceiling Toutatis had destroyed upon his arrival. Damien crouched down and found himself in Shadow Walker in the light of day. Sweeeet. Time to go with the indirect approach.

Walking while crouched was now as fast as a light jog. He rounded the column and found Toutatis standing in the center of the arena performing his best-known trick: spinning to win. The whirlwind was in its infancy but growing rapidly. Noigel hadn't seen this combat before. He didn't know what was coming.

Noigel, all minions back.

The minions were retreating behind their columns when Toutatis's rotation speed hit the threshold for the secondary effect to kick in. Most of his minions escaped, but a few of them were caught at the edge of the maelstrom and flung around within it helplessly. It didn't last long. Lightning bolts had begun striking the ground, each of them unerringly piercing an imp within the area of effect. Their ashes were added to the swirling mass of matter that continued to expand. Damien waited for Toutatis to lurch into a column. It took five seconds before Damien realized it wasn't happening. What he'd previously thought of as full power was nothing of the sort.

This was bad. Toutatis was spinning faster and faster and the whirlwind continued to grow. It was already twice the circumference Damien had thought was the limit and still expanding. If this went on, it would soon envelop the whole room. Damien doubted the lightning bolts cared if he was in stealth or not. Why wasn't Toutatis triggering? Last time he'd flung himself at Damien long before...ah, of course. He'd been too efficient. Toutatis needed a target. Damien would be damned before it was him.

Noigel, send out an imp!

The edge of the whirlwind had reached the foot of the columns when Noigel sent out his unwitting sacrifice. It was in the air, flying. Damien cursed. He hadn't been specific enough.

Noigel, put it on the fl—

There was no need. Toutatis was not deterred by his target being in the air and half the room away. Damien couldn't see Toutatis clearly through the dense cloud of sand, rubble and dust. He could only get an estimate of his opponent's speed from the shifting border of the whirlwind, although he did catch a brief flash of silver when the Warrior Champion of the Heavens made his move.

It took less than half a second for Toutatis to reach the target Damien had offered. Damien surmised that the longer he kept Toutatis waiting, the faster he'd spin and the faster he'd launch himself when a target did present itself. It was not the speed that shocked Damien, so much as the route: a straight line from the floor to the imp, halfway to the open roof.

Toutatis hit the wall behind the imp so hard, the resulting blast dispelled his whirlwind immediately. It made Damien's Ex-Imp-losion look like a popping balloon. It was as bad as the initial landing animation, which Damien had seen coming and had appropriately hidden behind a column for. He hadn't counted on a repeat performance, which was why he'd been crouched in plain sight, assuming he was safe.

The shockwave threw Damien past the column and into the wall a long way behind him. As the déjà vu settled in, prompting Damien to check his HUD for internal bleeding and broken bones, he became acutely aware he wasn't quite as OP as he'd thought. The power gap between him and Toutatis was almost unchanged. It was quite the time to have such a realization, given that the red eye had reappeared in his HUD.

Damien ran behind the column, feeling very slow, and crouched down again. Out of sight, his Shadow Walker was reactivated. He was sneaking his way around, expecting Toutatis to run for where he'd last been seen. Instead, Toutatis arrived in front of him and began methodically swinging his sword over the empty space. The minions that had been sheltering there fled without Toutatis paying them any notice. Not only had Toutatis predicted where Damien was headed, he knew he was in stealth and was searching for him to the exclusion of visible targets.

Uh-oh. Gotta go fast. Damien about-faced and rolled over and over like a florescent spiky erinaceidae with a crippling addiction to finger jewelry. It was the only way he could both stay in Shadow Walker and move fast enough to stay ahead of Toutatis's sweeps. If that's what it took to stay alive, no copyright law in the universe was gonna stop him. Toutatis was no sloth, but there was a lot of space for him to cover between the column and the wall. He was too slow.

Toutatis gave up his search and returned to the middle of the arena, where he began to spin all over again. Damien took control of an imp himself and placed it directly in front of a column. Sorry, dude. He prepared his weapons and edged closer, making sure he was close enough to engage while staying out of Toutatis's path.

Toutatis took the bait. While not as fast as the previous jump had been, it was still more than enough to squish the imp before it could manage a single wing beat. Toutatis's sword had sliced deep into the stone pillar and now it was stuck. The right kind of déjà vu. Since their last encounter, Damien had acquired better offensive options than a measured kick to an ill-defined pair of gonads.

Damien flung a kunai at Toutatis's bare back and it sank in with a meaty squelch. It did 4% damage, far more than the non-sneak 40%-debuffed hit he'd inflicted earlier but still nowhere near enough. Toutatis remained completely focused on heaving his sword from the stone. Damien had to make the most of this attack window. He pulled on the chain and hurtled headlong toward his target.

He cocked his second arm en route, the same way he did when possessing his wraiths, and put all his weight behind the other kunai's blade. It sank in up to Damien's knuckles, right between Toutatis's shoulder blades. It was a shame he couldn't use this technique in stealth, since he'd already broken it by inflicting damage with the first kunai. It was a critical hit though, deep enough to hit the heart from the back through Toutatis's considerable frame. Another 4% of Toutatis's hit points were gone.

Toutatis reached behind himself to grab Damien, the sword briefly forgotten. At least Damien had found the one place in the entire arena where Toutatis had no chance of seeing him, which was somewhat undermined by Toutatis knowing exactly where he was. Damien used his embedded kunai for leverage as he twisted his head out of Toutatis's grasping fingers. He couldn't stay here.

He twisted both kunai and kicked off Toutatis, rolling then preparing to throw again. Toutatis returned his attention to his weapon, pulling the first few feet of it free. The window of opportunity was closing. He hadn't done enough damage yet. Damien threw a kunai into Toutatis and pulled on the chain.

He knew the animation of the sword coming loose was a warning that time was growing short. After this column went down there would only be three more opportunities like this left, and no cover for him or his minions to hide behind. That was a significant concern. He had to milk this for all it was worth. As Damien's kunai sank in and he pulled on the chain, Toutatis immediately stopped trying to free his weapon, braced himself and kicked down the column.

This was definitely not what Damien was supposed to be doing. As the foot landed and the column began to tumble, Damien missed out on a critical strike because he was focused on leaving before he'd even arrived. He had to be. The column was collapsing on top of them. Damien kicked off again, jumping backward so he could see the blocks of stone that were threatening to crush him.

Toutatis had thoughtfully knocked him clear of this hazard when they'd first met, for the low, low price of breaking just about every bone in Damien's body. Damien was more than capable of avoiding them on his own. The quick jumps he'd practiced had turned out to be less useful than tactical rolls against the Cave Urchins, but with double stamina and agility they were very applicable here.

The last of the blocks fell and Toutatis appeared through the dust cloud, just before the debris around him started moving sideways. He was spinning again. Jeez, talk about a one-trick pony. The fallen fragments of the column were quickly disintegrated by friction and lightning.

Toutatis's hit points were at 84%. Damien was not on track to beating him with now only three columns left standing. Damien needed to up his game. He understood all the conditions of this fight. He knew how to draw his opponent, he knew the attack window, he had a baseline for how much damage he could do by himself. More importantly, Noigel had now seen all these things too.

Noigel, as soon as Toutatis hits the column throw everything at him.

Damien had one small problem to negotiate first. Playing matador. He was currently the only visible target. He was standing in the right place, directly in front of a column. Sending out even a single imp would be more complicated than it was worth. He wouldn't have time to judge whether Toutatis was attacking him or the imp. Which meant if Toutatis went for the imp, Damien would be in mid-dodge when Toutatis hit the wall and the shockwave occurred.

The imp would be destroyed, Damien would be knocked back and then he'd have to run the gauntlet of avoiding Toutatis again until he reentered stealth. Demon Gating to the imp would be even messier. Whether or not he died would be decided by a coin flip.

It was simpler this way. Not necessarily safer, but definitely simpler. If he could dodge Toutatis with a level 28 warrior, he could dodge him with a level 50 occultist. Probably. Damien waited, holding his nerve as the whirlwind expanded. The spin was counterclockwise, so his best chance would be jumping wi—

Toutatis hurled himself forward. Damien immediately regretted his decision. He'd been planning on neatly hopping sideways, but that no longer seemed sufficient. He threw himself away from the impact, arms outstretched. It wasn't as suave as he'd have liked but screw it, it worked the first time. The whirlwind picked him up, carrying him a little further and shredding him ever so slightly before Toutatis hit the column and Damien was dropped unceremoniously into the sand.

As one, all the minions emerged from cover and converged on Toutatis. Most of them were within range of at least one succubus and had been Bloodlusted. The succubi pointed at Toutatis simultaneously and two overlapping Circles of Hell appeared at his feet. Damien knew the armor-reduction effect didn't stack, but the damage did. Noigel was following his instruction to throw everything they had into this combat. Each of the succubi was also channeling a Chaotic Bolt.

The black flames engulfing Toutatis reminded Damien of an option he had yet to avail himself of. He had his own attack involving black flames now – 'Demon-Spear' – although it wasn't quite so easy to pull off and was as yet untested. No time like the present, especially since Toutatis was once again heaving on his weapon, exposing his ribcage. Damien rolled forward and flung both kunai, grabbing the chains tightly and raising his hands up. They felt hot for a second before he swished them down and two balls of black fire traveled side by side along the crest of the chains' wave.

Toutatis had turned his attention to the missiles lodged in his side, grabbing the chains with the intention of yanking Damien off his feet. The movement of the chains was halted around his closed fists but the fire riding the crest pushed through them, all the way into the blades.

Toutatis had already been burning from standing in two Circles of Hell. Damien had thought that the visual effect of his skill, especially when layered on top of similar effects, would be underwhelming. He was sorely mistaken. If Circle of Hell could be likened to a roaring fire in functionality, intensity and scale, this ability lay somewhere in between a dynamite plunger, a car battery and an incendiary bomb.

The two black sparks passed into Toutatis's body, and in the span of a low *whoomph* Toutatis was no longer simply on fire. His body was charred, cracked, blackened ash. The damage was hard to measure accurately since he was hit less than a second later by two Chaotic Bolts from two sides. He was already in a bad way, and now the rest of the minions were arriving.

Damien Demon Gated to the first of them: Noigel, who'd taken point and was dive-bombing the burning god with a pair of flimsy throwing knives raised above his head. It was ideal. Damien had no idea whether Noigel was setting him up for the switcheroo or if he'd been pulled out of a full-on Hail Mary, but either way his number-one imp was in danger of earning Damien's sincere respect. He earned a more immediate reprieve as Damien replaced him and followed through on Noigel's strategy with the agility required to make it work.

Circle of Hell reduced armor integrity by 50%. The Demon-Spear also reduced armor by 50%, if only for a modest five-second duration. He was pretty sure that since they were separate abilities their effects would stack, although he didn't know whether it was cumulative or multiplicative. Whichever it was, it was super effective. His kunai sank through the black tar, through the melted-slag remains of Toutatis's helmet and into his skull.

The imps and hounds arrived and were all over Toutatis a second after Damien had made his mark, alighting on Toutatis's body before raking every inch of him. Those that found space on his arms and legs only had a couple of seconds to do it with.

Toutatis's armor had been so diminished he may as well have been completely naked, which was saying something considering how naked he was already. Damien got the best of it, in pride of place over Toutatis's head.

Despite the unwieldy nature of his new weapons, he still managed to administer two more stabs before the Demon-Spear debuff was gone. He and his minions had inflicted colossal damage with still more coming. By the time the Demon-Spear debuff was over, Toutatis was long overdue for the next stage.

Toutatis wasted no time in kicking down the column to retrieve his sword, forcing Damien to jump clear. The imps and hounds remained where they were, savaging Toutatis from head to toe as the remnants of the column rained down upon them.

Now Damien was further back he could see the fruits of his labors. Toutatis was at 35% health and it was still dropping as the hounds and imps continued their assault. The next whirlwind would be brutal. Toutatis didn't wait for the column to finish falling to begin his spin. The imps and hounds were thrown off him in all directions, many of them getting sliced and diced before they were out of range. Damien pointed at the only imp yet to be thrown clear by the centrifugal force. There could only be one. Noigel had planted his knives in Toutatis's back and was clinging on for as long as he could.

"Imp-losion."

Much of the falling debris had been pulled into Toutatis's orbit by the winds, but not yet long enough for the twisting matter to grind it down. The whirlwind was culled in its infancy and Noigel was sucked into the portal that appeared. Then the whirlwind was sucked into the space Noigel had vacated. Damien corralled all his surviving minions to his side as he retreated to the center of the arena before turning to view the aftermath.

Somewhere between the first and the twentieth boulder, Toutatis's spin had been brought to a complete halt. He'd still been stood over the Circles of Hell when they'd collided with him. Toutatis pulled what remained of the helmet from his head, revealing his face: bald, bearded, warpainted and drenched in his own blood and brains, oozing from the four hideous wounds Damien had inflicted to his head.

8% health. Down to his last and looking meaner and more murderous than ever. This was exactly the stage Damien had been hoping to avoid with an expedient nuking. He probably should've waited until Toutatis's health was a bit lower before going all in. Toutatis reclaimed his sword and began running toward Damien at breakneck speed.

No Noigel to implement instructions. Demon Gate on cooldown. Stats cut by 40%. Damien threw all the minions at Toutatis, trying to slow him down as he bought time to figure out what to do. He knew it wouldn't work before they'd even reached the enraged god. The minions were useful for ambushes or applied at a point of weakness. Even a possessed incubus would not slow down an angry Toutatis one jot. There was only one skill he had left that was both useful and available. The question was how he himself might survive it.

Toutatis had already cut down a succubus and a hound without breaking his stride. He'd be on Damien in seconds. Better to die trying something stupid and learn from it than die doing nothing. Damien threw one of his kunai into his opponent's chest as Toutatis bounded across the open ground toward him, his sword raised to strike. Damien pointed his free kunai at an imp between them and braced himself. This had better work.

"Ex-Imp-losion."

Damien hadn't been counting his Imp-losions during his traversal of the Inner Circle and certainly didn't have time to check how many stacks the ability currently held. Not less than three. A more accurate assessment than that was difficult since he was currently being subjected to its effects.

The preexisting minions had all been packed fairly close together and were the first struck by the expanding shock wave. While they somersaulted helplessly outward, clearing the field, the newly remanifested imps were shot through or into them at full speed. It must've been quite something to go from nothingness to hurtling into existence in a hostile world. Their circumstances were completely out of their control unless they survived long enough for their lives to have meaning. Damien wouldn't be relying on them here.

The sand directly beneath them was forced out of the ground by pure air pressure to reveal the cold flagstones beneath. Sand is very shock-absorbent, but not Ex-Imp-losion-proof from a couple of feet away. The released air of all the Imp-losions passed unimpeded through the air far more quickly. Damien was blown backward, only to get held in place by the chain of the kunai embedded in Toutatis's chest.

All this in 0.3 seconds. At 0.31 seconds, the resulting pull on the chain reeled Damien in, through the outer shock wave toward his opponent. Toutatis had barely slowed, but had clamped his eyes shut against the blast of coarse, rough, irritating sand in that all-important moment. Damien planted his other kunai directly between them, all the way down to the back of the blade. Toutatis opened his eyes again, but even as he did so the color was fading out of them.

Toutatis keeled over backward with Damien on top of him and was gone before they hit the ground. The ten souls that flowed into Damien's soul reserve confirmed his victory. Damien twisted both kunai free and stood over his fallen adversary. Praise Be.

Ding.

A portal had opened in the center of the arena floor. Damien opened his HUD and checked his notifications. In addition to having leveled up for the fifth consecutive time this session and reached level 51, there was even better news. Bartholomew's quest was finally complete. All that was left was to go through the portal and meet Bartholomew's master. After he'd gathered himself and collected his spoils, at least.

Damien put his hand on Toutatis's body and thought 'Loot'. If he'd got all that incredible gear on the way to this, he could only imagine the reward for completion. He stared at the item that appeared in his HUD and frowned. Only one item with no name, just question marks. Why wasn't there any information about it?

He put it in his inventory and willed it into his open hand. It was a black gemstone. It appeared to be swallowing the light. It was noticeably darker around his hand. He analyzed the item and was still rebuked. Only a name and a description, both of which were comprised of question mark strings.

Well, so long as he took it with him he'd have time to figure out what it was later. He'd been playing for hours and was ready to put this behind him. He resummoned Noigel first, who arrived on his shoulder and cupped a hand around his own ear, leaning in to Damien's mouth.

"Nicely done, Noigel. I'm very pleased with your performance."

Noigel rolled his hand around before putting it back on his ear and leaning in closer. Damien had a look around. The fight had left him with only nine imps and a single succubus. Noigel couldn't speak properly. Excellent. Damien canceled his next imp summon.

"I'm so glad to have a second-in-command who'd put themselves on the line for me, out of the goodness of their heart. Your loyalty is its own re—"

"Pthbpthbpthbpthbpthb!"

Damien wiped the spittle off his face. He probably deserved that.

"I'm just teasing. Really though, great job back there. Nice use of the knives."

He shooed Noigel off him, only for Noigel to make a beeline for the surviving succubus. No thank you. Damien wasted no time in ordering everyone through the portal and followed through after them. He could finish up the livestream and go to bed. Huge success! Tomorrow he'd see how Lillian and Aetherius were doing, maybe go help them out since he'd finished—

He stepped into complete darkness. This was disturbing. Damien hadn't been blinded by darkness since he was made an occultist. He should've been able to see something. He turned to look at the portal and found that that was gone as well. Either that or he couldn't see it. There was no way of orienting himself.

He raised his hands to his face and felt his fingers there. He couldn't even see that close.

He focused on opening his menu, just to check he was still in game. The menu wouldn't open. Maybe there'd been some kind of glitch when he came through the portal. Great. He'd just finished fighting Toutatis and now he'd glitched out. His HUD had disappeared. There was no sound either. Where were Noigel and the rest of them? If he'd lost his minions to this glitch—

"You're late."

Damien's kunai slipped into his hands. At least now he knew he was still online. While it was better than being stuck in a glitch or a coma, it was still disturbing. Why couldn't he open his menu? He was trying once again when the voice rang out in his head. The words were threatening but the tone was silvery, self-assured and chiding. Whoever was speaking was close by and could clearly see him.

"Your menu privileges have been revoked. Continue brandishing my weapons and they'll be revoked also."

So whoever was talking to him not only knew about the menu, but also that he'd been trying and failing to access it. Damien put his weapons away. He wasn't in the habit of obeying strangers in the dark. He was very much in the habit of calculating his odds. He had a hunch who this might be.

"Are you Bartholomew's master?"

"I am the master of all in this world."

Yup. It was definitely him.

"I can see where Bartholomew gets it from."

Damien felt hot breath on his face as the air reverberated back and forth over his host's vocal cords. A carnivorous growling that held nothing in common with the creature's voice that was being beamed into his head directly.

"A poor comparison. I made Bartholomew everything he is, which amounts to precious little. The finest craftsman cannot mold a masterpiece from inferior clay. If not for me, he would be entirely without worth. The two of you hold that much in common."

Damien had been squinting, trying to make out anything at

all. This introduction was similar to how Bartholomew had made his acquaintance, though that had been considerably more short-lived. It took a few seconds for the words to sink in. When they did, Damien redirected his attention.

"I'd be worthless without your help? I've never even met you, let alone been helped by you."

"Your life was, is and always will be in my hands. Without my blessing, your journey would not have even begun. You're nothing without me."

"Back up a bit. Have we met? It's hard to tell when I can't see you, but I'm pretty sure we haven't. I'd remember someone with a throat condition as serious as yours."

"No, Damien. We have not met. But upon your every impure thought, self-serving deed or careless word, I was there to watch your fall from grace. Time and time again."

"Ooga-booga to you too, Mr. Mysterious. Really, it's lovely to meet you. I've come a long way to be here, but I've been playing for a long time and I'm just about ready to log off. If you'd be so kind as to give me my menu back, we can continue this tomorrow. Maybe you could pay your electricity bill before then, so I can actually see who I'm talking to."

"The bill comes due, Damien, but not for me. Indulge me. Allow me to show you what you owe."

There was a sharp rap on his forehead, a flick from a powerful hand. Damien staggered back in the darkness, his eyes closed and his hands stretching out for balance. He had no idea how much damage it had done with no active HUD, only that it hurt.

"Hey! What's th—"

He opened his eyes and could see, not that what he saw made any sense. He was at the bottom of the Downward Spiral. Bartholomew stood ahead, staring upward while the rats cut him a wide berth. Something was wrong with him. It took a moment for Damien to figure out, since this was the version of Bartholomew he was most accustomed to. His master had reverted back to how he had looked when they first met: a ghoulish corpse.

Had something happened while he was away? Why was he here at all? It was as his perspective shifted forward, even while he was stepping back, that Damien understood his situation. This wasn't his body and he wasn't in control. He could still feel his own body standing upright, but was looking through the eyes of another.

He was familiar with various gaits and walks, having used Possession on each of his minion types many times over. This movement wasn't any of theirs. It was as big as an incubus and quieter than a wraith. Big enough to loom over Bartholomew. Quiet enough to arrive at his back without him noticing.

"This is a poor reception, Bartholomew."

Bartholomew immediately turned and prostrated himself on the floor.

"My lord! You need not have come here, I—"

A cleft hoof, attached to Damien's perspective, arrived on the back of Bartholomew's head. It pressed his mouth firmly into the dirt, preventing further speech. The voice emanating from within Damien's head continued in the same lazy drawl.

"*I* don't need to do anything. It is *you* who must be spurred to action. There's a man up there who has piqued my interest. He'll be joining us shortly. You need to make a good first impression."

The foot was retracted, allowing Bartholomew to continue speaking into the floor. He was shaking. Bartholomew was afraid.

"My lord, I was already bested by him when I was whole, I'm no match for him in my current state. Not even if he's alone."

"You mean the mage? Trust you to misinterpret my intentions. No, I came for the one who arrived before him. The fresh meat. He shows promise."

Bartholomew staggered to his feet, his hands knotting into each other at his waist as he looked anywhere except into the eyes of Damien's host.

"Forgive my asking, Lord, but what value—"

The backhand echoed through the dungeon, knocking Bartholomew back to the ground before he'd even stood completely upright. Damien winced. This was excessive, even directed at Bartholomew. It was all the worse for viewing the attack from the perspective of the aggressor. It felt as though he were the one inflicting this sadistic punishment.

"Do not question me. You didn't think to question the value I saw in you, though you have long since worn it out. Why do you make it so hard to help you? Do you think you can continue abusing my hospitality without offering anything in return?"

Two massive hands appeared, hauling Bartholomew to his feet by the scruff of his neck before dusting him down, suddenly concerned with the vampire's well-being.

"There, all better. I'll give you one more chance, so focus on what you're supposed to be doing. No, look up! Half-wit. Where would you be without me? You'll need to put your Sin to good use, he won't be using the stairs. Oh, here he comes! Look alive, Bartholomew!"

His host's vision panned upward, in time for the silhouette of a figure to appear against the dull gray light. Whoever it was, they were plummeting through the darkness. They had already passed the third floor when Bartholomew stretched out his hands. One pointed at the falling figure, the other over a solitary rat in the middle of the dungeon floor. A portal appeared at each location instantly and the rat screeched as the figure landed on top of it, circumventing four floors of gravity. Before the rat's screech had been stifled, Bartholomew snapped his hands closed and the portals snapped out of existence.

As much as he wanted to, Damien could not look away. As if he hadn't been uncomfortable enough already. He knew the figure who'd just landed on the rat and was lying there, still assuming he was dead. It was him. This was his arrival in the Downward Spiral. A month ago.

He'd always thought he'd survived his fall by luck. He'd never conceived that Bartholomew had had any part in it. A heavy hand stroked Bartholomew's decrepit head, taking the credit for Damien's survival.

"Well done, Bartholomew. Perhaps you're not completely useless after all. Put him through his paces. Don't make it too easy, we need to ensure he can perform under pressure. You've got your first occultist student, all thanks to me! Do not fail."

Damien's vision went black. He couldn't tell if the vision was over until a face swam out of the darkness a few inches in front of him. If you could call it a face. It was little more than a skull. From its head protruded two curled horns and a thick head of golden hair. Damien had known he was hopelessly outmatched for a while now, but seeing was believing. The voice reappeared in his mind, speaking to him the same way Mordred had. The mouth remained still while fetid air rasped out between its clenched teeth.

"Without me, Mr. Arkwright, you'd have been doomed from the start. How conceited, to believe you could survive without my intervention. Bartholomew would've let you fall to your death. I thoughtfully came to ensure your survival."

Damien was distracted by the basic information that had appeared over his host's head. Not so distracted that he failed to notice the very formal use of his real-world name. He'd been interested to meet Bartholomew's master. Not anymore.

Lucifer – Level ??? – Archon

"Let's review your history."

Lucifer traced a rectangle through the air with his impeccably manicured, razor-sharp fingernails. The outline of a blue-tinged information screen appeared underneath them, within which Damien saw a reversed screenshot of himself followed by row upon row of inverted text. Lucifer scrolled down the list, picking out noteworthy items from it.

"It all started with a brief voice call from Aetherius, who sent you a location marker to the Downward Spiral. Shortly afterward, you left the starting zone with no class and no equipment. How bold. Then came the external call from CU, pertaining to your mother's condition and your subsequent, imminent placement in foster care. How unspeakably tragic."

All of this was being delivered in an incredibly flat tone. Lucifer peered around the information screen and his glowing eyes bored into Damien, his mouth still unmoving, as the voice lilted with mild interest.

"How is Cassandra *Brades*, by the way? I'm assuming her condition improved following my competition victory? I should hope so, given your drive to save her at all costs was in large part why I invested in you."

Damien was dumbstruck. This thing not only had access to his conversations and phone records, it also understood real-world infrastructure? The devil did not wait long for a response as Damien boggled at him, all thought of witty repartee a thing of the past. The darkness was slowly peeling back as the devil spoke, revealing more of Damien's unsolicited shadowy backer.

"Very good. I'm *so* glad everything worked out. All thanks to me, of course. But I digress; you performed passably well as my champion, yet have done little since then to merit my gifts. Already you have begun your descent into obscurity. Once again I find you in front of me, hoping I will make up for your lack."

Now the aura wasn't smothering him directly, Damien knew where he'd seen it before. It was the same aura that surrounded the forest marking the edge of Bartholomew's territory. It had been layered over him like a second skin, preventing him from seeing outside of its confines. The veil was being lifted. Lucifer was becoming more visible all the time.

While Damien appreciated having Lucifer introduced to him gradually, he would've preferred the veil not to have been lifted at all. He should've aborted after he acquired the final piece of Bartholomew's gear set. Or maybe after he'd beaten Toutatis. It's more comfortable not to know some evil exists. At the very least, Mobius could have added a 'skip' option to this dramatic, overbearing cutscene. Damien did his best to hurry it along himself.

"Can you get to the point? I know how you types like to talk."

The devil peered around the information screen a second time. He closed it with a rattling sigh and stepped toward Damien, hands raised.

"The point? The point is you need to understand our relationship if it is to progress any further. You are a vessel for my greatness. I saw your need and set you on the path which would fulfill it. You willingly signed yourself over when you applied your new name to the contract Bartholomew presented as my agent."

Lucifer placed his clawed hands over Damien's head, turning it forcefully this way and that. It was all Damien could do not to stab him, although the longer it went on the more he felt like doing so regardless of the outcome. Lucifer was kneading his head. Caressing it. Squeezing it. Allowing his thumbs to venture into Damien's mouth, pulling back his lips and running his fingers over his teeth. Exploring him, as if he were an interesting ornament.

"You are mine: your life is mine, your body is mine, your mind is mine. Your abilities are mine, your skills are mine, your possessions are mine. Your fans are mine, your goals are mine, your victories are mine."

Damien pushed the hands away. Lucifer was far stronger. Whenever he resisted, Lucifer would violently twist his head before continuing to pry, his voice continuing in Damien's head without pause and drowning out all protest. Lucifer pulled him in close, holding him tightly across the chin.

"Your flaws, your failures and your weaknesses are yours, and yours alone."

He released Damien, leaving him to sputter. While he'd been subjected to this disgusting act, the veil of shadow had stretched far enough to encompass a throne directly behind his abuser. Lucifer took a few steps back and reclined in his seat.

"Once you've got that through your head, which is mine minus any delusions you're harboring without my permission, I'll let you be on your way."

He stuck his elbow on the armrest, nestled his head in his hand and contemplated Damien lazily. Damien wanted out. Even without his menu he could attempt to log out verbally. It didn't seem likely that Lucifer would allow him to do so. Maybe he could try appeasing him?

"What do you want me to say?"

"Thanking me for all your success would be a good start. A promise to repay me for my favor would be sensible, although that won't mean much until you act on it. A paltry admission that without me you're worthless is strongly advised. Material offerings would be a more immediate way of demonstrating your subservience, although arbitrary since everything you own is already mine by default. I'm not sure what you'll have to do to retain my favor, but I'm very reasonable and open to further suggestions."

So much for that. Damien would rather die than take any of these options. It didn't sound like it would make much difference either way. Time to leave.

"I'll think about it. Nice to meet you. Log out!"

The Logout Sphere enveloped him. The feeling of relief had barely registered when Lucifer rose out of his chair.

"I haven't given you permission to leave."

"And yet I'm leaving anyway."

Lucifer strode in front of him while Damien stared in open defiance. He couldn't move while logging out, it wasn't as if there were anything else he could do. At the very last moment, Lucifer jabbed a pointed finger through Damien's shoulder. The Logout Sphere shattered, along with Damien's thin veneer of calm. He started yelling, only for Lucifer to drown him out with the voice in his head. Damien couldn't even hear himself and Lucifer wasn't listening either.

"I don't know why you're getting so worked up about this. You're being very unreasonable. Childish, even. After everything I've done for you, I never expected such ingratitude. Here, I tire of your insolence. You can show yourself out."

He set Damien down on the floor and nodded. A portal opened at Damien's back. Damien turned to look at it, then back to Lucifer again. Lucifer had folded his arms and was fixing Damien with his permanent, skinless skull grin. It was only as Damien turned and took his first step to freedom that Lucifer's voice manifested in his head once more.

"However, if you leave without acknowledging me I shall sever all ties. You will no longer be an occultist. Your level and experience will reset to zero. I will reclaim all the possessions you've accumulated for me, which you will have no further need of. If you wish to continue abusing my power—"

The devil threw out his arms and spread his huge leathery wings wide, his demand grating through his throat and rippling through the air. It was by far more horrid and visceral than the honeyed voice he'd projected into Damien's head.

"—*bow down and worship me.*"

25

TWO SIDES OF THE SAME COIN

Lillian refreshed Damien's livestream and received the same message again:

Daemien has entered a private cutscene. The stream will resume when the cutscene is over.

That could only mean one thing. Damien had finished his quest! In her excitement, Lillian voice called him and was greeted halfway through the first ring with a similar message in audio. She'd have to wait a little longer to congratulate him personally. The time on her own self-imposed challenge was about to reset. She'd started, now she had to finish. Even if most of her reasons for starting had since evaporated.

Lillian: Damien's all done. Our turn. Coming?

Aetherius: I'm already here. No sign of Hammertime. Too bad.

Lillian: On my way.

She logged in and opened her eyes. Andrew, true to his word, was waiting to greet her. The Lady of the Lake was standing to one side of the red carpet, allowing him passage to the throne that he was not willing to take. Upon Lillian's arrival, the Lady strode into the center of the aisle to block her path. It wasn't exactly polite, but it was better than being drowned or crushed in gallons of invisible water.

Andrew gave a crisp, disciplined salute, which had the desired effect immediately. Had Lillian cringed any harder her face would've cramped off and buried itself in the ground.

"Don't do that."

"By your command, Lillian the Im—"

"No, don't do that either. Come on, we only enforced that garbage when we had a bunch of randoms in the guild."

"Alright, we'll save the strict discipline for when we're on ceremony."

"We've got five people left including ourselves, I don't think we'll be worrying about discipline for a while."

"We might have to, once you clear the quest."

That was not as encouraging as Andrew thought it would be. Lillian didn't want to get into it. She didn't think he'd appreciate her having second thoughts. She deftly moved the conversation elsewhere.

"I've still got about two minutes before the next attempt. You said you had an idea. Did you find anything?"

"Of course I did."

Andrew sent Lillian a link. It went straight to an external web page, a long definition of the word 'pride'. Lillian was a couple of lines in before she looked up at Andrew without hiding her confusion.

"What does this have to do with anything?"

Andrew gawped at her.

"You remember I said each of the riddles was connected to a primary virtue? I'm still certain this last one relates to humility, which we covered pretty exhaustively over lunch. The opposite of humility is—"

"Pride. Yeah, you said. Sorry I asked."

That had been a bit terse. Andrew frowned but kept going.

"There was a paragraph in here that caught my attention. The site it came from is maintained by Mobius Enterprises, so with any luck they referenced it when...is everything okay, Lillian? You seem distracted."

"No, no, everything's fine. Thank you for this, it should be useful. I'll give it a quick read before I head in."

She looked up and gave him a smile, which she hoped looked more real than it felt. Andrew seemed skeptical, but nodded and moved away rather than hanging around to creepily watch her read. That was a relief. More than the opportunity to swot up on the challenge, Lillian needed time to clear her head and figure out what she actually wanted.

One of the lines in the article had enough buzzwords to interrupt her thought processes. She skipped back to read it from the beginning and realized this was the paragraph that had prompted Andrew to share the article.

'*Pride* is sometimes viewed as corrupt or as a vice, sometimes as proper or as a virtue. With a negative connotation, *pride* refers to a foolishly and irrationally corrupt sense of one's personal value, status or accomplishments, used synonymously with hubris. With a positive connotation, *pride* refers to a content sense of attachment toward one's own or another's choices and actions, or toward a whole group of people, and is a product of praise, independent self-reflection, and a fulfilled feeling of belonging.'

Did that mean she was supposed to avoid all pride in her second interview? Or just the negatives? She thought to ask, then realized it wouldn't serve any purpose. Andrew was just as much in the dark as she was. He hadn't set this task, he was just providing literature to inform her own decision.

That was big of him. Then she considered what it said in the paragraph – a content sense of attachment toward one's own or another's choices and actions – and could not prevent herself from smirking. He couldn't very well present her with this information only to ignore it himself. He knew she'd pick up on it and call him out. Smart boy. Classic Andrew. Smug git.

One small problem. Andrew's respect and what she was reading only made her sense of contentment stronger. Which defeated the purpose of taking on the challenge at all. She wrestled with her feelings for the rest of the article, not a single word of which arrested her so thoroughly as the core of valuable insight in the main paragraph. She was a long way from the end when she knew what she needed to do. Only one parcel of information was missing. A parcel of information only Andrew could provide.

"Hey, I finished it off. Thanks for sending it my way."

Andrew closed his menu and got to his feet.

"Damien still hasn't left that cutscene. I hope he's not in trouble."

"This is Damien you're talking about. If he could handle you, I'm sure he'll manage whatever he found through the portal."

"That's true, but he did have help dealing with me."

"Oi, leave off. I don't think I ever said it out loud, but...sorry. We made a hell of a mess, didn't we?"

"You did the best you could. So did I. Now we get to look back on our mistakes and laugh, a privilege I'm happy to accept."

Oh? Andrew had become quite the wise mage over the course of their adventure. Lillian didn't dare say it. She didn't have the heart to belittle such a pure sentiment, especially since it aligned with her one remaining goal so favorably. Step by step, Andrew was returning to the person she'd fallen in love with. That would have to wait. After a breakup as tumultuous as they'd shared, she'd be doing neither of them any favors by rushing back into it.

Andrew felt the same way, so far as she could tell. He'd been nothing but respectful when they had met up that afternoon and had behaved himself all the way through to the evening, aside from a few carefully measured, slightly misguided plays. They'd talked for hours without straying into sensitive topics. If it was right, it would continue to feel right indefinitely. However, they had a more immediate problem to deal with. A problem Lillian was no longer certain would be best resolved by further conflict.

"Andrew. I've got a personal question."

Andrew got to his feet and did some warm-up stretches, waiting for Lillian to lay into him. When he saw she was serious, the comedic routine ground to a halt. She waited for him to stop bouncing before she laid out her last and most persistent concern. The one that had been eating away at her since Damien first told her who Magnitude really was.

"I know you're here because you want to help me. I don't doubt that for a second. I also know you and Richard are...not getting along."

She'd only mentioned his brother's name, yet Andrew already looked uncomfortable. This was the right question. While the quest was not yet complete, Lillian had already inadvertently accomplished most of her personal goals. She'd been so focused on the task she set herself, she hadn't realized the quest was redundant until she and Andrew were on good terms again. She knew it wasn't the same for Andrew himself. His problem ran a little deeper. She needed to know how deep.

"It's one thing declaring war against a player blocking me and my guild's progress. It's something else entirely, helping you fight your own brother. I don't know if I want to be involved."

"It's a bit late for that, isn't it?"

"Everything's changed. We're talking again. Rising Tide has kicked the bucket, save for a small trusted group we can run dungeons with. Hammertime betrayed us, then I caught up with him and had my say. This is a turning point. We can walk away from this with our heads held high, leave everything in the past and get on with our lives. It's exactly the right time for this."

"I can't do that. I promised Richard he'd pay for what he did. I have to see it through."

"Why are you dead set on revenge? He behaved terribly, but so did we. He's still your brother! He killed you, after you'd already lost the competition, at a time when you'd have ended up dead pretty soon anyway. Is that really worth all this drama?"

Andrew was back to tapping his foot again, more violently than before. He was staring ahead, trying and failing not to look surly. She tried a different tack.

"We could stop investing all our time in Saga Online and play it rather than building our lives around it. Now we're back to where we were, we could find you something more realistic and less stressful to do with yourself. I'd even help you find your feet. Why not let Richard do whatever he's doing? It's only a game. You don't have to let your hatred define you."

Lillian hadn't even got halfway through before Andrew stopped tapping his foot and looked directly at her, his arms tightly crossed over his chest. He waited until she'd finished before refuting her.

"Firstly, we're not back to where we were. We're talking. I'm very happy about it, but it's not the same. Secondly, this isn't just about revenge. He can't be allowed to succeed. Not the way he's done it."

"It looks a lot like revenge from here."

"I don't want to get into this before you take on the challenge. It won't help—"

"I'll be the judge of what I want to hear. I'd like to hear this. If killing you and besmirching your glowing public image isn't the problem, what is?"

Andrew closed his eyes.

"It's staring you in the face. You have all the information you need already. Do I have to say it? Where do you think Richard got the gold to buy Carlisle from?"

"Enlighten me."

With his eyes still closed, Andrew took a deep breath and folded his arms. Then he did the opposite of enlightening her.

"Everyone assumes I stole the entire contents of Rising Tide's vault. I don't know how I'd manage that, even if I wanted to, but of course I didn't. Richard waited until I was in Aetherium's vault to use the Portal Scroll. The same Portal Scroll he used to summon Archimonde, in the footage Damien shared with you."

Lillian had already seen where this was going. Had Andrew's eyes been open, he'd have watched her face darkening and have known it. He almost certainly knew it anyway. But he continued to speak, and Lillian's 'live and let live' attitude continued to evaporate.

"Whenever I went through one of those portals to see him, it closed after I passed through. I assumed the target of the scroll passes through and it closes, just like the occultist ability. Except it turns out that's not how it works. That's just what he wanted me to think. The portals he's using work both ways."

Andrew had been reluctant to say anything before. Now he'd started, he couldn't stop. His foot was tapping relentlessly up and down, keeping time for his tuneless tale.

"Richard groomed me. He didn't just kill me instead of helping me, I might've been able to accept that. He used me to get access to Rising Tide's vault, robbed us blind and pinned it on me without having to say a word. He turned my loss into his gain."

All Rising Tide's accumulated effort. Not just Lillian and Andrew's, but that of the entire guild. Thousands of combined hours of toil. The guild that had been under her care. Until she'd stopped helping after Andrew followed through on his brother's prank, leaving Andrew alone and vulnerable. Lillian was already compiling a new flowchart in her head. Andrew kept on, venting everything he'd kept to himself for as long as he could until Lillian had invited him to share.

"He had to know I was in the vault before he used the scroll. I didn't share my recording, there was nothing about that night I wanted to share with anyone. I told the last players I was going into the vault, so more likely than not it was one of them. Whoever it was, it's probably the same player who told him you were coming online behind my back."

Lillian nodded thoughtfully. She summarized it as best she could, to make sure she had a handle on the whole affair.

"In addition to killing you instead of helping you, Richard tricked you into opening a portal into the vault so he could steal everything we built together over two months?"

"Yup."

"He then used the gold to buy Carlisle, demolish it and build the wall, thus preventing Damien from pursuing his quest, and anyone affiliated with the Empire from pursuing the Excalibur quest?"

"Correct."

"The quest I only needed to pursue in the first place because you lost the competition to Damien and Rising Tide fell apart?"

"With a helping hand from you for maximum irony, yes."

"I was still helping you, up to the last week. Which was around the time Richard started gunning for the prank. He didn't mention I was helping with your admin duties, I assume? Only that I was playing behind your back?"

"That's right."

"So Richard fed you the bad information while withholding the good, in order to coerce you into pulling a disgusting prank on me that was not only the death knell of our relationship, but which has also impacted my mental stability and my real-life work performance for the last month?"

"Lillian, you're starting—"

Yes. Lillian was starting. She was starting to see the threads Richard had been pulling on very clearly.

"According to you, Richard said I was drawing attention away from you just by playing. That's why I performed my duties covertly, so covertly even you didn't notice. But he drew your attention to me in such a way, you thought I was coming online between two and eight in the morning for *my* benefit?"

She was starting to rant. Andrew put his hands up and stepped away from her.

"Lillian, I'm really sorry, I was under a lot of stress at the time and I wasn't thinking clearl—"

"Don't worry, Andrew. I'm not angry with you. Yet. You said Richard was the one who brought the prank to you. Did you tell him about my family history?"

"Does it matter?"

"It matters to me. A lot. Did you tell him about it, yes or no?"

"No. I told him the prank was unacceptable but never why. You asked me not to share that with anyone."

"So he did his own research, then built that psychological bombshell around it?"

"You don't think it could be a coincidence?"

"No. I do not. After everything Richard's done since then, do you think it's a coincidence?"

Andrew paused. It had been a complicated story, but from Lillian's perspective she'd complicated it one step further than Andrew had managed alone. A very important step. Andrew stared over her shoulder, his hands slumping to his sides.

"No."

Lillian turned and walked down the carpet toward the empty throne. Andrew caught her by the shoulder, just before she passed water woman and went beyond his reach.

"Are you sure you're in the right mindset to do this?"

"I'm in the only mindset to do this. Wait here."

She pulled out of Andrew's grip and strode past the Lady of the Lake. Andrew's voice was cut off the moment she crossed the threshold. The strange silver-haired figure appeared in the throne in front of her when she was halfway to it, along with the heart rate monitor in the top corner of her HUD. It was at 68 beats per minute. Lillian hadn't been lying when she said she was calm. She was also angry, but she was more than capable of housing both states simultaneously. She was well practiced in that regard.

She drew to a stop in front of her interviewer and folded her arms, waiting somewhat impatiently for the first question. The mystery interviewer had steepled his fingers and was regarding her intently, waiting for her to make the first move. She refused to do so. She'd wait as long as it took.

Lillian was so angry, and so intent on containing it in her focused bubble of calm, she'd forgotten the first question was actually an order.

"Tell me about yourself."

There was one thing about Lillian that defined her above all others. Not a personality trait. Not a mindset. Not a core value. A mere event, the foundation upon which she'd constructed everything else.

"My father died when I was young. He was walking me to preschool when he was hit by a self-driving car. I don't know if you know what that is. Do you know what a car is? He was hit by a large mass of thinking, fast-moving metal, with people inside it. The car decided to veer off the road and murder us instead of putting the five people divided between itself and the other car in danger. An easy choice, especially since one of the passengers was pregnant."

Lillian nodded, her lips pressed together tightly. Her heart rate had barely risen, up to 76 beats per minute. She wasn't paying it any attention at all. She was so invested in her story, told without caring whether or not it was to her audience's liking, she didn't notice the lack of interruption. Her one-man audience was leaning in, compromising his completely rigid posture to bring his head just a little closer.

"It was an automated murder, plain and simple, but the company called it a "tragic accident". Then they praised their algorithm. Praised it! For a net increase in saved lives. Our family lost our primary source of income, but my mom got a heavy payout not to pursue the matter further. Considering how "logical" the algorithm was, we were lucky to get anything at all. *Justice is served.*"

She clenched her fists. Her bpm had risen to 83. They were entering the crux of it now.

"My mother waited until I was older, then used the money to send me away. She blamed me for what happened. She never said so outright but I know, because for a long time I blamed myself as well. There wasn't anyone else to blame. I went into medicine. Got a scholarship, so I wouldn't have to live off my father's blood money. I decided to spend my life inflicting meaning on a chaotic, indifferent world. If I can save just a few people from suffering like I did, maybe my life will have some purpose. That's who I am."

The figure on the throne turned his head to one side. Calculating. Of all the NPCs in Arcadia, she had to be judged by this one. Most of the NPCs were incredibly realistic, with mannerisms and turns of phrase that made it difficult to distinguish between them and regular players. This one acted almost exactly like a robot. Lillian wasn't even sure it would pass the Turing Test. She appeared to have passed the first section of her own test, though.

"Why do you want to wield Excalibur?"

Lillian didn't have to think about this question, either. She just said the first words that popped into her head.

"There's a man, called Magnitude. I need to kill him. Obtaining Excalibur is the fastest way of doing that."

This did not go down well. Lillian flinched as her judge, jury and executioner slammed his closed fist onto the armrest of his stone throne. It cracked under the force of the hit, the fracture running deep into the stone. Her host did not seem quite so robotic now. In fact, he suddenly seemed a great deal like her.

"Careful, Lillian. I was starting to like you."

"That's the most honest answer I have. I can explain myself if...oh, I see. The heart rate monitor isn't to see if I'm afraid, is it? Not exactly. You're also a lie detector."

Her interviewer suddenly sat bolt upright. It was only obvious how far he'd strayed from his rigid posture when he returned to it.

"That's impolite. I'm a truth detector. Besides which, discerning truth is only half useful. I also discern quality of truth."

"How's my quality of truth?"

"We'll find out, once you've explained why you deserve Excalibur for the sake of revenge."

"That's the thing. I don't think I deserve Excalibur. I first came to Arcadia to help someone else, but I've been doing everything out of self-interest for a while now. This quest, for instance. I wanted Excalibur for myself. I wanted to take back control. I forgot why I started playing, why I came to Arcadia in the first place. Which is why, until a short while ago, I was ready to quit this quest. More than that, I was ready to quit this world. Only, I couldn't convince my partner to come with me. Which made leaving pointless."

The silver stranger leaned back in. It was a good thing Lillian had built up enough credit with her first answer to survive her party foul.

"Go on?"

She turned and pointed at Andrew, who was standing half the room away, next to the Lady.

"You see that guy over there? He's the one who finally balanced me out. Most people learned to keep their distance, but he took a chance on me. He took the time to understand me and told me what I needed to hear. Magnitude turned us against each other, then stepped in and profited from it. I thought Aetherius wanted revenge, the same way you think I want it. I was sure that if he kept on this way he'd end up just as hollow as I am. Listening to him describe what was done to him, I realized revenge is the wrong word. It always has been. What he actually wants is what I've always wanted for myself. Closure. Meaning. Purpose."

"What closure, meaning or purpose could come through wielding Excalibur?"

Lillian laid out the conclusion of her verbal essay as honestly and concisely as she could.

"What Magnitude did to us, he's now extended to the whole Empire. If he succeeds through lies, manipulation and division, it will all be justified. Not only in his eyes, but in the eyes of everyone watching. I won't abandon Aetherius, and I can't stand by doing nothing in a world where inflicting suffering – for personal gain or out of so-called "necessity" – is regarded as the norm. I already have a world like that. Someone needs to give Magnitude's actions matching consequences, to inflict the order on this world that my own world lacks. That's something I'm prepared to fight for. Anytime. Anywhere."

Her host drummed his fingers on the armrest of his fractured chair as he scrutinized her. Lillian's heart rate was slowly dropping back to her resting rate. The heart rate monitor abruptly disappeared as her interviewer stood up. He walked rigidly down the steps to stand in front of her, looking her up and down.

"You're not perfect. But nor was Arthur. You'll do."

He put his hand out, still staring intently into her eyes. When Lillian didn't respond, he looked to his palm and then back to her. She put her hand out. He took it. They shook. He smiled.

"I look forward to working with you."

He held her hand tighter, still smiling, then blurred at the edges. His feet left the ground and Lillian was left supporting his weight. He was light as a feather. He was all quicksilver, his body compressing. His hand molded itself into a grip. His body straightened, becoming even stiffer and sharper than it was before. The transformation ended, the details wrought only after he'd returned to his true form.

Lillian was holding Excalibur.

A notification flashed belligerently in the corner of her HUD, just over the one declaring she'd reached level 51. The wording and the gilded presentation indicated it was not unique to her: a game-wide announcement.

Lillian has been judged worthy. Excalibur has consented to being guided by her hand. By divine right, she is hereby ordained Queen of Camelot. The Empire is hers to command.

As a person Excalibur had looked strange, as a sword it was excruciatingly wonderful. A hundred times more beautiful than she'd thought possible. She hadn't even been sure she wanted it. Now it was within her grasp, she thought her heart might break just looking at it. It was the most beautiful and the most famous sword in all the world. The stats it bore were no small part of its beauty.

Excalibur – Legendary Artifact
Level Requirement: N/A
Durability: ???/???
Damage: 510 (10 x current level) + (Strength x 3)
Stats: 255 Strength (5 x current level)
Description: The foundation of King Arthur's legend. A sword beyond compare. Can only be wielded by a noble soul.
Special Abilities: Divine Authority, Indestructible, Soul-bound

"Wow. Makes my artifact look like a toy."

Andrew was standing by her side, staring at Excalibur with

her. He reached out as if to touch it, then thought better and pulled his hand back, nursing his fingers as if he'd already been cut.

"You did it."

"No. We did it. Now comes the hard part."

26

DANCE WITH THE DEVIL

Damien had been trapped with Lucifer for at least half an hour. Not physically trapped, because the portal had remained open. He could only guess how long, since he couldn't open his menu. It was hard to keep time, with Lucifer interrupting him every few seconds by projecting into his skull.

"Come now, Damien. We both know you're being unreasonable."

Knowing the purpose of the messages was to aggravate him did not make them any more bearable. Much the opposite. Damien knew all he had to do to get out of this was submit. Every time he worked at the idea of it, Lucifer would pass another comment and Damien's inclination to make the smart choice would slip away.

"It must be a shock, realizing none of your success ever belonged to you. You'll have to get over it if you want our relationship to work."

Damien knew how important his character was to his new career. No one was coming to watch him. Not really. They were coming to see the occultist who'd won the competition. If his account was purged, he did not predict his viewers all transferring over to watch him start from scratch. Worse, he wouldn't be able to play an occultist again. If this was what awaited him, what would be the point?

"I have to say, you're the only person who's reacted like this to being told the truth. You're oversensitive."

Damien's thoughts were not on how to escape from this. That was easy. He could suck all this up, smile and nod, bow his way out and leave intact. He knew that. It would be so easy, so logical. He still had Magnitude and Archimonde to deal with. He might be able to go help Lillian and Andrew with their quest. It was the only sensible option, and rather than having to search for it he'd had it laid out in plain view. He just couldn't bring himself to do it. He'd rather die.

Magnitude and Archimonde represented significant threats, but this was a far worse problem. The two of them threatened to make the game unplayable for him if they weren't stopped. As his only path of progression, Lucifer made the game unplayable for him right now.

"You're the one who's forcing me to treat you like this. I'm not enjoying it any more than y—"

Damien spoke up for the first time since the portal had appeared.

"You can view private messages? That's a bit of an infringement on my rights, don't you think?"

"For hell's sake, now the boy's interrupting me."

It was projected into his head, just like everything else, but delivered as if it were an aside. Something Damien was not supposed to hear. It was almost comical, having a stage whisper beamed into his mind. Lucifer did not acknowledge the contradiction. He paced over to Damien, who raised his hands defensively and pointlessly. Lucifer stopped just short, placing his hands on his knees and stooping to Damien's level. As if he were addressing a toddler.

"Didn't your mother teach you to respect your elders? Am I to take it polite conversation does not form part of her curriculum? Or perhaps your bottomless entitlement indicates she's raised you poorly and isn't very good at her job?"

Damien had managed to control himself for a while. He'd avoided losing his temper at each and every one of Lucifer's unwanted intrusions. It was only an AI. What it thought didn't matter. What it said didn't matter. But even as Damien told himself this, he didn't believe it. This was the last straw. He may as well get an answer to his question before he headed on his way.

"I asked if—"

"Look at you! One mention of your mother is all it takes to turn you into a dribbling mess! You were even worse while she was in the hospital. You can barely do anything right without her holding your hand!"

The devil drew his enormous fists up to his burning eyes, twisting them violently in the angriest mime of mocking grief Damien had ever seen.

"My mahmee's in the ho-pi-tle. I'm shad, and angwee, and confustered, all at the saaaame time! I can't even get a Cowup-tion spell wight, and punching walls is my onwy way of conveying my emotions, because I wack the intelligence to expwess my feewings wike a normal person! Booo-hooo!"

Damien had obviously struck a nerve. Lucifer's rant had no end in sight. He'd stood up straight to cast his arms over Damien's head, the threat of violence kept in plain view without ever quite being fulfilled.

"I all but gave up on you after that introduction. The driving force I thought gave you a modicum of worth resulted in all kinds of idiotic mistakes. You were painful to look at. You indicated you were eighteen or over, but you behaved more like you were twelve, or younger. When your mother needed you most! What's wrong with you?"

If Damien had understood correctly, he was being judged as immature for not performing at 100% after his mom had nearly died in front of him. Lucifer's knowledge of these affairs was exactly what Damien had asked about, but Lucifer was paradoxically covering up the question by relentlessly attacking his character, using the very fact Damien had leveled against him as ammunition. If Lucifer saw the irony of what he was doing, he didn't make it known. If anything he was somehow inverting logic and passing it off as reason, redoubling his new unpleasantness to mask previous unpleasantness.

"You barely managed to scrape through, even though I thrust greatness upon you. All I ask is you show some respect, but you can't even manage that. You're an even bigger failure than Bartholomew. A laughable achievement, but the only one you've managed of your own accord."

Lucifer stopped ranting and gave a haughty nod. Asking more questions would only prompt similar non-answers. This was unsustainable. The only option Damien had left was to sever all ties. First, he'd feed Lucifer every single word and make him eat it. He had nothing to lose at that point anyway, except his temper. Damien could at the very least keep that.

"One thing my mother taught me: when a spoilt brat is having a tantrum, you let them tire themselves out first. If you're all tuckered out, it's my turn. I'm going to tell everyone you can access private messages."

Lucifer plucked up Damien by his throat. Damien didn't resist. He just smirked as his breathing became strained. He couldn't see his hit points, but they had to be dropping. In the real world, his apathy would be unfathomable. It didn't matter here. Not only because there was no actual threat of physical harm, but because Damien had decided to abandon his class.

If Lucifer killed him, Damien would be beyond his control. The same would happen if Damien left through the portal. Now it was only a question of which came first. Damien's victory was guaranteed. He didn't get guaranteed victories very often. Never, actually. He'd take his time enjoying this one.

Lucifer loosened his grip enough for Damien to breathe. He knew what Damien knew. He changed tactic, pulling Damien in close so his breath could rasp over Damien's face while he implanted new words in his mind.

"Go ahead. Tell anyone you like. I'll send out my own message, perfectly neutral, to counterbalance it. I might go with this one."

The words popped into Damien's field of vision of their own accord, the only trace of his long-absent HUD. They were not neutral.

We regret to inform our loyal player base that player

'Daemien' has knowingly abused a glitch in the occultist class without informing Mobius Enterprises. Saga Online does not tolerate cheating in any form, especially from a Mobius Enterprises employee. To serve as a warning, he has been stripped of his account.

Damien was still reading the words as Lucifer drawled over his thoughts.

"Yes, that should do nicely. When you start complaining, everyone will see you for the petulant, embryonic smear you are. No one will believe you."

He set Damien back down and dusted off his shoulders more forcefully than was needed, even if there'd been anything to brush away. He seemed confident the imbalance had been addressed.

"If you're done with your cute display of defiance, you can bow to me now."

The imbalance had become significantly more pronounced.

"Why? That doesn't change anything."

"Is that so? Your career ended, your legacy tarnished, all the progress I allowed you to make, lost. I have been a valuable, long-unappreciated ally. I've always been on your side. You do not want me as an enemy. Bow."

"No, I don't think I will. There's literally nothing you can do that will make me bow. I'm leaving. When you next see me, I'll be killing you. Goodbye."

He turned to walk through the portal and made it only a few steps before Lucifer blocked his path. Damien laughed at him as he threw Lucifer's words back in his terrifying face. All the threat was gone from it now he'd resolved to leave.

"What's wrong with *you*? You put this choice in front of me, so certain I'd do what you wanted. Now you're stopping me because my choice isn't to your liking?"

"I'm only trying to prevent you from making a mistake. Perhaps you don't believe these things will happen, but I assure you they will. You'll regret this."

Damien folded his arms and tilted his head, looking at Lucifer sideways.

"You're the one who's made a mistake. I don't "need" to play the game any more. I sorted my mom out, almost entirely on my own. No, wait, that's not true. I got a lot of help, but not from you. Bartholomew's "dark offering" to become an occultist doesn't count, because he threatened to eat me if I didn't accept. Pretty much the same method you're using. You said the two of you aren't similar. You're right: you're almost exactly the same."

Lucifer struck him across the face, sending Damien tumbling across the sand. Hmm. Yes. The floor was made out of sand over here, too. Whatever. His pain settings were as low as they could be. He'd have endured this at any pain threshold, or so he'd like to think. Damien continued talking from the floor without bothering to get up. Getting up would imply that's the state he'd prefer to be in when it really wasn't very important.

"I didn't have to become an occultist. I could've invested my efforts into saving my mom any number of ways, both in and outside of Saga Online. Occultism was the first option that came along I could work with. You were just lucky to pick me up early. Besides, you didn't draft me as an occultist to help me. You needed to draw attention to your undersubscribed class. Now you're framing it as though you did me a favor, when it is *I* who did *you* the favor. Don't be shy. You can say 'Thank you, Damien'. Maybe give me a little bow to show your grati—"

Lucifer picked him up by the top of his head and held him there.

"I can make this very unpleasant for you. I won't grant you the sweet release of death. I'll hold you here and make you suffer. That's my job. Unlike you or your dear meemaw, I'm highly proficient at it."

Could Lucifer do that? Not really. He could stop him from logging out directly with damage perhaps, but Damien could still die. Hopefully. It didn't make any difference either way. He'd already decided.

"You can't keep me here forever. You know that. This is only a matter of time. The longer you make it for me, the worse I'll eventually make it for you. I guarantee it."

"With no class, at level 1, no fanbase, no income for playing and no reason to continue? Forgive me for not shaking in my cloven hooves."

"I won't be playing professionally anymore, but I'll manage it in my free time. One day, someone will show up here. Could be anyone. You won't recognize them, because I'll change my face and keep my communications limited. I'll kill you and I'll make sure you know it was me before you go. You'll have that to look forward to for the rest of your short life, because of what you're about to do to me now. Have fun, while you can."

Damien wasn't looking forward to this, but at least he'd already secured his victory. Now he'd just have to pay back the debt. This was gonna suck. At least he'd already ensured he'd win. All that was left was to accept the consequences of his actions.

Lucifer raised his hand, claws bared, and Damien squeezed his eyes shut. He'd dealt with worse than this. The pain would be simulated. He wouldn't actually be harmed. That would be the first point he clung to, as the pain wore on. He'd not stand up to torture, but since he'd already removed the option of bowing his way out that didn't matter. He'd just have to endure as best he could and wait for an opportunity to end this encounter prematurely. He was still wincing in advance of the pain when Lucifer's voice blared into his skull.

"Your judgment has proven accurate, Bartholomew. He's insufferably arrogant. I'm most pleased."

"I did insist he was a worthy candidate, my lord."

Damien opened his eyes to find Bartholomew standing by Lucifer's side. Lucifer released his grip, allowing Damien to drop to the floor. Lucifer inclined his head, ever so slightly, and Damien's HUD was restored. Then he turned away, wiping his hand down on Bartholomew's robe.

"Had you put him forward for the role of Wrath, this would've been considerably simpler."

"That is true, my lord, but that position is taken. I felt you'd be more inclined to fill an empty seat. I also felt aiming for anything less than the top spot would not accommodate his full potential. I was confident Daemien would make the grade, given his past behavior and my interactions with him."

A quick check of Damien's long-lost HUD showed his live recording had automatically been stopped. None of this had been visible to anyone outside of this room. He didn't know whether to be relieved that his experience hadn't been shared, or perturbed that no one would believe him if he relayed it to them.

Damien had gone from being the object of Lucifer's unwanted attention to being completely ignored. They were talking about him as if he weren't in earshot, as if he simply did not exist. This was somehow worse than torture. He pulled himself to his feet while Lucifer continued chatting with Damien's former master.

"My doubts were valid, Bartholomew. It took a great deal of exacerbation to elicit the required—"

"Hi guys! I'm still here! Can someone explain—"

Lucifer raised a hand and placed the palm over Damien's face.

"Quiet, whelp. Grown-ups are talking. We'll let you know when you're allowed to speak."

Damien stepped back. Nah. He'd had it up to here. No more games.

"No thanks. Enjoy your chat."

He drew a kunai and turned its point toward his own chest, holding it in both hands. His health was still low from the ground slam. He was leaving.

"Damien, you passed!"

Bartholomew had blurted it out, the concern in his voice undeniable. Damien kept the kunai held over his chest. At least now he wasn't being ignored.

"He's just demanding attention, Bartholomew. Don't give it to him. It will only encourage him."

Bartholomew prostrated himself before Lucifer, clutching at his hooves and kissing them. Doing what his former pupil could not.

"My lord, please. You've already demonstrated his Sin. Pushing him further will only undo your expert work in drawing it out of him. I will take responsibility for his disrespect, since I was his teacher."

"Your former master knows his place, Damien. Perhaps you left his charge early. Fine. You shall have the attention you so desperately crave."

He held his hand out.

"Give me the item Toutatis dropped. I shall fashion it into a unique piece that reflects your...tendencies. Or just kill yourself. There are thousands like you I can turn to. I'm not fussed."

Nothing to lose, Damien supposed. He kept the kunai over his heart as he placed the black gem into Lucifer's outstretched palm. Lucifer cupped it in both hands.

"Bartholomew is familiar with this power. I loaned it to him in his battles against Aetherius. It was unstable, unrooted, he could only sustain it for a few minutes. Not least of all because he already harbors his own true Sin, which he refuses to use to its fullest extent. For you, it will be a perfect match."

Lucifer's hands were radiating immense heat. His fingers were glowing, the bones visible through his incandescent flesh. Damien could see the shape of the gem in the middle of them. It was becoming a pentagram.

"Remove your tunic, Damien. I will embed my Sin into you directly."

"You want me to strip?"

"I've seen it all before, Damien, your body is nothing special. I require access to your chest. In this instance, removing your tunic will suffice."

Damien looked to Bartholomew, who was cowering on the floor a few feet away. Bartholomew nodded, feverishly. Not exactly the best endorsement for having hands laid upon him by Satan. Part of Damien wanted to see where this led. If he was prepared to submit to potential hours of torture, this was a very short leap.

Damien removed his chest armor and put his weapons away. Worst-case scenario, he'd reject all this and go back to being tortured. There was no harm in checking this path before he reconsigned himself to the more difficult and less rewarding one.

Lucifer grabbed him by the shoulder and pulled his other arm back, the pentagram glowing in his hand.

"This will hurt. It's for your own good."

He thrust his palm over Damien's heart and pressed the burning symbol into his flesh. The only thing worse than the pain was the smell. Lucifer held it there as Damien gritted his teeth. He wouldn't give him the satisfaction of crying out. The prospect of enduring a few hours of this seemed quite silly, all of a sudden. The procedure had an absurdly efficient pain-to-damage ratio.

It took a whole five seconds, after which Lucifer released his grip and admired his handiwork. Damien looked down and found his body had been marked. It was a tattoo that was not a tattoo. It was hard, and heavy. He tapped it and it clinked to the touch, then pulsed painfully.

"Go on, take a look. Maybe you'll finally realize how favored you are."

Damien was in his menu in seconds, where two very peculiar notifications awaited his inspection. The first was flashing gold. The other was a deep shade of purple. He opened the gold one first.

Lillian has been judged worthy. Excalibur has consented to being guided by her hand. By divine right, she is hereby ordained Queen of Camelot. The Empire is hers to command.

She did it. Damien forgot where he was, everything he'd been through, and smiled. Lillian. Queen of Camelot. A reckoning was coming. If he'd got a notification, so had everyone else. Somewhere, out there, beneath the pale moonlight, Magnitude was thinking of her, and screaming into his pillow tonight.

"Is that all you can manage? A smile? For the greatest gift I can bestow?"

At least Lucifer couldn't see through his eyes. He thought Damien was looking at his own notification. Good to know.

Damien kept the smile plastered to his face as he opened the second notification. This one was personal.

You are the Sin of Pride. You have gained a new ability. Check your Skill List.

He did as he was told, scrolling down the list to find what was new. It was in the Demonology tree. As he read it, everything clicked into place:

Embodiment of Sin
Soul energy: 10
Description: You place a hand on your dark mark and speak the name of your Sin, whereupon you are transformed into its Embodiment, the unfettered form of one of the lesser demons in your thrall. Your physical form and attributes will be improved and new combat options will become available upon transformation. The transformation lasts until you are killed or the ability is canceled, which is performed through the same action as activating it.

"Bartholomew mentioned you're a slow reader. It has long been known your pride lies in your physical abilities, rather than your intellectual ones. Needs must, I suppose."

Damien reequipped his chest armor and closed his menu, the mark throbbing against the leather with each heartbeat. Hopefully that would fade after a while. Even if it didn't, it was worth it for this ability. This was why Archimonde looked the way he did. He was also an Embodiment of Sin. This is why Archimonde had tried so hard to keep him from entering the Dark Tower. Damien was all caught up. Now he could go to bed. He turned to his ungracious host.

"I'm quite tired. It's been *lovely* meeting you Lucifer, and to see you again, Bart, in these unexpected circumstances. If that takes care of everything, I'm off."

"We're not done here, Damien. I'd be remiss to allow your departure before you've paid your respects. Before, you were my far-flung underling. I am now your direct and only superior. You will enjoy superiority over all the lesser Sins. Bartholomew included."

"I'm Bartholomew's superior?"

If Lucifer had lips, Damien was sure they'd be twisting upward.

"You are. Of course, you fall below me in the hierarchy, so my orders will supersede any you give. Naturally. The hierarchy must be respected. I can perfectly understand why you were reluctant to submit to me before. Oh, yes. Quite understandable. But now I've granted you such a high honor, I remain hopeful you can see some sense? I can take the mark away, just as easily as I granted it. Along with everything else."

He put his head on Damien's shoulder and embraced him. Damien stood rigidly, with Bartholomew nodding at him fervently and throwing two thumbs way up from behind Lucifer's back. All Damien could manage was a pair of pats on Lucifer's shoulder while he tried to conceal how appalled he was with himself. It was enough. Lucifer drew back, holding his shoulders in both hands to look him over.

"Since you've proven yourself as Pride, I'll put this as gently as I can. I have guided you to become an occultist, which has turned out very well for you. I put you against Toutatis at the end of my dungeon, because I knew that would be your heart's desire. I accepted Bartholomew's request to consider you for the role of Pride, my highest honor. I subjected you to rigorous testing only to ensure you wouldn't be a disappointment. I got no pleasure out of it, I assure you. Isn't that right, Bartholomew?"

"Absolutely, my lord, no pleasure out of it whatsoever."

"Isn't that right, Damien?"

"I completely understand."

Lucifer ruffled his hair, making Damien's skin crawl.

"Spoken like a true aspect of Pride. I'm afraid, for my benefit, you will have to go against your tendencies to retain your position. You must show at least a little gratitude. Not only for all

I've granted you, but because your new position makes it a requirement. I believe I made it clear that you must bow."

Damien at least wanted to see what this transformation would do for him before he ran the threat of his character being wiped. He also wanted to see the practical applications of Lucifer's assertion of his superiority. At least now he had something of practical worth to show for his visit. This was his victory. That's what he told himself, not really feeling it, as he bowed.

"There, that wasn't so hard, was it? Well done. Good boy. Anyway, I tire of your presence, I have more important things to do. I believe you have some affairs to deal with before the end of this weekend? I shall summon you here again, after you've had time to enjoy your new position. I hope I shall find you more pliable when we next meet. Bartholomew, take Pride back to your dwelling with you."

Bartholomew snapped his fingers and a new portal opened. He grabbed Damien and wheeled him backward through it, bowing to Lucifer with every step. They passed through it into the Downward Spiral and with a final bow, Bartholomew closed the way through. He immediately turned to Damien and shook him up and down, laughing like a maniac.

"You did it! My own student, the Embodiment of Pride! I might be even more proud than you are! I kid, of course, that's not possi—"

Damien pulled out of his grip and began the log-out procedure. He spoke to Bartholomew through the ten-second timer.

"Don't talk to me. Don't even look at me. I'll be back here tomorrow, you can explain yourself then. Bartholomew, Scourge of the World, sending me to the devil without a word of warni—"

The logout ended. Damien was back in his room. Thoroughly annoyed, still not certain he'd made the right choice, he stared into the wall for a long time before he fell asleep. So much for his stable career.

27

THE TURN

"What time did you leave the game?"

Damien screwed his eyeballs shut to pump blood into them. It felt as though he'd fallen asleep minutes ago. Cassandra, true to form, had been banging on his door hard enough to make it rattle on the hinges. She'd probably been at it for a while. As soon as he answered, she'd taken one look and sent him straight back to bed. His breakfast arrived on a tray fifteen minutes later, a phenomenon usually reserved for when he was sick.

He was in no state to hide the truth from her. Especially since she knew something was amiss. She'd sat with him and started probing the moment he was sitting upright. It had taken minutes for her to pry the events of that morning from him. Damien kept his eyes averted as he continued playing down the events of that early morning.

"I can't remember. As soon as it was over I logged out, didn't look at the time."

"What's your best guess?"

"Maybe 1:30?"

"You were unable to log out for over an hour, while some garish version of a mythological evil figure psychologically tortured you."

"It was much less than an hour, I probably got the time

wrong. Most of it was just words, he only started hitting me toward the end and that didn't bother me. My pain settings were low, and even if they'd been high—"

Cassandra grabbed the back of his wrist and squeezed it.

"First and foremost, Damien Arkwright—"

Damien winced. She only used his second name, his father's name, when she had something very serious to say.

"Never, ever dismiss pain like that. Yours or anyone else's. I know how that works. Just because the pain is in your head, doesn't mean it's not real. That goes as much for what Lucifer said as for when he hit you. Don't play down what happened, like you're trying on me. I expect you to make a full complaint to Kevin, like you did for Lillian. Will you do that?"

Damien nodded, still keeping his attention completely focused on his plate. So much for getting his mom off his back. Cassandra waited until he was looking at her to speak.

"It's not just a game. This is the first time you've had some control over your own circumstances. I approve, for the most part. I hope after what happened to you this morning you don't mind if I voice my concerns?"

"Is there any way I can stop you?"

"No. But it won't make any difference if you don't listen."

Damien put the tray to one side and took his mom's hand in both of his. Cassandra shuffled up the edge of his bed to sit closer to him.

"You already know I've been watching you play. I have no idea what's going on but you're obviously good at it. They all die, you stay alive, most of the time. That's the idea, right? That's not what bothers me. You don't seem very happy when you're playing."

"That's not true! I love playing Saga!"

"Yes, darling, but you can love something without enjoying it."

"How does that make any sense?"

Cassandra gave him a wry smile.

"I love working as a kindergarten teacher. I don't enjoy it very much."

Damien was bewildered. She'd never said anything like that before.

"How do you mean?"

"Well, I teach because I want to help raise kids, to make sure they're getting everything they need emotionally and morally. It wasn't always that way, I sort of fell into the job. I started when we left your father because I needed to look after you and work at the same time. Kindergarten teaching was pretty much my only option, other than dancing on a table for money while you stayed in a back room."

No matter how many times she made variations of this joke, it was embarrassing without fail.

"Mom! Stop it!"

"No darling, I'm only joking, that was never going to happen. I applied to a place but they wouldn't take me. Heart condition. I might go for a career change, now you've got me a new one."

"MOM!"

Cassandra laughed hard and Damien's pang of annoyance was quickly replaced with contentment. He'd accomplished this. Not only had he managed to bring things back to normal, he'd improved their situation tenfold. A hundredfold. A thousandfold. More than that. It was immeasurable. The misery Cassandra had been carrying with her for well over a decade was all gone, thanks to his hard work. Now he just had to do whatever it took to keep it away. Cassandra took his attention again and continued where she'd left off.

"I understand how you feel. At least I think I do. I started teaching because I had to. Not the most noble reason for entering this vocation, but there you are. My health meant changing jobs wasn't wise, but that's not the only reason I stuck with it: I'm good at it. My children care about me and I care about them. That's something I can't say for everyone who enters this career, no matter how well trained they are or how many pieces of paper they have. I feel like I'm making a difference, that what I'm doing is important. I have the chance to change a lot of people's lives for the better. It's only for a little while, but it's a crucial time. If I do really well, the children take a piece of me with them when they go. Is your job like that?"

"If the people I work with take a piece of me when they go, that means I've made a mistake."

Damien thought it was funny, but it went straight over his mother's head. Maybe. Or perhaps she just was reluctant to give him an easy way out. Either way, she remained silent. Damien filled the void.

"Yeah, I guess some of it's like that. Don't know how important it is but it keeps the subscribers entertained. It feels like half of them are waiting for me to fail and the other half would support me no matter what I do. It's very strange."

Cassandra gave his hands a squeeze.

"At least you've got half your audience in the bag. That's still a lot of pressure to carry. I used to get anxiety standing up in front of kids to give a thirty-minute lesson! Mind you, they're better behaved than your audience. I've seen the comments section on your videos. Some of your viewers could do with sitting in on my classes."

"I'll let them know."

"I doubt they'd appreciate that."

Damien perked up a bit more. This conversation was proving much more restful than his sleep had been. He'd been preparing himself for a stoic defense of his streaming career, he hadn't thought they'd have an open conversation like this. Cassandra was expertly working him. Lulling him into a sense of security before she drove her point home. Every word drew her closer to her goal.

"I got past the anxiety of teaching the lessons pretty quickly. It's just a question of learning to hold their attention. The only difference between you and me is that I do it with about thirty kids for half an hour a day, whereas you do it with up to a million people at a time for anywhere between fifteen minutes and six hours. No big difference between us, really."

"Your job still sounds harder than mine."

"I wish that were true. Still, there's another area of overlap for us. After I got used to keeping the kids on the right track, I realized the real problem. Looking after the children is easy. They say what they want, they show how they're feeling, they push boundaries to see what they can and can't get away with. All very straightforward. Eventually, I get to know them well enough that I can see what will happen long before it occurs. Sometimes they try to catch me out, doing things in devious ways when they think I'm not looking, but they're not very good at it. I let them think I'm not looking, when I'm waiting to turn at the exact moment they snatch a toy, or spit in their neighbor's food just to make them cry. They haven't had enough time to practice, so I get the chance to guide them away from such behaviors. The real problem, and I'm sure you'll understand me on this, is the adults. The problem with adults, Damien, is they have agendas."

Damien's spidey sense was tingling. He didn't know what it meant.

"Why is that a problem?"

"A child can only think in the short term. Their wants are limited to their immediate futures, somewhere in the next five minutes or less. That makes them easy to predict. I can redirect them before they've started their plans, or have my own plan in place before they've taken the first step of their own. Sometimes I can even lay ambushes for them, which they run toward head-first without ever imagining I set it up to teach them an important lesson. Adults hide what they're feeling. They have hidden agendas, which they'll do anything to meet. If you block their path, they'll either force you to walk it with them or they'll remove you from it. They won't explain their reasoning, because their reasoning will often be indefensible and they know it. If they do it well enough, you won't know why. If they're *really* clever, you won't even know who."

Cassandra's voice had become increasingly urgent, her hands tightening as she spoke. Damien flexed his fingers and she somewhat relaxed her grip, though her eyes still watered.

"Your job is not easier than mine. There are people who've been doing this for longer than you who want you to fail. This streaming career has a good income, but there's a reason for that. It's extreme. It's competitive. And it's unstable because you're in other people's way. You've been exposed to a deeply unconducive environment. I'm worried it's having an effect on your development."

Too late, Damien realized where this was headed. She was taking the headset away again. She'd created a perfect choke point and he'd unwittingly been led straight down it. He was locked in.

Cassandra sprung her maniacal trap.

"If this goes wrong, I don't want you to imagine for a moment that it's your fault. You shouldn't have to think this way so soon. You're not a child anymore, but you're not quite an adult yet, either. That's why I went back to work early, so if it got too hard you'd know you don't have to do this any longer than you want to. I'll be here if you want a sounding board at any time, however things go, but the only person you need to answer to is yourself. I'll try to make sure you don't judge yourself too harshly."

Cassandra leaned forward and kissed him on the forehead. Damien sat in stunned silence, feeling as though the rug had been swept from under his feet and then somehow put back again.

"I love you very much. I'm late for work but we can talk about this tonight if you feel like it? Or earlier. Or later. I promise I won't bring it up again unless you bring it up first. Is that okay?"

Damien, jaw slightly ajar, nodded slowly.

"Thank you, mom. I love you, too. I promise I'll do my best."

"You don't need to promise me that, I know you will. Your best is more than good enough for me. Love you. Eat your breakfast before it gets any colder."

She blew him a kiss through the doorway and was gone. The front door to their house shut less than half a minute later, leaving Damien frozen in place. That put things in perspective. At least Cassandra wouldn't have to wait long. He'd definitely be talking about it with her, very soon. Right after he'd had some time to figure out what to make of it.

Damien picked up the tray and carried it to his work station. He could gaze into his screen, chew on his breakfast and ponder his mother's words all at the same time. Like multitasking, except he'd be doing all of them inefficiently at once. He jabbed at the screen with one hand as he fished for food and directed it into his face with the other, but hadn't finished the first mouthful before the front page loaded, taking up the entirety of his attention.

1. **War! Lillian begins conscription to fight Magnitude and the Carlisle-Elite.**
2. **Lillian, Camelot's new ruler. What does she know? Does she know things? Let's find out! Click here to see her profile.**
3. **Round Two! Daemien collects new gear and beats Toutatis at the top of the Dark Tower! Highlights**
4. **Carlisle-Elite open recruitment to all Empire heroes over level 40. Goooood morning Frozen Forest!**
5. **Do you want to train your very own baby dragon? You do? Well you're in the WRONG GAME. So says Beastmaster Cubbs in an interview explaining the finer points of his niche class.**

Damien had made it to third place on the front page. He could've been first, if not for Lillian achieving the ever so slightly more prestigious accomplishment of taking over a whole faction. Hmmph. He was happy for her. Shame Mordred had killed him the first time round, otherwise he might've been right at the top. He'd still attained a great deal of visibility for his channel. It didn't seem as important as it had before his talks with Lucifer and his mom respectively, but it was an accomplishment nonetheless.

A new class emerges. Hardly the most important thing going on, but interesting all the same. As much as Damien would've liked a baby dragon, he already had enough problems managing his own personal zoo. Which reminded him: Noigel was due his reward. He needed to have a word with Bartholomew. He needed to find out what was happening with Lillian. Andrew, too. He had no home base anymore, so he'd have to sort that out as well. Somewhere in the middle of all this he needed to review his footage and make his own highlights and commentary, to double down on the exposure he was getting.

He kept feeding himself as he went into his messages with Lillian. Their communication had been spotty over the last few days, to put it mildly. He suddenly felt a little guilty for not doing a better job of staying in touch. Then again, she'd been more or less the same. They'd both been busy. Now would be a good time to reconnect properly, although she was probably busier than ever. He brought up her chat box.

Daemien: Lillian, saw the notification yesterday and just saw the front page, congrats! What's happening in Camelot? I'd take a look myself but it's not really my scene. I guess you're pretty busy. Let me know when you have time to talk, we haven't caught up properly in ages!

That would do the trick. She'd probably get around to it sometime that evening, after she'd got a handle on running the kingdom. Damien was navigating to the Council of Nine page to get an unhealthy dose of adoration when the chat box blipped.

Lillian: Need you here. War prep. Sending a squad to pick you up. Where do they need to go?

Hell's bells.

Daemien: Where is 'here'?

Lillian: Camelot's War Room. Don't worry, it'll be a big squad.

Daemien: The Empire guards will kill me if I set foot in the city!

Lillian: The Empire guards are the ones coming to pick you up. Very busy. Tell me where they should get you from.

Daemien: I can get to the front gate myself. If they wait there for me I'll show up.

Lillian: When?

Damien was gobbling his breakfast down as fast as he could, alternating between stuffing himself and typing.

Daemien: As soon as possible. I'll message when I'm ten minutes out?

Lillian: Sure. Faster is better.

What did she need him in Camelot for? This would be an unexpected treat. He hadn't set foot there since he'd played as Scorpius, always thinking he could go back whenever he pleased. His first time in Camelot on this account, and he'd already hit level 50.

He finished off his breakfast, hastily mopped up what he'd missed and stuck his headset back on. The nodules comfortably refilled the indentations he'd accumulated over the course of wearing the thing for the last week. He'd been on it so often it was changing the shape of his damn head. No time to worry about that just now. He adjusted the pillow under his neck so the H4ckz0r might bite into his cranium a little less, and folded his hands over his chest.

He opened his eyes in the middle of Bartholomew's dungeon and found himself standing at the epicenter of a large pile of corpses, human and rat alike. It appeared the introduction of his Login Sphere to Bartholomew's carefully controlled occultist recruitment scheme had not come without consequences. Namely, all the would-be recruits' sneaking and patient waiting had been replaced with a no-holds-barred bloodbath, brought on by the arrival of his single light source.

"Winner, winner, craven sinner!"

Bartholomew began pulsing light and the lone, shattered-rib-equipped survivor limped his way over. They were not alone. All Damien's summons were stood neatly against the wall, the sole succubus and nine imps practically pushing their noses into the cold stone. Bartholomew had less patience for their antics than Damien did.

Damien had all but forgotten about them in the wake of yesterday's interrogation, followed by his need to get away from Bart himself. It was something of a relief to see they hadn't been lost. Not that it made up for what Bartholomew had done.

Bartholomew finished vetting his newest recruit and shut down his light display, floating over to where Damien was waiting for him. To his credit, Damien's first three words were on track for how he intended the conversation to go.

"Good morning, Bartholomew."

"Good morning, Daemien."

"No it isn't! Don't be polite! Not after everything—"

He caught himself, roughly folding his arms across his chest and grumbling in lieu of shouting more. The newly ordained occultist was tiptoeing around them, doubtlessly looting and collecting the souls of the fallen. Their quality was too low for Damien to perceive. Damien addressed them directly.

"Congrats on becoming an occultist. You might've found it hard but trust me, that was the easy part. Here's a tip: don't believe *anything* this guy tells you. He's the worst quest-giver of all time! I guarantee it."

The guy, named 'StabbyMcFace', stared at Damien open-mouthed for the duration of Damien's advisory. As soon as Damien stopped speaking, StabbyMcFace abruptly fled for the outer wall. Damien couldn't say he blamed him, although the advice had been sincere. Stabby wouldn't know until it was too late. Just another warm body for Bart's pyramid scheme. Damien took a deep breath and turned his attention back to Bart, who'd been waiting without so much as a word.

"The Path of Deceit is *your* path, Mr. "I hold liars in higher regard". This gear has your name all over it, literally."

"I'm flattered you chose my path. My "gear" looks good on you."

"Yeah, it does. Shame you didn't tell me it existed. You just sent me on my merry way with only the vaguest hint it might be worthwhile. That's bad enough, but it doesn't come *close* to signing me up for a one-on-one torture session with the devil."

Bartholomew touched down on the floor. Was it Damien's imagination or had he become...taller than his former master? Bartholomew had always loomed over him, though that was a given since the vampire usually hovered around. Now they were standing on even ground, Damien was the one looming over him.

The thought only entered his mind for an instant before

Bartholomew negated it. He was bowing. Just that was enough to make Damien reel. It went against every interaction they'd ever shared. It became worse when Bartholomew began to simper at him.

"I'm deeply sorry for the nature of your trial, but this is the world we live in. The devil is our master. The only way to advance is to court him. I did my utmost to push you as far as you could go, the purview of any great master. There is no higher station in the devil's employ than that which you have attained, and no other means by which you could have attained it."

He was keeping his head bowed. When Damien had been informed of his place directly under Lucifer in the hierarchy, he thought he'd enjoy his newfound superiority. It actually made him feel a little sick. This viewpoint was all too similar to what he'd seen through Lucifer's eyes. Now he was in Lucifer's position.

Worse than that, Bart was employing a tool Damien had seen him use only rarely: sincerity. Despite himself, Damien could feel his anger fading. However, he did his best not to let Bartholomew off the hook.

"All this time, you've either been lying to me or concealing things from me. You never even told me who we were working for."

"The master's job is not to tell the student what to do, it is to set them on the path to knowledge. What you have, you earned through your own hard work. A distinction your new master will not make."

Bartholomew tilted his head up ever so slightly to look at Damien's face. What he saw must have encouraged him, because what he said next sounded much more like the Bartholomew Damien knew.

"And while it's true I never explicitly mentioned the source of our power, it hardly merited explanation. Where did you think our abilities came from? The tooth fairy?"

Bartholomew had no sooner spoken the words than he hunched his shoulders and stared at the floor. Damien had accustomed himself to Bartholomew's humor over the course of his tutelage. It made him very uncomfortable to watch his mentor cower in front of him, just for being himself.

"Stop doing that! Just because I'm angry it doesn't mean I'll hit you."

"That's what they all say, at first."

This was impossible. Damien knew Bartholomew was just an AI, that he could technically do anything to him and it wouldn't have any meaning. But it would have meaning to Damien. He knew what he wanted now, far more clearly.

"Can we go back to talking the way we used to? I want a proper argument, not this kowtowing rubbish. If you say something that goes too far, I'll tell you."

Bartholomew hesitantly stood up straight. He still looked a little nervous.

"If that's your command—"

"Oh for— yes, fine, I *command* you to speak to me as an equal. Although I do have some questions I'd like you to answer. Honestly, if you can. If I'm Pride, what are you? Lucifer said you had your own Sin. What is it?"

Bartholomew's jaw unhinged and he stuck his tongue out. Damien thought Bart had drastically misinterpreted what 'equal' meant until he saw the black mark imprinted on his oratory organ. It was a pentagram, the same symbol Lucifer had imprinted over Damien's heart. Bartholomew's jaw snapped shut.

"I am Gluttony. I rank fifth among the Sins. It's a pleasure to finally introduce myself to you properly, Daemien. Or should I refer to you as Pride?"

"Daemien will do just fine, thanks. I have more questions but I also have the Queen of Camelot waiting for an audience with me. Thank you for your honesty. It must've been difficult."

"It's far easier to be honest than it is to lie, and far less rewarding. I don't hold liars in higher regard for nothing, you know. I may continue to indulge myself here and there."

That Damien could believe. While Bartholomew was superb at twisting words, no amount of verbiage would negate the difficulties Damien had encountered over the last week. Damien would not let that go unanswered. While they'd been talking, he'd been scheming.

Damien needed a new base, and Noigel needed his long-overdue reward. There was some definite overlap to be exploited here, as well as a precedent for Bartholomew fulfilling Damien's most basic need. Once he'd hit upon the idea, the rest of it came to Damien almost of its own accord.

He checked the wall, where Bartholomew had placed all his minions in permanent time-out, until he found Noigel. The imp was within earshot. Damien spoke clearly to make sure Noigel would hear him.

"Can you open up my old base for me? It'll only be temporary, I'll deconstruct everything and move out before the end of the week."

Bartholomew glanced at him sidelong.

"Is that a request? Or an order disguised as one? If it's a request, the answer is no. I still don't share living space. If it's an order, I'm obliged to do as you say. So, Daemien, will you order me to go against my wishes? Or will you change your plan on my account?"

Damien narrowed his eyes. Of course he could just order Bart to do it, but he wanted to outsmart his former master rather than playing the rank card and forcing his hand. Bart needed to make this mistake willingly.

"You're a piece of work, you know that? Neither. I'm not requesting it and I certainly won't order it. What do you want in exchange for letting me have my base here for a couple of days, Gluttony?"

"A favor in kind. A quest you will embark on in the future, for my own benefit rather than yours. That would fit your assertion that I'm the worst quest-giver of all time, would it not? Do you find that acceptable, Pride?"

Bartholomew had adjusted quickly to Damien's rank. He was still a little behind on Damien's intentions. Damien sealed the trap.

"Sure, one quest in exchange for housing my base to the end

of the week. It will be *my* base, though. No interfering in my affairs or the deal's off. Copacetic?"

Damien held his hand out. Bartholomew had always been reluctant to touch him, making a show of wiping his hands off on his robes afterward and complaining bitterly. Not this time. Bartholomew grabbed his hand and shook it firmly. Damien could get used to this 'Pride' thing.

"I return your demons to you. I won't demand reparations for having looked after them all this time, given the conditions you've been subjected to of late, but I trust you appreciate it has been an unwanted chore. Come this way, young master."

He waved a hand while speaking and Damien's minions returned to his Soul Summon Limit, with Noigel immediately jumping onto his shoulder and clinging to him. The imp seemed needy. Nine hours of being saddled with Bartholomew would do that to anyone.

Bartholomew carved open Damien's old space in his dungeon, inclined his head and left him to it. Damien wasted no time in putting his imps to work, taking the rubble left over from Bartholomew's handiwork to craft it into a Soul Well. With Noigel, eight imps and a succubus to Bloodlust them, it was quick work. When they'd finished the first tier, Damien dismissed two imps and tapped the Soul Well ten times to fill it with the soul energy from Toutatis.

It was great to have a high Soul Summon Limit, but his Soul Reserve was still unchanged. He could only hold 10 souls at a time. It was a good thing he'd preserved them rather than testing his new 'Pride' form earlier. He reopened his chat box to Lillian.

Daemien: I should be at the front gate of Camelot in about fifteen minutes.

Lillian: Faster, please. The squad will be waiting for you.

Alright. Only one thing left to do. He dismissed all his imps except for Noigel and one other. He needed one in order to be able to leave the dungeon without having to pick his way through Bartholomew's demons and traps, after which he'd dismiss that one too. Any demons would render the daytime stealth from his gear's 'Sunset Emperor' set bonus somewhat pointless. First, though, he bound Noigel and the succubus to the Soul Well before addressing his long-suffering minion.

"This is all yours until I'm back. The two of you can do whatever you want for as long as you want. You'll have the rest of the day, with more succubi added as we go, but you should have at least an hour to start with. Go nuts. Make as much noise as you feel like. Let me know if Bartholomew gives you any trouble and I'll tell him off."

He turned and walked through the archway, trying to leave before Bartholomew could figure out what he'd done. As planned, he sent his remaining imp flying up to the top of the dungeon to make an expedient getaway. It was not quite at the top when the first howl emanated from Damien's temporary base. It sounded like a cat in heat was being crushed by a pneumatic press. Perfect.

Bartholomew stared at the entrance to Damien's base in abject horror. He slowly twisted his neck to stare at Damien himself. Damien realized he was smiling a little too broadly. Oh well. Might as well own it.

"Remember Bartholomew, we have an agreement. No further interference in my affairs. If Noigel reports you bothered him I will order you to do everything you've already agreed to. I'm sorry for the nature of your trial but this is, as you put it, the world we live in. Good morning, Bartholomew."

He looked up and Demon Gated to his waiting imp. Noigel's howls were still audible from the very top of the dungeon. Damien knew Noigel was only making the noise for show. He was usually fairly quiet when he was fulfilling his "urges". Nor had Damien ordered Noigel to make noise. He'd simply encouraged him to do so, if that's what he wanted. It must've been very boring, standing with his nose pressed against the wall for nearly nine hours.

As soon as Damien's Demon Gate imp had returned to his side he dismissed it and set off through the trees. Noigel's howling faded as he pushed through the foliage. He crouched down in the warmth of the sun to check his 'Sunset Emperor' functioned as advertised before breaking into a run.

Damien could find cover and crouch if anything showed up, but Tintagel was a starting zone. He was probably the most dangerous entity here by a long way, although he avoided the roads to steer clear of any Empire NPC patrols.

Now he was alone, Damien could focus on himself. He was definitely bigger than he used to be. Not quite Hammertime-sized, but definitely bigger than when he logged out yesterday. His body was proportionally unchanged, so he didn't *feel* bigger. It would be more accurate to say the world felt smaller. More of the ground was passing under his feet with each step. Combined with his much improved agility stat, he was absurdly quick.

It was only when he passed a level 6 scout on the plains that he realized how much bigger he was. The guy barely came up to his armpit. As if the difference in power between them wasn't clear enough already. Damien gave him a cheeky wave as he approached, and after a brief pause the player holstered his crossbow and knelt down as he passed. It was a very simple way of conveying a message without words: please don't kill me.

It had taken Damien over half an hour to get from the starting zone to the Downward Spiral, back when he was level 1. Damien had drastically overestimated how long it would take to make the same trip. Camelot's main gate was a kilometer past the spawning point and he was traveling off the main road, so with his agility-based character he'd given a conservative estimate of arriving in half the time. However, hardly eight minutes had passed before he crested a ridge and found himself at his destination. He hadn't even been running in a straight line, or at his top speed.

This was ridiculous. Not as ridiculous as what was waiting for him in front of Camelot's main gate. Lillian said she was sending a 'squad'. He'd not expected ten 'Queen's Guard, an NPC he'd never even heard of, let alone seen before.

Although they all bore that name, there were three distinct kinds. The five in the front line were heavily armored, with shields and halberds strapped to their backs. Four were equipped with bows. The last was a priest, stood at the center of the back line. It was less a squad than an optimized ball of death. They were all level 50 and covered all the basic needs of a raid party, condensed to the simplest possible terms.

The squad was lined up in two rows and standing motionless. They'd attracted a fair few players, many of whom were pulling stupid poses in front of them as they took turns screenshotting each other. The Queen's Guard seemed not to care, until one of the players strayed a little too close. The priest immediately cried out.

"Close ranks!"

The overstepping player was punted backward by an iron-clad shoulder. The front line dropped to one knee and their shields locked together in front, forming an impenetrable wall. The rangers behind drew their bows and filled the gaps, with the priest glaring over the top looking for signs of aggression. All present were suitably chastened.

"At ease!"

The group returned to their previous formation in the span of a second. This was all very interesting, but Damien only had one concern. Their names, and the names of all the players around them, were red. They were all hostiles. He did not want his first act as 'Pride' to be getting annihilated by player and non-player alike.

Daemien: I see your squad, my HUD displays them as enemies. Are you sure this is a good idea?

Lillian: Of course not, I've never done this before. I'll tell them you're here.

Not encouraging. Damien was still typing out his reply when the priest yelled over the heads of the crowd.

"Daemien, step forward!"

At least they knew he was there. That didn't necessarily mean they wouldn't murder him on sight. Damien was higher level than any of the players congregating around the squad, in most cases more than twenty levels higher. He picked his way around all but the lowest-level players, who he could get within arm's length of without them even realizing he was there.

This gear bonus was incredibly useful. Still, it was not the same as true invisibility. He'd found a point of ingress through the crowd and was within ten meters when he and the priest locked eyes. The priest's diplomacy needed work.

"Target—"

The front line of warriors ran toward him while Damien was still figuring out what to do. By the time he'd decided to run, the option had been removed. The five of them encircled him, their shields locking him in.

"—acquired. We've been instructed to bring you in for an audience with her majesty, Lillian the Immortal. Do not resist. Quick march!"

The shield wall shifted and Damien was pushed forward into a jog. They were bringing him through the gate. Their movement was completely synchronized, even with half of them running backward. The pace was not quite a sprint, especially not by Damien's standards, but it was a fair bit faster than walking speed. The shield wall remained completely intact the whole time, with not so much as a chink appearing in the gaps.

This lot were even better coordinated than his own summons. Also quite a bit ruder, which was saying something with Noigel dragging the average up. On the one hand, Damien had never traveled more safely. On the other, he'd never traveled less efficiently or more uncomfortably. Trams during rush hour were roomy by comparison. Needless to say, he did not get a scenic view of Camelot on his way in.

Within a few minutes, which felt like far longer, the paved stone under his feet gave way to marble and they were walled in. They'd entered the castle proper. A minute later, the phalanx around him abruptly dispersed and took their places around the War Room.

The 'squad' that had picked Damien up was only one of five. There were fifty Queen's Guard stood all around, all with the same group composition. Lillian had acquired an instant guild of completely loyal NPCs, along with the undisputed best guild headquarters in the Empire. There were significant perks to being queen, another of which she was availing herself of at that very moment.

She was standing at the other side of the Round Table, over which a holographic map of Tintagel was projected. There were insignias scattered all across it, hovering over fortified positions that were marked out on the map. Damien recognized a couple of them. They were guild emblems, each marking out a guild headquarters. Basic information for each guild was displayed in text boxes next to them as Damien focused on them.

On either side of Lillian was another player. As Damien's escort dispersed, all three looked up from what they were doing. It was no surprise to see one of them was Andrew, but the second was Hammertime. Hadn't Andrew said he'd betrayed Lillian's party? The three of them were kitted out in new gear, very similar in style to what Lillian's Queen's Guard had equipped. Damien wasn't the only one boasting significant upgrades.

Lillian's basic information appeared over her head as she rounded the table toward him, leaving Hammertime and Andrew to themselves. It gave Damien quite a start when he spotted not only her newly added title along with her nickname and level 50, but also a *golden skull*. His HUD registered her as an epic boss. Lillian wasn't just in control of the Empire. She *was* the Empire, courtesy of the impossible sword that hung unsheathed at her side.

It was a lot to take in for Damien's first glimpse inside Camelot. More than he could manage before Lillian had closed in on him, her pace slowing and her brow furrowing as she drew closer.

"Long time no see! What happened to you? You're bigger than before."

She looked him up and down, grabbed him by the shoulders and examined him at arm's length. Most of it was surely for show, since he'd started shorter than her and was now at least a head taller. She finished her inspection and nodded at him, grinning broadly.

"Yup, definitely bigger. When did that happen? Is it a new trait?"

Damien twitched at the memory. *Nothing to see here. Move along.*

"Something like that. I like your table. What are you up to? It looks like you're planning a takeover."

"Not if I can help it. I already had to throw King Bedi—*former* King Bedivere into the dungeon. He refused to accept he wasn't king anymore, even after the NPCs saw Excalibur and stopped following his orders. We're hoping to talk some sense into the guild leaders but we don't think they'll be any happier than Bedivere. They weren't very kind to either of us in the last council meeting we had."

Yeah, Damien could remember. One part stood out in particular. He couldn't help feeling a little resentment, although he did his best to hide it in his tone if not with his chosen words.

"I think you'd be better off wiping them out and starting fresh. You shouldn't have to save those idiots from themselves."

Lillian raised her eyebrows and took a step back.

"Sorry, Damien, this requires a more delicate touch. We have a battle to fight this evening and battles need bodies. Living ones, to start with. I didn't do this to start another civil war on top of the one we already have."

"Are you sure? I'd happily pay the more obstinate council leaders a personal visit."

Lillian stepped back in, very close, staring straight into his face. The *clink* of armor echoed around the room as her Queen's Guard shifted.

"Damien? I forbid you to attack any Empire players today. I want everyone focused on the same goal. It's well known you and I have been working together, if you run around...oh great, here we go again."

Andrew was rounding the table to the pair of them, his eyes pinned to Hammertime as he traced his hands around the circumference of the best scrying table in the game.

"Gratz on your second Toutatis fight, Damien. Watching it almost made me gla—"

Andrew looked forward at who he was speaking to and stopped in his tracks.

"Is he bigger?"

"He's bigger."

"How did that happen?"

It seemed the change Damien had undergone was more obvious to everyone else than it was to him. He didn't feel like airing out his own drama, it might make him look unstable and he was dealing with plenty already. Not least of all, the shock of seeing Lillian and Andrew cooperating. He knew they had been, in theory. It just hit different seeing it in person.

"It's a long story, Andrew, I'll tell you about it later. Why's Hammertime here? I thought you said he was an enemy?"

At the mention of Hammertime, Lillian screwed her eyes shut and pinched the bridge of her nose. Andrew glared back at the man under discussion, who steadfastly kept his attention glued to the table as the puny mage vented at him from the other side of it.

"He still is, as far as I'm concerned. Lillian gave him a second chance. Suited him up in Queen's Guard gear, paid for a new weapon for him, full executive treatment. She's even tipped him to be Camelot's 'Warmaster'. Apparently she's adopted a policy of rewarding players who screw us over."

Lillian kept her nose pinched and her eyes closed as she directed her commentary at Damien.

"He came with us on the quest, making him the only other guild leader who had the foresight to see Magnitude needed to be stopped immediately. He helped us past the wall and saved you, Damien, from Archimonde in the process. He has his own mind, unlike the rest of the echo chamber council, and isn't completely incapable of changing it. Most importantly, he said he was sorry for what he did and got out of our way after I set him straight. If it's good enough for me, it should be good enough for anyone else. I've already explained my reasoning umpteen times today, always to the same person. Who doesn't seem to be interested."

"If I'd been swayed the first time I wouldn't bring it up umpteen times after. He's a mistake waiting to happen."

Lillian opened her eyes and turned on Andrew directly.

"Even if I didn't want him here, he's necessary. Not only is his guild the biggest since Rising Tide collapsed, we also had beef with him, which works in our favor now. It shows we're willing to cooperate with old enemies and we'll forgive the other guild leaders too, if they're not too stupid to live. Until we pull Rising Tide back together, he represents the only guild leader whose support is guaranteed. Let it go!"

Andrew looked to Damien, who gave him nothing. No way was he getting involved in this domestic. It was already a shock to see Andrew and Lillian talking, arguing even, without the whole interaction falling apart. He felt a pang of something he didn't immediately recognize, which heightened when Andrew turned away from him and gave his response to Lillian point blank.

"Fine. If the hammer you bought him ends up embedded in the back of your skull, I'll be standing over your corpse screaming 'I told you so'. Unless he kills me first, which seems likely. I'll stand with your guard until you're back, I'm not comfortable being with him alone."

Lillian let out a huff as Andrew haughtily strode to the wall, standing between two of the heavily armored guards. Damien didn't know Hammertime particularly well, so he couldn't vouch for which one of them had this right. All he knew was that Lillian would never let *him* talk to her like that. Which is when he realized what the uncomfortable knot in his stomach was. Jealousy. Huh. Damien was both glad and not glad the two of them were back on speaking terms. He filed it away for later consideration as Lillian made Andrew's excuses. Quietly, so Andrew wouldn't hear them.

"Sorry about that, he's had a pretty rough time of it."

It almost seemed like a personal insult, as if Damien hadn't had a "rough time" of it himself.

"Yeah, I'm sure. So, you were chewing me out for offering help stabilizing your kingdom?"

"I've got that under control. What I need from you is help negotiating with the occultists. Making a plea to them to cease player-killing activity today will make me appear weak and is more likely to encourage attacks, but I figure if you said the same thing it might work."

"I'm not sure why you think that. I'm a whole lot stronger but I'm not leader of the occultists."

"Maybe not, but you're the next best thing. You won the streaming competition and everyone watched you hit level 50 and beat Toutatis. I'd think your words would hold some sway."

Damien put a hand on the table and cupped the other under his chin. Would they? If he was telling them to coordinate an attack on a guild they'd probably all show up for the fun of it. Telling them *not* to attack was a different story. Although, he had an obvious starting point. He could work from there, but he'd need something to work with. Something a bit more tangible.

"I'm pretty sure I've got fifty occultists in the bag. I should be able to stop them from attacking for a day. If you give me some leverage I can do you one better: I might be able to bring them onside."

Lillian shook her head, her face an inscrutable mask of calm.

"I don't want them onside, I just want them to stand back until this is resolved. They already have motivation to do so: getting rid of Magnitude. He's blocking their access to the Dark Tower. The Carlisle-Elite opened recruitment to all Empire players over level 40, I'm sure you saw it. It's access to late-game content in exchange for leaving the Empire. That's bad for occultists too, since their targets—"

Damien had put quite a bit of thought into this. Now he could finally put his rumination to good use. Better yet, he could employ it on Lillian, who'd recently taken to speaking to him as though he were a child and she knew everything.

"You're not thinking like an occultist, and worse, you're not thinking like Magnitude. What if he appeals to occultists with a better offer than nothing? As you say, they'll all want past the wall now they've seen the Dark Tower. What if Magnitude gives it to them, as well as protection from Empire forces behind the wall, out of your reach? In exchange for killing Empire players, which is beneficial to occultists already?"

The smirk was fading from Lillian's face as he spoke. This was novel. He'd stopped her in her tracks. He pressed on.

"Short term, he has a new group of devoted player-killers on his side, with a common goal of killing Empire players. Long term, you're completely screwed. In a few days' time, you'll be dealing with packs of level 50 occultists, geared like me, roaming Empire space. I already did an online walkthrough for the Path of Deceit, so the best of the agility occultists could be done as soon as this evening. You need to stop ignoring us and hoping we won't get involved, before Magnitude starts paying us attention."

Lillian's smirk had been pulled into a tight, thin line.

"What do you want?"

"I think occultists should be treated as allies by the Empire. You're the Queen of Camelot, do you have the option of changing our 'Enemy of the Realm' status? That's the kind of leverage I'm looking for."

Lillian's eyes flashed, then returned to an intense stare.

"I have that option, but no plans to use it. A big change like that will cause a lot of upset to all the Empire players, at a time when I'm trying to promote unity. Maybe if the occultists hadn't been ganking Empire players left and right recently, I'd consider it. Not like this."

"Why not funnel them toward the *right* Empire players? Camelot puts out bounties on people who break the law. You have a class that gains experience from killing their targets, but we can't turn in bounties because being an occultist is (surprise!) against the law. Normal players kill each other all the time. It's not about the killing. It's about being an occultist. Even better, occultists don't get to party up with anyone else and if they try to grind regular mobs for EXP they get targeted, just for having picked that class! If we had any other reasonable options, maybe we'd do things in a lawful way."

"That's naive, Damien. If I made occultists 'legal', most of them would go about killing people all over the place with no repercussions at all."

"Lillian. You're not hearing what I'm telling you. If you had rogue occultists who ran around killing other players, you could send *your* occultists to deal with them. At least this way you'd have access to some on your side. Like *me*, for instance. I've been pretty useful in a party, haven't I? Worst-case scenario, you have exactly the same situation you started with."

"No, Damien. Worst-case scenario I piss off all the regular human players, none of the occultists show up and I end up with no one to help fight Magnitude. It's not as simple as you make it out to be."

"It's not as complicated as you make it out to be. Either you reach out to them, or Magnitude does. Which would you rather? You even have me as a buffer against public opinion, so you can blame me if it goes wrong. That's why you invited me here, right?"

It was only as he stopped talking that he realized the room was completely silent, and that they'd been getting louder and louder. Damien's words bounced off the walls, back onto him. The two of them stood there in silence, neither of them looking away. Lillian broke the stalemate.

"I'll put something on my channel, confirming that anyone who contributes will be suitably rewarded. Conversely, there will also be *suitable rewards* for players manipulating this situation to their advantage. And this is a crucial time when we should be working together, not fighting amongst ourselves. If you could convey that to the occultists, while I'm focusing on the other 99% of human players, that might be useful. I'll put Matthew's squad under your control for the next fifteen minutes. They'll escort you out of the city. You can leave."

She was walking back to Hammertime when she paused mid-step and turned back to him.

"By the way. I agreed with everything you told the Round Table Council in that council meeting. I felt exactly the same way. It doesn't mean venting your frustration at them made you look clever. Or considerate. We managed to fix that problem by the skin of our teeth. Don't kill any Empire players today."

She'd already turned her back on him before he could reply. Matthew's squad promptly moved in to surround him. The priest's nose was crinkled in obvious disgust.

"What would you have us do, Daemien the Low?"

Oh boy. Big mistake. Matthew had chosen a very poor time to hit the 'Low' button. Damien slowly turned his head to Matthew and fixed him with a glare.

"First, we're moving to the courtyard. No need to box me in this time."

Damien had a good opportunity to get a view of the castle's interior, which he did not take. He was focused on how he'd be spending the rest of that day. And more immediately, how her Queen's Guard squad would be spending the next ten minutes.

They made it into the courtyard and Damien waited for Matthew to pipe up again. It took a few seconds of standing around doing nothing but Matthew did not disappoint.

"And what would you have us do now, Daemien the Low?"

"You first. Sixty push-ups. Every push-up you don't manage is two for all your squad. We'll do the same again every time someone calls me 'Low'. That means now."

28

HEARTS AND MINDS

Damien had a great time for the next five minutes, setting increasingly impossible goals for his rude hosts. It was all in the guise of punishment while also testing their abilities at length. They were impressive, to say the least.

The priest might not have managed sixty push-ups but the warriors could do them almost indefinitely, even clad in heavy armor. Damien sat on one of their backs for a full minute without any recognizable effect on his subject's speed or stamina. The rangers were nearly as fast at jump-stepping as he was. He knew, because he set the pace for them and was surprised when they kept it up for two minutes.

Matthew got off pretty light after the initial corporeal punishment. Damien ordered him to divulge his abilities, most of which required damage to accurately ascertain. The best of them was a resurrection ability, which he could use exclusively on members of his squad. Not testable without potentially provoking a war, unfortunately. It had a remarkably short cooldown of thirty seconds, if Matthew was to be believed. Provided the priest was alive and had mana, the squad was a self-sufficient closed unit.

This lot were far more reliable than his own summons. And to think, he could've had far better minions if he'd decided to run Camelot rather than playing as an occultist. Darn. Missed opportunity. When he was satisfied Matthew wouldn't give him any more lip, Damien had himself escorted through Camelot's streets. He went through the inner, middle and outer quadrants in turn, each dingier than the last, before he reached the front gate. They'd gone much faster now his escort wasn't penning him in like cattle, but he had time to look around and give a few extremely perturbed players a wave. There's nothing quite like feeding your ego.

Once he got to the front gate he ordered Matthew back to the castle, crouched and made his own way to a safe distance. As he started the short jog back to Bart's, he made a mental checklist of everything he needed to do that day.

He needed to test his activated 'Sin of Pride' ability. Rebuild and upgrade his base structures. Bring his Soul Summon Limit to full. Visit Antonio's internet cafe and talk to Gian in person. Talk with the occultists in the Council of Nine, convincing them to join the fight against Magnitude. Edit his own footage of the Dark Tower and put it on his page, along with his own call to arms. Test his newest demon, the consumer. Avoid thinking about Lucifer, at all costs. Buy groceries.

It was a good thing his mom had forced him up that morning. He had a lot of tasks to do and little time to do them in. About seven hours, give or take. He rearranged them in his head as he went, putting them into some sort of priority order. They were all necessary. His main problem was his complete lack of resources. Much of his base-building would require a volume of raw materials he couldn't realistically farm in one day.

He'd had plenty of these materials stockpiled in his old base, but had given them all up to get past Archimonde and to the Dark Tower. Hindsight is 2020. It must've been a pretty terrible year to have a colloquialism dedicated to it.

He couldn't murder Empire players to get his hands on their armor for scrap and their souls for summons. Lillian had made it very clear she wouldn't take kindly to him slaying Empire players in advance of the fight against Magnitude. But he couldn't fathom where else he was supposed to get the resources from. Building a new Gateway with only Noigel, a few imps and a succubus would take time he didn't have.

As Damien shuffled his options around, deciding what to attempt first, a logical order presented itself. If it worked out, he'd exponentially increase his productivity. The problem was, it relied on the most nutty group of people he knew: the Council of Nine. He had other business with them anyway, so it made sense to start from there and see how many of his other problems he could eliminate.

He reached the top of the Downward Spiral, soaking up the memories as always as he summoned an imp from his 4 outstanding soul energy to assist him on his journey downward. He could still hear Noigel faintly warbling from the bottom. Damien Demon Gated to the lowest level, picked his way around the aspiring occultists killing each other there, tipped his fingers to a very unamused-looking Bartholomew and made his way into his base.

Noigel was grooming his succubus, lapping her hooves. He stopped what he was doing to shriek into the air. Damien coughed mid-shriek and Noigel sat upright, the horns rapidly receding back into his skull. Damien pretended not to notice as he positioned a Gateway blueprint in the same place his old one used to be.

"I'm upgrading the base. You do you, I'll be out of here in a little while."

He summoned three more imps one by one, each of them setting to work on the Gateway as they arrived. While he pointed at the floor and summoned them with one hand, he navigated to the Council of Nine page with the other. There'd been a lot of activity while he was gone. The page increasingly looked like a shrine to him, alternating between videos of his run through the Dark Tower and replays of the raids they'd conducted on Empire players.

Oh boy. If this got out, it would look really, really bad. Damien was doubly glad he'd assigned this first priority. He addressed his followers in the manner to which he was accustomed.

Daemien: Hello. (3:1)

No response. Huh. He knew occultists weren't stereotypically morning people, but he'd expected at least a couple of them to be online. The group was larger than it had been at the beginning of the week: there were now seventy-four players in there. Damien checked the discussion group and found they'd had one of their 'Low Priest' events yesterday, running 'til the early hours of the morning. Horded up, killed a bunch of players and got Daemiaemiaemien up to level 23. If he understood the timing correctly, they'd set out shortly after his broadcast ended.

They were active, which was definitely good news, but were still heavily engaged in mass Empire player-killing sprees on their Friday nights. Right. What Lillian said about Damien being naive was coming into focus a bit. On the other hand, that meant they should have a fresh supply of raw materials he could 'borrow'.

Daemien: I want to upgrade everyone's structures, in exchange for a proposition: I'll be fighting Magnitude this evening and want to see if anyone here will team up with me. I lost my base and need help getting ready as soon as possible. PM me your locations if you decide I can visit. (3:2)

While he typed, his minions had been working hard. The Gateway would take hours to complete, even if Noigel and the succubus were assisting. Although his imps' stats had improved with Damien's level, four of them were not the mighty workforce he needed.

With so much to do in so little time, he couldn't afford to sit in base watching over construction. The problem was, the construction was also important. That's what Noigel was for, ideally, but he'd promised Noigel a reward. He surely wouldn't take this well. Damien tried it on anyway.

"Noigel, I'm heading into the real world, I need you to do a bit of work while I'm gone."

Noigel couldn't speak properly since Damien didn't have ten imps, but Noigel had always been just as adept at showing as he was at telling. In this case, showing consisted of an expedient mooning, accompanied by a long slew of demonic curses that would make flowers wilt. Damien couldn't say he blamed him. He circled the Soul Well Noigel was balancing on until he wasn't in the line of moon-fire.

"Noigel, you've done a really awesome job. If I had it my way, you'd be in a fully stocked base with four succubi. That's not your fault. I hope you can see it's not really my fault either. You'll get everything I promised as soon as I can make it possible."

Noigel shuffled around with his head between his knees, aiming between his legs to put Damien back in his sights. Damien squeezed his temples between thumb and middle finger, simultaneously relieving pressure and covering his eyes to avoid Noigel's show. Today was all about multitasking.

"If I don't have an active Gateway, I can't cast Portal. If I don't have a Tier II Gateway, I can't Portal back to the one I built near the Dark Tower. I'm level 51, Noigel. I can't get any soul energy around here. Which means I can't summon the succubi you want. Or rebuild the rest of my base. Or do anything, really."

Noigel had stopped tracking Damien's movement. The imp was holding his pose but already looking quite defeated. Surly, but defeated nonetheless. Damien decided to give him the smallest mercy.

"I'll be back in half an hour or so. Do you want me to leave you with the succubus until I get back, or do you want me to leave you with the imps so you can front-load the work?"

Noigel's head flicked upward and he clung to the succubus. Of course. Front-loading his pleasure. How very familiar.

"Alright, then that's what you'll get. But when I come back it'll be building time. I won't forget the reward you're due. Keep reminding me, so you know I haven't forgotten. See you in a bit."

Damien logged out, two of the four building imps leaving with him since there was no space for them on the Soul Well, and ran for the shower. Ten minutes later he was out of the house. Five minutes after that he was standing outside the internet cafe. With any luck he'd find Gian inside rather than Antonio or his son; he'd sent Antonio the credits to pay off Gian's fine a few days ago, hopefully he'd be back on his day shift.

He was on his way in, his eyes adjusting to the light, but he stopped dead in the doorway. The pods were gone. His first thought was that CU had returned and impounded them. A quick glance around showed the reality was worse. They were still there, they'd just been moved up against the back wall. Where they should've been all along. That wasn't the only change. The red tape binding them shut had been removed.

Confusion gave way to disbelief, which gave way to Antonio's threatening voice from behind the counter.

"You're still not welcome here, get out of my shop."

There was a chance he'd misread this. Small, but possible. It had more to do with hope than reality at that point. Surely Antonio hadn't done what the evidence said he had.

"Where's Gian? Did you pay—"

"I said get out!"

There. Now Damien was 100% sure. Why he'd bothered waiting on the last percentile was already beyond him.

"I gave you the credits to pay Gian's fine. I made that very clear. Why did you spend it on the pods?"

"You're a child, I don't need to explain myself to you. Once you gave me the credits they were mine to do whatever I wanted with."

"That wasn't—"

"Not interested. Get out."

Damien had wanted to support Antonio's business to make amends. Damien was flexible. He wasn't averse to doing the same thing to show he was the better person.

"You're welcome. I'll be back later today."

"I didn't thank you. If I see you again, I'll physically remove you from my property."

"It won't be yours much longer without my help. Unless another *child* bails out your *business* before I do."

Antonio, his face visibly red even in the half light, jumped out of his chair and circled the desk. Damien was halfway down the street before his charity case was halfway to the door. Not all Saga Online skills translated into real life, but Damien's risk assessment was definitely improving. Once the adrenaline had worn off, he fumed the rest of the way home.

To think he'd given credits out of his own pocket. While he didn't much care for Antonio, he was compelled to do right by Gian. How could those two be related? His thoughts circled the drainpipe all the way home. It was only as the door slammed behind him he realized he'd forgotten to buy groceries. Quest stacking sure is complicated, especially when you're attempting it between parallel realities and you're running into resistance in both of them. So the private message from the Council of Nine page owner was a welcome surprise.

Vargus: We're sending someone to the Downward Spiral to pick you up.

Daemien: How do you know I'm in the Downward Spiral?

Vargus: There was a video of you arguing with Bartholomew this morning from a new occultist called StabbyMcFace, remember him? He recorded the whole conversation. You looked bigger, very cool, what's the deal? PB.

Great. The longer he talked to Vargus, the further behind he felt and the further behind he was still falling. Far too much was happening at once. All the more reason to get a move on.

Daemien: Who's coming to get me? How long until they get there?

Vargus: He's there already. Aren't you?

Which was when a separate chat box popped up. He shouldn't have been surprised.

Scorepeeus63: I'm outside your base. Your Noigel got angry and yelled at me. It looked like he and a succubus were fighting on your Soul Well. Wtf, man? Control yo ho, no offense. PB. Where you at?

Damien jumped up and ran for his headset. The last thing he needed was a horny Noigel picking a fight with an oblivious nine-year-old kill-happy occultist, or the other way round. He was back in under half a minute. Noigel didn't quite hiss at him when he arrived, but it was a close-run thing. A quick glare from Damien cut it off before it began.

"You know the score, Noigel. I order you to complete construction on the Gateway. When it's done, you'll be one step closer to your full reward."

He set the imps to work, swapping the succubus into his own Soul Summon Limit before escorting her outside. Scorepeeus63 was waiting for him, leaning against a wall with Bartholomew just barely tolerating his presence. As Damien approached quietly through the struggling occultist sign-ups, the mouths of both players dropped. It was hard to say who was more shocked by the appearance of the other.

While Damien's improvement was impressive, Scorepeeus63's was not far off: he was level 42. Four levels higher than when Damien had last seen him. He was also wearing new gear: a bizarre mix of mismatched equipment, evidence of the players he'd presumably murdered to get to that point.

The gear was serving a purpose. His Soul Summon Limit had hit 30, judging by the long line of minions standing unnaturally straight up against the wall. Bartholomew was glaring at each of them in turn, daring them to interfere with his initiates' ongoing trial. The vampire still made time to stare at Damien, the fury and weight of a minute's silent judgment packed into a half second, before he returned his gaze to Scorepeeus63's unruly minion horde. Scorepeeus63 proved himself more unruly than any of them.

"Woah! You look gnarly, my dude! Show me some skin! Like your new threads, yo. So tight!"

There was a gargled scream as a distracted initiate was stabbed through the throat with a rat femur, about ten feet away. Bartholomew's disdain was palpable. Scorepeeus63's gear and abilities were not in question, but his conversational ability made Damien feel like a socialite. Some things take longer to learn than others, he supposed. Damien reluctantly returned his mega-fan's fist bump, feeling a little dirty while he did it.

"Yes. Yo. Indeed. I hear you're escorting me to the H—"

"Shhhhhh! First rule of the Hub: we don't talk about the Hub!"

If anyone else had yelled such a contradictory statement, Damien would've assumed they were being "ironic". To Scorepeeus63, he attributed the outburst to being nine years old. It seemed mean to point it out, as annoying as it was. Scorepeeus63 had gone out of his way to help him before and was now doing so again. Damien could think of better ways to repay him than defining a logical fallacy.

His young guide motioned to Damien's base and the two of them picked their way back across. The two occultists moved quietly enough, but Scorepeeus63's demons thoroughly disturbed the initiates, who were having a very unique trial.

They entered the base, where Scorepeeus63 was better received with Damien by his side and Noigel working on the Gateway. At least insofar as being ignored constituted 'received' and kicking other imps constituted 'working'. Scorepeeus63 performed a familiar gesture and ten seconds later a portal appeared. It was strange to see the skill used by someone else.

"After you, Dark Lord."

Cringe. Considering where the portal led, he'd better get used to it. Damien ushered his succubus through and followed on after them, swapping one dark environment for another. He wasn't sure what he'd expected until his expectation was not met.

With a name like the Hub, Damien had subconsciously believed it would be a big space with the individual occultist structures arrayed around it, like a market square. The cramped dead end he was standing in, with demons pressed up against the walls and occupying every square inch of the structures, was not quite as glamorous as he'd expected.

"Welcome to mah crib, dawg."

The portal had closed after Scorepeeus63 passed through it and he was now throwing gang signs. All his minions were throwing gang signs in response, which meant Damien was receiving a great deal of sharp elbows at waist height, the worst place to receive sharp elbows. For all his talent using occultist abilities, it appeared Scorepeeus63 was more suggestible than his own imps.

Still, Damien couldn't deny that the structures were in good nick: everything was fully upgraded in line with Scorepeeus63's level. Since Damien had hit level 50 he could upgrade the Gateways and Demon Forges to the third tier.

"Do you mind if I upgrade your structures? I can get your Demon Forge and Gateway up to the next tier, then give them back to you."

"That'd be awesome, yes please!"

"Transfer ownership to me."

As soon as the Demon Forge's basic information turned blue, Damien focused on it and checked the upgrade cost. There was a strange requirement, a material he hadn't seen before: consumer iron. That was the name of his new demon. He'd seen Archimonde's version eating ore by the Demon Forge outside the Dark Tower. Simple enough, except the consumer cost 8 souls to summon. Back to the same problem: there's very little an occultist can do without soul energy.

Damien only had a succubus attached to him. Dismissing it at half cost would leave him 4.5 souls short. Scorepeeus63, on the other hand, had plenty of minions at hand. Hadn't Lucifer said Damien was now the highest authority, second only to Lucifer himself? Bartholomew had taken control of his minions on several occasions in the past.

The vampire had appropriated Damien's imps on his first day, allowing them to build his first Soul Well while he evaded the crappy child services. Just this morning, Bartholomew had babysat his minions after Damien had abruptly logged out following Lucifer's torture session. Archimonde had taken minions off him during combat. If they could do it, so, presumably, could he.

How?

He'd picked up the ability to give orders mentally by instinct. That hadn't worked out so well with the spells, but the management of minions had always come intuitively. He'd simply give

Scorepeeus63's minions orders. He stared at the back of an imp's head and thought at it.

I bind you to my will.

His Soul Summon Limit went up a point. Gnarly, my dude. He could take control of minions from other occultists, without their permission. Now he could see why Bartholomew had been so excited. This was extraordinary. He focused on the imp and the stat box appeared above its head.

The minion's level had gone up in line with Damien's. The stats had not. Hmmm. Hmmmmmmmmm. Would this work in reverse? If he gave Scorepeeus63 one of his minions, would the minion's level decrease but its stats remain in place? If Scorepeeus63 leveled up with the minion in his roster, would the minion's stats then continue to increase?

These were very interesting questions. There was only one Damien needed answered then and there. He brought the imp to his side and dismissed it. The portal it hopped through spat out a half soul in exchange. Aw yiss.

"Score, I'm borrowing some of your minions so I can build the structures. I'll also need access to your inventory chest for the raw materials."

He started by dismissing his own succubus for 3.5 souls. Then, without asking for permission, he picked out a wraith, a hound and three imps from Scorepeeus63's control and dismissed them all at half cost for the remaining 4.5. He had the 8 souls he needed. He pointed at the ground to summon a consumer. The rune burning into the flagstones bore the consumer's defining features: the outer edge of the circle was ringed with teeth, the middle was a spiraling corkscrew tongue.

The minions remaining in the enclosed space clambered onto structures to get out of the way. The sigil was as large as an incubus's. When the summoning was complete, the portal opened within it as usual. What was unusual was that rather than the consumer climbing out of it, the portal rose off the ground, with the consumer's feet appearing first as the portal drew upward.

The rift reached the top of the consumer's head and winked

out of existence. Its head and body were, broadly speaking, the same thing. Damien had seen this creature from a long way away and had even killed one in the dark, but hadn't had time to appreciate just how weird it was.

Two large black orbs sat on either side of the slathering maw, from which hung the slimy tongue. The arms were short, not even long enough to reach each other across the thing's front, but powerful. Damien opened the consumer's stat window to see how powerful it was and got a bit of a shock. This thing was weird across the board.

Consumer
Strength: 80**Agility:** 20 **Intelligence:** 20
Constitution: 250 **Endurance:** 80**Wisdom:** 100
Abilities: Feeding Frenzy, Tongue Lash, Mana Eater, Caustic Juices

No surprises regarding the theme of the abilities. Damien had seen at least three of them in action, two of them used by Archimonde itself: the Tongue Lash and Mana Eater. Caustic Juices was likely related to the behavior he'd witnessed in Archimonde's base, where the consumer was eating metal brought to it by imps.

Feeding Frenzy he wasn't so sure about. It sounded like a combat ability. Probably took effect after killing an enemy by eating it? In which case Damien himself had been used to trigger it on one occasion, he just hadn't lived afterward to see what it did.

None of the primary stats were particularly high. The one that stood out was constitution. The consumer had as much health as some base structures, around the same as if Damien possessed an incubus. The consumer would have 5,000 hit points if he possessed it. That seemed pretty unreal. He'd have to test it in a few situations to know how to use it properly.

"Score, I still need those materials. Score?"

Scorepeeus63 had become uncharacteristically silent. Damien turned to him and saw his mouth hanging open.

"Score, when you're ready I need twenty iron."

"Twenty iron...right, on it."

Scorepeeus63 dropped it at his feet and Damien chucked them one after the other into the consumer's mouth. After five chunks of ore the consumer's mouth clamped shut and it began to chew. Its mana pool began to drop steadily. That explained what the high wisdom stat was for: converting regular iron into consumer iron took both time and energy. How much time, Damien had no idea. That was a resource he didn't want to use inefficiently.

He turned his attention to the Tier III Gateway and found that would require consumer iron as well. Yikes. So from Tier III onward, his structure-building progress would be tied to this minion's ability to produce materials. Not a good prospect. He had to go collect more soul energy to get more consumers, so he could speed this up. Fortunately, Scorepeeus63 had given him possession of a Tier II Gateway.

"Score, I'm giving this demon to you. Make room in your Soul Summon Limit. I've got to get more soul energy, bring more consumers back with me. You take control of him for now. The Tier III Demon Forge needs twenty consumer iron total, so once he's done with that batch put your imps on construction and feed the consumer more iron. I'll be back as soon as I can."

He stared at the consumer and thought at it.

You belong to Scorepeeus63.

The consumer was far too busy chewing to acknowledge the order, but it left Damien's Soul Summon Limit. Scorepeeus63's happy squeal confirmed the transferal. Damien checked the consumer's stat window: the stats had decreased. Fair enough; if the stats hadn't gone down, that would've meant Damien could give a level 1 occultist a level 50 incubus and completely break the game. Not that Damien was averse to finding exploits.

Damien channeled a portal for the first time in four days and was presented with two options: 'Daemien's Gateway' or the 'Fields of Eternity'. His Gateway to the Inner Circle was still intact! Thank goodness there was next to no player activity there yet, and that he'd been so careful in choosing where to build it.

He channeled the portal and ended up right where he needed to be.

The next few minutes had a very different feel to them than when Damien had first passed through that zone. His ability to remain stealthed in the daytime, coupled with his mid-ranged weapon and much improved stats, made farming a very easy prospect. He snuck across the zone, killing anything on the way that looked like a good prospect. If there was any species he didn't like the look of, such as the large armored rhinos, he could either avoid or outrun them without difficulty.

It took him about fifteen minutes to get his hands on 10 souls, running in one direction and killing anything that looked appropriate along the way. Some mobs were now too low level to be of much use, not a concern on his previous trip. There was no shortage of enemies with question marks above their heads, with whom he maintained very safe social distancing practices. Especially Scolopendra-Millicornu, the massive flying bug, which occupied a vast territory. Stealthed in the light of day, it was not difficult to pick his moments.

Despite getting his 10 souls, Damien was reluctant to use them. If he summoned a consumer now, it would slow him down and he may well end up dying to try and protect it. He couldn't send it through a portal back to Scorepeeus63, because he couldn't transfer ownership without passing through the portal himself. He ran onward into a marshland, which was inhabited by a tribe of spear-wielding Lizard-Men all around the right level.

Most were higher than necessary, but it was the most consistent group of mobs he'd seen in the Inner Circle so far. There were pros and cons to this: since they were all the same, if he knew how one behaved he'd know how they all behaved. On the downside, they could use tools and displayed basic group intelligence. He'd have to watch their movement patterns for a while and cull them one by one without drawing attention to himself.

Damien took cover behind a tree, knee deep in water. The terrain was not ideal, especially for crouching around in Shadow Walker, but at least he could use his kunai to get around quickly by aiming at the trees scattered around. If that happened, it would probably be with a view to retreating. If he wasn't careful, they'd discern his whereabouts and he'd go from the hunter to the hunted. This much he knew from his interactions with predatory groups displaying basic intelligence in the past, both in game and out of game, both PC and NPC.

First he had an important decision to make: how to use the 10 souls before initiating combat. He could summon regular creeps to help with the process in the manner to which he was accustomed, he could summon the consumer and test it, or...he could test his activated Pride ability. If it were as circumstantial as Archimonde's it could make life a lot easier.

While a small voice in the back of his head told him to play it safe, a much louder one insisted he activate Pride. He'd wanted to do it for a long time, there were a large number of enemies here to collect souls from, and there weren't any players to see the ability in use. It was the right move. Said the loud voice that wanted to see what it did, come what may. Damien put his hand over his heart.

"Pride."

Damien hadn't thought this through. His body expanded so fast there was a rush of air, not unlike a minor Ex-Imp-losion. His head smashed into a bough of the tree he was sheltering behind, which snapped then tumbled off him to splash into the water. That alone would've been enough noise to alert anything within a hundred yards of his location.

Damien finished transforming, utterly disoriented. He was now approximately the same size as the tree his head had smashed into. It had been a small tree, but he was now a large player. Very large. Too large to hide behind anything in his vicinity. As if that wasn't bad enough, his entire body had turned bright red. Not optimal camouflage. There were screeches from all around as the Lizard-Men pushed in to remove the threat from their territory.

This was less than ideal. Damien didn't have time to check his new abilities. He knew the incubus abilities though, intimately. They weren't complicated: Charge and Enrage. One for covering distances quickly and adding momentum behind attacks, one that doubled his strength and endurance when he had less than half health.

His enemies were coming to him and ideally he'd rather keep his health high, so neither of those abilities was particularly useful right now. Better to stick to his weapons. He hurled a kunai at the nearest enemy, preparing to pull himself toward it to finish it off quickly. There was no need. His kunai passed straight through the level 53 enemy and into the ground behind it. He'd one-shotted it.

He pulled back the kunai, neglecting to twist to release since his enemy was hanging dead on the chain. He found himself hurtling across the ground instead. Apparently he'd thrown the kunai so hard it had passed through two feet of water and embedded itself deeply enough in Arcadia's surface to function as an anchor. He knew that technically Arcadia was still bigger than him, but Damien found this a little unfair. He hadn't been able to see the kunai through the murky water, let alone prepare himself for the unforeseen consequences.

Before his hand reached the kunai and his momentum was halted, Damien made a pair of linked discoveries: the first was that Lizard-Men had a lot of fluid inside them. The second was that it was blue. He discovered this because the chain led straight through the chest of the Lizard-Man in question. His closed fist, far larger than the kunai that had made the initial hole, made contact with the Lizard-Man at a speed the Lizard-Man's evolution had not accounted for. It exploded. He wouldn't be looting that enemy.

Fortunately the blue blood was washed away almost as soon as it had coated him: by rancid bog water. Damien was pulled headfirst into the muck. He twisted his kunai and raised his head out of the filth just in time to receive a spear thrust to the face. Then another one in the same place as he pulled himself to his feet. Which was when Damien's body bulked up.

Damien's new Enrage was "slightly" more visually pronounced than that of his regular incubus: his arms, legs and torso had nearly doubled in size to match the effect of the buff. He was massive.

It hadn't been as dramatic as his transformation into Pride, taking a full second rather than a tenth of one. Damien took stock of the situation and punched the offending Lizard-Man in the face, kunai first. Its crocodilian snout caved in like a crunchy accordion before the crumple effect proved insufficient to save the mind sitting behind it. The Lizard-Man's back hit the water so hard, what was left of it bounced off the surface like a skipping stone, high into the air. It may as well have hit concrete.

It died.

Damien shrank back to his original size, but that's not where his attention was focused. Everything he knew about this game told him that he was the one that should be dead. A quick glance at his health bar informed him that despite taking two critical hits to the face, he was nowhere near death. Not even close. He had almost half his hit points left. They were sitting at 3,297/4,800. He had nearly 5,000 hit points.

"Wha—"

Damien surprised himself with his own voice, not only because he could speak at all but because of the quality of it. He sounded almost exactly like Lucifer. It was the cherry on the cake: his voice was much deeper than it used to be, his body was going through rapid changes nobody had bothered explaining to him and it seemed everyone in his vicinity didn't like him.

Business as usual.

Damien recovered from the shock and arrived at a conclusion, based more on what had just happened to the two Lizard-Men than what was happening to him. This form was freaking sweet. However, he still stood a good chance of dying if he didn't get this under control. He sighted another lizard entering his attack range and threw a kunai straight through its head. Another one-shot kill. With the same throw aimed at the head it was hardly a surprise. What was a surprise was that his health bar jumped up. Not just a little, but a large chunk.

He must have seen it wrong. He did the same thing again, with the same result. His health was recovering in bursts each time he killed. Damien had thought he'd have to find an opening and make his escape, but this changed everything. He'd always played evasively, now he could play aggressively.

He Charged toward the next opponent, who was winding back his spear for a throw. He'd taken three steps when his speed abruptly increased and the world around him became a blur. He didn't have much time to recalibrate, but nor did the Lizard-Man who was halfway through throwing his spear. His braced shoulder collided with the Lizard-Man's neck almost as fast as he'd superman-punched the chest cavity of his Lizard-Man colleague earlier. The Lizard-Man's neck snapped and it was punted backward, flying across the swamp until the momentum was partially stopped by a tree. Partially, because bits of the Lizard-Man disconnected and flew out from either side of the tree it had wrapped around.

It died.

What followed was ten minutes of Damien stamping his authority over a culture he didn't understand for his own gain. Once Damien finished with the Lizard-Men, he found their village and killed not just the Lizard-Men, but the Lizard-Women and Lizard-Children, too. When he ran out of Lizards, he murdered the next thing that happened to fall into his line of sight, only stopping to recruit consumers when his Soul Reserve was capped. All thought of testing them in combat was gone. Sometimes he forgot to summon a new consumer when his Soul Reserve was capped, because an enemy had caught his attention and he wanted to sic it more than he wanted to achieve his actual goal.

He was having fun.

Damien was very pleased with the way he'd played his class. He wouldn't have done it any other way. But it had always been extremely mentally taxing. Small mistakes cost him dearly. Big mistakes cost him twenty-four hours and more. After playing so cautiously for so long, it was an untold joy to let go and mindlessly stomp around as an unkillable machine. Damien embraced it more with each preposterously easy kill until he was laughing the whole while, without a care in the world.

Eventually he ran out of space in his Soul Summon Limit and ran out of enemies to murder. He reluctantly ground to a halt. If only it had always been this easy to farm souls. He had five consumers taking up most of his Soul Summon Limit, and the remaining five slots were filled with imps. His Soul Summon Limit had gone up a point from 44 to 45, which implied his wisdom had increased. He paused to look at his stats to find out what on earth was happening to him. His stat page provided much of the answer in pretty simple terms.

Class: Occultist
Level: 51
Health: 4,800/4,800 **Stamina:** 4,450/4,450 **Mana:** 3,960/3,960
Strength: 290 **Agility:** 394 **Intelligence:** 70
Constitution: 480 **Endurance:** 445 **Wisdom:** 396
Stat points: 5
Experience: 28,650/110,000
Soul Summon Limit: 45/45 **Soul Reserve:** 10/10

His agility, intelligence and wisdom had only marginally increased. His strength, constitution and endurance had skyrocketed. In terms of raw stats, he was effectively in a Nine-Tenths of the Lore-buffed possessed incubus's body, *on top of* all his own character stats. Although he did not appear to be wearing his armor, the stats from it were still applied. Between the armor's defense and the stats, he'd take the stats any day. He promptly put his 5 stat points into wisdom, hoping his Soul Summon Limit would remain at 45 even when his Embodiment wasn't active, and continued browsing.

He was surprised his agility hadn't increased much, given the obvious buff to his attacks. His weapon was agility-based for damage, not strength-based. Nor did his stat page do anything to explain the health regeneration he was getting. He turned to his ability page and got a surprise. Pride had its own category at the bottom of the Demonology section, only visible when it was activated.

First Deadly Sin – Pride
What can men do against such reckless hate?

Might Makes Right: All problems are solvable through the liberal application of brute force. All your attacks and abilities factor strength into their damage in addition to their standard damage calculation. E.g.: Chaotic Bolt Damage: (Int) + (Str) x 0.2

Narcissistic Rage: "No one heals himself by wounding another." – St. Ambrose, who never met the Embodiment of Pride. The regular Enrage doubles your strength and stamina when your health falls below half. With Narcissistic Rage, your attacks also gain a 10% Life-steal effect for 10 seconds, siphoning inflicted damage back to you as healing.

Single-Mindedness: The regular Charge doubles your movement speed for 10 seconds with no stamina drain and increases the damage of the first attack made in proportion to your movement speed. With Single-Mindedness, your movement speed is doubled again and the damage of your first attack is increased accordingly.

Stagnation: While in your Embodiment of Sin form, you will not gain experience from any source. Soul energy will be calculated independently and may still be collected.

Ah. Damien could see why the combat had gone in his favor, despite not setting it up properly. He was broken. If this was what broken looked like, he didn't want fixing. Even without knowing what his abilities were he'd still laid waste. How much worse would it be when he was using them effectively, and in tandem? Much. Much worse.

This was a double-edged sword: Archimonde was similarly overpowered. Pride's abilities were derivative of his incubus abilities, or more likely vice-versa, from a lore standpoint. It stood to reason he could gain some insight into Archimonde by looking into the consumer abilities. If the model held, Archimonde would have a stronger version of whatever it was they could do. It was a shame he'd been too busy testing his own abilities to look into the consumer abilities in depth. He'd have to test that later.

The only negative was 'Stagnation'. He wouldn't be able to gain experience while using this. Shame. That would've been too easy, huh? He could still farm souls, though, so this would work well for bringing his Soul Summon Limit back up or as an emergency button if he was about to die. That would reduce the inconveniences of dying very nicely while also making that scenario less likely.

Damien had gotten what he came for and more besides. It was time to head back. He opened a portal to the Gateway he'd borrowed off Scorepeeus63 and sent his consumers and imps through first. He followed them in afterwards, immediately killing an imp on arrival by not watching where he put his feet.

The room had been pretty full before but now it looked like a beehive. It was chock-full from top to bottom with imps. Several hundred of them, at least. Most of them were on the floor, dragging resources to the fully constructed Tier III Demon Forge. Those that had wings were flying in and out of the room at speed, those coming back bringing more iron and those leaving presumably going to get more.

The consumer was bent over the forge, working tirelessly despite the appalling conditions. Succubi lined the walls, firing off synchronized Bloodlusts that sent the entire room into a frenzy. Three of them were positioned in front of the consumer. When one started channeling a spell, the consumer opened its mouth wide to accept the donation of mana before continuing on with its endless work.

It appeared that all the occultists had gathered their best building teams to help Scorepeeus63's construction efforts. That would explain why the Tier III Demon Forge had been completed so quickly. Damien had thought it would still be under construction by the time he returned, but instead they'd grouped together and set all their minions on it at once. This was an interesting benefit of them cooperating rather than killing each other. On the downside, Damien could scarcely breathe without inhaling imps. He sent out a very clear instruction to every minion in the room.

Everyone stop.

All the imps landed on the floor, creating a three-imp-thick carpet. Damien turned and was greeted by a gaggle of occultists. Greeted was not quite the right word: ogled. Absorbed. Disbelieved. Then, as Scorepeeus63 dropped to his knees, worshiped. His eyes rolled back into his head from pure excitement, his hands thrown into the air in ecstasy, Scorepeeus63 screeched out his adulation in a broken falsetto chime:

"Alllllll hailllll the Daaaaark Looooord!"

Then he threw himself at the floor, palms against the ground. That's all it took. The rest of them immediately got on their knees and followed Scorepeeus63's example. The cult had an established narrative, which was much easier to stick to than putting their own narratives together. The narrative was and always had been Damien. Him showing up as a giant demon in their base and taking control of all their minions simultaneously had not weakened that narrative.

This was the perfect opportunity for Damien to make a munificent display for his own gain. He picked out the highest-level occultists and shuffled their minions around for them where necessary, swapping out his five consumers for three succubi and nineteen more imps.

"Everyone who I gave consumers to, head back to your bases. We're fighting Archimonde and Magnitude today, so I'll be visiting all your bases to upgrade your Demon Forges. Then we'll start building minion equipment. Don't let anyone outside the Council of Nine know what we're doing or what I look like, I want the advantage of surprise. We have less than six hours. Put messages on the board if you have any questions and I'll try to answer them."

He started channeling a new portal, intending to return to the Downward Spiral. Only 'Daemien's Gateway', which was actually Scorepeeus63's Gateway that he'd borrowed, and 'Fields of Eternity' were available. Annoying, but fixable. He trudged over to Scorepeeus63, the imp carpet parting at his advance.

"I formally transfer ownership of my Gateway to Scorepeeus63. Can you make me a portal back to the Downward Spiral, please?"

Ten seconds later, the portal was active. Damien sent all his new minions through before stopping himself in the nick of time. There wasn't much point in telling the Council of Nine to be careful if he waltzed into an occultist trial as the Embodiment of Pride ten seconds later. He put his hand over his heart and canceled the form. No soul energy refunded. Shame, but not the end of the world. His Soul Summon Limit had remained at 45 following his investment into wisdom, even after the Embodiment was canceled. Excellent.

Damien ushered the minions into his base as quickly as possible. Noigel was still working on the Gateway, though construction ground to a halt when Damien appeared with three succubi in tow.

"Your reward is waiting for you, Noigel. I'll need you to finish the Gateway first, up to second tier, so I can give the one I'm using back to its rightful owner. Then I'll need enough soul energy to fill a Tier III Soul Well. I'll be here for a few minutes, talking to Bart, so make the most of the imps while you have them. The faster it's all done, the faster you get your reward. Chop-chop."

He walked out, taking all three succubi with him. He made it halfway to Bartholomew before Noigel's screams exceeded any fury that had come from him before. It was enough to make Damien wince and appeared to offend Bartholomew even more. Damien had some slight reparations to make.

"Bartholomew. Hello. I've tested the Embodiment I got, after the torture session you signed me up for. It's...it's quite good. I feel as though, maybe, leaving you to put up with Noigel's noise all this time *might* not have been entirely fair."

"You think, do you? I hadn't noticed."

"That's very funny, Bartholomew. Har-har. Is there some way

we can block the entrance so you don't have to put up with the noise?"

"Why, yes. I can seal it shut with everyone inside. I'd have done it earlier but you told me not to interfere with your base. It appeared that making me and all my initiates endure it was by design, so I didn't wish to invoke your ire by going against your instruction."

Damien thought about it. Once Noigel had finished the Gateway he'd be able to Portal directly in. It would be strange but functional.

"Sure, let me finish off my Gateway first and you can seal the entrance. And Bartholomew? Thank you. But next time, keep me in the loop? I might've taken the whole thing a bit better if you'd let me know what the plan was."

"You're my superior now, you need not ask such a thing. The ends justified the means, did they not?"

"Maybe. I guess we'll find out when we see what the ends look like."

29

QUADRUPLE JEOPARDY

The Frozen Forest was firmly under Lillian's control by noon. Having officially decreed Carlisle-Elites as 'Enemies of the Realm' and exiled them from her domain, any would-be defectors responding to Magnitude's recruitment drive would be forced to travel through the zone to physically find Carlisle-Elite members to induct them into their guild. Lillian's first priority was to remove that option. While she couldn't build a wall spanning the width of an entire zone in a single day, she had Godhammer, the newly reconvened Rising Tide and fifty Queen's Guard at her disposal.

Men fight with troops. Children fight with buildings. Lillian knew the strategic importance of both.

It had taken hours to clear out the Frozen Forest, a slow but inevitable process. Lillian could neither make her groups too small nor spread them too far apart, or else she'd invite a counterattack. She and her Queen's Guard were the most hardcore party by some margin and had taken the vanguard. The resurrection and healing abilities of her five embedded priests made taking them down next to impossible without improbably high sustained damage, which they were more than capable of returning in kind. Magnitude saw the writing on the wall and pulled all his incursion troops out of the zone.

With eyes on the no-man's land in front of Magnitude's wall, handpicked anti-scout teams from Godhammer and Rising Tide combed the forest in shifts. They were tasked to find players who hadn't got the memo, scouts who were hiding to provide intel or Carlisle-Elite parties who'd logged out with the intention of logging in again to attack from the rear. Tracks left in the snow meant such groups would be detected quickly and converged on soon after, if they were foolish enough to attempt such a thing. Lillian was leaving nothing to chance.

With the front line secured on both sides, the Empire NPC craftsmen came to the fore. First they built a joint encampment within the tree cover, a double-sized Tier I base that could be thrown together in under an hour. There was no shortage of timber to use for construction material, though the rocks for their Portal Stones had to be dug up, transported or both. They needed more rocks than that, though, because the scale of this conflict demanded they employ a tactic that had never been very popular. Siege weaponry.

The option had always been available, a tab in the Construction menu of every guild leader. Most had tried it once or twice before they understood it offered more problems than solutions: any siege weaponry constructed had to be transported, which was slow, difficult, boring and left the convoy vulnerable. Building it on site took time and was an invitation for the guild headquarters under 'siege' to swarm out while the attackers were focused on building. It's not worth much to break down a wall unless you can handle whatever's behind it. Equally, it's not worth much to build a wall unless you can prevent people from destroying it. It was usually easier to nuke the front gate with spells, gunpowder or brute force, even factoring in casualties, than it was to try and coerce impatient players into the work and preparation required for a long siege.

However, this situation merited siege engines' use, as the top of Magnitude's wall was out of range of conventional weaponry from the ground. Lillian wasn't sure if they'd be able to destroy the wall itself. If not, they'd at least provide the ability to fire back at the people manning it. She set Andrew and Hammertime to crafting as many siege engines as possible while she went online to harass more guilds into joining them.

She'd only been messaging for a few minutes when she heard Hammertime and Andrew arguing with each other. This time sounded a bit more heated than usual, which was saying something. Despite being smaller, Andrew was the louder of the pair. What he had to say explained the volume.

"Lillian made you Warmaster! You represent our military strategy. So *why* are you building catapults?"

He could not be serious. Lillian closed her menu and made her way around the campsite, her first Queen's Guard team forming up on her wherever she turned. It was Andrew who'd insisted she keep one group on her at all times. He'd posited, sensibly and calmly, that the easiest way for Magnitude to win this would be by killing her before the battle began. The same Andrew was now spitting over the beginnings of a catapult. He was serious. Even worse, Hammertime was defending his choice.

"—half as much time to build and nearly half the resources, because it doesn't need the massive counterweight. That means we don't waste time bri—"

"It doesn't matter if it takes less time and less resources if the end product is COMPLETELY USELESS! How can— Lillian! Tell this idiot that trebuchets are the superior siege engine!"

"That idiot is my Warmaster and I'll thank you to address him properly *in front of our combined forces*. You're the Court Wizard, not the court jester. Keep it civil."

Andrew wrung his hands.

"But Lillian, he's building catapults! It's like he wants us to fail!"

"I know. I'll talk to him. I'm less concerned with his choice of weaponry than your lack of tact. Come on, Andrew, we're all on the same team here. Hammertime, walk with me please."

She escorted Hammertime out of earshot, then immediately wheeled on him.

"Okay, dude. What the hell? I know we didn't use siege engines very often but catapults? Really?"

"They're much simpler to make, I used them effectively several times, that's my choice."

"Hammertime, I didn't make you my Warmaster out of sympathy or to say sorry or anything. I made you Warmaster because you deserve it. You're a smart guy and your heart's in the right place. So watching you build catapults is a real kick in the teeth."

"Aetherius is building trebuchets, I'm building catapults. He can sit in the back and lob stuff from the back line, feeling all smug about it. Meanwhile, I'll run the much more mobile catapults in to destroy the front gate with a concentrated barrage. We'll see who's an idiot then!"

"Hammertime, I can't let you do this. I want to give you autonomy to do as you see fit, but this is so black and white I just can't. A trebuchet can launch a 90kg projectile over 300 meters, with surprising accuracy. A catapult manages about half that, from less than half the distance. Assuming it gets within firing distance, which won't happen because they'll be the target priority. Please change the catapults to trebuchets so we have sustained supporting fire."

"Sorry, Lillian, I'm standing my ground on this one. We have to destroy the gate and a catapult rush is our best chance of doing that. Aetherius insulted me to my face, in front of both our guilds. I have to show him the error of his ways."

Lillian licked her lips and stared up at the tree canopy, contemplating. There wasn't any point in having Hammertime as her Warmaster if she couldn't let him know what was going on.

"Andrew was wrong to talk to you like that. I'll talk to him in private, like I'm talking to you in private. It's no excuse, but he's under excruciating pressure: Magnitude is his older brother. Magnitude also killed him on the day Aetherium fell. He stole everything in Rising Tide's vault and used it to build this wall."

"You're joking."

"I wish. Keep it to yourself. He was holding together pretty well, until he saw you building catapults. Let me put this in perspective for you: we'll get one chance at destroying this wall, and you, the Warmaster I've appointed despite our personal grievances, are insisting on catapults instead of trebuchets. When both Andrew and I are telling you, me slightly more politely than him, that they don't work."

Hammertime scratched the back of his head.

"Are you really sure catapults won't work? They always worked for me."

"You used them twice, and from what I saw of those battles they were window dressing. This is important, Hammertime, important enough to get upset about. If you insist on building catapults, I'll have you stake your reputation on it. I'll change your title from 'Warmaster' to 'Lord Catapult'. If it goes well, it will be an enormous compliment. If it goes the way Andrew and I expect it to, don't say we didn't warn you. Carry on."

She walked further away, far enough not to hear the boys if they went back to bickering, and returned to private messaging each of the guild leaders in turn. It was no good just posting it on her own wall or in the forums, they'd just pretend not to see it. She had to call them out individually.

Lillian was halfway down the list when she got a reply. She thought it would be more of the same sorry excuses from dithering, self-proclaimed leaders of men, so it was a nice surprise to get something from Damien instead. A brief release from her obligations. Then she read the message. It was a brand-new request on top of everything else she was dealing with.

Daemien: Hey Lillian. I know you must be super busy right now, but there's something I was hoping you could help me with? Message me when you're free.

Lillian: I'm free right now. As free as I'm gonna get, anyway. What's up?

Daemien: I'm hosting a party at the internet cafe near me and was hoping you could make it. Trying to get them some publicity.

Lillian ran it through her head. Nope, there was no way she could deem that reasonable in the context of reality.

Lillian: I'm kinda busy. Running a kingdom, preparing for a war, trying to stop Hammertime and Andrew from murdering each other. Then I have a work shift tonight. Don't think I can leave. Aren't you a little busy to be doing publicity stunts?

Daemien: You remember the goons who were chasing me? Think you called one of them 'pube-face'? This is the first internet cafe they followed me into. They impounded the pods and fined the employee who gave me shelter without ID. They're closing down next week.

Oh. Well then. Lillian forgot about what she was doing completely and focused entirely on Damien.

Lillian: You know it's not your fault, right? You didn't do anything wrong, you just did what you had to because CU wouldn't treat you OR your mom properly. They're the ones who killed that business, not you.

Daemien: I do know that. The place was already on the way out without CU's help. It would just be nice to make a positive change in the world, rather than everything I touch falling apart.

Lillian: Bravo. If Oscars were still a thing, I'd tip you for one. Where's the cafe?

Daemien: Thanks Lillian, having the new Queen of Camelot there will be awesome. I'll send you the address.

Lillian: I never said I was going, I asked where it was. There's a difference. You said it was a party? Who else is going?

Damien sent the address a moment later, then Lillian waited for his further reply. He'd been replying pretty quickly up 'til that point. Now it was total radio silence. It persisted long enough for Lillian to work it out for herself. About fifty occultists, he'd said.

Lillian: You're inviting me to an occultist party.

Daemien: Yeah. It's an occultist thing.

Lillian: Hard pass. I don't want to be surrounded by people who salivate at the thought of killing me.

Daemien: It's a game and they're real-life people. A bit weird, but definitely people. I think. It would be a good way of showing them you're a real person too, if you want their help. You said you'd suitably reward "anyone" who stepped forward to help in the fight. I've got them eating out of the palm of my hand, our support is pretty much guaranteed. This is a chance to kiss some real babies. And you'd be saving a family's livelihood. And you'd be helping me.

Lillian: One out of three isn't great. I'll think about it.

She closed the chat box down and allowed her role to settle back on her shoulders. Now it was even heavier, because she was weighing up the prospect of leaving her post for however long it took to get to the internet cafe. Things were under control here, but could she even get there and back in time to go to work?

This was a bonus objective, one she'd be annoyed to let pass her by if it was at all possible. She went into autopilot, copying and pasting the guild leaders the same message as she played out the timing in her head. It had to be at least an hour away. She could've given up on it right there, but she focused on it harder and found an uncomfortable solution: she could more than halve that time if she used the underground highway. Which would mean taking an automated taxi.

Really? Today? It seemed like a bad idea, which made Lillian even more determined. She was not a fan of obstacles. When they showed up in her path she was *more* inclined to go that way, not less.

Lillian's pestering was obviously working, because some of the guild leaders were finally responding. Lillian put her bonus objective on hold as she collected their ETAs and preassigned them different construction tasks, depending on their aptitude. While guilds comparable to Godhammer and Rising Tide followed their example, creating the trebuchets that required longer build times and greater artisan mastery, the lower-tier guilds were assigned to building preposterously tall custom ladders.

On the one hand the ladders seemed extremely necessary, in order to get players with no scope for versatility up on the ramparts. On the other hand, they seemed like a great way to get lots of her own people killed in extraordinarily inappropriately hilarious ways. Better to have them and not need them than the reverse. It wouldn't be much of a victory if they were still being murdered by enemies on and in the wall, or if Magnitude decided to take up permanent residence inside it.

When she'd finally finished issuing instructions to the arriving guilds, she returned to her encampment and found Hammertime presiding over the construction of several trebuchets. There were no catapults in sight. Thank goodness. That would make this chat with Andrew much easier.

"Andrew, I need to talk to you for a minute."

She led him away, taking a great deal more care to make sure they weren't heard than she had with Hammertime. Andrew was the first to speak.

"Thank you for talking sense into Hammertime. Sorry for losing my temper. If that's all, I need to get back to work."

"No, Andrew, that's not all. And even if it was, preventing me from speaking my mind will not make this faster."

"Alright, fine. What is it?"

"You're obviously stressed out, so I had to explain it to Hammertime. I told him who Magnitude is."

Andrew narrowed his eyes. Lillian stared back at him, waiting for something more concrete than an angry look.

"Why?"

"He needed a reason besides the two of you not liking each other to understand your aggression. Like it or not, he is now involved and needs to know the bare minimum. Knowing this fight is personal is the bare minimum."

"I disagree."

"He's making trebuchets, I must've done something right. Treat him like an ally rather than an enemy and there's a real danger the two of you will work well together."

"I won't hold my breath."

"That's fine, so long as you stop mouth-breathing all over him. I can't leave the two of you here alone if you keep fighting, I need to log off soon."

"Yeah, you need to eat. You haven't logged off since this morning."

"Neither have you...I'm not logging off just to eat. Damien invited me to an internet cafe for an event."

"With everything else you have on your plate?"

"Yeah, I know. But it's the right thing to do. He's trying to advertise an internet cafe so it doesn't close down. You have your personal stake in this, it seems this is his. Problem is, I'd have to go by automated taxi to get there fast enough. I know this is stupid—"

"It is stupid. I'm surprised you're even considering it, especially if you need to take an automated taxi. I know they're...you don't like them. We need you here and we need you at your best."

"If I don't do this thing that I know is the right thing to do, I won't be at my best. Besides, there will be lots of occultists there as well and we need to keep our options open. We'll need their help unless more players show up."

If Lillian thought casually dropping it into the conversation was going to make it hit more softly, she was mistaken.

"Damien is hosting an occultist party at an internet cafe, and you want to go?"

"I don't *want* to. I *have* to. We've been here for four hours and only six guilds have enlisted, with two hours to go. Since the Empire players aren't showing up, screw 'em. We need a safety net, Damien's providing one. That's worth a trip, don't you think?"

"I don't think putting you in an automated car to travel by yourself to a party full of weirdos, Damien included, is a good idea. And I won't pretend to change my mind to make you feel better about it."

"What if you came with me?"

"What, and left Hammertime in charge of the defense while we're gone? Are you out of your mind?"

"If he was as big an idiot as you're making him out to be, he wouldn't have given us half as much trouble when he was our enemy. Magnitude isn't sending anyone out, he's probably making his own preparations on the other side of the wall. Please come with me. I don't want to go alone, and I think it would be good for you and Damien to meet in person, as well."

Andrew drew his hand down his face.

"You're going no matter what I say, aren't you?"

"Yup."

"And if I don't help, you'll be traveling by yourself, by automated taxi, to a real-life occultist den, right before an endeavor that requires your complete focus."

"Concise and accurate. As expected of my Court Wizard."

"You're a pain. What food should I bring on my way to your place?"

It was 5:30pm. Damien's guests had been arriving for the last fifteen minutes, though he didn't know if his first choice of venue would have him. Its owner had chased him into the street earlier that day, after all. Hopefully Antonio would be a little less brash when there were witnesses who were also paying customers.

He'd managed most of the tasks set for him and a few more on top, although he'd not quite got around to groceries. He'd left his mom a note on the kitchen table apologizing, informing her he'd be home late and why. She'd understand. Right now he was a bit more preoccupied with what lay ahead.

He was sitting in the noodle bar window across the street, watching members of the Council of Nine enter. There wasn't realistically anyone else they could be, given he'd never seen anyone else go in there. Without that knowledge he wouldn't have had a clue, as it turned out occultists came from all walks of life.

Some were more or less what he'd expected, youths just like him. For each that came alone there'd be a pair traveling together, sometimes three or four. Interspersed between these arrivals were those he hadn't foreseen. Suited businessmen, coming straight from work. Suited businesswomen, doing the same. Middle-aged, pot-bellied men in jeans and T-shirts which were pulled up to expose their one-packs in the blistering heat, much to the chagrin of those around them.

The group he'd been dreading arrived toward the end: a put-upon lady with a floral dress and a strained smile entered, herding a gaggle of excited young children in front of her. Damien tried to make out Scorepeeus63 among them, but of course it was impossible. Scorepeeus63 had taken Damien's face on his avatar, after all.

When the kids entered, Damien decided it was time. If Antonio wouldn't have them, they needed to move to another venue before battle started. He'd have to give Lillian notice before they diverted to his second choice: the better organized, much larger pod hotel chain on the main road, about a ten-minute walk away. He could forgive himself for holding up the occultists a little, but something told him Lillian might not be so forgiving. She had a fair few more players to organize than he did.

It was a risk, but with a larger pod hotel nearby that was both willing and equipped to house them, Damien regarded it as a risk worth taking. That didn't make it easier to step through the door. He slurped down the last of his noodles, picked up his backpack and marched across the street through the internet cafe door, not allowing himself time to reconsider.

It was gratifying to see how many had shown up at his beck and call. He'd counted over forty people. The space was completely transformed by their presence. It was a bit crowded with the outdated cubicles taking up space, but everyone was gathered around and talking over them. Teenagers, moms, dads, suits, all happily chatting away. The youngest of them were kneeling on the chairs so they could see over the top.

Damien had been worried this would end up being awkward, but that couldn't have been further from the truth. There was one thing the group all had in common, besides their unwitting fealty to a manifestation of Satan: they all had sticker labels on the front of their clothing. Damien took a step closer and squinted at one of the businessmen's labels, reading, with some incredulity, 'BabySharkolomew'.

"Ah-hah, Praise Be. Guess I don't need to ask who you are."

Stood off to the side of the doorway was one of the unsuited, larger gentlemen Damien had seen enter. If Damien wasn't mistaken, he'd been one of the first to arrive. His poorly fitting T-shirt had been mercifully pulled back down over his front and was now adorned with a sticker that had his name on it. 'Vargus'. He was holding a pad of sticker labels and a marker pen. This was clearly not his first rodeo. He scrawled 'Daemien' onto the top leaf and handed it over.

"If you could sign my headset later that would be awesome, but I guess you've got other stuff to worry about right now. If you don't mind my asking, why did you bring us here? This shop's a bit small and this guy isn't prepared for us."

He tilted his head toward the back and Damien followed his glance. Antonio was carrying beanbags out of a back room five at a time (or he would've been if he wasn't wedged in the doorway). He ripped them through, and as the lousy furniture dropped to the floor, his contorted face appeared in the frame.

He was just about managing to force a smile, but it didn't take a genius to see he was on the verge of tears. He finally had customers and was trying his best to accommodate them, but there were too many and he was all by himself. The desks were no use to people who'd come to play VR, he'd have to move them out to make room for the beanbags.

At this rate, Damien would have to take everyone to the larger chain round the corner. What would that do to Antonio? It was his own fault. Damien had come that afternoon to try and give him advance warning and had been talked down to and threatened instead. Part of him felt this served Antonio right. The rest of him felt physically sick, watching a grown man trying to stave off a meltdown.

Well, it was all up to Antonio in the end. This would be Damien's last attempt to help someone who thought himself above Damien's assistance.

"Vargus...that feels weird...can you come talk to him with me?"

"There's a Dream Factory round the corner, why don't we go there? Bit more expensive but much better equipped, it's a good chain."

"No, if we help him out we'll be done in a few minutes.

Come stand behind me, please, I don't want to talk to him alone. He seems stressed out."

They made their way to the back of the room, the people in front making space for them. It wasn't long before Damien was recognized and the players started yelling out to him. The physical presence of children was enough to keep the ruder adulations out of the adults' mouths. The physical presence of a parent was enough to keep the ruder adulations out of the children's mouths. For Antonio, just Damien's name was rude enough.

He dropped the next installment of beanbags and turned, right as Damien stepped into punching range. Damien stared up at him, daring him to do it. With the rest of the group behind him only Antonio could see his face, but everyone could see Antonio's. As sad a spectacle as he was, Damien wouldn't let him off the hook without taking back some of the verbal abuse. He'd spent enough of his life being walked over without it coming from a would-be beneficiary.

"I see you're struggling, since Gian isn't around and I didn't get the chance to tell you we were coming. Do you need help? We all need to be online as soon as possible, so if this isn't sorted out in the next few minutes we're going round the corner to the Dream Factory. Can we help you move the furniture, or should we just leave?"

"...Okay."

Damien lowered his voice.

"Try 'Yes please', and 'Thank you'."

"Yes please."

"And?"

"Thank you."

"You're *welcome*! Hey, everyone, we need to help Antonio make room. I should've given him notice we were coming but I was too busy farming souls all day, let's not make him suffer for it. Move all the desks to one side, please! Vargus, can you go with Antonio to the back and help him get more beanbags out?"

Minion management in real life was not so different from minion management in game. The only difference was that

Antonio had been much more difficult to get under control than Noigel. Not being able to give orders sure made things tricky, but in the end it came down to the same crucial underlying factor: incentive.

Incentive to meet Damien got forty strangers to travel from all over the city to a place they'd never heard of before. Incentive to help Damien remove the chip from his shoulder had convinced Lillian to do the same thing, on the eve of the fight she'd been preparing for all day and working toward all week. And while goodwill, compassion, courage and patience had got him nowhere with Antonio, holding the incentive of forty-plus paying patrons over his head had done the trick. He was a hard man to help and a harder man to love.

"I can't believe you got me in an automated taxi for *this*."

She actually came. Damien had barely turned when Lillian embraced him in a bone-crunching hug and Damien's thoughts went completely parkour. They did an additional backflip when he saw who was standing behind her, his hands awkwardly jammed in his pockets. Her plus one did not cut quite such a dashing figure in person as he did in game, but Damien had seen his streams more than enough to recognize him.

Andrew pulled out a hand and held it to him, his eyes rising up off the floor to meet Damien's.

"Long time no see."

Damien hadn't counted on meeting Andrew in person, least of all as Lillian's escort. While both of them were a bit out of place in this company, Andrew was most definitely regarded by occultists as the enemy. Damien put on his biggest smile and grabbed his hand, shaking it as enthusiastically as he could.

"Andrew! So glad you could make it! I wouldn't have got through the Path of Deceit without your help, now you're kind enough to show up here!"

Andrew glanced around at the players, who were an even split of puzzled looks and stink eyes. He understood the game immediately and put on a matching smile of his own.

"And we wouldn't have got through our challenges without your help, either. Thanks for inviting me."

"Have you been looking after Lillian?"

"As best as I can, not that she needs looking after. What do you think, Lillian? Have I been looking after you?"

Lillian put a finger to her pouting lips and answered in the same stage whisper, for everyone to hear.

"Meeeeeeh. He's doing alright. Hasn't pushed me down any holes, recently."

She clamped her lips together and did her very best not to laugh. Freaking Lillian. She knew exactly what she was doing. Damien gave up on the act and turned to address the room directly.

"Everyone. These are my guests, and my friends. Be nice. After we're done you'll be able to get autographs from all three of us: the Queen of Camelot, the streaming competition winner and...uuuh..."

It was Andrew who chipped in to save Damien from his faux pas, his flaring eyes menacing even without their customary green tinge.

"And the Big Bad Evil Guy himself! Where's my one true nemesis, Scorepeeus63? Is he here?"

One of the boys ran up to him and thumbed at himself, his feet planted wide. Scorepeeus63 acted almost exactly the same in real life as he did online. It was not endearing.

"Here I am! You screamed like a big girl and I killed you stone dead!"

Oof. This appeared to be one level past Andrew's tolerance threshold. Lillian didn't seem thrilled by the 'big girl' reference either, but Andrew was taking it a bit worse, his teeth grinding together.

"You certainly did, you little—"

Lillian elbowed him in the ribs, her eyes wide and warning.

"—man. It was a good kill, you caught me off guard. Can I get *your* autograph after we've finished up here?"

That was all it took. Score's face lit up and he puffed out his chest.

"S-sure! If you pay me."

Score's minder swept in, mouthed an apology and dragged

Score to the other side of the room by his arm, through the laughing plainclothes occultists. Lillian rubbed Andrew's back, soothing him and hurting Damien in equal measure.

"You did good. Nice touch, asking for his autograph. Very clever."

"None of our autographs will be worth much if we don't win this fight."

"True enough. Damien, hope you don't mind, but is there somewhere we can bed down separately? I'm used to playing in the privacy of my own home, you know? Damien?"

"Sorry, I was just...yeah, there are some pods available, as it happens. I'll talk to Antonio and let him know we're using them. Maybe after this is all over the three of us can sit down and have a chat?"

"No can do, I have a make-up work shift tonight. Not sure how I'll manage but I'll do my best. Maybe if I can stomach traveling alone you and Andrew can have at it? I'm sure you have a lot to talk about."

That was one way of putting it. Andrew spoke for both of them.

"One crisis at a time. I'm getting in a pod before any more children attack me. See you in there, Lillian. You too, Damien, maybe."

He gave them each a nod in turn and made for a pod, trying to give the occultists he was trapped with as wide a berth as possible. He clambered in and closed it before anyone could tell him not to, leaving Damien free to ask Lillian the burning question.

"So, you're seeing Andrew again, huh?"

"No! We're still clearing the air. Getting Excalibur with him gave me a lot to think about. How come you didn't freak out when he showed up?"

Damien thought back to the night they'd got past Archimonde, the state Lillian had been in and the action Andrew had taken.

"I kinda did. If you thought I'd freak out you could've at least told me he was coming! What's the deal?"

"I don't like traveling alone and I didn't want Andrew to be alone tonight either. I know there's a lot at stake for us, but he's even more worried about this than we are. You're still helping us, right? This isn't some occultist plot to stab us in the back?"

"Stab players in the back? Me? Never! Not you, anyway. Everyone here is showing up to the battle, and there are a few more logging in to join us from their own homes. You should log in as well, I'll message you in game."

He led her to one of the pods and gave her a nod. Lillian squeezed him by the shoulder before he could get away.

"Good luck."

"You too."

Lillian logged in and opened her eyes on her frontline encampment. The Queen's Guard squad hadn't moved an inch since she'd logged out, so she'd fallen right back into formation. Saga Online was moving into the evening stage, the light turning from clear and bright to the dimmer, golden hue. It was joined by the hubbub of conversation, construction noises, the sharpening of weapons, the crackling of campfires and the squelch of footsteps, all blending together in a single roar. The sound of a thousand raid parties, all raring to go.

Fifteen minutes left.

Lillian went straight to Hammertime and found Andrew already there, grilling him. Hammertime was standing stiffly, his arms tightly folded across his barrel chest, but he could barely get a word in as Andrew assailed him with one question after another. Their exchange looked every inch like a miniature poodle trying to intimidate a good-natured St. Bernard.

This was exactly why Lillian had always dealt with the people side of Rising Tide and had left Andrew with the numbers. Hammertime saw her squad coming and looked visibly relieved. Lillian tapped Andrew on the shoulder midrant.

"Thank you, Andrew, I'll take it from here. Please take a party outside and give me a status report, I want a rough estimate of how many players there are and their state of readiness."

"But Hammertime's already done that through messages!"

"Yes, Andrew, and I want you to physically look and tell me that what you see matches the information other guilds have been sending him. Now, please."

Andrew stalked off, messaging to pull a Rising Tide party onto him before he reached the gate. Lillian waited until he'd passed through to start conferring with Hammertime.

"Anything to report?"

"About an hour ago, Magnitude sent three battalions of NPC Carlisle-Elites in front of the wall. We prepared to defend our position, but they never came this way. My best guess is they've been put there to slow us down so the enemy gets more time to fire on us before we reach the wall. Most of the guilds still haven't shown up and I don't think they will."

"How many do we have?"

"Twelve."

"Twelve? Out of the twenty-four in the Round Table war council? On a Saturday evening? With the entire Human Realm at stake?"

"Yeah, I wasn't pleased, either. Most of them are low-tier guilds looking to get the rewards you promised. Those who answered are here in full force, but a lot of the guilds not participating are the highest-tier ones."

Lillian had figured out the reason why while Hammertime was talking. It's much easier to rationalize a ridiculous thing that has happened than a ridiculous thing you thought had no chance of happening.

"They'd rather sit on the fence and see who wins than participate and risk being on the losing side. Cowards."

"Yes, but technically, no. While you were out, I recruited several thousand new members into Godhammer."

Lillian couldn't see his face underneath the helmet, though she wished she could. He'd delivered the line as if he were making a statement about the weather, or noting he'd completed a milk run.

"Where did you get several thousand members from?"

"It turns out most players wanted in on the combat. The problem was that their leaders forbade it, on pain of being kicked from the guild. So I made a post, offering anyone in a nonparticipating guild to join Godhammer, under Camelot's new Warmaster. It went viral. You're looking at the leader of the largest guild in video game history."

"You've always been good at pinching other guilds' players, but this is a masterstroke."

"I just opened a door, they're the ones who used it."

"And now I've sent Andrew out to check on our forces, and in addition to whatever other players have shown up he's going to find several thousand Godhammer guild members?"

She didn't need to see his face to read this reply. Hammertime could only just about hold back his laughter, his answer coming out as a strained yelp.

"Yup."

"Well, he shouldn't have much to complain about, but he probably will anyway. Good work. How many players would you say we have, altogether?"

"It's over nine thousand."

"What, nine thousand? There's no way that can be right! Can it?"

"I think it's right. After all, you're probably thinking of high-level, serious players. I'm afraid most of these players are less—"

Hammertime's voice trailed off and Lillian turned to see what had stopped him. Andrew was marching toward them from the gate, his hands behind his back and a wan smile on his lips. He turned to Lillian, ignoring the person he was talking about completely.

"Hammertime has amassed a fine army of filthy casuals. Noobs, as far as the eye can see."

"Andrew, don't be negative. He's done great."

"Did that seem negative? That wasn't my intention, I guess it comes naturally. He's done well, I'm very impressed."

He managed to turn his head to Hammertime and inclined his head ever so slightly before continuing.

"I need to get Rising Tide formed up. In the battle, I suggest you give orders to guild leaders and we relay them to our own troops. We'll operate better with the people we're familiar with, our players are more likely to respond to us and we can give more precise instructions. You give us objectives, we'll decide how to carry them out. How Hammertime will manage that with thousands of new recruits, I have no idea. Should be interesting. Now might be a good time for the two of you to figure that out."

He reached up to slap Hammertime on the shoulder, thought better of it, gave him another curt nod and then left to gather up his raid party. His suggestion was a lot better than what Lillian had been thinking of doing. Hammertime, his whole body encased in armor, was unmoving and inscrutable. Nevertheless, Lillian could hazard a guess as to what he was thinking about.

"You don't know how to manage several thousand players simultaneously, do you?"

"Not as such. Do you?"

"Nope, I had one bad idea for myself until Andrew suggested delegating responsibility. I guess it'll have to do for you: stick them all in a separate raid group, designate yourself and me as the only people who can speak and order them like that. They won't win any synchronized dancing competitions, but it's enough to tell them to go forward or back."

"What if they don't listen to me?"

"Guess you weren't thinking about that when you recruited them, huh? Don't worry, in Rising Tide I had to deal with large amounts of new recruits all the time. I recommend shouting very loudly, possibly cursing as well. Either it works, or you feel a little better when it doesn't."

"That's not encouraging."

"Unless you think of something better in the next few minutes, that's all I have for you. I'll be front and center with my Queen's Guard, going for the front gate. If I die, you're in charge. That means you'll stay at the back, with your core guild members operating the trebuchets."

"You want me in the back? I thought as your Warmaster we'd be fighting side by side."

"I'd much rather have you on the front line with me, but I need you to do something far more important: be my eyes. We'll maintain communication at all times. Tell me everything you see. Movements on the wall, where the line is weakening, any opportunities that present themselves."

She paused, waiting for some sign of acknowledgment from Hammertime. A few seconds passed before his helmet faded from view. The last time he'd done this, it had been to show Lillian how completely unfazed he was by her verbal assault. Now it was the complete opposite. He was afraid. It didn't sit right on his ruggedly handsome tailored face, which only made it more apparent.

"I've never done anything like this before, Lillian. Most units I've ever managed in combat was about a hundred, and that was against you. This isn't a guild fight, this is a war. The scale is too big. I don't know if I can handle it."

"Don't worry, Hammertime. We'll figure it out together. I know you'll do your best. I don't think there's anyone else out there who could do better. I trust you."

She stuck her hand out and Hammertime shook it, his face hardening back into the confident expression he'd crafted it with the view to expressing. However, she didn't want him to be *too* comfortable.

"I trust you, except for your choice of siege engine."

"Nobody's perfect."

That came out of nowhere, and so quickly. She gave his hand a squeeze to mask her surprise.

"You're damn right, but we're more than good enough. I'll give you some time to prepare. Keep an eye out for my voice chat invitation, then keep an eye out for me."

Lillian did not share Andrew's reservations. She smacked Hammertime on the shoulder and was both surprised and pleased when Hammertime smacked her back. She couldn't keep herself from smiling. This was a relationship that might outlast this conflict, whichever way it went. She turned and called all her Queen's Guard onto her location as she invited all the guild leaders into a group. They were quick to accept, and she was quick to get to the point.

"No more typed messages to me, anything you need to share comes through here. Urgent messages only. Not everyone came, but you did. Thank you. Good luck out there."

To her annoyance, while she'd been talking there had come an incessant string of chat box *pings*.

Daemien: Yo.

Daemien: Yoyo.

Daemien: Yoyoyo.

Daemien: Yoyoyoyo.

Lillian: WHAT?

Daemien: Yoyoyoyoyo.

Daemien: We can't get anywhere near the front line, we're blocked by thousands of red names. If you want us to help, you need to cancel our 'Enemies of the Realm' status! We're literally here to fight for the realm!

Lillian: Wait.

How to balance this out? Lillian didn't want to use the occultists unless she had to. Nor could she afford to offend them, in case she needed them. In which case, she could hold them in reserve with Hammertime. Lillian called her Warmaster and he immediately picked up.

"I'm getting them lined up as fast as I—"

"There's something else. Damien is behind us with an occultist raid party."

"Should we call off the attack?"

"No! They're here to help. When we move in for the attack, I'll tell him to move the occultists up. If you see us struggling somewhere, send the occultists in before you go yourself. I'm rescinding their 'Enemies of the Realm' status for this fight. If they do something stupid, let me know."

"I hope you know what you're doing."

"If they wanted to screw this up, Damien wouldn't be telling us where they are. I'd rather be diplomatic than encourage a bunch of battle-ready occultists to attack us from behind. Damien won't, but I can't speak for the rest of them. Your role just became even more important. Try to be friendly.

I'll make sure Damien listens to you and hopefully they'll listen to him."

"Understood."

"Keep this line open. Wheel the trebuchets into the open the moment we move out. Call for silence on your group chat. It's time."

Lillian went onto her guild leader channel.

"Everyone take your positions. Sixty seconds, then we charge. If we wait until everyone's ready we'll be here all night. Put me through to all your guilds, now. I need to say something before we go."

She went into Damien's chat box.

Lillian: I'm removing 'Enemies of the Realm' from occultists now. You're hanging back with Hammertime. Wait until he orders you to move in. Follow his instructions as if he were me.

The multitasking required for this was insane. Lillian had just thirty seconds left to run her checks on herself, now she'd finished helping everyone else. She opened her stat page.

Class: Paladin
Level: 51
Health: 2,050/2,050 **Stamina:** 2,050/2050 **Mana:** 1,550/1,550
Strength: 635 **Agility:** 60 **Intelligence:** 60
Constitution: 205 **Endurance:** 205 **Wisdom:** 155
Stat points: 0
Experience: 14,158/110,000

Nope, she was still fine. The level 50 gear she'd commissioned herself in Camelot with her newfound wealth was a big part of it, but Excalibur granted her 255 strength all by itself. With a 3 x strength multiplier on her weapon and 510 base damage on top, there was only one way to describe her: obscene. Let alone if she activated Divine Might. A single Divine Might-buffed hit with Excalibur would do over 4,000 damage, if Andrew's calculations proved correct. Closer to 8,500 if it was a critical hit, which was very much the basis on which she played with bladed weapons.

She was a one-shot killer queen. She'd leave the dynamite and laser beams to Trinytea and Andrew, respectively.

Lillian wanted to do away with the prefight tension and get stuck in, but there was one task left: she had to properly motivate her army. The guild leaders had patched her through to their combined forces. She was going out live to some ten thousand players.

What could she say to so many people, from so many walks of life, to strike a chord with as many of them as possible? To instill the spirit required for this endeavor? Not too cringy, not too careless, not too boring, a speech that united all of them?

It was a tough one. A lot of these players were about to face twenty-four-hour death timers and would likely accomplish next to nothing through their individual sacrifices. Yet to most of them, this was just a game. She'd alienate just as many of them by taking it too seriously.

Then a name had come to mind. Someone she'd often been associated with before she'd learned to do what she did without dying. A long-revered name, likely more legendary to this group than Excalibur, King Arthur and the Knights of the Round Table combined.

"This is Lillian. You have ten seconds to turn down your chat volume before I give my prebattle speech."

Everyone had heard her speak, softly though it may have been. The forest fell silent. With nothing but a flick of her head, the occultists were removed from her list of 'Enemies of the Realm'. The Carlisle-Elites were now alone in that regard. She closed her menu to find all had turned toward her, waiting to hear what she had to say. Lillian took a deep breath, thrust Excalibur above her head and screamed out her chosen words.

"Alright, let's do this: LEEEEROOOOOOOOOOOOOOOOOY—"

The solemn silence was replaced with uproar, much of it laughter. There were winces from those who hadn't taken her volume advice seriously. There was mild confusion from those who had yet to stumble across this most ancient of memes, but there was also a resounding roar in reply from those who knew it well. Those who didn't would surely look it up after this. There were enough who did that her call was joined by thousands upon thousands of ecstatic voices.

"—NNNNNJENKIIIIIIINS!"

She turned and ran into the no-man's land, her Queen's Guard flanking her on either side and the largest army ever to grace Saga Online stampeding behind her.

30

FAITH, STEEL AND GUNPOWDER

Damien was still typing out his unmeasured response when the horde of red names in front of him turned green. Seconds later Lillian's war cry rang through the forest, followed by a wall of noise as almost everyone else took it up with her. Then the snow slid from the trees as thousands of footfalls shook the earth.

He'd spent all day getting ready to help Lillian and she'd left him on the bench. He closed the chat box and yelled into his comms at the fifty occultists he'd handpicked for the fight.

"They've started, everybody move up to the battle line as fast as you can! Control your own minions for now."

Damien had been able to get closer than the rest of them, since he could Shadow Walk in daylight. His 'Sunset Emperor' ability didn't work while he was in his Pride form, but having finished farming he'd reverted to his original state. This was very much intended. He had the 10 soul energy in his Soul Reserve required to transform back, a surprise tool that would help him later. If the battle wasn't over before he even got there.

The first explosion echoed through the forest, then a whole series of them on top of each other. He ran forward through the trampled mud, looking for Hammertime. No sign. He sent Noigel up a tree at the edge of the clearing and Demon Gated to his position, then scanned the battlefield left and right to find his liaison. He hadn't managed a full sweep before the scene in front of him captured his attention and would not give it back.

What lay in front of him was barbarous insanity. Combat had started less than half a minute ago and already the ground was littered with bodies. There were so many, both standing and fallen, that you couldn't see the snow. The wall was a perfect staging ground from which to rain projectiles down upon them, whittling their numbers down wherever they'd been left unprotected.

When Damien and Lillian had made their first assault, the wall was only operating at a fraction of its efficiency: there'd been NPC guards lining the top and NPC archers firing through embrasures across the middle. Three more rows of embrasures were now being utilized, running all the way from one side of the wall to the other.

Now Damien was bearing witness to the firepower of a fully armed and operational death wall. It was no longer manned with NPCs, who were instead serving as cannon fodder in front of the gate. Their positions had been taken by the ostensibly thinking and breathing player characters who'd opted for immediate gratification.

The wall allowed the tiny fraction of players who'd most effectively murdered their kin in the Frozen Forest to take full advantage of their betrayal of the human race. Their protected vantage points meant they were free to strike at those arrayed below them with complete impunity, ensuring through their combined efforts that their immorally obtained advantage was preserved. All they had to worry about was who to target.

Exploding arrows, fireballs, lightning bolts and worse descended into the massed ranks of those their achievements drove them to see as less than them. The level 50 abilities were particularly obvious, unleashed upon droves of dissenters that didn't even know their names.

Slow-moving orbs of electricity shot out tendrils of jagged blue light in bursts at all in their proximity until the orbs hit the ground and exploded with horrific consequences. Towering walls of ice blocked, froze and impaled those around them, funneling the masses into choke points for effortless extermination. Flamethrowers emanating from the lowest floor of the wall created an impassable blanket of fire that scorched everything in their path, slaughtering both the attackers and the allied NPCs locked in combat with them.

From the top of the wall rained down concentrated streams of arrows and gunfire, which were still less horrible ways to go than what some of the assassins now had access to: clouds of yellow death, spreading from poisonous bombs lobbed over the front line, scalding all they touched inside and out.

Their new allegiance had availed these players the privilege to obtain great power. Power they intended to maintain. Power that was only power, in relative terms, if it was kept beyond the reach of those who came after them.

Yet even in the face of certain destruction, Lillian's forces advanced. Everyone who'd answered her call knew why they were there: death, glory or both. The bodies on the field remained unlooted. Sanctuary spells overlapped each other on the front line, keeping as much of the onslaught at bay as possible. When one went down, another went up in its place.

The hardiest tanks had survived the initial barrage and were now forming a strong front line, the unrelenting heals landing upon them meaning only a one-shot kill would bring them down. The enemy had plenty of those, but were instead focusing their fire on the squishier players behind them.

"Keep pushing forward! Ladders at the ready! Suppressing fire! Treb support is coming!"

Damien tore his eyes away and found Hammertime. He had to be talking to them over comms, but his bellows seemed intended to make himself heard over the din of battle from half the field away. He was pushing an enormous trebuchet out from the forest with a team of ten Godhammer guild-mates, though he was all but pushing it by himself as the rest of them struggled to keep up with him.

As Damien descended the tree, Hammertime let the machine roll forward and twisted to check on the remaining four trebuchets still approaching their positions. Then he looked over the battlefield and saw what Damien had just seen. He cradled his head in his hands, struggling to comprehend the catastrophe unfolding in front of him.

"They need support, loose! *Loose!* That means *fire*, you shit-wits! LOOSE!"

The trebuchet arms whirled round in deceptively lazy arcs, but the boulders in the slings were moving anything but lazily. There was a low *whomph* as they hit top speed and were released to hurtle over the battlefield. They'd been used a little hastily, but the wall was a large target. The *clangs* were abrupt, the *screech* of metal heinous, even over the cacophony of battle emanating from a quarter kilometer ahead of them.

Ten seconds later, five more vacuums created by five more preposterously fast-moving boulders stirred the air. The impacts rang out, creating five gaping wounds in the wall's outer layer and exposing the players within. Hammertime yelled in triumph and the struggling players across the battlefield echoed his call. This seemingly impregnable defense could be hurt. The players behind it were not untouchable. The shift in morale was not just audible, but palpable.

Damien jumped to the floor and ran up, hoping to catch Hammertime before he started yelling again. He'd nearly made it and Godhammer had almost finished resetting when a projectile tinged off Hammertime's helmet. He took no damage, but precious few of his players were wearing heavy armor and none of them were level 50, unlike Hammertime himself. Damien stopped in his tracks as two other players in Hammertime's personal group fell to the ground.

This was monstrous. The trebuchet's ranged superiority was being rendered moot. The Carlisle-Elite didn't have the ability to destroy siege engines at this range, yet their superior technology allowed them to kill the teams operating them without warning.

Hammertime stared at the freshly made corpses of his teammates in disbelief as another projectile tinged off the back of his head. He had no priests. They'd all embedded themselves in the attacking force, where it had been thought they'd be most useful. The other teams were also under fire, yet they did not stop until their leader ordered them to.

"Anyone not in heavy armor, retreat to the forest! Oh for f— I'm talking to the treb teams, not you in front! Attacking force, keep advancing! Treb operators in light armor, find cover!"

In the time it had taken him to address this problem, more of his team had been wiped out. Such a simple mistake, resulting in so many wasted lives. His lightly armored units fled for the forest, the shots mostly missing now they were aimed at moving targets rather than sitting ducks standing at their posts. The damage was done. Without enough players left to operate them, the trebuchets may as well have been destroyed.

While everyone else had retreated, Damien had sprinted forward and taken cover behind a sturdy wooden strut on Hammertime's personal machine. Damien's stats might have significantly improved but his armor was still not designed to keep out bullets. He had no desire to get done in by campers. He twisted his head around the corner and found Hammertime trying to operate the trebuchet entirely by himself, apologizing to whoever was on the other end of his comms.

"Our teams have been compromised, I'm so sorry, please hold on, I'll make it work. All armored core Godhammer units, come to my location. We have to keep firing at least one!"

Damien could fix this.

"Hammertime, cancel that order. I can—"

"Damien, I'm busy! I'll deal with you in a minute!"

As usual, a demonstration would be necessary for anyone to have any faith in him. Damien tersely got on his own comms, his finger pressed to his ear.

"Nine-year-olds, don't come out of the woods yet. Snipers. Send all the incubi out where I can see them. Noigel, where are you? Stop messing around and come here!"

Damien's entire personal lineup was composed of imps, both to ensure Noigel was on form and to fuel Damien's many imp-related abilities. Unfortunately, high intelligence was no substitute for enthusiasm. Noigel slowly and deliberately weaved back and forth through the air as bullets whipped all around him, keeping his movements unpredictable to avoid taking any hits. It was effective in many regards: he was trolling not only the players aiming at him, but Damien too. By the time he landed between Damien's legs, it would've been quicker to have dismissed and resummoned him.

"Noigel, how much do you know about the operation of siege engines and can you convey it to a horde of incubi?"

They eyeballed each other as sniper shots thudded into the ground all around them. Damien only looked up when his incubus platoon arrived from the trees as instructed. He had the Soul Summon Limits of fifty occultists to draw from. Under his instruction, they'd shared their gear so that their Soul Summon Limits were maxed. Given that none of them were level 50 and thus his 'Legion' trait was an impossibility for any of them, that represented a combined Soul Summon Limit of 1,500. A little more than Damien was used to handling.

This was more than high enough to justify a very satisfying fifty incubi. It was also more than high enough to justify Damien boosting Noigel's intelligence stat as high as possible, since he'd be micromanaging considerably more minions on Damien's behalf. The problem was, Damien had never dealt with Noigel when he had such high intelligence. Which, coupled with his imp's well-documented aggravation at not receiving his rewards, had some drawbacks.

Noigel was not speaking. Damien had thirty-five more imps than the required amount for him to do so. Noigel was being a dick. Damien drew breath for a follow-up question.

"Would you like me to grab you by the throat and hold you out for target practice?"

"It's a trebuchet. It chucks rocks at idiots, for idiots. It's not brain science or rocket surgery."

"I'll take that as a yes. I want ten incubi on each trebuchet in the next ten seconds, or else I'll perform brain science or rocket surgery on *you*."

Noigel screeched directly into Damien's face without looking away. It seemed most of it was for effect. The incubi started moving as Noigel uttered the first syllable and split up perfectly into their separate teams long before he'd finished.

As they started winching, greasing and loading the mechanisms with Hammertime gawping at them, the snipers tried their luck on the new targets. Their bullets could pierce the incubi's armor no more easily than they could Hammertime's.

This was where the majority of the Council of Nine's efforts had gone: dressing fifty incubi 'to the nines', as it were. The latest in incubus fashion had not come cheap or easy, but it had proven manageable once a dozen occultists had converted their bases into imp/consumer sweat shops. The Tier III Demon Forges had provided a considerable upgrade, one Damien felt was long overdue. They offered minion gear with stats.

While minions gained stats every five levels, they still fell far behind the stat gains of players. Even less balanced, the gear players wore scaled higher and higher as they progressed to each level, making the minions less and less useful as they did so. Damien found it quite reasonable that at the high threshold of level 50 he should finally gain access to comparable amenities for his own minions, keeping them competitive at the cost of the preparation time and material requirements that seemed to go hand in hand with being an occultist.

However, he was willing to concede he'd been surprised he could deck out *any* occultist minion in Tier III Demon Forge gear. The stats on the gear simply scaled with the level of the minion wearing it. It could've been better, if they'd all been able to equip gear with level 50 stats. It would've been considerably worse if none of them could wear it at all. Damien wasn't about to complain about the compromise Mobius had made.

Damien's only regret was that he couldn't wear it himself in his Pride form. He'd tried. Repeatedly. He imagined Archimonde had tried too, and given that Archimonde would have access to better gear and was higher level it was probably just as well.

Damien gave up on outstaring Noigel when the trebuchets fired for the third time. He had better things to do. He possessed a passing incubus so he could see what was happening without putting himself in danger. The third round of boulders punched into the wall either near or directly on top of the initial impacts, causing vastly more damage to the already compromised structure. It didn't look quite so impervious now.

The army had made their way through NPCs and suppressing fire and were now crowded against the wall. Though they were still under attack they'd thoroughly embedded themselves, none more so than Lillian's personal team: her Queen's Guard had formed a solid layer of shields blocking out the view from all sides. The fifty of them had to be crammed in there like sardines, but they were certainly all protected. In addition to the wall of armor covering them, the bright golden domes indicated three of the five priests had active Sanctuary spells.

Damien didn't know how Lillian would swing her hammer in the middle of this group, but she could only be working on bringing the gate down. She'd breached the wall with Rising Tide the first time round, had cleared it all the way through with ten players on her second attempt and was leading this third, considerably larger offensive now. She was the undisputed authority on breaking through Magnitude's wall. Whatever she was doing in there, it would work. It was only a matter of ti—

Far back from the front line, something was happening: a gap appeared in the crush of players, a gap that widened as everyone in the vicinity drew away from the disturbance. A single orb of blue light was the cause. A lone Login Sphere, in the middle of the no-man's land. Whoever it was, they were alone. Which was when Damien realized, even with the distance between them, that the sphere was much, much larger than regular size.

There was only one player it could be.

Damien turned to yell a warning at Hammertime before remembering he couldn't currently speak. He canceled the Possession just as Hammertime started bellowing again, at what sounded like everyone. He'd figured it out as well.

"Lillian, it's Archimonde, Archimonde's logging in from the center of the field, all guild leaders stop what you're doi—"

The sphere cracked open and dissipated to reveal what was inside: pus, oozing from a burst cyst. Archimonde had arrived on the field of battle. For the first time, Damien could see its level: it was at level 58. A myriad of portals appeared all around it, but before any of its minions had stepped through Archimonde was already flicking its wrist at one target after the next. Archimonde had only flicked its wrist a few times, but the Corruption was spreading quickly. Archimonde had taken the 'Contagion' trait, allowing Corruption to spread by touch. These conditions, with so many people crammed so close together, were an ideal breeding ground.

While Archimonde's wrist continued to flick, some of the more optimistic players ran in to engage the creature in melee. Archimonde's other hand pointed at the floor beneath its feet and a Circle of Hell appeared there. All players within its confines were snared and set ablaze, which is when the armored hell hounds began to savage all around them.

It appeared Archimonde had also dressed his minions for the occasion. Damien focused, trying to give them new orders, but it didn't work. Every time he, Archimonde or Bartholomew had employed this undocumented skill, the minions had either been freely given or were in close range. He'd have to get closer. Damien was more than willing, since he couldn't beat the shit out of Archimonde without doing so.

There was no time to Shadow Walk there. Nor could he transform and Charge, because Archimonde was surrounded by allied players who'd break the Charge on impact. Damien rounded the trebuchet he'd been using as cover and immediately broke into a run. Other players had taken a similar view and were starting to react. Ranged abilities thudded into Archimonde's vast consumer body, doing little and sometimes even healing it if they were carelessly cast at the gaping maw. The tongue flicked out and caught a priest spamming Dispels.

As she died in Archimonde's jaws, the mouth opened even wider and two more tongues lashed out of it, wrapping around anyone in the vicinity and drawing them in before they knew what was happening. For the regular consumers, successfully eating one enemy doubled the speed, range and draw strength of Tongue Lash – 'Feeding Frenzy'. Compound interest. Archimonde's Sin of Greed-based version was at least three times more effective, based on the proliferation of tongues.

Damien was not deterred. In the ten seconds since Archimonde had arrived, nearly a quarter of Lillian's army had been infected and Corruption was still spreading. Archimonde pointed at an imp flying toward the front of the army, his tongues apparently seeking targets of their own accord while he focused on other matters. The Imp-losion overhead scattered players all around it. The Corruption was spread even to those who'd been careful, starting new blooming points.

From overhead, on the wall, it would've been similar to seeing a bacterial culture blossom on a petri dish. Which was likely close to how Magnitude's forces viewed the players opposing them in the first place. It wasn't killing everyone, but it was killing a lot of them and weakening all of them to further attacks from other sources. A single spell, cast a handful of times, could do this much damage in the right conditions.

Meanwhile, Archimonde was feeding itself so quickly, standing so firmly in the center of the Circle of Hell and eating so rampantly, that nothing could kill it fast enough. All the while, the influence of the Embodiment of Greed was reducing pressure on the attack on the wall. Damien was halfway there when Archimonde spotted him. Damien had him right where he wanted him: as far as Archimonde was aware, he'd be just another easy meal. Damien was nearly close enough to hit Archimonde with a kunai. His transformation would be almost instantaneous. Archimonde would have no time to react.

Damien was putting his hand over his heart when Archimonde stabbed a finger into the air. Damien couldn't hear what he was saying over the hubbub, nor did he need to. He stopped and looked up, where the black ball of nothing appeared in its infancy and started to grow. When he looked back down, Archimonde was already facing the wall. Where Archimonde's imps had been flying. A second later, Archimonde was gone, standing on the damn wall. Replaced with a paltry imp.

Why had Archimonde fled? This was supposed to be it! Yet the moment it had seen Damien, Archimonde had immediately abandoned what it was doing, despite having no obvious cause for concern. The damage was done. The entire battlefield was stampeding away from the wall as the Dark Omen in the sky grew. It wouldn't be long before it tore into the ground, sucking in a huge number of players with it. They had to get clear, but the person with the furthest to run was Lillian, who'd been attacking the front gate.

Damien started running forward, against everyone else. He wouldn't leave her there. It was only a few seconds before she passed him, effortlessly outrunning everyone nearby. She did not look happy, but she was very much alive. Her Queen's Guard were nearly keeping pace with her, covering her escape to their own cost. Most of the wall was firing at her location, attempting to bring her down while her back was turned. Ironically, much of their ordnance was sucked into the Dark Omen forming overhead, but the same could be said of the trebuchet shots being fired to cover the army's escape.

Damien ran back the way he'd come, fighting the instinct that he was running the wrong way. Lillian retreating made it easier yet harder at the same time, given the look on her face. He got a good view of it once she stopped and turned, prompting him to turn with her, right as the Dark Omen plummeted into the earth. Players who hadn't got clear were sucked backward into it, along with many of the corpses that had been littering the ground. What little was left of the evening light grew even dimmer.

The entire offensive had been interrupted at the critical moment. While they'd done a little damage to the wall and Lillian may have done some damage to the gate, their casualties were obscene. They'd have to start again. A new defensive line had formed outside the gate, only visible now the Dark Omen had passed.

This time it was Carlisle-Elite players rather than NPCs, the big guns. There weren't as many of them, but they were all over level 50. That wasn't the most offensive thing about them. Not even close. They were squatting down, looting the bodies during the lull in combat. They'd suffered next to no casualties and were already profiting from their tactic.

The equipment of those who opposed them would be distributed to fill the gaps in their gear or melted down to reinforce their wall. The potions would become fuel to kill the next wave. The gold might well fund the next place Magnitude enacted this strategy. Compound interest, fed by the exploitation of the living with a view to turning them into the dead.

Lillian's army was in complete disarray. Many of the players were still on low health with no potions and not enough mana between the healers to get everyone combat-ready. Sniper shots were ringing into the assembled masses even as they paused for breath. It was obviously time to pull the occultists off the bench. Damien walked up to Lillian as she shouted orders.

"All healers with no mana or mana potions, report to the supply chain! Any party with less than twenty-five players dissolve yourselves and join other groups! I need anyone with a shield to join my Queen's Guard and make a defensive line, we're still taking fire from marksmen!"

There wasn't time to be polite. The longer they waited, the longer Magnitude would have to take advantage of their absence. Damien's forces were still fresh and the way to the gate was clear. He could go all out. He pulled Lillian's arm away from her ear and stared into her eyes.

"We need to attack now, the occultists are ready to go. Or do you want us—"

—to keep cheerleading from the back, is how he'd have ended the sentence, if Lillian hadn't interrupted him by pulling her arm away and pointing a finger in his face. And then she just wandered away from him, shaking her head in disbelief. She regarded him as a burden.

Fine. Damien was past asking for permission and did not require forgiveness. He put his hand over his heart and muttered his Sin under his breath.

"Pride."

He exploded into his true form, the players on all sides of him falling beneath his lofty perspective, then cracked his neck each way. This body had already become more comfortable to him than his normal one, having spent hours abusing its benefits during that day's grind. It was not quite so comfortable for the rest of the human race arrayed around him. They were cutting him a wide berth, much as they had Archimonde. Damien couldn't care less what they thought. This was how he operated, now. No more slinking in the shadows. Instead he'd throw some shade.

He'd turned away from player-killing. He'd advocated cooperation. He'd been patient. Even a personal relationship with the Ruler of the Empire hadn't been enough to grant him due consideration. He paced up and down to avoid the sniper shots now trained solely on him as he publicly adopted the only operable position he'd been left with. He was ostensibly talking to his occultists, but everyone heard what he had to say.

"Occultists, forward. Battle formation as discussed. I'll go first to prevent more looting; no one loots Empire corpses except us. We need to defend our protection racket, since they can't defend themselves."

The snipers had hit him a couple of times while he spoke, tracking his movement. Damien was a large, large target. Irritating. Actions speak louder than words. Damien paced a little longer until a final shot dropped his hit points just below 50%. When his body bulked up as his Narcissistic Rage kicked in, he faced the wall and Charged.

When he'd been in Possession of a regular incubus, Damien had been able to get halfway across the no-man's land in the ten seconds following his Charge but had then been forced to plod the rest of the way over with regular movement. However, his new body retained his agility stat and 'Single-Mindedness' doubled the speed of his Charge after twenty feet, a distance he could achieve in a single stride.

Damien was the only player present who was not surprised when he cleared the length of the battlefield in just a shade over four seconds.

He'd chosen his target arbitrarily, since it didn't make much difference what he decided to hit. They all looked pretty much the same. He honed in on the largest blob in the middle of a long line of indistinct figures. It was BiggusDickus. Who was looking rather flaccid at Damien's approach. He fluffed himself up a bit right before Damien reached him, grounding his shield in the dirt and bracing himself behind it.

This would've been very effective against a conventional Charge. However, when the devil grants you a body that weighs approximately a ton and has a top Charge speed in the region of 50 meters per second, most of these details work out in your favor in the majority of circumstances.

Damien's Charge was ended the moment his shoulder connected with the shield. All the kinetic energy had already been transferred. BiggusDickus's health was already low as he flew backward into the gate. His flight was short, his end was not sweet. The gate did not fare well, but it fared better than BiggusDickus did. Fare-poorly, BiggusDickus.

The players around Damien were not attacking, for some reason. In fact, they were running toward the gate, which remained firmly closed. Those who arrived there first were screaming and pounding on it, even. Damien needed to get his health back up before the ten seconds of life-steal were depleted. He threw a chain kunai at one of the runners, then pulled them into his melee range. His second kunai ran them through on arrival.

The chunky design of the kunai traded off quick attack speed for better armor penetration and more damage. This was not a problem when most things Damien attacked died in either one or two hits. It was even less of a problem when Damien had the size and strength to wield them as if they were regular daggers. His health was now above half and his strength had dropped back to pre-Enraged levels, but he still did more than enough damage to put most of the enemies away in one, two or three hits, depending on whether he managed a critical strike with either or both of his first two attacks.

It was a shame that the 'Stagnation' effect while he was using Pride prevented him from getting experience. He'd never killed so many players with so little effort. It did not take long. It didn't take much longer for enemies in the wall to start firing back.

The most noteworthy disadvantages of the Pride form were twinned. His lack of armor and preposterously large character model were an extremely poor combination. Damien's health was as high as the sturdiest tank, yet he had no armor to make the most of it. While his life-steal was superb for sustainability it only lasted for ten seconds after he went below half health. He'd still die if he was hit by enough attacks simultaneously, or if he didn't get his health back above 50% before his Narcissistic Rage effect ended.

All he could do was keep moving as unpredictably as possible. A second standing in one place would invite death. He'd acquired a variety of new dodging mechanisms on the Path of Deceit, and the rest of them he'd been practicing for his entire play-through. So long as he wasn't jumping straight toward or away from the players aiming at him, any movement was good movement.

He had a lot of different factors to look out for, including keeping an eye on the wall to evade the larger, nastier spells being thrown his way. So it took him a few seconds to find a spot where he was comfortable enough to answer Lillian's voice call.

"I'm busy, Lillian."

He hung up. That felt good, until he remembered he was about six feet away from her in real life. No time to think about it now, he was running out of prospects to attack on the ground level but there were still plenty of projectiles coming his way. Some of the players aiming at him were doing so through the holes that had been left by the trebuchets. Mistake. He feinted toward a player on the ground, then jumped up and hurled both kunai at a mage who'd been channeling a spell in plain sight. One hit sufficed.

It was a shame he couldn't pull himself toward players lighter than him without canceling his Pride form, but there was no way he'd deactivate it to try. Even his human form would weigh more than any clothies or leather wearers, since his Sin of Pride had come with a free growth spurt. He'd die pretty quickly if he didn't succeed the first time. Besides, he already had a plan for that bit. If Noigel and the occultists ever showed up.

Damien had been concentrating so hard he had no idea how long he'd been there. Long enough to kill the entire platoon who'd been on looting duty, but that didn't tell him very much. Long enough that his stamina was starting to run low. He couldn't look away from the wall, otherwise he wouldn't see the projectiles coming. He couldn't ask the occultists what was happening without entering his menu, since he'd set the chat so he was the only one who could communicate through it. It had all seemed like a good idea at the time.

Damien found a concrete answer to how long he'd been there when his Charge came off cooldown. It had been thirty seconds. It felt longer. He could always use it to retreat. And face thousands of people who'd rather watch him die alone than help him achieve their goal?

He wouldn't give them the satisfaction.

Damien set his sights on the gate and was positioning himself to Charge it head-on when a loud noise, far away but quickly drawing closer, caught his attention. It was a human cry. Deep, sonorous, angry, scared and...coming from somewhere high above? The players in the wall had been looking down on Damien, but the noise and the spectacle drew their gaze away from him and onto this UFO. The scream grew louder and they began firing at it. It was only as it passed directly overhead that Damien dared glance up. What he saw so confused him that he drew to a stop.

Hammertime.

Godhammer's guild leader was curled up in a bright-red glowing ball, the light of his Berserker Rage trailing a blood rainbow across the sky in his wake. It was handily displaying his trajectory, which was a small price to pay for the full minute of regeneration and damage reduction he'd be receiving from it. He'd need it. He was heading straight toward a pristine section of the armor-plated wall.

That wasn't the strangest part. Hammertime was spinning. It looked a lot like one of Toutatis's spins, only vertical instead of horizontal. A Whirlwind attack. That was a pretty cool ability and this was a pretty insane way to put it through its paces. It was only when Hammertime hit the wall at full tilt, tearing a wider hole in it than any rock could, that Damien realized how Hammertime had achieved such airtime in the first place. The madman had fired himself out of a trebuchet.

It did not take long before the screams of squishies and the dents appearing all along his level of ingress indicated Hammertime was very much alive. He was exactly the kind of player this construction was supposed to keep ranged units safe from. Now it was trapping them in close proximity with him.

The floor Hammertime had "infiltrated" went completely dark. There were no more attacks coming from anywhere on that level. Yet despite Hammertime no longer being a target, not all the remaining players were firing at Damien. Many of the shots were going high over his head. Damien moved out of their line of fire and glanced behind him.

Fifty incubi were pacing slowly down the no-man's land in a long line, a walking wall of consumer iron armor. The occultists hid behind them, one each, as the armor-coated wall of flesh turned away arrows and bullets. Twenty-five consumers were spaced out at intervals between them, stepping forward whenever a magic ability was cast in that direction in order to eat it raw.

Over six hundred imps were split between the air and the ground, filling the battlefield with their screeches. They frustrated any attempt to make a meaningful dent on their army or their own numbers, leaping or swooping in front of single-target high-damage spells, only to part when large AoE abilities were sent their way.

Twenty-seven succubi flew with the airborne groups, each with an orbiting imp-meat shield. They were the only other minion type Damien had seen fit to construct armor for, and were clad in consumer steel. The consumers were already protected by the armor-clad incubi and would also recover health and mana every time they successfully ate a spell.

Noigel had outdone himself, wherever he was. Damien's top

imp took it to the next stage when the line reached the halfway point. The closer they got to the wall, the easier it would be for enemy players to aim over the armored front line. The second half of the battlefield had to be traversed as quickly as possible. But not by everyone. Just the imps would suffice. The succubi all cast simultaneously and almost every single imp was Bloodlusted. They swarmed forward.

The imps bobbed and weaved, their numbers dropping rapidly now their mandate was to close in. However, they were not dying fast enough to prevent them from accomplishing their purpose. Intelligence-based occultists and the succubi provided covering fire, flinging Chaotic Bolts or casting Corruption through breaches in the wall's defense. The imps flew into every nook and cranny then made themselves visible, poking their heads out of the arrow slits and screeching to draw attention. The occultists were scanning the wall, looking out for the blue headers of their own imps in the sea of green as they continued to move forward behind their troops.

Not all occultists who'd taken the 'Hell's Angels' trait, imbuing their imps with wings, were built for physical damage. However, all occultists who were built for physical damage had taken the 'Hell's Angels' trait; the remaining level 10 traits were 'Contagion' and 'Controlled Chaos', imbuing Corruption and Chaotic Bolt respectively with bonus effects. The utility of these traits was less than apparent for anyone built around the lost occultist art of stabbing people.

For this reason, most of the imp army being fielded had been allocated to these physical damage oriented occultists, along with one succubus each. This was not simply because their imps could fly. Their handlers also possessed the knowledge and experience required to implement the tactics Damien had employed over the course of his career. Only this time it would be on a much larger, coordinated scale.

The melee occultists pointed. The imps Imp-loded all across the wall, from the inside, pulling it in on itself across the middle. Like crushing a tin can. Each Imp-losion was accompanied by a hard screech of the metal wall and a softer clatter from the cogs in the machine being thrown around inside it.

The brittle caster classes were being smashed into the walls of their defense turned prison. More imps continued infiltrating the structure in their wake, at which point the same occultists who'd triggered the Imp-losions Demon Gated in to finish what they'd started.

The succubi flew upward and assailed the ramparts, where the snipers and rangers had congregated. They covered the platform with Circles of Hell and rained Chaotic Bolts down upon their enemies. Their stats were considerable, now they were wearing consumer steel. Those arrows and bullets that did manage to thread the imps orbiting them either had their damage significantly reduced or turned away entirely by the high-grade armor Damien had insisted the succubi be coated in.

In the span of five seconds after the first imps had reached their destinations, the wall was warped, twisted and filled from top to bottom with dagger-wielding melee players, supported by any surviving imps. It must've been cold and dark within the wall for the Carlisle-Elite, the only light sources either tiny slats from which to view their enemies or massive holes in their defenses created by those who wanted their advantage destroyed. They'd defended it to the last even when they had to know what they were doing was wrong, or hadn't bothered thinking hard enough to know why it was wrong. Now they were all dead. How sad.

Damien opened his menu.

"Alexa, play 'Despacito'."

He hung back as the occultist line moved past him, checking everything was working as it should. He had no complaints. The only remaining attacks were coming from the top of the wall, where the snipers and rangers were located. Damien was still watching, allowing his stamina and health to regenerate passively, when Lillian's second voice call blared into his ears.

He eyed it up. The only thing worse than answering it would be not answering it. Not a whole lot of choice, then. Damien cut the music track off and picked up, diplomatically deciding to let

Lillian speak first. He hadn't let her speak at all the first time. She probably had a lot to say. She did, it just wasn't what Damien had been expecting.

"You must think I'm a complete idiot."

"I have no idea what you're talking about."

"Yeah you do. You could've done that this whole time, and I was too focused on what I was doing to listen."

"Y-you were very busy. I thought I should step in."

"And that speech you made? Calling the whole Empire your 'protection racket'? Genius! You really got them riled up. I had no idea how to get our players back in the field after those losses. After what you said, it was a struggle to stop them from running in to kill you before we were ready!"

Lillian had handed Damien a way out. He seized it with both hands. For a deeply self-involved moment, Damien had been certain he'd been left to die alone. Thanks to Lillian, he could pretend it was all calculated.

"What can I say? Happy to help."

"Okay, cool. Because I told them to go for it. Look behind you."

"You what?"

Which is when Damien registered the thundering of feet. Lillian was flanked by her Queen's Guard front and center, her sword raised over her head and her eyes locked onto him. He could see her lips moving in time with the words echoing in his head. Damien started running forward, looking over his shoulder as thousands of human players advanced on him with wild abandon. Disturbingly, every single last one of them was grinning at him manically as they brandished their weapons and ran toward him.

"Yeah, no, I mean, you must've known that's what would happen. Right? Since the wall is done for, you're the biggest threat to the Empire and we're all conveniently gathered here to deal with you. I offered 1000 gold to the player who lands the killing blow."

As powerful as Damien had become, he didn't really have the capacity to fight thousands of players at once. Assuming he wanted to, which he didn't. That was more Archimonde's scene, with the Contagion trait and the consistent spell-vamp, and even Archimonde hadn't attempted to go for Lillian directly.

Damien scanned the wall, looking for an imp he could Demon Gate to while glancing behind him to make sure the army hadn't caught up yet. His imps were all suddenly unavailable. Better yet, Hammertime had extricated himself from the wall and was running toward Damien from the other direction, his Berserker Rage still up. Damien could probably handle him, but he didn't want to do that either.

Damien had no way out that didn't involve killing. Lillian's army was getting pretty close, and the wall in front of him and the army of players behind his Charge wouldn't help either. Damien twisted each way, waiting for a sensible course of action to reveal itself.

"Lillian, you've got to be joking, right?"

"Everybody stop!"

Just like that, the entire army drew to a halt. No confusion, no one falling out of line. They all stopped dead. Yet if anything, their grins had become even more manic. Some of them were laughing. Lillian turned to address them, which is when Damien spotted that she'd made a friend. Noigel was clinging to her back, a living rat-skin backpack. The imp slowly turned his head 180 degrees and delivered unto Damien a scathing, malicious grin.

The pieces had started falling into place even before Lillian addressed her troops, her voice still ringing out loud and clear in his head through their voice call.

"Good job everybody, he was properly terrified. Go finish off the wall, I'll be with you soon. I need a word with my friend."

They cheered and filed past Damien in a much more orderly fashion, still giving him a wide berth. Reactions to him were mixed. Most of them ogled him in awe, while some of them stuck their tongues out at him only to quickly set their gazes forward when Damien glared back at them. As the throng moved around him, Lillian set Excalibur at her waist and entered his personal space, alone. She reached behind her, plucked Noigel off her back and extended the imp to him.

"This is yours. He's great, that whole trick was his idea. If he wasn't already helping you out I'd offer him a seat at the Round Table. I need smart advisors."

Damien plucked the imp up between his thumb and forefinger, resisting the urge to squeeze, and dropped him on his own shoulder.

Lillian grinned. "I patched the first call through to the entire army, so they could all hear me formally recognize occultists as allies of the Empire. They all heard you blow me off instead."

Damien, the Sin of Pride, smacked his open palm into his face. It would've been comical had he not been so embarrassed.

Lillian took a step closer. "I needed to get you back or I'd have lost them forever. I'd like a fresh start. Clean slate. We square?"

Damien drew in a huge breath and rattled out a sigh, prompting the human players still passing to give him a few more feet of leeway. He extended his hand and frowned. These hands were designed for breaking, not for shaking. He was gingerly sticking out his pinky when Lillian seized the top of his palm and grabbed it tight. Her hands were smaller, but that didn't mean they weren't built for breaking. Damien couldn't even move his hand.

Lillian dialed down her power to the point where they could shake hands as equals. Well, that was a reality check. Lillian let go and looked him up and down.

"I thought you'd be stronger. Size isn't everything, eh?"

"It's more about how the abilities stack on top of each other. Maybe when we're done here we can trade notes?"

"Or just have it out in a duel, if you're up for it?"

Two reality checks, right on top of each other. Damien wouldn't go one versus one against Lillian under any circumstances.

"Maybe just trade—"

There was a tumultuous crash from the front line, loud and sudden enough to make Damien wince. He swiveled and saw the gate had been utterly destroyed. The enormous doors had been rent from their hinges and knocked over onto the players standing in front of it. There had been a lot of them crowded there, each looking to make their own mark on this auspicious moment in gaming history. Yet as happens all too often, history had instead made its mark on them.

Hundreds were crushed under the weight of the doors as the gates were knocked down from the other side. Magnitude was standing in the gap they'd left behind, cutting an imposing figure in spite of his diminutive form. This was partly down to the two vast stone columns protruding from the floor on either side of him, the battering rams that had destroyed the gate. They were already receding back into the floor. His health regeneration was more imposing than that. He had 65% of his hit points by the time Damien spotted him and was back at full only a few seconds later. But the most imposing thing about him by some margin was his level, which Damien could see for the first time. He was level 60.

31

WHY DO I HEAR BOSS MUSIC?

Magnitude put his hands above his head, the symbolism of which was somewhat marred by the previous crushing of hundreds of players, preceded by the wholesale slaughter of thousands.

The players were hesitating. Everyone wanted to go in, but no one wanted to go in first. Damien could only just about perceive Magnitude's level, and to the rest of these arrayed players it would simply be question marks, same as his class name. He did not imagine knowing their opponent was only level 60 would provide them with a great deal of comfort.

Nevertheless, it was a large group of players. Only one of them had to step out of line. It was Hammertime who broke rank first, his hammer raised high. The moment it happened, three followed him. Then a dozen. The bystander effect was broken until all the players were running into range to make their attacks.

Magnitude did not move as they came for him, his hands remaining above his head. It was only as they drew very close – close enough for the first of them to stop – that they saw what was arrayed behind him in the distance. It was only then that Magnitude's hands clapped together and he hopped up. The players at the front had been trying to force their way backward, while the players behind had forced them onward. Damien was tall enough to see over the top of them. He saw when Hammertime stopped running and allowed the head of his weapon to hit the dirt. Damien couldn't argue with his assessment.

Cannons. Gatling guns. Mortars. The bleeding edge of dwarven tech, operated entirely by their creators. The dwarven forces all wore the same armor and flew the same banner. Clan Eitri. Lillian was not the only one who'd brought a major power to bear. Magnitude was halfway into the ground when the salvo started.

Hammertime evaporated. The players at the front were mown down in droves. The cannon fire wiped them out in long steady lines of obliteration while the Gatling guns finished off what little was left. The wall was no longer manned, but it was far past having served its purpose. Lillian's huge army was being funneled into a tiny space, upon which outrageous ordnance was being unloaded.

Lillian did not know what was happening. She could only tell her forces were being obliterated from the sounds. The situation was grim enough without the leader remaining unaware. Damien hoisted her up over his head, just in time to watch the second wave of her army running in. Her complaints at being so handled stuck in her throat as she saw the extent of the carnage. Then she saw the players heedlessly running in. Then the extent of what they were running toward.

"Everyone stop! They're using—"

Her words were drowned out by whistles overhead, prompting both her and Damien to look up. The mortars were not limited by the wall. They'd fired over it and their payloads were on the way down. Into the massed troops. With seconds to spare, Lillian yelled even louder. Trying to substitute urgency in place of expediency.

"Sanctuaries up, shields up, evasi—"

The rest of it was lost to the roar. A few moments ago, everyone had thought the battle was all but won. Their guard had been down. Even Lillian thought she'd had a spare moment to talk with Damien before they wrapped things up. At the very moment they'd relaxed, her army had been decimated.

Their levels counted for nothing. Their experience counted for nothing. Their cause counted for nothing. Heavy ordnance does not discriminate between right or wrong, skilled or noob, team-oriented or self-serving. Only between those who are lucky and those who are in the wrong place at the wrong time. Lillian's army was in the wrong place at the wrong time.

This was a poor scenario in which to have a large character model and no armor. Damien dropped Lillian and yelled as he smashed his open palm over his chest, reverting back to his human form. He was still trying to decide where to run when Lillian landed on her feet and forced him to the floor by the back of his head, then held her shield over them both. She was shouting something Damien couldn't hear, not even as she screamed directly into his ear.

The explosions abated and she hauled Damien to his feet, still shouting into his face. It was all white noise. She scanned the battlefield, her lips still moving even as she assessed the damage. Damien looked across the battlefield with her. They'd been shattered. It was over. A dozen craters were scattered all around them, the players pointlessly running from the points of impact as if those particular areas were dangerous, not the projectiles that had caused them. The bulk of Lillian's army had become an illogical, fearful mob. If her hand hadn't been on the back of his head, Damien would've been among their number.

The players had lost all sense of direction and purpose. Some were fleeing, some were advancing through the gate only to being mown down by the cannons trained on it. The guild leaders had more sense, guiding their troops to the edge of the wall where the mortars' trajectory made it nearly impossible to strike them. They'd already sustained heavy casualties. The damage had been done.

"—occultists are left? Damien!"

She shook him and Damien's head snapped back.

"How many occultists? How many demons? Damien!"

"Uh, I don't know, let me—"

"Incubi and the fat ones on either side of the gate, take the succubi, imps and occultists to the ramparts."

"I don't understa—"

"Tell Noigel to follow my orders."

"I don't know if tha—"

The hollow *thunks* of a second round of mortar fire echoed from beyond the wall. Lillian burst into white light, grabbed Damien by the collar and dragged him toward the wall. He didn't slow her down in the least. Her speed was not as dramatic as his Charge, but it was considerably faster than his own unaided movement which he'd been so proud of. It was more useful here, because while Damien would lose momentum as soon as he made contact with something, Lillian's regular movement had no such restriction. She could force her way through the crowd with impunity, and she could drag dead weight behind her with no loss of momentum whatsoever.

They made it, crowding into the mass of bodies of those who'd also sought refuge there. Lillian took Damien's collar in both hands and shook him like a rag doll as the second wave of bombs fell.

"Leave Noigel here and tell him to obey me. Take the occultists to the top of the wall and fire back! I'll send Andrew to help."

"I have Demon Gate, how is Andrew going to ge—"

"Stop thinking and do what I tell you! This is a battle, not a discussion forum! You wanted to be part of the Empire, that means you follow my orders. Go! Now!"

Damien had still not recovered. He was too used to everything going to plan. Lillian was frustrated, but very much engaged. She'd already started yelling into her comms. Not desiring a third briefing and without any plan of his own, Damien submitted to her instruction.

"Noigel, stay with Lillian, do whatever she says. Send all the other imps and the succubi to the top of the wall. Occultists, are you the— ah, crap you're all muted – okay, any of you who hear this, head for the top of the wall. Take control of your minions as need be. I'm on my way."

Noigel had moved to Lillian's shoulder before he had finished the first sentence. There was an imp ready for him just a few seconds after that. Damien Demon Gated and pulled himself over the edge of the ramparts, just as the rest of the forces were arriving: 'Ninja' trait assassins with wall-walking, cloud-riding lightning mages, ice mages creating their own platforms, double-jumping rangers exploiting the holes in the defense.

No priests, no warriors, no paladins. Only rangers, mages and assassins, limited to those with the necessary traits to reach the top of the wall. And of course the occultists, whose ability to reach out-of-the-way places was built into their skill set. Damien examined his Soul Summon Limit and found his imps had taken their share of hits: twenty-six of his forty-five imps remained. He was nonetheless doing better than most of the occultists arriving.

He estimated they had a total of sixty imps, not including his. More or less. Maybe a dozen succubi? He checked the occultist raid group and found just over half of them were still alive, though he had no way of knowing which minions had been lost with them. In the past, he'd always been able to adapt because he still had some idea of his available resources. At this scale, it was impossible.

If managing the occultists and their remaining minions was difficult, he had no chance of dealing with the assassins, rangers and mages. One of the mages stuck his head over the top of the parapet, trying to understand what the situation was on the other side. He promptly found out when his head was blown off. Snipers, again, trained on the top of the wall. Lovely. He kept his head down as he made his way through the rabble to the center, trying to warn away others from suffering the same fate.

"Everyone keep your heads down! Wait until we get—"

A ringing ran through his head, a voice chat invitation from Lillian to a group chat called 'Carlisle Raid'. The sound had completely cut through his train of thought, but no one had been listening to what he was saying anyway. The same thing was happening over and over again, all along the breadth of the wall. Players assuming they were somehow special, that they knew how to peek over a wall better than the person who'd just died doing the same thing and that what had happened to others who'd done exactly that, sometimes even within their view, would not happen to them.

Damien had nearly made it to the center when he joined the group to the sound of Lillian shouting:

"Hammertime is dead, Aetherius is in charge of the new recruits now! Andrew, I have eyes down here, we need you up there to guide the support."

Andrew's voice cut in over her just before she'd finished:

"That won't work, Lillian, I can't get—"

"Hold on tight."

"Hhhhhnnnnnnnngggg—"

The strained yell cut out and a second later Andrew appeared out of Blink before tumbling onto the ramparts in a heap. He took a moment to lie facedown on the floor, mumbling into both it and the comms.

"I hate when you do that."

"You're alive, good, get in position."

Then he was up and assessing the wall. He braced himself against the stone, failing to make the same mistake as the players he was now in charge of. Damien crouched down next to him as he and Lillian took it in turns to shout over the same connection.

"Everyone keep your heads down until Lillian gives the go order—"

"Noigel, put the demons on the sides of the gate, Queen's Guard and tanks fall in behind them—"

Andrew looked directly at Damien while still talking into the comms.

"The imps will go out first to draw fire, any that make it should Imp-lode over the front line. While they're en route, the assassins will run down the wall—"

The hollow *thuds* of another round of mortar fire prompted Lillian to talk even faster and Andrew to match her. The shells thrummed through the air in front of the wall and the two of them struggled not to overlap their speech as they raced to finish before the shells dropped.

"—Tanks and melee go straight for the cannons, ranged units go directly left or right when you get through the openi—"

"Anything that flies goes out in a straight line to take pressure off the kill zone—"

Damien was handing out his imps into the Soul Summon Limits of any occultist he could see, trying to spread them out evenly as he conveyed Andrew's instructions to his out-of-the-loop occultists while adding a few specifics.

"Occultists, control your own succubi and imps, leave the incubi and consumers to Noigel, Imp-losions over the heavy artillery, fly the succubi overhead and use all their mana as fast as possible, Circles of Hell starting from the front line and moving back, then drain the rest of the mana with Chaotic B—"

Lillian had already started counting down:

"—two, one, GO!"

The imps went over the top and the bullets immediately started flying all around them. As soon as the first salvo was over the assassins went over the wall and began hurtling down it. The mages followed after them, lightning mages on their thunder clouds and ice mages stepping off the ramparts to create slick sheets of ice which began at the ramparts and which they rode on the balls of their feet. The succubi flew overhead and began pointing with one hand while charging bolts with the other. The back of the ramparts was crowded with rangers firing volley after volley. The roar of cannon fire meant that down below, Lillian's group was also on the move.

Damien remained stood back from the edge, watching the imps fly outward. Now the minions had cleared the wall and were directly over Magnitude's forces they were being largely ignored. The dwarves had their hands full suppressing the more immediate threat of the players coming for them. The cannons could not aim up, but the snipers, rifles and Gatling guns could. They were doing their utmost to mow everything down before anything was close enough to do damage. Ignoring the imps.

"All imps dive, break the front line!"

Damien sent his own imps streaking to the ground and moments later the rest of them dive-bombed. As his remaining five imps reached the correct point, right over the middle of the cannons, Damien pointed and his first imp Imp-loded. The two cannons he'd managed to encompass within the effect rocked backward off the floor and crashed back down again, trained in the wrong directions. The dwarves loading them and the line of gunners stood behind them were tossed through the air, creating a hole in the middle of the defense. The rest of the imps began arriving soon afterward, each Imp-losion breaking the formation a little more.

Archimonde appeared, Demon Gating in from further back. He cast back his hoggish head and glared upward at the approaching waves of imps. They immediately pulled out of their dives and flew instead toward the gate. They were now enemy imps. Go figure. Archimonde intended to use them to suppress Lillian's advance. Just one Imp-losion in that choke point would cause untold mayhem. It was a good thing Damien had spent a week preparing for this. He stared at the imps as they drew closer to the gate, thinking the same thing over and over again.

You're mine. Come here.

Their names turned blue and they flew up onto the wall before landing behind it. Damien looked out at Archimonde, which had watched their approaching flight. Nine imps recycled. A crushing Imp-losion/Corruption combo culled in its infancy. It was a shame Damien couldn't see Archimonde's face clearly over the distance and through the gunfire smoke. He'd just have to superimpose the despair he imagined Archimonde was feeling onto the creature's piggish features with his imagination. It wasn't hard to imagine, given the despair he'd felt when Archimonde had done the same to him. He stuck his arm above his head and gave his rival a hearty wave, rubbing it in. How do you like it?

Noigel's intelligence wouldn't be much use to Lillian with so few imps, but it didn't seem like she'd asked him to do anything complicated. The incubi and consumers had a very easy role to play in her plan: cannon fodder. Their muscular armored bodies and immense bulk respectively made them ideal to both draw concern and absorb heavy ordnance. They faded away to dust shortly after being killed, which was just as well considering the number of corpses already piling up. Lillian scaled the pile of corpses, followed immediately by her Queen's Guard, with the survivors of the mortar assault piling through after her and fanning out as they passed through the gate.

The Gatling guns that had not yet been put out of commission all stopped what they were doing and fired on the approaching squad, with little effect. Lillian was running with her shield in front of her, the bullets echoing off it. The effect of those that penetrated both her shield and her armor was mitigated by the heals landing on her from her retinue and the healers who'd passed through the gate and panned out to the sides, reducing pressure on the choke point.

If she and her Queen's Guard made it into melee, removing them would be next to impossible. Magnitude clearly thought the same. He rose out of the ground in front of his tattered vanguard and drove his fists back into the earth from which he'd so suddenly appeared.

Damien watched his hit points plummet until the ability that was draining them obscured him. A solid slab of rock shook itself free of the earth and rose up, blocking the valley from one side to the other. It stopped suddenly at just five meters high. It would not be high enough to stop Lillian from jumping over it, but enough to divide her forces between those who could scale it and those who couldn't, in so doing blocking line of sight for the healers.

At the very moment Lillian had put them on the back foot, Magnitude had presented yet another obstacle. He was buying his army time to regroup, preventing Lillian from hitting them while they were out of formation. She'd got what few players remained through the choke point. Yet if the cannons could all be pointed back in the right direction and the gunners could be regrouped into their formations, and if they all fired simultaneously when Magnitude lowered the wall, the damage would be catastrophic.

Andrew's voice came calm and clear over the chat, just a fraction of a second after the wall stopped rising.

"Lillian, the wall's thin, you can smash it. Do it."

While the other players had faltered, Lillian and her Queen's Guard had not slowed down. When Andrew said "Do it", she sped up. Divine Might enveloped her and she leaned into the run, leaving everyone else behind. Damien held his forehead and forced himself to watch, the spectacle turning him into a spectator. Andrew was already firing Arcane Bolts, arcing them over the wall to soften up her targets before Lillian did what she'd always done. Just before she reached the wall, Damien noticed Magnitude running back to the safety of the rearguard. Andrew grunted, but kept his suppressing fire arcing over the wall rather than chasing Magnitude with it.

Damien had seen Lillian go through thicker walls when she was more than ten levels lower, before she had a legendary weapon. Excalibur remained firmly in her grasp as she raised her shield, braced behind it and slammed into the slab at full tilt, more bloody-minded and destructive than any cannon ball.

Lillian was not a good choice of target for a bluff, least of all with Andrew providing oversight. She burst through and the whole facade cracked and came tumbling down.

Oh yeaaaah.

Through the rubble and dust, Lillian set to work. The Queen's Guard and battle-worn players were soon to follow. Magnitude's dwarven reinforcements were not melee combatants and his remaining Carlisle-Elites were not Lillian. Now they'd finally got into melee range, this battle was going one way and one way only. Upon watching his safety net collapse and the fighting break out, Magnitude turned and vanished into the ground, repeating the move three times to get all the way to the back line. Archimonde was waiting for him.

Magnitude turned to Archimonde and shook his head. Archimonde extended out its palm and it glowed purple. The creature was summoning a portal. They were leaving! Just like that. The very players who'd precipitated this war didn't intend to see it through. It had all been fun and games while they had held the advantage, but now they were happy to let the players they'd led into this situation die in order to cover their escape.

On the plus side, if they were leaving then the battle was all but won. That was good, right? It would be better to let them go, rather than drawing this out. Damien wasn't too pleased with the idea.

"Andrew, your brother's leaving. Is that alright with you?"

Andrew's eyes darted upward. He took it in, then his fingers twitched. The Arcane Bolts he'd been guiding into the front line curved upward, flying straight over their heads toward the only two players who were not in combat. Archimonde was concentrating on making a portal. Magnitude was not. He drove his hands into the earth and a new wall appeared. The first two Arcane Bolts collided with it. Those that followed curved up and over, then burst on the ground behind it. Andrew began screaming into the comms.

"Lillian, Richard is escaping! Catch him! Don't let—"

That was enough for Damien. Nine imps took to the sky. He looked up and appropriated the nearest succubus into his Soul Summon Limit, immediately ordering it to Bloodlust. It didn't have enough mana. For crying— he possessed it and its wisdom stat doubled, along with its remaining mana. Just enough. Bloodlust. Cancel Possession. The red mist chased the imps out and their movement speed increased. They were nearly there.

Had Andrew's bolts connected? Even if they had, how long would it be until the game defined those hit as 'out of combat'? Always with the details. More Arcane Bolts overtook his imps on either side, curving around the wall before colliding with each other to keep the targets pinned. Just before Damien's imps disappeared from view he Demon Gated, his kunai raised over his head, and dropped down.

He'd had eyes on the wall the whole time yet they were gone. He looked all the way to the end of the valley, just in time to watch Archimonde plod past the edge of the valley wall and out of sight. Demon Gate and that stupid ground-tunneling ability.

Damien sprinted after them. The movement speed he'd been so proud of was not fast enough. He put his hand over his chest and transformed back into his Pride form, his long strides covering the ground much faster. What would he do if he caught up with them? Fighting one or the other would be difficult, fighting both of them together would be nightmarish. He'd have to at least keep them busy until more players arrived. That he could probably manage, if he was careful.

It was such a long way. Every second felt agonizingly slow. Damien came out of the mouth of the valley and saw them. Right as Archimonde finished summoning the portal. Magnitude turned as Damien arrived, his annoying sixth sense preventing Damien from catching him unawares. He was only a few feet from safety. Archimonde followed his gaze, turning its back on the portal.

The portal would either close the moment the caster passed through it or a few seconds after the caster first entered combat. If Damien attacked Archimonde to try and prevent their escape, the portal would still take ten seconds to close. Archimonde was standing right in front of it. Preventing it from leaving would be next to impossible. Magnitude wasn't using his own Portal Stone, and during his long run Damien had figured out why. It was likely attached to the wall. That's why he was relying on Archimonde to make his exit.

Put it all together and Damien only had one option.

Damien Charged straight at Archimonde. Magnitude had already curled his hands into fists and was driving them downward. Too late. Damien's kunai went straight through Archimonde's head as it turned to face him, a perfect combat initiation. He'd almost expected to kill Archimonde outright, but no such luck.

The damage had to be extreme. He didn't have time to assess how extreme, because Archimonde was falling back through the portal. Damien immediately pulled on both chains and was dragged through after the creature.

The portal snapped shut behind them.

32

ORDER VERSUS ORDER, CHAOS VERSUS CHAOS

Lillian had activated her Divine Might as Damien had Charged past the edge of the valley and out of sight. It had not been difficult to extricate herself from combat: most of the opposing forces fled at her advance, only for Lillian to pass them. There were some who had attempted to block her, assuming that since they were comparably leveled they'd also be evenly matched. Quickly turning Divine Might on and then off again a few seconds at a time allowed her to disillusion them without compromising on speed. She jumped over them or cut them down, as if they weren't even there.

When you're really powerful, you get to pick your fights, a fact Magnitude and Archimonde were inverting in their favor. Which was interesting, considering Damien and Lillian were picking a fight with them.

Damien had dropped in front of her just as she passed Magnitude's last line of defense. With her stamina low and Damien both fresh and ahead of her, Lillian slowed to his speed and allowed it to tick back up. Even when he changed back into his demon form, Lillian still felt it was prudent to let him stay ahead so she could recharge. It was only when he Charged out of her field of view that her concern outweighed her pragmatism.

She rounded the edge of the valley, fully expecting to dive

straight into combat to help Damien against not one, but two high-level special-class enemies. She arrived and found Magnitude all alone, staring into empty space. Where did Damien go? Where did Archimonde go, for that matter? In the time it took Lillian to figure out what had happened, Magnitude caught sight of her.

He froze. Lillian deactivated her Divine Might. Magnitude was already at full health, but her stamina and mana would take a while to regenerate. She needed to buy time.

"Hello, Dick. We have something to discu—"

Richard's hands clapped above his head and the ground swallowed him up. It's not so easy to goad enemies into maniacal speeches revealing their master plans when their master plans have already collapsed. He reappeared a short distance away with 85% health, his hit points already regenerating.

Lillian watched Richard's health bar, timing his regeneration as she pursued him across the Wastes. This movement spell was essentially Blink with a different flavor. The only real differences were that it cost health rather than mana and that the caster came out of the ground rather than appearing in midair. To most players, the health cost would be a disadvantage. Not for Richard. Despite his legs barely carrying him any additional distance at all, he was at full health and back in the ground before Lillian reached him.

Richard's Blink either had a preposterously short cooldown or no cooldown at all. That wasn't the worst part: he was regenerating 5% of his health per second. Richard could go from nearly dead to full health in twenty seconds. How do you fight something like that?

Lillian had something in mind.

Richard had evaded her for the third time when Lillian activated Divine Might and sprinted full-on. It only took a second to reach him. She thought she might catch him out with the pattern he was displaying: four seconds then a dive, maintaining his health as much as possible. Magnitude clapped his hands above his head as soon as he sprung from below, merging the end of his first tunnel with the start of the next. He hadn't even looked at her. That lined up with what Damien had shown her in his footage: Magnitude had known Damien's location even when he was out of line of sight. A sensory ability, related to his earth mage theme.

Keeping Divine Might activated, Lillian continued her blitz. Magnitude responded the exact same way. So it hadn't been a fluke. He definitely knew. Lillian's mana had been low even before this started. Magnitude was always moving in a straight line, always the same distance away to what Lillian assumed to be the maximum range of the ability. Behaving so predictably was a cardinal sin in PvP. As much as Lillian wanted to keep this up and let Richard drain his own health some more, it wasn't viable. She'd run out of mana before he ran out of health, assuming he didn't change tactic. If her mana dropped any lower she wouldn't be able to enact her plan. Enacting it right now would give her less than five seconds of full use. Deactivating Divine Might so her mana regen could kick in would allow Magnitude to draw further ahead and fully regenerate. She had to make this work now.

Lillian planted the balls of her steel-plated feet deep into the floor. Her toes curled into the ground, through her steel boots, searching for purchase to propel her forward to where Richard would next appear. With Excalibur in hand and Divine Might activated, her strength was high enough to damage her own gear if she didn't exercise restraint.

The situation did not warrant restraint.

Magnitude's head disappeared from view and she launched, leaving a pair of craters where she'd expended maximum force. In flight, she activated her level 50 trait. Uriel's Blessing. Excalibur glowed white hot, then burst into flame.

Uriel's Blessing: Mana cost: 510, Damage: 50 + (Str x 0.1) per second for 10 seconds, Effect: Armor Piercing 50%
Uriel, the angel of repentance, bestows holy fire on your weapon for 30 seconds. Cooldown: 5 minutes.

This was only the third time Lillian had activated this ability. The first had been a private test on a fully armored training dummy in her Throne Room, to see whether it was really as good as it claimed to be. It was. The second time was in battle, when she'd been using it to sear through the gate. She'd simply pierced it with Excalibur up to the hilt and dragged it across the middle. It had been working, until Archimonde had showed up. It would've worked afterwards, too, if Damien were capable of not being himself for five minutes. That had turned out alright though, in spite of everything.

Lillian had not chosen this trait because it sounded cool and looked pretty. Whatever Magnitude was, this trait was the cure. It would kill plenty of other things as well, but this unknown class in particular. Richard's pudgy little body had at least one useful benefit besides magic resistance. He was completely encased in his jade armor. There were no gaps to exploit. The armor piercing would allow Lillian to create her own gaps. The burning effect would prevent Magnitude's natural healing. That she could house these effects in an indestructible legendary sword was the stuff of nonsense.

Magnitude popped out of the ground right in front of her. He wouldn't know where Lillian was, because she wasn't touching the ground. It only took him a fraction of a second to realize something was terribly wrong. Because Lillian ran him through.

Magnitude skidded through the dirt as the rest of Lillian collided with him, Excalibur cutting a furrow through the earth where it protruded out of his chest. His health was at 32% and dropping fast. Lillian's mana was nearly completely empty from activating Uriel's Blessing, and she only had a few seconds of Divine Might left. She didn't waste time activating Numbers:14. All that was left was the killing blow.

She was withdrawing Excalibur to administer it when Magnitude's health dropped to 19%. His right hand swept through the ground and up, backhanding a boulder into Lillian's face. One second of space was all he needed.

"Renewal!"

Magnitude's health was restored to full and the burning

effect was gone. Lillian had only just reopened her eyes when the light of Magnitude's activated artifact blinded her. She'd really hoped to kill him before he could use the damn thing. She set her shield in front of her, protecting herself from any boulders that might be coming. Two slabs of rock smashed into her on either side instead. Her mana bar empty, Divine Might fizzled out. Her armor had shielded her from some of the damage, but now it was a crumpled mess and her health had been cut down to 60%. Magnitude had 85% health and rising.

At least she'd tried. Which is when Andrew spoke to her over the voice chat. It was so long since he'd spoken she'd forgotten it was still active.

"I saw the **pip** flash, I'm on **pip** my way, how **pip** it looking over **pip** there?"

Lillian was too busy to wonder why Andrew's voice was cutting in and out. Now Magnitude had gotten her in this position, he was pressing his advantage. Magnitude threw another boulder at her as she advanced on him, and she sliced it in half with her still-burning sword, marking the end of her stamina. He only had one resource to worry about compared to Lillian's three, all of which were low.

Now he had control of this, Lillian would never get it back. Her burst strategy had failed and he was wearing her down by attrition. If Andrew showed up, that just meant Magnitude would get both of them. Andrew wouldn't have been able to keep up with them once Magnitude had started running anyway. He had to stay away.

"Don't come, I—"

Magnitude placed his palms on the floor. Lillian jumped backward just in time to avoid being crushed, but her stamina was now so low she couldn't maintain balance. She hit the floor and rolled to her knees, panting. She only just managed to raise her shield in time to block the next boulder thrown at her, which protected her from most of the damage but sent her tumbling further.

"—I tried, I couldn't beat him. Defend the wa—"

Magnitude's palms hit the floor again. His health was low,

but he was intent on finishing her off. Lillian activated Divine Might a fraction of a second before the slabs hit and braced. It wasn't worth much with her stamina so low, but it was the best she could do. She reduced the damage, but not by much. If only she'd started this fight with full stamina and mana, things might have been different. They'd won the war, but she'd always regret not making Magnitude pay for what he'd done. Andrew's voice, oddly demure given the circumstances, came back over the chat.

"Don't be **pip** so dramatic, I'll **pip** be there soon to **pip** sort this out."

No! Why was he coming here? He had to know he couldn't handle Magnitude in a one-on-one fight. The only reason Lillian wasn't dead yet was that Magnitude had run out of health to attack her with. He was down to 18%. He was biding his time, allowing his health to rise back up now he was in control. Lillian staggered to her feet and adopted her combat stance. She had to kill Magnitude before Andrew got there.

She took a step forward and Magnitude took a step back. Really? Still afraid of her, even only a spell or two from victory? Which is when Lillian heard the faint, rhythmic *pips* from behind her. She couldn't turn her back on Magnitude to see what it was. She didn't have to: Andrew Blinked to her side and twisted his wrist. It shone green and a circle of glowing runes appeared in his palm, turning anticlockwise. His other hand held out a health potion in front of Lillian at chest height.

"Drink."

Magnitude raised a hand, as if to ward his brother away.

"Andrew, I don't want to fi—"

The moment Lillian took the potion Andrew Blinked again. He was standing right in front of Magnitude. His right hand twisted and the green circle glowed and span in his palm. His left index finger jabbed Magnitude on the nose. He uttered a single high-pitched syllable as ridiculous as the gesture it accompanied.

"Boop."

Magnitude seized Andrew's hand in one of his and was cocking the other one back to punch his younger brother into tomorrow when Andrew Blinked again. His third Blink in five seconds. It was supposed to have a thirty-second cooldown. That glowing green circle had to be his level 50 ability. If Lillian had understood what it did correctly, it was pretty mint. He was resetting the cooldown of his Blink instantly. Why he'd gone to all that effort just to boop Magnitude on the nose was—

Magnitude screamed. Lillian stared at him dumbfounded. He had a single scratch on his face. A tiny slither of blood was trickling out of it. His health was no longer regenerating. It was frozen, at 48%. Even that tiny cut was enough to cancel out his health regeneration. Andrew tipped a mana potion to his lips, mumbling to Lillian in singsong over the comms from behind it.

"Stop gawking and drink the potion, please."

Lillian tipped the bottle up as fast as she could and started drinking it down. Magnitude had the same idea. A potion appeared in his hand, but before he could drink it Andrew had flung an Arcane Bolt and steered it into the potion. It exploded in Magnitude's face. Andrew nonchalantly finished off his own potion, then went back to staring at his brother.

Magnitude completely lost it. With a scream of rage, he dug his hand into the earth and hurled a boulder at Andrew. Andrew Blinked through it and was standing in front of Magnitude again. Wrist twist–

"Boop."

In the second it took Magnitude to equip his pickax weapon, Andrew had already Blinked back to Lillian's side. A second cut had appeared on Magnitude's face and he was down to 38% health, mainly by his own hand. Whatever spell Andrew was using, it was hardly doing any damage at all. Andrew drew another mana potion and thrust that at Lillian, too.

"Drink."

Magnitude turned on the spot and tunneled away from them. He emerged, his health at 18%, and thrust his hand out for another potion. Andrew was on him in two Blinks and a twist of his hand. He fired a single-handed Arcane Beam directly into Magnitude's face. It was just a short burst, but more than enough to break a glass bottle.

"*Boop*. Lillian, I need some muscle. Come here, please. *Boop*."

While the show had been going on, her stamina had regenerated a great deal. Lillian jogged over. Magnitude was trying to run while Andrew kept pace at a brisk walk, periodically jabbing the back of his brother's head with a single outstretched finger.

"*Boop*. You hear that, Richard? *Boop*. That's the sound of all your plans. *Boop*. Dying. *Boooooooooooooooooop*."

Magnitude turned and took a swing at Andrew. Andrew took a step back, then stepped back in and deftly tapped him on the head yet again. Lillian walked past Magnitude, her sword drawn, and blocked his path. Andrew didn't take his eyes off Magnitude as he gave his instructions.

"We don't know what the cooldown on his artifact is. *Boop*. I'd rather not do this again, so take it off him, please. *Boop*."

Every time he tapped his brother Andrew made the same ridiculous high-pitched noise, jarring completely with the gravity of the situation. It was annoying Richard to no end, but there was nothing he could do about it. All his points were in strength or constitution. Without the stamina or agility to support running and without the necessary health to use his personalized Blink, he couldn't even get close enough to Andrew to hit him.

Lillian had to remind herself what Magnitude had done, in order to reconcile it with what Andrew was now doing. Cornering a player and stealing his artifact was pretty low, even on Andrew's worst day. Magnitude backed away as Lillian advanced on him. Andrew lost his temper.

"I'll make this simple: give me the artifact or Lillian will take everything on your person and kill you where you stand. *Boop*. If you give us the artifact, I'll give it back when I'm finished talking to you and I won't kill you. *Boop*. As a bonus, if you cooperate I'll stop 'booping' when I do the spell. *Boop*."

Magnitude swatted his hand away and sneered at him.

"How da—"

"AH-AH-AH! Don't talk to me, we're long past that. Shut up and do as you're told. *Boop*."

Magnitude glared at him, his fists shaking in impotent rage. He'd stopped talking, but he didn't hand over the artifact.

"Okay. Lillian, remo—"

Magnitude thrust his hand out and a piece of artistry appeared within it. His artifact looked a great deal more elaborate than the one he'd given Andrew. Just a day ago Andrew's artifact had seemed so incredible, yet now items which far outclassed it were appearing all the time.

Andrew didn't seem to care much. He tapped the underside of Magnitude's hand, reapplying the same spell again but without 'booping' him this time, and leaned in to examine the artifact. Lillian examined it with him.

Gaia's Embrace: Upon the verbal command "Renewal", your hit points are immediately restored to full and any adverse effects on you are removed. Cooldown: 10 minutes.

New information. That's nice to have. Andrew took it one stage further.

"The artifact you made for me granted a level 50 arcane mage trait. I guess this one's a minecrafter trait?"

Lillian heard the word and furrowed her brow. It had come out of nowhere. She hadn't realized what it meant yet. Magnitude did. He looked horrified. Andrew glanced up at Magnitude, nodded in satisfaction at his turmoil and then looked at Lillian.

"Oh, sorry, didn't explain that properly. Richard is a *minecrafter*. That's the name of his class. I saw Damien's guesses and did some research – the armor made of precious minerals, the pickaxe as a weapon choice for a caster, the magical manipulation of the ground, overlapping the dwarven lore so neatly. Yeah, Mobius Enterprises pulled a fast one on us. Until now."

Lillian looked at Magnitude, knowing his class name, and it appeared above his head. The question marks were all gone. Magnitude's biggest advantage was lost; he was now a known entity that could be researched, recognized and understood by all. Andrew kept blithely talking, as if he hadn't undermined his older brother's efforts to remain a mystery with a carelessly uttered word.

"You can take the artifact back, we won't be here that long. Keep your hand out though, unless you'd rather I went back to poking your face."

Magnitude numbly dropped the artifact into his inventory. Andrew was already talking again. Dismantling.

"The spell I'm using is called 'Inflict Wounds'. There's a reason for that: it inflicts a bleed for ten seconds on top of the initial damage and has a one-second cooldown. Shorter than the duration of the bleed, which is all that matters."

He was periodically tapping the back of Magnitude's hand as he spoke.

"I always thought it was a joke ability. No mage wants to get within poking distance of their enemies. It has at least one very useful function, though: making your construction-based class completely useless in combat."

Lillian wondered why he was explaining it in such detail. Then it hit her: he was broadcasting this information live.

"Any damage-over-time spell will work. Corruption from an occultist is a surefire winner, for example. I picked this lame, ignored, easily accessible ability because I wanted to show everyone how vulnerable you are."

Andrew had been talking long enough for the Inflict Wounds spell to bring Magnitude down to 5% health. Four whole percentage points after four minutes of affliction. Yet Magnitude was completely crippled by it.

"If you had healers with you they could Dispel these effects and this would've been more complicated. But your recruitment strategy for the Carlisle-Elite stipulated prospective members had to kill Empire players. The Carlisle-Elite had no dedicated healers! Bit of an oversight, don't you think?"

Magnitude swung at him out of nowhere, only for Andrew to Blink out and then back in again behind him, poking the back of his head for good measure. Magnitude had completely lost any semblance of control over his fate, or anyone else's. Andrew was drawing this out. Lillian understood, but she still felt it was enough.

"Andrew, you've got him where you want him. He's taken enough of our time."

"Sure, sorry. I'm about ready to wrap this up."

Andrew pulled a utility belt out of his Bag of Holding, then swapped them around. The Bag of Holding was in the palm of his hand.

"Disconnect from inventory."

He tossed the Bag of Holding in Magnitude's face.

"I don't need any "gifts" from you. Or anything else. The artifact you crafted from my material is gone, but seeing how you stole from Rising Tide's vault and framed it on me, we'll call that even. You have no reason to contact me, so don't. Have a nice life. I wish you the best of luck."

He grabbed Richard's limp, outstretched hand and shook it. Reapplying Inflict Wounds for the last time. Andrew released him and stalked away on foot, equipping his utility belt. Lillian took his place in front of Magnitude. She only had a few seconds to make a very important decision.

"You're really not killing him?"

Andrew looked Magnitude up and down, then back to Lillian, and shrugged.

"He's dead to me."

That was all well and good, but thousands of players hadn't shown up that day so Lillian could preside over a metaphorical death. She drew her sword, immediately activating Uriel's Blessing and Divine Might. Magnitude stood motionless. It wouldn't have made any difference if he ran, but he had no will to survive. He'd been keen enough to submit his artifact before. Now he was past caring.

Lillian almost felt sorry for him. Almost. She planted her feet.

"My heart isn't as big as Andrew's."

Richard's health had just started ticking up again when Lillian dragged Excalibur across her body at waist height. A quarter of her full stamina was expended in a double-handed, stone-crunching, flesh-searing blow. Richard's head rolled across the floor. His body teetered forward and hit the ground with a *thud*. Game.

Lillian swished Excalibur over the body, discarding the blood, and slotted the naked blade back onto her belt. Andrew listlessly stared at the corpse Lillian had created. Having pursued this goal for so long, Lillian had thought she'd be pleased once it was accomplished, to put it mildly. She was usually happy and relieved to have dealt with a powerful adversary. Andrew's talk, which he'd purposefully publicized, put the whole thing into perspective. This wasn't a victory for him. He'd accomplished a deeply unpleasant task. She knew, because she'd been in that position herself not too long ago.

Lillian decided the rest of this conversation was not for other people's ears, assuming any of it ever had been.

"Magnitude is dead. I'll be back shortly to help secure the wall. Thank you for your service. The Empire owes those who participated a great debt, which will be paid in full."

She closed the group down. Then carefully walked over to Andrew, examining him to make sure he didn't reject her approach. He was still staring at the body. She gently put the palm of her hand between his shoulder blades, and when he didn't reject that either she settled it there and rubbed his back as platonically as she could.

"You did the right thing."

"I don't know. What if I'd—"

"No 'what if's. You can't fix other people. They can only choose to fix themselves. That's a lot harder when they're being rewarded for terrible behavior."

Andrew snorted, his eyes still not leaving the headless corpse she'd created.

"Is that why you came after me with Damien? Because you wanted to 'fix' me?"

"Nope. I was filled with rage and misery and wanted to completely destroy your life. My actions had zero moral bearing. Redeeming you came later, but that had nothing to do with me.

you did it all by yourself. Maybe, in time, Richard will understand as well. Like you did."

"Or maybe he'll be the same manipulative turd for all eternity."

"Maybe. That's on him. Not you."

She patted him a couple of times and dropped her hand back down. The situation was already uncomfortable without inadvertently signaling she wanted to hook up. Change of subject.

"Sorry I killed him. I know you said we wouldn't—"

"I never said that. I said *I* wouldn't kill him. I was very careful with my wording, since I knew you'd probably do it when I didn't. Just don't loot the body. We don't need anything from him."

Fair enough. Lillian turned and stared at the body with him. Magnitude had constituted such a huge threat for such a long time. Now it just looked sad. So much for an epic final battle. They couldn't just leave it there, though. It wasn't that far from the wall and an enterprising player might swing by and loot him after they'd left.

"Andrew? Do you want to bury the body?"

"Seems appropriate."

The first thing Damien noticed was the heat. It smothered him as soon as he passed through the portal. Then he was smothered by Archimonde, which was considerably worse.

Damien knew just how quickly portals closed after their casters passed through them, hence his haste. He'd just about made it through, but his landing had been less than controlled: he couldn't see where he was going until he'd arrived. In this case, his "arrival" consisted of whapping into Archimonde's front with a slick slap. He was wrapped around a sweaty, turgid ball of flesh, and it was biting him.

He'd twisted the kunai to break free when Archimonde had executed a pro-gamer move: rather than supporting Damien's weight or trying to push him off, the demon had collapsed on top of him. Before Damien could break free, it pointed at the floor next to Damien's head and a Circle of Hell formed around them. Damien was being cooked and eaten, both of which were healing Archimonde, and he was pinned by Archimonde's bulk from above and the root of the circle from below.

Damien's elbows and the back of his head were among the extremities that were now locked to the ground. This was a situation where brute force would not work. He cast his eyes around, looking for what he needed. They'd passed through Archimonde's portal. They were in Archimonde's base. Bases have—

You're mine. Come here.

Demon Gate was still on cooldown, but any extra help was welcome at that moment. A consumer was the closest. The tongue lashed around Archimonde's neck and drew it backward. Archimonde was seven levels higher than him and the consumer was as strong as it could be under Damien's control, yet it wasn't anywhere near strong enough to pull Archimonde off him. It was strong enough to lever its former master's head up, prompting Archimonde's hands to reach for its own neck instead of keeping Damien's arms pinned down. Just as Damien's Narcissistic Rage activated and the root ended.

Damien swung his weapons round, skewering Archimonde's head between them. He was pretty sure he felt the blades scrape against each other, inside Archimonde's head. That's a lot of damage. Yet not enough: Archimonde still had two-thirds of its health.

Since when did stabbing something in the head, twice, not even bring it below half health? It was ridiculous even without considering Might Makes Right and the resulting carnage. Each critical strike had inflicted over 2,500 damage, over 5,000 damage together. Archimonde had something in the region of 15,000 hit points. Which were continuing to go up as Damien's went down.

The root was gone from his arms but the fire hadn't stopped burning and the teeth hadn't stopped churning. A damage race, then. Archimonde was already being laid into by a flock of newly winged imps at its back, the consumer's tongue wrapped around its neck and two succubi, all forcibly donated into Damien's Soul Summon Limit fund. Between them and him, one way or another this battle would be over in seconds. Either the increasing damage of Archimonde's Circle of Hell and the teeth being raked across the front of Damien's torso would overtake him, or Damien would finish this in the next couple of blows.

He twisted the kunai and was drawing them back when the minions broke off their engagement with Archimonde. They were fleeing to the back of the cave. They'd left Damien's Soul Summon Limit and were no longer under his control. A gnarled, immaculately manicured hand seized Archimonde by the top of its head and yanked it out of range before Damien's kunai could swing back into its temples. The second hand seized one of Damien's horns and discarded him outside the circle.

"Why can't they ever play nicely without adult supervision?"

Lucifer may have been wearing his permanent unskinned grin, but he did not sound happy. Enraged Damien was tank-sized, larger and more impressive than Lucifer physically, if not quite so terrifying to behold. Looks can be deceiving. Lucifer had manhandled both him and Archimonde with ease.

"Archie baby, you know how this works. Fights between Sins in Hell have strict rules. Give me one good reason not to revoke your standing."

Damien was still balking at 'Archie baby' when Archimonde pointed a finger into his face. Damien swatted it away, earning a growl from Lucifer for each of them, as Archimonde scapegoated his problems away.

"I had to defend myself from this noob. He followed me through my portal, took control of my minions and tried to kill me."

Damien stared at the creature. Archimonde sounded pretty normal when it wasn't doing its dodgy weaboo speak. Lucifer nodded sagely, then turned his attention to Damien.

"Damien. As the first Sin, I expected better from you. That's not how we do things here."

"How am I supposed to know something I've never been—"

"Always with the tiresome excuses. Your mistakes never have anything to do with you, do they?"

Complete shutdown. A line composed of utter tripe that was impossible to defend against. Archimonde continued slathering its tongue up and down its savior's backside.

"Thank you for setting him straight, my lord. As you can see, Daemien has encroached on my base in Hell's Hunting Grounds *and* attacked a fellow Sin in your domain without going through the proper channels. I demand punishment."

Hell's Hunting Grounds? This was Hell? It was hard to tell in this cave, but that at least explained the heat. Damien lacked the capacity to be both curious and angry at the same time. He fell into the latter.

"I have no idea what the rules are here. Archimonde killed me first, I'm returning the favor. It's that simple, what's not—"

"Not knowing the rules is not a defense against following them, and no one is obligated to tell you what they are. Be quiet."

"So where can I find the rules? Are they written down somewhe—"

"I make them up as I go along! This is my domain! Silence!"

Damien couldn't believe it. What point was there in being the Embodiment of Pride when the very entity who'd granted him it wouldn't let him accomplish his goal? Every fiber in his being wanted to erase Archimonde from existence, yet Lucifer had prevented him from exacting his revenge and was now apparently about to punish him for attempting to do so. It didn't seem very satanic from where Damien was standing, but Lucifer dressed it up well enough.

"You have disobeyed the laws of Hell. You have trampled on my authority as sovereign and questioned my judgment in front of my subjects. There is no greater crime."

This didn't sound good. Archimonde was grinning broadly, with both mouths. Its stomach looked like a zombified smiley emoji. Lucifer pointed at Damien.

"I shall now pass sentence. Your punishment is—"

His hand swiveled round and suddenly Lucifer was pointing directly at Archimonde instead.

"—to fight Archimonde to the death in 'Mortal Sin Combat'."

Damien had to think fast.

"Uuuuh...oh, no. Please. Anything but that."

Off to his right, Archimonde started to stammer.

"B-but my lord, you sai—"

"B-b-but my lord! You said— SHUT UP, Archimonde. Nobody likes a suck-up, not even me. If you're so keen on seeing Damien punished you can do it yourself. I've already set the stage."

A portal opened behind Lucifer as he came to the end of his sentence. Either he could manifest them instantly or he'd started ten seconds ago and it took him next to no concentration whatsoever. Lucifer shoved Archimonde through first, before the creature could weasel its way out of it. Damien passed through immediately afterwards of his own accord. Lucifer came through behind them, took one of each of their hands and raised them up to cheers, screams and thunderous applause.

They were standing at the center of a giant coliseum, more than twice the size of the space in which Damien had fought Toutatis. It was large enough for armies to fight in. The only feature was a gigantic skull throne in the very center, which they'd arrived in front of. Damien recognized it. This was where he'd first met Lucifer. Everything beyond the throne had been veiled before, but he could see it all clearly now, illuminated by a blood-red sun that scorched overhead.

No stone columns and no prebattle ceiling in here, but there were other similarities. Once again the floor was densely packed sand and the battlespace was circular, hemmed in by stone walls from atop which the shrieks of the audience rained down upon them. This audience was strange, to say the least: the stands above the walls were filled with thousands of demonic minions of every kind.

This seemed like a good time to be livestreaming. Damien double-checked he was still rolling. Win or lose, this would get a lot of views. It wouldn't be worth as much to do his good deed, putting Archimonde in his place, if there was no one watching.

Lucifer turned to his combatants.

"Rule one: No enthralling your enemy's minions. That means you, Damien, since you're the higher-ranking Sin."

Damn. That was his biggest advantage over Archimonde gone. He could see why Lucifer required his highest-ranking underlings to settle disputes this way. That didn't mean he liked it.

"Rule two: Any and all abilities are allowed, with one exception: you may not summon Noigel. Summoning Noigel will result in your immediate disqualification, automatic forfeiture of the match and subsequent execution, by me."

Now Damien's *second-biggest* advantage over Archimonde was gone. He had a Soul Summon Limit of 45, but controlling all of his minions simultaneously would be a difficult prospect without Noigel's help. He was about to ask why but managed to bite his tongue. Debating it would only result in derision and lost favor, at best.

"Rule three: You have one minute to select your full Soul Summon Limit's worth of minions from my personal retinue. You may not attack each other, or each other's minions, until after the minute has passed."

The four gates at each compass point of the coliseum opened and demons began pouring out of them, gathering around the outer wall. They all had green writing above their heads. There were hundreds of them, all filing around the edges before standing perfectly still at equal distances. Lucifer's personal retinue was akin to a small rapture. They continued to assemble as Lucifer moved on to the next rule.

"Rule four: When your opponent is on the verge of death, I shall disable them and cry "FINISH HIM", at which point you must dispatch them in the most brutal way you can imagine. Brutal enough to constitute a Mortal Sin. If it does not please me, both of you will be deemed losers."

Damien turned and stared at Archimonde. He had no problem with that rule. It didn't even need to be stated, considering what he was getting Archimonde back for: humiliating and eating him, then using an ability on Lillian that practically broke her. There wouldn't be much point in Damien going through with this unless he repaid Archimonde in kind.

Archimonde glanced back at him, then quickly set its gaze

ahead. The blubbering and stammering were gone, but the anxiety was bubbling just below the surface. Was Archimonde really that scared of a twenty-four-hour death timer? The battle was already done, this was just the fight at the end for the cherry on the cake. Surely for Archimonde, who was seven levels higher than him and obviously had vastly better gear, this was a good prospect. So why was the creature not into it?

Lucifer spoke the final rule and Damien found out.

"Rule five: The loser, or losers, will be stripped of their Sin. Your time starts now."

Lucifer took his seat and the crowd of demons fell deathly silent. Waiting to be picked. Only now the fight had started did Archimonde's reluctance make sense. Damien had only just got this form, he hadn't realized he could lose it this way. He'd wanted to one-up Archimonde, he didn't think there'd be anything more permanent than death on the line. Now he was at personal risk.

Wait. Never mind the risk for himself. The odds may have been stacked against him, but now he could really hurt Archimonde. If he got this right, Archimonde would never be a threat to anyone again. Only as a regular occultist anyway, which was nothing compared to what the creature was now.

If Damien had been given this as a choice, he'd have probably taken it. It was only because it was being foisted on him at the last moment that he wasn't sure. This was by design, to throw him off. An advantage for Archimonde, who already knew the rules of this engagement.

He needed minions. What to pick? Know your enemy. Archimonde was a magic-user, so the first pick was easy. Damien glanced at a consumer at the outer wall and it began to trundle toward him. Archimonde wasn't picking. It was watching. That was part of the game too. Regardless of what Archimonde eventually picked, there were certain things he'd absolutely—

Which was when Damien realized something important: his health wasn't at full. He'd been regaining it slowly, but it was only at 2,827/4,800. Damien's health had been low when Lucifer had brought the fight between him and Archimonde to a halt. There hadn't been enough time to fully regenerate.

The same went for Archimonde, right? Damien quickly turned to look at his competitor and realised the creature had been flicking its wrist while he'd been looking away. Archimonde's health was rising rapidly. Damien followed Archimonde's gaze and found several of the minions at the outer wall on fire, burning from Corruption. Archimonde was using it in combination with its spell-vamp to economically restore its own health.

The rules had stipulated they couldn't attack each other's minions, it didn't say anything about attacking Lucifer's. The burning minions were just standing there, taking the damage without becoming hostile. Archimonde had tried to do it without Damien noticing to gain a decisive advantage.

What kind of deathmatch starts with the players at less than full health? A deathmatch in Hell, with Lucifer adjudicating. The demons in the stands were whooping and hollering. This was part of the entertainment. Never mind which minions he'd pick for now, Damien needed to get back to full health. His inventory was absent while he was in this form, so potions wouldn't cut it. If he changed into his normal form to drink potions, he wouldn't have the soul energy to change back. He'd have to follow Archimonde's example.

He picked out an incubus off to the side that Archimonde hadn't selected yet and ran toward it, kunai raised. Thank goodness he'd noticed this problem, otherwise he'd have started with an enormous handicap. He'd nearly reached the incubus when he realized there was another problem. His health was above half and he didn't have Narcissistic Rage enabled. Archimonde's spell-vamp appeared to be constant, whereas Damien's life-steal was only active for ten seconds after dropping below half health.

Desperate times, desperate measures. Damien took his kunai and cut himself, trying to measure it out so he'd remove only as much health as necessary. Down to 2,330/4,800. As soon as he bulked up, he turned on Lucifer's incubus. Right as he stabbed it, it ignited in black flames. The fire spread to him as he touched it. That was an attack! Archimonde had attacked him! He looked to Lucifer, waiting for the announcement that Archimonde had forfeited the match. Lucifer was sitting quite still, his head propped up on his elbow, staring straight at Damien with that permanent grin. He'd seen it and approved. He was allowing it.

Archimonde had a way to inflict damage on Damien without attacking him directly. The Corruption was doing approximately 50 damage a second and the timer indicated it would last twenty-five seconds. Around 1,250 damage over the duration. On one spell. That Damien couldn't get rid of. No wonder Archimonde had caused so much chaos with Corruption and the Contagion trait in the battle. Up until recently, Damien himself had had fewer maximum hit points than that.

At least Lucifer's incubus had a lot of hit points too. Damien was already on fire, he may as well drain this minion before he moved on. Except before he landed his second pair of stabs, the basic information above Lucifer's incubus turned red. Archimonde had drawn the same incubus he'd set on fire into its own Soul Summon Limit.

Lucifer's disapproval boomed across the sand as the icon denoting Damien's Soul Summon Limit flashed and changed: it read 8/22.

"Damien, you have attacked one of Archimonde's minions. You may now only select half your Soul Summon Limit's worth of minions. One more instance of cheating and you will forfeit the match."

What a dirty, clever, honorless, rotting kumquat Archimonde was turning out to be. First the creature had set the incubus on fire and let Damien attack it, then it had taken control of the same minion to get Damien penalized. It was a whole lot better than losing the match outright but still terrible. If Archimonde could force another error, Damien would lose on a technicality. Archimonde was doing everything it could to end this fight before it began.

Damien really needed more healing and his Narcissistic Rage would only last another five seconds. He'd regained 10% of the inflicted damage from his four critical strikes on the incubus.

The first two hits had granted 500 hit points back as life-steal, the reward for two perfectly executed critical strikes dealing 5,000 damage. But when Archimonde had taken the incubus over, the incubus's hit points had dropped: it had defaulted from Lucifer's unknown level to Archimonde's and the stats had dropped accordingly. Leaving it with less health for Damien to drain.

By the time the Corruption on Damien was over, he'd be back to less than half health. Yet if he made a move to attack anything, Archimonde could take control of his target almost instantly and get Damien disqualified.

Damien could see a way that this could work to his advantage, if Archimonde thought little enough of him. Damien ran toward the next incubus and raised his kunai over it. Then pulled back at the last second. As expected, the name above it turned red. Archimonde had been so desperate to get him disqualified, it had now taken two incubi into its Soul Summon Limit. Greed had been too greedy. Damien could use the incubus to life-steal some of his health back after the fight started, without breaking any rules. It was a poor investment for Archimonde.

Archimonde made the same judgment call. It dismissed the incubus it had just taken off Lucifer's hands, only for Lucifer to clarify the rules.

"The two incubi you appropriated both count toward your full complement of minions, Archimonde. If you decide to set them on fire before you enthrall them or dismiss them after, that's your choice. But you won't be getting any more."

Hah! The devil's in the details. Archimonde had taken 20 souls' worth of minions into its Soul Summon Limit and both of the minions were gone already, one now dead from Damien's rule breaking assault and Corruptions flames, the other dismissed. Damien knew Archimonde couldn't have the Legion trait, because he had access to the Dark Omen spell, which was another level 50 trait. He only had 10 minion slots left.

It was a definite victory, but with a trade-off. Damien's Narcissistic Rage had ended. No more life-steal for the time being. Although the Corruption he'd been afflicted with would leave him with less health than he'd started with, it did serve a purpose. Not only would he drop below half health and regain his life-steal in a matter of seconds, but crucially it also helped him keep track of time. Lucifer was not providing a timer for when the minute would be over.

Damien had been blindsided by the last rule, revealing his Embodiment was on the line. He therefore hadn't thought to count the seconds down himself, but knowing the Corruption lasted twenty-five seconds he estimated they were coming up to the halfway point. His best guess was that it had taken him fifteen seconds to come to terms with the stakes, reach an incubus at the outer wall which was around a hundred meters away, inflict damage on himself and then attack it. So once Corruption was completely over, there'd be around fifteen seconds left before the preliminary stage was over.

They were locked in an unspoken stalemate. Archimonde only had 10 Soul Summon Limit left to employ, yet Lucifer had said that if Damien attacked one of Archimonde's minions again he'd be disqualified. If Archimonde's timing was better than Damien's, Archimonde would take the minion as Damien was attacking it and Damien would lose for the stupidest reason.

What to do? His health was about to drop below 50%, which was a big problem. His life-steal only operated for ten seconds after he dropped below half health. If he didn't get back above that threshold before the effect wore off, he'd have no life-steal for the duration of the deathmatch.

Then it occurred to him. He was playing defensively, when he needed to be playing offensively. Archimonde had obligingly demonstrated how. Damien's main problem was getting into attack range, but it wasn't actually a problem at all. It was effortless. If neither of them could attack the other's minions until combat began, Damien had an enormous advantage. Instead of worrying about getting his health back to full, he needed to apply pressure. These rules worked in his favor, if he could be sick-minded enough.

Damien enthralled a single imp as he moved to the next high

health minion in line. A consumer, which would have more health than an incubus, but at a price. One of the biggest advantages of the consumer had not been apparent to Damien until now, when it was crucial. Their heads were also their torsos. They had no throats. The only evident critical strike points they had were their tongues.

Archimonde had an orc head on the top of its larger-than-average consumer body, but the lesser version had no immediately accessible weak point. Damien could get more health from this thing, but it would require more attacks. The flurry of blows this would require put him in greater danger of Archimonde enthralling the minion as he attacked, ending the fight. Damien himself could enthrall the consumer and then stab it, circumventing the possibility of a TKO. This was problematic, not only because it would leave him with only 5 more Soul Summon Limit, but also because the consumer's hit points would drop to 2,500. 250 health would not be sufficient. Which was why he was preparing a countermeasure.

Damien stood behind the consumer this time, making sure he could see both the consumer's basic information and Archimonde itself. As his imp flew toward Archimonde from behind Damien's health dropped below 50% and Narcissistic Rage was reapplied. He held his kunai behind the consumer and prepared to strike, keeping his kunai hidden behind the consumer's bulk.

If Archimonde was stupid enough to enthrall this consumer before Damien attacked, Damien would surely win outright. It would take up 8 of Archimonde's remaining 10 Soul Summon Limit on top of the two incubi that had been killed or dismissed. This would leave Archimonde with nothing but a single consumer, whose benefits Archimonde's own body already housed, and two final slots. Which was not what Damien wanted.

Damien had no intention of winning, or indeed losing, his fight with Archimonde based on a technicality. If Archimonde made a misstep that was its own fault, but Damien wouldn't force an error. Even though there were plenty of ways he could. He was more than capable of putting himself in a position to beat Archimonde legitimately, even while Archimonde strained to beat him by abusing the rules.

While he stared at Archimonde across the gap and Archimonde stared back, no doubt trying to gauge when Damien would strike so he could enthrall his target at the optimal moment, the solitary imp Damien had taken control of hovered in front of Archimonde's face. At Damien's behest, it screeched at maximum volume, loud enough to reduce its own stamina. As Archimonde's vision was blocked and its attention diverted, Damien plunged his kunai into the consumer's back.

Damien had learned plenty about watching where other characters were looking from fighting Mordred. If Archimonde wasn't looking at the consumer, the creature couldn't take control of it. As the kunai sank in, Damien's hit points went above 50% and the Corruption on him spread to the consumer he was attacking. The Corruption was reaching the end of its duration anyway.

As his health went back above 50%, Damien lost the strength bonus from Enrage. However, he still had ten seconds to make the most of his activated life-steal. His damage dropped about 300 points per strike, but it was still nearly 1,000 damage with each hit. Damien made up for it with more attacks. Just like old times.

Archimonde made to attack the imp, then realized its mistake. Archimonde wasn't allowed to attack it, even while it screamed into its face. It would be the easiest thing in the world for Archimonde to destroy it, had Damien's foe not been bound by the exact same rules it had just abused to Damien's detriment. Damien stabbed as fast as he could until Archimonde turned back, then distanced himself from the consumer. His hit points were at 3,805/4,800. That was manageable. Fifteen seconds left to go. More or less.

The Corruption on Damien had ended and around half his time was gone. He needed to sort his own minions out before it was too late. He didn't know what Archimonde wanted to do with its remaining 10 slots, but he knew very well what he wanted to with his remaining 13. His main difficulty was getting into range. That was easily fixed.

He'd crapstacked imps against Andrew to great effect and saw no reason why it wouldn't work here. All he needed to concern himself with was getting into melee range with Archimonde and staying there. Any amount of time spent at a distance would be in Archimonde's favor. Damien ran around the outside of the wall and manually picked out imps, changing the location he drew them from each time to ensure Archimonde wouldn't take control of any of them right before he did. Then he manually spread them all over the arena. He couldn't keep them bunched up, or else a single Corruption/Imp-losion combo would deal with them all. Wherever Archimonde went, Damien would be there not long after.

Ten seconds left. Ish. Damien had already picked and positioned his minions. There was no reason for Archimonde not to select its own, now the creature could see what Damien was intent on doing. The imp Damien had put on screaming duty was panting and the screaming had been reduced to a hoarse yell. It was completely out of stamina, which went some way to illustrating how much force Damien had put into the order.

Damien had Demon Gate and Charge as his gap-closing tools. Archimonde only had Demon Gate. Which should he go with first? The Single-Minded Charge was his best damage ability and he needed it to connect. If he used it first, Archimonde could evade it by Demon Gating, assuming Archimonde took any imps. Then it occurred to him that there was a much easier way to close the gap. He could start the battle right next to Archimonde. According to the rules, Archimonde wouldn't be able to do anything about it.

Damien started running back to where Archimonde was, staring his enemy down the whole way. Archimonde took a moment to register what he was doing, then started waddling away. It was the most desperate, terrified waddle Damien had ever seen. He grinned. He'd stand right in his enemy's face until time was up.

"Rule six: Do not approach your enemy until the battle begins."

Damien stopped running and stared at Lucifer. Was his entire goal to make this difficult? Silly question. Of course it was. If Damien started next to Archimonde, that wouldn't be entertaining.

Lucifer snapped his fingers. All the remaining minions Damien and Archimonde had not availed themselves of were sucked into portals as they were dismissed. A few imps in Archimonde's vicinity remained behind. It turned out Archimonde had selected its minions after all, it had just kept them standing in line so as not to draw attention to them. Damien had barely registered this fact when he was once again engulfed by the black flames of Corruption. He looked to Archimonde and saw the creature was channeling a Chaotic Bolt with one hand and throttling Damien's imp with the other. It was already dead. Opportunity missed.

The battle had begun. Damien sent all his imps flying toward Archimonde and called the consumer to himself, closing the net and preparing his defense. The way things had developed, he hadn't thought the consumer would come into play. If he hadn't been distracted by Lucifer – or heaven forbid had been provided with a countdown – Archimonde wouldn't have been able to kill his first imp before Damien could Demon Gate to it. Now it was slightly more complicated.

Archimonde discarded the imp corpse and twisted its wrist at every imp coming its way. They were dying in seconds. Damien was running toward his consumer, which was moving far too slowly to rely on. He glanced between the imps and Archimonde as he ran, waiting for the Chaotic Bolt to be fired. Archimonde could release the bolt any time it pleased within five seconds. Even if the bolt wasn't fully charged, his enemy would hit Damien with it before he got to safety.

Still running, Damien threw a kunai. At his own consumer. He yanked the chain back just before Archimonde released the second-fastest bolt in the known game. The consumer's health went up and down like a yoyo as first it took Damien's hit with the kunai, then smacked into Damien's front with its gob open wide, eating Archimonde's magic attack in a demonic enactment of 'Get down, Mr. President' protocol. As the consumer landed in front of him, Damien found what he was looking for: a burning imp that had less time to live than a moth at a candlelit vigil. It had drawn close enough for Damien to apply pressure.

Damien Demon Gated and threw a kunai as he arrived, piercing Archimonde's shoulder. It was wide of the target, but considering the expediency of his throw Damien was glad to have hit his enemy at all. Especially when Archimonde abruptly burst into black flames. Connecting with the chain kunai qualified for Corruption spreading by touch. It wouldn't do much damage to Archimonde's enormous health pool, but Damien would take whatever he could get. He was drawing himself in on the chain when Archimonde looked past him and was replaced with an imp.

Archimonde had used its only escape. Damien's window of opportunity had arrived. The chain snapped back into his hand and he rolled as he hit the floor, mitigating most of the collision damage. Archimonde's imp helped a little in that regard, offering about the same impact resistance and resulting mess you'd expect from a piano landing on a water balloon.

Damien turned, sighted Archimonde at the far end of the arena and Charged. Archimonde's imps were moving to block him, but Damien was far too fast for them to intercept. He was over halfway there when a Chaotic Bolt thundered into his torso, but his speed was not compromised. His Narcissistic Rage was triggered by the damage. Archimonde had done him a favor: his strength had been increased for him right before he pulled off his biggest attack.

Damien drew his arms back, waiting for the last moment to thrust so he could get the full momentum of the Single-Minded Charge behind both kunai blades. Nothing he'd hit with this ability so far had survived. He had no idea how much damage it would do when his weapons were boosted by the impact damage.

Archimonde was a sitting duck. Without a Demon Gate on standby, there was no way the creature could remove itself from Damien's path. Yet there was something Damien had not taken into account. Archimonde could throw something into his path instead.

Archimonde hurriedly raised a pointing finger. All Damien could think of was getting to his enemy before it cast any more bolts. His strides were long enough to cover an enormous amount of ground extremely quickly, but they were not long enough to step over Archimonde's Circle of Hell. Damien's stride faltered as his first foot was rooted and then the next one stamped down in front of it to maintain balance. His health was deteriorating from the damage over time of both Corruption and the circle. He'd been relying on the Charge damage, but now his Charge was gone and he was rooted in place.

Archimonde began channeling a Chaotic Bolt in each hand. Damien would be rooted for five seconds, the bolts would be ready to fire in three. He had no way of dodging either of them. Between them, the Corruption and the increasing damage of Circle of Hell, Damien would be dead before the root was over.

No imps nearby for Imp-losions. No Demon Gate. Archimonde was a long way away. Damien had only one offensive option left. He braced his right arm and hurled his kunai as hard as he could. He had increased strength on his side, which would be worth nothing without accuracy. At least he was standing still for it rather than either he or his target being in motion.

The chain extended seemingly without end, the loops on Damien's arm running forward and backward and forward again with more chain appearing underneath in layers each time it unraveled in the opposite direction. It was completely impossible. If there'd been as much chain covering his forearms as the distance of his throw implied, they'd have been layered ten feet thick. It was a VR-enabled optical illusion, appreciated only through Damien's peripheral vision. However, his focus was entirely on whether or not the blade would land. It did, and considering the nature of Archimonde it was no surprise where he'd connected: right into the center of his foe's guts.

The chain had stopped unwinding and gone taut. The kunai had found purchase. Damien was still rooted to the floor, he wasn't going anywhere. He instinctively seized the chain in both hands, totally unnecessarily given the mechanics of his weapon but understandable given what he knew would happen next. He dragged the chain back, hoping he was in time to interrupt Archimonde's dual-cast Chaotic Bolts, and yelled out his most heartfelt desire.

"GET OVER HERE!"

The Embodiment of Greed was yanked forward off the ground, the Chaotic Bolts misfiring left and right as Archimonde's arms whiplashed behind its body. Damien cocked his left hand and braced the back of the other kunai against his palm, guiding it between his middle and ring fingers to turn it into a vicious knuckleduster. As Archimonde reached him, Damien twisted his right hand to release the chain. The kunai in his closed fist glided into the bottom of Archimonde's jaw, powerful and well timed enough to send his enemy upward and back the way it had come.

As Archimonde was pummeled into the air, the root of the Circle of Hell ended. Damien threw a kunai into Archimonde's open back, then pulled. Airborne Archimonde was not a stable grounding point. Damien orbited Archimonde from underneath rather than traveling to him directly. Damien's hour of training as he had ascended through the overlapping beams in the Dark Tower's Path of Deceit made what to do in this situation a matter of course.

He twisted to release exactly as his momentum carried him upward and Archimonde was pulled back down to Hell. Archimonde was yet to hit the floor when Damien hurled a kunai into his enemy's throat and pulled. His knees landed on Archimonde's chest as his second kunai plunged through Archimonde's forehead, then Archimonde smashed into the ground and was crushed between it and Damien.

Three noncritical strikes for 1,000 damage each. Three Enraged critical strikes for 2,500 damage each. A generous portion of impact damage from the fist behind Damien's kunai, Damien's knees connecting with his enemy's chest and Archimonde hitting the ground to be crushed under his Enraged bulk. Plus whatever damage Archimonde had taken and was continuing to take from its own Corruption. Damien's life-steal was finished, but he'd regained over 1,000 hit points and was on top of his stunned foe. Archimonde was less than a single critical strike away from death.

Which was when Archimonde played its last resort. Before Damien could land the last hit, Archimonde pointed a shaky finger at his head.

"Shedim!"

Damien lost all vision. He'd been blinded. Experiencing it was different from knowing about it in theory. Blindness in and of itself was pretty scary, but temporary in this case. Nothing Damien couldn't handle. He'd dealt with worse. He just had to keep his cool. Everything had gone completely dark, darker than if he'd closed his eyes. Then there was color, blurred but clearing rapidly. It was irrelevant. Whatever nightmares this ability gave him, they wouldn't be real. Damien had recomposed himself and was raising his hand for the final blow when the voice cut into his head.

"It's not your fault. I love you very much."

The hairs on the back of Damien's neck stood on end. The details were starting to fill in. It was only his vision and his hearing that were affected. He could feel Archimonde lying below him. He could feel that his own hand and the heaving chest beneath it were that of his Pride form. What he was seeing and hearing told a different story.

"It's not your fault. I love you very much."

He was back in Central Union. In his house. Although he hadn't lost his simulated sense of touch, his audio and visuals had been taken from him, hijacked to replay the worst seconds of his life in a loop. He could see the profile of his feeble arms stretched out in front of him. He put the palms of his hands over his eyes, but it did nothing to prevent the scene from repeating. The more details he recognized, the more of them started filling in. He was in his house. On his kitchen floor. There was a figure lying prone in front of him.

"It's not your fault. I love you very much."

It sharpened, starting from the most important details and

then expanding outward like tissue paper set on fire. The first part that cleared was his mother's face. She was gaunt, almost skeletal, exactly as it had been on that day. Worse still, she was smiling at him. Separate points began from which the scene gained yet more clarity. Her hand squeezing his, though he could only see it, not feel it. The broken bowl with the chicken pasta in that miserable splat on the floor.

"It's not your fault. I love you very—"

Which is when Damien realized he was punching Archimonde in the face. He'd already struck his enemy three times before he realized what he was doing. Conscious thought streamed in afterwards, lagging behind his instincts. So this was why Lillian had become a gibbering wreck. This is what Archimonde had done to her, and what Andrew had halted before Damien could. He'd hated it even before he had understood it personally.

Damien picked up where his instincts had left off and methodically continued his assault. He still didn't have the wherewithal to take hold of his weapons. However, Might Makes Right and his retriggered Narcissistic Rage ensured he accomplished his goal, despite having lost his mind.

"It's not your fau—"

His closed fist descended on where his sense of touch told him Archimonde's head was for the sixth time when the vision faded. Suddenly, Damien was deafening himself with his own roar. So he'd been screaming, as well. He hadn't registered that either. He awakened to find his knuckles embedded across Archimonde's face, which was little more than a bloody pulp.

It wasn't enough.

He'd buried his fists in Archimonde's face a dozen times more, now consciously choosing not to use his weapons to drag it out as long as possible, before Lucifer split them up and dragged Archimonde to its feet. It stood in a stupor.

"Finish him."

Damien hadn't put a great deal of thought into how he'd dispatch his enemy. He'd only known it would fit Lucifer's criteria of being as brutal as he could imagine. Having been subjected to his worst fear in excruciating detail, Damien's horizons had been broadened. Necessity is the mother of creation. Damien needed Archimonde to suffer. He held his hand out and waited for a few seconds before his nearest imp landed on top of it.

Damien wished he'd taken the 'Shedim' trait so he could force Archimonde through what he'd just been subjected to, if only for a few seconds. His own abilities would have to suffice. Given what he now had in mind, his genius almost frightened him. Not enough to dissuade him from seizing the imp and plunging it into Archimonde's gaping, unresisting stomach.

Damien grasped the upper and lower lips of the mouth that had once consumed him and pulled them open wide, granting him a clear line of sight to the imp that would execute his grand design. He pointed with his index finger without releasing Archimonde's lips:

"Ex-Im—"

He pulled the lips over each other, sealing the only exit.

"—p-losion."

Damien knew all about the perks of good preparation. His Ex-Imp-losion was fully charged. It was dangerous enough at close range without being activated *inside* the object of his wrath. Archimonde's body swelled up and air rushed from its flaccid maw on either side. Damien clenched his fists together tighter to try and prevent it, but the pressure escaping soon found new avenues from which to be expelled: the five imps that had been charged by Damien's Imp-losions burst out of Archimonde's body in all directions, reducing it to a gory party popper. Archimonde's head disconnected from its mangled body and soared into the air on a fountain of blood, and the rest of its internal workings left its body via the holes the imps had torn out of it.

It wasn't enough.

Damien released what little remained of Archimonde's body, allowing it to topple into the sand, and flung his kunai at the exact moment the head hung in midair. Accuracy was no longer a concern. Damien hadn't even questioned whether he could hit such a small target. He'd previously worried if he was capable of hitting Archimonde's entire body at a comparable distance. Now he had no doubt.

He struck true, then whipped his arm downward and twisted to release. Archimonde's head hit the compressed sand with a *thud*, a *crack* and a *squelch*. It was obliterated. Now Archimonde's head was the miserable splat on the floor.

It wasn't enough. It would never be enough. But there wasn't anything left for Damien to take his anger out on, so it would have to do. For now.

Lucifer traced his hands over his own blood-drenched body, licked Archimonde off his fingers, then grasped Damien's hand and thrust it into the air. He was pleased.

"Fatality. Damien wins."

33

CONQUEROR'S WILL

Lillian had arrived at the wall with Andrew in tow, only to find everyone left alive standing among the bodies. Gormlessly staring into their menus. They'd stopped everything to watch Damien's livestream. Lillian became equally gormless when she set eyes on Lucifer, gathering the situation Damien was in by degrees. The rules had already been explained at that point and the preliminary stage had begun. It didn't make a whole lot of sense to Lillian, but Lucifer's referencing of his own rules as Damien fell foul of them, coupled with the *oooohs* and *aaaahs* of the players surrounding them, had given her enough information to get the gist.

Then the combat had started. This Lillian could follow. Damien didn't have as much raw power as she did, but he had some pretty disgusting combat options with his new form and weaponry. It took him fifteen seconds to get Archimonde on the floor and at his hypothetical mercy, alone. Lillian couldn't have been happier. Which was when Archimonde pointed into Damien's face and spoke the magic word.

Her blood ran cold. Damien's greatest fear was about to be displayed on a livestream. Lillian couldn't imagine sharing what she'd been subjected to with an audience. It wasn't that she didn't want to show fear; she was just as entitled to be afraid of things as anyone else, especially when it was the worst thing that had ever happened to her. It was the intimacy of it. It was private. So when Damien's vision remained intact, for a brief moment Lillian was relieved. She thought he'd dodged the bullet entirely. Yet when he had stopped attacking and released his weapons, allowing them to dangle from his wrists off their chains, her perspective changed.

It took no time at all for Lillian to realize what he was seeing, because he'd already told her all about it. Damien's worst fear was strikingly similar to her own. Now she had to watch someone else suffer what she'd gone through. So when Damien's pained breathing was broken with a primal roar, melding seamlessly from pain to full-blown rage as his fists descended into Archimonde's face, Lillian's triumphant scream drowned him out entirely.

"Get him! Take him do—"

She remembered where she was and cleared her throat, catching a few bemused glances from outside the bounds of her spectating window. Not so many as she'd expected. Most of the crowd were fixated on the fight and some were shouting even louder than she was, be it in joy, amazement or horror. The joy was split between the latter two shortly afterwards, when Archimonde Ex-Imp-loded.

Lillian was neither surprised, nor fussed. When in Rome. She knew most of the viewers around her wouldn't see it that way, but they didn't know what she knew. She was more concerned with Damien's well-being. While the plethora of demons in the stands were showering him with praise, Damien himself was very quiet. He was in the wrong company. She tapped out a message while Lucifer paraded him around the arena like a prizewinning dog.

Lillian: You did amazingly well. I'm sorry Archimonde did that to you. I'm logging out now, have to leave for work soon. I'd like to see you before I go if you can manage it.

She watched him open his menu and saw her own message there. Good. Then she tapped Andrew on the shoulder to get his attention.

"I'm logging out to get Damien. I've sent for the Empire Artisan's Guild already, they'll make short work of the wall but we need some players watching over them, just in case. Sort it out for me, please. Also, please send Hammertime a message, he should get the word around his own guild. I'll wait for you for fifteen minutes; if I don't see you by then I'll head off alone."

"Don't go without me, I'll be there."

Not a word of complaint about sorting out her duties for her. Even more incredibly, not a word of complaint for Lillian suggesting he contact Hammertime. Maybe because dealing with Hammertime was small potatoes after handling Magnitude. Maybe because he was aware Damien's need outstripped his own comfort. Lillian didn't fancy pulling on either of those threads when he'd given her the time she needed.

She'd have to get a move on. Damien had already finished summoning his own portal. He then made his excuses to Lucifer, who was not best pleased, but Damien brushed off the Lord of Hell and stepped away. Then he just stood in his base, doing nothing, saying nothing. He had to know he was still livestreaming, because just before Lillian logged out he cut the feed.

She was out of her own pod in seconds, only to end up waiting for Damien for minutes. It was a bizarre situation: there were occultists lying down everywhere, arranged precariously on beanbags or lying down on yoga mats. A number of them were already waiting and some of them were just waking up, but Damien's pod remained firmly closed. Unable to stand around doing nothing any longer, Lillian went to make herself useful.

"How much for the three pods?"

"You're Lillian? *The* Lillian?"

Lillian glanced at the monitor set to the side behind his desk. He was watching her stream on repeat. This wasn't the first time Lillian's actions in Saga had gotten her attention, but it was the first time she'd seen a stranger watching her actions through her eyes, out in the real world.

"The one and only."

He leaned sideways to look at the line of pods, his eyes widening as he connected the dots.

"And that's Aetherius, in the pod next to yours?"

"Yup. Damien invited us along to hype this place up. I'll put out a message on my profile saying this is where we fought the battle, if that's alright by you?"

"That would be amazing! Thank you!"

"Don't thank me, thank Damien. He was very persistent about getting me here. Sorry, I want to pay up. How much?"

"Free of charge. If you're sending business my way that's more—"

Lillian clacked her credit card onto the desk. The idea of depriving a venue which was making do with yoga mats and beanbags of her custom was ridiculous, almost as ridiculous as the idea of going there in the first place.

"I wasn't invited here to take advantage of you, don't offend me. Ring me up."

There were scattered cheers and Lillian turned to find Damien climbing out of his pod. He was wearing the fake smile Lillian was so well acquainted with from her own time in the streaming competition. Damien didn't wear it quite so well as she or Andrew could. Practice makes perfect. His closest fans didn't seem to notice. One of them was already thrusting out a marker pen and a headset, blathering on about how awesome Damien was without noticing he looked anything but.

Lillian left her credit card behind to extricate Damien from the rapidly forming dogpile. If he felt half as bad as she had after being targeted by Shedim, this was the last thing he needed. It was a lot harder to push her way through a crowd out here than it was in Saga. By the time she got to Damien, he was signing headsets as they were thrust under his nose, and the cafe was full of noise.

Lillian had had it with these savages. She got to the front and grasped Damien by the arm as he continued scrawling his best pass at a signature on whatever was handed to him, this time a Saga merch T-shirt. He didn't look like he wanted to be there, at all.

"Hey, do you want to get some air with me?"

"I've got to do this first. Can you help me out?"

It wasn't the way she wanted to help, but it was what

Damien was asking for and she could do it. Lillian stood next to him and doubled down on his signature on everything that was passed in her direction, making everyone there happy except herself. It was only when she noticed people returning with new objects to sign that she decided enough was enough. She put on her showman's smile.

"Thanks so much for helping today, you guys were great, enjoy the signatures. I have to go and I need Damien to escort me, so see you next time! Bye-bye now, goodbye, GGWP, bye-bye."

She grabbed Damien firmly by the shoulders and led him past the desk, where her credit card was being held out by the store owner lest she had forgotten. She hadn't. In fact, she had a request for him.

"When An...Aetherius gets out of the pod, can you send him...Damien, where are we going? Somewhere nearby we can talk while we wait for Andrew."

"Noodle bar opposite."

"Can you send Aetherius to the noodle bar over the road for me? Thanks, appreciated. Damien, say goodbye to all your fans. No, that's not a threat, just give them a wave for— okay, good. Bye everybody! Thanks for everything!"

And they were outta there. Lillian frog-marched Damien over the road and into a seat at the window. It was a clever choice for the situation, almost as if he'd done this before. She ordered two chicken satay bowls for herself and Andrew and a miso for Damien, thinking something hot to drink would do him a world of good. It wasn't much good if he wasn't drinking it.

"Do you want to talk about it?"

"No. I mean, why not? We won, right? I'm guessing we won."

"We won."

"Oh, good. That's good."

"That's not what I was asking, and you know it."

Damien set his eyes back out the window. He was putting on the same fake smile for her that he'd been putting on for his fans. It annoyed Lillian intensely. She stared at him for a while, waiting to see exactly how uncomfortable he was. The silence got long enough for her to decide to guide the whole conversation without Damien's help.

She'd cut right to the point. After all, a proper introduction was long overdue.

"Here's what I saw when I got Shedimmed: my father was walking with me when an automated car veered off the road and ran him down. His final act was shielding me from harm. They failed to revive him in the hospital. I was six at the time."

She didn't know how Damien would take this. At least the shock factor got his attention.

"Why are you telling me that?"

"Because you were living through your worst fear when we first met and you told me all about it, even though you didn't *have* to tell me the truth. You could've just lied. I avoid—"

Damien sat bolt upright and stared at Lillian, mouth ajar.

"Did everyone see—"

"It's okay, it's okay, don't worry. We didn't see anything. I don't know for certain how it works, but my best guess is it triggers traumatic memories. It blinds and deafens you but we saw and heard everything as normal. I only knew what you'd seen because I was there for both of them. It couldn't have been anything else."

She slurped down some of her noodles, giving Damien the opportunity to correct her if she was wrong. He didn't say anything, but he started drinking his miso. A good sign. Lillian pressed her advantage.

"I understand why you're pretending everything is fine. I avoid telling people about my past. It changes the way they look at me. The way they treat me. You don't need to be embarrassed about it with me. You handled it better than I did, that's for sure! I enjoyed watching you beat the crap out of Archimonde."

"You'd have done the same. I was lucky he used Shedim while I was right on top of him."

True enough. Andrew had just come out of the internet cafe and was heading straight for them. Time to go. Lillian clapped Damien on the back as she stood up and gathered her things.

"I'm glad I came, thanks for having me along. Do me a favor. Go home and have a rest. Give your mom a hug, make that bad dream disappear for one of us. Next time we hang out let's do something other than Saga for a change, how's your karaoke?"

She'd sandwiched the heaviest part of her message between softer niceties, but it made for pretty poor camouflage. It wasn't designed not to be noticed so much as not to be replied to. Damien took the hint.

"Yeah, karaoke would be great."

She gave him a hug, which he returned with feeling, when Andrew scooched in next to Damien. He stuck out his hand.

"Well done. That wasn't an easy fight."

Damien took his hand and they shook. Not like before, when they had done it for the benefit of onlookers and it had been overenthusiastic and showy, but slowly and deliberately.

"Thanks. And thanks again for looking after Lillian."

"It's a two-way street. Speaking of which, I'm under orders to take her to work and it's been a difficult day for both of us. Let's have a proper meeting next time."

"Sounds good."

Damien followed them out and the three of them gave each other nods and small waves, each preoccupied with their own thoughts, before Damien went in the opposite direction. It was only when Lillian settled into the automated metal box of total lack of control that her train of thought completely fell to pieces. Andrew stuck his hand out for her to take, his eyes set straight ahead of him.

Lillian hesitated for a few moments, but took it pretty quickly when the car started moving. The mild irritation was a good secondary distraction, which Andrew was keen to capitalize on.

"Didn't think you'd take it, after you clung to the handrail all the way here."

"It reassures me that if someone pushes a pram out in front of us, at least you'll die with me. If it happens while I'm holding your hand, I'll have a crack at breaking your fingers before we hit the pavement."

"What an honor. So glad I'm still useful."

Nope, visualizing the worst-case scenario was, surprisingly, not calming Lillian down. She screwed her eyes shut and tried to think about something else. It was only when they reached the elevator to the underground highway about ten minutes later that she could open her eyes again. She quickly released Andrew's hand and dropped it into his lap before looking out the window at the lights blurring by.

They were moving at maximum speed, but the ride was smooth and the path was clear. Lillian didn't have any problem with automated vehicles, in and of themselves. It was when automated cars had to make sudden choices stemming from the actions of a stupid human that things got dicey. Since the tunnel could only be accessed by automated cars, this was the fastest yet safest part of the trip.

She turned back to Andrew while she could still think. His answer would determine whether or not her campaign had been a success.

"What will you do now?"

"Go home and eat my noodles."

"I mean after that."

"Go back online, double-check the wall's secure, put some posts on the Rising Tide page."

"No, Andrew. I mean after that. What's next?"

"Oh, you mean long term? Well, once you've got Camelot under control I'll be resigning as your Court Wizard."

Goddammit.

"Why? We've just fixed—"

They emerged from the tunnel and shot out into the unpredictable world again. Lillian stopped talking and stared at her feet. Why was it that most of the car had to be see-through? She'd rather not have a clear visual of her impending doom. Andrew stuck his hand back out and she grasped it, then squeezed. Her grip wasn't nearly as strong here as it was in Saga, but it was more than enough to convey her sentiment. She had a lot more to say, but this was one of the few places on earth that rendered Lillian silent.

The car stopped in front of Jefferson Hospital and the doors swung open. Lillian opened her eyes as Andrew let go of her hand and climbed out. He didn't have to, there was plenty of space for Lillian to get by. He was just doing it because it was the right thing to do, or so she thought. As soon as she stepped out, the doors closed and the car rolled away. She turned to him, puzzled.

"Wait, how are you getting home?"

"Tram service around here somewhere. I'll find it. Goodnight, Lillian. Thanks for everything."

Lillian stepped after him and tapped him on the shoulder. He was practically running away from her.

"You think I'll let what you said slide? We just fixed everything! What the hell are you talking about?"

"We didn't fix it, not really. What I did to you is completely unforgivable, and I deserved everything—"

Lillian thought they were past this.

"You did it to me! I decide if it's unforgivable! Not you!"

"No, Lillian, that's not true. You can forgive me all day long, but if I don't forgive myself it doesn't mean anything. I'm an adult, remember? I'm responsible for my own choices, I don't get to blame Richard for doing things I shouldn't have. Your words. Not mine."

"That was about playing Saga instead of studying for the tests, this is different."

"It applies just as much. I ruined the best thing I had going for me. I don't intend to linger on it, which is pretty hard to do while I'm your underling. I'll resign as Court Wizard and hand off Rising Tide as soon as you've established control."

Lillian folded her arms. She could feel herself becoming unreasonable, but there wasn't much she could do to stop herself. Andrew had started it.

"Thanks for making this easy. I don't accept your resignation."

"And I don't accept your lack of acceptance of my resignation. Sorry, Lillian, but I need to move on with my life. You said so yourself, that I'm too clever to live off your back, that it would destroy me – except it turns out I'm not, and it didn't. I don't need saving. I'm glad we've made amends and I'm sure we'll see each other again."

He leaned forward and kissed her on the cheek.

"Goodbye, Lillian. You're not perfect, but you're pretty damn close and a lot better than I deserved."

He took a few steps back and stared at her, taking her in. He gave her his very best fake smile, so good Lillian wasn't sure if she'd classified it correctly. Then Andrew turned on his heel and walked away without turning back.

Andrew had shown his value by walking away. She couldn't believe it. She remained frozen in the street until long after he'd passed out of sight, waiting for him to look back. He never did.

They'd arrived at her work ahead of schedule. Her shift would begin in thirty minutes. She'd be working until 1am. If the necessary arrangements were to be made, she had to begin immediately.

She marched into Jefferson Hospital, pulling her headset out of her satchel as she went. She went straight to the nearest broom closet.

Lillian scrolled through her missed voice chats, arriving at the one she'd received not long after she'd taken Excalibur. It hadn't seemed like the right time for the call back then, with Magnitude still posing a threat. Now was the right time. She dialed back, not entirely sure she'd receive any response at all. The call was picked up after two rings.

"Congratulations on your acquisition of Excalibur, Lillian Meridian. And your victory earlier this evening. I was wondering when I might expect your call."

"Hello, Mr. Adler. Thank you. We need to talk."

It was 5:30pm the next day by the time Damien had finished cataloguing his journey in a single highlights stream. It was comprehensive: the attempt to join forces with Empire players to run a dungeon, ending in their deaths. His jaunt through the Frozen Forest, including his encounter with Aetherius. His and

Lillian's first failed attempt to get past the wall, completed by his two "interactions" with Magnitude and Archimonde. The successful second run through the wall with unlikely allies and the second appearance from 'Archie baby'. The slog through the Inner Circle to the Dark Tower and the diversion to get past Archimonde. His prolonged, purgatorial dealings with Cave Urchins, Mordred and Toutatis. The preparations with his occultists. The war. And the final battle with Archimonde.

Busy week. The only part he'd edited heavily was Lillian's episode fighting Archimonde. It had been a lot simpler than he'd expected: just a quick blur to a half second he'd glanced at the ground, a little blur effect as he was looking back up to remove a few seconds from when he was Charging in, some overlaid sound effects to replace Lillian's screaming and hey presto. Reality had been altered.

The conversation with Lucifer didn't come into question, since Lucifer had cut all the recording of it. There'd been a lot of personal stuff, so Damien wouldn't have shared it anyway, but he did regret not having it available. He had no proof of what had happened, nor did he have any way of explaining how he'd become Pride. He'd said it was a private cutscene, that anyone who wanted to understand would have to go through it themselves although he didn't recommend it, and had left it at that.

He logged back into Saga, arriving in the temporary base Bartholomew had loaned him for the weekend. He'd put it to good use. Noigel had been receiving his promised reward for coming up on eight hours. Four succubi and a single imp had been attached to the Soul Well along with him. Damien had only been joking about adding the last imp, but Noigel had insisted.

The extra imp was sitting in the corner, playing patty-cake with the wall. It seemed more bored than envious of its superior, but Noigel was too preoccupied to notice. In addition to feasting on succubus fur being fed into his mouth like grapes, his head was too heavy to lift up and look across the room. His horns were now larger than he was. Each of them. So long as they reverted to their original size when Noigel was done, as had always happened before, Damien wasn't too fussed.

Damien rolled the stone blocking his base away and then rolled it back again after he and his personal posse emerged. He'd rather not have any sudden jarring noises in the background while he spoke to Kevin. No occultist trials today, everyone was avoiding death timers in order to enjoy the festivities in Camelot.

When Kevin didn't pick up the first time round, Damien called again. He wanted to give Kevin a chance, so he was relieved when his call was answered almost immediately on the third attempt. If Kevin was upset about being contacted on one of his days off, he didn't show it.

"Damien! How's it going?"

"It's going well! Did you catch what happened yesterday?"

"Did I! I caught the whole thing. You played remarkably well."

"Thanks. In particular, did you catch the end of my fight with Archimonde?"

"Yeah, you really gave it to him, huh? Maybe a little over the top there, at the end, but that's what the combat sequence was designed—"

"I meant the part just before that. Do you remember the bit where Archimonde used 'Shedim' on me?"

"I did, didn't see it do anything though. Whatever it was, it clearly wasn't enough to stop you! I was really worried you were getting in over your head with these characters, but you sure proved me—"

"Kevin. Shedim is the ability I asked you to raise alarms about. I sent you video footage of what it did to Lillian earlier this week and told you to get it checked. Urgently."

There was a pause. When Kevin came back, all the panic was gone. He was in full-on professional mode. *Colder.* Not what Damien was looking for. Not what he'd expected, either.

"Damien. I do apologize, but the issue you voiced was not within my purview. I'm your PR manager now. As a former beta-tester, you know a single case study observed in another individual rather than personally experienced does not justify the diversion of time and resources—"

That was Damien's limit. As much as he didn't want to keep interrupting Kevin, it would've helped if Kevin had opted to meet him halfway by actually listening to him. Damien kept his tone as civil and amenable as he could, though he felt like yelling down the line. He contented himself with talking over Kevin until he relented, about three seconds in.

"I can tell you exactly what 'Shedim' does now, since I was targeted by it. It triggers traumatic memories. For me, it picked out when my mom was having a heart attack. It played the worst part of it, in my head, on a three-second loop. It was worse for Lillian, from what I hear."

Kevin scoffed over the line.

"Th—that's impossible! The skills are all carefully vetted, none of them have that effe—"

Warmer. Still in denial, though. And in so doing, he was calling Damien a liar.

"Oh they do, and there's worse on the way. How many case studies do you need? Because I know at least fifteen occultists who hit level 40 yesterday, some of whom are minors. They'll give you plenty more case studies. Is this a path you feel Mobius Enterprises wishes to explore in depth?"

"Of course not! When you said it was urgent, I thought you meant a minor glitch, not any—"

Warmer. Still not the words Damien was looking for.

"I said it was urgent. A week ago. I showed you Lillian's reaction. What part of that looked like a minor glitch?"

"I thought it was an isolated case, it looks like I should've called it in, but like I said, I've been so busy, that's why—"

Hot. Still all those unnecessary 'buts', though. Come on, Kevin, you can do it. Just one last push.

"Kevin. Next time I say something's urgent, will you take me seriously? It's not like I'm unfamiliar with headset technical issues, is it? My mom isn't the only one who ended up in a hospital that week. I know what 'urgent' means."

"N-no, it's not. I mean, of course you do. I'm sorry."

Well done, Kevin. For a moment there, I thought we weren't going to make it.

"It's fine. I'm just concerned, because I'd like to make a stable career out of this. I can't do that if our headsets keep turning everyone's brains inside out. Oh, and while we're on the subject: do feel free to send me a message before you doctor my gaming footage and put it up on the official channel in future. You may be my PR guy, but it's very much my channel. I don't need you deciding my direction without my input. Let's work a little more closely. Copacetic?"

A final pause before Kevin came the rest of the way over to Damien's side.

"Loud and clear."

"Thank you, Kevin. I'll call tomorrow to ask what progress you've made on the 'Shedim' problem. Have a good night."

Damien hung up. He'd been so naive to think he could rely on other people, in game or out. He was starting to get the hang of dealing with them, though. Of course, he'd already issued strict instructions on the Council of Nine page not to take their level 40 trait until further notice. There was an ability patch in the works. No loose ends.

He'd cemented his position as a Saga streamer, had claimed the Embodiment of Pride and had helped Lillian – one of the only players who'd been open-minded enough to cooperate with him from the beginning – into a position of power. With occultists no longer 'Enemies of the Realm', Magnitude and Archimonde out of the picture and this final impending potential PR hazard dealt with, his long-term livestreaming career prospects looked pretty rosy.

"That's a very evil look, Damien. I haven't seen an expression on your face quite like that since your skirmish with Godhammer and Rising Tide."

Even now, Bartholomew still knew how to push his luck but Damien was in far too good a mood to care about being snuck up on.

"I'm filling the shoes you had Lucifer fit me for, Bart. We have to play the hand we're dealt. You dealt me a good hand. I intend to play it."

"I'm glad you finally appreciate what I did for you. Although it does come with some additional responsibilities. Lucifer requires your attendance. You left rather suddenly following your victory yesterday and there are matters he wishes—"

"I have something else to do tonight. I've been invited to a party and it's important I show my face. Lucifer shall have to wait."

"He won't like that. I was instructed to send you as soon as you returned, and he's superior to both of us. Tell him yourself."

"I'm not attending Lucifer to tell him I'm not attending him. My not showing up will speak for itself. I'll be back to remove Noigel and the base before midnight and our agreement will be at an end, as promised."

"Not quite. You'll still owe your side of the bargain, which is as yet undetermined."

"Yeah, yeah. Well, you earned it. I'm heading out. Have a good night, Bart."

He sent an imp up to the entrance of the Downward Spiral, the rest of his minions either flying up after it or running around the traps. Bartholomew tutted at him just before he left.

"Should Lucifer come asking, I won't cover for you. There's no point when he knows everything."

"No need to cover for me, I'll handle it myself."

He Demon Gated up and picked his way to the edge of the forest, then checked the time: 17:45. He was surprised Lillian hadn't contacted him already, as they were supposed to be at Godhammer's headquarters by six and she'd definitely said she was picking him up. He was supposed to help her keep Andrew preoccupied.

A few minutes later, hoof-beats echoed from down the road. The entirety of the Queen's Guard were all on horseback, along with Andrew and Lillian herself at the front. Damien left the forest and struck out to meet them at the side of the road, so he was waiting by the time they got there. Lillian looked him up and down, then investigated the minions behind him. Damien remembered this part.

"Let me guess: I need to get rid of all my minions for now?"

"No, it's alright. Your minions don't draw unwanted attention anymore. The hounds can run alongside, if they can keep up. The imps and succubi can ride with my priests, maybe teach them a little humility. Matthew! Mark! Luke! John!...Derek."

Four stately priests rode up to the front, along with an unkempt, slightly smelly, unambiguously happier-looking priest than the other four. He looked like a goblin that had been recently transformed into a human and was still working out the kinks, but was just incredibly grateful to be there at all. He sounded like a goblin, too:

"*Derek!*"

Lillian scratched her head. Every chain has a weak link.

"Yes, Derek, very good. The five of you shall provide Damien's demonic horde with transportation on your own horses. Damien, I've brought you a gift."

She waved her hand over her shoulder and a pitch-black steed was wrestled to the front by a pair of bemused-looking warriors. It was neither as robust as Lillian's speckled 'Boudicea', nor as aesthetically pleasing as Aetherius's shimmering 'Butt-stallion'. But Damien preferred it to either of them. It was a lean, mean, pitch-black ground-covering machine, with glowing red eyes and a temperament to match. It was called 'Shadowmere'. A bit pretentious for Damien's tastes, but not a dealbreaker. He'd never had a mount before! He was going up in the world.

"Thanks! This is very cool."

"Yeah, we thought you needed an upgrade to your status. A horse is kinda like a car, just relatively more expensive to buy and marginally cheaper to maintain. Don't worry, now you're not an Enemy of the Realm we can help you look after it. Right, Andrew?"

"If he doesn't cut its head off, that would be a good start."

Andrew was looking a bit sour. Given his itinerary, Damien could understand why. Damien himself had been informed already, not only as to what Andrew thought was going on, but about what Lillian actually had planned. It was one of those rare instances where Damien could concretely say he knew more than Andrew did, the kind of experience he hadn't enjoyed since he'd abused his as yet unknown class. It was important he didn't give the game away.

"In fairness, Andrew, I wasn't trying to maintain your Pegasus when I did that. Much the opposite."

"The way things are going, it seems like my head is next. Did Lillian tell you what we're doing today?"

"Yeah. She told me all about it. How are you feeling?"

Lillian cut in before Andrew could answer.

"Let's talk on the move, boys, we're already running late. I'm going ahead to make sure everything is in order. Matthew, Mark, Luke, John: you escort our guests. I expect you to make decent time. Derek, with me."

"Derek!"

Off Lillian went, with five warriors, four rangers and a demented priest in tow. Derek was clearly the most chill of Lillian's five priests, which was probably why she'd left Damien and Andrew with the rest of them. The other four were still arguing about which of them would provide rides to the two succubi. Lillian's order that they make decent time forced a decision and the group rode on. Damien couldn't help but notice that the four Queen's Guard units had encircled him and Andrew as they headed off again. He leaned in to Andrew and whispered in conspiratorial tones:

"So, how are you feeling?"

Andrew was not quite so reserved.

"Annoyed. Lillian's always been a bit of a control freak. It's funny, really. I'm sure she knows I could ditch these clowns if I wanted to, but that doesn't stop her from trying. Unless...she hasn't put you on trial as well, has she? Have you done anything to annoy her lately?"

"I could write you a list, but I don't think she wants me dead just at the moment. I'm sure she's just ordered them to encircle us for our protection."

Damien didn't believe it even as he said it, but it was the best he could come up with. Andrew raised his eyebrows, apparently putting even less stock in Damien's words than Damien did himself.

"It's not like either of us needs protection. You could murder most of these guys in a heartbeat. I could use 'Blink' with 'Time-Skip' and be over the horizon before they even flinched. That's why you're here, right? To chase me down if I try to run? I bet you'd enjoy that."

"Funnily enough, I wouldn't. Not at all. If you try to run, I won't do anything to stop you. I'm just here for...you know...emotional support."

Andrew, not finding the fight he'd been looking for in Damien, turned instead to the Queen's Guard.

"It's just as well I don't intend to run. The thing that's making my palms itch is having these guys covering me so closely. Ordering them to encircle us is a show of weakness, more than anything. It makes me feel like demonstrating how easily I can escape them, then deciding whether or not I'll come back afterwards."

Andrew hadn't bothered keeping his voice down while he delivered this statement. The riders around them drew further away. Ain't modern AI something? Andrew was very talkative today. Damien knew, vaguely, what Andrew had been told was happening. He wanted to know what Andrew thought of all this, from his perspective.

"If you're so sure you can get out of your trial, why are you still going?"

"I messed up, Damien. I messed up bad. You know that better than anyone. I thought I was doing the right thing. Everything I did, I thought it was exactly what anyone else in my position would've done if they knew how. Now I know better. This trial is my chance for me to move on. I don't know exactly what punishment Lillian has in mind, but after it's done we can all call it quits. Did you know this only happened because I told her I was quitting?"

"She might've mentioned it, yeah."

"If I hadn't, she'd have let me stay on indefinitely. She wanted to reward me, for "loyalty". She said I'd redeemed myself. Do you feel like I've redeemed myself? Have I redeemed myself by tagging along with you and Lillian, just to get the bag you took from me and because we had a common enemy?"

Damien hadn't expected to be put on the spot, at least not this way round. If anything, he'd expected the reverse. Damien didn't have any prepared statements for this scenario. He'd never considered Andrew might want to be judged. He did his best to roll with it.

"You're not really doing yourself justice here, Andrew. You might've tagged along with us at the start, but nobody forced you to stick with Lillian afterwards. She already told me she couldn't have done this without you. If you hadn't come, we'd never have spoken like this. I'd never have seen you as a human being, rather than as a half-human, half-troll."

"Thanks."

"You're welcome. I didn't like being allies, at first, but I'm glad it happened. There was more to you than I realized. If you haven't redeemed yourself yet, you're well on the way."

"Maybe. Hopefully the trial will fast-track the process and I can move on. I hope we stay in touch, though? I could use your help tracking down Magnitude's party. Even if you don't want to do that, we could still talk. If that's alright?"

"Let's see how this goes, first."

They continued riding in silence. Damien knew he was supposed to be keeping Andrew preoccupied, but Andrew was doing a better job of preoccupying himself than Damien ever could.

They made it to Godhammer's guild headquarters twenty minutes later. Damien could still remember when this had been under Rising Tide's control and he and Lillian had laid waste to it. Lillian, mainly. It looked no less imposing than the first time he'd laid eyes on it. The circular parapets set into the slanting walls were now well manned by rangers, who watched their progress as they rode over the open ground to the gate. The gate was closed. The sun was going down. Aside from the *clop* of horses' hooves, there was total silence.

While the rest of them dismounted, Andrew stared at the gate and shook his head.

"Why did it have to be here? Nothing good has ever happened here...oh, I see. She's cementing Hammertime's authority in my absence. Clever."

Damien couldn't bring himself to say anything. He was too afraid to ruin it. All he could manage was a shrug. Andrew dismounted, brought his gaze back to Damien and sighed.

"You coming in with me?"

"I'll stay out here for now. They're waiting for you, not me. I'll follow in after."

"Alright. Wish me luck."

"Good luck, Andrew."

Andrew nodded and paced toward the gate, his arms tightly pressed against his sides and his shoulders hunched up around his silly, pointy elf ears. The moment he turned away, Damien went into his chat box.

Daemien: 10 seconds.

Lillian: Thank you.

The gates swung open and Andrew crossed over the threshold. He'd taken a few steps inside, his eyes cast to the floor, when all the lights came on. Andrew's head snapped upward as the noise hit him. Damien saw over his shoulders as they slumped down. The courtyard was lined with lanterns, magical lights and fireflies. There was a huge banner spread across the entire courtyard, the letters within it flashing with bright magic that lit up the players arrayed around it. Godhammer and Rising Tide players, all. Lillian and Hammertime stood in the very center, at the edge of a huge custom-built stage. The banner hanging over their heads bore a single word:

CONGRATULATIONS

Lillian was in her menu. Her hand swished, and swished, and pointed. A notification appeared in Damien's HUD, the same type as had appeared when Lillian had taken Excalibur. It was a global notification. Every player in Saga received it simultaneously.

'Due to work constraints, **Lillian, Queen of Camelot**, is unable to bear the burden of rulership alone. She has appointed **Aetherius** as **King of Camelot**. Should **Aetherius** accept, he and **Lillian** shall rule Camelot as equals. They will share a single, sponsored Mobius Enterprises channel and revenue from this channel shall be evenly split between them.

Thank you for your attention,

Mr. Adler.'

Godhammer was clapping politely. Rising Tide was less reserved. They'd truly risen from the ashes. They were whole again. Lillian dropped down from the platform and headed toward Andrew as Hammertime spurred his guild to match the enthusiasm of their former rivals. Andrew hadn't moved since he'd looked up. He was frozen on the spot. They'd got him. A hell of an achievement, with so many players who needed to stay quiet. Lillian moved in close and embraced her prospective partner.

"This is what you deserve, and what I deserve. Better late than never, right?"

Damien nodded to himself. Check, and mate. Lillian had done exactly as she'd said she would. She was way out of his league, anyway. He could only hope Andrew had the common sense to make the right choice.

The global notification was extended by a single flashing line.

'**Aetherius** accepts.'

Done. And there was much rejoicing. It may not have been exactly what Damien had wanted, but he couldn't deny how perfect it was. Andrew's guild had surged forward to throw their guild leader in the air. Damien passed them by and walked into the compound, straight to the extremely long table Lillian had set aside. This was the time for his class to represent, while there was nothing that could bring them down. He put a hand to his ear.

"Everyone, move in and mingle. Through the gate, *walking*, please. We don't want it to look like an attack. Lillian told the guards you're coming, act like you belong."

The occultists filed out of the trees where they'd been waiting for his order. The furor was just dying down as they came in. Damien waved a hand and they huddled together and ran for him. They had green names now, so hopefully their presence wouldn't cause too much of a disturbance. However, the minions, Damien's included, sort of gave them away. A group of Godhammer players came walking over, looking quite nervous. Damien's guard went up, then they spoke and his guard went all the way down.

"Could we take screenshots with you guys?"

Bingpot. The Godhammer party gathered behind Damien, with all the occultists crowding in around them and filling every spare inch of space. This was new territory. Damien was certainly used to attention, but none of the occultists were used to being appreciated. As soon as the first batch of occultist tourists left, another took their place. It wasn't long before almost all the players were lining up for their own picture opportunities with the former outcast group. They were a novelty and an oddity, but it was a start.

Hammertime was explaining the criteria for a dueling tournament when Damien received the call that cut his celebration short:

Voice Chat Invitation: Lucifer, Gamer ID 000666, A/D

This was new. Damien figured he should probably take this. While many of the occultists were lining up to surround the stage and hear the rules for the tournament, Damien rose, then veered out the now open gate and around the side. He answered the call.

"Lucifer, I'm kinda busy. What's up?"

"Either you come to me, or I come to you. Your choice."

The call was ended. A second later, a black orb pulsed in front of him and expanded to a swirling disc, two meters high and one wide. It was a portal. Apparently Lucifer could conjure them to players, rather than being limited to Gateways. Huh. Like the scroll Magnitude had used to summon Archimonde.

Andrew's party was going well. Lucifer showing up might put a crimp on things. Possibly. Damien called his minions to him, sent them through the portal and followed on after them himself.

He arrived in front of Lucifer's throne. Lucifer was holding up an orc by the back of its head. Archimonde did not look quite so threatening in its regular form. Damien had been there. Archimonde had not made peace with its circumstances. The orc was kicking, struggling and pleading, to no avail. Lucifer hummed over Archimonde in a deep baritone.

"How nice of you to finally join us, Damien. I didn't want you to miss this."

"What's 'this', exactly?"

"An example."

Lucifer twisted Archimonde round in his grip, the fingers of his free hand clenching together to lock the sharp nails together. His arm uncoiled, piercing into Archimonde's stomach. Archimonde's screeches became a little higher. Lucifer's eyes did not leave Damien's as his hand rummaged around within Archimonde's core.

"Listen well. You have only one master. I will not compete for your attention, because there's no competition to be had. You remain my property, an unruly pet yet to be properly trained. I've allowed you a fair amount of freedom as you came to grips with your power, so you could learn to appreciate what you have to lose if you go against my wishes."

He pulled his hand out of Archimonde's guts. It was holding a small, black sphere. Lucifer held it out for Damien's inspection: it was the unknown black gem, the material for Archimonde's Embodiment. Now Damien knew why he was here: he'd been uncordially invited to Archimonde's un-knighting ceremony. He felt his own Embodiment pulse painfully. The Embodiment disappeared from Lucifer's grip to who knows where, be it his inventory or the ether.

"If you fail to follow my instructions in the future, you will be discarded. Those who cannot obey are less than useless to me. I demand your unwavering obedience in the future, or else."

Lucifer's hands coiled again and struck Archimonde straight through the top of its head. Archimonde sustained the second of its back-to-back death cooldown timers.

"Copacetic?"

Lucifer couldn't stand to let him think he'd won. Right when

Damien had felt as happy and secure as he had in a long time, Lucifer had been compelled to ensure Damien didn't get too comfortable. That's how he worked. Damien wouldn't let it spoil his evening, if he could help it. This was a problem for another day.

"Yup. Crystal clear. Is that all? Great. See you later."

He'd have to walk all the way back to Andrew's party. For the sake of this stupid little hazing ritual, he'd been forced to stop everything he was doing. At least with his Embodiment switched on it wouldn't take long. He messaged Vargus to see if he could build an emergency Gateway with the other occultists. They had a lot of imp power between them and plenty of resources in the environment around. That would be even faster. Maybe he could get back in time for the dueling tournament.

He sent the message and summoned a portal back to his base, which he ushered his minions through. Just before he passed through it himself, Lucifer suddenly spoke again.

"Do be a dear and tell Noigel I wish him well. It's incredible he managed to achieve his own Embodiment at all, considering your lack of imagination."

The portal Damien had conjured shimmered and almost died. He barely managed to hold it as he glanced back at Lucifer, unable to hide his confusion. Lucifer was undeniably sneering, just slightly more malignantly than his immutable resting-sneer-face could account for. Damien braced himself and stepped through the portal.

The succubi were no longer gathered around Noigel. The four of them were cowering at the edges of the walls, covering their faces and weeping. Damien's own summons had joined them. Something was standing on top of Damien's Soul Well. It was slightly larger than a succubus, about the same size as Damien with his Pride-acquired extra inches of height. It looked more or less like a succubus from the back as well. Damien checked Noigel's basic information:

Noigel – Invidia

Noigel was an Embodiment of Sin. Damien had never even considered the possibility. Of course he hadn't. It was ridiculous.

How could this have happened? More than that, how had he not noticed? It had seemed so obvious Noigel was just getting his kicks from cavorting with the succubi, yet all this time he'd been covertly pursuing this goal? All the signs were there, why had Damien missed them?

Noigel twisted his head, then turned all the way around. There was enough of Noigel left that it was undoubtedly him. Rather than the horns reverting, he'd grown into them. They curled from the top of his forehead into tight circles, like those of a ram. His hairless head was now matted with short, thick black fur, no different from that covering his hooves all the way up to his waist.

The most prominent new feature was embedded in Noigel's forehead: a glowing red eye, set sideways. Unlike the eyes Noigel had started with, this one had a pupil. It was even more disturbing than the black orbs Damien had accustomed himself to seeing in demons, not least because it was staring straight at him.

Noigel jumped down off the Soul Well and cantered toward Damien, who was so taken aback he activated his Pride form immediately. Noigel drew to a stop in front of him, put his hands on his hips and began tapping a hoof as he continued glaring at his master. He was waiting for Damien to speak, but Damien had absolutely no idea what to say. He started by checking Noigel's stats, looking for more information:

Noigel – Embodiment of Envy
Strength: 40 **Agility:** 320 **Intelligence:** 385
Constitution: 310 **Endurance:** 320 **Wisdom:** 310
Soul Summon Limit: 14/15
Soul Summon Cost: 10
Abilities: We Are Many, Forbidden Knowledge, Evil Eye, Chaotic Bolt, Bloodlust, Circle of Hell, Bite, Leap, Claw

What in the name of Todd was this? Noigel was more powerful than most players. Now his intelligence would always be high. He'd have Forbidden Knowledge all the time and had picked up all the succubi's magic abilities, plus this Evil Eye thing which was creeping Damien out no end.

Much of this was imposing, yet all of it still paled in comparison to the part Damien could not easily understand: Noigel had his own Soul Summon Limit? What? Noigel's own Soul Summon Cost had risen to 10, and he'd taken two of Damien's succubi into his own Soul Summon Limit while Damien was absent to prevent them from becoming untethered.

With Noigel as his underling, all this was great news. On paper. So why did Damien have a pervading sense of dread? Because he'd been very comfortable in his superiority over Noigel and now they were nearly equals. That's why. Damien asserting himself over Bartholomew was one thing, as he didn't have to rely on Bartholomew and travel with him wherever he went. Somehow this seemed less a blessing than a cleverly disguised curse.

One thing was certain: this would require further testing. It's a shame that's the direction Damien chose to pursue in his first interaction with his irate, newly descended minion.

"Can you still speak? Or did—"

"You're pretending this isn't a thing? If you hadn't reduced my Embodiment requirements to a punishment/reward system, I could've reached this form before the battle and might've been able to actually help! All that time you treated me like a dirty little gremlin who wanted to have a cheeky—"

Damien put his fingers firmly in his ears and closed his eyes. His question had been answered. Noigel could still speak. Damn. There's always something, isn't there?

EPILOGUE

PPMD: I told you not to involve your brother. Are you satisfied now?

Mango: He was on track to win the streaming competition. Helping him at that stage both cemented his victory and meant we'd take the credit for it, in his eyes. It would've simplified the last stage of the plan, the most important stage.

PPMD: Simplifying the last step isn't useful when it complicates all the steps in between. It doesn't matter how or why my misgivings proved correct, only that they did. It's unfortunate retrieving Excalibur ourselves proved impossible, but that doesn't excuse you. Your skills made you perfectly designed for this task. The fiasco you caused between Andrew and Damien ironically destabilized the Empire and made it easier, yet you still mismanaged it.

Mango: I did the best I could with what I had. If Hungrybox and I had been supported by you, Armada and Mew2King, we'd have won easily.

PPMD: Which would've shown all five of us acting in tandem in the early game, as well as drawing us away from our own tasks. You don't solve complications with more complications, Mango. That's a losing line. Hungrybox was assigned to deal with Damien because he had the most at stake and was best equipped to handle him, even though it wasn't his responsibility.

Armada and Mew2King have been diligently pursuing their own tasks, as have I. We haven't had any unforeseen problems, because we didn't create any. Your insistence on backing Andrew for the streaming competition, which was never a priority, means we failed to keep the occultist class suppressed. Hungrybox has lost his Embodiment. He confirmed it, just now. You've jeopardized a crucial pillar of our team.

Mango: That's unfortunate.

PPMD: That makes it sound like luck was involved. It's not unfortunate. You steered him into an avoidable disaster.

Mango: There was no way any of us could've known what would happen.

PPMD: You're absolutely right, it was unpredictable. That's why I was against it. That's why there are only five of us: fewer moving parts. But each of us needs to do their part to the fullest, and now Hungrybox can't. You haven't just weakened him, you've weakened all of us. It's up to you to fix the mess you've made. In addition to catching up on your lost progress in Ragnar-Rock over the last week, you'll also be helping HungryBox reclaim his embodiment as fast as possible.

Mango: What about Camelot?

PPMD: I'll deal with it, along with my own affairs. You'll put me in touch with our contacts and I'll run the interference, so you can focus on helping Hungrybox.

Mango: Thank you, that's very kind of you.

PPMD: No it isn't, I'm not happy to be picking up your slack. I was already overworked, now I have to shoulder your responsibility. Three strikes and you lose half your cut. You're on strike two. The rest of the group is aware of that much. Do as I tell you so if anything goes wrong it's my fault, not yours. Understood?

Mango: Yes, PPMD.

PPMD: It'll take time to come up with an airtight solve. Try not to screw up before then. No more improvisation. Stick to the plan and we won't fail.

Mango: Hindsight is 2020.

PPMD: Foresight is 20XX.

AFTERWORD

Thanks for reading! If you enjoyed my work and would like to show your support, please leave a review on Amazon.

Thanks to the incredible Portal Books Team, especially my long suffering Editor Michael R. Miller and shorter but more intensely suffering Copy-Editor Richard Ridgwell, for their outstanding work whipping this into shape. Last but not least, thank you to Adam Sims for reprising the role of the books 'soul' for everyone who enjoys the audio version.

For more stories like this, you can sign up to the Portal-Books mailing list at https://portal-books.com/sign-up to get updates on new releases and 80,000 words of free reading material, including a 30K prequel on Rising Tide's heyday.

Praise Be.

If you prefer Facebook to email you can join the Portal Books Facebook Group where you can interact with authors and readers alike

www.facebook.com/groups/LitRPGPortal/

For more general discussions about the genre, these groups may be useful to you:

www.facebook.com/groups/LitRPGsociety

www.facebook.com/groups/LitRPG.books
www.facebook.com/groups/LitRPGGroup

If you want to find more great LitRPG Books check out the Amazon store - www.amazon.com/litrpg

Best wishes,
Oliver and The Portal Books Team
www.portal-books.com

JOIN THE GROUP

To learn more about LitRPG, talk to authors including myself, and just have an awesome time, please join the LitRPG Group.

Published by Portal Books, 2021

www.portal-books.com

Printed in Great Britain
by Amazon